THE LIFE SHE LEFT BEHIND

As a young widow, Glenda McKinley is torn between remaining at her beloved estate in the Scottish Highlands, and following the plans her deceased husband made to go to America. When the family doctor suggests her daughter Caitlin's health would improve by moving, the family prepare to go to Colorado. This is a blow to Ros, the eldest girl, who has fallen in love with Clive, son of their estate manager. But for her sister's sake, she agrees to try life on her uncle's cattle ranch. When a gentle cowboy falls for Glenda, she is inclined to stay, but Ros yearns to go back. Can they ever find true happiness?

THE LIFE SHE LEFT BEHIND

THE LIFE SHE LEFT BEHIND

by

Jessica Blair

Magna Large Print Books
Long Preston, North Yorkshire,
BD23 4ND, England.

British Library Cataloguing in Publication Data.

A catalogue record of this book is
available from the British Library

ISBN   978-0-7505-4566-2

First published in Great Britain in 2017 by Piatkus

Copyright © 2017 by Jessica Blair

Cover illustration © Malgorzata Maj by arrangement with
Arcangel Images Ltd.

The moral right of the author has been asserted

Published in Large Print 2018 by arrangement with
Little, Brown

Magna Large Print is an imprint of Library Magna Books Ltd.

Printed and bound in Great Britain by
T.J. (International) Ltd., Cornwall, PL28 8RW

For my great-granddaughter
Imogen Raisbeck, born 20 June 2016

Also, remembering a happy life with Joan

And for Anne, Geraldine, Judith and Duncan

And for Jill, a dear friend,
whose interest in my writing has
encouraged me to keep going

1

'One last wave!' forty-two-year-old Glenda Mc-
Kinley instructed her daughters as she drew her
thick plaid shawl more tightly around her shoulders against the chill that had arrived with the
lowering of the sun on this April day of 1878.

Her eyes were fixed on her husband John whose
strong arms were sending the rowing boat scud-
ding in the direction of the tiny island in the loch,
near to its opposite shore.

He was still thin after a severe chest infection
and Glenda now recalled the handsome strong,
young man with slightly curled dark hair that had
first won her heart. He was still relatively young at
forty-two years of age but he was leaner and his
hair and beard now had streaks of grey; his skin
dark and tough with the wind and sun that also
gave these Highland mountains their wonderful
subtle colours.

'Just a little longer, Mama,' pleaded sixteen-
year-old Caitlin.

'There's a lot to do before your father returns,
and that won't be long with the light fading,'
countered her mother.

'He should have gone earlier as you suggested,
Mama,' put in nineteen-year-old Rosalind, a little
tetchily.

Glenda knew what was upsetting her eldest
daughter but, deciding this was not the moment to

chide Rosalind, held back a reprimand. Instead she said, lacing her words with encouragement, 'Come on, let's see how Mrs Lynch is getting on with the cooking. When we've done that we'll go and dress ourselves in our best attire.'

'We'll give Papa the surprise of his life,' laughed Caitlin.

'Are you sure he knows nothing of your plans?' asked Rosalind.

'Yes,' replied her mother. 'He doesn't suspect we are doing anything special. The staff have been sworn to secrecy.'

'This is so exciting!' cried Caitlin quickly, putting aside any sorrow she felt on leaving.

'So don't you give it away by over-reacting,' warned her sister.

'I'm not stupid,' snapped Caitlin.

'Now come on, let's not bicker.' Glenda waved her daughters into the house and headed for the kitchen. Within a few minutes Mrs Lynch was reassuring her that the celebratory meal would be ready by the time the master was ready to sit down.

'So there is nothing more for us to do?' Glenda enquired.

'Nothing, Ma'am. You and the young ladies should go and enjoy getting ready.'

Glenda and her two daughters hurried up the stairs to their rooms. Twenty minutes later they all reappeared on the landing.

'Oh, Mama, you look wonderful,' gasped Rosalind, looking with both excitement and sadness at her mother's beautiful peacock-blue gown that complemented Glenda's Celtic red hair and emphasised a still trim figure.

'You do, you really do!' added Caitlin, not wanting to be left out.

Glenda laughed. 'You've seen this dress before. The present situation did not warrant my buying a new one.'

'I know, Mama, but you seem to glow and make it look special on what is really a sad occasion. Our last night at home.'

'Thank you very much.' She stepped back a little and took in her two daughters, Ros, so much like her father with her high cheek bones that were accentuated whenever she smiled and Cat, the young 'tom-boy', whose love of the outdoors had tanned her pale skin; but her real beauty shone from within, lighting up her hazel eyes. 'You two look just as lovely in those dresses; perfect to walk down the stairs with me when your father comes in.'

'Should I start my lookout now, Mama?' asked Caitlin, her tone filled with the expectation of how her father might react when he saw the three of them standing on the stairs dressed in their finest just for him and for the dream they were to follow.

'Why not?' replied her mother. 'We don't know exactly when he will leave the island, except that he won't be late.'

'I'll get the best view from here,' announced Cat, heading for the window seat at the end of the landing.

'A good loud shout when you first see him,' said Rosalind. 'Don't miss him by daydreaming about the future.'

'As if I would,' muttered Caitlin, as she ran to

the seat and settled her gaze across the loch towards the castle that stood, a half ruin, on the tiny island a short distance away. She followed the sun's rays touching the mountain-tops with an ever-changing light that also took every opportunity to spread enchantment into the glens and, closer to home, the trees her father had planted when her and Ros had been toddlers. She smiled at the memory of them insisting that he should name them all. She must not miss the first signs that her father was heading home.

Glenda smiled to herself at her youngest daughter's determination to play her part in the surprise. 'Come, Rosalind, we may as well be comfortable while we wait.'

They went down the stairs and settled on to a comfortable, slightly faded sofa in front of the blazing log fire in the sitting room. Glenda looked at her daughter, staring at the leaping flames as if they were not there. The sparkle had faded from Rosalind's eyes recently.

'Still worried about leaving Scotland?' Glenda asked her gently.

Rosalind screwed up her face. 'Not exactly worried but I don't really want to go. I love this land. I love our Scottish mountains. I love my home, all our memories of every room in this house. I want to take them all with me.'

'So do I,' said Glenda. 'I'm locking them away in my memory so I'll have them with me wherever I go. You try and do the same, then you and I can share them whenever we want.'

'So why are we going?'

'You know the last few years have been difficult

for us, Rosalind. Your father and I are getting older and have no son to take on such a large estate with challenging farming conditions. Your father's illness last year took a lot out of him and now he feels he wants a better life for us all and believes that we can find it in America. He has not taken this decision lightly. He has consulted your Uncle Gordon who's been in America for sixteen years now. He tells us there is good land available from which we can live well. We should be able to build ourselves a solid and profitable future. We are lucky to have his advice from which to profit.'

'I know, but life there won't be the same as it is here.'

Glenda smiled. 'It won't, but it might be better; Uncle Gordon believes so. After moving around he has now finally settled in Colorado. He also agrees with your father's decision not to sell up here, so that if ever any of us wishes to return, we can do so. That's why we are leaving the furniture, our best clothes and so on. We have to see what life in America is like before we make a final decision.'

'Is that a promise, Mama?'

'You know it is, and also that the estate is being placed meanwhile in the capable hands of Mr and Mrs Martins; Jessie will keep her eye on the house and Greg will look after the estate helped by his son. Your father has given Greg and Clive carte blanche to do as they think best to keep the estate a viable proposition. So, you see, you can be re-assured once again that Pinmuir House, Loch, its castle and lands, are being looked after...'

Her words, which she saw were reassuring her

eldest daughter, were cut short by a piercing scream that echoed through the house.

Glenda started. A chill ran through her at the sound of further screams. The colour drained from Rosalind's face. 'Caitlin!' she cried, leaping to her feet. Her mother was close behind her as they reached the hall.

'Mama! Mama!' Caitlin, racing down the stairs, was shaking so much she could barely get the words out. She flung herself at her mother.

Glenda grabbed her by her upper arms and shook her slightly. "What is it, Cat? What's wrong?'

Caitlin gasped, 'Fire ... fire!'

Glenda released her, turned and rushed to the front of the house. She yanked open the oak door and even as she plunged outside saw dark smoke and flames rising from the castle. She started towards the loch but after a few steps realised it was useless – John had their only boat!

'Papa!' gasped Rosalind, following her mother. She was aware of someone beside her, turned, grasped his arm and said, 'He's over at the castle, Clive! The boat is still tied up there. Get help ... quick!'

A shocked Clive acted immediately. Thankful that he had come from his home on horseback, he sent the animal galloping in the direction of their nearest neighbour, a mile along the shore of the loch.

There was still enough light to distinguish any movement on the island but all Glenda could see were the devouring flames, their macabre dance reflected in the still waters of the loch.

Caitlin clung to her mother, and Rosalind

huddled close to them both. Glenda felt the weight of the inevitable settling over her, even though she tried desperately to cling to some last shred of hope.

2

Glenda waited on the shore. She resisted Mrs Martins' attempts to persuade her to return to the comfort of the house, and found strength in Rosalind and Caitlin's refusal to leave her side.

'Mama, will Clive be long?' The plaintive note in her youngest daughter's voice tugged at Glenda's heart.

'I hope not, love,' she replied.

'He'll be as quick as possible,' said Rosalind. 'I hope he finds Mr McBain at home.'

'Won't Mr McBain have seen the fire?' asked Caitlin.

'Not from where the family live,' said Glenda. 'The spur of the mountain protrudes into the loch and masks their view in this direction.'

'Come on, Clive. Hurry up, hurry up!' chanted Rosalind, half to herself, but Caitlin caught the words and joined in.

Glenda moved restlessly from one foot to the other, wishing there was something more she could do. She knew the people who had gathered by the lochside would wait until news arrived and be ready to help if needed. She wanted the Mc-Bains to arrive with their boat and then she could get to the castle, find John alive and unharmed, safe from the fire that still gnawed at the stone walls as if seeking their complete destruction.

The minutes passed by slowly with people speculating as to what the delay might be. Tensions were mounting. Then the sound of a galloping horse penetrated the gloom. The suspense eased and hope balanced on a knife-edge.

'The McBains are on their way!' yelled Clive as he hauled his horse to a halt. He swung out of the saddle and ran to Mrs McKinley. 'They shouldn't be long, Ma'am.'

'Thank you, Clive,' she returned, anxiety in her voice.

He glanced at Rosalind who echoed her mother's words almost silently, which he acknowledged with a small reassuring smile.

'How many boats are coming, Clive?' asked his father.

'Two,' he replied.

'Good,' said Greg Martins, who started choosing the men he would like to accompany him over to the island.

'I'm coming too,' Glenda announced firmly.

'No, Ma'am. You'd be better here, looking after your daughters.'

'No!' screamed Caitlin. 'I want to go too. I want Papa!'

'The wind is too strong for you to go. You stay here and look after your mother,' said Greg in a gently persuasive tone. 'You'll be doing an important job.'

His eyes met Glenda's and she nodded.

'You'll do that for Mr Martins, won't you?' her

18

mother asked the girl.

Caitlin tightened her lips and bowed her head in acceptance.

'We'll do it together, Cat,' said Rosalind.

Jessie Martins stepped out of the group of people who had gathered in spite of the cold when news of the fire had spread among the estate workers. She turned to the cook. 'Mrs Lynch, let us go into the house. We'll make a warm drink for everyone.'

Glenda nodded her approval but she herself stayed close to the water's edge. 'Off you go and help, girls,' she said to her daughters.

'No, Mama. Mr Martins wants us to look after you,' said Caitlin.

'Very well.' Glenda allowed herself a little smile at her daughter's acceptance of her role.

With every passing minute their attention veered between the direction from which the boat would come and the spectacle of the burning castle nearly a mile away. Horror filled Glenda's eyes at the realisation that the timbers, supporting the stone walls, had started crashing to the ground, and without them parts of the roof had started to cave in also. Her eyes were now fixed on the disintegrating building and she saw the sudden leaping of flames and dust thrown up to the sky.

Glenda flinched. 'John, John ... where are you?'

'The boats! The boats!' There was hope in the cries that went up, started by Caitlin.

Men rushed into the water, ready to grab and haul in the boats as soon as they reached the shallows. Shouts rang out, orders were willingly taken, the beach came alive with willing would-be rescuers, but then words of warning were uttered as the early-evening sky over the island filled with billowing smoke. Another castle wall had collapsed and the danger they faced was emphasised once again.

'No, Mrs McKinley. No!' Glenda had stepped determinedly towards the boats as soon as they touched the shore. Mr Martins' attention was on her at once. He reached out to stop her, stumbled but managed to grab her arm and hold on as he fell. Willing hands hauled them both to their feet.

'Take your daughters into the house. You can do no good here, Ma'am. The men will do their best.'

'Come, Mama,' said Rosalind, taking her mother's hand.

As Glenda felt her other hand taken by Caitlin and heard her younger daughter's sobs, she nodded towards Greg. They watched the boats leave and then walked slowly to the house.

Glenda sank on to the first chair she saw, took her two daughters in her arms and then succumbed to the ministrations of Mrs Martins, who said gently, 'You must be exhausted. I know it will be hard but go to your room and try and get some sleep, Ma'am. I'll keep my eye on what is happening here.'

Glenda nodded and reluctantly went to the room she shared with her husband. Her daughters followed her.

Two hours later a noise disturbed Glenda. She woke with a start, trying to grasp where she was and why. After a few brief moments realisation dawned with a sense of alarm and an intense desire to see John. So as not to wake her sleeping daughters she slid carefully from the bed. She threw a shawl around her shoulders and stepped over to the window. She eased aside a curtain so she could look out. There was no movement on the shore so she knew the men were still on the island. She still expected John to come back, striding in the side door of the house, casting off his old tweed jacket in the lobby to go and settle inside his study. Surely she would once again walk in to see him with a glass of whisky in his hand, turn to smile at her before he settled down to work. She would kiss him again, wouldn't she? Her wait would have to continue.

Clive and his friend Tim, with four other men, having quickly gathered provisions in case they needed to spend the night on the island, started to move along the shoreline away from the castle. Their knowledge of the loch and local conditions had led them to believe that if John McKinley had fallen into the water, in an attempt to leave the burning castle, he could have been washed ashore further along the lochside. With light fading from the sky they made camp in the shelter of some rocks and held on to the hope that a new day might yet bring success.

A bright morning sun heightened their expectation and they lost little time in renewing the search.

Clive called out, 'There's an outcrop of rocks ahead that should give me a good view. I'll push on and scale it.' With the approval of the others, he left them at a quick trot and, reaching the mound, started up it. From the top he signalled to the search party.

Clive surveyed the jumble of rocks beneath but nothing claimed his attention. He decided to move further to the right before continuing along the shore. After a hundred yards he stopped on the brink of a gully that dropped sharply to meet the waves of the incoming tide. His eyes widened. Excitement gripped him. Was that a rock ... or clothing?

He yelled to attract his companions. 'Here, over here!' He pointed where he wanted them to go.

Tim signalled their acknowledgement. They closed ranks as they moved closer and closer to the gully. Clive held his position. If the bundle was not what he thought it was, his guidance might still be needed. Anxiety gripped him as he watched. He held his breath when he saw them reach the heap and bend down to examine it. One of them straightened up slowly. 'It's John!'

Then any hope Clive still had was dashed as two of the men gesticulated with their thumbs down. He scrambled back in a cascade of rocks, heedless of the danger. Suddenly he was on the shore and running towards the grim-faced group.

'Dead when we found him,' one of them reported. 'With the strengthening wind he's taken a beating on the rocks.'

Words lodged in Clive's throat at the thought of breaking the news to the McKinleys. How could he face Rosalind and Caitlin? What could he say?

As the boats neared the McKinley home the men saw Glenda and her daughters rush to the shore.

Eyes met and held. That brief moment of time marked the last moment when there were still those who believed that John might yet be alive.

The men carried him carefully, a blanket over him, towards the group of onlookers on the shore.

Glenda felt her elder daughter's grip on her tighten and knew Rosalind had guessed the truth: this could be no one but her father. A choking cry came from Caitlin as she too realised what lay so still beneath the blanket. All three of them stood without moving, frozen by grief.

A dreadful silence prevailed as the estate workers watched the rescuers approach Glenda McKinley and lower their burden gently to the ground at her feet.

Mrs Martins and Mrs McBain came close to Rosalind and Caitlin to hold them back. Turning and resting her head on Jessie Martins' shoulder, Caitlin sobbed uncontrollably for the father she had loved.

Glenda, with tears streaming down her face, fell to her knees and folded back the blanket from his face. There was a moment's pause. Then, as she took her husband in her arms, the cry of a haunted soul reverberated across shore, loch and hillside. 'Oh, John, why? Why, why, why?' There was no answer, only shuddering sobs from Rosalind and Caitlin.

After a few minutes Glenda kissed him, laid him gently down, and stood up. The men dropped the blanket over him again but as they lifted his body one edge slipped and, in the seconds that it took to re-cover him, Caitlin turned and saw a horribly deformed face, covered with lacerations and bruises, and barely recognised it as belonging to her beloved father. She tried to cry out but no sound came. She was transfixed by the horror of what she had seen. Then she was aware of her mother holding out her arms and indicating to her daughters to walk beside her. They led the sad cortege to the house where Glenda directed them to lay John on his bed.

Tears stained the paper on which Glenda wrote to her husband's brother in America.

Dear Gordon,
   It is with an aching heart that I write to tell you that John died yesterday. He had gone to the castle in the late afternoon. It seems that he fell and probably injured his leg knocking over an oil lamp that started a fire from which his only escape lay in the loch. Sadly that and the rocks were too much for him.
   The tragedy is still too recent for me to write more now, except to say that, our American dream is shattered and will remain unfulfilled.
   God keep you at this tragic time.
   Your loving sister-in-law,
   Glenda

3

'It has been a hard day, Ma'am,' said Mrs Martins as Glenda and her daughters came into the house after seeing the last of the mourners leave. 'I told Mrs Lynch to prepare some tea for you. I'll let her know you are ready for it.'

'Thank you,' said Glenda, weary after a day when she had been obliged to act with composure despite the wrenching sorrow inside her.

As they were settling themselves Caitlin asked, 'Mama, don't you think your relations could have come to Papa's funeral?'

'I agree with you, Cat,' put in Rosalind indignantly. 'You and I don't know them but they could have come, for Mama's sake.'

Glenda gave a weak smile. 'I didn't expect them to, not after all these years.'

'Why? It's not as if they live far away – only ten miles or so as the crow flies.'

'The rift has become too wide. Your grandfather was adamant that if I married your father, I would be an outcast as far as the rest of my family was concerned. I was cut off without a penny. No one else dared to contest that, and they were all banned from contacting me in any way.'

'But you didn't obey him,' pointed out Rosalind.

'I loved your father too much to lose him.'

'What exactly happened when you said you

would marry Papa?' asked Caitlin.

'I had to leave home immediately, with only what I stood up in.'

'That was cruel,' said Caitlin in disgust.

'What did you do then, Mama?' asked Rosalind, who had always wondered about her scarcity of relatives.

Glenda paused. She had never told her daughters the full story but now felt it was the right time. They were older and needed answers to the questions she had previously shrugged aside.

'Your father was angry when I told him that I had been cast out. He was all for confronting my father there and then, but I persuaded him not to. It would only have led to more trouble.'

'What happened to you then?'

'Your father persuaded me to go home with him.'

'To this house?'

'Yes. Your uncle Gordon and your father were living here together. Immediately your uncle was aware of the situation, he invited me to make my home with them. I have ever been grateful for that invitation. Your father and I married immediately, to avoid any scandal, and were very happy.' Her voice caught in her throat at the thought that her life could no longer be the same.

'If you were all happy together, why did Uncle Gordon leave?' asked Rosalind.

'Didn't he like children?' Caitlin suggested.

'No, no, no!' Glenda protested quickly. 'He loved the two of you; spoiled you as if you were his own.'

'So why did he go?' pressed Rosalind.

'Your uncle believed that if he left, life would be

easier for us as a family. We tried to persuade him to stay but he was adamant. He insisted on signing over the estate to John so that your father was free to work it as he saw best. And, well, you know the rest. Gordon found himself a new life in America, worked hard to make it a success. You've read in his letters how he moved around, always seeming to do well for himself in spite of the harsh conditions. He is now settled in Colorado where his cattle ranch is thriving. He realised from your father's letters to him that our estate here was stagnating and advised us to follow him. He believed we could make a good life in America.'

'Can we?' asked Rosalind.

'I don't know.' Her mother shook her head from side to side, and fought back further tears as she added, 'We will have to see. There will be much to decide, but for now we have to observe mourning conventions. You two will wear black for a year ... two years for me.'

The sisters pulled faces. 'Do we have to?' moaned Caitlin.

'Yes. We do from respect for Papa.'

'Does that mean we'll be staying here now?' asked Caitlin.

'Certainly for the present. For now I think it best if we follow the plans your father left for the estate. Because we were going to America, he put a lot of thought into them.'

'Does that mean we might still go?' asked Rosalind.

'Not necessarily, but it does mean we have time to grieve, sort ourselves out and consider our next move. The Martins will look after the estate for

27

now. Neither of you should worry. We will see how life works out for us.'

Seeing her daughters were reassured, Glenda left them to mourn in their own way. She went to her own room craving silence and memories, knowing the future would seem for ever empty. Lying on her bed, her face in the pillow to silence the racking sobs and tears, she fought back screams until she felt exhausted but she arose knowing her first task was to inscribe the date of John's death in the family bible. She brushed down her black skirt, went to the study and took up her pen. Once that was done she decided she would write to Gordon. It was the next day before she composed the final script.

Dear Gordon,

I thought you would like to know that John was laid to rest in a simple service conducted by Rev. Kintail, whom you won't know as he came to Gartonhag long after you were gone. He could not have been kinder or his address more apposite. The weather was warm and dry. I'll swear the hills and mountains remembered how you and John enjoyed sharing their beauty and put on a special display for him. A lone piper played a lament that I will hear again every time I stand at the grave side.

The girls and I miss him as we missed you when you left for America.

Keep us in your thoughts – we face an uncertain future.

Glenda

After finishing the letter she sent for her daughters. When they entered the room a few minutes later Glenda remarked, 'Those mourning dresses suit you, they fit well.'

They both pulled faces and muttered, 'Black, ugh!'

Glenda, recalling how she had felt at their age when having to wear black, gave them no reprimand but merely said, 'The time will soon pass but it is up to you to live your lives as normally as you can. Enjoy yourselves, in fact – I place no restrictions on any activity, except to say you should wear black whenever you are in company.'

'We will, Mama,' they both promised.

'Good. Now, we should settle back into our lives here. It is fortunate we have only our personal belongings to see to. I suggest we do that straight away.'

'May we go riding, Mama?' asked Caitlin.

'Get your things unpacked and you can go tomorrow morning.'

'Good, good!' cried Caitlin excitedly. 'Are you coming too, Rosalind?'

'Of course. Let's see to our clothes now and then we'll find Clive and tell him to have your Pearl and my Freya ready for us in the morning.' She enjoyed Clive's company. They had been brought up together, her father having no son had taught him to shoot and hunt. He found himself the envy of the other boys at the local school. Afterwards John had taught him further on subjects while his own father instructed Clive on all practical estate work. He had grown into a handsome, young man of twenty-one with ambition to become a gentleman.

On returning from their ride the next day they led their ponies to the stable where Clive commented, 'I'm so pleased you are able to exercise your fine pair of Highland ponies. They are strong and sure-footed, but need more daily exercise than I am able to give them with all the other work I have to do.' Looking at Rosalind he added, 'I thought your riding might be restricted at present.'

'I think Mama sees it as a way for us to take in some fresh air and be out of our black for a while.'

'I'm glad she does,' said Caitlin, screwing up her nose as she added, 'I really don't like black. We must keep to the estate, though, for our rides.'

'I'm sorry I can't accompany you. Father's already drawing up a plan of work now your mama has left the running of the estate to us.'

'Are you pleased about that?' asked Rosalind.

'More than pleased,' replied Clive enthusiastically. 'I think we can make improvements even though we are restricted by the lie of the land. But we'll see.'

'You really do like working here then?' queried Rosalind.

'Yes.'

'Wouldn't you like to work on a bigger estate, with better land?'

'Not really. I can see the potential here. Your father had ideas but his illness restricted how much he could do himself.'

'And your father and you believe you can make improvements?'

'We'll try, as a tribute to him.'

'That is very thoughtful of you. Papa would

have been touched,' Rosalind said.

'We'll do our best for him. And, of course, for you.'

She smiled to herself when she saw Clive was embarrassed by having made this last observation aloud. 'Thank you,' she murmured.

'And if we do go, you'll take good care of Pearl and Freya won't you?' asked Caitlin.

'Of course.' Clive smiled at her. 'Haven't I always?'

'Yes. I didn't mean you hadn't,' she added with embarrassment.

'Come on, Cat, we'd better be getting back,' Rosalind told her.

As the sisters turned away, Clive caught Rosalind's eyes. 'I'm glad you aren't going to America now,' he said.

She gave a little nod of her head in acceptance of his remark without making any verbal acknowledgement of it. After they were out of earshot, Caitlin said in a hushed tone, 'I think Clive has a crush on you. You'd be a fool to pass him up!'

Life gradually slipped back almost to the normal, though they were acutely aware of the yawning gulf left by John. Glenda found great comfort and support in her daughters' company and in the loyalty of her staff, especially that of the Martins who all worked hard to keep Pinmuir a successful estate. But Glenda realised that, sooner or later, she would face some difficult decisions about whether or not this place was the best one for a widow and her two unmarried daughters. And when she did, she must take these decisions alone.

A letter arrived from Gordon.

Dear Glenda,

Thank you for your correspondence and particularly the information about John's funeral. I am glad it was a fine, typical Highland day. I could picture it all so vividly. I remember such days when the three of us were together walking in the hills. Those were wonderful times.

Of course you are ever in my thoughts and you know if I can be of help to you, despite the distance that separates us, you only have to ask. Or if you wish to resume your plan to visit me here, maybe even consider making the move permanent, you will always be welcome.

Yours with brotherly affection,
Gordon

Glenda replied:

Dear Gordon,

I thank you for your offer of help. The distance between us is a hindrance but it is comforting to know that I can seek your advice if I can't cope or make a sound decision by myself. I fear nothing can be decided about the possibility of coming to America until after our mourning period is over.

The Martins have sought my reassurance about their future. I've told them to carry on in the way agreed with John. I was sure you'd approve of that, even though you relinquished any right in the estate when you emigrated.

I am still prepared to contemplate a move to

America in due course, subject to whatever the future may hold for Rosalind and Caitlin. As you know, the Martins are devoted to us and that makes things here a lot easier. We will allow ourselves a period of calm reflection before making any definite plans.

Ros and Cat send their love.

I hope you are well and that life in America continues to suit you.

Glenda sat for a moment with her thoughts drifting to her brother-in-law, wondering if Kirsty McLain was the reason he had left his beloved Highlands so suddenly.

Then, annoyed with herself for wasting time speculating about something that did not concern her, she picked up her pen and signed the letter with a decisive flourish.

4

Glenda gathered the four small stacks of papers from the top of her desk and secured them together. She breathed a sigh of relief that this, the fourth of the quarterly accounts she had supervised, had been completed. She was thankful that the first yearly report since John's death showed the estate was financially stable; previous accounts had showed some disturbing losses. Although she would have preferred to record a profit, she was satisfied. So long as things remained stable she could see their lives taking a satisfactory course. But dare she hope there would be no further upheaval? Could she really expect that? She placed the papers in a folder, secured it with a green ribbon and placed it in a drawer of the desk that she locked.

Believing she had earned a cup of chocolate, Glenda went to the bell-pull to summon the housemaid.

'It is a pleasant morning, Paula. I'll be on the veranda.'

'Yes, Ma'am.'

Glenda strolled outside and paused to enjoy her first glimpse of the sun. It was warm and comforting, seeming to draw a special beauty out of the green clad hills, displaying them to advantage against the majestic backcloth of the harsher slopes beyond.

She sighed as she sat down and drove away the sorrow that dogged her. The sense of loss she felt was almost overwhelming, but she knew that she could not afford to succumb to that feeling – John would not want her to, and she had her daughters and their young lives to consider.

Rosalind and Caitlin had gone riding as they did most mornings. She was pleased they had this interest; it gave them something on which to focus and enjoy in the fresh air, some comfort for the loss of their father. Her own loss was eased somewhat by the way her children were coping and their solicitude and support for her. So, in spite of the shock that had almost overwhelmed her, Glenda concentrated on living day by day.

She stirred her hot chocolate, took a sip, pursed

her lips in approval and picked up the novel she had started yesterday, believing it would refresh her mind after the figures she had been dealing with. She settled down to prove that *The Scarlet Shawl* by Richard Jefferies would do just that.

She had read four pages and drunk half her chocolate when she was disturbed by the sound of a galloping horse approaching the house. Alarmed, she rose from her chair and moved to the balustrade from which she could gain a better view of the rider.

Caitlin! Panic seized Glenda. Where was Rosalind? Seeing her mother, the girl veered Pearl away from the track to the stable yard and made for the front of the house, bringing the horse to an abrupt halt.

'Where's Rosalind?' Glenda asked, her eyes expressing concern.

'She's with the lady!' gasped Caitlin, trying to get her breath.

'Lady?' Glenda frowned in surprise.

'Yes! Yes!' snapped Caitlin, with marked irritation.

'Calm down, Caitlin! Who is she and what does she want?'

'I don't know who she is. She wouldn't tell us, but she asked to see you.'

'Me? Didn't she give a name?'

'No, she wouldn't, but she obviously knew you because she said she wanted to give you a surprise.'

'Surprise? Who would want to give me a surprise? Is Rosalind with her?'

'Yes. Ros signalled to me to ride ahead and tell

you that you are going to have a mysterious visitor.' Caitlin revelled in emphasising the word 'mysterious'. 'Who can it be, Mama?'

'How should I know?' Glenda responded. 'I haven't even seen her yet.'

'Someone bringing us lots of money perhaps.' Caitlin's eyes widened in anticipation.

'I shouldn't think so, and we are perfectly well provided for,' Glenda reproved her daughter.

'I wish they'd hurry up,' said Caitlin, steadying Pearl, who was scraping one hoof over the grass. The moments seemed to drag by, testing their patience. Then, 'Mama, they are here!' announced the girl.

Curiosity overtook Glenda. The riders were still a little way off. She shaded her eyes against the sun.

'Oh, my goodness!' she gasped. The surprise of what she saw drained her face of colour. The woman, riding sidesaddle, held herself with perfect poise, and her gentle touch on the reins had sufficient control to lead the grey to do her bidding. Glenda knew the new arrival would be revelling in the impression she made and enjoying showing off her eye-catching blue velvet riding habit; she suddenly felt drab in her mourning black. How she wished she could throw it off and meet the other woman on an equal footing. Then Glenda stiffened herself against such frivolity in a widow.

As she brought her horse to a halt in front of her mother, Rosalind said, 'Mama, Caitlin and I met this lady and she asked where she might find you. I requested her name but she would not give

36

it nor reveal why she wished to come here. I thought it best to accompany her and send Caitlin ahead to inform you that someone had requested to see you.'

Sensing her daughter was wondering if she had done the right thing, Glenda reassured her. 'You acted perfectly properly, Ros. I suspect the lady in question held back information in order to surprise me completely. And she has certainly done that. Rosalind, Caitlin ... meet your Aunt Fiona.'

The two young sisters looked aghast. '*Aunt Fiona?*'

They saw little resemblance to their mother, Fiona having fair hair and a pale complexion with pink cheeks rather than the freckles of their mother. Only their eyes and proud demeanour showed a family resemblance.

The stranger laughed as she slid from the saddle and settled her feet firmly on the ground. 'Yes, your mother's sister.' With her eyes fixed on Glenda, eager for a reaction, she held her arms wide. Glenda hesitated for a moment then, cautiously, stepped into her sister's embrace.

'Relax, Glen. I come on a mission of peace, with news that should please you,' Fiona whispered close to her ear. 'Let us have a private word and then I'll officially meet my nieces.'

Glenda gave an almost imperceptible nod and said to her daughters, 'Go and tell Mrs Martins that we have a surprise guest for lunch. And we would like another pot of chocolate now.'

The girls were moving off when they were halted by their aunt. 'Tell Mrs Martins, whoever she is, that I will have a whisky instead of the chocolate.'

They looked questioningly at their mother. 'Chocolate only!' Glenda commanded.

Rosalind turned to Caitlin. 'You tell Mrs Martins. I'll tell Clive to see to the horses.'

Once the girls were out of earshot, Glenda bristled and glared at her sister. 'I don't know why you are here but never, if you come again, countermand any order I give to my children. And certainly don't indulge yourself in drinking spirits or wines at this time of day.'

'I'm sorry,' muttered Fiona, though her apology carried little real regret. 'I thought they looked old enough...'

'Maybe they are but John and I set them an example about drinking. I won't have that undermined. They are approaching an age when they will be able to make their own judgements on these matters and I don't wish any of their decisions to be influenced by bad examples.' Glenda left a slight reproving pause then added, 'Now, Fiona, let us begin again. Why are you here? It must be over twenty years since we saw each other so I don't believe this is a social call. You wouldn't dare do that in case Father heard of it.'

'He won't hear of it because he can't – he's dead!' replied her sister crisply.

For a moment Glenda did not respond to the news in any way. Then she said calmly and precisely, her eyes never leaving her sister, 'Why should that interest me after what he did to me?'

'He was your father, after all.'

'True, but he destroyed any love I had for him

38

when he refused me permission to marry John. When I defied his order he cut me off completely, and none of you had the courage to disobey his ruling, which, as you all knew, was breaking my heart. None of you gave me any support. I was cast out because I went against his wishes and authority – I lost you all and any right to a share in the family fortune, part of which should have come to me on my marriage. Father changed everything between us by annulling that right. Did you even dare to challenge him about it?'

Fiona answered her. 'We tried, Glenda, we really did. But you know Father would brook no opposition to his authority.

'Once I became the only girl I bore the brunt of it, Roger helped me as best he could and, for a while, I blamed you, but I gradually realised if the same chance came my way I'd have done the same thing.'

Glenda recalled John as he took her away ashamed and penniless to become his wife. He often told her it was the best decision of his life when he made Pinmuir her home. Would she really ever leave it?

Paula appeared with the pot of chocolate and cups, placing the tray on the table that Glenda had been using and removing her mistress's dirty cup; a simple, everyday action that allowed the two sisters a moment in which to reflect.

'Would you like your drink here or inside?' asked Glenda.

Fiona gave a little shrug of her shoulders. 'Wherever you wish, but I would definitely like to see my nieces again.'

'You shall, but first tell me: why are you not in mourning for Father?'

'Black is so drab; it does nothing for me,' replied Fiona in an offended way. 'I'll follow convention when necessity demands it, but otherwise I'll please myself.' The shrug of her sister's shoulders told Glenda that was the end of the matter, so she asked, 'When is Father's funeral?'

'It is two months since he died. You missed it.'

'And no one thought to let me know?'

'It was mentioned, but Roger was adamant that Father would not want you there. Besides, would you have come? None of us thought so. Neither you nor John tried to make amends or get in touch with us, even when Mother's grandchildren were born. Estrangement works two ways, Glenda.'

She stared hard at her sister but decided there were things they would never agree on.

'So why are you here, Fiona?'

'I heard a rumour that you were leaving for America but had lost John. I heard no more until a couple of weeks ago when a question about you arose at a dinner party I was attending. I wasn't able to give an answer, but the query set me wondering.'

'And you thought you'd like to know the truth,' said Glenda, a chill in her voice.

'You'll remember I was always noted for my curiosity,' replied Fiona, twitching her lips with a trace of amusement.

'You always were like a dog with a bone: holding on for all it was worth. Well, I'll tell you – it's no secret. When John died we were preparing to

40

visit Gordon at his invitation, to sample life in America.'

'From what I remember of him, he was always seeing opportunity in unlikely places. What scheme was he filling John's head with this time?'

'John was always cautious; he would never be drawn into any unsound proposition,' snapped Glenda defensively.

'So this one was good enough to draw you into the unknown?'

'Don't insinuate that Gordon was seeking to profit from our move. You may not know this, or have dismissed the information in a fit of jealousy, but my brother-in-law has done well for himself. He owns a big ranch in Colorado and runs a large herd of fine cattle.'

'And this is what he used to tempt you all to America?'

'There was no temptation involved.'

'You were all going?'

'Only on a visit, to see if we liked what life there had to offer.'

'And I suppose that plan has been set aside after John's death?'

'Not completely. We may still consider it.'

Fiona's look of surprise could not disguise her interest. 'You would still go without John? Without the company of a man?'

'It would only be a visit. At first. We could review other options when we were there.'

There was silence for a few moments before Fiona announced: 'Well, if you do decide to move to America after a visit there I would be most interested in buying this estate and all its assets.'

Glenda gasped at this unexpected offer. She gave her sister a doubtful look.

Fiona picked up on her incredulity. 'You look as if you don't believe me?'

'Well ... how...'

'The offer is quite genuine. I have the means to honour it. You see, Father left me a sizeable fortune that includes a part of what you surrendered! Glenda, I'm a very rich woman.' Her sister gave a delighted chuckle. 'If you accept my offer, you'll get part of what could have been yours by right, if by a different route ... a smack in the face for Father after his treatment of you.'

'I'm not interested in that aspect of the offer,' countered Glenda sharply.

'But you are interested in selling?'

A door had opened unexpectedly and widened the possibilities for Glenda's future and those of her children. Who wouldn't be interested in such a proposition? She thought of John – what would he want her to do?

At that moment the terrace door opened and Rosalind and Caitlin came out.

'Hello, girls,' Fiona greeted them brightly. She caught the glance Glenda shot her and read in it a request not to divulge her offer. She gave her sister a reassuring nod.

The girls returned their aunt's greeting, then Rosalind added, 'As we came into the hall, Mrs Martins saw us and asked us to tell you Mrs Lynch will have lunch ready in five minutes.'

'Very good,' said Glenda. She rose from her chair and Fiona did likewise. 'I'll show you where you can refresh yourself,' Glenda told her sister.

42

Ten minutes later they were all enjoying vegetable soup, freshly made to the special recipe of the McKinleys' cook.

The two girls were soon at ease with their new-found aunt and Glenda marvelled at the way in which her sister, who had never had any children of her own, was totally at ease with them. Would it be a good idea for them to get to know Fiona better? Could it lead to reconciliation with the rest of the family? Glenda decided she could test the attitude towards her if she made the first tentative moves through her sister. But was that a good idea? Fiona had been the only one to make contact after their father's death. Could anything worthwhile be built on that or was she seeing light where there was very little? Were Fiona's pleasantries based solely on her desire to own what was currently her sister's? Glenda wanted to know but deemed the best way to find out was to extend the olive branch.

'Fiona, do you have to be back home today?' she asked tentatively as lunch was drawing to a close.

'No, I'm a free spirit. I come and go as I please. But I am careful not to overstay my welcome whomever I visit ... then I can visit again.'

'So why not stay with us for the night?'

Fiona turned to her nieces. 'Would you like that?'

'Yes, yes!' they both agreed, excitement in their voices and smiles.

'It isn't every day that we discover an aunt we did not know,' added Rosalind.

'Then we'll make it a memorable event. You'll

be able to show me around. I saw two men planting trees about half a mile along the road to the
house.'

'That would be Mr Martins and his son Clive,'
said Rosalind.

'We are doing some afforestation along that hillside,' said Glenda. 'Something Greg ... that is, Mr
Martins suggested a couple of months ago. The
Martins are a loyal family. Mrs Martins ... Jessie ...
is my very efficient housekeeper and amanuensis.'

Glenda felt herself thawing towards her sister
and sensed that the feeling was reciprocated. The
two of them took a walk in the afternoon during
which Fiona learned more about the Pinmuir
Estate.

'This may be an indelicate question but I have
to ask it. Have you ever thought of demolishing
the castle after what happened?' she asked.

'No. I haven't found it troubling even though
its destruction took my beloved John from me. In
some strange way, I find it a fitting memorial to
him and what he was doing here.'

'Do the girls talk to you about him?'

'Rosalind, yes. Caitlin very, very, rarely. You see,
she was the one who first saw the fire and raised
the alarm.'

'Is that why you still entertain thoughts of what
Gordon can offer – a life completely different
from the one you lead here, a new life that could
help erase the bad memories?'

'Yes, and to fulfil John's last dream, but I think
it wise to hang on to the estate meantime, just in
case I or the girls should wish to return.'

'Very sensible,' agreed Fiona. 'But may I ask,

should the time ever come that you wish to sell, will you give me first refusal? You could always retain the house – I shan't need that.'

Before Glenda could answer, the strains of music from a piano flowed through the house. Fiona looked at her sister. 'Who's playing?' she asked.

'It will be Cat,' replied Glenda. 'They both play but Cat has the most delicate touch and she loves Chopin.'

The sisters sat quietly listening, enjoying the impromptu recital that seemed to put the finishing touch to their reconciliation. But Glenda also wondered whether she had done the right thing in involving Fiona so closely in their lives.

5

Glenda did not sleep easily that night as her mind dwelt upon the many aspects of her life that had been thrown into question by the un-expected visit from her sister.

Twenty years since they had last met, Fiona seemed still to have the same effervescent person-ality, one that would kick over the traces if it suited her, though always cautiously and in such a way as to preserve her safety and status. She could be a rebel but was able to control the tendency if it meant her actions might rebound on her. Glenda sensed her sister was still a good judge of character from the way she'd spoken to Rosalind and Caitlin and elicited information without causing offence.

She always had an eye out for the main chance, though. Now Glenda wondered if Fiona's tacit support of her defiance of her father's objections to her marriage had been purely for her sister's own ends; after all, hadn't she admitted she had inherited part of what would have been Glenda's?

Unable to sleep she lay wondering how she would tell Rosalind and Caitlin of their aunt's proposal to buy the estate. What would they have to say to that? After all, it would affect their lives and, as young as they were, she knew she should listen. But that would have to wait until after Fiona had left. With that thought Glenda finally fell into a shallow sleep in the early hours of the morning.

She awoke with her soft feather bed encouraging her to enjoy its warmth a little longer, but the sunlight streaming in across her room called to her to enjoy the day out of doors. Since the previous year when she had reduced staff numbers, Glenda had done without a personal maid and so she dressed herself. Twenty minutes later, when she entered the dining room, she was surprised to find Fiona, Rosalind and Caitlin already enjoying breakfast.

'Good morning, Glenda,' Fiona greeted her brightly. 'I peeped out when I woke, saw it was a lovely morning and decided to go riding.'

'Aunt heard us moving, poked her head into our rooms and invited us to accompany her,' explained Caitlin, excitement gleaming in her eyes.

'Come with us, Mama,' put in Rosalind. 'It will do you good.'

It took Glenda only a moment to consider this.

46

'Thank you, I will. I'll have a quick breakfast, get changed and join you at the stables in forty minutes.'

'I'll go and tell Clive to have your horse ready,' said Rosalind. 'I've already told him about ours.'

Forty minutes later they were all taking charge of their horses while Clive oversaw the stable boys, to make sure everything was as it should be for the riders. He paid particular attention to adjusting Rosalind's stirrups to her liking.

'Comfortable, Miss?' he asked.

'Yes, thank you, Clive,' she answered with a smile.

'Where are we heading?' asked Fiona.

Glenda looked thoughtful.

'Can you still get to Eishken Loch?' Fiona queried.

'It's a long time since I've seen it,' Glenda replied.

Before she could add to that, Caitlin said, 'Ros has been there.'

Her revelation brought her a sharp glare of hostility from Rosalind, who hoped her sister's disclosure would pass unnoticed. It did not.

'I warned you of the dangers of the terrain around Eishken Loch and forbade you to go there alone,' said Glenda, coldly critical.

Before Rosalind could offer any explanation, Caitlin explained, 'Clive knew you had told her that, so Ros asked him to accompany her.'

Glenda raised an eyebrow but refrained from further comment. Her look was reprimand enough for Rosalind and her mother did not wish to spoil the day for them all, so when Caitlin said,

'May we go, Mama? I've never been?' Glenda could do nothing but agree.

'Very well, but don't stray. Follow the rest of us carefully and keep close. I remember there are some tricky stretches to negotiate.'

'If the way is as I remember it, your mother is right,' agreed Fiona.

'You've been before?' asked Caitlin, somewhat surprised.

Fiona gave a little laugh. 'Oh, yes, when we were younger. In a group that included your father.'

After securing their horses, they all walked to the lochside, found some flat rocks and sat down to chatter and enjoy the sunshine.

After a while, seeing her mother and aunt absorbed in conversation, Rosalind stood up and said, 'I'm going to have a walk. Want to come, Cat?'

She scrambled to her feet, saying, 'Yes, I want to see the ruined kirk.'

'Very well,' said Ros. 'Let's go. We will be back soon, Mama.'

'There's no rush,' said Glenda. 'Your aunt and I are quite happy here.'

She received a nod of approval from Fiona, who realised her sister had seized on this chance for them to have some private time together.

Once the girls were out of sight Glenda asked, 'Fiona, you want first refusal on the estate ... are you genuine about your offer to buy it at the price you quoted me last night?'

'Yes. That was a serious offer, should you decide to settle in America.'

'I must point out that the estate was barely paying its way before John's death, though there are signs that the Martins are turning things round again. I don't know how I would have managed to get through this last year without them. I would wish for reassurance about their continued employment here should I ever decide to sell to you.'

'You may have that. I am sure that something could be written into the articles of sale to guarantee their continued employment. And, as I said, if you do not wish to sever all connections with Pinmuir, you could always retain the house for a lesser sale price.'

'This is a very generous attitude you are taking.'

'If that is a trace of suspicion in your voice, you can eliminate it. I seek only to salve my conscience for what Father did to you.'

Glenda nodded thoughtfully then said, 'I will speak to Rosalind and Caitlin and let them know of your offer. This is their home and they should be consulted.'

'That suits me,' replied Fiona.

'If you are not tied to any other engagement, why not stay on for a few more days?' A teasing twinkle came to Glenda's eyes as they met Fiona's. 'It might give you time to change your mind.'

Fiona smiled as she said, 'I don't think I will even though staying on would give me the chance to get to know my delightful nieces better. I hope to see them again.' Then a more serious expression returned to her face. 'With what I'm offering you, you would be free to follow in John's dream.'

'You mean I could live it for him ... be reunited with Gordon?'

'Yes, and get away from the stark reminder of John's death that stands still in Pinmuir Loch.'

Glenda tightened her lips thoughtfully for a moment, gave a little shrug of her shoulders and said, 'We shall see.'

Fiona nodded. 'Think carefully. Any decision taken now will affect my nieces' future. Especially Rosalind, who, it seems to me has a particular interest in Clive.'

Glenda looked startled by this then gave a dismissive smile. 'They've been friends since childhood. Besides, Ros has always said she will marry a rich laird.'

They heard laughter and saw Ros and Caitlin coming back from the loch.

'Have you had a good time?' asked Fiona.

'Lovely,' replied Caitlin. 'The old kirk is so mysterious.'

'I'm glad you enjoyed it,' replied her mother. 'Now we must get back. Your aunt must be away.'

They lost no time in reaching the house where Ros asked, 'When do you want your horse, Aunt? I'll tell Clive to get him ready.'

'Thank you.' Fiona glanced towards her sister and gave a knowing smile that was answered by a shrug of the shoulders.

A few minutes later Clive appeared. 'Your horse is ready, Ma'am.'

'Thank you for looking after him, Clive.' Fiona could see how attractive he was, having an air about him that generated confidence and trust; Rosalind could do worse, she thought.

Fiona hugged her nieces. 'Look after your mother,' she said meaningfully.

'Please come again,' Caitlin requested.

'I shall.' Her aunt smiled at her.

'Yes, do,' said Rosalind.

As Fiona embraced her sister she said quietly, 'Thank you for having me. A bridge has been repaired; it has taken us a long time. Don't let us be parted again.'

'I won't,' replied Glenda, 'but what about the rest of the family?'

'I can't speak for them but I'll do my best to cauterise their minds of the bitterness Father instilled in them.'

'Thank you. It is good to have your friendship again,' Glenda conceded. With her daughters beside her she watched her sister ride away.

'Did you like your Aunt Fiona?' Glenda asked her girls.

'Yes,' said Rosalind. 'She's very agreeable.'

'I liked her too,' put in Caitlin. 'I wish she had stayed longer.'

'She might come again,' said Rosalind.

'I hope so,' added Caitlin with enthusiasm. 'Do you think she will, Mama?'

Glenda hesitated for a moment. Was this the right time to put Fiona's offer to them? Why not? Her sister required a decision, so why not seek the girls' thoughts?

'Let us stroll beside the water. I have something to ask you.'

'That sounds mysterious,' said Rosalind as she fell into step with her mother.

'Your aunt has offered to buy the Pinmuir Estate if we went to America and decided to stay.'

Caitlin raised an immediate objection. 'Even

51

the horses? She can't have Pearl! She can't!'

'It would give us a chance to carry out the plans your papa made for us all, and we'd have the help and support of your uncle so would not be alone.'

'What do you want to do, Mama?' asked Rosalind.

Glenda gave a little smile but said only, 'I want what is best for all of us.'

Ros quickly added, 'I'm sure Cat will agree with me that we want you to be happy in whatever we do.'

'That is very thoughtful of you both. If we decide to follow your father's dream, we need the decision to be unanimous.'

In the thoughtful silence that followed Glenda thought she saw doubt overcoming her younger daughter. 'What is troubling you, Caitlin?' she queried gently.

The girl bit her lip and then, with a sorrowful look in her eyes, said quietly, 'I don't want to leave Papa.'

'Oh, Cat, nor do I. But we must believe that, whatever we do, he will be watching over us.'

Cat pursed her lips thoughtfully, then gave a nod of acceptance. 'If that is so, I don't mind if we stay here or go to America.'

Glenda glanced questioningly at Rosalind. She saw that this daughter too was grappling with doubts. 'I love where we live. I love the mountains, the lochs, the wild countryside. Like Cat, I don't want to leave Papa but I can accept your explanation that he will be with us wherever we are, if we keep our memories of him strong and try to do what he would want us to do. I'm sure he'll keep us safe and guide our lives.'

'And what would you miss most if we left this life behind?'

'Lots, but along with the usual things it would be the Martins. They have become much closer to us since you included them in our household after Father died. I know they had been involved with the estate and our lives before that, but now they seem part of the family don't they? I'll miss them all, but if we are making a visit to America merely to test how we like it, then I am in favour of going for a limited period.'

'And I!' shouted Caitlin.

Rosalind watched for her mother's reaction.

Glenda nodded slowly and then smiled warmly as she said, 'We won't rush into a decision. There is no need. Besides, I still have nearly a year's mourning to observe.'

'Do you have to, Mama?' asked Caitlin. 'Ros and I are free from that now.'

'Yes, I must,' replied Glenda firmly. 'The time will pass quickly and it will give us the opportunity to consider the merits and demerits of a journey to America.'

6

'Off to sleep, young lady.' Glenda swept a rebellious strand of hair from her daughter's forehead. Cat returned the smile and nodded. Glenda gave a tug on the eiderdown; her heart was full as she straightened up and turned to the door. One year and one week since the fire had taken John from them. During the past seven days Ros and Cat had refrained from mentioning the tragedy, and Glenda knew they had done so for fear of upsetting her. Her throat tight with emotion, she turned the oil lamp lower and slipped quietly from the room, leaving the door slightly ajar.

A lamp burning at one end of the landing cast shadows along the dark red carpet, contesting the slow movement of those created by the pale moonlight shining through two mullioned windows. Glenda paused at the first one to look out at the moon coating the lawn and a stand of firs with a silver sheen. 'Oh, John,' she whispered, allowing a tear to run down her cheek as she recalled nights when they had needed no words to express how much they loved each other. She stood lost to the immediate world, minutes passing by, until a slight movement from the next room along the landing attracted her attention.

She stepped over to the door and pushed it open gently, at the same time asking, 'Are you awake, Ros?'

'Not in bed yet, Mama. Come in.'

Glenda stepped into the room, closing the door gently behind her.

'I was engrossed in this book,' said Rosalind.

'What is it this time?' asked Glenda, pleased that her eldest daughter's love of reading complemented her love of the outdoors.

'*Far From The Madding Crowd.*'

'Are you enjoying it?'

'Oh, yes,' replied Ros enthusiastically. 'Hardy is

54

such a good writer, I get totally engrossed in his characters and drawn into their story.'

'Good. I'm pleased you are enjoying it. I wish Cat was as interested in reading as you are.'

'It will come, Mama.'

'I hope you are right. Now, put the book down and come and look at the wonders of the night with me.'

They crossed the room together and each drew aside one of the velvet curtains, allowing moonlight to bathe the room with its bewitching glow. Gazing out into the garden Ros commented, 'I'm sure the fairies will dance for us tonight!'

'I wouldn't be surprised at...' Glenda's sentence was left unfinished, cut off by the unearthly scream that shattered the peace. Painful memories were instantly revived.

'Cat!' Ros was already heading for the door. Glenda was only a stride behind. They burst into Cat's room to find her standing stiffly near the window, her wide eyes drenched in terror, screams issuing from her lips.

'What is it?' Glenda asked, dropping to one knee beside her daughter.

Ros put her arm around her sister's shoulders, hoping the contact would reassure Cat.

Caitlin gulped and trembled. 'Mama...' Tears streamed down her face.

'What is it, love?' asked Glenda.

'The fire!'

Glenda automatically glanced out of the window. Puzzled, she said, 'There is no fire, Cat.'

'There is, there is!' Her voice rose higher with every word.

'No, there isn't,' added Rosalind firmly.

'There is! There is!' screamed Cat.

'All right, Cat.' Glenda hugged her daughter close. 'You've been dreaming, that's all. There is no fire, I promise you. Now calm down. Ros will get you a hot drink.' She glanced at her eldest daughter, who nodded, rose to her feet and hurried from the room.

Glenda smoothed Cat's hair as she held her, humming a gentle tune and hoping that the soothing sound would combat her distress.

'There is a fire, Mama,' insisted the girl. She raised her head to look into her mother's eyes. 'I saw it very clearly. I was trying to warn you but you...'

'Hush, hush. You were dreaming.'

The last three words were delivered with a firmness that made them lodge in Caitlin's mind. She gave a deep sigh.

Glenda seized her opportunity. 'Come and see.' She eased her daughter to her feet and, hand in hand, led Cat to the window. 'See, there is no fire.'

Cat shuddered. Bewildered, she said, 'But there was, Mama.'

'Yes, there was, but that was a year ago. For some reason it came to your mind while you were asleep and you thought it was real and happening now.'

Before Caitlin could comment further the door opened and Ros came in, carrying a tray with cups of chocolate on it.

'Here you are, this will help you sleep,' she said with conviction. She placed the tray on a table near Glenda for her mother to take charge. The chocolate and biscuits began their soothing effect and the scare that had woken Caitlin was not mentioned again.

Twenty minutes later she was warm in her bed once more and hardly responded to the gentle kiss Glenda placed on her forehead.

Ros stopped her mother when they left the room. 'I'll sit with her in case she wakes again. You get some sleep. And don't worry, I'll stay with her.'

'Thanks, Ros, but wake me if she is disturbed again.'

'I will. I don't suppose it will happen a second time.'

'I hope not. Strange that it has taken over a year for her to be disturbed by dreams of the fire. Let's hope there is no repetition.'

Two days later when Glenda said goodnight to Caitlin she was relieved that the day had ended with a warm smile from her daughter and no mention of any bad dreams haunting her. Cat seemed relaxed, chattering about the day's activities and especially their morning ride.

'Can we do it again tomorrow, Mama?'

'If the weather holds good,' replied Glenda.

'Then I'll ask God to make it so.'

Glenda kissed the now seventeen-year-old Caitlin on the forehead and said, as she had done so many times throughout her daughter's life, 'Sweet dreams.'

Glenda and Rosalind were both fast asleep when the grandfather clock in the hall struck midnight. Used to it, neither of them heard it, but they did hear the scream that followed the last stroke. They were awake immediately and knew that the scream had come from Cat. They scrambled from their beds, pulled robes around themselves and ran from their rooms. Neither of them spoke as they burst on to the landing. A few strides brought them into Cat's room where they found her standing, looking out of the window. Her wide-open mouth screamed in alarm at what she was seeing.

Glenda dropped to her knees beside her and put her arms around Cat in a protective way that she hoped would ward off whatever was alarming her. 'What is it?' she asked, trying to sound gentle and not cause any further alarm.

Cat pointed at the window. 'There! Someone's trying to take Papa away. I can't stop them!'

Ros looked out. 'There's no one here, Cat.'

'There is!' snapped the girl. 'Stop them! Please stop them!'

'I can't,' returned Ros. 'I would if I could but I can't even see them.'

'You've let them get away!'

'I couldn't see them.'

'Let's you and me look,' suggested Glenda. She eased Cat closer to the window. 'There you are. There is no one.'

Cat shuddered and tears rolled down her cheeks accompanied by great gulping sobs. Glenda held her tight and stroked her shoulders. As Ros left the room to fetch warm drinks she wondered what had caused the nightmare to erupt again. Would her sister ever escape the horror she had witnessed?

7

Rosalind, disturbed by the same noise, came half awake. For a week now she had heard the movement of padding feet coming restlessly from Caitlin's bedroom in the early hours of the morning. This latest disturbance had started a week after her sister's last nightmare, at a time when Rosalind and her mother had believed the horrors in Caitlin's mind had finally been conquered. Now Rosalind wondered if the sound of her sister walking the floor was a forerunner of a new cause for concern. Not wanting to spark off any untoward reaction, Rosalind lay still, listening to the movement in her sister's room; always the same rhythm, step after step, then a short pause that Rosalind judged to be in front of the window. Finally the pacing stopped, bringing silence to the house except for the creaks and night sounds that were familiar to them all.

When her mother did not speak about hearing Caitlin's footsteps, Rosalind decided to remain mute about them. But after another week, in which the pacing became more agitated and on two occasions she heard her sister whispering something in an argumentative tone, Ros decided to mention Cat's disturbed nights.

'Mama, I've finished,' said Caitlin, moving her breakfast plate away from her. 'May I be excused?'

'Are you riding?'

'Yes, Mama.'

'Are you going too, Ros?'

She was quick to seize her chance. 'I've not finished my breakfast yet. You go, Cat. Stay in sight of the house and I'll join you when I'm ready. Then we'll take a ride into the hills.'

Cat gave her a grin, eyes widening in anticipation of the pleasure ahead.

'Off you go then,' said Glenda, 'but wait around for your sister.'

'Ask Clive to saddle Freya, please,' called Rosalind as Caitlin ran from the room.

'I will,' called Cat. 'He'll like doing that.'

Ros automatically glanced at her mother and the eye contact caused her to flush.

'Do you like Clive?' Glenda asked.

Ros's colour deepened and she answered shyly, realising what her mother was implying, 'Yes, Mama. I don't meet many men my own age, and of course he's always so helpful.'

'So he should be,' replied Glenda. 'You've known him all your life. You've played together, grown up together. Your Aunt Fiona thought there might be more to it than that, but I said you were intent on marrying a rich laird.'

Rosalind said nothing but looked at her fingers resting on the table. Glenda knew it was best to say no more at this moment – the ice had been broken. She took a sip of her coffee and Ros did likewise.

As she placed her cup back on its saucer, Rosalind asked, 'Mama, have you heard Caitlin during the night recently?'

Glenda's expression immediately grew alarmed. 'No. Have you?'

'Yes, but I'm next door to her and you are further along the landing.'

Glenda nodded. 'Go on.'

Rosalind quickly told her about Cat's disturbed nights.

'You should have come to me before this,' her mother said.

'I didn't want to alarm you. The nightmares seemed to be over, but I thought you ought to know when this carried on for so long.'

'I'm glad you have.' Glenda pondered for a moment or two. 'I think I should consult Dr Hamley, merely as a precaution so that he will be forewarned if there are any further developments. You are going riding with Cat so I'll go to see Dr Hamley while you're out. Don't say where I have gone. Tell Cat I decided to take the opportunity to see Mr McBain about repairs to our boat. It's time we started using it again.'

Glenda usually enjoyed the ride to the small neighbouring village and, whenever she came this way, resolved to do it more often. Today, though, she barely observed her surroundings, too worried about Caitlin.

The doctor's house was set at the opposite end of the village so there was no evading the questioning gazes and whispering tongues of folk not bothering to hide their curiosity about the presence of this widow still in mourning black. Glenda kept her back straight and her eyes fixed firmly ahead; she did not wish to be drawn into

61

idle conversation.

'Soon be there, Bess,' she whispered to her horse.

A few minutes later they reached the last house on the street. Trees had been cleared from the hillside so as to build the doctor's residence. Dr Hamley had had the plot landscaped to a design drawn up by his wife, blending it in with the rising ground as if it was part of the mountain.

Glenda slid from the saddle, tied Bess to the nearby posts especially placed for patients visiting the doctor, brushed her skirt and then walked briskly to the front door. Her tug on the bell-pull was soon answered by the housekeeper, neatly attired in black skirt and white blouse, her hair pinned carefully at the crown of her head.

'Good day, Mrs McKinley,' she said brightly.

'Hello, Iris. I'd like to see the doctor, please.'

The housekeeper moved aside to allow Glenda to step in. After closing the front door, Iris opened one that revealed a comfortable waiting room.

'I'll let Dr Hamley know you are here, Ma'am. As you see, there are no other patients so I'm sure he will be with you in a few minutes.'

Within three he had joined her.

'Mrs McKinley.' The doctor, while speaking brightly, was making his private assessment of Glenda. He stood tall in his grey tweed suit, extending one hand to her. As she took it she felt his comforting touch. 'It is good to see you. I hope your visit is not of a serious nature,' he said.

'Thank you. I am very well,' she replied.

'Good, good. I am pleased you seem to have

got over your terrible ordeal but I do know how much you suffered, both bodily and mentally. You have done exceedingly well to recover so fast.' He indicated for her to sit down as he asked, 'What brings you here?'

'It isn't for myself, Doctor, it's about Caitlin.'

He raised his eyebrows to query this.

'She started having nightmares a while ago,' Glenda explained.

'She's the youngest girl?'

'Yes.'

'Are these nightmares related to anything specific?'

'The events of just over a year ago; the fire in particular.'

He nodded thoughtfully. 'Describe to me what happens. And does anything you know of bring them on?'

'I really don't know. She goes to bed quite happily and then wakes up screaming. It takes some time to calm her down.' Glenda went on to describe the nature of her daughter's nightmares and what she and Rosalind had to do to calm her. 'Yet the following morning she never mentions the terror she felt. It is as if she doesn't remember anything at all.'

'Has that continued to be the pattern?'

'Oh, no.' Glenda went on to describe how the disturbances had taken a different form recently.

When she had finished Dr Hamley looked thoughtful for a few minutes. Glenda remained silent and still while he reflected.

'Little is understood of the mind and its workings. I have read some of the new theories and drawn my own conclusions, whether right or wrong I do not know. I can only outline to you what my opinion is and from that offer a suggestion of what you can do ... no, no... I should say what you can try to do, because I cannot offer any guarantee that it will be the solution to your daughter's problem.' The doctor paused, his eyes fixed on her. Glenda knew he was weighing up how much hope he could give her that Caitlin's nightmares would stop.

Dr Hamley went on to explain what he thought might help Caitlin. 'Having a change of environment might be beneficial ... in fact, probably will be. Removing her from the scene of the trauma should help her mind adjust to other things, though when she returns home again I cannot say what her reaction might be. I'm sorry, Mrs McKinley, you will need to remain vigilant and then act in the best interests of your daughter.'

Glenda considered his words.

'Thank you, Doctor, you have been most helpful.'

'I don't know what I have done except to talk. I wonder if I even made sense?'

'I think you did. I will take what you have said into consideration and act upon it.'

'I hope you do, Mrs McKinley. You deserve to find peace again. And if you ... no, when you do ... I will rejoice with you.' He took her hand as she stood up. 'God go with you and with your family, Mrs McKinley. When you find the solution, let me know.'

'I certainly will, Doctor.'

'Better still, when you decide on the path you

will follow let me know and thereafter keep me informed of any progress you make – you could be doing a service to others.'

On the ride home, Glenda turned her thoughts to all the aspects of what the doctor had termed 'Caitlin's illness'. She pulled Bess to a sudden halt. Why hadn't her husband suggested the obvious remedy? 'John, why didn't you speak to me before now?' Glenda said aloud. She eased herself on the saddle and cast a glance at the gathering rain clouds. She patted her horse's neck. 'Come on, Bess, beat the rain home.'

The horse interpreted the urgency of her tone and in a matter of moments was stretched into a gallop along the track for Pinmuir House. Because the weather had taken a turn for the worse Glenda knew her daughters would have returned early from their ride.

The sound of a fast-approaching horse brought Clive and Rosalind hurrying from the stables.

'It's your mother. I'd better make myself scarce,' he commented.

'No need,' answered Rosalind quickly. 'I'm sure she suspects there's more than just friendship be-tween us. Stay. She'll need you to look after Bess.'

'If you say so. I've never seen her arrive home at this speed. Something must be wrong.'

'It can't be Caitlin, she's inside playing the piano,' Rosalind pointed out.

Anxious about what such haste might herald, they watched her approach.

Glenda pulled Bess to a halt that tore up the ground. Clive ran forward to grasp the bridle and counter the nervousness he detected in the animal.

'Thank you,' called Glenda.

Ros took her arm and ran with her into the house. Glenda changed out of her wet clothes and seated herself in a comfortable chair in the drawing room.

'I'll ask Mrs Martins for some tea,' said Caitlin, who had come to see what had caused the commotion.

As the door closed on her, Glenda straightened and took hold of Ros's arm. 'I might have a solution to stop these nightmares of your sister's.'

Ros was about to say something but was stopped when Glenda said, 'It concerns Cat so let's leave it until she comes back.'

'Mrs Martins has told Cook, who promised us some biscuits she has just made,' Caitlin informed them on her return.

'Now you can hear what I learned,' Glenda announced. She looked at Caitlin. 'I have been to see Dr Hamley about your nightmares.'

'Why, Mama? They've stopped,' Cat said, a touch of indignation in her tone.

'You haven't thrown them off completely, Cat. Ros has told me you wake every night and walk about your room, sometimes for as long as an hour.' She saw Cat frown and give her sister a hostile glance.

'Don't blame her for telling me. She did the right thing. In view of the more violent nightmares you had, I thought it wise to seek help from the doctor.'

Caitlin looked sullen. 'What did he tell you?'

she asked grumpily.

'He was very helpful even though he could not guarantee a full cure, telling me that in the medical profession little is known about the mind and how it works. He suggested possible avenues to go down. Of these there is one I think should help you.'

Glenda paused for a moment as if considering carefully what she should say next. 'He suggested we should move away from the area where the tragedy occurred since it acts as a constant and generates bad memories for you.'

'But I don't want to leave,' Cat objected.

'Nor do I,' Ros pointed out, 'but if it will do you good, I'll go.'

'I don't want to be done good to,' Cat snapped.

'Of course you do,' countered Glenda. 'Don't you see that the doctor's suggestion is an attempt to make you better? To rid you of these nightmares and let you lead a normal life? Besides, not long ago you were excited by the prospect of going to America. Please let us give it a try.'

Cat did not reply immediately but continued to look down at her hands, resting in her lap, then said, 'Will these fingers ever play a piano again?'

A little surprised by this question, Glenda seized on it. 'Of course they will. We'll come back here with you fully recovered and those keys will ring to joyful, triumphant notes.'

Cat looked thoughtful then said, 'All right,' though still a little reluctantly.

'Good, I'm sure you have made the right decision,' said Glenda enthusiastically. 'I think we should take up your father's plan to visit your uncle Gordon.'

'But didn't Father want to settle there?' asked Rosalind, seeing the possibility of the ties between her and Clive being torn apart. With a sudden jolt she realised the true extent of her feelings for him. It wasn't just flirting and friendship, but something much deeper. Would that last with her in America? What would a different life there bring?

Ros quickly turned her attention to her mother as Glenda said, 'Settling there was a possibility, certainly. It can remain a possibility. I have decided to keep the estate for now.'

Rosalind seemed satisfied by this. She and Caitlin exchanged quick glances of approval.

'Very well, Mama, if going to America honours Papa's plan for us and helps Cat, then we both agree.'

Glenda looked relieved, a new light in her eyes. 'I'm sure your decision is a wise one and will help all of us. And I promise, if anyone wishes to return home they can do so.'

8

Rosalind went to her room deep in thought. America? A new life? The enormity of her decision to accompany her mother and sister struck her anew. Her future was turned upside down when all she had wanted was for her life here in the Highlands to endure. Clive! The coming separation struck even harder now she had realised her love for him. She was overwhelmed by the prospect of telling him of the impending visit to America and the other changes it might bring about. But there was no point in putting it off; she didn't want him to hear it from anyone else first. As she crossed her room to the wardrobe she glanced out of the window. The rain was ceasing and the clouds were breaking, allowing the sky to brighten – could she take this as an omen for her future?

She slipped her feet into her black leather boots, quickly laced them up, shrugged on a green calf-length coat and left her head uncovered for Clive, who loved her flame-coloured hair. She tripped quickly down the stairs, out of the front door and over to the stables. Her hope of finding him there was answered.

'Clive, walk with me,' she said.

His surprise gave way to joy but he had to admit, 'I must finish this grooming first but it'll only be a few minutes. I'll see you in the usual place.'

'All right, don't be long.' Ros left the stable. Once outside she turned away from the house and took a familiar path on which she was soon out of sight of Pinmuir's buildings. She walked briskly to the top of a rise from which she headed into a small, secluded valley where a dilapidated stone building nestled close to the mountainside. A well-worn wooden door still hung from its iron hinges. It creaked when Rosalind pushed upon it. She smiled to herself, recalling the day she and Clive had found this place, and her recollections continued to the occasion when they had made it a little more comfortable with some hay... Here they had talked, laughed and shared dreams. Now she nervously settled to await his arrival.

Clive speeded up his grooming without neglecting it. Satisfied with the result, he grabbed the jacket he had thrown over the partition between two stalls. He swung it round his shoulders and slid his arms into the sleeves as he walked outside and took the path after Ros. Eager to be with her and discover what lay behind her request that was unusual for this time of day, he lengthened his stride.

Ros recognised his footsteps and was on her feet when he pushed the door open.

She crossed the stone floor quickly, flung her arms round his neck and kissed him fiercely on the mouth in a way she had never done before. His hands, broad from outdoor work, spanned her waist and held her tightly to him when she would have broken away. They swayed together, enjoying the sensations that coursed through them, until finally Clive pulled away a little and asked hoarsely, 'What did you want with me?'

A mischievous twinkle came into her eyes as she replied, 'Couldn't you tell?'

'I meant, why did you want to meet today?'

'It may not be what you want to hear,' she replied.

Alarm bells started to ring when he saw her serious expression. 'What is it, Ros?' he asked.

She tried to stop the tears from coming but failed. It was no good holding them back. The truth had to be told. 'I'm going to America.'

Clive's shock was total. 'No! No, Ros, you can't!'

She gave a little nod. 'I'm afraid it's the truth,

and I can't alter it.' She felt as if her dreams had been torn out of her heart and now lay scattered across her beloved mountains. There was no solace left for her.

'When? Why?' he cried.

'Mother has talked to Dr Hamley about Cat's troubled condition and he suggested a change of environment would help, so Mother thought it a good idea to visit Uncle Gordon as Father planned before he died.'

'But why do *you* have to go? *Why?*' he protested.

'I can't let Mother travel alone with Cat, who truly is not well. There might be problems. I would hate myself for not accompanying them if anything happened to either of them.' She hesitated, to let the words sink in. 'Please try and understand.'

Grim-faced, he sighed. 'I don't want to, but I do,' he said with obvious sadness. Clive felt his whole world was collapsing just when it had been beckoning him on to a joyous future. America! The name thrust insidiously into his mind. It settled there, mocking everything that had been born with the realisation that this beautiful girl had become much more to him than a childhood sweetheart.

Ros saw distress tearing him apart. Now was the time to show him what he really meant to her. She reached out, took his hand in hers and drew him to her. She kissed him. She felt his lips tremble and then they were both swept away by a passion they had never felt before. They lingered, not wanting to interrupt the sensations that flowed

71

through them and imprinted on their minds another kiss they would treasure forever.

'The memory of this will remain with me until we meet again,' he whispered close to her ear.

'As it will with me,' said Ros, then added, 'and there can be other things to remember.' She leaned back against his arms so she could look into his eyes and seek agreement.

She found it. Together they sank down upon the hay.

As they were leaving the house she pulled on his sleeve and smiled at him. 'Don't look so solemn, Clive. I'm not going yet. There is a lot more we can do first.'

'I suppose so, but you *are* going.'

'And I'll be coming back.'

'Who knows? America might change your mind,' he said doubtfully.

'My heart is with you, here in the mountains that I love as much as you do. I will carry our love in my heart, and America won't steal it from me. Let us make the most of our time together until I have to leave.'

Clive looked wistfully at Ros. 'I don't want you to go but I understand why it has to be.' He kissed her, not with the passion that had recently flared between them but with regret that they were having to part. They must keep alive the flame of the love they had kindled today.

They shared a silence as they started to stroll again until Ros said, 'I expect Mother will tell your parents of her decision, so please don't mention it to them before then.'

He met the pleading in her eyes. 'My lips are sealed,' he said.

Glenda's mouth tightened in an attempt to stop her head from buzzing with all the things that needed to be done before they left for America, but there was one thing that must be tackled first. She went to her desk picked up her pen and began to write:

Dear Gordon,

I will come straight to the point of this letter and the request it contains.

Since witnessing her father's death, Caitlin has been suffering from bad nightmares in various forms. I have consulted our doctor and he has suggested a change of environment might help. A move of that sort would take her away from daily reminders of the tragedy and hopefully let her see that life must go on without dwelling on the past. Colorado might provide the answer and I wondered if you would allow us to resume John's old plan? I intend merely a visit, though should life there suit us I do not rule out the prospect of settling there permanently.

If you have to refuse my request for any reason, please say so. I will understand.

I hope all is well with you.

With respect,

Your sister-in-law

Glenda signed the letter, read it one more time and, in the hope that the answer would be favourable, sealed it in an envelope that she had already addressed, thankful for the new speed with which letters to America travelled since the Transatlantic crossing time had been improved.

At lunch she told Ros and Cat what she had done, then added, 'Please don't tell anyone else what we intend until we have Uncle Gordon's agreement. Only then will I break the news to the Martins.'

'Oh, Mama, I've already told Clive,' Ros blurted out guiltily, but quickly added, 'I did ask him to keep it secret until you had told his family yourself.'

'I hope you didn't mention my nightmares,' said Cat.

'Of course I didn't,' replied Ros, crossing her fingers.

'I'm sure Clive is honourable enough to keep your secret,' Glenda told her. 'I suggest we live our normal lives until we hear from your uncle. It is no good making plans until we know with certainty whether he is still agreeable to our going to Colorado.'

They waited anxiously for his letter in reply. When it came three weeks later Glenda opened it in front of her two daughters.

Dear Glenda

Of course you must come. All of us must do our best to enable Cat to regain full health without any worries. Start making your arrangements to come as soon as possible. I will do the same here. When you have your sailing date and the name of the ship, please let me know so that I can be at the port to meet you.

Looking forward to seeing you again, Glenda, and to meeting my grown-up nieces.

Gordon

'Now we can really lay our plans,' she said as she put the letter aside. 'I will tell the Martins this evening, and tomorrow I will write to the shipping company.'

'Which one is it, Mama?' asked Caitlin.

'It was founded by Samuel Cunard and is commonly known as the Cunard Line. It is noted for its punctuality, comfort and safety so we'll be in good hands.'

'How long will we be at sea?' asked Cat.

'I think the crossing will take thirteen days from Liverpool to New York,' said Glenda, 'but I will get all the information when I write to Cunard's. We must decide on a date as soon as possible so I can let Uncle Gordon know the crossing details.'

Glenda, who had begun to have some doubts as to whether she was doing the right thing, was gratified by the reaction of her daughters. 'It's getting exciting now you are going to apply for berths,' said Caitlin.

'And we'll be able to see the mountains Uncle Gordon says are bigger than our Highlands, unless he's teasing us,' said Rosalind.

Glenda laughed. 'I don't think he's doing that, Ros, and I'm just as eager as you to see them.'

The following day Glenda made it her first job to write to the Cunard Line supplying possible sailing dates. Excitement took over at Pinmuir when, ten days later, she received word from the shipping company.

'Hurry, Mama,' urged Cat as her mother took up a letter opener to slit the envelope.

Ros watched intently, knowing that the letter's contents would announce the day she must part from Clive.

Glenda withdrew a sheet of paper and scanned it quickly. 'We sail from Liverpool on the twelfth of July in the *Malta*,' she announced, her voice trembling a little. 'I must write to your uncle immediately.'

Glenda grew anxious when July arrived with no further communication from her brother-in-law. Finally a brief note arrived that she was able to read to her daughters: 'I will meet you at the *Malta*'s berth in New York. Regards, Gordon.'

Brief though this was, Glenda found it reassuring.

Ros felt the void that had been deepening in her grow almost overwhelming.

The thought that Ros seemed to be moving out of his life worried Clive as the day of their parting drew nearer. With only their pledges to hold them together, could they stand the strain of parting?

Caitlin hid her worry. She was so tired of the long nights spent lying awake dreading the images that might penetrate her sleep if she dared to close her eyes. Her only hope lay in the doctor's suggestion, but would the unknown that lay ahead be enough to save her?

9

After the arrangements were made the enormity of her departure for America with her daughters had begun to weigh heavily on Glenda's shoulders. Leaving her beloved home for an uncertain future was so hard. If it hadn't been for the need to help Cat perhaps she would have changed her mind. She felt in need of some relaxation and good company away from Pinmuir.

She hurried to the stables and called, 'Clive!' sending his name echoing through the building.

'Ma'am,' he called back as he lowered a horse's hoof that he had been examining. He stepped out of a stall.

'Clive, have my horse ready in half an hour, please. Not side-saddle,' Glenda said briskly and hurried away.

As good as her word, she reappeared at precisely the time she had indicated.

'Bess is in good shape, Ma'am.'

Glenda patted the horse's neck. 'So you are,' she said lovingly.

Clive held the horse steady as Glenda swung into the saddle. Taking the reins, she brought the animal under her control. 'Clive, if you see my daughters, tell them I've gone to see their Aunt Fiona. They can expect me back when they see me.'

'Yes, Ma'am.'

He watched her ride away, admiring the way she handled the horse. Wondering where Rosalind might be, he picked up a stiff broom and started to clean out the stall just vacated by Bess.

Five minutes later Caitlin interrupted him. 'From my window I saw Mother leaving; did she say where she was going?'

'Yes. To your Aunt Fiona's.'

'Thanks,' said Cat. 'That gives me the opportunity to start packing my bags for America, without Mama breathing down my neck. If I see Ros I'll let her know and she can do the same.' Cat didn't wait for any comment from him.

As he watched her hurry off in the direction of the house, Clive thought now would be a good time. He cast his eyes across the valley where they had agreed pre-arranged signals that meant only one thing: I am here. There was no such signal yet.

He stamped his foot in frustration and brushed the ground harder. Nearly ten minutes later he saw the desired signal. He threw down the brush in its usual place, acknowledged Ros's sign to him and rushed from the building. There wasn't a moment to lose! She would be waiting at their secret rendezvous.

Ros was standing in the doorway when he came in sight.

Her heart beat faster with desire. She opened her arms wide. He did not slow his pace. She braced herself but allowed him to carry her down with him, tumbling into the hay.

When they finally lay quietly in an atmosphere of joy, Clive gave Ros the message from her mother and told her that her sister was packing. These messages sobered them both until Clive raised himself on one arm so he could look into her eyes.

'I love you, Ros, so very, very much.'

She reached up and touched his lips with her fingers. 'I will lock away those words in my heart until I return. I will think of them every day.' She kissed him. 'And you can do the same.'

'Your kiss and your love are already imprinted on my heart,' he whispered as he ran his fingers down her neck.

Their lips came together again and they allowed time to stand still.

Glenda slowed her horse to a walking pace when she caught her first glimpse of Fiona's house, which she remembered in her childhood days being a lodge for the gatekeeper. The front façade was much as Glenda recalled it: a central front door with sash windows to either side. There were three windows on the upper floor, set symmetrically. She could see an extension had been carefully matched to the existing building and now included a round tower of two storeys with a conical slate roof. The additions had, to Glenda's mind, improved the look of the building, which now had the air of being truly cared for.

'Who can this be?' muttered Fiona, and added a curse as she laid her book down on the small table beside her wing chair, placed to catch the light streaming in through the bow window. 'Just when I was enjoying *Barchester Towers*.' Hearing the horse's hoofs slowing, she added to her displeasure with an uncomplimentary, 'Front-door visitors too! I'm not expecting anyone who merits that!' She went to the window, peeping out so she would not be seen.

'Glenda!' Fiona's tone changed completely; the day had even brightened! Her sister's visit could only mean that they had set aside the bygones that had marred much of their lives. Once more she darted a glance out of the window. What was Glenda wearing? Fiona gave a short gasp. A beautifully cut dark green riding habit with split skirt... 'Oh, my goodness, she has been riding astride!' Not that Fiona was being critical. She knew Glenda had flouted a great many polite conventions after their father had disowned her. She strode out of the room and was at the top of the stairs just as her butler was opening the door to Glenda. 'Good day, Ma'am,' he said, politely curious.

'Mrs McKinley calling on Miss Copeland,' Glenda informed him.

'Thank you, Ma'am. I will see if...'

'No need, Charles,' called Fiona, running down the stairs.

The butler kept his surprise under control, as he replied, 'Yes, Ma'am.'

He stepped to one side to allow Glenda to enter the hall, saying, 'Please come in, Ma'am.' He closed the door behind her and moved quietly away to the rear of the house.

'Glenda! My dear, this is a pleasant surprise. It is so nice to see you again. You look ravishing. That colour suits you and the cut of that riding habit is just right for you. And not side-saddle, I note!'

Glenda laughed at her sister's enthusiasm. 'It's good to see you so approving.'

'Anything my little sister does I approve of, even shedding widow's weeds a little early.' Fiona linked arms with her. 'Come in. Sit down. Fancy a drink?'

'Chocolate, please.'

'Nothing stronger?'

'No, thank you.'

Fiona went to the bell-pull, calling over her shoulder, 'Make yourself at home.'

Glenda slipped out of her jacket and sank on to the settee, thankful to have thrown off the need to make any decisions for a while.

'You've made a few changes to the old lodge as I remember it,' she commented.

'Roger inherited Father's house and moved in with his family so I decided to move out, though he tried to get me to stay. He was seeing me as an amanuensis to his wife. Unpaid naturally.'

'Typical,' commented Glenda. 'He always tried to boss all of us about when we were children.'

'Well, I was not having that. I don't like his wife anyway, and his children are all snobs, really stuck up.'

The chocolate arrived and as the door closed behind the maid, Fiona, whilst filling two cups, said, 'I hope this visit will take us even further along the road to reconciliation and we can smooth the future ahead of us.'

'Me too,' returned Glenda. 'But it may have to wait awhile.'

Fiona looked startled. She paused with her cup halfway to her lips, then returned it slowly to her saucer and settled her eyes on her sister as she said, 'Why?'

'We are going to America!'

Fiona sat up, eyes wide with the desire to know more. She sat enthralled without interrupting Glenda's flow of information as she told of her consultation with the doctor and his recommendation for a change of environment for Caitlin.

'It could be just what Cat needs,' Fiona agreed.

'I hope so.'

'You are going to Gordon's then?'

'Yes. It was what John had planned and Gordon has welcomed us to take up his offer.'

'Your plans are thrilling,' said Fiona. 'Are you looking forward to your adventure?'

'I don't know that I am really,' said Glenda with a doubtful grimace.

'Oh, come on,' returned Fiona, disbelief edging her words.

'I'm doing it for Cat. I'd do anything to rid her of the horrors she witnessed. If this is what it takes then I'll do it.'

'What about Ros?'

'She is in agreement, for the sake of her sister.'

'But what about her relationship with Clive? Surely that is blossoming into something serious?'

'I think you are seeing more in that than there really is. I grant you that there is a stronger feeling than I first thought when you mentioned it to me, but Ros was all for helping Cat. If strongly in favour of coming back again!'

'And she's willing to risk a new life in America changing her mind?'

'Look, Fiona, both Ros and Cat are young women now and what they make of life is up to them.'

Seeing how firmly decided Glenda was about this, Fiona let her opinions about her nieces' future go unspoken. 'And you?' she said to her sister. 'What might the future hold for you when you see Gordon again?'

Glenda bristled. 'What are you implying?'

Fiona shrugged. 'You two were always so close as children.'

Glenda responded sharply, 'Yes, as children. Then I grew up and fell in love with John and married him. He will always remain the love of my life.'

Fiona gave a little smile. 'We'll see what America does for you all.' She changed the subject quickly before Glenda could make any retort. 'Have you given any further consideration to my offer to buy your estate, except for the house and the small parcel of land on which it stands?'

'Yes. The answer is still the same: I'm not selling anything. The house remains with the estate. As I have indicated before, we want somewhere any of us could live if we chose to return.'

Fiona nodded. 'I'm disappointed, but I understand. I will say it is a wise decision. If ever circumstances change and you decide to sell, I would still like first refusal.'

'You have it,' said Glenda firmly, rising from her chair to shake her sister's hand, a gesture that sealed an unwritten contract.

'Thank you,' said Fiona. 'You can be certain that I will keep my eye on the house and property.'

'I don't mind that but I will brook no interference with the Martins family whom I am putting in charge, as of now. You must understand that. They have supported me, with understanding and loyalty, through the loss of John. I am leaving them in full charge. They can make any decisions they see fit for the betterment of my property. I will draw up an agreement between them and me, officially signed. Copies for them, for me and for you.'

Fiona looked thoughtful then after a few minutes' consideration she agreed. With the situation settled, Glenda accepted her invitation to stay for lunch.

The sisters enjoyed their time together. It was obvious to both of them that they were trying to make up for their lost years.

When the time came for Glenda to leave Fiona said, 'As we have been talking, I have been considering your sailing date from Liverpool.'

'Yes, the twelfth of July.'

'I will accompany you there, to see you off. You will have no one else to do that, will you?'

'No. But there is no need for you...'

'I must do it. I cannot let you leave without someone being there to see you off,' Fiona interrupted. 'You can leave the organising of getting us all to Liverpool to me. I will arrange accommodation there for three nights, and an extra one for myself before I return here.'

'This is so generous of you but I shouldn't accept.'

'Of course you should,' Fiona insisted. 'Say no more. I will see to that side of your departure. You will be busy with all the other things you have to manage.'

'This is so very generous of you,' returned Glenda. 'It will be more than comforting to know that accommodation in Liverpool is taken care of. Your presence as we set sail will be a tremendous boost. I am sure Ros and Cat will appreciate your kindness too. May I ask that you book them a double room at the hotel in Liverpool? It is what I have done with the shipping company for our berths on the ship, just in case Caitlin can't settle.'

'Of course. It shall be done,' replied Fiona.

10

'Mama! Aunt Fiona's here!' Caitlin's cry rang through the house.

'I'm coming!' Glenda's acknowledgement was accompanied by a quicker footfall as she crossed the hall to meet her sister. She opened the front door and stepped outside, to see Fiona's head-groom driving the coach along the road that swept the side of the loch. Today it was ruffled by small waves that seemed to lap against the shore with a melancholy sound. The groom turned into the driveway and almost before he had brought the vehicle to a halt an under-groom had jumped down from his seat and was opening the door for the passenger. Fiona gave him a nod of thanks then turned to her sister whose arms were held out in welcome.

'The great day is here,' said Fiona as they embraced. She turned to Caitlin. 'Are you ready for this big adventure?'

'Yes, Aunt,' replied Cat. 'I am.'

Fiona was pleased to detect excitement in her niece's voice, and hoped this would be Cat's attitude to the whole expedition.

'Where's Rosalind?' she asked as they were walking into the house, leaving the servants to see to the luggage.

'Saying goodbye to Clive somewhere, I expect,' replied Cat.

'She'll join us soon, no doubt,' said Glenda, without further comment.

Clive's fingers were entwined with Rosalind's. Their sadness was mirrored in each other's eyes. 'I'm going to miss you terribly,' he said, a catch in his voice.

'And what am going to do without you?' she replied. 'I so wish I hadn't to go.'

'I know,' he said, 'but I suppose you must help Cat, and be there for your mother. You'll remain in my thoughts every day.'

'And you in mine.'

Their lips met in a kiss that expressed their feelings for each other. They lingered, not wanting to separate, not wanting to part and place thousands of miles between them.

Tears dampened their eyes as she went to the house, and he to the stables. They paused and looked back at each other. The temptation to cross the space that separated them was almost overwhelming. As the one who was leaving, Ros knew she had to be the one to stay strong. She blew Clive a kiss, turned away and disappeared into the house. He stood staring at the blank space where she had been and only became aware of his tears when he felt them streaming down his cheeks. He was startled by the emotion that burned through him. Grown men did not cry! He brushed away the tears and walked into the stables.

Ros dried her eyes and hurried to the room where she knew her mother, Caitlin and her aunt would be. Recognising there had been tears, Glenda gave her daughter a hug of understanding but made no comment, allowing the activity in the house to divert Ros's mind from the sadness of parting. First love was always hard.

As the servants carried the hand luggage to the coach, where the groom oversaw its packing, Jessie Martins said to her husband, 'I hope all those trunks that have already been sent are safely stored away in the ship's hold.' The groom also saw that the coach was being made as comfortable as possible for his passengers. Mrs Martins fussed over her employer's needs, making sure that nothing was left behind, while her husband helped with the luggage that had been packed for the journey.

Finally all was ready and farewells had to be made. Glenda looked across the loch and the rising mountains, and recalled John's love for them and for her. Caitlin wondered what might lie in store for her in a foreign land. Apprehension cast a shadow over her enthusiasm for the journey so that she had to force it from her mind and concentrate only on her hopes for a cure. Ros could hardly bear this parting from everything she held so dear but kept telling herself it might not be for too long. They all took their places in the coach.

The groom called to his team of two and flicked the reins. The carriage lurched forward. They were on their way. Good wishes were finally called and hands waved in goodbye.

Hurt stabbed at Rosalind's heart. Clive had not appeared for the final parting, to wave them off. She had seen the look of disapproval on his mother's face. Ros felt limp with disappointment. Her whole world was crumbling around her. Had the kisses of a few minutes ago meant nothing? She sat quiet through all the commotion. The roadway dipped along the lochside then turned towards the valley, striking up through rising terrain, but Rosalind was seeing none of it through her damp eyes.

'Ros, look! Look!' Cat's shout startled everyone. They sat up, staring in the direction she was pointing.

'Clive!' Ros's voice was joyful. 'He came.' Her expression was radiant with relief. 'And he's brought Freya to say goodbye!'

'And he has my Pearl,' enthused Caitlin, seeing her horse held on a long rein by Clive's side.

He matched the pace of his two horses to that of the coach and stayed there for half a mile before he signalled that he must return to Pinmuir. He gradually dropped behind, waving until the track turned a bend and the coach was lost to his sight, leaving him with one thought. I wonder when I will see Ros again ... if ever.

'That was a wonderful thought of Clive's bringing Freya and Pearl to say goodbye,' commented Glenda with an approving smile that lightened Ros's grieving heart.

The girls settled down for what to them would be a journey of discovery. Fiona knew a great deal about the way to Liverpool so was able to keep up their interest in what they were seeing. Glenda was glad she had at last chosen to make the passage to America; by doing something John had set his heart on, she felt closer to him.

The miles sped away; Fiona made sure no one felt bored or overwhelmed by the travelling. She had purposely split the journey into three stages with very good nightly accommodation to ease its rigours before their final destination, the Adelphi Hotel in Liverpool.

As they moved into the outskirts of the town Cat uttered her surprise. 'Mama, so many houses!'

Fiona smiled. 'You'll see many more before we reach our hotel, Cat. At the moment we are in one of the better parts of Liverpool.' They passed close to a development that was a maze of streets with rows of houses facing each other, making Cat ask where all the people were and what they did for a living.

'There is a part of this town that is known as Sailors' Town, so that tells you what some of them do,' answered her aunt.

'Will we see Sailors' Town?' asked Rosalind.

Fiona shook her head. 'No, your mother wouldn't thank me for taking you there; it's a rough and rowdy area. You'll maybe catch a glimpse of it when you embark the day after to-morrow. I don't know what quay we will be using but that information will be waiting for us at the hotel.'

Their coach came to a halt and they heard the groom asking for directions to the Adelphi. A moment after receiving these they were moving on and in five minutes were at their destination.

'It looks as though the hotel has had some work done recently,' commented Glenda. 'In fact there's outside work still awaiting completion.'

Their arrival had drawn a plethora of liveried hotel employees to greet them with offers of help. Luggage was brought inside, the coach and horses taken care of, registration completed efficiently, bell-boys were called and handed keys to the rooms the new arrivals would occupy. The head 'boy' supervised the care being given to the new guests and oversaw them being directed to their allocated rooms. He efficiently passed on any information he thought necessary and finally wished them an enjoyable stay.

Rosalind and Cat excitedly conducted a quick examination of their room and ran into their mother's and aunt's, giving them the seal of approval.

With the stage set, Glenda and Fiona joined in the excitement, pleased that both young women seemed to be taking pleasure in their future.

That continued the following day when the four of them perused Liverpool's shops, relaxed after tea, and finally retired after an exceptional evening meal that seemed to be especially for guests sailing for America the following afternoon.

At breakfast Fiona announced, 'I have asked reception to hire a cab to take us to the dock from which the *Malta* is sailing. You have to be on board by two for a three-thirty sailing.'

'Fiona, thank you for that. In fact, I cannot thank you enough for all the trouble you have taken in organising everything for the first stages of our journey.'

'Please don't. It is something I have enjoyed doing, and a gift from me to see you on your way. Remember me to Gordon. I hope you find him well and thriving.' She left a slight pause then added, 'All I ask is that you keep in touch regularly so that the bond we have reforged won't be broken again.'

'You have my promise,' Glenda assured her.

Although there had been some doubts in the McKinleys' minds when the visit to America had first been mooted, now the time for leaving England was close, excitement was beginning to replace any other feeling; even Ros was now looking forward to this new experience.

Glenda bustled Ros and Cat when she poked her head round their door. 'Get those bags shut, *now!* The porter will be here any moment to take them to the cab your aunt has hired. Then come down, ready to leave.'

An air of rising excitement was palpable as several other people assembled for the cabs they too had ordered. A few minutes later the commissionaire announced, 'Cab for the McKinley family!' Waiting bell-boys whisked their luggage away, leaving the family to follow them. Once outside they were in the hands of a cabbie, who quickly had them settled in their seats. A

91

moment's check satisfied him that they and their luggage were all ready to leave. He climbed on to his box, took the reins and called to his horse. The animal responded and was skilfully guided through the traffic that was almost filling the way to the docks. The hustle and bustle of central Liverpool changed to the more industrial aspect of a town thriving on its growing wealth.

'Mama, look at all those ships!' called Caitlin when she saw the docks seemingly choked with so many vessels; sailing vessels, some with sails furled, others with them ready to try and make their way among the throng needing to sail down the Mersey before heading for their destination. There was movement on all the quays as cargos were dealt with by beehives of men, whose shouts were barely recognisable in the general cacophony of sound that swept over the quays.

'It's unbelievable,' gasped Ros. 'How can they ever tell where things should be put?'

Fiona laughed. 'They find a way. Any ship held up here is losing its owners money, and time spent idle in port does not put wages in its crew's pockets.'

'How on earth do we find our ship?' asked an incredulous Glenda.

'The cabbie knows which quay is being used by the American packet ships,' Fiona reassured her.

A few minutes later they turned on to a quay alongside which was moored a three-masted ship, with its sails furled.

'Why the sails if we have a funnel?' asked Caitlin, a little indignant at the thought that they might use an old-fashioned method of locomotion – the wind.

'For added speed,' said Rosalind, 'The captain will order their use if he thinks the wind will help.'

The minutes ticked by relentlessly until the order 'Ten minutes to sailing time' rang through the ship.

Fiona said, 'Well, this is it,' as she turned to Rosalind and took her into her arms. 'I should have known you long ago, but from what I know of you now I am pleased you are my niece.'

'And that you are my aunt.'

'Take care of your mother and Cat.'

'I will.' A tear trickled down Ros's cheek. 'Give Clive my love.'

'It is as good as said,' replied Fiona. She turned to Cat and hugged her. 'Enjoy yourself, and get better.'

'I will, Aunt, I will.'

Glenda looked deep into Fiona's eyes. 'Look after yourself.'

'I will, and you do so too.'

Their eyes spoke so much to each other that they both knew there was no need for more, except an extra hug when the words 'All ashore that's going ashore' rang out. The ship became alive with people heading for the gangways as the crew supervised the exit. The quay once again became crowded, as did the rail of the ship. Shouts filled the air with orders for the crew competing with passengers' goodbyes.

When the powerful engines were engaged the ship began to move slowly away from the quay. The McKinleys waved vigorously and Fiona responded with equal zest.

Under the captain's supervision, the gap between ship and shore widened steadily. She took to the sea as if that was the place she needed to be, and, with each passing moment, as she ploughed steadily through the Atlantic waves, the time came nearer and nearer when she would dock in New York.

11

They stood watching the great city draw closer. 'Will Uncle Gordon be on the quay, Mama?' asked Caitlin when she saw the line of docking places assigned to passenger vessels.

'I would have thought so but maybe not; his last message to me was merely that he would meet us in New York.'

Caitlin's brow furrowed. 'We won't know where to go if he isn't here, and from what we have seen of all those buildings he will be difficult to find.'

Rosalind smiled at her sister's doubt. 'I think Uncle Gordon will be more considerate than to leave us high and dry, wondering where we are supposed to go.'

'I'm sure he would have left a message somewhere if he was not able to be here,' Glenda added to reassure Cat. 'Look, even from here, we can see lots of people gathering on the quays in use, especially the one we seem to be heading for. Let's keep a lookout for him.'

'But I don't remember him,' moaned Cat.

'Then I'll look out for him,' said Glenda, crossing her fingers behind her back and hoping that her brother-in-law had changed little in twenty years.

The quays drew nearer and nearer as the *Malta* was skilfully manoeuvred under the watchful eye of her captain, now dressed in the official Cunard uniform for the ship's arrival in her home port.

The number of people on the section of the quay allocated to those meeting passengers was growing all the time. They all strained to identify relatives and friends and readily gave way to their feelings when they saw anyone they recognised. The McKinleys felt lost in the welter of sound that sprang up from the passengers at the ship's rail.

Glenda's attention was caught by a hansom cab coming at speed on to the quay. It was turned and backed into a special area for cabs. A sense of relief flooded over Glenda when she recognised the passenger who sprang out of it. 'There he is, there he is!'

'Where, Mama?' Ros and Cat chorused together, excitement mounting in their voices.

'He's getting out of that cab that's just arrived.' Glenda's eyes fixed on the figure, now searching the people crowded along the ship's rail. Then an arm was raised.

'There he is,' said Glenda. 'The man who has removed his hat and is waving it at us.'

'Seen him!' called Ros.

'So have I,' added Cat.

Their waving became even more vigorous. They

95

were rewarded by an equally energetic response, accompanied by a broad smile.

Oh, John! The words stayed silent on Glenda's lips as her eyes fixed on the man whose presence was reviving so many memories for her of his brother.

The gangways were dropped. 'Mama, Mama, people are being allowed on board,' said Caitlin.

'Gordon's heading for our nearest gangway,' said Glenda. 'We had better stay here, he's seen where we are.' She tried to disguise the tremor of nervousness that accompanied her last observation but she need not have worried: each of her daughters was determined not to lose sight of him.

They watched Gordon stride up the gangway and slip past anyone who appeared to be blocking his way. When he reached the deck below them he disappeared from view momentarily only to step on to their deck a moment later and start towards them with a broad smile of welcome on his face.

'Gordon!'

'Glenda!' He took her in his arms and embraced her. 'It's so good to see you. After all these years, you bring a breath of Scotland to me.' He slackened his hold to turn to his nieces. 'And you two also. Ros, you were only a wee lass of three years when I left ... and Caitlin, the little babe, has already grown into a young lady.' He hugged them both and they held on to him a shade longer than was usually deemed polite, but nobody worried; they were all smiling happily, feeling that surely they were not strangers to each other even though, for many years, they had met only through the letters they exchanged.

'There is so much we have to say to each other, but that will all have to wait. We must get you settled into your hotel first.'

'I'll have to find one,' said Glenda.

'It is already taken care of,' Gordon assured her.

'How?' she asked.

'When you gave me the name of the ship I checked it out at the Cunard offices where I am known. They have always been very helpful. They made the hotel bookings for me. You have no need to worry about anything. It is all paid for; you are my guests for as long as you are in America. The bookings are for a week's stay. I thought you might like to find your land-legs again and see something of New York before we head West.' To lighten the moment and ease the tears he saw forming in Glenda's eyes, he added, as he turned to Ros and Cat, 'You'd like that, young ladies, wouldn't you?'

'Yes, please, Uncle Gordon,' replied Cat.

'This city looks so big,' commented Ros recalling the interest it had stirred in her as they approached the docks. 'It looks different from anything I've seen before.'

'It's a little bigger than Pinmuir,' said Gordon with a teasing smile. 'It's an interesting, vibrant place, but I'm always glad to get back to my ranch and see the mountains. I think you'll like those too, but for now we had better get you settled in your hotel.' He led the way down the gangway but on the quay diverted them away from the officials supervising the queue of passengers. He had a brief word with the officer in charge, who nodded and, with a smile, said to Glenda, 'I hope you and your daughters enjoy your stay in America. You are

97

in good hands with Mr McKinley.'

'Thank you,' replied Glenda. She was about to ask about their hand luggage when the officer raised his hand. 'Ma'am, if you are concerned about your luggage it has been taken care of. Hand luggage is in your cab and that which you sent on from England is already on its way to Mr McKinley's ranch. It should be delivered before you arrive.'

'Thank you,' replied Glenda, feeling dazed by what was happening to them and thankful she had someone here who was familiar with the city and its ways; many travellers on the boat weren't so lucky. As she started to look around Gordon appeared beside her. 'Just follow the man heading for us. He's the cabbie who will soon be depositing us at the Grand Union Hotel.'

'Good day, Ma'am,' the cabbie said, touching his forehead with his index finger, but it wasn't his politeness that caught Glenda's attention.

'You aren't from these parts,' she commented with a smile.

'No, Ma'am, I originated near Kelso. Do you know it?'

'Ah, the Scottish Borders. What brought you here?'

'Seeking a better life for my wife and four bairns. A lot of Scotsmen came over at that time.'

'Have you found it?'

'It was hard when we first came. There was some antagonism but we stuck it out and managed. I was lucky to find a job here as a cab driver, then our luck changed completely when Mr McKinley hired me by chance. A Scot helped a fellow Scot.

He set me up with this cab, recommended me to his friends and hires me himself whenever he is in New York. I've never looked back.'

'Good luck to you,' said Glenda.

'Don't forget, a week today, Sam,' Gordon reminded him.

'I'll be here on the dot,' he replied, and helped his passengers into his cab. In a matter of moments Sam was showing his expertise as he drove them through the crowded streets to the Grand Union Hotel.

As they progressed there were constant expressions of surprise and interest from Ros and Cat, and the same disbelief in what she was seeing from their mother.

'I never expected New York to be as big as it is,' she commented. 'Who runs it all?'

Gordon was pleased with their reactions for it meant their minds were diverted from the tragedy that he felt sure still shadowed their lives. With so many more new experiences that he knew were coming their way, he hoped the past could be left behind in the country across the sea.

Sam guided the carriage into a drive and through formal gardens that fronted a huge building of four storeys. Four rectangular towers, one on each corner, dominated the hotel's façade, one of which was a floor higher and topped by a rotunda. Eye-catching flags flew from each tower.

'What a wonderful building,' commented Rosalind, in awe of what was to be their home for nearly a week.

'It was constantly improved and enlarged by its owners, the Leland Brothers, who bought it in

99

1864 and changed its name five years later to the Grand Union Hotel.' Sam was slowing the cab down as they neared the front of the building.

'Well, that's enough of a history lesson for today,' said Gordon. 'Now it's time to enjoy yourselves.'

'I like hearing all these facts,' said Ros.

'With everything so different and ever-changing as you cross America, you'll hear plenty more while you are with me.'

'Ros loves reading,' explained Glenda, 'She has a good memory too. They both ride but it is Caitlin who is a natural in the saddle.'

Conversation faded as Sam brought his cab to a halt. He jumped down from his seat as several bell-boys hurried from the hotel to take charge of the newcomers' luggage.

Sam bade his passengers goodbye and left them in the care of the hotel where the receptionist greeted the new arrivals.

'Good day, Mr McKinley. It is swell to see you again and to have you and your relations staying with us.'

'The only place in New York for me,' he replied with a smile, and went on to introduce Glenda and his nieces.

'Your first time in America, I believe?' said the receptionist.

'It is.'

'Then I hope you enjoy your stay. I am sure Mr McKinley will be a wonderful host.' He dealt with the necessary registrations quickly then signalled to two bell-boys who were standing close by. 'Suite Three,' he said, handing over the necessary keys.

The bell-boys took charge of the luggage and

led the way to the lift.

Caitlin paused warily at the small box-like room she was to step into.

'Come along,' said Glenda. Cat frowned and gave a slight shake of her head.

'It's all right,' said Ros, gently persuasive.

Cat still hesitated but a quiet, 'Excuse me, Miss, may I help?' delivered politely by one of the bell-boys, dispelled Cat's wariness. She gave the boy a little shake of her head as she said, 'I'll be all right, thank you,' and took her mother's hand to step confidently into the lift.

Within a matter of moments the luggage was loaded and then, with everyone inside, a bell-boy closed the door.

It was the first time both girls had been in an elevator and they felt mixed emotions of fear and enjoyment.

Glenda smiled at them and silently mouthed the words, 'It is only a short ride.'

As if on cue a bell-boy set the lift in motion. Nervously Cat glanced at him. He gave her a warm smile and winked. Embarrassed, she blushed, but her attention had been diverted and she was unaware that the lift was coming to a stop. The door slid open. One bell-boy stepped out and assisted his passengers to their suite while the other saw to their luggage.

On stepping inside the room Glenda had to stifle a gasp; it wouldn't have been lady-like to reveal her surprise in front of a hotel employee. The room, part of a suite, was large, far bigger than she had expected. Two long sash windows flooded it with light and each had heavy velvet curtains held back by matching cords. Armchairs were placed near each window, leaving the centre of the room dominated by two sofas, with small tables conveniently placed at each end. Potted palms were placed to give maximum effect to the light oak woodwork and walls of subdued blue.

'Would Madam like me to show her the other rooms?' A query from the bell-boy refocused Glenda's mind.

'Yes, please.'

Rosalind and Caitlin, equally astonished, followed the bell-boy's tour. 'Your room, Ma'am.'

The large double bed looked so comfortable, Glenda want to flop on to it and stay there. A mahogany wardrobe with matching chest of drawers, and dressing table with mirrors and chair, did not diminish the feeling of space and yet there was everything to hand for a guest's comfort.

The bell-boy indicated a door. 'For the convenience of you all, Madam, and this other door leads into your daughters' bedroom.' The atmosphere became charged with excitement when Rosalind and Caitlin expressed their delight while simultaneously trying to choose the bed they particularly wanted. The room was furnished similarly to their mother's except that it had twin beds.

'If there is anything you need during your stay there is a bell-pull beside each bed and a porter on duty all night. A maid will be with you shortly to help you unpack.'

Their luggage was brought in and they were left to express their delight at the luxury all around them.

They had arranged to meet Gordon in the

Palm Court in an hour and were pleased to see he was already seated at a table. Ros and Cat were fascinated by the foreign plants that stood by so elegantly, like soldiers keeping them safe.

'I have ordered tea for you. It was the first thing I missed when I came to America, but now I can't be without coffee. Is everything to your liking?' Gordon enquired.

'It's wonderful,' replied Glenda, 'and your nieces are overwhelmed and excited about the luxury of everything, as am I. We didn't expect this sort of reception. You shouldn't have gone to so much trouble, and in such a fine hotel.'

'You three deserve it and I am more than satisfied that you like it. It is so wonderful to have you here. Now I thought you might like to ask me about the city before you see it tomorrow, and of course anything else you would like to know.'

They asked him about the hotel that seemed like a palace to them, what they could and couldn't do, and Ros wanted to know more about the city and its inhabitants. After they finished their warm and very welcome drinks, Gordon said, 'Just get yourselves settled here for now. We'll talk more after our meal this evening, if that suits you?'

'Of course it does. Whatever you think best; we are in your hands.'

'Good. I'll call for you at six.'

'Thank you so much, Gordon. I just wish John was with us.'

'So do I,' he replied, with feeling in his eyes. 'It was one of my dreams that we would be together here, and I was thrilled when he said you would all come and see what you thought to my proposal.'

Glenda, giving a wistful smile, said, 'But now we must make the best of what life has brought us.'

Gordon nodded. 'You always were the wise one.'

She gave a little shake of her head but made no comment.

They rose from the table and Gordon, indicating where the elevator was, said, 'I will leave you in peace.' He allowed them to step inside and, before the bell-boy pressed the button for their floor, said, 'Remember, I'll call for you at six.' Then he was gone and the door closed.

For a few moments Glenda stood deep in thought. Gordon was so like John in his looks but she wondered how much life in America had changed him. Gordon certainly hadn't left any-thing of their arrival to chance she thought, slightly irritated by his efficiency, confidence and display of pride in the way he was known in this city. She remembered him as a carefree boy that just let life take its chances; something her quiet John had still managed to do alongside his estate work.

12

'My three young ladies look very glamorous this evening,' commented Gordon as soon as he set eyes on them.

'I don't know about that,' replied Glenda, 'but

we thank you all the same.'

Ros and Cat echoed the remark and Ros added, 'We only had our travelling clothes, the others are in our trunks somewhere in America.'

'Heading for Colorado,' put in Gordon, and then added, 'I hope!' He screwed up his face thoughtfully. 'Maybe we'd better go shopping to-morrow.'

Cat's face lit up with surprise and hope. 'That would be thrilling,' she commented.

'It would be good to buy some new clothes,' Glenda agreed, 'but let us enjoy this evening first.'

'Are we ready to go down now?' Gordon queried.

They all nodded, and, when they reached the sweeping curve of the wide staircase, Glenda gratefully took his proffered arm. Ros and Cat followed.

A young footman met them at the bottom of the stairs.

'Good evening, Mr McKinley. It is a pleasure to have you with us again and to meet your lovely ladies. I see you are dining with us this evening. Would you like to go to your table now?'

Gordon cast a questioning glance at Glenda.

'Yes, please,' was her reply.

The footman escorted them to the restaurant where a waiter, immaculately dressed in white shirt and black suit, took over. Once again Glenda noted the respect the staff showed to Gordon at all times. 'You seem well known here and the staff are quick to respond to your requests.'

He smiled. 'I have always maintained that people

in service are better on your side; they are a wealth of knowledge about who is who and what is going on. Treat them kindly, but keep them in their place without appearing to do so, and you'll always be well thought of. I put that into practice from my very first step on to American soil and it has paid dividends ever since. It has helped me to move up in the world in all sorts of ways and enabled me to occupy the place I have today. But you don't want to hear about me.'

'I do, but perhaps not just now.' Glenda cast her eyes in the direction of her daughters, which Gordon interpreted as meaning she wanted to speak to him on her own. He met her gaze and gave a little nod to show that he had understood.

At that moment the head waiter came forward and showed the same pleasure that other members of staff had expressed on seeing Gordon again. He presented the four of them with menus.

Ros and Cat were flattered by all the attention. Finally they had all made their choices, which, as the evening wore on, proved to be more than enjoyable. Gordon used the time to get to know about his nieces and was delighted that they were of a lively disposition, with interesting and enquiring minds. Remembering what Glenda had told him, he talked about riding, reading, and had his own questions ready to elicit further information on their interests.

As they left the dining room, Ros said to Caitlin, 'Let's you and I go to our room and have a game of cards, leaving Mama and Uncle Gordon to have a chat. They must have such a lot to talk about.'

'Let's,' Cat agreed.

When they had gone Glenda and Gordon settled down in comfortable chairs in the lounge and she said, 'I'll come straight to the point while we are alone.' He made no comment. 'I am concerned about the cost of our visit,' she went on. 'Everything so far has been paid for by you. This cannot go on.'

He held up his hand to stop her. 'Glenda, don't scold me for something I want to do. When you indicated that you wanted to come, I was delighted. It gave me a chance to do something for you and hopefully to help find a cure for Caitlin's problems. I want to be part of that. In the short time I've known her I can see she has a wonderful personality. So has Ros. I would like to be part of their lives even if you are not going to make a permanent home here. I don't want you to have any financial worries. Let me start by paying for this visit, no strings attached.'

Glenda sat assessing this proposal.

'I am more than grateful to you, Gordon,' she said finally. 'We all are; I appreciate what you are doing for us, but if we are to be here for any length of time we need to be able to pay our way in some form or other. At the very least let me look after your house and do some cooking. In the last year Jessie Martins has taught me a great deal. My daughters would like to help, too, and it would give us the opportunity to weigh up our futures.'

Gordon looked slightly uneasy as he said, 'You have every right to be cautious. You are a very astute woman, John would be proud of you. Now, let us have a glass of champagne and drink to the future.'

They raised their glasses in the hope and belief that all would be well.

Caitlin stared at her cards with a vacant expression and yawned.

'I think it's time you went to bed,' said Ros. 'Shopping tomorrow is likely be a long and tiring day.'

Cat nodded and wearily answered, 'Are you going to bed too?'

'Shortly. First I want to write a letter to Clive so that it will leave tomorrow. Goodness knows when I'll have an opportunity to post another once we leave New York.'

Cat nodded and mumbled, 'Don't wake me up when you come.'

'I won't. Sleep well.'

'Say goodnight to Mama and Uncle Gordon for me.'

'I will.'

Ros settled at the card table and wrote:

Dearest Clive

I am writing to you before we move on from New York, which we will be doing in six days' time. It seems strange to be writing to you from this distance. The whole journey has been a wonderful experience but my heart ached because I was leaving you behind. The sea voyage was invigorating and it was a blessing that none of us were seasick, though some of the other passengers were very poorly.

Thank goodness Uncle Gordon was here to meet us, knowing exactly where we would be; he had a cab organised to take us to ... the largest hotel with the finest reputation in New York! It is all very interesting, though I am looking forward to moving on. I want to be where I can see the open views and big skies they talk about. I want to leave all the city people behind; they jostle and bump into one another because they seem always to be in a hurry.

I am looking forward to seeing Uncle Gordon's ranch in Colorado. He won't tell us anything about it. I think he wants it to be a surprise. It is hard to imagine we will be travelling for at least four days before we get there and will be still in the same country!

Mama is in good spirits and Cat is coping well. I think the new experiences are keeping her mind occupied. On the ship she had restless nights but no real nightmares. Who knows? Perhaps we will return sooner than we thought. Oh, how good it will feel when we are together again.

I am missing you and still picture you with Freya, watching us leave. It brings tears to my eyes, and will be with me every day until I see you again.

Take care of yourself and look after Pinmuir and Scotland for me.

My love as always,

Ros

The following morning a sharp knocking on the door woke Ros and Cat at the same time.

'Who on earth...?' Ros muttered as she pushed the bedclothes back. Then she saw the time. 'Oh, my goodness!'

'Are you two up?' a voice asked from outside the door.

'Yes, Mama,' Ros responded.

'Breakfast's in forty minutes, don't be late.'

Footsteps faded away down the corridor.

'Come on, Cat,' Rosalind urged. 'It's dress-buying day!' Her sister swung out of bed. 'Can't keep Uncle Gordon waiting.'

They prepared themselves for the outing whilst speculating what attire they might look for. Ros kept her eye on the clock and, within a few minutes of the time appointed by their mother, they headed downstairs and into the dining room, where some of the hotel guests were already eating their breakfast.

The sisters saw Gordon coming towards them to take them to a table where their mother was already seated. Greetings were exchanged.

'Did you both sleep well? Were you comfortable, Cat?' asked Glenda, but glanced at Ros who quickly nodded and said, 'Yes, Mama. I woke only once and Caitlin was sound asleep.'

Cat put in, 'No nightmares last night, Mama,' clearly in a jovial mood, ready for their day out.

'I have been in touch with Sam, and hired him to be with you until you have finished shopping for your dresses and anything else you may want,' said Gordon.

'Won't you be with us?' asked Glenda, a touch of concern in her tone.

'No. I have some business to see to before we leave for Colorado. Sam is hired for the day, so make the most of him for your shopping; he knows where I have accounts. He'll drop you here at the hotel when you finish and I will see you for our evening meal at the usual time. I shall expect the three of you to be looking glamorous in your new purchases. Have a happy shopping day.' Smiling, he rose from the table and bade them good day.

'I think I've nearly had enough of New York City,' said Ros as she placed her purchases on the floor and flopped on to the bed with a deep, contented sigh.

'So have I,' agreed Cat, kicking off her shoes and rubbing her feet. 'New York pavements are a bit too hard. Thank goodness for Sam driving us the longer distances.'

'I have enjoyed it but the buildings seem to be crowding in on you. I like more space,' said Ros. 'I'm looking forward to seeing the wide open prairies.'

'Hopefully from a horse.'

'Definitely.'

'And giving it its head.'

'The thrum of its hoofs! With wider spaces than we had in Scotland, we will get a really good gallop.'

'We'll have to wait a while for that. Uncle Gordon has planned some sightseeing.'

'Five days to get there, if we don't run into any trouble.' Cat raised her eyes to the ceiling. 'I just want to be there now!'

'The sooner the better.' Ros's words faded away. Cat covered her sister with a blanket, seeing she was already asleep.

Caitlin stirred. Her eyes flickered and then closed

again. She could make no sense of anything except that she was lying in a comfortable bed – but where? For a few moments she tried to answer her own question. She was getting nowhere with the answer when suddenly her mind cleared. Cat sat up, caught sight of the clock and quickly rolled out of bed. She shook her sister, still sound asleep, and called, 'Ros! Ros! Get up!'

She woke in an instant and was thrown into panic. Was her sister having a nightmare? She flung her blanket aside and was on her feet before she spoke. 'Cat, are you all right? What's the matter?'

'Nothing. But it's time you and I were dressing for dinner or we'll be late.'

Cat quickly dressed and was soon priming her hair in front of the dressing-table mirror. Ros cast off her clothes but had difficulty deciding on which new outfit to wear. 'That one,' said Cat impatiently. 'Now hurry.'

Ros was just pinching her cheeks for the last time, to give her skin a healthy glow, when there was a tap on the door. Cat hurried to open it.

'Come in, Mama.'

'Are you two ready?'

'Nearly,' called Ros. She swung round on her stool. 'There. It's been a rush but will I do?'

Glenda gave them both a critical glance then said, 'Stand together.'

As they shuffled towards each other, they smoothed their new clothes to make a few last adjustments.

'You both look wonderful. The ideal choices for wearing both here and at the ranch,' Glenda told them. 'Your skirts fit perfectly. The green suits your complexion, Cat. And you, Ros, look very engaging in that deep blue.' She smiled at her eldest daughter and said, 'I wish Clive could see you now!' Her pride in them both was obvious.

They were flattered by their mother's compliments. 'You are too kind, Mama,' said Ros. 'That scarlet blouse of yours is sure to attract attention.'

'And I love the beautiful red shoes peeking out from underneath your skirt,' said Cat. 'You outshine us, and I'm sure Uncle Gordon will think the same.'

When he saw them coming down the stairs he was briefly struck silent.

'I shall be the envy of every man dining here this evening,' he said finally. 'I am privileged and delighted to be your escort. You have certainly had a good day, choosing these flattering outfits. You'll have to tell me all about it as we enjoy our meal.' He escorted them into the dining room where some of the other guests turned their heads in admiration.

'No one can match you,' Gordon whispered to Glenda as he sat down beside her.

Once Cat had nearly finished her main course she asked, 'When and where do we eat on our way to Colorado?'

'On the train,' replied Gordon. 'We have a Pullman compartment. Let's save the details as a surprise for you.'

'But we are going soon?' asked Cat.

'Yes,' replied her mother. 'And Uncle insisted we had the best means of travelling so that we can enjoy everything about our journey into a country we don't know.'

'It sounds so exciting,' said Cat, with an enthusiasm that Glenda saw as a blessing. She hoped her daughter's recovery continued.

But first they had New York City to explore.

The McKinley women were not used to sightseeing and though they were over-awed by the new Statue of Liberty, the mansions of the Robber Barons and a night at the ballet, it was the open-topped carriage drive through Central Park that they enjoyed the most, an anomaly in the centre of such a bustling city. It was good to feel the breeze freely blowing on their faces again.

After five days they found they had grown tired of the jostling people with their long drawling accents and, sometimes, uncouth ways. It was hard to get used to city life as well as the change in culture. Colorado beckoned.

13

'Just a few instructions before we set out on our adventure,' said Glenda when they were nearing the end of their breakfast a few days later. A glance from her told Gordon to take over.

He cleared his throat. 'Today will be the start of a long journey for you – in the region of two thousand miles, which will take maybe four days on the train. There will be plenty to keep you interested, though the prairies can become monotonous so have something to do with you, a book

114

to read or cards to play. However, I think you will find plenty to hold your attention. As I told you, we will be travelling in a special Pullman carriage that I have booked. It will be exclusively ours, to sit in comfortably and take all our meals, served by attendants employed by the rail company. It will be just as if we are in a first-class hotel. Enjoy it.'

'Will other people be travelling in Pullman coaches?' asked Ros.

'Yes. At what grade depends on how much they pay. Other passengers travelling first- or second-class use a separate part of the train. They are not allowed to enter the Pullman coaches, though those travelling like us have the freedom of the whole train. However, I will say it would be best to keep to our carriage. The rest of the passengers will be a very mixed lot. There will be people from all walks of life: salesmen coming to peddle their goods in the rough, raw West, cowboys looking for employment, professional gamblers, wives going home after visiting relatives in the east, soldiers returning to their posts, miners and their families hoping to change their circumstances. There will be a whole galaxy of the people who make up this expanding country.'

'You make it sound so colourful,' said Rosalind.

'It is. America has unlimited potential that makes it truly exciting. You're going to love it.'

The pointers on the hall clock were nearing one-thirty when the McKinley party assembled in the hotel's ornate entrance hall.

'Everyone happy?' Gordon asked breezily.

115

Responding to his mood, the women chorused, 'Yes.'

Sam appeared in the doorway and started to gather their luggage. Two bell-boys hurried to take the rest of their belongings to the cab. With tips in their hands they bade the party goodbye. After checking that his passengers were comfortably seated Sam climbed on to his seat, took the reins and, with a call familiar to his horse, sent it on its way. As they approached the station the road became more and more crowded with passengers due to take the same train as the McKinleys.

'Coach three,' called an official, when the driver asked which coach his party was to take.

Sam drove alongside the train until he reached Pullman car three.

Seeing the cab slowing, a smartly dressed steward instantly stepped out to open the cab door for them. He assisted the new arrivals to the ground and waited while they made their farewells to the driver.

'According to the information I have been given, Mr McKinley, you have exclusive use of the whole of this carriage, and we are all ready to serve you at any time,' the steward said.

'Thank you,' replied Gordon, while Glenda and her daughters offered friendly smiles.

'I will let you get settled in,' said the porter, going to the door. 'Make yourselves comfortable and enjoy your time with us.'

'I'll leave you to it, if you don't mind,' said Gordon to the women. 'I'd like to get a couple of business letters off before we leave. I'll ask our steward to give you a conducted tour of the carriage. I'll be in the next compartment and will rejoin you shortly.'

'Very well,' Glenda told him.

Once the door closed behind Gordon, Glenda, Ros and Cat let their excitement spill over.

'This is simply out of this world!' Once again Glenda wondered how her husband's brother had made this amount of money; but he had always been more ambitious than John, she thought.

'This is so unexpected – it's magical! How can I describe it to Clive?' said Ros.

Cat flopped into one of the four armchairs arranged so they did not impede passage through the car or the use of the window seats. 'Ooh, that's so comfortable,' she said as she reclined against the back of the chair.

'So is this,' said Ros, who was trying one of the window seats. 'Imagine sitting here and watching miles and miles of countryside go by.'

'No expense has been spared to make these cars special,' commented Glenda as she glanced around and stretched her hand towards the wall. 'These mirrors must be French plate and they shine as if new.'

'Excuse me but you are quite right, Ma'am,' said the steward as he came back into the compartment. 'I just caught your comment. The three chandeliers will interest you too. All of these delicately coloured fittings are especially created for the particular carriage in which they hang. The furniture and its coverings have all been made to Pullman exclusive designs. Some of the individual seats are swivelled so passengers can swing round to see the view on both sides of the train.' He

117

demonstrated and smiled at the expressions of amazement on their faces. 'The next car, towards the front, is similar to this, and beyond that is the kitchen car. Your meals will be served in this, your exclusive carriage.'

'What about other passengers, where do they eat?' asked Glenda.

'First- and second-class passengers can take their meals in what we call hotel cars, very similar to dining in a static hotel. Those travelling in the lower-class accommodation take meals as they can, buying something from the refreshment services at stations where we stop; that can be a bit of a rush and a crush though.'

'I can imagine that, having seen so many people gathering on the platform,' commented Glenda.

The steward continued his conducted tour, allowing his passengers to pause to examine the black walnut woodwork and luxurious red Brussels carpeting.

As he brought his tour to a close in the main room of their car Glenda pointed out, 'You haven't shown us our sleeping accommodation.'

'No, Ma'am.' The man gave a little smile. 'It is here, in the full length of your car.'

The three McKinleys looked a little confused.

'Here, Ma'am.' The steward reached up to the carriage panelling and pulled down a section to reveal what could be used as a bed.

'How ingenious,' commented Ros.

'Wonderful!' said Cat, but at the same time wondered if she would be able to sleep when the train was moving.

'Privacy?' questioned Glenda.

'The hanging curtains at each bedhead can be drawn to make that complete.' He showed them.

'Thank you,' said Glenda, and added, 'whoever thought all this out deserves a medal. It is marvellous, so much thought for passenger comfort over long distances.'

'Mr Pullman was the brains behind it and other railway companies clamoured for the carriages. Mr Pullman built more, leased them to interested companies and made a fortune.'

Gordon had caught his comment as he returned to their car. He corroborated the steward's information and thanked him.

'No trouble, sir. It is good to show people around who are interested. I will bring you a menu and return for your order after you have seen what the chef is offering this evening.' He glanced at his watch. 'We should be leaving in fifteen minutes.'

14

Dearest Clive,

We are on our way in a Pullman train after leaving New York at 3 p.m. today.

You would not believe the luxury of our carriage (or car to use the American term). Uncle Gordon booked the whole carriage so we have it to ourselves: a living room with sections that let down to make comfortable beds although Uncle Gordon has a small private bedroom to himself, of course. We dine here on meals supplied from a special kitchen carriage. The stewards on the train are very attentive and eager to please. It should all make for a pleasant journey.

The land we have seen so far reminds me of the border country between Scotland and England, gentle and undulating, mostly cultivated fields but some woodland. From what I hear the drama in the landscape will come later.

How I wish you were here to share everything with me. It would make life so much more delightful. I try to make it so by holding you in my thoughts and remembering the days we spent amongst our beloved Highlands. I look forward to the day when we can do that again.

My love,
Ros

She addressed an envelope and made it ready to post at the next opportunity.

That came the following morning when passengers who were travelling with no eating facilities were informed there would be an hour's stop for refreshments at the next station: 'Ladies have their own refreshment room. Gentlemen, please observe that distinction. If you don't you will be ejected and thrown in the caboose!' Female cheers rippled through the train at this threat.

Ten minutes later metal clattering on metal announced that the train was slowing. This brought many of the passengers travelling without dining facilities to their feet. The train jerked as brakes were applied. People stumbled, grabbed the nearest passenger or sought the back of the closest seat for support. Everyone wanting to be first at the serving points started to claim their supposed right before the train had stopped. As soon as it did people spilled out on to the platform, eager to appease their hunger.

The McKinleys watched it all and enjoyed their tasty lunch from the comfort of their own carriage, ignoring a group of five urchins who pulled faces at them through the window, until a railway official scattered them with a swirl of his heavy cape.

'He's done that before,' commented Rosalind with a smile.

The platform had become a moving stream of people making sure, in one way or another, that they would be prepared for the next stage of their journey.

Ten minutes later three unmelodious blasts from the train's whistle signalled that they would be moving out in fifteen minutes. Some passengers from the first class carriage rushed to reclaim their seats, causing confusion when they sat themselves in the wrong places. Arguments that made the air blue ensued until a railway official cooled tempers and set the mistake right. Two more blasts warned passengers that their train would leave in ten minutes. This brought even more panic when a mother and father announced that their three young children were missing, causing confusion and a hasty search until someone shouted, 'Here ... they are here!'

A waiter from the cafe appeared, leading the children who were innocently eating ice cream. Their parents, scolding them mercilessly, bustled them back on to their carriage, their ice-cream cornets scattered in the dust. The next hoot startled everyone still immersed in the uproar. Three young men, a little unsteady on their feet, grabbed at the iron railings on the end of the final carriage. Amidst a crescendo of encouragement they managed to haul themselves on board. They rolled over the railings, grasping the flailing hands of their friends. Their success brought cheers from those who had witnessed it.

'That was a close call for them,' said Ros, laughing as she leaned out of the window to watch.

'Is this journey always as exciting as this?' queried Cat.

'It might get even more so.' Gordon smiled.

The train, puffing hard from its unusually shaped funnel, picked up speed, leaving a plume of black smoke marking its passing.

Once more the McKinleys settled down to enjoy the luxury of their carriage and relaxed as the train ate up the miles towards Colorado. While they were enjoying their evening meal Gordon informed them, 'Tomorrow we will see the prairies.'

'Will there be buffalo?' asked Cat.

'We might see some but there won't be the large herds there once were.'

'Why? Did the Indians kill them all?'

'No. They killed only what they required for their own livelihood, but that was always a sustainable kill because there were so many buffalo. The coming of the railways caused the real slaughter and decimation of the herds. The large numbers of workers needed to be fed as they laid the railroad tracks, and the buffalo were a handy food supply.'

'I hope we see some.'

'I hope you do too. They are fine animals and a large herd of buffalo, and I mean large, is a wonderful sight, especially if they are in a full stampede. The ground will shake, as you've never felt it, and clouds of dust rise so thick that you don't want to linger near them or you'll choke.'

'Ros, we must keep our eyes open tomorrow. I want to see a herd of buffalo!' called Cat, in a manner that said there would be disappointment if her wish were not fulfilled.

She went to sleep that night recalling the excitement of a day she had thought might be dull. And tomorrow, with any luck, could turn out even better – buffalo!

A shrill scream fought against the rhythmic clatter of the wheels. The dim night-light sent shadows dancing across the carriage in time with the swaying of the train.

Glenda woke abruptly, aware that Cat was in trouble. She flung off the bedclothes, sending them tumbling to the floor. Someone beside her was also struggling to their feet. 'Ros!' she called.

'I'm here, Mama.' Ros reached out to her mother, just as another scream split the air.

'Buffalo!'

Glenda slid her arms protectively around her younger daughter.

'It's all right, Cat, Ros and I are here.'

'You've just been dreaming,' Ros tried to reassure her, rubbing her arm gently.

Cat gave a deep sob that ended with the muttered words, 'The buffalo!' She eased herself away from her mother to look at her with baleful eyes.

'The buffalo were coming. I couldn't escape.'

'But you did. You are safe here with your mother and sister. It was only a dream.'

There was a tap on the woodwork. 'Is everything all right?' asked a worried voice.

'Yes, come in, Gordon,' replied Glenda, and slid the curtain back for him. 'Cat's had a nightmare.'

'I was being charged at by a herd of buffalo, Uncle Gordon.'

'Only a dream, my dear. Remember, I told you there weren't any on this part of the prairie,' he said, with such conviction in his voice that she nodded her head meekly.

'Now, back into bed, Cat,' said Glenda, gently persuasive.

She scrambled between the sheets and Ros tucked her in.

'Sleep soundly,' said Glenda, kissing her daughter on the forehead.

Cat nodded and gave her uncle a sheepish grin, saying, 'Silly me.' He pressed a reassuring hand on Glenda's shoulder. 'She'll be all right, but call me if there is any cause for worry.'

'Thank you,' Glenda replied. 'Ros and I will sit here until she's asleep.'

'By the look of her that won't be long,' said Ros, noting how her sister's eyelids were drooping.

The next morning, as planned, nobody mentioned Cat's nightmare. Nor did she display any adverse reaction to it. In fact, it appeared as if nothing had occurred.

They finished their breakfast and settled down to observe the passing landscape, which rolled away into the distance broken only by oak savannahs and anaqua trees seeking water from the occasional stream.

'Is this the real prairie, Uncle Gordon?' asked Ros.

'Yes, as far as your eyes can see.'

'Clive would love the carpets of flowers and all the colours in the different grasses; he would look in wonder at how thick and tall they are.'

'Then he would probably be struck by the wealth of game there is here too: quail, turkey, deer and antelope.'

'I'm sure he would,' said Rosalind, 'but he'd also miss our deer, game birds and mountains.'

Glenda tried to divert Ros's thoughts. 'When you first came to America, Gordon, you wrote now and then but we learned very little of what you were doing. It was only after you had started ranching that you told us more, when you were trying to persuade John that there was a good life to be made for all of us here if we joined you. But what did you do before ranching?'

Gordon gave a little smile at her curiosity. 'There's no secret about it, Glenda. I wasn't a good correspondent, I know, and I'm sorry for that now; perhaps if I had been John would have been persuaded to come here sooner.' He gave a little shake of his head and tightened his lips for a moment. 'I was a stranger in an unfamiliar land when I first arrived. It was so different from everything I had known in Scotland. To be honest, I nearly came straight back, but that would have made me look foolish and I told myself there was a big adventure ahead of me if I wanted it. Eventually I decided to go West, probably believ-

125

ing that if I put as much distance as that between myself and Scotland I would be less tempted to give in and return. I worked here and there as I moved on. I lived frugally but in most places food came with the job because generally people were open hearted towards strangers. Of course there were those who tried to get more out of me than I was being paid for, and others who just didn't like a Scotsman. I stood up to them. Either I got the sack or I told them I was moving on.'

He paused, but seeing he had a rapt audience, went on. 'I reached the Mississippi and got work on one of the steamers plying its trade as a passenger and goods boat. Its captain and owner was Ed Berry, getting on in years but reluctant to give up. The river had been his life. He had lost his wife and young son in an accident I was told wasn't his fault, but Ed blamed himself. I had been with him three years when he told me he was dying and that he was leaving his boat to me. He hoped I would still run it in his memory for at least two years. I think he limited it to two because he saw I had the wanderlust, but also that I desired to better myself. After that time I sold the boat and all its trappings for a very good price and headed West, over the Rockies into Colorado, which wasn't a state then, and on to Denver, a rough town at the time. Because of the proximity of the silver mines in the mountains, I saw there was a good chance to make money there. That is exactly what I did.

'Four years ago I sold everything I had in Denver and bought land and started ranching – longhorns – beef cattle for the markets back east. There are a lot of mouths to feed there and they

126

love a good juicy steak.'

'But how do you get the beasts there?' asked Caitlin.

'Drive them.'

'What? Walk them all the way?'

Gordon smiled at her incredulous expression. 'Not all the way, but to one of the railheads, which has a direct link to the eastern stockyards handling cattle.'

'Don't you lose any on the way?'

'Yes, but that is inevitable. Generally it doesn't affect our profits because most of the cattle survive. They eat well and actually put on weight during what can be a thousand-mile drive.'

'Just a bit different from driving cattle at home,' commented Ros. 'Clive won't believe me when I tell him.'

'And that is it?' said Glenda. 'That is what you are still doing at your ranch?'

'Yes. It has been a profitable move, but I've been wondering if I'm wise being so committed to cattle trading with the eastern market. I've always left myself something in the bank to fall back on in case of a setback to what I'm doing.'

'Can't you do something about that?'

'Yes. I could scale down my cattle business a little and replace it with horse-trading.'

'Why horses?'

'They are easier to work and control when driven on the trail, as they would be if I raised horses to sell. There will always be a market for them if you analyse their main uses, such as Army needs and ranch work, as more and more smaller ranches are appearing.'

'Would you consider no longer ranching cattle?'

'Oh, no. There'll always be money to be made feeding the population in the east. I suppose I am looking to expand into horse-dealing because they are always needed and I just like horses.'

'I'm glad you do, Uncle Gordon,' said Caitlin with a joyful smile.

'When you get to my ranch you shall have your pick of my horses.'

'What?' Cat's eyes opened wide in disbelief.

'You can choose the one you want and it shall be yours for as long as you are with me. That also goes for Rosalind and your mother.'

'Gordon, you really should stop spoiling us,' Glenda chided him.

'I'm not spoiling you. The horses cost me nothing: they were wild on the prairies, a large herd that I was able to round up, break-in and sell at a good profit bar those I chose for ranch work. So, you see, I lost nothing and gained a great deal. We always have mustangs at the ranch that are already broken in and well trained, so you can have your pick of those. Apart from that there are two things you will also need to consider. First, they are used to being ridden astride; and secondly, you'll have to learn to use the American saddle.'

'The first won't be a problem. We have all ridden astride,' said Glenda.

'I prefer it,' Rosalind supported her mother.

'I do too,' agreed Cat. 'Much more control, especially at full gallop.'

'Good,' said Gordon. 'And my cowboys will soon have you weaned away from the saddle you have been used to. They are a good crew and loyal to me. Perhaps that's because I treat them as equals in work and in play, but they know the consequences if they step out of line. I listen to their suggestions and opinions and sometimes use them. They appreciate the recognition.'

'It sounds as though you are a good man-handler,' commented Glenda with an admiring smile.

Gordon gave a little smile and a dismissive shrug. 'Maybe born in me, but I reckon I learned as I went along. But whatever, it has paid dividends. I am not boasting about my achievements; other men have done the same and more. All the land you can see from this train now is mine and all that we have travelled through for the last three hours. What you will see until we are an hour from Denver also belongs to me.'

Mother and daughters stared at him in disbelief.

'But...' began Glenda.

'There are no buts about it, Glenda. It's here to see and can be verified in the Land Office in Denver.'

'Are you driven to want even more?' she asked.

'In the beginning I was, but since I have achieved all I wanted to, I am contented as I am. I love being a cowboy, if I can consider myself one.'

'I am sure you can,' commented Glenda. 'The amount of land you have, the herds of horses, the huge herds of longhorns you mentioned plus the English cattle you have introduced, could never have come about if you hadn't worked your way up from learning the life of a cowboy and immersing yourself in it.'

129

'Maybe,' he said casually, 'but you need luck as well.'

'But you've got to grasp luck as soon as you recognise it and make it work for you,' said Rosalind in admiration, 'otherwise it will pass you by.'

'Very true, young lady. You are wise beyond your years.'

'I heard my father say something like that to a young Scotsman once. It stuck in my mind and I recalled it when I was listening to you telling us how you achieved your dream.'

'If you would allow me to add something – I would say, in working towards your goal, don't let anyone else get hurt. Rather, offer them a helping hand towards achieving their dream. It is up to them if they accept it or not.'

'Yours was a good dream, though,' commented Caitlin, who had listened intently to all that had been said. 'Not like mine.'

'You'll soon be rid of yours,' said Glenda, her eyes flooding with sympathy. 'Don't think about that. Let it go. Replace dreams with thoughts of what Uncle Gordon is bringing to our lives.'

Caitlin nodded her understanding. 'I will try, if he will tell us more about life at his ranch.'

'I will, my dear,' he said. 'We will be there the day after tomorrow unless there are any delays. And if there are, we'll take them in our stride.'

As they settled down again, Rosalind's mind drifted back to her uncle's life and she wondered if Clive, given the same chances, would have achieved all that Uncle Gordon had.

15

'Did you finish your letter?' Gordon asked Rosalind the next day after they had enjoyed a tasty breakfast.

'Yes and no,' she replied with an impish smile.

'Yes and no! What's that supposed to mean?' chided Cat.

'It means I'm not sure; if I get time to add a note I will, if I don't then the letter can be posted in Denver as it is.'

Gordon gave a silent curse, but added for all to hear, 'I should have told you – it will be best if you post any letters at Cheyenne. They will leave there sooner than from Denver. We change trains at Cheyenne because Denver was missed out of the direct north–south line, which means, unfortunately, we have to interrupt our schedule and change trains. There is talk of putting this right, but as yet nothing has been decided. So, if you let me have your letters, I'll see they are taken at Cheyenne.'

As the train slowed on approaching the station, he took their letters and told them on which platform they would board the train for Denver. Their train awaited them and when they found their new carriage and all were settled, Gordon said, 'The good thing is that this line between Cheyenne and Denver gives you better views of the Rockies.'

'How close will we get to them?' enquired Ros.

131

'The nearest is about twelve miles away, when we are at Denver, which lies at the confluence of Cherry Creek and the South Platte River. Just remember, although there are plans afoot for its development, Denver is still very much a mining town, rough and tough; a boom place that attracted all manner of people eager to dig a fortune in silver out of the ground.'

'Did they?' asked Cat, with an excited gleam in her eyes.

'Some did, some didn't. Many left, some stayed. A town built on mining is a town built on luck.'

'Did you ever try it, Uncle?' asked Ros.

'Yes, I did, but I soon realised it wasn't for me. Underground has never attracted me; give me wide open spaces any time – that's what I chose and they were kind to me, and still are. I hope you won't be disappointed by what you see later today,' he said.

Thoughts about what the ranch would be like were pushed to the back of their minds when Gordon announced, pointing his finger, 'You can get a good view of the Rockies now.'

The silence that enveloped their carriage was palpable, not even the rhythmic rotation of the train's wheels marred it. The distant mountains, forming a jagged skyline, were holding all their attention.

Glenda wondered what John would have made of this new land. Would it have taken a hold on him and never released him? Would the Rockies have triumphed or would the memories of their Scottish Highlands have been too powerful? And how would the magic of these mountains, already reaching out to her, influence her own future?

Ros's reaction was tempered by a feeling of resentment. Even from this distance she saw them as a formidable foe, trying to drive a wedge between her and Clive. They were higher, more powerful than her Highlands and she sensed she would have a fight on her hands resisting their allure.

Cat's eyes were wide with wonder as she linked the horses she had seen on the prairies with this landscape of foothills and mountains – a land with so much beauty and adventure, to be explored from the back of the horse Uncle Gordon had promised her. She couldn't wait.

With every mile their excitement and interest in what lay ahead gripped them tighter. A little relief came when the train began to slow and a steward entered their carriage to announce, 'Denver in ten minutes.' He helped them with their luggage and had it assembled by the time the train finally stopped at the platform. Gordon was first off the train once the steward had opened the door, and, at his signal, a cowboy hurried over to him.

'Welcome back, sir. I hope you had a good journey and all went according to plan.'

'It did, Mark, thanks,' Gordon said. 'Meet my relations. Mrs Glenda McKinley, my sister-in-law, and her two daughters Rosalind and Caitlin, better known as Ros and Cat.'

'Pleased to meet you all. Ma'am.' Mark touched the brim of his Stetson to Glenda. 'I hope you have had a good journey and it has not

133

been too tiring for anyone.'

'It has been most pleasant. We have been well looked after all the way, thanks to my brother-in-law's splendid planning,' replied Glenda.

'Mark is my manager so you will likely see a great deal of him,' explained Gordon, slapping his hand on the cowboy's shoulder. 'He has been with me ever since I moved into the cattle trade. He helped enormously to make the Circle C what it is today. I wanted him as a partner but he preferred to remain an employee.'

'That way there would be no reason for us to fall out,' Mark explained. 'Gordon's the boss and the final decision on any policy regarding the ranch is his.'

Glenda liked the openness she could sense in the relationship between these two men, even in this short exchange. She guessed their friendship would have been almost instant, born out of immediate respect for one another.

She judged Mark to be about fifty years old, the same age as Gordon; six foot tall, well built, but, through the nature of his work, always retaining his leanness and strength. It was his grey eyes that caught her attention more than anything – they were alive, alert, with the power to command attention. Yet she also saw gentleness and consideration there. Here was a man of many parts but one who had earned the respect he was given.

Her own thoughts startled her and Glenda drew back into herself momentarily. It was unusual for her to consider any man in this way apart from her own beloved husband.

Then she saw Gordon helping Rosalind and

Caitlin into a horse-drawn vehicle and Mark was standing beside her.

'Can I help you in, Ma'am?'

'Thank you,' she said, taking his hand.

He steadied her on the iron step that hung from the door level and only let go when she had sat down, facing forward, beside Caitlin.

'Comfortable, Ma' am?'

'Yes, very, thank you. This is not what I expected.'

Mark gave a little smile. 'Everyone who takes a first ride in this says the same. It was specially built to my specifications – thought them out one day when I had used the stagecoach into Denver from Cheyenne. It wasn't a very comfortable ride. But you'll be all right in this one.' He glanced over his shoulder on hearing footsteps. 'Ah, here's Boss-man,' he added jokingly on seeing Gordon.

He opened the door and Gordon stepped into the coach and sat down beside Rosalind.

'Everyone settled?' he asked. There were no dissension so he added, 'All right, shotgun, let's away.'

Mark closed the door and climbed up the outside steps to get to his seat beside the driver.

'Don't worry about that term,' said Gordon with amusement as he saw their questioning faces. 'We still have these so called "shotguns" on out-of-the-way trails, but attacks are now infrequent. Our Indian troubles are close to being solved and almost all outlaws have been accounted for. But there is still an outside chance of flare-ups and criminal activity. If the times are volatile then it is wise to have someone ride shotgun. I don't think we'll have any trouble today, so enjoy the view.'

The three women sat back, lost in wonder at the scenery as the trail swung through the foothills of the Rockies while making a steady climb. Every twist and turn brought a fresh breathtaking aspect or gave them a different angle on the landscape they had already passed through. The climb became steeper; the two horses strained in the harness to keep the coach moving. So far they had needed no cajoling. It was as if they knew the terrain and what was expected of them.

When Rosalind commented on this fact, Gordon gave them all something to think about. 'They are a good pair,' he said, 'but they always pull with extra strength in this section of the climb. I reckon they know they are nearing home where food will be waiting for them, but I also believe they know they are nearing the top of the ascent and the strain will soon be over. They always automatically stop there for a rest. Not one of my four drivers, like Lance who has the reins now, objects unless there is an emergency. The driver will then use a different tone of voice to order them on.'

Some time later the passengers felt the coach slowing and finally come to rest.

'Everyone out!' called Gordon.

Mark, who had dropped from his seat before the coach was truly stationary, was already opening the door and was by the steps to help the passengers to the ground.

Gordon, wanting to help, slipped smoothly out of the coach the moment it had stopped. He was eager to watch the expressions of the women as they saw his ranch for the first time. He nodded to Mark and held out his hand to assist Glenda.

As her feet touched the ground she said, 'Thank you, that was a most comfortable...' The word trailed away as amazement at the view silenced her.

'Welcome home,' said Gordon, with a genuine feeling of pleasure, 'and welcome to John. I know he is here with us in spirit.' He turned to come face to face with Glenda. 'My dream has finally been fulfilled,' he added.

A lump came to Glenda's throat; she could not stop the tear that trickled down her cheeks.

Mark had been helping Rosalind. 'Welcome to the Circle C,' he said quietly. She made no reply but her eyes expressed astonishment, which pleased him. Next he helped Cat out of the coach. Her eyes widened and her pulse raced at the sight of all the horses. 'So many,' she gasped as she watched them for a moment, moving around in their corrals.

'And one will be yours, I believe,' said Mark. 'I think I know someone who will help you make a good choice.'

Cat glanced at him with curiosity. 'Who?'

He gave a little laugh. 'You will have to wait and see. Your uncle is wanting to say something.'

Gordon looked at his relations. 'You have already seen much of the land and the cattle and horses that form the Circle C ranch. The mile-wide valley that stretches before you is its heart. This is some of the best land, as you can no doubt judge from the luscious grass before you. The fences you see are to keep cattle and horses off the best growth, from which we derive excellent hay to be used when needed. The barns built away from the other buildings are there for storage purposes. A little further round from them are the stables in which we can house fifty horses. We can quickly erect more stabling if necessary. We have wood already cut for that purpose. That has come from the woods and forests you can see along the mountainsides.' Gordon pointed further round. 'Close to the stables, you can see the blacksmith's forge. Two men are employed there, shoeing and making any metal parts we require on a working ranch. A hundred yards further round you see my house and a hundred yards beyond that you see a replica that was built when I expected John and all of you to be coming a while ago. If you would rather not use it as it is we can change it.'

Glenda looked at him. 'What did you just say? Did I hear you right?'

Gordon repeated what he had said, emphasising this extra house had been built just for them but could be altered. 'No, no,' she replied resolutely. 'It looks too good to think of any changes. But, Gordon, you have gone to so much trouble just for us. I can hardly believe it.'

He smiled, ignored her remark and added, 'If you do want any adjustments made after you have lived in it, we can do them. I'll take you into mine in a moment then you can see what it is like living in a wooden ranch house. The other buildings I haven't yet mentioned are Mark's house, very similar to my own, and the two long buildings beyond the forge are the bunkhouse for our cowboys and their dining area with its own kitchen.'

'Almost like a little town,' commented Rosalind.

'Yes,' replied Gordon. 'But Mark and I insist that whoever works for us must keep the whole area tidy so the view across the valley is un-marred.'

As they had been looking at all Gordon was pointing out, Glenda had been astonished to see an encampment of about twenty Indian dwellings. 'What about the tepees?' she queried.

'The same ruling on neatness, cleanliness, etcetera applies to anyone working on the Circle C. They know from the start they have to abide by our rules. If they do they are treated like our other employees.'

'You have Indians working for you? Don't the cowboys object to them?'

'No, they recognise the contribution the Indians make to the ranch. They and their families have all been handpicked. They are from a very noble race, the Arapaho, who are the dominant tribe in this area. As you can see from the rows of fruit trees, we have an orchard that needs care. The Indian women enjoy this part of our enterprise and have become expert in the care of trees, but we use the men for all other work, especially where the horses are concerned. They are fine riders as you will see and are essential to us at round-up and branding times.'

Glenda felt uneasy. Gordon had written to John regarding the terrible fighting between the Indians and the white settlers ... but her thoughts were interrupted by her daughter's observation.

'I think the decoration on their homes adds

'colour to their area of the ranch,' said Cat.

'Be sure and tell them that,' said Gordon. 'They'll be pleased.'

'How can I tell them when I can't speak their language?'

'Most of them speak some English, but not so many of the older ones. They pick it up from the cowboys, so you do get some strange words and phrases. I know some of the younger ones will like practising their English on you and they'll attempt to teach you their language.'

'I'd like to try it,' said Cat, 'wouldn't you, Ros?'

'It could be interesting but I'll see,' she said with less enthusiasm, as she tried to take everything in. It would take a long time to adjust to life here, she felt.

Gordon made no comment but said instead, 'Should we move on and I'll show you my house?'

Everyone returned to their places on the coach and Lance started off at a gentle pace down the track. On reaching the bottom they swept round a small rise and came up before the houses, to stop at the one belonging to Gordon, who was quickly out of the coach. He opened the door for Glenda and, when everyone else was on the ground, started up the path towards his own front door. As they neared it the door opened and out stepped a straight-backed young lady with jet black hair tied in a neat roll at the back of her neck. Glenda was enchanted by her beautiful smile as she said, 'Welcome home.'

Her pronunciation gave Glenda a surprise; the faint Scottish twang in its tone told Glenda that Gordon had taught this young woman to speak

English. If she needed any proof of that, the truth of it was confirmed when he said, 'Glenda, Ros, Cat, meet my wife!'

16

Dear Fiona,

A short while ago I received a terrible shock. We finally arrived at Gordon's ranch where we were introduced to his wife: an Indian, not much older than Ros! I did not know what to do. It was not so long ago that we heard these people were killing settlers in the most brutal of ways.

I almost left, there and then, but I had nowhere to go. I realised I was dependent on Gordon who, I must say, has been kindness itself since he met us in New York. Here at the ranch he has built a replica of his own house for us; both are made of wood, and he has furnished ours for us and promised to alter it in any way we want. I really could not throw such kindness back at him, so I am faced with adapting to present circumstances, at least until the girls and I decide what else to do. I know they were as shocked as I was, but we need time to consider our future.

However, since the first surprising impression I received of Zalinda, I have found her to be a charming young woman; she speaks English and is friendly towards us. Her tanned skin is smooth, hair almost black and her eyes dark brown, but it is her smile that is her most winning feature. She is the daughter of Chief Ouray, leader of the branch of the tribe to which Gordon has given some of his land. I just find the situation very unexpected and am sorry that my brother-in-law didn't prepare us better for it.

I cannot write more now but will do so soon.

How is Scotland?

Love,

Glenda

When that letter was sent to be posted in Denver the next day, it was accompanied by another addressed to Clive in Rosalind's handwriting.

'A letter for Clive Martins!' The shout came across the heather-clad terrain that tumbled into a shallow dip where Clive, who was planting some recently purchased fir trees, also enjoyed the warmth of the morning sun. Recognising the voice of the man with the post, he straightened quickly, dropped the spade he was using and ran towards the postie's Highland pony.

'Good day, Mr Macaulay,' panted Clive, rubbing soil from his hands.

'Couldn't get here fast enough, I see. One for you from America.' The postman held it out to Clive, but just as he was about to take it, Macaulay held on to it teasingly. 'Or maybe I should deliver it on my return?'

'Nothing of the sort, Mr Macaulay,' rapped Clive. 'I'll take it here and now!'

Macaulay steadied his horse, restless to be on its way. 'Wait, wait, Hughie. This young man wants his letter.' The postman flicked the letter over and glanced at it. 'Says on the back "Rosalind for Clive". Seems like it must be meant for ye.'

'Aye, it does,' snapped Clive. 'Now hand it over.'

Macaulay gave a shrug of his shoulders. 'I suppose I should, though it seems likely ye'll not tell me what she says?'

'Don't be nosy,' said Clive, grabbing the letter. He was away back down the hill without another word.

As Macaulay rode off he looked back at Clive, smiled to himself and wished he were young again.

Clive had only a few moments to wait until the postman was out of sight and then he raced to the building that had been special to him and Ros. As he dropped on to the hay so many memories came racing back but they did not stop him from ripping the envelope open and extracting a sheet of paper. New words in Rosalind's handwriting banished his memories.

My dear Clive,

The news I write here will surprise you: Uncle Gordon is married to a Red Indian. He had never breathed a word about it until we arrived at his ranch and he introduced us. Not one word until this young woman, maybe only a year or two older than me, stepped out of the house to greet and welcome us.

At that moment you could sense the shock we all felt. There were a few seconds in which no one spoke; possibly we were all wondering what to do. Then, Mother trying to hide her surprise, stepped forward and held out her hand to Zalinda (that's her Christian name). I could see relief on her face as she warmly took hold of Mother's hand in return. We were invited inside and Zalinda clapped her hands to summon three nearby Indian girls, each around the age of eighteen; they came in to take our outdoor clothes and escort us to a room where we could refresh ourselves and get rid of our travel dust. Then, in the main room, we found tea and cake served in the British manner, to make us feel at home. It did the trick up to a point; the atmosphere began to grow more easy.

There is much more to tell you, much to decide after we get used to the situation here. No doubt we will consider in due course which way of life, here or in Scotland, will work best for us, but there is one thing I do know: I love you and *will* return, and nothing will change that.

Love,
Rosalind

Fiona finished reading the letter from her sister then sat and absorbed the news. Gordon and his Indian bride... Fiona tried to put herself in Glenda's shoes but soon knew that she couldn't and could only speculate as to how she might have reacted to the way in which he had broken the fact of his marriage. Surely it would have been kinder to mention it before their arrival? And why had he chosen a Red Indian... Love? Personal gain? Even as she considered these points Fiona knew she would have an irritating wait before she received more details.

Her thoughts were interrupted by the sound of a

galloping horse. Someone in a hurry! She crossed to the window and recognised the rider immediately – Clive Martins. She swung round, hurried to the landing and ran down the stairs. She was on the stone veranda just as Clive brought his horse to a gravel-churning stop. He swung from the saddle and flung his reins over the wooden post. He took the steps to the veranda quickly and was breathing hard when he faced Fiona.

'Sorry, Miss Copeland,' he gasped.

'Come, sit down.' She grasped his arm and led him to a nearby chair. 'I think there's only one reason why you would ride to me at such a pace. News from America!'

He nodded. 'Have you heard?'

'Yes.'

That one word from Fiona sent relief surging through him – he wouldn't have to break the news that Mrs McKinley's brother-in-law had married an American Indian!

'My letter from Rosalind gave me no details,' said Clive.

'Nor did mine from my sister except to say that Mr Gordon's wife is the young daughter of an Indian chief. What it will mean for my sister and her girls, I can't even guess. You and I will have to wait patiently until they have sorted themselves out. Nobody locally knew what the McKinleys wanted from this visit to America but it certainly wasn't this! The next letter might tell us more. All we can do is wait.'

'Will you be answering your letter soon? I'm not sure if I should give any opinion on the matter to Ros; it is hardly my place.'

'Yes, I will answer it. I will be non-committal but will show interest in what they are doing on the ranch and talk of life here. I suggest you use the same tactic until we learn a little more.'

In the time these letters had taken to reach Scotland, life in Colorado had settled down somewhat.

Zalinda had ordered that the visitors should be allowed to unpack, settle in and recuperate from their days of travelling. Although eager to explore the Circle C, they appreciated the thoughtfulness and the quiet time she had allowed them, even though they knew that she too must be curious about Gordon's relations.

A few minutes after she had woken on their third morning at the Circle C, Glenda heard a tap on her door. In answer to her, 'Come in,' the Indian girl who had been appointed her personal maid entered the room.

Not used to British ways, the girl spoke first. 'Good morning, Mrs McKinley. It is a beautiful morning.' She drew back the curtains and warm sunshine flooded in.

Glenda realised things were going to be very different here. 'Thank you, Namia. Are my daughters awake?'

'I heard talking coming from both rooms but that has stopped. I think they must have gone down to breakfast.'

'Then maybe I'd better hurry.'

With her toilette completed, Glenda chose a closer-fitting yellow cotton blouse and a light grey skirt that fell neatly from the tight waist to the tops of her buttoned black leather ankle boots. She knotted a silk tartan scarf at her throat, examined herself in the mirror, gave her hair a final pat, thanked Namia for her help and left the room to face their third day at the Circle C.

As she walked down the stairs she admired the construction of the building and thought how thrilled John would have been by it. She looked forward to seeing the other buildings. That amused her because she couldn't remember ever having felt that way before. By the time she had reached the bottom of the stairs she thought it must be because she had never lived before in a completely new construction; Pinmuir House had been built in the eighteenth century, and the castle long before. Reaching the hall, she paused and looked back up the sweeping staircase. Gordon had certainly put a lot of thought into this building, but then he had believed they were coming to live here permanently while John was alive.

Chatter and laughter coming from the dining room reminded her of the decisions she would have to make. She stepped quickly to the dining-room door and walked in to find her two daughters seated with Zalinda and Gordon at the long oak table. Glenda remembered then that when they had dined next door for yesterday's evening meal, she had invited her brother-in-law and his wife over for breakfast.

'Good morning,' she said. 'My apologies for being late.'

'No, no, you are not late,' said Zalinda, her tone banishing any guilt Glenda had felt. 'Gordon has always said breakfast is an open meal – have it when it is convenient.'

'But don't be too long, Mama!' urged Caitlin. 'Uncle Gordon's going to let us choose our horses.'

Glenda smiled at her younger daughter's enthusiasm. 'You shouldn't spoil us so,' she said, glancing at her brother-in-law.

'I told you there would be a horse for each of you. You need one when you live here. They help you to see all that this place has to offer.'

'Please don't refuse,' put in Zalinda, and added, with a touch of amusement as she glanced at her husband, 'When the chief makes such a gesture it would be bad medicine to say no.'

Glenda replied, 'All right, I won't make bad medicine. Thank you very, very much, Gordon.'

'Then eat up. Your daughters are eager to make their choice.' He pushed himself up from the table. 'If you'll excuse me, I'll get my two fastest horsemen to cut out the best animals and drive them into an empty corral where you can take your pick.' He looked hard at Cat and Ros whom he could see were restless to be looking the horses over. 'And you, young ladies, don't rush your mother, let her enjoy her breakfast. Come with me. I'll show you where to wait on the veranda so you can see my cowboys driving the horses into the corral.'

The two young women rose eagerly to their feet to follow him.

When they had gone Zalinda offered more coffee, which Glenda accepted. 'I presume there are riding clothes in the luggage you sent ahead?' the young woman queried.

'Yes. We have brought split skirts.'

'Good. As you are obviously aware, they will be much more convenient for ranch life and will give you the opportunity to do more riding. Anticipating that you would have brought little else for riding, I have provided each of you with a leather waistcoat, slicker and Stetson, which is what the cowboys wear.'

'Zalinda, thank you, but this is far more than being hospitable. We will ever be in your debt.' Glenda was beginning to wonder how she could pay her way. It now seemed a long time since New York when she was suggesting she could repay him by looking after Gordon's house. She felt slightly irritated by the recollection until she heard Zalinda speaking.

'Don't thank me, just be happy with us and for us. Gordon's hopes are fulfilled now that you are here. Of course he always had high hopes that his brother would join him, but he would never have pressured him to do so. Then fate stepped in. He thought all his plans for the future were in vain. I can tell you truly that your decision to visit us with your two daughters has given my husband great joy and healed a wound that was eating at him.'

'Was he really hit so hard by the loss of John?' asked Glenda.

'Oh, yes. You see, marriage was a big step for both of us. When Gordon allowed my father and some of his people to live on his land, my father, as the chief, arranged for the marriage to take place in order to seal the contract between our two peoples. Gordon believed that the presence of his brother and his family would help to quell

149

any antagonism there might be to our marriage. I'm sure your presence here will do much to ease those attitudes.'

'I hope it does. I believe John would not have raised any objection to his brother's marriage to you.'

'I thank you for your support. There were at first strong objections from within my tribe. But even though I am much younger than Gordon, we now have a relationship built on love and the Arapaho and the Circle C employees understand that peace between them is possible. Hopefully that will continue when my brother takes over as chief. I will take you to meet my family sometime in the future, if you are agreeable?'

'Of course. I look forward to it, and no doubt Rosalind and Caitlin will do too. Though it had better be after we have chosen the horses!' Glenda drained her cup and rose from the table.

As they reached the door she stopped and gave Zalinda a warm smile. 'Thank you so much for all you are doing for us. As you will know from my letters to Gordon, Caitlin was badly affected by her father's death and I was advised to take her into a new environment.'

'Gordon told me everything. I hope the spirits of my world can help her. I believe they will, particularly if you believe it too.'

'I will trust that your spirits will unite with my God, and that their union will be enough to help my child make a full recovery.'

17

On hearing footsteps coming on to the veranda from the house, Caitlin and Ros spun round.

'Mama, how are you going to choose from all these horses?' asked Caitlin.

'Your uncle has certainly set us a problem but no doubt we'll hear some good advice,' Glenda replied.

'You will, and maybe even from me,' laughed Zalinda. 'I was hardly ever off a horse until I met Gordon. Even then we rode often together and, because I know this country, I was a great help to him. Well, I like to think I was.'

'Looking around, I'm sure you were. I didn't expect the Circle C to be as large as it is nor to find it so well organised.'

'It has to be if you run as many cattle as we do, as you will see in the fall when many of them will set out for the eastern states. It's a stirring sight, hundreds and hundreds of steers under the eyes of as many as sixty cowboys. Today some of those men will be eyeing the horses for the purpose of that cattle drive and may select some from those mustered in the big corral for you and your daughters to choose from. Would you like to look them over now?'

Glenda nodded. 'This is going to be so interesting and so different from home. Our ponies are bred for hardiness rather than speed.'

'Don't worry, when it comes to horse-talk the men here are not shy in coming forward with advice, particularly when they are offering it to such pretty listeners! But, whoever you listen to, make sure to let the final choice be yours. After all, you are going to be the horse's rider.'

As they watched the horses Ros commented, 'They look a wonderful herd, I wish Clive could have seen them.'

'Is that your man?' Zalinda asked her casually.

'Yes,' replied Rosalind, smiling at the Indian's turn of phrase.

'You'll have to bring him here one day.'

'I'd love to do that,' she answered wistfully.

'We must bear it in mind,' promised Zalinda. 'What is his work?'

'He's employed on our estate. At present he and his father are looking after it for us.'

'You must tell me about that sometime. I have only heard about it from Gordon so far and it must have changed since he left Scotland.'

Before any further exchanges could be made, Caitlin interrupted them. 'Look we have to go. Uncle is waving to us from the corral.'

'He must be satisfied with the horses Spike and Joe have assembled for you.'

Glenda and her daughters matched their pace to that of Zalinda as they hurried to the corral in high spirits.

'How many horses do you think they have in there?' asked Ros. 'I've been trying to count them.'

'Impossible when they're on the move.' Zalinda considered then said, 'But I reckon close on thirty-four.'

Gordon was waiting for them at the corral gate. 'All ready?' he asked. They nodded while eagerly eyeing the horses. 'Good, here's what we do. The adjoining corral is the one in which Spike and Joe will assemble your choices as you make them. After you have done so they will see that the others are returned to the herd. Take your time, there's no rush, make sure you have the one you really want.'

'What if we both pick the same horse?' asked Ros.

'I don't think that is likely but, if it does happen, Spike or Joe will remove it and replace it with another.'

'So neither of us will get our first choice?'

'Doing it my way saves any dispute. You accept that?'

'Yes,' the three of them chorused.

'Very well, let's get on with it. Look them over.'

Cat climbed up the pole rungs of the fence to the top one, on which she settled for a better view of the horses. She knew for her this was going to be a difficult task.

Circle C cowboys began to drift towards the corral when they realised what was taking place.

'Do ya reckon they'll know what they're about?' asked one cowboy. His face, battered by the wind and browned by the sun, betrayed time spent in Colorado's hills and mountains.

'They've dressed as if they do, but I reckon some of those horses will think different.'

'Who are they?'

'I had time off like you. I was in Denver but heard tell of them when I got back. The Boss's sister-in-law and her two daughters are here for an indefinite period.'

'Husbands?'

'She's a widow; her daughters are single.'

'Mm, fancy-looking pieces, all of them.'

'Get that out of your mind. Don't fall foul of the Boss or you'll be spitting blood somewhere out on the prairie. He'll not pull his punches if you step out of line. And remember, I don't want any backlash, which there'll be if you cause trouble – I recommended you to the Boss because you're a damned good cattleman, but that will count for nothing for both of us if you try anything on. Keep your nose out of the Boss's family life.'

'All right. Quit worrying. I ain't goin' to upset this outfit. And we might be in for a show now.' The man nodded in the direction of the corral where Glenda was making her choice of horse.

She was glad John had taught her what to look for in their ponies and horses even though they did not keep many back in Scotland. After looking at one or two and comparing their points, she noticed a beautiful grey that reminded her of John's horse when she'd first known him. First she checked the animal's teeth; next she gently ran her hand over its forelegs indicating that she meant it no harm, yet with a touch firm enough to judge the animal's strength. The grey's hide was healthy and its skin revealed continuous care. Glenda stood back from it and took in aspects of its stance and the way it held itself. She particularly liked its lithe yet strong body. She voiced this to Gordon, who had been standing close by without expressing any opinion.

154

'You are right,' he replied. 'She is one of my best six mares. This breed was Spanish in origin and mixed with good racehorse stock.'

'And what was the outcome?'

'They had the strength and staying power of our general working horses, but from the imported stock gained speed and agility. They can outrun stampeding cattle and are agile enough to get in the most awkward places, to stop the animals from straying when we are driving them to cattle towns. You couldn't imagine the work they get through. The cowboy spends long hours in the saddle; his horse is so much a part of his life that it is held in great affection. We call them quarter horses because in some parts they were raced over a quarter of a mile.'

Glenda nodded with interest and was truly satisfied with her choice. Then she noticed her eldest daughter. 'I think Ros is near to making a decision too. She's in serious discussion with your manager.'

Gordon nodded. 'She's in good hands. Mark taught me a lot when I came into ranching. My niece will find no one better to give her advice about the horse she has chosen.'

Rosalind had taken the horse's bridle, Mark beside her, and they were approaching Gordon and Glenda.

'Miss McKinley has made her choice,' said Mark. Ros was pleased with the admiration heaped on her horse, a lean, shapely animal that seemed to be enjoying hearing its praises sung. Ros also showed delight at what was being said, for it confirmed that she was a good judge of horses even though her experience had been on a smaller scale in Scotland. She wondered what Clive would think, seeing so many horses, one of which was a beautiful dun colour and would, in a few minutes, be hers.

'Ready, young lady?' The query from Gordon startled her, cutting into her dream world. 'Is this the one you've chosen?'

'Yes, Uncle. And thank you, not only for the horse, which I will call Brandy to toast this wonderful day, but also because you have widened my eyes to the variety within this world. It has been fascinating and I already love my new mount.'

Gordon called to the limping cowboy who had taken over the charge of Glenda's choice. 'Another one for your stable, Buck. Reckon you can manage these two, Suzie and Brandy, for some lovely ladies?'

'Just try me. They both have an eye for outstanding horseflesh. It will be my pleasure to look after their mounts.' Buck touched the brim of his Stetson as he inclined his head to each woman in turn.

'Right, that's settled,' said Gordon. 'Now for Caitlin,' he added, looking around for his younger niece.

'As a matter of fact, she seems to be talking about a horse now,' said Rosalind.

Glenda and Gordon glanced across the corral to the group that had gathered when Caitlin left her perch.

'Maybe I'd better go to her,' said Glenda.

'It strikes me she is holding her own with Sid, who is an expert on the type of horse she looks to be interested in. Leave her to put her own questions. Zalinda is with them but she'll see Caitlin makes the right decision, without appearing to intrude.'

Glenda's lip tightened. Gordon had no right to interfere in what was a matter for mother and daughter. Then another thought struck her – was that what John would have said? She bit her lip, feeling a pang of jealousy at the way Zalinda appeared to be usurping a role she herself should be taking.

'What do you think, Cat?' Zalinda asked the girl.

'I certainly like the look of her. Her brown and white coat is so different and those eyes are so appealing, as if she's pleading to be mine. But is she on the small side?'

'That doesn't hinder her capabilities, as you will see.' Gordon called to the young Indian brave who was standing with the horse. 'Ahote, ride Gila for Miss McKinley to see how she performs.'

'Yes, Boss,' Ahote replied with enthusiasm. He tapped the horse as he turned and sprang in one quick movement on to its back. The horse took his weight without flinching and waited for another command. The Indian whispered something and Gila started walking. Ahote guided the horse with care through the throng of people, and then with the open space before him put the animal into a trot, holding that pace until they reached the end of the corral. There he turned the horse and brought it to a stop. The Indian surveyed the area before him. As if the audience had read his mind they cleared a space for horse and rider. No one could hear what was said then but whatever it was brought an instant reaction from Gila. In a flash she was into a gallop. The earth flew beneath her hooves, faster and faster, until people said she covered the ground without touching it.

About two hundred yards from the end of the corral, Ahote whispered an order. Gila almost simultaneously came to a halt. After a moment the Indian gave another order. The horse turned on the spot; another order and it stepped sideways. It kept moving that way until ordered into another manoeuvre. The demonstration of the horse's capabilities went on until Gordon called a halt.

'There you are, Caitlin. A horse that has been trained to move and herd cattle, and one that has picked up, on her own, how to negotiate all manner of obstacles in the landscape in all weathers. You might never need that, but on the other hand one day your life could hang on it. Better to be prepared. What do you think? Is she the horse for you?'

Gordon had barely finished speaking before Caitlin was saying, 'Oh, yes, please, Uncle Gordon. Yes, please!'

'Very well, she's yours. But there is one condition.'

'Anything, Uncle Gordon, anything!'

'I see great disappointment on the face of that young Indian who has an attachment to Gila. I don't want any ill feeling to be caused by my giving her to you, so I am making Ahote responsible for looking after Gila for you. The skewbald is also known as the Indian's horse in these parts and Ahote has trained her well.'

The concern Ahote had felt disappeared in a

flash. There was relief and joy in his dark eyes.

After most people had dispersed, Glenda waited for Caitlin. She did not like her being alone with a man who came from people who had, until fairly recently, waged war against the white man. She watched closely as Caitlin turned to Ahote and said, 'I admire the way you rode like that without a saddle. I will keep her name as Gila, and I thank you for training her so well. You must let me know what commands you use for her.'

She looked thoughtful as she gazed at a horse she had already fallen deeply in love with. Ahote stood waiting, gently stroking Gila's neck, and nodded in understanding.

Glenda called, 'Caitlin, come, we have things to discuss.'

'Take Gila to her stable,' said Caitlin to Ahote. 'We'll talk again soon.'

'Yes, Miss.'

'And no more "Miss". Between you and me it will be Caitlin ... oh, no, better make that Cat, it will make things easier.'

He took the reins and led Gila away muttering to himself, 'Cat.'

18

Fiona was surprised to see a dejected-looking Clive leaning on the open gate leading to Pinmuir. He should have been working outside on the estate, taking his chance while the fine weather was still with them. He must have heard her horse approach and would normally have been instantly alert to find out who was coming. But not today. The hunched shoulders, his body slumped against the gate, told a different story.

Since the family had left, Fiona had become a more regular visitor here and did not show the airs and graces she might once have done. 'What's wrong with you?' she called as she brought her horse to a stop. There was no reply. She swung from the saddle and dropped to the ground. 'There should be no time for displays of misery on such a fine day as this. Whatever is biting you wants dealing with. Come on, tell me.' As he turned to lean his back against the gate, she saw his miserable expression and made a guess as to the reason. 'Bad news from America?'

'Not really, Miss Fiona, although I haven't had a letter from Ros for a long while and that isn't like her. Maybe she's getting to like America too much. However, my immediate trouble is, I've no horse. Bonnie died four days ago.'

'One day's mourning then get on with life. We can't stand still because an animal has died.'

'That's harsh. Bonnie has been with me a long time, my constant companion. Besides, animals are kinder than humans and serve us without complaint,' answered Clive.

'There are plenty of other horses. We'll find you one. We have to or you'll be stuck here and won't be able to give the McKinley Estate the attention it deserves. Apart from that, I need you to have one.'

'Please don't start talking in riddles, Miss

160

Fiona, I'm in no mood for them.'

'Nor am I. And I've told you before, forget the Miss – in a funny way it reminds me that I'm missing out on life. Now, young man, first we must deal with the horse problem.' There was no doubt Fiona was taking charge. 'Let us go to the house. Perhaps you could ask Mrs Lynch or your mother to make us a cup of tea, which we can enjoy outside while I make you a proposition.'

Once the tea had been organised and Fiona and Clive were settled outside she took up her story again.

'I was coming to tell you that my niece, who has just arrived back from touring Europe with family friends, is intending to stay with me for some time while her father's away and I hoped you would entertain her and remind her of our countryside. She is a little younger than you, a nice-looking girl but is a bit of a snob. She has no real reason to be. Gets that from Roger. It wants stamping out of her if she is to...'

'And you expect me to do that?' Clive interrupted, showing incredulity at the request. 'I have plenty of work to do here.'

'Don't be too obvious about it. Anyway, it won't be every day; only on days I won't be around and the weather is fine. I think knowing you and being with you will do the trick ... put her down a peg or two. Now, don't look so doubtful. A fine young man like you should have no difficulty in entertaining my niece and I dare say you might even enjoy it. I'll finance any expenses you incur. I expect co-operation and help from you. You need a horse, don't you?' The tone with which she put

161

the question and gave him an encouraging smile left him in no doubt as to her inference.

'You're putting me in a corner – the offer of a new horse in exchange for my help?'

Fiona said nothing but gave a little nod.

'How do I explain it to my parents?'

'What is the point in trying to keep it a secret? Tell them the truth, a friend is helping a friend.'

'I suppose there's no harm in it, when you put it that way.'

'Then we have a deal?'

'Yes, but there is a condition.'

'What is that?'

'No word of this must reach Rosalind.'

'I wouldn't dream of writing to her about our arrangement.'

Clive hesitated for a moment then held out his hand to accept Fiona's, sealing the agreement.

'I'll return tomorrow morning at ten o'clock. Then we'll go and find you another horse.'

Fiona was as good as her word; she arrived at Pinmuir House just as the hands on the mantelpiece clock reached ten o'clock.

'Good morning, Mrs Martins.'

'Good morning, Miss Copeland, you have brought a fine day. Please come in and enjoy a cup of tea before you set off.'

'That is very kind,' returned Fiona.

Mrs Martins stepped to one side to allow her to enter the house. As Fiona did so she said, laughing, 'I'm going to follow my nose. There's such a wonderful smell of baking.'

Mrs Martins raised her eyebrow as Fiona

headed for the kitchen. 'Mrs Lynch isn't very tidy. It's a mess in there,' she said, with a small note of protest in her voice.

'I don't mind, I don't expect tidiness in a kitchen,' called Fiona, continuing on her way.

In a few moments she was seated at the table, taking her first sip of tea.

'This is very kind of you, seeing about replacing poor old Bonnie. She had a long life,' said Mrs Martins.

'And I'm sure a good one,' commented Fiona.

'Clive thought the world of her. He was wondering what he was going to do without her. He could have borrowed Rosalind's Freya but she's too delicate for the kind of work he sometimes has to do. Your kind offer has eased his problem. The laddie needs a strong horse, and we had thought that he and his father could share, but that wouldn't have worked. You've stepped in at the right moment. My husband is sorry he isn't here to see you but he had work started at the northern limits of the estate that he hoped to complete today.'

The chat continued after Clive had joined them but having finished her tea Fiona was eager to be away.

Clive borrowed Freya and as they set off, Fiona said, 'I have four horse dealers in mind. Three of them combine their trade with farming, the other is a case of dabbling; if he sees a good horse, which he believes he can sell on at a good profit, he buys it. He knows good horseflesh is more expensive but you'll know you've bought good stock. We'll leave him until last.'

163

'I've always been pleased with the trader we've dealt with in the past,' said Clive, with slight annoyance in his voice. He intended to make sure he remained in charge.

So the hunt for a horse started, with Clive's mind set on obtaining a good-tempered mount, strong, capable of hard work in all weathers, and agile enough to meet with hazards of the Highland terrain.

They had visited two of the dealers but written one of them off as they were not impressed by the horses he had on offer. Fiona and Clive rode on to Glentorrent, the village five miles further on, and then she turned her horse towards some level ground behind the Trooper's Arms, a coaching inn.

'I hope you are as hungry as I am,' she said, drawing her horse to a halt.

'I hadn't thought of it,' Clive replied, following her, 'but now you've mentioned it, I wouldn't mind something.'

'Then let's away in. I have been here before and had an enjoyable meal. Let's see if we can say the same this time.'

Clive helped her from the saddle and looked a little embarrassed on following her into the inn.

'Where do I want to be?' he whispered.

'Right opposite me when we sit down.'

'But...'

'No buts about it,' she replied. 'Get used to it. One day you could be Laird of Pinmuir. Practise on my niece Adrianna. She wouldn't hold back but have the servants at such a place running around like scalded cats. You must teach her to do it in a more pleasant way.'

'Seems to me, Miss Fiona, you've all this worked out.'

'It's a good idea to keep one step ahead. I'm going to enjoy today's venison pie,' she said, indicating the board behind the bar. 'You relax and do the same.'

Clive's sharp mind helped him to observe closely and to keep what he'd learned in mind. He left the inn feeling more confident about the life that could await him when Rosalind returned from America.

Whether it was the result of the food or the relaxed atmosphere neither of them could decide but, whatever it was, at their next destination they quickly found a horse they both liked and thought would be ideal for work around the McKinley Estate. Clive felt sure his new acquisition would also become a favourite with Rosalind. He must start singing its praises to counteract the comments she was making about the horses on her uncle's ranch.

On their return Clive put all three horses in the stable, giving the name Merlin to his new mount.

'Did you succeed?' asked Jessie.

'Yes, we did,' replied Clive. 'Third place we visited. Struck a good bargain, didn't we, Miss Copeland? Well, you did.'

'Of course, always leave bargaining to the ladies.'

'Come in, Miss. Mrs Lynch saved some scones for your return but I can get you something else, if you wish.'

'No, thank you. We had a splendid lunch, but you do tempt me with your scones.'

They settled down to tell her about their day and to wait for the return of her husband. Time slipped away unnoticed until Jessie exclaimed, 'Oh, my goodness, it's dark. I wonder where Greg is?' She automatically left her chair and started closing the curtains. 'It's too dark for you to be venturing home, Miss Copeland. I've a bed made up if you'd like to wait until morning.'

'That is extremely kind, and I won't say no to you. I can't say I'm too fond of travelling in the dark.' After a slight pause she added, 'Please, my name is Fiona.'

'Did Father arrive after we had gone to bed?' asked Clive when he came into the kitchen the next morning.

Jessie gave a little shake of her head. 'No. I expect his work kept him too late to get back. He'll have stayed somewhere close to where he was working.'

That morning Clive chose to work near home and be there for his father's arrival. Fiona said she would check things were in order on the estate as she had promised to write to Glenda. She had expected to talk to Greg Martins concerning the book-keeping.

But that expectation weakened as the day wore on.

Fiona could wait no longer to return home and, as she was leaving the Martins, could see anxiety beginning to creep into Jessie's mind.

'As I am standing in for Glenda, please get word

166

to me if your husband doesn't arrive tonight,' said Fiona. 'It doesn't matter what time, day or night. I'll come over. One of the footmen can accompany me.' When Jessie hesitated, she added firmly, 'Promise, or Glenda will never forgive me.'

'I'll have Clive, but I promise I'll call you if necessary. I'm sure Greg will be back soon.'

But when darkness began to close across the Highlands, Jessie was not so certain.

19

'I'll have a quick breakfast then go and look for Father. I know where he was working.'

Clive's mother's usually bright and cheerful face was now cloudy by concern. Her face was drawn and pallor had overcome her familiar bloom.

'I'll tell Mrs Lynch to pack you some food.'

'Don't bother. I'll have my breakfast and if I need anything later I'll get something elsewhere.'

'Very well.'

Clive hurried his breakfast. He drained his cup of tea, grabbed his jacket and cap. 'I'll get Merlin ready,' he said, and hurried to the stable.

'Your first job for us is an errand of hope,' he said as he patted the horse's neck.

Five minutes later he hugged his mother, Merlin waiting patiently beside them.

'Find my Greg,' she whispered in Merlin's ear. The horse nodded its head as if it understood.

'Get word to Miss Copeland if you need her for

anything at all,' said Clive.

His mother patted his arm and said, 'I will.' Then, with hope in her heart, she watched him ride away.

After riding three miles he voiced his praise for Merlin. 'Good boy. Already I can feel you are at home with us.' He was grateful to Miss Copeland for making a keen assessment of the animal and advising him to buy it. Clive had feared that when the McKinleys had left for America she would interfere in the running of the estate, but she had not; shown interest, yes, but did not attempt to alter the arrangements left in place by her sister. Clive showed keenness and ability but he and his father approached Fiona for advice if it was a decision of financial importance. Now he was pleased he had done so over the choice of the horse.

He rode at a steady pace on a trail that took him northwards towards the area he knew his father had been working in. Although he felt sure Greg would have a good reason for not returning home yesterday, something was telling him that all was not right. This was further than he would normally have gone and he was leaving Pinmuir land. Clive reached a tiny village he thought his father would have used as a base and decided to seek news of him there before venturing further.

He halted Merlin outside an inn that looked as if it had seen better days. Clive secured the bridle to a hook in the wall, gave Merlin a friendly pat, and went in to seek information. The taproom was gloomy but tidy. A well-built man was leaning on the counter talking with three men seated at a

168

table on which stood tankards of ale. Clive did not recognise any of them. One of the men was wiping foam from his lips. The conversation ceased as they all turned their attention to this stranger who had interrupted their drinking.

'Good day,' said Clive, a little tentatively, feeling eyes boring into him.

'Good day to you,' returned the landlord. He reached for an empty tankard in anticipation of an order as he looked enquiringly at Clive.

Though he wanted information and then to be on his way, Clive thought it best to acknowledge the landlord's gesture, so he nodded.

'Riding through?' queried the landlord as he prepared to pull a draught of ale.

'I'll be able to answer that if you can answer my question.' Clive made his request in a friendly tone and noted the suspicion in the landlord's eyes lift a little.

'What might you be wanting to know?' he asked.

Clive became aware that the three men at the table had stopped talking. His exchanges with the landlord must have caught their attention.

'I'm from the Pinmuir Estate and I'm looking for my father. I know he was working near the northern boundary; he had expected the job to take only a day and a half but he has not been home for nearly three days now. My mother was getting worried so, as I said, I've come to find him.'

Knowing that he had captured their attention, Clive turned so that all the men were in his field of vision. He caught reactions that made him believe these men knew something. He was about to

169

tackle them when the landlord spoke up, 'Aye, I reckon we do. Angus here will tell you the story.'

The other man averted his eyes as he spoke.

'It isna a pleasant tale, mind... We, that is Jock and I ... found him this morning. We were late leaving home so took a short cut. It is not a good idea unless you know the track. It's narrow and treacherous in parts, with some nasty drops. One false step can be fatal. Jock and I spotted a figure at the bottom of a precipice. It took us twenty minutes to get safely down to him. Before we drew near we could tell the accident had killed him. We got back here as soon as we could.'

Clive could barely take in what he was hearing. There had to be a mistake surely.

The landlord took up the story. 'We laid your father in one of the outhouses and reported it to the local constable. He took the matter in hand.'

'Has my father's body been removed?' asked Clive automatically, not knowing what the procedure would be.

'No, but we are expecting information about that very soon.'

'May I see him?'

'I would let you but the constable was very firm – no one to see him until I receive permission to release the body.'

Clive nodded, feeling numb with grief and shock.

The landlord drew another ale and put the tankard in front of him. 'Drink that and follow it with this.' He poured a whisky and put the glass in front of Clive. 'You look as though you could do with it.'

170

He was halfway through his ale when the door was opened and a burly man strode in.

'Constable said you have a body here that needs removing. Anybody know where to?' When there was no immediate response the man barked again, 'Come on, somebody must know something. I have a coffin ready; it's outside. I want this job finished so I can get back to my home.'

Clive straightened. His eyes steely, he rejoined, 'I know about the body. It is my father's and you'll show him proper respect throughout.'

The other man was about to reply, but under the accusing gaze of the occupants of the bar, thought better of it. 'Where is he?' he grunted.

'Locked in one of my outhouses,' said the landlord.

The undertaker gave a little mocking laugh. 'Did you think he was going to run away?'

Clive scowled. 'What did I tell you? Respect the dead.'

The landlord led the way to the outhouse and within fifteen minutes the coffin was on a cart and underway. The so-called undertaker grumbled complaints about the time it was taking.

When they were in sight of Pinmuir Estate, Clive gave the man final directions to reach the McKinleys' house and then rode on to forewarn his mother.

Five days later, Greg Martins was laid to rest by the Reverend Kintail in the tiny cemetery at Gartonhag, with only Jessie, Fiona, Clive, the doctor and a few villagers in attendance.

That evening three letters were written at Pinmuir.

20

Glenda and her daughters settled into ranch life. Some of the cowboys had married quarters, which were central to the daily life of all. Glenda was welcomed in to their rooms by the wives and found they were meeting places for knitting, sewing and quilt-making groups, while other women shared their kitchens for baking and jam making. Glenda, however, soon discovered they were really places where friendships were built and laughter shared. Gordon had built a wooden schoolhouse where Mrs Bradley took charge of about thirty children for a few hours a day. She welcomed the input by Rosalind, whose stories of her own land with its green hillsides and frequent lochs filled the children with delight. Cat followed the daily chores of the ranch alongside the cowboys, riding Gila whenever she could.

Zalinda joined in the frequent activities when she could but today was a special day for her and the McKinleys.

'Uncle Gordon and Zalinda are arriving at eleven o'clock. We must see that our horses are ready and all of us prepared for the ride, which might take an hour at a good pace,' Glenda instructed. 'It would not be polite to arrive at the Arapaho encampment late; in fact, they would take it as an insult if we do. Your uncle would not want that after all the hard work he and Mark have 'put in, encouraging the chief to establish this settlement on friendly terms. Mark will be riding with us.' Glenda glanced at the wall clock. 'We have an hour and a half to get ready.' She rose from the table and left the room.

'This is the start of an exciting day,' said Caitlin. 'Are you looking forward to it, Ros?'

'Yes, I am. I didn't think I would be at first but I am curious as to how the Arapaho live, especially as they're our neighbours.'

'There's twenty miles or so between us,' Cat pointed out.

'I know, but no one else lives on that stretch of land. Hasn't Ahote offered to take you to their village?'

Making sure she was out of hearing of her mother, Caitlin answered, 'I asked him but he refused, telling me it would not be right until the chief had made his formal invitation and we had met the whole tribe.'

'So he sticks to tribal rules and Indian law?'

'Of course, but he also appreciates what Uncle Gordon has done in mending the tribe's relationships with the white man. He goes along with Uncle Gordon's philosophy of the best thing for his land being harmony, as does their chief now.'

'All very noble but will that ever be totally achieved?' said Ros doubtfully.

'Who knows?' said Caitlin. 'But it is up to everyone to try.'

'Yes, I agree,' said Ros. She made no further comment, but was struck by the thought that she had not until then realised that her sister had truly grown up or that this young Indian had made such

173

an impression on her. Now she was looking forward to the coming visit with even more interest and ran to the stables, followed by Cat, to prepare Brandy and Gila.

With Gordon in charge, the party set out for the Arapaho encampment.

Although they had been aware of the magnificence of the distant Rockies, they were nevertheless struck by the spectacle as they rode out to an escarpment in the foothills. Though still thirty miles away, it was as if the mountains had suddenly risen from the ground to remind intruders of the power they held over them.

Glenda automatically halted her horse to look at the view. Gordon, alongside her, was quick to react. 'Ten-minute break!' he called.

They swung to the ground and walked the few yards to the point he had indicated would give them the best view.

When they reached the position Caitlin gasped, 'What a glorious sight!'

'Yes, quite wonderful, but no better than the views we've seen in our own Highlands,' commented Rosalind.

'Don't be stupid,' snapped Cat. 'You've never seen anything like this at home.'

'I'll grant you that. All I'm saying is that, in their own way, the Scottish Highlands can be just as impressive.'

'I think you've got a case of sour grapes because you aren't with Clive,' snapped Caitlin, feeling nervous at the prospect of this meeting with Ahote and his people.

'Rubbish! Say what you like, but I think you are becoming...' Rosalind's retort was cut short by her sister.

'There are no buts about it. You were obsessed with Clive before we left home and you are carrying him around in your mind even now.'

'No, I'm not,' said Rosalind, crossing her fingers behind her back at the lie.

'Oh, shut up and enjoy the scenery.'

Rosalind made no reply, nor comment, but silently agreed that from here the foothills made a wonderful introduction to the sweeping panorama of the mighty Rockies. The different shades of green, brown and yellow that dressed the lower slopes gave way to darker tones of brown, grey and black as the great mountain range soared above them, topped by splashes of snow that had found shelter from the sun.

Rosalind gave a silent sigh, wishing that Clive were standing beside her now, the beauty they witnessed drawing them closer and closer.

Their mother, who had caught some of the girls' conversation, allowed her lips to twitch in amusement.

Mark, standing close by, had also caught the sisters' exchange. As his lips curled into a little smile he saw Glenda too had been amused by her daughters' repartee. 'Does this often happen?' he asked.

She grinned. 'Reasonably often, but it never gets out of hand. They are the best of friends usually.'

'That's good,' he said.

'I'm thankful for it.'

Zalinda then came over to them and said,

'Gordon says we must be on our way again.'

At that they heard his voice shout, 'Mount up!'

Gordon's call had shattered Rosalind's dreams of Clive's arms around her.

'Boss is eager to be on,' commented Mark. As he walked with Glenda to her horse, he said, 'I've noticed you've been handling your horse very well. It's not always easy with a new mount but you have a natural gift, as do your daughters, most notably Caitlin.' He helped Glenda mount, which prompted him to say, 'Are you comfortable with our American saddle, Ma'am?'

She waited until he was on his own horse and Gordon had shouted 'Let's ride' before she answered.

'Yes. It was a little strange at first but after a few attempts I felt at home. I can understand why you cowboys need the design you use.'

Mark smiled. 'Today you may witness how the Indians ride, without any saddle, just as Ahote did the day Cat chose Gila. She and that horse hit it off straight away. It was good to see,' he said 'and it hasn't taken you long either to get used to our way of life.'

'Yes, I do enjoy watching you cattlemen working with the steers.' She left a fraction of a pause then said, 'If I am to call you Mark, which I prefer, then if you have no objection you should forget Ma'am and call me Glenda or Glen, I don't mind which.'

Mark touched the brim of his Stetson with two fingers and said, 'As you command, Glen.'

She saw relief in his smile and the atmosphere eased.

'By the way, Glen, that young man Ahote... I noticed you were a little worried about the attention he has been giving Caitlin and how she responds. Don't let it cause you any alarm. He is an honourable young fellow. You can see that from his attitude when your daughter chose the horse he had trained and adored. I rather think Ahote had hoped he would one day have done enough to keep Gila for himself. That was why, when Cat chose her, Gordon put him in charge of the horse, so that there would be no cause for jealousy. You need have no worries about him, Glen.'

She smiled at him warmly. 'Thanks for the reassurance, Mark.'

They rode on without speaking, each sensing that they could enjoy silence together.

After ten miles riding through the foothills Gordon led the way from the escarpment into a grassy valley. In four miles it widened and the trail became more marked. When it turned, to be close to the flowing waters of a wide stream, they were met by the sight of twenty tepees spaced around and close to a rising mound that gave them shelter from the prevailing west wind. The tepees, with their colourful decorations, showed no sign of life.

Zalinda slowed the visitors to a walking pace as they approached the middle tepee. After a few moments the covered entrance in the side was drawn back. Zalinda and Gordon brought the party to a halt. At that moment an Indian stepped out. He was wearing a fringed and patterned buckskin tunic. On his head were two or three feathers and around his neck were beads of bright colours. He drew himself up proudly, feet set slightly apart, perfectly balanced. His dark eyes shone with pleasure at seeing his daughter again.

He stepped forward and held out his arms to Zalinda, who rested her head against his chest, as she had while a child. He moved her aside and held out his hand in welcome to Gordon's party.

'I am Chief Ouray.' Then, sweeping his arms to indicate the members of his tribe, who had appeared outside their tepees, he said, 'I and my people welcome you to our humble homes. Mr Gordon's relations are our friends. I hope your stay in our country is without care. I will meet each of you now and then we will feast.'

He made a gesture to indicate they should go inside his large tepee. In the centre was a hearth where meat was cooking. Smoke rose up to escape from a central hole. The chief signalled for the party to sit themselves down on the buffalo hides spread out on the ground before them. Young women brought in a variety of food. The wild turkey and deer meat were supplemented with herbs, prairie turnips and potatoes. At this sight Glenda realised how hungry she was.

When all was ready, six sharp beats on a drum signalled the time to eat but also brought silence from the few Indians and cowboys who had gathered together. Chief Ouray spoke a few words in his own language.

Cat glanced at Ahote, who had joined her. 'Thanks to Manitou, the Great Spirit, for this food and for our friends,' he translated in a whisper.

Heads were still bowed and Gordon also gave thanks; then they ate. Rosalind, Cat and their

178

mother exchanged looks as they picked up their food with their fingers.

'What a wonderful gathering and greeting,' said Cat to Ahote. 'Don't you think so, Mama?' she added, turning to her mother.

'Yes, I do,' she replied, then curtly acknowledged Ahote without any real warmth.

'Mr Gordon is good to us,' said Ahote. 'He handed over land for us to live on when other people of our tribe were being sent to reservations. Although we used to be a nomadic people, Mrs McKinley, your brother-in-law helped us by teaching our men to do ranch work. Now Indians and cowboys work alongside each other with the cattle and horses. Mr Gordon has a huge area of prairie and wonderful grassland that spreads into the foothills of the mountains. You must let me show you some time.' As if to emphasise that, he added, 'You know how to choose a good horse, Mrs McKinley.'

'Thank you, Ahote. I noted your pleasure in the one my daughter chose; you too have an eye for a good horse.'

'They have been and always will be my life.'

'I would like to meet your mother and father, are they here?' asked Rosalind.

Ahote shook his head as sadness came to his eyes. 'Alas, no, they were killed by another tribe who raided for gain. I was only a baby then. An Arapaho found me wrapped in a blanket and hidden under a tree trunk. My mother must have quickly put me there out of sight. I am ever grateful to her for doing that and to the Arapaho chief of that time for adopting me.'

'So you are not related to Zalinda?' asked Rosalind.

'No. She is Chief Ouray's daughter,' he replied.

After the meal a display of Indian skills on horseback held them enthralled. Glenda was so absorbed by them that she had been unaware of Mark joining her. She started when he said, 'Did you enjoy that?'

'It was breathtaking. They are such wonderful riders, you'd believe they were born in the saddle.'

He smiled as he said, 'Without a saddle!'

She laughed. 'Yes, you're right, of course.'

'Chief Ouray is sorry he has to leave you now to talk with Gordon before we return to the Circle C, but gave permission for me to show you and your daughters around their encampment. They will welcome you, especially if you are with me.'

'You are close to them?'

'I like to think so. They are good people.'

Glenda sensed a deeper understanding developing between her and Mark, but it was to be interrupted by the arrival of two letters the following week.

21

Dear Mrs McKinley,

I am sorry to be burdening you with bad news at this time. My beloved Greg has died as the result of a fall while working in a remote region at the northern end of the estate. He was working alone

180

and not found for three days. Clive went in search of him and was able to return with his father's body.

The funeral has taken place in Gartonhag. Reverend Kintail conducted the service and spoke well of Greg. The attendance was small but we expected no more from the remote area in which we live.

With your permission, if this loss will mean changes for you, Clive and I will carry on until we hear from you.

In sadness, my regards,
Jessie Martins

Dear Glenda,

You will no doubt have received a letter informing you of the terrible tragedy that has befallen Mrs Martins and Clive. From what was gleaned when Clive went to look for him, it appears his father took what he believed to be a short cut, but unsure of the changing terrain, fell down a precipice resulting in his death.

Mrs Martins and Clive are bearing up very well. I have assured them that you would wish for them to carry on while you consider the situation. I hope I did right?

I have our niece Adrianna coming to stay with me for a few weeks whilst her father has to be away. She has recently returned from abroad and it seems she is growing up too fast for Roger's liking. He wants me to take over the role of mother to her! What does he expect me, a maiden aunt, to do with her? She is a high-spirited girl ... or should I say young woman? Ah, well, life can bring unwanted tasks! We have to cope with them and hopefully gain something from them. My competence will be severely tested, no doubt.

I do hope life in Colorado is proving interesting. My love to you, to my two nieces and to Gordon.

Your sister,

Fiona

Glenda's immediate reaction on reading her letters was, 'I should be there. I must go. Oh, why am I so far away when I'm needed?' Irritated, she stamped her foot. But this was no way for her to be acting. Nothing positive could be achieved here. That could only be done by going to Scotland. There would be much to decide and act upon. It was no good expecting problems to solve themselves. Plans must be made. She called out to one of the Indian servants, who appeared as if from nowhere.

'Namia, please find my daughter Rosalind and tell her I want to see her as quickly as possible.'

Namia sped from the house. She had seen Rosalind heading for the stables. In a few minutes the message had been delivered and the girl was hurrying to the house.

'You wanted me, Mama?'

'Yes. Bad news, I am sorry to say.'

'What's wrong, Mama?'

Without considering the contents Glenda held out the letters from Mrs Martins and Aunt Fiona. 'Read these.'

Rosalind took the letters and read the one from Jessie first. She paled at the tragic news. Then she read the letter from her aunt. She saw confirmation of the news about Greg and her aunt's description of Adrianna. A lively young lady in the vicinity? Was she the reason Clive had not corresponded with Ros lately, not even to report his father's death? Had he already met Adrianna and become mesmerised by her? As hard as Rosalind tried to dismiss this idea the more it persisted, taking precedence over what her mother was saying.

'Ros, I fear I must return to Scotland immediately. Changes will have to be made at Pinmuir. Do we wish to return there permanently or to move here? I had not expected to have to face such a choice until we had given life here a full test. Nor did I wish to do so until I was certain that Cat was completely cured of her nightmares. Though she is sleeping better there are still times when I hear her having uneasy nights. She has been doing well, but this news of Mr Martins might just tip the balance again. I don't like leaving her but I feel I must attend to Pinmuir's future in person.'

'Oh, Mama, please may I go too? I am sure Caitlin will be safe here. Besides, you will need a travelling companion. Please, please.'

Her daughter's plea was difficult to refuse, but Glenda answered by taking Ros's hands in hers and saying, 'Oh, my dear, dear girl, I know you want to go back. You love Scotland so much, and besides I know you will want to support Clive, but I need you here. Yes, Cat's nightmares are a part of it but I worry also about her getting too close to Ahote. I am not happy about her forming a loving relationship with an Indian. There is too much that could stand between them.

'I'm sorry, Ros, but if you stay it will take a weight off my mind. I could ask Uncle Gordon and Zalinda but they are not familiar enough with Cat's problem to cope with it alone.'

Rosalind looked crestfallen. She so badly wanted to see Clive again, to hold him and for him to remember what he had been missing. She needed to detach him from this cousin of hers as quickly as possible. Tears of frustration filled her eyes. Cat was a grown woman, let her get on with her own life, thought Ros, but then remembered how her sister had needed her in the past. There was a long pause while she composed her thoughts then she said 'Think no more about it, Mama. I will be here for her. All I ask is that you take a letter from me to Clive.'

'Of course I will. You get it written. I'll find Uncle Gordon and Zalinda and explain what has happened, seek their advice about travelling, but first I must explain to Caitlin.'

Glenda guessed rightly that she would find her daughter at the stables. Caitlin and Ahote were grooming Gila when her mother walked in.

'Good day, Mrs McKinley.' Ahote smiled at her.

Glenda nodded. 'Hello, Ahote,' she replied. 'I need to talk with Caitlin for a few minutes.' She looked at Cat who laid down her brush. 'Should we walk?'

'Very well, Mama.' She glanced back at Ahote and left the stable with her mother.

Caitlin, though shocked by the news of Mr Mar-

184

tins's death, met it with a calmness her mother had not expected.

'I will be returning to Scotland,' Glenda informed her, and went on to explain why she needed to go and what arrangements she intended making for the time she would be away. Then she added, 'I know Ahote is a good friend, Caitlin, but that's all it can be – friendship. It is still early days in the peace between the Indians and the ranchers and we don't understand all the Indian ways. Please don't do anything foolish in my absence. Remember, I trust you to keep your father's good name.'

Cat looked her mother in the eyes and decided it was better to make no objection to this.

As Glenda went on to see Gordon and Zalinda she thought of Caitlin's meek reaction. Her daughter was quickly absorbing the Colorado way of life so perhaps this was truly the solution to her troubled mind.

When Gordon and his wife received Glenda's news they expressed their sorrow for Mrs Martins and Clive, but also concern about Glenda travelling alone.

'You really should have an escort at least until you have found a passage to Britain,' said Gordon. 'Let me take you, I can always mix it with business.'

'I will be perfectly all right,' Glenda insisted, but Gordon would not hear of it.

Zalinda, not happy to be seeing her husband leaving her again, came up with what she hoped would be the solution. 'I believe Mark is due a break even though he hardly ever seeks one. It would do him good to get away for a while, and what better way than to make him feel useful? He hates time off unless he has a purpose in mind.'

'Splendid idea,' Gordon agreed. 'I'll send someone to find him right away.'

A quarter of an hour later they heard the sound of a horse approaching at a gallop. Gordon got to his feet and went outside on to the veranda. Mark, with a query on his face, greeted him from the saddle.

'Here I am, Boss, what have I to take on board?'

'Get out of that saddle and come inside, I have something to ask you.'

'Something troubling you? You rarely call me in from the range. A good job I hadn't ridden further away.'

Mark took off his Stetson, slapped dust off it and then gave his shirt a brush down and unfastened his chaps.

'Forget all that,' Gordon told him. 'We aren't house proud, I've told you that before.'

'Yes, Boss.'

'And I've told you, I'm not your boss.'

'Yes, Boss.'

'Aw, get inside. There's a job for you. If I'm your boss, I'm ordering you to do it. If I'm not your boss, you have a choice – do it or don't do it. So decide what I am.'

'After I've heard what the job is.'

'You're a real cuss.'

Gordon opened the door and Mark followed him inside. He dropped his Stetson on an oak chest and was only a step behind when they entered the large room furnished with two settees,

186

a round table and six accompanying tall-backed chairs. He hid his surprise at seeing the two ladies and acknowledged them with a friendly, 'Good day.'

'Sit down,' said Gordon. When he had settled Gordon continued, 'We are seeking your help, Mark.'

This raised his curiosity, especially as Glenda was there and therefore the request must include her.

'Mrs McKinley has received news from her native Scotland that requires her immediate return. She wishes her daughters to remain here, which presents no problem. The trouble is that, although she insists she will be safe travelling alone, Zalinda and I do not think it a good idea.'

'So you are going to...' Mark stopped talking. He looked askance at Gordon, and said thoughtfully with a little nod, 'Boss or not Boss?'

'Your decision,' said Gordon.

Mark had made up his mind but hesitated deliberately, in order to annoy Gordon. Mark glanced at the two ladies who looked puzzled, not knowing what this banter was about.

'Not Boss,' said Mark, a note of defeat in his voice.

'The full sentence, please,' said Gordon.

Mark pulled a face at him. 'You are not my boss!' he said firmly.

Gordon slapped his thigh in delight. 'Ladies, you witnessed that statement. "You are not my boss."' He looked hard at Mark. 'Remember that in future. We are now partners, signed and sealed by your words in front of witnesses. That's far more binding in my mind than any piece of paper lodged in a Denver safe. This deserves a toast!'

Once the glasses were filled and the toast was drunk, Zalinda said, 'Now that is settled I think, Gordon, you had better relieve Glenda of her problem and convince Mark he wasn't brought here merely for you to trick him into making that admission.'

Gordon chuckled. 'I think we had better do that, but first I believe Mark wants to make an offer.'

'Mrs McKinley, I would be honoured to escort you to New York and see you safely on board a ship to take you home.'

'I am grateful to you, Mark, and it will be a pleasure for me to have you as my escort.' Glenda inclined her head gracefully with her eyes meeting his, expressing thanks and pleasure.

She sought out Rosalind and Caitlin, and received their approval of Mark as her escort.

'Have you anything in mind about the estate?' asked Rosalind.

'I'm not sure. I really need to assess the situation when I get there. I have no doubt that Clive will have learned much from his father, but whether he is capable of running Pinmuir should I decide to settle permanently in Colorado, I will have to see. I think he will be eventually; if he had had more time with his father, I'd be certain of it. What do you think, Ros?'

'He was always interested in the estate and talked a lot about future developments; he seemed keen enough and I think he spoke to Caitlin about it too, but things change and that may just have been pie-in-the-sky. The whole situation has been altered by his father's death. I'll go along with whatever you decide, Mama.'

'So will I, Mama, but I do love it here,' said Caitlin.

Glenda wondered why Ros had been so luke-warm in her opinion but thought it best to let the matter rest. Glenda looked ahead: she would have plenty of time on the journey to think over the future, though she could not of course ignore the handsome cowboy who would be escorting her to New York. Not that she had any desire to do that.

22

'Thank you, Mark, for all your help. It has not only been reassuring to have you with me, it has also been a pleasure.'

Mark took Glenda's hand in his. 'It has been a delight for me too. You have been wonderful company. Perhaps we could spend more time together after your return?'

She smiled and looked deep into his eyes, nodding and answering, 'That could be a possibility.' Glenda was not going to allow herself to appear too keen. Who knew what lay ahead?

'When you know the date of your return to New York, let me know and I'll arrange to meet you here.' Mark gave a little smile. 'And the boss won't be able to say no. After all, I'm officially his partner now.'

Glenda laughed. 'So you are.' She gave him a light kiss on the cheek, turned and hurried up the gangway on to the ship. She found a place against the rail among the other passengers calling good-byes to friends and relations on shore. Glenda saw Mark smiling at her as he touched his cheek where she had kissed him.

The ship left the dock on time, but Glenda and Mark stayed where they were until both were lost to view.

Glenda heaved a thoughtful sigh. Mark was recalling where life had taken him since Glenda and her daughters had arrived at the Circle C. He would carry in his mind a picture of the lady on board that ship for a long time to come. Would she return or would the power of Scotland prevail?

The next day, as Glenda's ship met the Atlantic waves, Caitlin searched for Ros and found her with Zalinda in the house. 'Ros, please may I have a word?' They walked on to the veranda.

'Ahote has asked me to go riding with him and I thought I would let you know.'

Ros remembered her promise to their mother. 'Where are you going? How long will you be away?'

'He hasn't told me.'

'Cat, I know you have a strong friendship with Ahote, but be careful. Don't get too attached. You've never experienced love with a man before and we may, after all, be returning to Pinmuir soon.'

'But I could stay. What is there at home for me?

You have Clive. If I go back, I'll end up an old spinster!' Cat's voice was angry now, which antagonised her sister.

'My relationship with Clive is none of your affair,' Ros shouted, releasing the anger generated by disappointment at having no letter from him recently.

Zalinda, hearing raised voices, came out and asked for an explanation after which she took hold of Ros's arm gently and said, 'Cat is only going for a ride with a friend. Ahote will do nothing wrong; he is a good man. Don't get so worked up about it.'

Ros ignored Zalinda, looked to the ground and then at her sister and said, 'Cat, Mother asked me to keep an eye on you. I know you can take care of yourself, but she is worried. Remember, it was not long ago that these people were known as savages. No offence to you, Zalinda, that's just the way it was.'

Cat gasped. Zalinda looked sad, restrained her anger and said, 'Unfortunately that's true, Cat. Your sister is asking you to be careful, for the sake of your mother. Why don't you ask Ahote to speak with Ros before you go?'

Caitlin and Ahote turned their horses in the direction of the foothills and the Rockies beyond. They rode at a steady pace, at one with their mounts, ready to talk or prepared to share the silence.

'Where are you taking me, Ahote?' asked Cat after they had ridden some distance.

'To a beautiful secret place that I have locked in

my heart, a place I have shared with no one else, but would like to share with you.'

'Where is it?'

'It wouldn't be a secret if I told you now.'

'Then let's get there quickly.' Caitlin laughed, happy that Ros had, in the end, agreed to this outing.

'No, no! The ride there is beautiful. We have plenty of time, and we will be back before dark as I promised your sister.'

'We'll think about the time later,' she said, a mischievous challenge in her eyes.

'As much as I might like what your eyes are telling me, I made a promise and I will keep it. Besides I want a good report about us waiting for your mother when she returns.'

'She need never know what we do.'

'True, but we will do nothing we might be sorry for and that could result in me being cast out by family and tribe. I can't risk that. Besides it would tarnish this ride in our memories and we would lose our respect for each other.'

'You talk like a parent.'

'What is wrong with that? What they say and teach us is for our own good.'

'Nothing, I suppose,' Cat quietly agreed. She pulled her horse to a halt. Ahote drew up beside her.

'Get down,' she said.

He sensed determination in her voice so did as he was told.

She got to the ground and stepped quickly over to him. Before he could do anything, she pulled him into her arms and kissed him on the mouth, holding her kiss beyond the moment when she felt him relax and respond to her.

'Ahote, I love you. I have done since I first saw you riding Gila.'

'Love is too strong a word, Cat. We haven't spent enough time together for that. But when I recognised your riding ability, I realised you were a special woman, and more so when I witnessed your love for Gila, which meant a lot to me. My heart sank when you chose her, but then watching you I recognised your love for her, and from that came respect and a real liking for you.'

Cat was disappointed by his measured response but knew time had to be on her side. She looked into his eyes and smiled.

'This is a memorable day,' she said. 'Now take me to this beautiful secret place you want to share with me.'

'And with you only.' Ahote smiled at her, his dark eyes deep and warm.

They rode on, content in each other's company.

Ahote guided them carefully on a track that grew narrower and narrower, never widening more than the width of a horse and rider. The huge wall of rock, seeming determined to block their way, rose higher and higher and began to weigh on Cat's feelings. She swayed in the saddle, starting to feel short of breath. The walls of rock began to spin. She tried to call out but no sound came. Ahote, in front, glanced round. The sight of a deathly white face drew him out of his saddle. In three paces he was reaching up to Caitlin, grasping her before she could collapse and taking her full weight, steadying her then lowering her to the ground. Alarm surged through him. He cradled her in his arms.

'Caitlin! Caitlin!' Over and over her name came from his lips as he gently rocked her. 'Speak to me. Speak to me! Cat! Cat!' He felt strongly about this young woman, more than he had indicated to her. He pulled her against his chest, gently supporting her.

How long they remained that way they never knew. Ahote felt her stir against his arms. He straightened up and looked down into eyes that were flickering open.

'Cat, speak to me.'

Looking bewildered, she asked, 'Where am I?'

'Safe with Ahote,' he said gently.

'But where am I?'

'In Colorado, America.'

She looked beyond him and then shrank back against him. 'What is that towering over us?'

Ahote was puzzled but realised it was no good trying to deceive her. 'A mountain in the Rockies.'

She nodded. 'Now I remember. You brought me here to show me something.'

'My secret place.'

'Yes.' She looked hard at him. 'Please take me there.'

'Wouldn't you rather go back and see your sister?'

'I will in due course, but first show me your secret place.'

As they had been speaking she was scrutinising his face. He sensed that whatever seemed to have been troubling her was slowly receding. He waited until she felt ready to stand.

'Come then, I will take you there.' She took his

outstretched hand and felt kindness and safety in his touch.

He held her hand as he led her through a gap in the wall of rock. Ahote thanked the Great Spirit that Cat did not have another reaction to the towering walls. Whatever had sparked that darkness had been vanquished!

Ten yards further on the gap widened enough for them to step out on to a rocky shelf that gave them a perfect view across a tranquil deep blue lake into which, on the opposite side, a narrow waterfall ran, light catching its downpour in a series of dancing rainbows.

Ahote felt in Cat's touch that the magic of the place was affecting her just as it had done to him the first time he had seen this hidden masterpiece of nature. He had sworn then never to reveal its presence to anyone, but now he no longer held the secret!

He realised she must have read his thoughts when she stooped down and scooped some water from the lake into her left hand. She dipped her right fingers into it and made a blessing on his forehead, saying, 'Your secret will also be mine until the end of time.'

He pulled her towards him and kissed her brow.

23

The sound of horses approaching drew Rosalind's attention away from the book she was reading. She looked up from the veranda where she had been sitting in its shade. A sense of relief sped through her. Caitlin was back. Then her eyes were drawn to her sister. Something was different about her. She seemed to be more assured, relaxed and totally at ease in this land. Ros felt a lightening of her spirits. The promise to her mother was still binding but it looked as though Cat was managing life here perfectly well already.

Something had happened on this ride, something Ros was eager to know about. Even before she halted her horse, Cat called out, 'Ros, we have had a wonderful ride! Somehow I've come back lighter of heart.'

She was out of the saddle almost before her horse had halted. Ros was out of her chair. They met at the top of the veranda steps and Caitlin locked arms with her sister.

'I've been in such a wonderful place. I had a terrible fright getting there, but that disappeared when we arrived. I feel my bad memories of Father's death have finally left me.'

Ros saw tears welling in her sister's eyes. What had happened to her? It must have been while she was with Ahote but he had ridden away to the stables as if he did not wish to become involved.

Anger and suspicion rose within Ros. Their mother had told Cat she did not wish her to develop a relationship with him yet their day together seemed to have brought them closer. Ros thought of the trouble that lay ahead when her mother returned and felt annoyed with Cat for putting her in this awkward situation. She held back the words that were forming on her lips, words that would wound. She was all too aware that Caitlin's emotions were fragile still.

'I think we had better go inside,' said Ros.

The coldness in her tone needled Cat. 'What do you think I've done?' she demanded.

'You tell me,' rapped Ros and stepped past her sister.

Cat followed her, slamming the door shut. 'You think the worst because I've been out with an Indian!'

'Yes, I think the worst because you are disobeying Mama's instructions not to get involved with Ahote. You dare to do that in spite of my reminder to you. You are placing me in an invidious position when Mama returns. I don't suppose you ever gave that a thought. You were only thinking of yourself.'

'I was not! I was not!'

'Then you were letting Ahote take advantage of...'

'No! You are wrong ... terribly wrong. Why are you condemning me without hearing my side of the story?' Tears started to stream down Cat's cheeks.

Angry with herself Ros snapped, 'Well, tell me what really did happen!'

A downcast Cat said nothing.

'What is this all about?' Ros said in a more patient tone. 'Begin from the moment you rode out from the Circle C today.'

Cat steadied herself. At least her sister sounded calmer and was now trying to be helpful. Cat described her ride with Ahote and the visit to the hidden lake.

'Is that all?' asked Ros. 'You're sure you've told me everything? You say Ahote held you in his arms ... did anything else happen?'

'No,' replied Cat ingenuously.

Ros let the silence stretch and then said, 'I will send for Ahote.'

'No, please don't,' Cat requested.

'I must.'

Cat started to plead but nothing could prevent Ros from pursuing this matter and she believed she must speak to Ahote.

On his arrival, Ros plunged straight in. 'My sister tells me that you were with her when, for some reason, she fainted.'

'That is true, Miss.'

'What happened then?'

'Nothing happened except that I held her in my arms and prayed to the Great Spirit for her recovery.'

Cat quickly continued. 'When I came round I realised I'd fainted because, in my nightmares, I sometimes relive what Father must have gone through ... walking over rocks while feeling the castle walls tumble around him. As you know, my bad dreams have nearly disappeared but now I feel Ahote has finally helped me put the terror

198

behind me. I felt light at heart again.'

Ros looked hard at her sister and then at Ahote. She recognised in them the feelings she had shared with Clive before she'd left him to come West. She was happy for her sister then but felt the contrast with her own situation. Ros went to her and embraced her, saying, 'I am glad you seem well again, Cat.' She glanced towards Ahote. 'Thank you for helping my sister.' He nodded in acceptance of her words and said, 'I must get back to my work.'

As the door closed behind Ahote, Cat said, 'I wish Mother had been here.'

'She will get a surprise when she returns,' commented Ros wistfully.

'It's too difficult to explain by letter,' said Cat. 'Besides I want to be quite sure the nightmares have gone. Let's surprise her with my happiness with Ahote.'

'Are we sure she will come back? She will have much to see to in Scotland during which time I think she will have to consider her plans for the future. Maybe she will choose to stay there,' said Ros.

'What will you do then, Ros?' asked Cat

'I don't know,' she replied. 'There have been times recently when I have thought Clive's feelings for me are not what they once were, though he has never said so. He has not written as often as I'd hoped, but then I haven't communicated with him as much as I used to. Maybe we have both let other things crowd our lives. Everything here has been so new to me, and Clive must take on many extra responsibilities since his father's death.'

'Clive still loves you, I'm sure of it. You were always the one who was so adamant that you would return to Pinmuir,' Cat pointed out.

'True, but life has a habit of changing our outlook. Who ever would have thought you would fall for a Red Indian and do it in defiance of Mother?'

Cat smiled at her. Ros was changing her attitude a little; their mother's return though would prove more testing.

24

Glenda hired a coach in Fort William to complete her journey to Pinmuir. The horses swung round a bend to break away from the encroaching mountains and embrace the widening panorama of the view along Loch Pinmuir and beyond. She was home! The world had spun round and brought her back. White clouds parted to allow the sun to shine on her. She sighed contentedly but it was laced with regret that Ros and Cat were not sharing this homecoming with her.

Then at a glimpse of the ruined castle sadness choked her throat. If only John had not decided to pay it a final visit before they left for America.

A tear slid down her cheek and she forced herself to rein in her emotions. There was a future to be grasped here and choices to be made.

The driver manoeuvred the horses and carriage through the gateway, which she automatically noted had been widened since she'd last passed this way. She had no time to consider anything else; the coach was coming to a halt close to the front door.

Jessie Martins, ever alert for unexpected sounds, came to see who was calling at Pinmuir House. When she opened the front door she stopped as if she had hit a stone wall. Her eyes widened in disbelief.

'Mrs McKinley!' she gasped.

Glenda smiled. 'Yes, it is me, Mrs Martins. I am so sorry for your loss.' She noticed a thinner woman than she remembered, the traces of her recent grief showing in Jessie's face.

'Thank you for your letter. You have arrived sooner than expected but it is so good to see you again and be able to say "Welcome Home".'

'I'm sorry I could not give you an exact date. It's good to see you too. How about a cup of tea for both of us? I'll see to my luggage and pay the coachman and then I want all the news of Pinmuir.'

Mrs Martins bustled back inside and a moment later a maid appeared to help her mistress.

Within a quarter of an hour something nearing normality was restored; the coach had gone and the baggage had been deposited in Glenda's room. When she had refreshed herself, she walked downstairs into the small sitting room where Mrs Martins immediately started to pour the tea.

'Ah, scones! I must thank Mrs Lynch. I have not encountered any to match them on my travels. It feels as if I am truly home.'

'That sounds reassuring, Ma'am.'

Glenda gave a weak smile. 'Not so fast, Jessie. Presently I am here to assess what will happen to this estate. My daughters are still in America and their opinions and suggestions are important to me. After all, they are the ones who will inherit Pinmuir. Apart from that, I expect there will be the accounts to see to and payments to be made. And we must discuss plans for the future, for everyone's sake including yours and Clive's. How is he?'

'Losing his father has thrown a lot more responsibility on him but he has managed quite well. He was upset for a while when Bonnie died but Miss Fiona helped when she bought him Merlin, a strong working horse.'

'Has he taken on anyone else to take care of the maintenance work Greg was doing on the estate?'

'For two months Clive went out on his own but found the work too difficult to get through. He tried hard to find someone and then he heard the McBains were selling up and moving on. You'll remember them, they lived at the end of the loch?'

'Yes, of course I do. They helped in finding John. A good family.'

'Well, their son Tim wanted to stay in the area. When Clive heard this he jumped at the chance to employ a friend. Tim was pleased by the offer and they seem to be working very well together.' Jessie hesitated momentarily then said, with a touch of regret in her voice, 'I'm sorry to say, though, that Clive's work has suffered recently.'

'Well, if Tim is the cause he had better go,' said Glenda crisply.

'Oh, no, it's not that. Clive is managing much better now that he has Tim to help.'

'So what is it? What does he want? I thought Clive would spend the rest of his life here?'

'That is what I have always thought and hoped too.' Jessie tightened her lips and shook her head. 'No, Ma'am, it's because of that Miss Adrianna, your niece who is staying with Miss Copeland. Your sister requested that Clive should accompany her niece on her rides round the area and now she's turning his head. It's a pity that young miss ever came on the scene. I've talked to him, pointing out the pitfalls if he gets involved with someone who thinks she can have everything her way and tries to make us all jump to her bidding. Oh, dear, you don't want to listen to a fussy mother. But I don't want him getting in over his head with Miss Adrianna, nor do I want Miss Rosalind to be hurt. Has she heard anything about your niece from Clive?'

'I don't know. If she has, she has not mentioned it to me. She was very upset when I insisted she must stay with Cat instead of coming here with me, but I do have a letter from her for Clive.'

'He sleeps back at our cottage but will be here for his evening meal, so you could give it to him then,' replied Jessie. 'I'm afraid this evening it will only be a potato and onion pie.'

'Excellent, Jessie. Potato and onion pie was always a favourite with John and me. In America it seems to be nothing but beef. It will be good to have a change.'

Feeling weary, Glenda added, 'I think I am now ready for a rest after my long journey.'

Jessie smiled and said, 'I prepared your room as soon as I received your letter, Ma'am. Now I suggest you have a good sleep. The maid will already have unpacked your things.'

'Thanks, what would I...'

'No need to say another word, Mrs McKinley. It's good to have you back. No matter how long it's for, it will be a pleasure to have you here again.'

When Glenda opened her bedroom door, the comforting feeling of being back home swept over her and she could not resist opening the window.

The colourful hills with their mountainous backcloth seemed to fill her mind and draw her thoughts away from America. She breathed in deeply, the clean air tinged with moisture reminding her of harsh dry days when the prairies gasped for water. As she settled under the eiderdown she gave a little smile. In the forthcoming days there was much to decide: the Highlands or the Rockies, the prairies or the gentle valleys, and would she find love again? Could Mark fill the void left by John? How did her daughters wish to spend their futures and would she ever be free from worrying about them?

Glenda decided there was nothing for it but to sleep, and later this evening she would assess whatever trouble Adrianna had brought in her wake.

25

Jessie had informed Clive that Mrs McKinley was returning to Pinmuir for a while but he had not expected it would be almost immediately. As he sat down for his meal with them Glenda greeted him warmly and was pleased that he immediately enquired after Ros.

'She is well and wanted to come back home with me but I insisted she stay to look after Cat. Ros was very upset. I know she wanted to see you very much, Clive ... oh, but I nearly forgot, she has sent you a letter.' Glenda pulled it from her skirt pocket and watched him put it in his jacket, hopefully to read later.

This he did in the stables that held so many happy memories.

Dear Clive,

It was with shock and a heavy heart that I learned of your father's death after your mother and Aunt Fiona wrote to us. I was surprised that you did not write to me yourself rather than letting me hear about it from others, even though I know I haven't written so frequently lately. Maybe you had perfectly good reasons but I was hurt by the omission. I know it will have been a trying time for you although it does not take long to send a brief word. I felt you left me out and ignored the saying, 'a trouble shared is a trouble halved'.

Did you not think I would have sympathised with all my heart? Or have you found consolation with someone else? I miss you and wish I could be there to help.

Rosalind

He clutched the letter to his chest then slowly screwed it up.

Clive's lips tightened. He did not like being scolded. Did Ros expect him to be always at her beck and call? He did not care for her insinuation that he might have found someone else. Was that just probing or had she heard about his meetings with Adrianna?

His mind flew back to the last moments he had shared with Fiona's niece. He had wanted to know all about her and she told him about her days in Europe and especially Paris, where politics, art and literature were discussed in every street café, frequented by people of all ages. He was fascinated by these glimpses of, what seemed, another civilisation ... and she had been sharing it with him. Adrianna had slid her fingers between his. He had not pulled away; in fact her boldness made him wonder what might happen between them next time they met. He knew she was tempting him, but ... why not? Adrianna was here now; Ros was far away and might never come back. Was she looking for a reason to sever their relationship, or was her final sentence really how she felt?

Why did Ros have to go? He stood up and went over to Freya, put his head against the horse's neck and whispered, 'You're all I have of her now.'

The following day Glenda felt she needed to clear her mind so that she could concentrate on the books that would reveal the condition of the estate's finances. She informed Mrs Martins she would go for a walk; it seemed a long time since she had roamed these hills and glens and today's sky held the promise of a good day. She put on her ankle boots and wool jacket and went in search of solace.

Glenda kept to a leisurely pace and enjoyed her surroundings. After a quarter of an hour the path climbed a small hummock that hid the creek from view. Reaching the top, she stopped to regain her breath and admire the vista that held so many memories for her. John and she had done their courting in these surroundings. Nostalgia swept in with such a force that Glenda had to stop it overwhelming her. She realised she was not alone. A figure she did not recognise had appeared in the far reaches of the wood. What was a stranger doing on her land? Glenda stepped back so as to be hidden. She felt guilty about her action but really did not want to meet anybody now and hoped whoever it was would quickly leave her in peace.

She saw a young lady walking with a purposeful stride. Glenda began to suspect who this was. She glanced around her and, seeing an outcrop of boulders, stepped into a more secure hiding place from which she could keep an eye on the stranger's movements.

She could see that the young lady's clothes were of good quality and fitted so well that Glenda immediately assessed they had been tailor-made for the wearer. She was around eighteen, with beautiful chestnut hair. Her face was gentle with a smile that seemed to be recalling a private secret. She was slim and straight-backed and radiated a beauty that Glenda reckoned could play havoc with any young man's feelings.

This must be Adrianna.

No wonder Clive's mother was worried.

Now Glenda was alarmed too. Ros was so far away. It was always said that absence made the heart grow stronger, but being apart could work the other way too. Had it done so in Clive's relationship with Rosalind? Glenda wondered if she should interfere. Maybe not directly. But how?

She tried to remember the landscape of this area. She needed to recall the quickest path to where she had last seen Clive working. Adrianna seemed confident of the route she was taking but appeared to be in no hurry. Maybe the rendezvous was some time away. Glenda made another survey of the landscape. Then she started off.

She was soon breathing heavily and cursing herself for not doing more walking in America. After nearly half an hour she wondered if she had strayed from the path she had chosen. Espying a rise in the ground a short distance ahead to her right, she took a detour to it. She breathed a sigh of relief when it gave her a wider view and she recognised where she was. A quick survey revealed no evidence of Adrianna, but that did nothing to calm her mind. She resumed her walk at a rapid pace.

Soon Glenda saw two figures working side by side in a small plantation of firs. There was no one else nearby. Though she was relieved Glenda did not slacken her pace.

She saw Clive straighten and look in her direction, surprise on his face. He spoke to Tim beside him and he also pulled himself up, his face too expressing surprise. She saw them exchange a brief word and then Clive started towards her.

'Mrs McKinley! It is a pleasure to see you up here. Is there anything wrong?'

'I just came for a walk to prepare myself for all the paperwork I have to do while I am here. John and I walked here sometimes and I thought it would bring me peace to see it again.'

'Then Tim and I will leave you. We both have other things to attend to elsewhere.'

Glenda saw her opportunity. 'Please would Tim go back to Pinmuir House and tell your mother I may be late for lunch before he starts work elsewhere?'

Clive looked at him and nodded. Tim gathered his tools with a promise to look at some trees they had previously spoken about.

Clive watched him go and said, 'I hope you enjoy your walk, Mrs McKinley. And thank you for Ros's letter. I will send one back for her with you when you return to America, if I may?'

Glenda nodded and stood a while as she watched him walk away in the direction from which Adrianna was approaching. Had they a secret hideaway?

Once Clive had almost disappeared from view she followed him, keeping her distance. It was not long before he turned north to the outer reaches of the estate. Glenda hid behind a tree and watched him leap down into what she remembered as a small hollow. She crept after him quietly.

'Well, if it isn't the Laird of Pinmuir!' Adrianna teased as she held out her hands to grasp Clive's.

He thought how beautiful she looked and in a low voice said, 'We'll have to be careful in future. Mrs McKinley's back and she likes walking this way. I've just spoken to her where Tim and I were working.'

'She's back from America?'

'Yes, but I don't think it will be for long.'

Glenda was seething inside. Hadn't Ros's letter meant anything to him? And what was that about the Laird of Pinmuir? Was Clive getting above his station or was it just Adrianna's wishful thinking? Should she interrupt them? But the couple moved closer and Adrianna put her fingers to his cheek. 'Kiss me, Clive. I hardly slept last night for thinking of you.'

Clive's eyes met hers. Recalling the way Ros had chastised him in her letter, he pulled Adrianna roughly to him and kissed her passionately. Glenda turned and ran down the low hillock, tears for her daughter starting to fill her eyes. Ros did not deserve this.

26

Over lunch Glenda was quieter than usual. When should she approach Clive, if at all? The problems seemed insurmountable. They had just finished their meal when they heard the sound of a horse approaching.

'Miss Fiona, no doubt,' commented Mrs Martins. She glanced at her son. 'You be careful what you say.'

Clive made no reply to this but went to open the front door ready to greet their visitor. His mother proved to be right. Fiona was slowing her horse. He went out to help her from the saddle.

'Good day, Fiona,' he greeted her amiably.

She gave him a nod and asked, 'Is my sister inside?'

'Yes.'

'Please tell her I am here.'

'Certainly.'

He turned away, but before he could reach the front door, Glenda appeared.

'Hello, Glen,' Fiona greeted her. 'Thank you for your letter. If I had known the exact day of your arrival, I could have arranged to meet you. And why didn't you let me know you were back?'

'Because I've only just returned,' laughed Glenda, 'and wasn't sure of my plans. There's a lot to see to here, as I'm sure you can imagine.'

'Well, no matter. I was hoping to bring

Adrianna to meet you today but she had other arrangements. No doubt you will meet her soon.'

Glenda, relieved not to have to face her niece, answered, 'Don't worry, I am sure she has a lot to do now she's home again from Europe. Besides, her father disowned me so she has no reason to seek my acquaintance now.'

Fiona quickly changed the subject. 'It's good to see you looking so well. American life must suit you. You must tell me all about it. And perhaps you might invite me to experience it for myself sometime.'

Glenda gave a short smile. 'I'm not sure you would fit into their way of life! It's hard, dusty work, and we all pull together for the good of the rest.'

'I won't know until I try it.'

'Knowing you, you will probably jump in without thinking, but don't do any jumping yet. I'm not sure I will be remaining there.'

'Are you serious? Will you be here some time, or perhaps permanently?'

'That remains to be seen. There's more than one life to be considered.'

'I expect there is,' Fiona agreed.

'Cup of tea, ladies?' Mrs Martins called from the doorway.

'If it's accompanied by one of Mrs Lynch's scones,' said Fiona with an anticipatory smile.

'Already warming in the oven.'

The sisters settled to enjoy their time together, and once they had grown accustomed to each other again, Glenda decided this might be a good time to bring up the subject that had been prey-

212

ing on her mind.

'Fiona, Mrs Martins mentioned you had asked Clive to partner Adrianna on her rides. Why was that?'

'So that she would rid herself of this high-and-mighty way of behaving she has. It isn't attractive and she will soon be in the market for a husband. She'll never get anywhere with men, acting like that.'

'You never contemplated that something might develop between her and Clive?'

'No... Never.' Fiona looked surprised but from her sister's expression realised something must have happened. 'Surely not? It can't be...'

Glenda raised her eyebrows. 'I happened to come across them together while I was out on a walk. I don't know how serious their relationship has become but it has certainly passed beyond being good friends.'

Fiona looked truly shocked. She buried her head in her hands for a moment. 'Oh, Glenda, I am so sorry to hear this and will try and stop it immediately. I'll have words with Adrianna when I return.'

'That might just make her more rebellious. She has that same impulsive streak I had at her age. I was hoping the letter from Ros I brought for Clive might have helped, but I fear not.'

'Glenda, I'm sure Clive really loves Ros.' But while she spoke Fiona recalled the times Adrianna had talked of the handsome young estate manager. How could she have been so blind?

Glenda went on, 'I think Ros will return to Pinmuir sometime in the future. She does not share

Caitlin's enthusiasm for America. I will tell you all shortly but I realise now that I need to consult a solicitor about the future of the estate and to make sure the girls are taken care of no matter where we decide to make our home.'

'So it looks as if my offer to buy Pinmuir is blown away.'

'More than likely, but who knows what tomorrow may bring?'

'Remember you promised me first refusal, if selling becomes a possibility.'

'I will remember.'

'Now tell me all about America.'

Jessie Martins could hear the chatter and laughter coming from the sitting room. It was good to have the house come alive again. She hoped Glenda would decide to make a permanent move back here within the year.

27

Anxious to see her future settled, Glenda set about putting things into place.

Wanting the girls' inheritances settled, she consulted her solicitor. He agreed with her suggestions for making the legacies of Rosalind and Caitlin watertight provided she did not leave herself destitute in doing so.

'I'm sure my daughters would see that did not happen, Mr Fielding,' Glenda countered his cautious approach.

'From what I know of them, I'm sure you are right, Mrs McKinley,' the solicitor hastened to reassure her, but he added, 'New ways of life change people. I'd advise you to be cautious in your disposition of your assets. First and foremost you need to provide for yourself and think in the long term. You are still a young woman. From what I hear your estate seems to be thriving now and you are comfortably off; you have cash and land to provide an income for you in the years to come. Think carefully about all this and come and see me again.'

'I will, Mr Fielding, and I will make it soon because I don't want to delay too long before I return to America.'

'Very well, Mrs McKinley, I know what you are trying to do. I will have the necessary documents drawn up for your approval, shall we say three weeks from today?'

'That would be splendid. Thank you. I look forward to seeing you again then.'

On reaching home Glenda asked for a fresh horse to be ready for her when she had finished a light lunch. She had decided that with the weather holding fine, she would look over the estate and see the progress Clive and Tim had achieved during the time they had been working together. As her ride progressed, she became increasingly impressed by what they had achieved.

New plantations had been established in places where she would not have seen the potential. The sheep seemed to be thriving and there was a stone fold behind one of the new stands of trees, providing shelter for the flock. Rocks had been dragged from the riverbed and a small waterfall now made a picturesque approach to the front of Pinmuir House. She halted her horse and sat drinking in the view, marvelling at what the two young men had achieved already.

Glenda let her thoughts drift. Though her immediate future was mapped by the return to Colorado – what then? Return to what she was looking at, to what she still thought of as home? Or was there something new that was tugging at her – a new beginning in a new land, perhaps with another person's encouragement. How much did she love the handsome, kindly American cattleman? Would she ever feel for him as she had for John?

'Hello, Mrs McKinley.'

She started on hearing a man's voice and turned quickly, 'Oh, hello, Tim.'

He smiled. 'You were far gone, Mrs McKinley.'

Glenda laughed. 'I was, wasn't I?'

'Somewhere nice, I hope,' he said politely.

'It might be ... I don't know. Do you know where Clive is?'

'He should be the other side of this hill, on the flatter ground. Would you like me to ride with you, to see if he's still there?'

'That would be kind. I've been on my own since early afternoon.' Glenda wondered if she would find Clive working or maybe with Adrianna.

As they rode together Glenda took the opportunity to ask Tim, 'Do you like working at Pinmuir?'

'Oh, yes, I do, Mrs McKinley. It was a godsend to me that Clive was looking for help when my parents decided to move nearer Edinburgh. I didn't want to go. I love this part of the Highlands. Anywhere else would have been a foreign land to me.'

'So you are settled here?'

'For as long as you wish to employ me, Ma'am.'

'I'm pleased to hear that, Tim. I am busy making plans for the future.'

He looked startled and concerned. 'You aren't thinking of selling, are you?'

'I'm not fully decided yet but I think the answer will be no.' She could not mistake the relief that came into his face then.

They had topped the rise. 'There he is, Ma'am,' said Tim, pointing ahead to his right.

'Seen him,' Glenda answered, relieved that Clive was on his own.

'Would you like me to leave you, Ma'am? Do you wish to speak to Clive alone?'

'No,' she replied. 'Stay.'

'Yes, Ma'am.'

In a few minutes greetings were being exchanged with Clive.

'I've been riding round the estate,' said Glenda, 'and I met Tim. When I asked where you were, he offered to escort me. There's a big flat-topped stone over there. Let's sit down and talk.'

Clive swung from his saddle, wondering what was coming.

When they were at ease, Glenda said, 'I am very pleased with what I have seen today. Your work and ideas are splendid. Far better than I could have directed you to do.'

The young men murmured their thanks, but inwardly they were feeling delighted by the praise.

'Have you further plans?' she asked.

'At the moment we tend to act on short-term improvements,' said Clive.

'Not a bad idea but you must not forget the bigger picture,' Glenda pointed out. 'With the progress you have made I think you could start looking into increasing income from the estate.'

'Tim and I have discussed that.'

'We have two small plantations of pines we believe are ready for felling,' said Tim enthusiastically. 'Clive has been sounding out a local timber dealer.'

'And he has promised he will have a look and give us his opinion within the next week.'

'Well done! It is good to see all the enthusiasm you have put into looking after the estate. You have enhanced its beauty, but also viewed it as a paying enterprise. Keep on this way and you will not go unrewarded.'

As she left them Glenda felt more convinced about her decision to keep the estate. Now she would consult Mrs Martins about the accounts, visit the solicitor with the books and then her work would be done.

'I may be able to return to America sooner than I thought,' she told Jessie later.

'I see. Does that please you, Ma'am?'

Glenda screwed up her face doubtfully. 'I don't know. I don't seem to be able to make up my mind.'

'Something will happen to make everything slip into place exactly as you want it,' Jessie told her encouragingly.

Glenda sighed.

'You have great faith, Jessie. I hope you are right.'

28

The next morning Glenda rose early and after breakfast wrote to the shipping company, reserving the best cabin available on the first liner sailing from Liverpool to New York the following month.

She went over the accounts closely with Jessie and went to see the solicitor, who seemed impressed with what he saw. 'The villagers thought that once your husband had gone and the family and you left for America, the estate would die. You have two good workers there by the look of it,' he said and Glenda was gratified to hear it. If only Adrianna were not around, causing complications.

The reply from the shipping company came a week later informing Glenda that she was booked first-class on the *North Star* leaving Liverpool for New York on the fifth of August. Her ticket and sailing documents could be picked up there.

She immediately penned a letter:

Dear Mark,

I write to tell you that I would like to avail myself of your kind offer to meet me in New York on my return to America. I have taken passage on the

219

North Star. I leave from Liverpool for New York on the fifth of August. All being well I should arrive in New York a week later, I hope this is suitable for you. If not, please say so.

I look forward to seeing you again and hope all is well at the Circle C.

With my thoughts and good wishes,
Glenda

She then wrote to both Rosalind and Caitlin informing them of her plans for returning to the Circle C, ending the letter:

…It will be good to see you both. I have much to tell you. Everything has gone smoothly here so I am able to return earlier than expected. I hope all is well with you and that life at the ranch is still enjoyable.

Love,
Mama

Even though she was busy with her preparations to leave Scotland, Glenda found time to be with Fiona. Adrianna was not mentioned and Glenda did not press the matter, wanting Rosalind to settle everything herself. Glenda's last days before leaving were spent absorbing the changing spirit of Pinmuir. One day her attention was drawn to two figures, hand-in-hand, climbing a distant slope. Clive and Adrianna! What had Ros's letter said to Clive that had driven him into another girl's arms? Glenda waited until they had passed from her sight then she hurried home. She was due to leave Scotland in a couple of days. Clive had told her to tell Ros that he was only halfway through the letter he was writing her and would post it shortly. Glenda would more than likely reach Colorado before it arrived. She dreaded what it would say.

When Fiona came to bid her sister goodbye and a safe crossing of the Atlantic, Glenda could not restrain herself. 'Did you mention Clive to Adrianna?' she asked.

'Yes, I did, and she said there was nothing serious in it.'

'But they seemed very close when I saw them together two days ago.'

'Adrianna assured me it was just simple companionship on both sides. She has few acquaintances here since she's been abroad so long. Let her live a little, as we did at that age, Glenda. Remember, you had just met John when you were Adrianna's age.'

'But...'

'Oh, don't worry so! Clive *does* love Ros,' Fiona told her impatiently, then changed the subject. 'Are you being met in New York?'

'Yes.'

'By Gordon's partner at the Circle C, the man you mentioned escorting you on your way over?'

'Yes. He's called Mark. You'd like him.'

'Seems to me he's made for you,' commented Fiona, with a sidelong look.

Glenda smiled.

'We'll see.'

'Whatever you say, but take notice of your sister's advice: follow your heart.'

That advice was still ringing in Glenda's mind when all she could see was the ocean stretching around her.

She'd hoped the Atlantic crossing would give her an opportunity to resolve her problems but it did not. The week on the liner passed quickly and she enjoyed meeting new people. What would she tell Ros when she saw her, though? And how would she feel about Mark after her time back at Pinmuir. Glenda felt herself becoming despondent as the ship drew nearer and nearer to the quay.

She scanned the crowded dockside for a sight of him. Her eyes searched the crowd again. Her heart missed a beat. But two people were waving frantically as if trying to capture someone's attention. It couldn't be... It was! It truly was! Her heart brimmed over with joy – Ros and Cat were here. But how? Why? Their faces were wreathed in joy as they made their way nearer the ship's gangway. Then they were battling against the tide of passengers pouring on to the dockside. In a few minutes Ros and Cat had their arms locked round their mother, and the three of them wept with happiness.

Then the questions. How did you get here? Why aren't you at the ranch? Did you have a good voyage? Is everything all right at Pinmuir?

Then Glenda heard: 'Welcome back.'

The deep drawl brought her spinning round. 'Mark! This was your doing?'

'I thought it was what you would want.'

'It is, it is!' There was no denying the pleasure he had brought her. 'This is such a wonderful surprise.'

'Well, I'm delighted you approve. I'll escort you all to the hotel. We have a compartment booked on the train for Denver the day after tomorrow.'

'How thoughtful. It's so good of you to take all this trouble.'

'My pleasure,' replied Mark, with a little bow of his head. 'But let me say, here and now, that Gordon insisted on paying for the hotel and train travel. I protested but he won. He usually does.' Mark cut short the topic by waving to Sam, who drew up in his cab.

'Good day, ladies. I'm happy to see you once more,' said the driver as he climbed down to help with the luggage.

'Sam!' gasped Glenda. 'We meet again. Another splendid surprise.'

'Kind of you to say so, Ma'am.'

Mark rode outside with the driver as they left the docks, allowing the women some privacy.

As soon as they were seated, Glenda said to her daughters, 'You both look well. Colorado life must be suiting you.'

Neither of them took up this observation, merely replied, 'We'll tell you all about it at the hotel.' Glenda realised she would have to take her chance then of telling Ros the distressing news about Clive. So far she had passed over it by telling her of the letter that would soon be arriving and of all the work he had done on the estate.

At the hotel Mark left them to settle in. Glenda's daughters, as prearranged, came to her room to exchange news.

'What have you to tell me?' she asked when they were sitting comfortably.

Both of them talked animatedly about life at the Circle C.

'Yes, but how have *you* been?'

Ros and Cat looked at each other.

'Mama, you asked me to take responsibility for Cat's welfare, and to watch out for any signs of her illness recurring. Well, I must report there have been no nightmares,' Ros told her. 'However, she fainted while she was out riding...' Ros hesitated for a moment.

'Go on,' Glenda prompted her.

Ros continued without expanding on all the circumstances. 'That's it,' she said, when she had finished. A momentary silence filled the room.

'You are telling me that Cat fainted because she was in a narrow space?'

'Yes, Mama. I believe it was a form of claustrophobia that caused me to faint,' Cat confirmed.

'Did you fall ... hurt yourself? Where were you, Ros? What did you do?'

There was a short silence. Caitlin decided there was no use trying to cover up the incident. 'No, Mama. I slid out of the saddle rather than fell. Ahote had seen me fainting. He caught me and stayed with me until I felt well enough to return to the Circle C. By the time we reached it I was feeling perfectly well. Much, much better than I have done since the tragedy at Pinmuir. It seems like a miracle.'

Glenda hid her surprise at Caitlin's open recollection of the tragedy in Scotland and its outcome. 'And that was it?' she asked.

'Yes.'

Glenda approached her elder daughter and

looked at her closely. 'I'll ask you again: where were you, Rosalind?' she asked, rather accusingly.

'Back at the ranch, Mama.' Ros hung her head momentarily.

'What?' Glenda exploded. 'I told you to look after Cat while I was away. It seems you took no notice.'

'I was looking after her,' countered Ros quickly. 'I judged Cat to be strong enough for the ride and believed the fresh air would do her good.'

'But out alone with an Indian ... you can never tell what might happen. You seem to have forgotten, it's not long since they were killing General Custer and his men.'

'Mother! That was during a war! We are at peace now.'

'And look at the Indians on Uncle Gordon's land,' put in Caitlin. 'They are peaceful and friendly enough. Besides, if Ahote hadn't been with me I might have lain there until I died from the heat. It wasn't a place other people go.'

'So why had he taken you there?'

'To show me a beautiful secret place.'

'Secret? *His* secret, Cat, so anything could have happened and nobody would have found you.'

An angry tone came into Cat's voice. 'I am disgusted if that is what you think of him and of your own daughter. Ahote is an honourable young man and would never allow any harm to come to me. I suggest you forget your anger with Ros and with me, and realise that there is good in everyone – even those who aren't white.'

Cat stormed from the room followed by Ros, who looked back over her shoulder, calling out,

'You've only yourself to blame, Mother,' before slamming the door behind her.

Their words shocked Glenda. She sat quite still for a few minutes, expecting the girls to come back. They did not. This was not the reunion she had expected. If only John were here. He would have handled this far better than she had done. Glenda sank on to her bed and wept.

29

A restless night did not solve Glenda's problems. She woke after a short shallow sleep wishing she was still back at Pinmuir. She realised it was up to her to make peace with her daughters and there was still the conversation about Clive that she must have with Ros.

She realised she must re-examine her attitude towards Ahote. Had she properly examined her feelings towards him? She had observed what was happening between the Indians and the white men on the Circle C. Efforts were being made to forge an alliance. Now, when she really considered the situation, she realised how deep her intolerance was, and how it was all she had ever known; people of different races weren't really understood in the Highlands. She knew she must put a stop to this way of thinking if she wanted to repair the damage she had caused between herself and her daughters.

There was a new day to face.

When she walked into the dining room she

found Ros and Cat already at the table with Mark.

'Good morning to the three of you,' said Glenda brightly.

'Good morning, Mama,' replied Ros and Caitlin politely but she could hear the underlying ice in their tone.

'Good morning, Glenda,' Mark replied with a smile.

She wondered if her daughters had mentioned anything to him about the disagreement, but she guessed they would not have done.

Breakfast was a slightly stilted occasion. Mark noticed that something was amiss, though he was gentleman enough to make no observation. Instead he tried to take the conversation along a different tack and was immediately successful.

'First thing we do this morning is go shopping. I am going to buy three dresses or three riding outfits for three people, not far away. It has been my pleasure to escort them so far and I hope it will continue to be so all the way to the Circle C.'

He was pleased to see his offer had brought the bright light back into Rosalind's and Caitlin's eyes.

'You are being far too generous. You shouldn't spoil us,' Glenda protested.

'My pleasure,' he replied. 'Now which is it to be?'

'Riding clothes, please,' Rosalind and Caitlin replied without hesitation.

'That was a quick decision,' commented Mark. 'What about you, Glenda?' Seeing her hesitate, he quickly added, 'I won't take a refusal. You must make my pleasure complete by accepting my offer.'

'Then I agree. What I would really like is a good outdoor coat ready for winter.'

'It shall be yours,' he replied, with undisguised pleasure in his eyes.

So began two days of enjoyable shopping and fine dining at some of the best restaurants in the city. A joyous spirit enveloped them and Glenda hoped their disagreements had been exorcised by their time spent together in New York. It seemed to be that way on their train journey west. There was plenty to keep them occupied and more than enough for them to see. All three women had much to consider as they sensed their arrival in Colorado would lead to a watershed in their lives.

Gordon and Zalinda welcomed them all back with an invitation to dinner. There was much conversation about Circle C, New York, Pinmuir, the horses and cattle ... topics ranged far and wide. But between Glenda and her daughters there was still a slight air of restraint.

The next morning Rosalind and Caitlin left the breakfast table to see their horses and used the time together to talk over their future.

'Do you think Mama has got over her prejudice against Indians and especially Ahote?' asked Caitlin, hoping that her sister would not brush the question aside. Caitlin desperately wanted Ros's advice. She felt relief surge through her when her sister answered.

'I knew you would eventually ask me that. It's a question we both have to face and better two minds than one.'

'I don't want to hurt Mama but her attitude

towards him is just blatant prejudice.'

'We have to try and put ourselves in her shoes,' said Ros. 'It must be a shock to her on many counts. Remember, none of us faced the question of race before coming here, and we are young and open to new challenges. She cannot understand your growing friendship with Ahote. She also believes that I disobeyed her instructions to look after you while she was away.'

'But can't she see it from another point of view? Can't she see the example of Uncle Gordon and Zalinda?'

'But remember how shocked we all were on our arrival, when we first realised they were man and wife. I suppose the difference is that they were already married and we just had to accept that. It would have been worse for Mother than it was for us as Uncle Gordon had not made any attempt to tell her and they are old friends. She must have felt betrayed. Also, Zalinda is no common Indian, but what we might term royalty within her tribe. I suppose Mama sees Ahote as merely an Indian brave who is taking her daughter away from her.'

'So what can I do?'

'Be patient. Let her see there is no harm in your friendship with him.'

'Do you think that will work?'

'You and Mama must try and see things from one another's point of view.'

'Ros! Can I talk to you about something?' called her mother, coming out on to the veranda.

Both girls turned to her.

Catlin nodded thoughtfully to Ros. 'You'd better go. We don't want to upset her further.'

'Can you get Brandy ready for me?' Ros asked.

Caitlin gave her sister a quick hug. 'Of course! Thanks, sis. You are a Godsend.'

Ros approached Glenda.

'What is it, Mother?'

'Ros, sit down. Have you received a letter yet from Clive? Gordon and Zalinda went into Denver yesterday and I wondered if they had collected one for you?'

'No, Mama, but you did say he was busy.'

'I have something I need to tell you. I am only sorry I have not been able to confide in you before now. I know it will upset you and while we were in New York I wanted us all to enjoy ourselves.'

They sat down. Glenda took Ros's hands in hers. She told her daughter what she had seen at Pinmuir: 'But your aunt seems to think it will soon blow over when Adrianna's father returns. She implied there was nothing serious between our niece and Clive, just a deep friendship.'

Ros sat in shocked silence. Glenda rose and rested her hand on her daughter's shoulder. 'Think hard about what you want to do. You can build a good life here for yourself and I'm sure you will fall in love again.'

Ros raised her head and looked her in the eyes. 'I didn't want to come here, Mother, but I did it for Cat. This is not the place I want to be. I long to breathe the Scottish air and scramble through the rocky glens again. I was happy there with Clive. I believed in him and he in me. Coming here, so far away, was bound to cause problems.

I don't know what has happened with my cousin but I still believe he and I can have a future together.'

'But...'

'Yes, it means I must go home to Pinmuir.' Relief surged through Ros as she said those words. She rose from her seat decisively and added, 'Please don't oppose me. I will ask Uncle Gordon to arrange the travel side of things, but, Mother, I want to go home as soon as possible. Don't let the Martins or Aunt Fiona know.'

Glenda paled at the thought of losing her eldest child. 'Ros,' she pleaded. 'You mustn't be so hasty. This is what you feel in the immediate aftermath of hearing about Clive. Think again, discuss it with Caitlin, and if your answer is still the same in a few days, ask me then about going back. I need to think about how it will affect Cat and me.'

Glenda was certain that Cat would want to stay in America. If Ros went back to Scotland, where did that leave her mother?

30

Later that night Ros told Caitlin of her plan. Her sister was upset but they had begun to realise their lives were taking individual paths. Although the parting would bring great sorrow, each would know the other was living as she chose. In one thing they were united: they would not allow their mother's prejudices to colour their own attitudes.

Neither of them spoke to her about this but Glenda sensed the unease they'd felt since the argument in New York.

Eventually she broke the ice. 'I need to say something to you both now that you're setting out on the courses you will take. I would like to say that I am sorry I upset you both on my return. I should not have criticised you in the way that I did. I should have listened more to what you had to say. In my defence, and after due consideration, I believe my extreme attitude was probably caused by the way I was brought up and the problems I have had to face over the last four years. I will learn to adjust to life as it is now but it will take time. Please will you forgive me and let us start again?'

Ros glanced at Cat, who nodded at her to speak for them both. 'Of course we will, Mama. And we have something to discuss with you, so let us start with a clean slate.' They rose from their chairs and set a seal on the peace between them by exchanging kisses.

When they were settled once more, Glenda asked, 'Who wants to be first?'

'I think I had better be. I intend to return to Pinmuir.'

'Very well,' Glenda conceded. 'And I take it you still want to be reconciled with Clive.'

'Oh I do, so very, very much,' replied Ros fervently. 'I will brook no opposition from Adrianna, if she is still around.'

Glenda approved of her elder daughter's determination. 'Then we had better get organised, telling your uncle, packing your things for shipping, booking your passage – oh, so many things to see to! I'll come with you to New York. You'll be able to manage by yourself from then on, I'm sure.'

'And I'll come with you, Mama, then you'll have company for your return to the Circle C,' offered Cat.

'That's very thoughtful of you, dear. Thank you. It will be hard watching Ros leave but we'll make the best of it and try to enjoy another visit to New York.'

Glenda fixed her attention on Cat then. 'That's Ros settled as far as we can see. There'll be a lot left for you to do when you get back to Scotland, Ros, but I know you'll succeed. What about you, Cat?'

'I want to stay in Colorado.'

Glenda felt a pang of disappointment; she had hoped they would all stay together but it was evident now that this was not to be. She warned herself to be careful how she expressed her opinions this time. 'Very well, Cat. What do you intend to do here?'

'I'll sweetheart Uncle Gordon into allowing me some land to start a horse breeding business, particularly quarter horses. There'll always be a market for them as long as cattle-rearing thrives. I can see no reason for it not to succeed.'

'You are serious in this?' queried Glenda.

'Oh, yes! You know my love of horses. But I'll seek Uncle Gordon's advice and guidance.'

'I'm sure he will help. I think Mark will be interested too. One thing I would ask of you: don't just rely on their charity. I would...'

'I would never do that, Mama. If they see the possibilities, I would wish everything to be placed on a business footing, drawn up legally so there can be no argument about anything in the future.'

'Sensible young lady,' commented her mother. 'Now, I've got to ask this and please don't think I am trying to derail your plan ... I just want to be clear about everything so you won't be upset if anything goes wrong with your scheme.'

'Nothing will go wrong, Mama. I'll make sure it doesn't. But what do you want to ask me?'

'Where does Ahote stand in your plans?'

Caitlin did not make an immediate answer but after a moment's silence she said, carefully and deliberately, 'Mama, this idea was not a sudden whim of mine. I worked carefully on it before I confided in you. Knowing Ahote's love of horses too, and the special affinity he has with them, I told him what I intended, making him promise to tell no one else. I know he has kept to his vow as I would always trust him to do.

'There is something else you should know. Contrary to what you imagine, nothing happened between Ahote and myself while you were away. I say again, it did not. Neither of us would have allowed it to. If we had it would have destroyed the special relationship we have. These are the terms on which I desire to stay in Colorado.'

Silence reigned for a few moments before Glenda spoke up. 'Cat, you have been very forthright with me and I thank you for that. I most humbly apologise for thinking ill of you and Ahote. Please forgive me.'

Cat jumped up and rushed to her mother, to hug her and say, 'Of course I do, Mama.'

'Ros, you will find when you get home that

there is a great deal of legal work to be studied and documents to be signed. I went into it all when I was last there. I had also to consider Caitlin's rights in the estate. That has all been settled with the necessary documents. I hope you will agree that the provisions I made are fair to you both, and will not impinge on any future developments in your lives. Should you and Clive decide to marry, your future at Pinmuir is assured.

'Now all I can say is: remember I am here and will help you both in any way I can, even though that might be difficult at times when there are thousands of miles between us.'

'We'll manage somehow,' said Rosalind.

'Yes, we will,' Glenda agreed. 'But your situation is the one that requires immediate attention. We'll concentrate on that for now. Start packing whatever you will need with you. Everything else can be consigned for shipment to Pinmuir. Cat, for now please help your sister. I know you will want to see your business started as soon as possible but it must not be rushed.' She looked thoughtful for a moment and then announced, 'I think we will arrange to have a family meal in a few days' time and celebrate your plans for the future. So there will be we three, Uncle Gordon, Zalinda...'

'And Mark,' cut in Cat. 'He'll be needed for escort duties, Mama, when we go to see Ros set sail for Pinmuir.'

'I'll have you for company,' Glenda objected.

'But you'd like him along too. If you aren't going to ask him, I will.'

Glenda capitulated with very little protest. She

then said, 'If Ahote is going to be involved in your project, Cat, he had better dine with us too.'

Cat's eyes dampened as she silently mouthed, 'Thank you.'

31

Zalinda, impeccably dressed in a close-fitting housecoat that matched the colour of her hair, hurried into the room when the maid informed her that they had visitors. Her broad smile and open arms expressed a warm welcome as she hugged each one of them in turn. 'This is a lovely surprise,' she said. 'And so early in the morning.'

'I hope we are not intruding?' said Glenda.

'Of course you aren't. You know you are most welcome any time.'

Gordon walked in dressed for the outdoors, carrying his Stetson and wearing the heeled calf-length boots that showed some part of his morning would be spent in the saddle.

'Great to see you all,' he said, smiling. 'Stay and have some coffee?'

'Thank you, but we have just had breakfast. If you can spare the time, we have something to ask you,' said Glenda.

'Anything for my dear sister-in-law.'

'I must tell you that Ros and Cat have made some decisions about what they want to do with their lives. I'll let them tell you. First Rosalind.'

At a nod from her mother Rosalind announced,

'I am returning to Pinmuir.'

'For good?' queried Gordon.

'Yes. Although hopefully I'll have the option of visiting you in the future.'

'And is the young man I've heard talk about still in the picture?'

'He'd better be or else I'll want a very good reason why not.'

'Be wise about it, Ros,' said Zalinda in her quiet way. 'Don't rush in too quickly. You have a long future before you; choose your man carefully.'

Ros nodded her acceptance of this advice.

'Now you, Cat,' Glenda prompted.

Cat swallowed, a little embarrassed now to reveal the scope of her ambitions.

'I want to stay in Colorado.'

Nobody spoke. Zalinda glanced at her husband, who for a moment looked a little bemused by this bald statement.

Cat then broke into a torrent of words as she outlined her scheme. When she paused for breath, her uncle said, 'If I understand you rightly, Cat, you want to spend your life here, in Colorado, raising horses?'

'Yes, Uncle Gordon. But I'll need your help.'

'I understood that,' he said with a wisp of a smile. 'What does your mother think to this idea?'

'When we decided to take up your offer and visit you, that is all we had in mind – just a visit, but I did say if it led to any of us wanting to stay permanently I would support that choice. Now you've just heard the decisions of my daughters and I will stick to what I agreed with them.'

'And you ... what have you decided to do,

Glenda?' asked Zalinda.

Glenda gave a little shake of her head. 'I don't know. I'm torn between the two options. Ros must go as soon as possible. I have been to Scotland recently; all is in order there regarding the estate, so she can easily move in without my being there. For the moment I will see how Cat fares and whether she still wants to settle here once she has tried horse-rearing.'

Gordon nodded his approval. Turning to Ros, he said, 'First, all of us on the ranch will miss you, Mrs Bradley and the school children especially so. Zalinda and I are sorry you will be leaving and wish you every happiness in the future. Pinmuir is clearly the place for you and in that you are more like your father than you realise. I think he might have done the same thing after visiting us a while.'

Zalinda added, 'Please don't ever forget us, Ros. May the Good Spirit be with you for ever, and may you always walk in happy shoes.'

Ros's eyes were damp as she hugged her aunt and uncle.

'Now, Cat, have you thought your idea through?' Gordon asked her. 'You do realise you still have much to learn? Rearing horses can be physically draining even for the cowboys, and there's a lot of mental strain too. Above all you must understand quarter horses: their way of working, their physical make-up, character, and what makes them differ-ent from other breeds plus, of course, gaining an affinity with them. That can mean spending long days in the saddle, no matter if the weather is searing hot, blowing a gale or thick with snow. You'll also have a business to run and accounts to keep. But the work can bring you much joy in the friendship and love you gain from horses.'

'I will take notice of everything you have said and make sure I don't let any of you down.' Cat looked to her mother who gave her a nod of approval.

'If I could say a word?' said Glenda. 'No one else knows of our plans so may I ask you not to breathe a word of them for the moment? I would like to give Rosalind a farewell supper at which Cat can announce her plans to all those who will be included in them. Shall we say six o'clock in three days' time?'

A murmur of agreement was given.

'If you need any help, I'll make myself available,' Zalinda offered. 'And I am happy to accompany you on the journey to and from New York.'

'Thank you. That would be most helpful,' said Glenda. 'And our further thanks to you and Gordon for making our time with you so enjoyable and now fruitful.'

'Your family is our family,' replied Zalinda, 'and always will be no matter where we are.'

32

It was a busy three days for Glenda and her daughters and they were grateful for Zalinda's help in organising the preparations for the celebration meal. This resulted in a splendid array of choices for each course, which brought praise from every guest there including the senior cowboys, their wives and Ahote as well as the McKinley family.

When they had all been served coffee, Glenda rose from her chair. Silence settled in over the room.

'I want to thank you all for being here to bid farewell to Rosalind. She is returning to Scotland to see to the running of the McKinley Estate. She has my full support and blessing for the life she will lead in the country she loves. I'm sure we all wish her well in the course she has chosen.'

Clapping broke out and good wishes were called out across the room.

As the sound faded, Glenda resumed: 'You now know what Rosalind is doing but what about Caitlin?' Glenda allowed her audience to consider this then she said, 'You need to hear from Cat first and then from her uncle.'

Cat stood up. 'I will come straight to the point. I wish to remain in Colorado to work with horses, eventually to breed them.' She paused for a moment to allow a buzz of speculation between the guests to die down. 'I approached Uncle Gordon for advice. He pointed out the pitfalls but said that if this is what I really wish to do then he will support me. For that encouragement I thank him.' Cat sat down amidst clapping and good wishes.

As it died down Gordon stood up. 'Tonight is Ros's chance to say farewell to all those who have helped her over the past few years. Let us raise our glasses and wish her God speed.' Everyone raised a glass and said, 'To Ros.'

She nodded her thanks and added, 'I have loved the time I have spent here and I am sure I will visit again in the future. So thank you from the bottom of my heart.'

During the celebrations that followed Gordon sought the chance to tell Glenda, Mark, Ros, Cat and Ahote to stay behind when the others were leaving. With that accomplished, once they were all settled comfortably with more coffee available, he said, 'I asked you to stay behind because I had more to say to you, which the others need not hear.

'Since the moment Cat first sought my advice, I have given her idea much thought. I believe it could be a viable consideration but it will need your help in various ways. The land needn't concern you; that will be for me to deal with. I will put Cat under the care and instruction of the most-skilled person I know at getting the best out of any horse – Mark.'

Congratulations and cries of approval rang out across the room.

Mark nodded his acceptance. 'From what I have seen of Cat's dealings with Circle C horses, I am sure she will succeed in what she dearly wants to do. I look forward to teaching her all I know.'

'Mark, in this venture Ahote will be your assistant. He has a natural affinity with horses. I have rarely seen such a special gift among white men so perhaps we will all learn something too.'

Murmurs of approval rang out again, and Ahote's expression revealed how he felt about his appointment. Amidst the excitement, he and Cat managed to exchange glances.

Gordon added, 'I had hoped that one day I would share all this with my brother. Sadly I can't, so helping his family is the next best thing.'

As hard as everyone tried to ignore the coming departure they found it impossible to do so. Zalinda insisted on accompanying the party travelling to New York. But once bookings for the sea passage had been made and they had reserved their rail travel and accommodation in New York, they were able to concentrate on their final days together in Colorado. They were thankful for the fine dry weather, which enabled them to enjoy riding in the mountains and store away memories of sharing the wide prairies together. Cat noticed how her mother and Mark seemed to be growing closer and thought their three futures at the Circle C were assured.

There were times when Mark, accompanying them, took the opportunity to study Caitlin's riding and handling of her horse, though he never made these outings into serious lessons. That would begin once Rosalind had left for Scotland.

Although eager to be on her way to Pinmuir, Ros had to curb her desire until all the necessary formalities were completed. She held back from writing to Clive to tell him she was coming home. She wanted nothing to prepare him for her arrival. She sensed she would know at their first meeting if Adrianna had taken her place. If she had done, what would Ros do: accept it or fight for him? Then she remembered what she

had told her mother and that stiffened her determination to vanquish her rival. But, of course, it
was Clive who would make the final decision.

33

Although everyone tried to enjoy the train journey
to New York it was overshadowed by the thought
of Ros's departure. Having observed Glenda sink-
ing deeper and deeper into silence as the train ate
up the miles, Zalinda took the opportunity to have
a chat with her.

'Need company?' she asked.

Glenda nodded and smiled weakly. There was a
part of her that would have liked to travel the return journey with Mark alone, but Ros had
wanted her 'aunt' there, thinking it would make
the parting from her mother easier to bear, especially when going back to the Circle C without
her.

Zalinda sat by Glenda's side and said, 'It is not
easy to make light of parting with a loved one, no
matter what the circumstances,' Zalinda sympathised. 'You are sure to miss Ros, even though
you'll still have Cat.'

'I know,' Glenda agreed. 'This will be the first
time we have been truly parted. I sometimes
wonder if we did right coming to Colorado.'

'You must look at that with a positive attitude
and count the blessings it has brought you all.
You still have your children, no matter what the

distance between you and no matter where they are. I have sensed a strong bond between you all that will last throughout your lives. They are two wonderful young women.' Zalinda added with sadness in her voice, 'I envy you.'

Those three words startled Glenda. She eyed Zalinda as she tentatively asked, 'You mean...?'

She nodded. 'Twice. We lost them both at birth.'

Glenda took her hand. 'Oh, I am so sorry. I did not know.'

'There was no need for you to have our sadness thrust on you. You were far, far away. As it had been a secret for so long we saw no reason to disclose it later.'

'And you have both had to observe my relationship with my daughters. It must have tugged at your hearts?'

'It did, but we thrust that aside. The past is the past and we must dwell in the land of the living. As well as my own joy in having Ros and Cat with us, I know that Gordon has derived much pleasure from having them here. He thinks the world of them and, having no one else to help in the same way, wishes to do all he can for them.'

Glenda gripped Zalinda's hand. 'Thank you both again. I won't breathe a word of what you have told me, but I am glad you did.' The look of sympathy in her eyes changed to one of query. 'Zalinda, do you mind if I ask you about someone? If you would rather I didn't, do say so. I will understand and won't mention it again.'

Zalinda gave a small smile of anticipation. 'Mark, you mean?'

With a slightly embarrassed note in her voice,

Glenda said, 'Yes.'

'I thought there might be something blossoming there. And why not? You are both free agents. Mark has never been married. He's a good man, considerate towards people he takes to, hard-working, shrewd, but doesn't enjoy fuss well, you saw that when Gordon tricked him into admitting he is his own boss.

'They met while they were young, when Gordon was new to America. They were friends from the start, both wanting to make their fortunes, so decided to do it together. Mark is a naturally loyal and generous man. You need fear nothing from him and he will always respect you. Remember, when he abandons his role as a hard-working cowboy, he is a quiet man. There may be times when you have to do the roping.'

Glenda smiled at this. 'Thank you, Zalinda, I am grateful to you for speaking so openly.'

'Do you believe you might have a future with him here in Colorado?'

'It's a possibility. It depends...'

The following day dawned dull. Grey cloud persisted but the folk from Colorado did their best to try to make light of Ros's departure. Hugs, kisses, tears, good wishes, last-minute advice, were all exchanged before the watery distance between solid land and the unsteady ship widened, leaving no alternative but for them all to accept the parting.

34

An hour before the ship was due to dock in Liverpool Rosalind sought the help of a ship's officer to arrange a coach for Scotland. He gave her message to a driver and his young assistant, who welcomed the thought of a long journey and were happy to see a pleasant young lady safely to her destination.

An overnight stop was taken at a country inn north of Glasgow where Rosalind was thankful to be free from the movement of ship and coach. A sound sleep saw her ready to welcome and be welcomed by her beloved Highlands. The good weather helped her to relax as she watched the countryside go by. With the flat land left behind, the steepening hills painted in autumnal yellows, browns and greens seemed to be welcoming Rosalind back to the land where she belonged. The sense of coming home intensified as they approached her final destination among the mountains. But Rosalind held back from the decisive moment. Instead of taking her directly to her home, she ordered the coach driver to deposit her at the Trooper's Arms, a coaching inn she knew of but had never visited.

The rumbling of a vehicle stopping brought the landlord James McLaren to a window. 'Maggie!' he shouted, sending his voice echoing around the stone building huddled at the foot of a rocky hill.

'Coming!' The acknowledgement came

quickly; Maggie had recognised the tone in her husband's voice that indicated a female customer was arriving, and a lady too since she was in a carriage. Maggie wiped her hands on her apron, unfastened it, threw it into the kitchen, patted her hair and hurried to the front door where her husband was already stepping outside to assist the newcomer.

'Good day...'

Maggie cut in quickly with '...Miss' to complete his greeting, having noted that the young lady wore no wedding ring. Maggie was curious – a young lady travelling alone in this remote area? Who was she? And why pay the driver as if she had no further need of the coach? 'The young lady's bags, Mac,' Maggie prompted her husband.

He nodded, took them and bustled inside.

Ros exchanged a few words with the driver and his assistant and then turned to Maggie, hovering nearby and wondering what would happen next.

Ros gave her a pleasant smile and, concealing her local knowledge, said casually, 'This is beautiful countryside. Have you a room for tonight?'

'How long would you want it for, Miss?' asked Maggie, as if letting the room depended on that answer.

'I'm not sure at the moment but let us say three nights. It could be more.'

'Very good, Miss. I'll give you one at the front, the one with the bow window, it will give you a better view of the mountains.'

'Splendid,' said Ros, not saying it would also give her a clear view of anyone coming to the inn.

'Will you be wanting to take your meals here?'

asked Maggie.

'Certainly.' Ros smiled as she added, 'I don't want to starve, and walking makes me hungry.'

'You are here for your health then, Miss?' Maggie queried.

'No,' replied Ros. 'I enjoy walking and it does me good. I love this part of the world.'

'You've been here before?'

'Not here, but nearer the coast.'

'I am sure you will enjoy our countryside just as much.'

'I hope I shall.' Ros decided she had said enough. 'The room, please,' she said pleasantly.

'Of course, Miss. Follow me.'

Maggie led the way up the stairs to the landing, which was flooded with light from two sash windows. She opened the first door on the left and stood back for Ros to enter. She found herself in a square room of generous proportions.

'You have an attractive establishment. I hope it is well patronised?' said Ros.

She was pleased when her fishing for information made the catch she'd hoped for.

'Locally, no. We draw more local trade from Glentorrent, which is only five miles away. Some of the younger ones like the walk and enjoy using the time to do their courting.'

Ros gave a little smile of satisfaction. This inn was certainly convenient for Pinmuir, yet sufficiently far away to allow her privacy from prying eyes.

'Thank you. I look forward to my time here,' she said.

When Maggie McLaren left her, Ros took

another look out of the bow window, summing up the lie of the track along which she hoped she might soon espy Clive and have her first glimpse of Adrianna.

35

For four days Rosalind kept vigil, either from her window while reading *Agnes Grey* or else discreetly when she went out walking. She remained alert for any movement in the landscape but her disappointment mounted when the sightings were of nothing more than deer or birds. She'd wanted to see Clive and Adrianna together but was also relieved she did not, even though the wait prolonged her anguish. Ros tried to tell herself that whatever romantic involvement they might have had must now be over.

Then on the fourth day, while striding up an unfamiliar hillside, she realised she was about to break the skyline. She stopped for a few moments to catch her breath. Hearing a slight rustling of leaves she moved cautiously, copying the way the Indians stalked deer on the hillsides of Colorado.

She lay flat on the ground, listening. Nothing. Using her elbows, she propelled her way forward. After a few yards she stopped. She strained her ears to catch any new sound. She could hear whispering. She edged forward, easing herself up until she could see over the rim of the hill. The ground in front of her dropped away gently and into her view came two figures, their arms around each other, lips touching.

Clive and ...? This could only be Adrianna! Ros's lips tightened in anger. It took all the strength of mind she could muster to keep her presence unknown. She didn't want to be accused of spying. If that happened the whole situation could rebound unfavourably for her. Was this situation of Adrianna's making and Clive too weak to resist or had he seen his chance to take advantage of a young lady? Either way Clive must be shown that he was in the wrong. Ros shrank into the hillside and moved quietly backwards until she knew she would not be seen. She paused to calm herself. That would only alienate Clive in a way that might thrust him back into Adrianna's arms. If she shouted at them now, lost her temper, she would risk all. She had come all the way from Colorado to claim the man she loved. Adrianna must be erased from his mind. If she wanted Clive's future and her own to be as one, together here in the Highlands where they had shared so much, she had to be dignified even though she did not feel like it. She felt numb and hurried in controlled temper back to the Trooper's Arms where she would await their arrival, certain that this would be their destination. Ros went straight to her room, changed into more suitable clothes, tidied herself and sat in the window to wait.

The minutes ticking by felt like hours. Then doubt began to creep in. Maybe they weren't coming to the inn... Then two figures came into view. Ros stiffened. The lovers were walking hand in hand, laughter on their lips and in their eyes.

Automatically she inched back so she would not be seen but they were so intent on each other they would never have noticed the unexpected. Ros guessed Clive would take Adrianna to the small room they called the snug.

She let them settle in then stood up, brushing down her green skirt, a colour Clive had always liked to see her in. She took a deep breath, instructing herself to be dignified at all times, then she negotiated the stairs and the short passage leading to the snug. She took hold of the door handle and strode abruptly into the room.

Startled by the unexpected intrusion into their privacy, Clive turned towards her and Adrianna started to protest. Clive looked at Ros in disbelief, his elbow catching his tankard hard sending ale swilling across the table to drain like a small waterfall into Adrianna's lap. This could not be happening he thought; Ros should not be here.

'Clive! I'm soaked. Whatever...' Adrianna stopped protesting, noticing his pallor and the look of shock on his face.

'Ros! What...? I don't understand,' Clive exclaimed.

Ros gave a little smile, pleased by the turmoil she had created. 'Don't look so shocked, Clive. This truly is Rosalind standing in front of you, all the way from Colorado in the heart of America.'

'But ... why?' Slowly he began to gather his scattered thoughts.

Adrianna stared at her cousin and rival.

'I am back for good,' replied Ros firmly, believing she would hold the initiative by coming straight to the point.

'What!' Clive's face blanched. He rose from the table.

'I am back for good,' Ros repeated emphatically. 'I have come home. So there are some things that you and I had better sort out and one of them is this young lady. She appears quite dumbstruck by learning who I am. I think the first thing for us to do is to take this fly-by-night safely home to our Aunt Fiona.'

'Now hold on!' put in Adrianna, realising she should strike back. She glared at Ros. 'Don't you start trying to throw your weight around! You disappeared from Clive's life. You can't just come barging in again, thinking he has held a torch for you. You ran out on him!'

'I did not! It was always my intention to come back.'

'You never made that clear,' blustered Clive, adding, 'your letters were mainly about your new life and the people around you. Your interest in Pinmuir seemed to vanish. What was I to think?'

'I did tell you I would return to you, repeatedly, but obviously this hussy here intervened and you ceased to pay attention.'

'Don't you dare use that term about me,' snapped Adrianna. 'You left Clive. I'd been away for years and when I returned he offered to show me round the area. We became friends and I wasn't going to pass up on a chance like that.'

'So you admit you set your cap at him?' Ros challenged her.

'Of course. An eligible young man – how could I resist?'

Ros glared at Clive. 'So she replaced me, did she, even though you were still writing me love letters?' She gave herself a moment to calm down, regain her dignity, and let the idea of the 'love letters' register with Adrianna. Her anger hung on the air for a few seconds and then she shouted, 'Well, Clive, which of us do you want? You had better make up your mind about the future. Do you want to spend it with me or with her? I need to know. I have to start working on my plans for Pinmuir. I want you there with me but I need love and loyalty. You'd better say where your feelings lie.'

'And I want the same,' rapped Adrianna. Her sharp tone left him in no doubt where she expected his choice to lie.

'She's right!' put in Ros, much to his surprise. 'It is your decision.'

Clive's eyes narrowed as he stared at the two young women, momentarily lost for words. He straightened his back and walked over to the door.

'Very well then. Tomorrow. Eleven o'clock. I will have reached my decision by then.'

He made his retreat speedily, not wanting to be around when the two young women decided to voice their opinion of each other.

36

Thousands of miles away, two friends rode slowly beneath the Colorado sun.

'I don't like it, Boss.' Mark looked up from the ground he had been grubbing with his hand. He held up his fist so Gordon could see what happened when he opened his fingers. The earth he had held sifted through Mark's fingers to be caught by the hot breeze that sprinkled it across the parched grassland.

'Nor do I,' agreed Gordon with a worried frown. He looked over the countless cattle, listless in the heat that shimmered across the prairie. 'They need water and so does the grass. It's far too dry, been that way too long. We need rain or there'll be no food for the animals.'

'Even the storage tanks we put in are nearly dry.'

'It's gotta rain, it must!' Gordon stared into the sky. 'Rain! Rain!' he yelled at the heavens as if he could command clouds to appear and pour life-giving water over the parched land.

'In all my time in the West, I've never seen a November start as dry as this,' said Mark, tipping his Stetson towards the back of his head so he could wipe the sweat from his forehead. That done he added, 'Let's get home and out of this damned sun.'

When they reached the ranch their first

thoughts were for their horses. They rode them into the stable. Gordon and Mark slid thankfully from their saddles and immediately started to relieve the animals of their harness.

Two cowboys ran into the stable. 'We'll take over, Boss!' they called.

'Thanks.' Gordon and Mark waved their appreciation. 'When's this damned weather going to change?'

A week later the question was answered.

The wind that had helped to dry out the prairie began to exert a different influence right across the grassland. Clouds gathered and thickened, massing around the foothills of the Rockies. The sky darkened.

'Rain!' yelled Gordon, as if he could command a deluge, but all that happened was a drop in the temperature that, with the help of the wind, singed the land completely dry.

The weather remained like that for four days, never fulfilling its promise to revive the land, never allowing the clouds to release the water they carried. Passing by seemed to be the game they were playing, to irritate everyone and leave them wanting and restlessly waiting. Glenda and Cat found it difficult to breathe and recalled the cool of Scotland with longing.

Midway through the fifth day of this, one of the cowboys who had been checking cattle on the prairies reported to Gordon and Mark that the Indians had left.

'Gone?' Their surprise was evident.

'Yes,' came the reply. 'Everything's gone, with barely a sign they were ever there.'

255

'I don't like this,' said Mark. 'It's a bad omen when they move everything so quickly, and at night too. Another sign of urgency.'

'Does anybody know where they go to?' asked the cowboy uneasily.

'No,' replied Gordon. 'It will be the foothills of the Rockies or even into the mountains themselves. Their trails are secret. They'll know if you try to follow them and they'll lose you. They don't use the same route every time, that's part of the mystery, but it's no secret that within three days of their moving, bad weather sets in and remains with us until spring. Sometimes longer. So let's get back and organise animal feed.'

The three men turned their horses round and put them into a gallop. The urgency of their arrival at the Circle C alerted the cowboys; even the women came out of their houses to listen to what was being said and contingency plans were immediately put into action to ease the trouble they all knew was coming.

A rolling rumble disturbed Glenda's sleep. For a few moments she could not identify it. The low sound came again. This time Glenda identified it as thunder bouncing off mountains and rolling along valleys. She had heard similar sounds in the Highlands near Loch Pinmuir only this was much deeper, as if determined to make itself known. Another crack from the heavens shook the timbers of the house. Now wide awake she swung out of bed just as a shout came from Cat, a frightened scream. Glenda's thoughts raced. She ran to her daughter's bedroom and reached

Cat as another clap of thunder broke over the house. But Glenda had her daughter tight in her arms and was saying in a quiet voice, 'It's only thunder, Cat. Don't let it frighten you. It won't harm you. You're safe with me.'

Cat nodded. They waited together, warm and comfortable until the rumbles became distant as if at last acknowledging defeat. Cat sighed and sank deeper into her mother's arms. In a moment she was fast asleep. Glenda breathed a sigh of relief and laid her daughter on the bed before she went quietly back to her own room.

The thunder slowly faded away.

Glenda lay comfortably on her pillows looking out of the window. Moonlight brightened the sky but the cloud thickened and began to sprinkle the countryside, prairie, mountains and valleys, first with a delicate film of white until it gave way to torrents of snowflakes, large and unyielding, forming ever-deepening drifts.

In the Scottish Highlands Ros had risen early. She had struggled to sleep, recalling the look on Clive's face as he first saw her. It was one of disbelief and horror rather than the love and excitement she had expected. Ros was no longer feeling as confident as she had been. Would she, as Mistress of Pinmuir, be able to throw Clive off the estate if he chose Adrianna? Mrs Martins would most likely go with him, so would Ros have to return to Colorado? Aunt Fiona would then buy the estate and Adrianna would have a claim on it... No, Ros had to stay at all costs. Clive *had* to choose her.

When she had arrived at her aunt's the previous

257

evening, Adrianna had asked her aunt to reason with Clive on her behalf but Fiona refused, saying the girl had to stand on her own two feet. Now Adrianna had another plan.

That dull November morning each young woman prepared to outshine the other.

The time was approaching when Clive would normally have been leaving to work with Tim on the fencing surrounding the outskirts of a maturing stand of Scotch pines. It was a job that needed completing before winter settled in. He had dressed accordingly; no fancy clothes to try to impress; the young women would have to take him as he was – dressed for work. Not wanting his mother to influence his decision, he had not even told her that Rosalind was back at Pinmuir.

'I'm off, Ma,' he called as he picked up the box of sandwiches she had prepared for him. He went to the stable, collected Merlin and wished women were as uncomplicated as horses. He sighed as he mounted and was thankful it was a fine morning with a warming sun. Clive fished his pocket-watch out of his waistcoat. He was early. Twenty minutes to wait. He entered the inn and a few minutes later, carrying a tankard of ale, returned outside. He took a swig to bolster his confidence then sat down to try to relax, but there was no chance of that; his mind was awhirl as he tried for the umpteenth time to convince himself that his choice was the right one.

Then his thoughts were frozen by the sound of horses' hooves. He stared at the rider as she came into sight. Adrianna, smart in her green split skirt, blouse, checked jacket and small but attention-grabbing hat, cut a figure that made Clive's heart miss a beat. By her side she led a horse that reminded him somewhat of his Bonnie. A lump came into his throat.

'Good morning, Clive,' Adrianna called as she dismounted and turned a radiant smile on him.

'Good morning,' he returned, then let his eyes slide towards the horse she had brought with her.

'A present for you,' she said.

'No, no,' he protested. 'I cannot accept.'

'Yes, you can. It is my gift to you, hopefully to seal a future between us. But, if not, Erelin can be a reminder to you of what we once shared.'

He was about to object again but was suddenly aware of movement elsewhere. He turned and saw Rosalind appear on the slope behind the inn. He noted how she paused on first seeing them. She must have summed up the situation quickly. Her stride became more purposeful.

'You must be short of confidence,' Ros taunted her cousin, 'resorting to a bribe.'

'You're wrong there,' countered Adrianna. 'Clive knows I love him and Erelin is my gift to him, no matter what the outcome this morning.'

'Love? You know nothing of love. Would you have waited as long as I have?'

'*You* may have!' Adrianna jeered. 'What do you think *we* were doing while you were in America?'

For a moment Ros froze. Her inner certainty failed her. She must cover it up quickly. But Adrianna had already sensed the doubt she had stirred up in Ros. 'Did you expect Clive to be a monk while you were thousands of miles away?

Let me tell you, he was far from that.'

Clive stepped in between them, arms and hands outstretched to stop them trading any more insults. 'You two had words last night. Don't say anything else you might regret. Besides, I really don't like what I see in either of you right now. I think it's time we finished this.' He bit his lip as his eyes switched from one girl to the other. 'I don't want to hurt either of you but it seems I can do no other. I respect you both and hope, in return, you will respect my decision.'

37

Two impatient young women forced themselves to stay silent. Search as they might they could learn nothing from the inscrutable expression on Clive's face. He began to speak.

'Adrianna, your aunt asked me to reacquaint you with our country again and I have enjoyed our days together far more than I ever thought I would. You are beautiful, fun, and one day some other man will take you to his heart and deserve you far more than I do. You are not right for me, and I think you have always known as much deep in your heart.'

She took a step towards him. 'No, Adrianna,' he said, holding out his arm to fend her off, 'it is Ros I choose. I know now that I might have used you to take my thoughts off Ros, and for that I am ashamed. I am sorry. Believe me, you will always have a special place in my thoughts.'

Tears streamed down her face. Earlier that morning she'd thought she would return to her aunt with her future settled. Yes, Clive was below her in status, but he hadn't bored her like the men she had met abroad. She turned to go and saw him step towards Rosalind. Adrianna envied her deeply at that moment. Ros stood in front of Clive and looked deep into his eyes. 'I missed you, Clive, and I trusted you. I could have had the pick of men in America, but I kept true to you. Can I ever trust you again?'

Clive hung his head in shame and shook it from side to side. 'I wouldn't blame you if you walked away right now, Ros, but I love you and always will.'

Ros took his head in her hands and kissed him passionately on the lips. The years she had been away disappeared in an instant and a bright future beckoned.

Clive heard the horses move, separated himself from Ros with difficulty and ran to Adrianna, helping her into the saddle. 'Take Erelin back,' he said. 'I know he was a favourite of your aunt's but she would never tell you that. Thank you, though. Now go gently and forget about me.' His eyes were sad as let her go, knowing of the hurt that was in her heart whilst he held such happiness in his.

He turned back to Ros. 'I never was her lover. You may not believe that right now, but it is true. When I saw you in front of me again yesterday, I immediately knew it was you; always you for me.' He stroked her cheek. 'Come, let's away from this

261

inn,' he said to Ros, 'it is no place for us right now.' They led their horses to the special place that had remained only theirs and Ros knew she had come home for ever as they sealed their love. Afterwards all thoughts of Adrianna were gone; they were reunited and their time apart forgotten.

'I wonder if we will see my cousin again?' said Ros.

'Probably not,' said Clive, 'I think her father is returning soon anyway. Let's surprise my mother with our news,' he urged. 'She doesn't even know you are in this country.'

With joy surging through them they hurried hand in hand to Pinmuir House, where they found Clive's mother seated at a table in the study sorting through some accounts.

'Hello, you two,' she greeted them absently and then looked up from the notebook in her hand. Disbelief filled her face. 'Ros! Are you real?' she gasped.

Jessie Martins was on her feet, arms held out; then she stepped back keeping hold of Rosalind's arms and saying, 'Let me look at you.' She eyed Ros for a moment, nodded her head and said, 'Yes, America hasn't marred your bloom, but I think you've fined down a little. Mrs Lynch will soon put that right. How long are you here for?'

'Forever, I hope,' replied Ros.

For a moment Jessie didn't pick up on her statement. 'Forever?'

'Yes. I've come home for good.'

'Oh! Then I must see that your old room is got ready for you!' She took a step towards the door. 'I'll get you moved back into your rightful home while I return to the cottage with Clive.'

'You can't do everything at once, Jessie. I will keep my room at the Trooper's Arms for tonight, so you'll have plenty of time.' Ros saw Jessie was going to protest so stopped her by saying, 'Mrs Lynch will be spared cooking for us this evening. You and she must eat with Clive and me at the inn in celebration of my return to Pinmuir. Then I can fill you in on all that has been happening back in Colorado.'

38

Cat twisted and turned in her bed, wondering at the strong light streaming into her room. Her eyes flickered open. She sat up, threw off her blankets and slipped out of bed, shuddering as the cold air touched her skin. She grabbed a shawl and swung it round her shoulders. Moving quickly to the window, she pushed back the curtains. Fully awake in an instant, she gasped at the wonderland she had revealed.

Snow sparkled as the sun shone brightly in a clear blue sky. The frosty air brought a sharpness to the scene that tantalised the eye. Circle C waited to be noticed.

The door of Caitlin's bedroom opened and her mother walked in, elegant and comfortable in the dressing gown she had had sent from New York via Denver.

'Something wake you?' Glenda asked brightly.

'The bright light,' replied Cat. 'The snow has turned everything into a beautiful winter picture. I must go outside ... I really must.'

'I'll come too,' agreed Glenda. 'We'll go for a walk together.'

'Maybe a ride?' suggested Cat.

'Depends how deep the snow is. Wrap up well. Breakfast in a quarter of an hour.'

Eager to be outside they both took a light breakfast. With help from their maids they donned their outdoor boots and warm clothes, adjusted earmuffs to their liking and were finally helped into their overcoats.

Cat was first to the door. She gripped the knob. 'Ready, Mama?'

Glenda nodded. Cat opened the door.

An icy blast surged at them causing them to catch their breath. Glenda cast a look at her daughter and then raised her eyes heavenwards as much as to say, 'We are stupid to be going out in this cold.'

Wondering where Ahote was and how he and the tribe were coping with this cutting wind, Cat said, 'You'll soon be used to it, Mama. The Indians manage.' The young woman laughed at her mother's antics as she tried to stay warm and upright. Cat sped away in front, taking no notice of the snow and icy patches.

Glenda, envious of her daughter's confidence, watched her go.

'Come on, Mama,' urged Cat. 'You've never been bothered like this before.'

'I'm certain you haven't,' said a quiet voice behind her.

Startled, Glenda almost lost her footing. She felt strong hands grasp her. She looked up and saw the amused expression in Mark's blue eyes.

'It's all right for you – you have more experience of Colorado weather,' she protested.

'I thought you would know deep snowfalls from Scotland?' he said innocently.

Glenda's lips tightened with annoyance at herself for overreacting. 'Sorry,' she said, through gritted teeth.

'Take my arm,' he offered. 'You'll be safe with that to hold on to. Besides I won't let you fall.' His eyes were fixed on hers.

'Thank you,' she replied, and Mark was instantly overwhelmed with happiness. He almost let go of her arm as the shock of it hit him. He had never felt this way before about a woman.

'Doesn't your daughter mind the snow and ice?' he asked, for something to say.

'She's young, doesn't see the danger in falling.'

'Exactly. You should start thinking the same way.'

'It never used to bother me.'

'Then think the same way now. Come on, let's walk together. Don't think about falling, and when we get going let your hold on me gradually diminish, until you aren't holding me at all.'

She saw he was right, and, knowing that, could not reject his offer.

Glenda found herself soon adopting the way she had dealt with the snow and ice of the Highlands. There she had had John's help and now it was that of a cowboy she figured was about the same age. She pulled her thoughts up sharply.

She should let their relationship mature rather than push it. She felt certain Mark would prefer it that way too.

Any further talk between them, which both were enjoying, was interrupted by Caitlin's return. The happiness she was feeling shone in her eyes and was reflected in the way the frosty air had brought a bright glow to her cheeks.

'Will we be able to ride tomorrow, Mark?' she asked.

'This sun is just warm enough to be giving us a slight thaw. If that continues and we have no more snow during the night, I think there is every possibility of a ride tomorrow. We will have to judge then.'

'If we can, will you come with us?' Cat asked. 'You'll know the best trails in the snow.'

'Wouldn't miss it,' he replied.

Cat was out of bed early the next day. Her heart raced with excitement when she drew back the curtains and saw there had been no snow during the night. The clear sky offered a chance to fulfil her desire to ride in the snow.

She and her mother were just finishing their breakfast when the maid, who had answered the knock on the front door, announced, 'Mr Mark is here, Ma'am.'

'Show him in.'

Mark came in breezily. 'You two ready?' he asked.

'Soon will be,' replied Cat. 'Would you like some coffee?'

'Please. I've just been seeing to the saddling of

the horses. I thought you'd be keen to ride when you saw we had the ideal day. The others weren't too pleased with me as in this weather there's a lot to do but I argued that some of the horses needed exercising anyway.'

'It's a glorious morning,' commented Glenda.

Settled with his coffee, Mark issued a warning. 'It does appear so but we did have a fall of snow during the night ... not much but it could have made one or two places a little tricky. The main thing is, be sure to stick to the trails. I will be taking you on those used mostly by our cowboys so there should be little difficulty, but you're sure to meet something that isn't straightforward.'

'Cat, don't get too far in front,' warned Glenda as they walked outside to the horses that had been brought to the front of the house by three cowboys, who helped them into their saddles and adjusted their stirrups.

They moved off at a walking pace, allowing their horses to get used to the conditions. The surface was slippery, with yielding softened earth beneath.

'The horses are coping well with changes along this track,' Glenda observed to Mark. 'Will it be like this wherever you take us?'

'No. When we get to the treeline the bad conditions will ease. The snow wasn't deep enough to penetrate the foliage. There we'll find the best riding. We will not venture any further up the mountain than there. Only expert riders trust themselves and their horses to venture higher.'

They rode on in silence, Glenda wondering what Mark had in store for them. She soon found out.

Ten minutes later the treeline ceased, leaving them to gaze across an open expanse of black rocks. Beyond that the ground rose steadily for about half a mile into a huge peak, its pinnacle proudly thrusting skywards. Mark checked his horse. Glenda pulled to a halt on his right-hand side and Cat positioned herself to his left. She leaned forward and patted her horse's neck, saying softly, 'Well done, Gila, enjoy your rest.' She turned to Mark. 'This is truly magnificent. It really is.'

He looked at Glenda, who had said nothing. He waited, trying to interpret her expression. Then she said, as if to herself, 'Awesome ... overpowering ... frightening.' She drifted into silence. Mark let it stay that way. He glanced at Cat and saw that she was completely lost in admiration of the whole landscape, as if she was saying, You are mine. You'll never escape me. And I'll always be here. Mark looked back at Glenda. Her expression had relaxed into contentment, as if she was now accepting the life the gods had allotted for her.

She sighed aloud and Mark asked, 'Something wrong, Glen?'

She caught the worried frown that furrowed his brow. 'No, no. Nothing. It's just the wonder of all this and what it has given me. Thank you so very much for bringing me here.'

She offered no more but Mark reckoned it had been enough. He would let this relationship proceed at its own pace; he knew she still thought often of her husband, and the shock of her loss had not been completely obliterated, maybe never would be, but he sensed she was leaving the door ajar in case someone else wanted to step inside,

268

with care and respect for her feelings.

'We'll ride a little further along this track around the lower slopes of the mountain,' he called. 'Don't get too far ahead, Cat. I'll be taking you on another trail back to the ranch that will give me a better chance to size up the weather.'

She acknowledged his instructions and rode on ahead.

'Your daily predictions have been right on the nail,' Glenda said. 'And I know Cat has appreciated being able to exercise Gila.'

'I'm glad she has enjoyed it and I hope you have too.'

'More than I can say.'

A few minutes' silence was broken when she asked, 'How many mustangs do you normally round up from the wild?'

'We have the *remuda,* which Gordon and I like to keep at about one hundred.'

'And those are the mustangs from the open range from which you replenish your stock?'

Mark smiled as he said, 'You're learning. We'll make a cowgirl of you yet.'

Glenda was beginning to worry about Cat whom she hadn't seen for a while but she did not voice that to Mark, who had not expressed any concern. She did not want to appear over-protective. Another quarter of a mile and the trail swept round a stand of firs. Glenda felt relieved to see Cat there, sitting quietly on her horse.

'Hello, you two,' she called out. 'I thought this might be the split in the trail you told us about so I'd better wait here.'

'Quite right,' Mark praised her.

'It's wonderful,' Cat enthused. 'I saw a small herd of buffalo back there, about a quarter of a mile away.'

'You were lucky. That was an unusual sighting for this part. Overall there are not many left. Hunters slaughtered the herds for their hides and left the carcasses to rot. The Indians traditionally used the hides for clothing but lost that supply as well as an important source of food. It led to trouble but that is settling down now and hopefully won't be the cause of further hostility.' He eased himself in his saddle, surveyed the land and then said, 'Right, let's head home for the Circle C. But this time, Cat, stay with us.'

'You think we might run into trouble?'

'Of a kind,' was all he said.

Cat was about to ask what it might be but caught her Mother's glance indicating that Cat should press him no further.

They rode on. No one spoke. Glenda noted that Mark was casting his gaze in a wider arc than he usually did. Something must be troubling him but she knew better than to query what it was. If he thought they were in danger he would make it known. He put his horse into a gentle trot and mother and daughter matched his steady pace.

Forty minutes later he drew to a halt against a board nailed to a post on which was roughly painted the words, **You Are Now Trespassing on Circle C Land**. As Glenda and Cat stopped beside Mark, Cat observed, 'That notice is old and flaking. It needs painting.'

'Tell your Uncle Gordon, he might take notice of you.'

'I will!' promised Cat.

Another half hour's riding brought them within sight of the ranch buildings. Glenda slowed her horse and stopped. Wondering why her mother had done so, Cat did likewise. Mark turned his horse to stop beside her.

'Something wrong?' he asked.

'What's been the matter, Mark, you've hardly spoken since we headed for home?'

'Sorry. I was bothered about the weather.'

'It's been a beautiful day. Still is,' said Glenda.

'You're right, but haven't you noticed the wind is changing direction?'

'No, but I had no cause to.'

'True. I should have thought of that. It has started to veer to the north. Blowing from that direction, the temperature could drop drastically at this time of the year.'

'Are you saying it's likely to happen?'

'Yes, and along with other signs, it worries me.'

'Such as?'

'The cattle are getting restless. Horses arc heading for the shelters provided for them. The sun is losing heat and cloud is thickening on the horizon, which is not a good sign, particularly if the wind direction doesn't change and I don't think it will. The birds and the rest of nature don't take easily to what is happening. I just have a feeling we're in for some very bad weather.'

As if in answer to his observation, the wind sharpened accompanied by a cold blast that penetrated their clothing, making them wish they had put on their thickest coats.

'Ride!' Mark yelled above the howl of the wind.

Glenda and Cat reacted instantly. Hoofs beat a tattoo on the land. With darkening clouds driving in from the north on the strengthening wind, the three riders urged their mounts on.

'Stables!' yelled Mark.

They raced towards them. Gordon and the Circle C hands were already shepherding horses out of the paddocks and into shelter. Gordon grabbed Cat by the arm as she dropped from the saddle. He pulled her round towards the house. 'Inside, now!' he yelled. 'And don't come out until you're told!' He pushed her towards the building and she ran, hunched into her coat.

Glenda swung out of the saddle. Her feet had hardly touched the ground when a voice called out and a hand gripped her arm. 'House!' She ran, fighting the wind that would have swept her away, thankful for the help that someone was giving her. A scarf was wrapped around her. She pushed it away from her eyes – Zalinda's. Glenda knew she would have been blown off her feet but for this help and the reassuring grip on her arm from someone who had left the safety of her home to come to her aid. They ran together, Zalinda in command, urging Glenda and Cat to her house. They were almost there when the door opened. The maids reached out to them and swiftly helped them out of their coats. Relieved, they drew warm air deep into their aching lungs. Soon hot coffee was ready; it soothed away thoughts of what could have happened if they had been caught for long in the ferocity of the wild wind.

Zalinda calmed such thoughts even though she was willing Gordon to walk through the door. She knew Glenda was feeling the same, and saw in Caitlin's restless pacing to and fro in front of the large window, worry for the horses. Some time later all anxiety fled when Gordon and Mark walked in, showing the after-effects of battling against the wind while keeping a weaker section of corral fencing in place to prevent horses escaping.

Coats were shed and the two men sat down to revive themselves with the food the servants brought. It was only then that Zalinda put the question that was on everyone's mind. 'Is this going to get worse?'

Gordon's expression was serious. 'I am not going to hold back on this one. I am afraid it is. I talked with Mark and he thinks the same.' He allowed Mark to take over.

'If it stays this way we are in for bad time. Experience tells me we'll have bitter winds and a lot of snow.'

'How bad?' Zalinda urged him.

'Difficult to say but we would be wise to lay in as much food as possible and anything that will keep us warm. We'll keep our eyes on the weather and, if there is any sort of lull, take the chance to stock up.'

'What about the men?' asked Glenda.

'They know what is required of them and have already started on that,' replied Gordon. 'I have also told them to slaughter several steers so we should be all right for meat. We must work together and stay indoors as much as possible. Inform someone if you have to go outside and report back when you return. I have delegated two men to keep the necessary paths usable.'

'Is one of those between our house and Glenda's?' queried Zalinda.

'Yes,' replied Gordon.

'Good,' said his wife. 'We should be able to overcome any difficulties that might arise.'

'You really are expecting a bad time?' asked Glenda.

'It is best to be prepared for the worst,' replied Mark. 'It could start any time.'

'But, listen, the wind has lost some of that disturbing howl.'

'Don't be deceived. We'll be lucky if this is the end of it. I seriously don't think it is.'

They could never have foreseen what was to come.

39

The weather eased. The wind still reminded them that it was there but it had relinquished a few degrees of cold. As if it was rejoicing the sun rose into a clear blue sky, tempting the people on the Circle C and those beyond to venture outside.

Zalinda, using the path that had been cleared between the two houses more than once, hurried to Glenda's. 'Gordon is sending two men with a wagon into town to obtain more supplies, if the road is still passable and if there is anything left there. Is there anything you desperately want?'

'More flour and butter, if possible. Oh, yes, and matches. I almost forgot.'

'Will that do for you?'

'It's only guesswork, on top of what we have and your advice on what we should stock.'

'I'll instruct them to do their best.' Zalinda looked out of the window. Glenda came to stand beside her.

'It looks settled,' she said.

'It does but it could turn again. Anyway, I'd best get back with your list of requirements.' Zalinda hurried away.

Glenda and Cat watched from their window and saw her have a few words with the two wagon men before she went inside her house.

'Mama, I'm going to the stables to see if Gila is settled and warm,' said Cat.

'I was hoping you might help me with some baking.' Seeing disappointment in Cat's expression, Glenda added, 'All right, I'll get Namia to help me. Off you go. But if you see the weather changing, get back here quick.'

'I will.' Cat shrugged herself into her outdoor clothes, crammed a hat on her head and slid her fingers into gloves. She ignored the frosty snow that glistened in the sunlight and strode quickly in the direction of the stables. This is not much worse than I've experienced in Scotland, she thought.

With the large double doors to the stables closed, she used the small door cut out of the left-hand side. It squeaked and groaned as she pushed it open. She stepped inside and turned quickly to close the door again. A middle-aged cowboy stepped out of one of the stalls to see who had come to disturb him.

His smile on seeing Caitlin was broad and furrowed a face that was badly weathered from a life spent outdoors until the day he was injured in a fall. Now he was only fit for less strenuous work but still managed to help out among the horses he loved.

'Hello, Miss Caitlin,' he greeted her.

'Hello, Buck,' she replied with a smile. 'How are you today?'

'Better than the weather, Miss.'

'It's a lovely day, Buck, the sun is shining,' she contradicted him gently.

'Aye, it is, Miss, but the wind bites and that ain't a good sign. Heed my words, there's more bad weather coming.'

'I've heard this before so I'm going to change the subject to a better one,' she said with a smile. 'How's Gila today?'

His eyes lit up. He liked this young lady who had learned quickly and put into practice all the knowledge about horses he'd willingly planted in her mind. Because of her, he paid particular attention to her horse and she appreciated that.

Cat wandered off to Gila's stall, leaving Buck to get on with his routine work; she knew he didn't like being interrupted for too long. Grateful for Gordon's kindness to him after his injury, he liked to be on top of his work. Cat sang quietly to Gila as she gently rubbed her down. The horse nuzzled her fondly.

After half an hour Buck came to her. 'I'm going to stable two,' he said. 'Shan't be long.'

Cat settled herself on a heap of hay, content to be with Gila. She became lost to time until the stable door crashed open. Startled, she jumped up.

'Miss, Miss,' panted Buck. 'Sorry I've been a while. My opinion was wanted. Took longer than expected.'

'It's all right, Buck. Get your breath back.'

He leaned forward, hands on his thighs, taking his weight, as he drew air into his lungs. He gave a little shake of his head. 'It's not all right. It's beginning to snow big flakes. The wind is strengthening from the north. You'd better get back home.'

'I hadn't looked out, Buck. Thanks for the warning.'

'I'll see you safely home, Miss.'

Cat was at the door. She opened it wide enough to look out then shut it again quickly. 'I'll be all right, Buck. You get off back to your cabin. By the look of things outside you shouldn't linger.' With that she was gone.

The sky was darkening. Snow whirled down thickly and the wind was strengthening by the second. Cat pulled the neck of her jacket tighter, and bent herself against the gale, thankful there were still traces of the track home visible. She stamped the snow off her boots on the porch and stepped inside, closing the door as quickly as possible. She took off her coat and sat down on a bench arranged against one wall. She was taking her snow-boots off when her mother bustled in.

'Thank goodness you're here,' she said, her expression full of concern.

'Did the wagon get back?' Cat asked

'Yes, but without the goods. The conditions got so bad they turned round.

'It's getting worse out there, the clouds look heavy with snow and look set to stay. Come and have a warming drink.'

But by the time Cat had had her coffee the weather was contradicting Glenda's observation. The falling snow had all but stopped and remained at bay throughout the rest of the afternoon and into the early evening, when it ceased completely. The contrary wind had finally made up its mind to stop playing with the window shutters that Glenda and the maids had closed before dark. Thankfully it had changed its yowl to a gentler note, as if it no longer wished to disturb the people living on the Circle C.

After checking they were not required the two maids retired, leaving mother and daughter quietly reading by the light from their oil lamp.

An hour later Glenda caught herself nodding off. Rousing herself, she said, 'I'm off to bed.'

'So am I,' said Cat. 'I was only waiting for you to wake up!'

'I wasn't asleep.'

'Yes, you were.'

'No, no, I was only resting my eyes.'

'Oh, so that's what you are calling it now,' laughed Cat.

Glenda stood up without replying. Instead she said, 'Are you coming to look out?'

'Of course.' It'd become almost a ritual that on the way to bed they looked out of the window they left unshuttered so that they never felt completely cut off from the outside world. They went quietly to another bedroom and drew back the curtains, allowing light from a bright moon to flood the room. They both gasped with surprise. In marked contrast to the wild day, night and moonlight had brought a serene stillness to their world.

'Oh, Mama, that's just so wonderful,' said Cat quietly, not wanting to mar the peace surrounding them.

'I judged the weather wrongly,' Glenda admitted.

They stood for a while, lost in the wonder of the night, then a little reluctantly left the mesmerising vision and went to bed.

They slept the sleep of contentment.

'Mama! Mama!' Someone was shaking Glenda awake.

'What is it?' she asked, alarmed to find Cat standing beside the bed.

'Come and see.' The urgency in her voice caused Glenda to swing quickly from her bed, grab her gown and follow her daughter to the window.

'Where on earth did all that come from?' she gasped.

'Not the earth!' laughed Cat.

Snow was piled as high as the window frames and they were on the side of the house most exposed to the wind, which they both realised was now beginning to strengthen and driving the fresh falling snow across the land like an engulfing shroud.

'It looks as though we will be prisoners in our own house for a while,' commented Glenda. 'We won't be able to go outside until it's safe to do so.'

'But I'll have to see Gila is all right,' Cat protested.

'Don't you dare think of that.'

'But...'

'No, Cat, there are no buts about it. I'm sure Gila will be all right. You said yourself that Buck was looking after her, along with other horses in his care.'

'But will he be able to get to the stable?'

'There'll be others to help him. They'll do all they can for the horses. Just settle down and don't worry. This weather can't go on forever.'

Two days later it appeared as if it would do so. The snow had not stopped and the howling wind curled itself around whatever was in its way; together they sought to destroy all before them. Marooned indoors the womenfolk watched the drifts getting higher and higher, except in places that were sheltered. The hope that the direction of the wind would not change was uppermost in everyone's minds. In even the slightest respite from the weather, the men of the Circle C battled with the snow to keep communications within the ranch as open as possible. They fought the elements to reach the stables and lavish care on the horses. They regretted they could not give the same attention to the cattle. On the open range the animals had to take their chances with whatever the weather threw at them.

Apart from her own concerns Glenda tried the best she could to keep Cat's thoughts away from Gila. Whenever he could get word to Cat, Buck informed her that her horse was coping well with the lack of exercise. Mark and Gordon tried to visit regularly and to be reassuring, though Glenda wondered how much of the true situation on the Circle C they were not revealing.

Zalinda also tried to visit Glenda whenever she could. Nor could she give a positive answer to Cat's query, 'There is never any news of the Indians that used to be on Circle C range; how will they be in this?'

'I'm sure they will be safe. They always find a way. Indians know all about the weather. That is why they will have moved earlier than usual.'

'Where do they go?'

'It is a different place every winter. Before I married I used to be with them, but once I became your uncle Gordon's wife, I was excluded from knowing where they would be going. They took the view that now I had your uncle to look after me. Don't you worry about them. I'm sure they will reappear after the winter passes.'

So the freeze went on and on, causing concern to all; the womenfolk found cooking tasty meals more difficult as their meat, vegetable and herb supplies began to diminish; tedium set in to home life and even the most experienced men were heard to say, 'Never known one like this.' 'This will leave terrible destruction in its wake.' 'It will break many ranchers.'

On hearing that last assessment, Cat was prompted to ask, 'Will it break you, Uncle Gordon?'

'It is impossible to answer that yet. We'll need to make an assessment once the situation improves.'

Another two weeks passed before the weather showed some reluctance to continue along the destructive path it had chosen. There was a glimmer of hope. But the conditions were still treacherous, particularly where ice was covered by snow.

Cat woke early. Her first thoughts were for her horse. She was tired of not being able to see Gila. She slipped out of bed and went to the window. The sun was just lighting an eastern sky free from cloud. It promised to be a nice day. This must be a turn for the better. Maybe the winter was being dismissed. Perhaps this was her chance to see Gila. She listened. No sound. The house was not yet stirring for the day. She dressed quickly, put on her outdoor clothes and silently left the house. The cold air still bit at her lungs but that was to be expected after being closed in for so long. She felt free.

Excited by the thought of seeing her beloved Gila again she headed for the stable, expecting to see Buck. She knew he was an early riser, but there was no sign of him outside. Maybe he was in the stable. She pulled up short at the horror of what had only just impinged on her mind. The corral gate and stable door stood open! Panic seized her. Where were the horses? She ran to the stable, only just managing to stay on her feet. She burst into the building. The horses? Gone! Gila? Gone!

'Help! Help!'

The call startled her. Buck!

She ran, glancing in each stall as she passed it. The fifth one brought her to a halt.

'Buck! What happened?' She was on her knees beside him, looking into a face that was bleeding from several cuts. Then the sight of his right leg, twisted badly beside him, gripped her attention.

She was about to try to lift him when caution prevented her.

'Buck, I'll get help.' She rose to her feet.

'The horses, Miss. They...'

'Never mind them. I'll be back. Don't try to move.' She grabbed a slicker that hung in one of the stalls and laid it over him. Once again she commanded firmly, 'Don't attempt to move until I'm back.'

Buck winced.

'Don't move!' With that Cat was gone. She ran out of the stable. She slithered on some ice, crashed through some small snowdrifts, veered away from the large ones that would have stopped her in her tracks, but all the time she propelled herself in the direction of her uncle's house. She was breathing heavily with the air burning her lungs by the time she reached it. She supported herself against the wall as she hammered on the door while trying to call out, 'Uncle Gordon! Uncle Gordon! Aunt Zalinda! Aunt Zalinda!' Her voice strengthened. She heard movement in the house. Then the door swung open.

Her aunt and uncle, shocked by her distress, helped her over the threshold.

'Hot drink!' Zalinda called to one of her maids, who had been woken by the noise. The other was already bringing two blankets.

Zalinda asked, 'What's happened, Cat?'

Gordon was asking the same question.

'It's Buck. He's badly hurt in the stable. Come quickly!'

'What!' gasped Gordon.

Concern clouded Zalinda's eyes. Calling new

instructions to the maids, she headed for the stairs followed by Gordon. In a few minutes, swathed in his outdoor clothes, he was leaving the house. Mark was called to attend to the injured man. After seeing to Buck, he called the men to assemble and told them what had happened.

'Buck came to the stable as usual and because the weather was more favourable, and showed signs of improving, he decided to let the horses have a run in the corral. They had been cooped up for so long that he rightly thought it would do them good. What he hadn't banked on was weakened fencing. Once the horses had found it they were able to break out. Buck only just managed to fling himself out of their way but he took some hefty blows.'

'Are we going after them, Boss?' someone asked.

'Sure, there's money roaming around somewhere out there. Thank goodness there was only the one corral affected. We'll start on that immediately in organised groups so we cover an area systematically. As we search for the horses we'll keep our eyes open for cattle. Goodness only knows where any survivors will have got to. A word of warning – don't take any risks. Watch out for wolves and grizzlies, they could be mighty hungry and hunting for food. Remember, it will be icy in patches so it will be dangerous riding. One other thing: take plenty of ammunition. Usual three shots if you've found something.'

As the men were dispersing, a distressed Caitlin confronted her uncle and Mark. 'My Gila's gone!'

40

Cat was almost inconsolable. When she expressed her desire to ride with the men searching for the missing horses, Glenda found herself agreeing but adding, 'And I will ride with you.'

A surprised hush descended on the men of the Circle C, busy gathering into search parties, when they saw the two women approaching on horseback, their intention obvious.

Gordon and Mark saw them at almost the same moment, looked at each other and immediately rode to meet them.

'What are you two doing?' demanded Gordon.

'Helping you find Gila,' replied Cat.

'No, no,' he answered. 'We want no more casualties.'

'We won't be any bother,' Cat shot back.

'We can't risk it. We'll be searching in some awkward places.'

'We can help without going into them.'

'You can't guarantee that. Situations develop and have to be dealt with there and then.'

'Uncle Gordon, please don't refuse me. I want to help find Gila.' A pleading note had come into Cat's voice.

Gordon looked to Glenda for assistance, but knowing how deeply her daughter wanted to be part of the search, Glenda gave him a neutral look and shrugged her shoulders helplessly. Gordon cursed under his breath but then decided if Cat was to learn more about horsemanship and conditions, he had to give way.

'All right,' he said reluctantly. 'Keep out of trouble and don't take any risks. Join the group Mark is assembling.'

Glenda saw his signal acknowledged but Mark's face looked like thunder; he was being made responsible for his friend's niece and sister-in-law in frightening conditions. Glenda knew then she should not have let Cat have her own way.

When the women reached him Mark informed them that his party of ten riders would search in an area that included a section of the foothills. The conditions had eased and visibility had improved. There was speculation that they might have had the worst of the weather but all hopes were dashed when the late afternoon brought a change that none of the searchers liked. The skies had darkened and sleet began to fall, stinging their faces and making visibility difficult again.

Mark called his party to gather around. 'I'm calling the search off. We have had a modicum of success, finding those ten horses in a coulee. They should be safely back at the Circle C now. I think it wisest to return to the ranch and hope this weather does not worsen.'

While he had been speaking Cat had brought her horse closer. 'No, Mark, no,' she protested. 'We can't give up. Gila must be...'

'Stop,' Mark cut in sharply. 'This weather is changing for the worse and that could endanger the men. I can't and won't put them at risk. We return to the ranch, now!'

Glenda saw defiance in Cat's eyes and could sense her daughter was on the point of arguing with Mark, and even continuing to search for Gila on her own. 'Cat! Don't think about it. Mark is in charge. He knows what is best for us.'

'I want my horse,' she said defiantly.

'You won't find her today. Now do as I say, young lady,' rapped Mark. As if on cue a drop in the temperature changed the sharp sleet into a thickening white blanket of falling snow, with the winds starting to whip it into a frenzy. 'Home!' Mark shouted in a manner that told everyone he would stand against anyone who said otherwise. He added quickly, 'And stay close together so no one strays in the white-out that is coming.'

They had to match their pace to the depth of the snow that was becoming harder to overcome. Horses fought against the deepening drifts. The riders huddled in their saddles and battled against the biting wind. Snow turned them into ghostly figures. The riders relied on Mark's knowledge of the terrain to get them back to the Circle C. All were relieved when they became aware of shadowy shapes emerging through the falling snow. A few more yards and the outlines of Circle C buildings were visible. The riders vented their feelings in thanks to Mark. He raised his hands in acknowledgement as he guided his horse towards the corral where he expected to find the ten horses his men had found. His tension eased when he saw them safely inside the repaired fence. They looked bedraggled and miserable, seeking shelter in the stable attached. He started to turn his horse away but pulled it sharply to a halt.

'Cat! Caitlin! Glenda!'

The call came again and again.

'Did you hear that, Mama?' she queried.

'Yes. It was Mark.'

'What on earth can he want? He knows you and I are back safely.'

'Cat! Cat!'

'That call's coming from the corral we were using,' said Glenda. 'Better see what he wants.'

Thankful that the snow in this section was not too deep, they covered the ground quickly.

The corral and horses appeared out of the swirling snow. Mother and daughter saw a skewbald horse nuzzling Mark.

Excitement surged through Cat as she pulled her horse to a halt. She dropped from the saddle almost before the horse had stopped.

'Gila! Gila!' Cat hugged her. 'How did my Gila get back here?'

'I don't know,' said Mark. 'It's a mystery to me. It doesn't look as though Gordon is back yet so I must have counted wrongly when we found those horses in the coulee.'

'I counted them with you,' said Glenda. 'There were ten and I would swear Gila wasn't among them.'

'I agree but here she is,' said Mark. 'Perhaps she was separated from the herd and decided to come back on her own, but I doubt it in these conditions.'

'In that case she must have been brought here.' Glenda paused then added thoughtfully, 'There's only one answer – Ahote.'

'You think he found her?' queried Mark.

'It's possible,' said Cat. 'Gila would trust him. Ahote would want to get her back here before he might be seen at the ranch and in case he was followed afterwards by someone wanting to discover the location of the Indian camp.'

'Well, we'll have to wait for better weather to find out if Ahote is the answer,' said Mark.

The other search parties were returning, only one more reporting success in finding and rescuing twelve horses.

'This has been a tiring but fruitful day,' commented Mark. 'We'd better get some rest. If the weather is suitable tomorrow we'll search for the other horses and see how the cattle are surviving in this cold.'

But the next morning despondency fell heavily on the whole of Circle C. Snow was billowing in the wind now, blowing with more ferocity. The intense chill attacked anyone who dared to venture outside. All the Circle C hands and their families were prepared for a bad winter but as the days dragged on and on, with little let up in the bad weather, despondency began to set in. Were they never going to be visited by the sun, a blue sky or a moon to brighten the night? Were they never again going to be able to walk or ride through the valleys, climb ridges, relax by water tumbling over stones? They relied on their belief that nature doesn't stand still.

But after nearly two months even the best of relationships were growing frayed. Tempers snapped, mild criticisms struck deep, and apologies were not easily made. Wives and husbands found faults they would never have noticed and children were more miserable and argumentative. Everyone longed for a change in the weather so that they could look forward to better days. They waited and waited. They bemoaned the fact that they were isolated, with more rain, frost, ice and snow, and the ever-blowing wind cutting deep into their minds, causing them to dub this the worst winter in living memory.

Then one morning Glenda woke to find the wind no longer howled. She looked out of her window and saw the shape and size of the drifts had not increased. The sky was no longer shedding snow. Clouds were parting to allow a glimpse of the sun. A new day, a new time, had been born.

Hope was revived. Shovels came out and were used with new enthusiasm to clear pathways and entrances to homes and buildings essential to the resurrection of the Circle C. Any item that could be set alight was burned to hasten the melting of drifts blocking movement around the land.

Gordon and Mark took stock of the essential tasks to be tackled first. They quickly drew up a rota of fences to restore, buildings to repair, anything and everything that would bring normality to the Circle C. They delegated men to work teams, drew in the women to see that food supplies were restored.

Satisfied with the organisation at the ranch, Gordon and Mark turned their attention to forming search parties to look for the missing horses and, more importantly, cattle. The future of the Circle C depended on it. The severe weather must have taken its toll on the cattle exposed to the elements but they were still hopeful of finding a surviving core from which the Circle C could expand again to its usual four thousand head.

41

The next day the air was full of tension. Eight men were chosen to search with Gordon and Mark. Some of those left behind assembled to see them off. All had a premonition that today would decide the Circle C's future.

Gordon called out to those who were to wait at the ranch: 'I can't say how long we will be away. You will realise from the food and spare clothing we are taking it may be some time.' He turned to his search party. 'Listen up! Until we are all back here, care is a priority. No one is to search by himself. Danger might lurk anywhere and a fall, if you're alone, could mean death by freezing. That is why I have instructed you to ride in pairs. We will use the usual system of three gunshots to raise the alarm if necessary. Take care, each one of you is more important than the cattle.'

Zalinda laid her hands on Gordon's shoulders and looked deep into his eyes. 'I love you. My spirit will ride with you and be by your side to keep you safe.' She kissed him and they held each other close for a few moments.

Mark swung down from his saddle. He threw his reins to a twelve-year-old standing with his mother to see the riders leave on their mission.

'Keep him quiet, Jed.'

'Sure will.'

Jed liked to be around the cowboys and they appreciated a youngster who wanted to follow their trade.

Mark turned to Glenda. 'Good to see you looking so well and pretty in the nicest of ways.'

'I think your eyes are deceiving you. But thank you.'

'My pleasure,' he replied, eyes fixed on her as if he was trying to imprint a picture on his mind.

She laid her hand on his arm. 'Promise me you'll take care? Don't try anything foolish. The land will be treacherous.'

'I know it like the back of my hand.' He gave a little smile. 'And I have an incentive to return – you.' He kissed her gently on the cheek.

She eyed him with a directness that had something in it he had never seen before. 'I think we can do better than that.'

'I think we can,' he said. Pulling her close, he kissed her for a long time, only stopping to say, 'I'm lucky to have you.'

'Take care on this search. I need you to come back safe and sound.'

'I will. Nothing is more certain, knowing that you are here for me.'

She kissed him again. 'Now go, before I persuade you to stay.'

The searchers knew the cattle would head for shelter but after two days and no sight of even one steer, Gordon and Mark began to wonder what condition the animals would be in after having endured such harsh freezing conditions for so long.

'Don't worry, they'll be fine. It will be the weaker ones we'll have lost,' said Mark. Gordon gave a thoughtful nod. He had expected to hear some kind of signal from the others by now.

It was midday on the third day when Mark called out to Gordon, riding a parallel track a short distance away. Gordon's hopes rose. He rode as quickly as the patches of deeper snow would allow him. Then he saw Mark, a dejected figure, sitting in the saddle awaiting his arrival.

Gordon swore when he pulled his horse to a halt alongside Mark. This was precisely what he had feared. Steers had piled on top of each other in their attempts to force their way over a fence before succumbing to the inevitable. They lay, rigid in death, stark evidence of the ferocity of the storm that had swept from the north during the last few months.

'Some of them were set on by hungry wolves,' commented Mark, having read the evidence in the torn bodies.

'We can't do anything here, we'd best ride on,' said a dejected Gordon, 'but I don't hold on finding any change of fortune.'

Over the next four long days they found nothing to raise their hopes, and reports from other searchers were equally gloomy. They were all feeling drained and longed for decent home cooking. Suddenly a gunshot echoed through the snow-covered hills. Their horses raised their heads and both men looked at each other with hope in their eyes. Another shot echoed over the hills.

'There!' yelled Mark, pointing towards a rock

face that had been to their left for the last mile.

They turned their mounts and quickened their pace as much as they dared. At one point the snow deepened but the horses showed no fear. The riders urged them on, anxious to see why there had been a signal. Another hundred yards and they rounded an outcrop of rock where one of the Circle C hands awaited them.

'There's cattle trapped in there.' He indicated a cleft in the rock face. 'Goodness knows how they got in.'

'They'd be desperate for shelter from the storm,' said Mark. 'Thought of food would come later. What matters now is, can we get them out?'

The two Circle C hands who had been riding together had already examined the site. They quickly passed an assessment to Gordon and Mark. 'The main problem is caused by a fall of rock, which must have happened after the cattle had squeezed in and injured some of them. They were trapped. We tried some of the rocks but two large boulders were too much for us. Three or four of us might be able to manage them.'

'Right,' said Gordon. 'Let's get on with it.'

The four men, having sized up the situation, worked with the shovels, picks and sledgehammers from the ranch. It was back-breaking work; sweat poured from them but, when enough groundwork was done, they pushed the boulders out of the way inches at a time. With the unfamiliar activity and their lack of food, the trapped cattle grew more and more unsettled. They were becoming a danger to their would-be rescuers.

As the work became harder the four men took

breathers more regularly. During one of these Mark scrambled over some rocks to a higher position. From there he believed he would be of more help in directing the final clearance of the area where twenty steers were held prisoner.

Having weighed up the possibilities from his position he called out, 'Work to your right. You should be able to clear a passage wide enough for one steer at a time to pass through. Then we can hold the cattle in that area until we make the final clearance.'

'We'll get on it,' called back Gordon. 'You stay up there and advise us.'

Mark acknowledged the order. With him able to see the whole picture and direct operations the men worked more eagerly, knowing their job must be nearing an end. Mark relaxed a little. It was going well. His thoughts flew to Glenda and the diamond ring he had placed in a drawer before he left on this mission.

'Keep on the same track but aim ten yards to the left,' he called out. 'You should find the final clearance easier for the last twenty yards.'

Gordon called out his acknowledgement. The other two cowboys whooped at the prospect of rest.

The sound of hammers and picks rang out in the clear air.

Mark straightened, eased his back and flexed his legs.

An unearthly scream rent the canyon. A thud and an ominous silence followed, leaving a crumpled body to mark a place of death among the rocks of a Colorado canyon.

42

As she was crossing the room Glenda glimpsed a movement outside. She automatically crossed to the window.

Cat, who was reading, noticed her mother's action and asked, 'Who is it, Mama?'

'Four horses but only three of them being ridden. The fourth has something tied on its...'

The room was suddenly charged with a sense of deep shock. Cat jumped to her feet and in a few strides was beside her mother just as words poured from Glenda's lips.

'No! Oh, please God, no! No ... not again!'

Her cry resounded through the house.

Cat stared out of the window. A group of slow riders ... Mark's horse, a covered bundle tied across its back.

Cat was beside her mother, grasping her, giving her support against the grief that was overwhelming her.

'Mark?' Cat queried what she was seeing, not believing it, yet knowing the truth – the lifeless form was his.

Glenda had moved towards the door. Cat quickly grasped her hand and went with her.

Gordon took the reins of Mark's horse and the eight cowboys continued to escort them to his house. Gordon's bowed head slowly turned and gave Glenda a nod of condolence as they passed.

Word spread through the Circle C ranch like a devouring prairie fire and everyone, dazed by the news, gathered in silent disbelief.

Zalinda sized up the situation quickly and came to join Gordon. A few words of explanation about the way Mark had died passed between them. In a moment she was with Glenda and Cat. Zalinda knew words of comfort would be useless at this moment but nevertheless she reassured them they were not alone; the whole of Circle C shared this loss.

Cat felt her mother tremble as they watched Mark's body eased from the back of his horse and taken inside by four broad-shouldered cowboys.

Zalinda quietly asked Glenda if she wanted to follow them. She nodded. Cat took her mother's arm.

Gordon led the way into the house with so many memories of times he and his friend had spent here together, laying plans to become the owners of one of the largest ranches in Colorado. Was the Circle C's future threatened by Mark's untimely death?

Mark had been laid on his bed, wearing the clothes in which he had been brought home. The traces of rock and soil on them hid a body broken by his fall. The shock hit Glenda hard. Silent tears streamed down her face.

Zalinda stood aside, allowing Glenda to mourn in her own way. Zalinda too grieved for a man she'd respected in many ways but mostly as her husband's friend. She knew she would have to be strong and help Gordon when the realisation of the scale of his loss hit him.

Later that day Zalinda informed the doctor of the tragedy so that he could write a death certificate and, together with her, lay out the body in preparation for the mourners who would pay their respects until the day he was buried.

Four days later Mark was laid to rest in an area of the Circle C set aside for such a purpose.

'You and Catlin cannot be on your own tonight,' Zalinda insisted. 'You both must continue to stay with us for as long as you like.'

'I seem to be too numb to think ahead,' said Glenda sadly.

'Take all the time you need,' said Zalinda, a statement that was backed whole-heartedly by Gordon who had met the loss of his friend and partner stoically while drawing on the strength of his wife. Her support was a prop for them both and they willingly let that spill over onto Glenda and Cat.

But mother and daughter knew they could not remain under the shadow of a friendship that was helping them deal with the tragic loss. Life had to go on. Everyone had problems but they put them aside. Cowboys' wives kept their meetings but respected Glenda's need for quiet until the time was right. Even the children learned to respect Mark's memory and mourn the loss of their friend.

The day after the funeral, Gordon decided he would deal with his friend's belongings. It was a simple task for he found in a drawer only one bequest – a small package on which was written, 'For Glenda'.

He took it with him as he left Mark's house. When Gordon walked into his home he was pleased to find Zalinda, Glenda and Caitlin waiting for him.

'Finished?' asked his wife.

'Yes. What little there was has been dealt with. It will be collected tomorrow.' His words caught in his throat. 'It seems an end not only to a life but to a vibrant personality who should still be with us.' He recollected himself, realising it was no use bemoaning their loss. 'Glenda. It's meant for you.'

'Me?' She took it from him, looking surprised. She removed the wrapping paper to find a small box. On opening it she gasped at the sight of a ring. A central diamond was set with three smaller diamonds to each side. Mark must have been saving up his money for a while to pay for this, she thought. For a moment there was silence. She was suddenly aware that a ring like this could only have been bought in New York all those weeks ago yet he had not shown his true feelings for her until their last goodbye. Now it was all too late.

'Oh, Mark! If only...' The tears had started to flow.

'Were you going to marry him?' asked Cat.

'I don't know. He never asked me.'

'It looks as though he was going to,' said Zalinda.

In a few moments, when it became obvious that Glenda wanted to drop the subject, the others let it go. But it rose again when mother and daughter went to bed.

'Would you have married him, Mama?' asked Cat.

Glenda's face was filled with regret and a trace of guilt. To have accepted a proposal from Mark would have felt like a betrayal to John. And yet…

'The truth is, I don't know,' she confessed. 'But I would certainly have considered it. He was a fine man.'

Lives were in turmoil. The devastation caused by Mark's accident and the severest winter for many years had to be put right. Recognising her husband's dilemma Zalinda quietly suggested to Gordon, 'Mark would have expected you to get on and rescue the Circle C from ruin. You owe it to him to do that. Aim with the accuracy of an arrow hitting its target.'

'I know what I must do but first we'll have to find the cattle to form the nucleus of a new herd and that won't be easy. It will take time to achieve that again.'

'You've done it once, there's no reason not to do it again.'

'And maybe face a winter as deadly as this one? Is it worth it?'

'Am I worth it?'

He took her in his arms and kissed her. 'You are worth so much more … and then all of it again and again and again.'

'If you think that then you'll do it. You can and you will.' Zalinda kissed and held him, promising love through the testing times to come.

43

Glenda saw the strong sunlight streaming into her bedroom. How long was it since she had seen that? It seemed to be calling her to a new life. But did she want one? No. She wanted the old one. But which one? She shook her head. The truth was, she could not regain either of them. John and Mark were gone and would not want her to mourn and be miserable. She must face a new future and come out better for doing so.

'Good morning,' she said brightly when she saw Zalinda and Gordon having their breakfast. 'The sun is glorious after that testing winter. Is it here to stay?'

'The signs are good,' replied Zalinda.

'Are you are going riding?'

'Yes. I'll help with any cattle that need to be brought into the pens.'

'Then I'll change and help too.'

'There's no need, if you don't feel up to it.'

'I want to keep busy,' replied Glenda. 'I want to help.'

'Then you shall,' said Gordon. 'Ride with Zalinda.'

'And so will I,' said Cat, who caught her uncle's underlying instruction to look after her mother.

He left the table to glance out of the window. 'Tom's getting the men organised. I'll have a word with him; tell him he has three other riders

301

to employ.' With that Gordon was hurrying from the room.

'Good morning, Tom, you're in good time.'

'You know me, Boss. Don't believe in hanging about if there's a job to be done. I think we're in for a very unpleasant one, so the sooner this is out of the way the better.'

'Right. I have three more riders for you: Zalinda, Glenda and Caitlin,' said Gordon. 'They insisted on working with us. Let them help the riders who are dealing with bringing loose cattle to the pens. I reckon they'll be pleased to be back in the corrals and will be easier to handle.'

'They're good horsewomen so I reckon they'll manage the lone critters. But I'll keep a couple of men working with them, just in case.'

'Sounds good,' said Gordon. 'You have the rest of us well organised.'

'Thanks, Boss. Let's hope we've seen the last of the freezing weather for this year.' Tom wheeled his horse around and galloped away. He cast his eyes over the whole assembly. Satisfied, he made the signal for them to start for their allocated areas.

They rode off in high hopes but the sight of circling buzzards left them with no illusions about the scale of the devastation they faced. Time and time again stock running before the thunderous wind had come up against fences that held them back. In panic steers and cattle had flailed and struck each other in their attempts to get through the living barrier that was holding them back. Wherever the cowboys rode, it was the same story. Animals piled high, unable to save themselves, having to wait until the cold agony took them away into the comfort of death.

Any survivors were rounded up, fed and taken into care or, where possible, allowed free range but kept under daily supervision. The dead animals had to be disposed of chiefly by fire, a task the cowboys abhorred though they put their personal feelings aside for the sake of the Circle C. The smoking pyres did not augur well for the ranch's future.

The losses had been greater than anticipated. Even Zalinda, who had tried to keep everyone's spirits up, was beginning to agree with Gordon's gloomy view of the future.

'I must tell everyone here to look for jobs elsewhere, with my blessing. They should take any opportunity that arises.' Gordon's attitude disappointed Zalinda but she knew he had to be practical about the situation; she would support him in whatever he did. They broke the news to Glenda and Cat at breakfast the next morning.

'You are the first to know,' Gordon concluded. 'I would be grateful if you kept it to yourselves until I have broken the news at a ranch meeting. To give me the chance to summon them all, we'll have it in two days' time.'

'This is terrible news,' said Glenda. 'What can I say? Sorry is not strong enough. I just wish there was some way I could ease things for you. I know Cat will be feeling the same.'

She nodded. Her eyes were full of tears as her dreams of life on the ranch lay in ruins.

Glenda saw her daughter's disappointment.

She wanted to reach out and comfort her but knew the gesture would be too much for Cat to bear with composure.

'Gordon and I have much to consider,' said Zalinda. 'We must decide where our future lies. Until we make a decision you are more than welcome to stay with us or else remain in the house Gordon built for you. You don't have to rush into making up your minds.'

44

'Oh, Mama why did this have to happen?' asked Cat. 'Just when everything was going so well for us here... How strange to think that Ros doesn't even know.'

Glenda smiled weakly. 'Yes, I'll write to her within the week but for now we mustn't sit moping. There is still a whole world out there with new places in it for us. We just need to claim them.'

'I thought I had claimed my place,' said Cat sadly.

'Would you still remain here if you could?'

'Yes, and I was certain while Mark was alive that he would have tempted you to stay.' Cat thought too of Ahote and the bond they had shared. She had always hoped it would have led them to become more than just friends. But had he now deserted her? The Indians were still nowhere to be seen.

'You must not let me influence your decision,'

said Glenda. 'It is your life and if you wish to rear horses you can still do so even if the Circle C no longer exists. Just follow your dream.'

'But that will not be easy if Uncle Gordon and Zalinda are not here at the ranch.'

'Let's wait and see what happens. We'll know in two days.'

It was mid-morning when the ranch hands and their families gathered to hear Gordon's decision on the future of the Circle C. The buzz of hope alternating with doubt fell away when he and Zalinda walked into the barn. They read nothing good in his expression. He had a brief word with Tom then turned to face the cowboys. Silence settled over the gathering.

Gordon cleared his throat. 'This last winter has been hell for us all. I for one would not wish to live through it again. I must be frank with you. It would not be fair of me to allow you to cling to any hope that we can continue where we were before the weather turned so deadly. It has torn the Circle C apart. After the last few days we now know our cattle losses are far greater than we had anticipated. For me to replace them fully would be financial ruin. We have looked at every angle and can see no way...'

A distant rumbling sound drowned out his words. The noise continued. The onlookers exchanged glances of disbelief. Most of them had heard similar sounds before, but now ... and here? The uproar drew nearer and nearer and the earth resounded beneath their feet.

'Cattle!' The word was on everyone's lips.

The cowboys followed in Gordon and Zalinda's wake rushing outside to verify the unbelievable.

They poured out of the building and stood in amazement. Almost two hundred longhorns were pelting forward with Indians manoeuvring each side of the herd while others ahead were forcing it to slow down. At the right moment they split the herd into two, and urged them into two large corrals. The ranch hands watched in awe at the skill of the Indians.

With everything under control the chief brought his riders to a halt and watched proudly as they formed up behind him.

Gordon and Zalinda hurried to greet him, their faces joyful. Chief Ouray dismounted and with a broad smile opened his arms to his daughter whose eyes were filled with tears of joy. He hugged her to him.

'Thank you,' she whispered. She had no need to say more – all her joy and relief were expressed in those two words. A thousand cattle plus the few hundred Gordon and the men had reclaimed would be enough to keep them solvent for the year ahead. Then they would build on that, and build again.

Her father smiled his love for Zalinda then turned to Gordon and took his son-in-law's outstretched hand.

'If I read correctly what you have done, all of us at the Circle C owe you an everlasting debt of thanks,' said Gordon.

Chief Ouray, waving this away, smiled and said, 'You owe my people nothing, we are only returning what is rightfully yours. No doubt you are curious, so let's you and I walk a little. My ageing legs need stretching.'

'Very well,' Gordon agreed. They signalled to their respective parties to take a break.

'You most likely wondered why we moved our camp earlier than usual. I sensed a change in the wind and knew the spirits of my ancestors were telling me to seek shelter in the foothills. The sky signalled great trouble ahead. I said nothing except to order my people to break camp. I led them to pastures in a secluded valley we had never visited before. The Great Spirits were guiding us, but first they told us to take sufficient cattle from the open range to ensure our own survival and the Circle C's. I took only cattle wearing your brand. We found the sheltered place from instructions handed down over generations and it was good. We survived the storm that destroyed so many without a single loss.'

'A miracle,' said Gordon.

'Call it what you will. I believe that my ancestors wished the Circle C to survive, for the sake of both our peoples.'

'It will not be easy to keep going after all we've lost,' said Gordon, 'but together we can do it. Please, move back on the land that you rightfully occupy and, in thanks for your actions, I will add more to your holding.'

The Indian chief bowed his head. 'You are a generous man, Mr Gordon. My people will sing your praise forever. I will go now and announce your generosity to them.'

45

Ahote, after helping to settle the cattle, rode into the ranch, looking for his friend. He halted his horse. 'Where is Mark?' he called to Zalinda. 'He wasn't with Gordon or Chief Ouray when I saw them.'

Zalinda placed her hand on his horse's neck and said, 'I have bad news, Ahote.'

Cat came up beside her but did not speak.

He turned his eyes to Cat and, alarmed by the great sadness he saw, asked, 'Tell me what is wrong?'

Zalinda went on to explain the loss of their beloved friend.

Cat reached up to take his hand but Ahote immediately jerked the reins to put his horse into a gallop. Cat was brushed aside.

'Let him go,' said Zalinda. 'He needs to mourn in his own way.'

Dear Ros,

I do not know if your Scottish newspapers reported the terrible winter we have had here. I have never experienced anything like it. There were extremes of frost and blizzards that kept us inside for at least two months. Some of the townfolk did not survive, even Lily who ran the store, do you remember her? The freezing conditions are only now beginning to yield to warmer weather. It almost destroyed the cattle. Uncle Gordon has lost more than three-quarters of his herd and there are still more that may not survive. However the Indians, who as usual had moved their encampment for the winter, we knew not where, appeared two days ago as if from nowhere with the makings of a new herd. Suffice it to say they have saved the Circle C from ruin.

However I have worse to tell you. Mark fell to his death while trying to rescue some cattle trapped in the mountains. Everyone on the ranch was devastated, but, needless to say, this has hit Mother hardest. I think you and I had detected a certain closeness between her and Mark, but it had evidently grown into something much deeper. She did not know until after his death that he had bought her an engagement ring. This tragedy will affect her future, just when I thought everything was looking bright for her.

Hopefully when the winter finally lifts mail will start to reach us again, so please write soon. I hope all of you at Pinmuir, and Aunt Fiona, are well.

Your loving sister,
Cat

Ros opened the letter and read Cat's words with astonishment and grief. She had wondered why the number of letters had dropped off but had expected it was the Scottish weather that had held things up. But for them it had only been a normal Highland winter, nothing like the one her family had been living through in Colorado. She was glad she had come back to Clive when she had.

Ros went to her writing desk and wrote to her mother, expressing sorrow at the death of Mark.

He was a fine man and how I feel for the loss felt by everyone on the Circle C, but especially you. I am sure you will miss him sadly. I sense there was a strong bond between you and I think my father would have been happy for you. Remember, you have shown strength and endurance in such a situation before, and I am sure once the shock fades, you will look to the future with hope once more.

Now I know that you will receive letters again after your 'big freeze' interrupted services, we can resume more frequent correspondence.

We too had a bad winter if not on the scale of yours. Our sheep are hardy and found shelter where they could. We lost a few but nothing out of the ordinary for a Highland winter. Clive and Tim kept checking those they could find and I don't know how they would have managed without the collies. Clive did not want to retire old Bob, his father's dog, whose legs were getting unsteady, but needs must. Bob now sleeps in front of the hearth, keeping Mrs Lynch company in the kitchen. You would have laughed at the way she objected to him at first but now she has grown to think of him as her own. Clive and Tim have constructed a new barn so that the sheep may take shelter nearer to the farm if they want to. They both have more ideas for developing the Estate, which I will write about in a separate letter when I have more details. It could turn out to be an exciting time for Pinmuir. Things are going well here.

Finally, may my love give you the strength to face the future without Mark, whatever it may hold.

Your loving daughter,
Ros

Glenda put the letter down. She noticed the sun trying to break through the clouds, and feeling she needed some fresh air, put on her well-worn coat. Zalinda watched from her window as Glenda walked in the direction of Mark's grave, knowing life would never be the same again for any of them.

On her return, Glenda decided to put pen to paper and wrote a brief note in answer to Ros's letter.

Dear Ros,

It was good to hear all your news after so long and we look forward to hearing from you again more often. The truth is, I am in limbo. I don't know what I want to do. It was all so easy when I had Mark. It is true we had a special partnership.

At the moment Cat and I are living with Gordon and Zalinda. As good as they are, and insist we are no trouble, we feel we should be moving back into the house that they built for us.

On the ranch Uncle Gordon has had to replace Mark with Tom Harley, so he and his wife have moved into Mark's house. Tom is taking to the new job well but his wife Sara feels rather shy towards me. Everything has changed.

Cat still wants to develop her plans for horse breeding, so Uncle Gordon is going to contact an expert he knows who will advise her further now

that Mark cannot.
I must go now.
Write soon,
Your loving mother

46

The evening sun touched the hills around Pinmuir with a delicate light that lent them an extra beauty and the mountains beyond a magic that dazzled Rosalind. The loch lay peaceful with only enough movement to flicker the water into dazzling diamonds.

She slipped her fingers between Clive's. Not a word passed between them but their touch spoke for them.

A few more steps then Clive stood still, released his fingers and, putting his arms round her waist, drew Ros closer. His lips met her willing acceptance and he prolonged the kiss until finally she let their lips part. Clive looked into her eyes.

'Ros McKinley, will you marry me?'

She threw back her head and laughed. Then, with tears of happiness welling up, she answered, 'I was longing to hear that. The answer is, yes, Clive. I will.'

Joy swept through them both, bringing passion in its wake that made them remember these moments all their lives. Happiness still filled them as they strolled beside the loch. Ros sensed the spirit of her father nearby.

'Let's go and tell your mother,' she said.

Clive kissed her on the forehead and smiled. He turned for home eagerly, pulling her behind him.

They quickened their pace, which broke into a run as they neared the house. Laughing, they swept into the sitting room. Their sudden entrance brought Jessie spinning round from the window where she had stood admiring Clive's latest work in the garden.

'What's got into you two?' she asked as her son embraced her and lifted her off her feet.

'I've just asked Ros to marry me and she's said she will!' He gave his mother a kiss on her cheek. 'Be happy for us, Mother.'

'I am! I am!' gasped Jessie, her tone expressing all the joy she was feeling. She hugged her son and when she turned to Ros and let her tears of joy flow they knew they had her approval.

Jessie produced a bottle of brandy. 'I've been keeping this for just such an occasion.' She called in Mrs Lynch to break the news to her. After their cook had expressed her delight she added, 'I'd like to arrange a special meal in celebration tomorrow evening. Just tell me how many might sit down at the table.'

'I think we can do that here and now,' said Ros. 'There will be we four, plus Aunt Fiona and Tim.' She glanced at Clive, seeking his approval.

He nodded and the arrangements were quickly settled. 'I'll see Tim now and get him to take a message to your aunt right away,' said Clive.

An hour later Tim returned with the news that the invitations had been accepted.

'I wish both your fathers had been here to

witness your happiness,' commented Jessie, sadness in her voice.

'They will be in spirit. I felt it when we were walking by the loch today,' Ros assured her.

Jessie nodded then asked, 'Have you decided on a date?'

'Not yet. It will depend if my mother and Cat, and maybe my uncle and aunt, can manage it.'

'We'll work out a schedule and then ask them for possible dates,' suggested Clive.

'I'll write to Mother and Cat tomorrow with the news of our engagement and see what might suit them.'

Dear Mama,

Yesterday Clive asked me to marry him and I said yes! Your approval would crown my happiness. Please, please approve. We have thought about dates, which can only be finalised after we have seen Rev. Kintail, but we are looking ahead to, say, six months' time so that you and Cat can make all the necessary arrangements to be here. We can't have the wedding without both of you.

We will also invite Uncle Gordon and Zalinda, and hopefully they will be able to say yes too.

No more for now.

Your excited daughter,

Rosalind

She wrote a similar letter to Cat, adding, 'Knowing your desire to stay in Colorado, I hope you and Ahote are remaining good friends but perhaps by now you have your eye on a handsome young cowboy working on the Circle C!'

In Colorado mother and daughter opened their correspondence at the same time and expressed delight at the news. 'We will be going, won't we, Mother?' exclaimed Cat. 'We *must*. Ros wants me to be her bridesmaid.'

'I wouldn't miss it for the world, and nor will you.'

Cat hugged her mother.

'We'll have to be careful with our money but we should be able to manage it. I'll be able to assess our financial situation properly once we are at Pinmuir and have seen the accounts. But don't let's worry about that now and spoil the happiness of the occasion.'

'I wonder if Uncle Gordon and Zalinda have received their invitations,' said Cat.

An hour later they arrived and were shown into the sitting room. Glenda thought they looked a little solemn but made no comment. She offered them coffee but they refused.

'We have had a letter from Rosalind with an invitation to attend her marriage to Clive of whom we heard when she was with us.'

'Good,' said Glenda. 'I am so happy with their decision.'

'We are flattered that they want us there but sadly we won't be able to attend,' said Gordon.

'Oh, no!' said Glenda.

'No!' protested Caitlin.

'Sorry, but we cannot afford the time away from the ranch after the problems the freeze caused,' Gordon told them. 'I must be here to see that the recovery is handled in the right way. I believe we

315

can survive but it will take time and need to be carefully supervised. We have not been able to get enough done so far to leave Tom on his own. He is a good man but there are still things he needs to experience before he can maintain Circle C as a top ranch.'

'Then get somebody in who has the experience so you can come to the wedding,' said Cat.

Gordon gave a wry smile. 'It wouldn't work, Cat. Tom would be hurt and it might push him into resigning. I don't want to lose him; he's shaping up to be a man who, in the future, could bear sole responsibility here. He is good with the Indians, who have settled in again; I don't want that putting at risk. So I'm afraid our answer to Ros's invitation will have to be no. I've suggested Zalinda goes but she says she would not feel comfortable in a strange country without me.'

Zalinda raised her hands to Glenda and Cat. 'Please don't try to persuade me. I know it would be a delight to share your wonderful day but I can't leave my husband. After all, he has made me a ranch manager now.'

Glenda's nod of understanding was replicated by Cat, who added, 'Although I know she'll be disappointed, Ros will understand.'

47

The days passed and the wedding was a major topic of conversation between Glenda and Cat. Glenda was happy for both her daughters. They all had learned much by living in America and with that knowledge she knew Ros and Cat would be all right, but what did life hold for her? The problem of her future began to weigh heavily on her. Bereft and bemused, she had only her daughters to consult but did not want her troubles to encumber them.

First, she had to decide where she wanted to be. She had no doubt that Gordon and Zalinda would want her to stay and live in the house they had built for her and her daughters; the friends she had made and who had taught her new skills would want her to stay, but Scotland drew her. She recalled the purple heather, the mists that curled round the mountain-tops, the laughter of a tight-knit community and the Scottish voices as they sang with the local fiddlers and pipers. But then she remembered the occasional barn dance where Mark and she had laughed at his dancing antics. Now it was the beautiful prairies with their backcloth of the Rockies that beckoned her. Both good days and hardships were recalled until she realised that she had better focus her mind on doing some work. After all, John's plan had been that they should come and help Gordon.

She felt it was only fair to both her daughters that she should have made up her mind about her future before the wedding. She had not done so as yet but there was still time.

In the coming days possible solutions came and went in Glenda's mind until one morning her determination to make a choice was so strong it could not be ignored. To be sure, she would think the alternatives over once more; observe the loved ones here in America and remember the family back home. Without fully realising it, excitement crept into Glenda's mind as the answers became clear to her.

'What am I going to do about my bridesmaid's dress, Mama? Can I take one of the dresses Uncle Gordon bought for me in New York?' asked Cat the next day.

'Yes, but just in case Ros wants you dressed in something else, I think it will be best if you go early. Say a month or two before the wedding, depending on when you can get a passage.'

'It's sounding as if you are not going with me?' queried Cat.

'I have things to see to here, and after all that has happened I'd like some time to myself. You can be more of a help to Ros, deciding on dresses for you both.'

Train times to New York were studied, passage on a ship from New York was booked, and this information was conveyed in a letter to Fiona, who offered to meet Cat when the ship arrived in Liverpool.

When the time for her to leave was nearly upon

318

her she went to say goodbye to Gila in her stall. As the horse nuzzled her she sensed someone behind her.

'Are you ready to go?' asked Ahote.

Cat smiled. 'Yes, I think so. But I would so like to have a last gallop on Gila before I leave.' She stretched out her hand to him. 'Come on, let's ride together.'

They rode at a leisurely pace before breaking into a thundering gallop. Cat knew Ahote's horse would outpace hers so urged Gila to a breakneck speed. They ran neck and neck, hooves beating a thunderous tattoo on the firm ground. Ahote noticed that Gila was going to overtake his Palamino so pulled the stallion up sharply, making the horse rear and dust cloud the air. Cat turned Gila around, almost slipping from the saddle.

'What's wrong?' she cried. Ahote's face was full of rage that sent a chill running through her.

'You stupid woman!' he shouted. 'Even our Indian squaws know a mare should never be ridden so hard unless it is in danger. You know I am the best horseman on the ranch. Do not mess with me, Cat.'

She was shocked by the way he was staring into her eyes and for a moment silence hung between them. Suddenly Cat was pleased to be going away. She kicked Gila into a trot and headed back to the stable.

On the day of her departure from Colorado Glenda accompanied Cat to the local station. They were informed it was on time and should arrive in ten minutes. Glenda, like every other mother, issued last-minute advice to her daughter, but Cat was not listening, still dwelling on Ahote's criticism of her. She was hurt he had not said goodbye.

She looked at the station clock. It ticked away precious moments of her life. Then a distant rumble grew louder and louder. The train would be here at any moment. She flung her arms around her mother's neck. Over her shoulder she saw the face of an Indian brave.

'Ahote!' she whispered. Her mother caught the note of relief in her daughter's voice and released her hold on Cat.

Ahote walked towards Cat and took her hand in his. 'Don't forget me when you are away. Come back to me.'

Caitlin smiled, touched his cheek and said, 'Wherever we are, our spirits will be bound together. So you see, Ahote, I have to return to you.'

She made her goodbyes to her mother and boarded the train for New York with a lighter heart. She watched the two people who loved her best leave together.

48

It was a warm morning in the Highlands and an expectant air hung over Pinmuir House.

'Welcome, Aunt,' Caitlin greeted the arrival of Fiona. 'This is exciting.'

'So the first fitting of the wedding dress should be. Have you the pictures from the magazines I loaned you?'

'I have them,' put in Ros, and ran to the window on hearing a trap pulling up outside.

'Mrs MacNicoll the dressmaker is here.'

Ten minutes later a pale mauve corded silk dress was laid out on the bed for them to see.

'It's beautiful,' Cat enthused. 'It will really set off the colour of your hair, Ros.'

Mrs MacNicoll smiled. 'Your sister chose the colour for that reason. Now she needs to tell me of any embellishments or changes that are required.'

Ros reached for the fashion pictures and discussed some trimmings she had seen there, with Mrs MacNicoll and her aunt.

Once tucks had been pinned in place and the trimmings finalised, other fittings were arranged. Suddenly feeling weary, Ros sighed and said, 'I wish Mother had been here.'

'Have you heard from her recently?' asked Fiona.

'We received a letter only three days ago,' said Cat. 'I'll fetch it for you.'

A few minutes later she read it out.

My dear girls,

I hope you are enjoying your time together and I am sorry I am not yet with you for the wedding but I hope to see you soon.

Life at the ranch is recovering well. Uncle Gordon has bought more cattle to swell the herd. Some of those the Indians saved have now calved. This all promises well for a cattle drive next year, even though the herd will be a smaller one than we've had in the past. Time will lead to expansion.

Tom relishes his job and Sara is now fully settled; Gordon made a good decision.

Both he and Zalinda send their love.

Gila and Ahote miss you, Cat.

All my love,

Mother

'Where can Mama be?' There was a snap of annoyance in Rosalind's voice. 'Aunt have you heard anything since we had this letter?'

'No,' replied Fiona.

'But she promised!' There was irritation in Ros's attitude as well as her tone. 'She knew I wanted her here for the last fitting of my wedding dress! Where is she?'

'I've never known her to break a promise to do something,' said Cat.

'It looks as if she's going to break this one.'

'Don't take on so,' said Cat, trying to calm her sister. 'And don't get wedding nerves now. You've three weeks yet.'

'But she might still be in America for all I know,' moaned Ros.

'You don't believe that,' rapped Cat.

'I may as well. If she cared, she'd be here by now, helping me!'

'We'll do that,' said her Aunt Fiona. 'Mrs Mac-Nicoll will have plenty of time if there are any further adjustments to be made. You must have your wedding dress just right so that you delight

Clive. Now go and put it on.'

After a few minutes Ros appeared in her wedding dress, followed by the dressmaker.

'Are you having your hair up or down?' asked Fiona.

Before Ros could reply, Cat interrupted, 'Oh, you must have it down, Ros.'

'I'll have to have it that way! I've told you before, I'm wearing a lace veil with an orange blossom headband,' she snapped.

'Then you definitely need a slightly darker ribbon on the bodice,' said Fiona. 'Don't you think so, Mrs MacNicoll?'

'Yes, I do.'

Ros, who was standing close to the dressmaker, was startled. Mrs MacNicoll had not spoken!

Before Ros could make any query the door steadily opened, drawing everyone's attention.

Glenda walked in!

'Mama!' Ros ran and hugged her mother as if she would never let her go. 'Where have you been?'

'I promised I'd be here, didn't I? So here I am.'

Before she could say any more, Cat and Fiona gathered round, and laughter and chatter were ringing through the room.

Glenda held up her hands. 'Stand back, Ros, let me look. You are gorgeous and that dress makes you glow. I couldn't have made you look any better if I had been here earlier. Clive will be so proud of you.'

Cat put her arm around her mother's shoulders. 'It is wonderful to have you here, Mama. Ros was beginning to feel on edge.'

'I will leave you now,' put in Mrs MacNicoll. 'I

should not intrude on this wonderful reunion. If it is all right with you, I can return the day after tomorrow?'

'That would suit us very well,' said Ros.

Mrs Martins was called to escort the dress-maker out, whereupon Glenda said, 'Thank you, Jessie, for keeping the timing of my homecoming a secret.'

That evening when mother and daughters were relaxing after dinner, Cat said, 'This is just like old times. We will remember this when we are back in Colorado, won't we, Mother?'

Glenda gave a little smile. 'I love both of you and never forget that. It has taken me a lot of thought to decide what I want to do with the rest of my life. I still had not made up my mind when I stood with Ahote on the platform and watched you leave, Cat. I am lucky enough to have lived in Scotland and Colorado, but it is the Highlands that have won my heart and, with no disrespect to Mark, I am making plans to settle here finally, to be near the man I first loved and who is still bound up in my heart.'

Her daughters looked at each other, rose from their seats and together hugged her, saying, 'Wherever you are, Mama, be happy.'

'I will. I am sure, Cat, you are going to be a very successful woman with the help of Gordon and Zalinda, and you are lucky enough to have found a true soulmate in Ahote.' Then, turning to Rosa-lind, she said, 'Be happy with Clive. I am relying on you both to take care of Pinmuir and the land I love. There is much for us all to sort out. I promise I shall not interfere in your lives, but if ever you need me, remember I will always be here.'

Acknowledgments

I must say thank you to my family, who have always encouraged me to follow the wonderful life of a writer. The horizons are far and wide and contain so much magic. I consider myself lucky to have walked there and met so many interesting and wonderful people whom I would never have known if I hadn't put pen to paper.

There are always those who make a special impact on the publication of a book.

I can still hear the words of encouragement my late wife Joan gave me when I stepped on to the rocky road to a writer's life. That encouragement has been kept up by Judith, one of my twin daughters, who reads every manuscript as I write.

Geraldine, her twin sister, prefers to read a book when it is finished, before it goes to my publisher. Anne and Duncan are always keen to show interest and carry that on beyond publication.

I must, as always, thank Lynn Curtis who was involved in the birth of Jessica Blair and has copy-edited every Jessica Blair title. Thanks, Lynn, for that and for your friendship.

And thanks to all the Piatkus staff, past and present, who have looked after my writing in the topsy-turvy world of publishing, especially Dominic Wakeford, my editor.

The publishers hope that this book has given you enjoyable reading. Large Print Books are especially designed to be as easy to see and hold as possible. If you wish a complete list of our books please ask at your local library or write directly to:

Magna Large Print Books
Magna House, Long Preston,
Skipton, North Yorkshire.
BD23 4ND

This Large Print Book for the partially sighted, who cannot read normal print, is published under the auspices of

THE ULVERSCROFT FOUNDATION

IMPROVISATION IN A RITUAL CONTEXT
The Music of Cantonese Opera

IMPROVISATION IN A RITUAL CONTEXT

THE MUSIC OF CANTONESE OPERA

SAU Y. CHAN

The Chinese University Press

ISBN 962–201–457–7

THE CHINESE UNIVERSITY PRESS
The Chinese University of Hong Kong
SHATIN, N.T., HONG KONG

The photographs on pages 2 and 21 were taken by
anonymous photographers and used with the kind permission of
Miss Alice Yung. The one on page 95 was by Sau Y. Chan.
Others were by Mr. Kenny Ip and reprinted with the kind
permission of the Chinese Opera Research Project,
The Chinese University of Hong Kong, which received
generous donation from Kodak (Far East) Limited
that supported the production of some of the photographs.

Printed in Hong Kong by Nam Fung Printing Co., Ltd.

Contents

List of Photographs

List of Tables

List of Figures

List of Music Examples

List of Examples

Map of Hong Kong

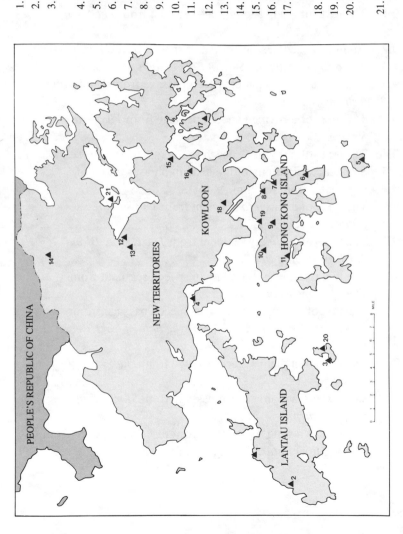

1. Sha Lo Wan
2. Tai O
3. Sai Wan, Cheung
   Chau Island
4. Tsing Yi Island
5. Po Toi Island
6. Shek O
7. Chai Wan
8. Shaukeiwan
9. Happy Valley
10. Sai Ying Pun
11. Aberdeen
12. Tai Po
13. Wun Yiu
14. Ping Che
15. Sai Kung
16. Pak Sha Wan
17. Kau Sai Wan,
    Kau Sai Island
18. Ping Shek
19. Causeway Bay
20. Tung Wan, Cheung
    Chau Island
21. The New Village of
    Sam Mun Tsai

Preface

This book is based on a doctoral dissertation that I completed in 1986 at the University of Pittsburgh. Professors Bell Yung and Deane Root were my co-advisors and Professors Arthur Tuden and J.H.K. Nketia sat on the dissertation committee. Professor Nathan Davis was responsible for teaching me the fundamental techniques and concepts of jazz improvisation.

Special thanks have to be expressed to Bell, who guided me into the field of ethnomusicology and allowed me free access to his extensive field data and recordings. The present study would not have been fruitful without his pioneer work on Cantonese opera.

There were about a hundred informants who generously and patiently answered my questions during my fieldwork research, among them the late Mr. Wong Jyt-seng who was also my Cantonese operatic song teacher. Those whom I must specially acknowledge include Zeng Mung-wen, Zeng Wen-fei, Loeng Hon-wae, Men Cin-sey, Jyn Siu-fae, Ziu Sek-men, Siu Kae-nam, Wong Wae-soeng, Wong Dek-zing, Cen Gim-sing, Mek Wae-men, Jip Juk-jin, Jip Siu-dek, Loeng Siu-sem, Loeng Jy, Loeng Ben, Loeng Gyn-gyn, Loeng Wae-hung, Ze Syt-sem, Loeng Fung-ji, Lem Mei-mei, Ng Jim-hung, Ma Lung, Zung Wae-ming, Ng Sau-fong, Sou Yung, Lung Gwun-tin, Sung Gem-wing, Zoeng Jim-hung, Gwan Hoi-san, Sen Ma Si-zeng, Leing Ci-bak, Jy Gai, Nam Fung, Men Bou-sem, the late Men Coi-fung, Gwok Fung-ji, Wen Juk-jy and Cen Zi-hung.

Not being a native speaker of the language, the experience of writing a book in English has been challenging throughout and frustrating at times. I am indebted to Professor Deane Root who introduced to me the basic concept and practice of scholarly writing during my graduate study at the University of Pittsburgh, and to Mr. Andrew Kwong of The Chinese University of Hong Kong who gave me valuable suggestions on the final revision of the manuscript. Among my colleagues at the Department of Music, The Chinese University of Hong Kong, I am indebted to Professor David Gwilt, Drs. Daniel Law, Harrison Ryker and William Watson, who were my teachers during my undergraduate days. Four students at the University, Miss Leung Kan, Miss Ho Po-kum, Mr. Kenny Tsui and Mr. Leung Sau-seen have assisted in the preparation of the manuscript. Dr. Larry Witzleben, Mr. Alan Hirvela, Mr. Yu Siu-wah and Mr. Kyle Heide have also commented on my writing.

Finally I wish to mention friends and colleagues who have supported my work with their warm encouragement. They are Professor Rulan Pian, Dr. Yung Sai-shing, Mrs. Ruth Kwong, Dr. Paul Kwong, Dr. Joseph Lam, Dr. Larry Witzleben, Dr. Benny Tsao, Dr. Eric Zee, Mr. Andy Tse, Mr. Li Siu-leung, Mr. Andrew Kwong and Miss Jip Juk-jin.

Sau Y. Chan

SAU Y. CHAN received his doctoral degree in ethnomusicology from the University of Pittsburgh in 1986 and started teaching at the Department of Music of The Chinese University of Hong Kong in 1987. His publications include several articles and three other books on Cantonese opera.

Romanizations and Transcriptions in This Book

Romanization of most of the Chinese terms appearing throughout the present study are according to the Cantonese dialect and based on the system in Wong Lik's *Guangzhou wa cin syt* 廣州話淺說 (*Introduction to Cantonese*, reprinted in 1957). For names of communities and streets in Hong Kong the official romanized forms are used, while names of cities, provinces and dynasties in mainland China and Chinese history are romanized according to the *hanyu pinyin* method. However, names of Hong Kong communities that do not have official romanizations are romanized according to Wong Lik's system. The names of Chinese authors and informants are also romanized within this system unless they have other better known names in English.

Certain spoken Cantonese syllables have no corresponding forms in the written language. In such cases, no Chinese characters are provided following the romanized syllables.

Nonsense syllables, the romanized form of which are mostly composed of vowels, are often added in speech for filling gaps between structural syllables, and in singing to facilitate the vocalization of the melismas. They are also not represented by Chinese characters.

However, some particles in speech and singing are phonetically close to, and are hence romanized in the same forms as some nonsense syllables. For example, "*a*" is often used as a nonsense syllable, but it is also the romanized form of a particle that is represented by the Chinese character 呀 . Such particles often appear at phrase and line endings and occasionally within other syntactic components. According to Kwok (1984:6), particles in spoken Cantonese do not have independent grammatical status and are often semantically unimportant, though most of them have some contextual meaning (1984:41–94). Luke (1990) refers to such particles as "utterance particles" or "modal particles."

Cantonese operatic music is performed at slightly higher pitches, usually about twenty vibrations per second, than those found in the equal-tempered system (see Chapters 3 and 5); transcriptions cited in the present study do not give the absolute pitches but the equal-tempered pitches closest to the performed ones. The female voice sings an octave higher than the male voice. Passages sung by the male voice are notated with the treble clef, an octave higher than as performed. Unless they are cited to illustrate ornamentation, minor melodic inflections are omitted from the music examples. The lyrics are given in Chinese without English translation if they are not relevant to the discussion.

Percussion music often occurs in complex forms in Cantonese operatic music. The present study transcribes only the simple percussion patterns that are played on more than one instrument, usually by more than one player. The transcriptions will give the composite rhythm, which is abstracted from the different rhythmic patterns played by each of the instruments. Under each attack, the most prominent sound is represented by mnemonics. The resulting transcription looks similar to the first line of Music Example R.1, which shows the rhythms for each of the instruments playing the percussion pattern *Pok deng ngo* 撲燈蛾 (see Chapter 5), as given in the book *Jyt keik lo gwu gei co zi sik* 粵劇鑼鼓基礎知識 (*Guide to Percussion Music of Cantonese Opera*, 1979:30–31).

The first line of the music example gives the mnemonics of the prominent sounds which help the players in memorizing the percussion patterns. As a professional practice, different percussionists employ slightly different systems of mnemonics. The present study adopts the system used in the *Guide*, slightly modified:

1. *guk* 局 :   a single stroke played on the large woodblock
2. *dek* 得 :   a single stroke played on the medium woodblock
3. *dik* 的 :   a single stroke played on the small woodblock
4. *cep* 揖 :   two strokes played simultaneously on the medium woodblock
5. *coeng* 昌 : a single stroke played on the small gong
6. *pong* 旁 :   a single stroke played on one of the gongs excluding the small gong
7. *ca* 查 :   a single stroke played on one of the pairs of cymbals
8. *cang* 撐 :   the sounding together of *pong* and *ca*

The playing of fast and repeated strokes on the large, medium and small woodblocks are transcribed as tremolos in the present study.

Music Example R.1   The percussion pattern *Pok deng ngo*

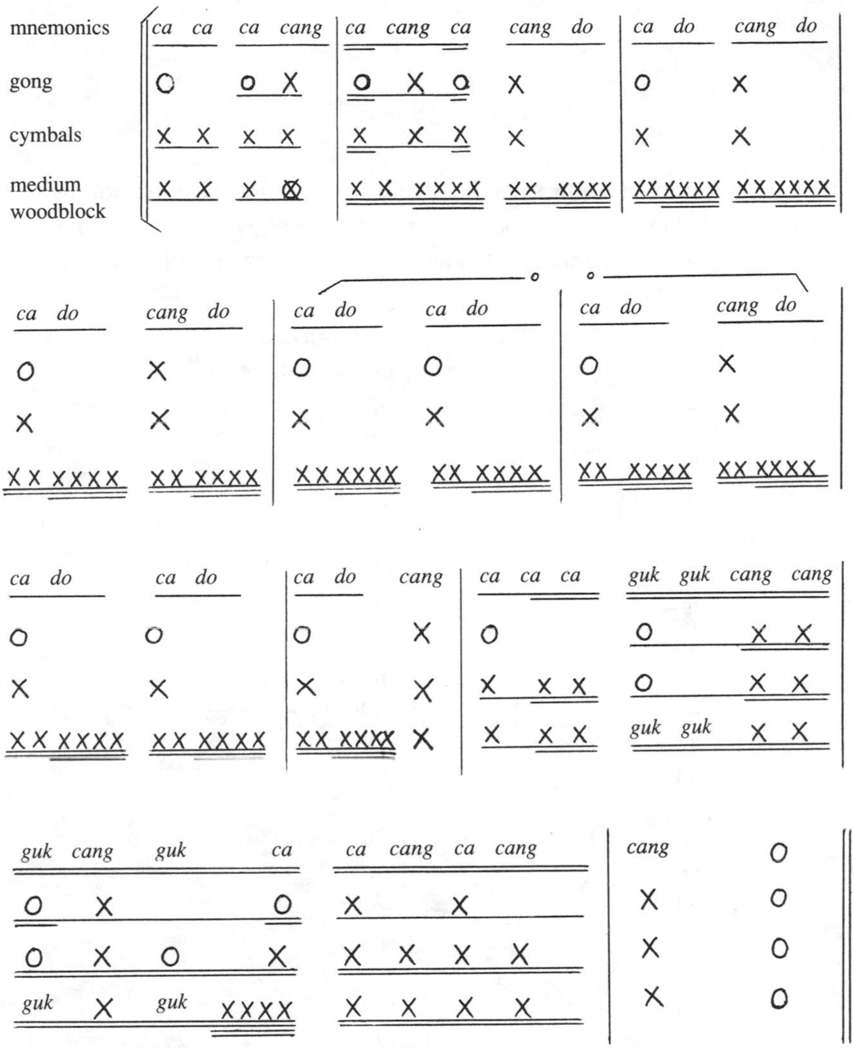

Meanings of Symbols

     ○ : rest

     ✕ : stroke

     ⊗ : two strokes played simultaneously on the medium woodblock

   —○○— : repeat for any number of times

Guide to Pronunciation for the Cantonese Dialect

Wong Lik's romanization system as used in the present book adopts the International Phonetic Alphabet in most of its initials and finals. The following is a guide to the most often used and exceptional initials and finals.

A. Initials	As in
c	no English equivalent; similar to *ch*urch with no "h" sound
gw	s*qui*ll
j	*y*es
kw	as*k wh*y
ng	si*ng*
s	*s*ee
w	*w*et
z	*j*ust

B. Finals	As in
a	f*a*ther
ae	t*i*ght
ai	*eye*
am	p*alm*
ang	s*oun*d
ao	c*ow*
ap	h*arp*
au	s*ou*th
em	s*um*
en	s*en*
eng	h*ung*
ep	*up*
et	n*ut*
o	s*aw*
ou	s*o*
ung	*own*
y	"ü" in German

1. An Introduction to Cantonese Opera

Brief History

Cantonese opera is one of the fourteen theatrical genres performed in Guangdong 廣東 province of southeastern China, not including the puppet genres (Loeng, 1982:4), and one of the 365 or so regional genres of opera in China (Zoeng, 1982:35). Historians have traced the origin of Cantonese opera back to the Ming dynasty (1368–1644) (Loeng, 1982:144), but some of the most prominent stylistic characteristics of the 1980s originated in the 1920s and 1930s. During these two decades drastic changes took place in the genre, among them the introduction of the Cantonese dialect in both sung and spoken passages, the incorporation of Western melodic instruments, the creation of new aria types, and the employment of traditional Cantonese fixed tunes and singing narratives in the vocal music (Soeng, 1981:72; Gim, 1980:44; Yung, 1976a:55–88, 1989:9). Before the 1920s, Cantonese opera resembled the styles of the regional genres that flourished in Guangdong and neighbouring provinces; since then, the genre has developed more distinctively Cantonese characteristics (Soeng, 1981:71–72). From this point of view, we can say that Cantonese opera is a young theatrical genre, though some of its performance practices, especially those related to the use of improvisation, are from an earlier period of time.

The changes mentioned above were introduced as innovations when the genre started to appear in commercial productions staged in permanent theatres in the cities of Guangzhou (the capital of Guangdong province) and Hong Kong during the 1920s and 1930s. While most of the productions were still staged in ritual contexts in the rural areas of Guangdong province and Hong Kong, large troupes began to make the city theatres their bases. Even now the genre continues to be disseminated chiefly through productions staged for the celebration of traditional and annual festivals, within the ritual context, in rural, temporary theatres, and for making a profit, within the commercial context, in urban, permanent theatres. Ritual performances are known as *Sen gung hei* 神功戲 (performances for the deities as a charitable and pious deed) in the profession of Cantonese opera. Productions within the commercial context are referred to as *Hei jyn hei* 戲院戲 (performance in a permanent theatre), since most of the performances in permanent theatres are for commercial purposes. These two types of productions are referred to as ritual and theatrical performances respectively in the present study.

The appearance of the new theatrical performance context enabled some of the actors to become stars. Some actors, probably influenced by Western opera and Peking opera, worked with their accompanying musicians to create their own personal singing styles. For some individuals, the genre was a means of gaining wealth and fame; for the entertainment entrepreneur, operatic productions were a means of collecting profit when the genre became the most popular form of entertainment before the introduction and widespread use of radio, television and motion pictures. While

The renowned principal male role actor Sit Gok-sin (1904–1956) performing at a theatre with an unidentified actress. The orchestra is seen at stage right. (c. 1935, theatre unknown, Hong Kong)

most of the troupes performed with no scripts, but only with outlines, before the 1920s, some of the urban troupes would hire scriptwriters to write playscripts for their productions. Since competition among the urban troupes was keen, new works were constantly produced by rival troupes to attract audiences.

When Cantonese opera was at its peak of popularity in both the urban and rural contexts in the 1930s, Cantonese operatic song emerged as its subgenre. Originally, most of the operatic songs were excerpts from operas and were performed by professional singers at tea houses and restaurants, venues collectively known as *go tan* 歌壇 (singing stage). (Before the popularity of operatic songs, performances of singing narratives were already common in tea houses and restaurants.) Later, writers wrote pieces in a style similar to opera excerpts, but which were intended to be sung without costume, stage setting and acting. Nevertheless, singers sometimes incorporated stylistic gestures from opera to enrich the visual effect. The introduction of commercial recordings enhanced the commercial value of operatic songs and added a new medium of dissemination.

The performances of Cantonese opera in its traditional context was highly improvisatory and flexible, whereas a gradual trend towards limiting the use of improvisation started in the 1920s and has continued to the present. This trend was brought about by the appearance of new means of dissemination, as well as by the subsequent changes in ideology, attitudes and tastes within the profession. After the mid-1950s, it was further reinforced by the belief that Cantonese operatic music was declining in popularity. Ideas expressed about revitalizing the genre often favoured the practices of assigning artistic directors, rehearsing before performances, eliminating improvisation, the use of a conductor and even pre-composing instrumental and vocal music.[1]

Cantonese Opera in Modern Hong Kong

In Hong Kong, operatic song is referred to as *jyt kuk* 粵曲 (Cantonese song); Cantonese opera is referred to as *dai hei* 大戲 (grand opera), due to the usually grand scale of production. In the 1980s, a medium-sized troupe performing for a traditional Chinese religious ritual celebration might involve up to thirty-five actors, ten accompanying musicians, and more than twenty backstage workers who would be responsible for stage settings, stage property, controlling the lighting and sound systems, cooking meals for members of the troupe and providing costumes.[2] Operatic performances usually involved elaborate and colourful costumes, heavy facial makeup, loud percussive music, comic episodes, acrobatics, dance, both realistic and symbolic acting, singing and spoken passages. Stage settings were sometimes elaborate, but usually simple enough for the workers to change the set within a short time between the acts and scenes.[3]

In the 1980s, Cantonese operatic music could be heard on television, radio, in theatres, ritual celebrations, tea houses,[4] restaurants,[5] in theatres located in amusement parks, at fund raising shows, art festivals presented by both private organizations and the Urban Services Department, occasional student performances and through commercial recordings. From August 1984 to the end of July 1985, a total of 415 days of performance were recorded (different troupes performing on the same day in different places were counted separately); 164 of them were in permanent theatres, 251 were for celebrations of rituals.[6] These figures exclude amateur and student performances and performances sponsored by the government or those at the amusement park where there were nightly and Sunday afternoon performances during the early 1980s. Singing sessions of operatic song were organized by amateur and semi-professional music clubs.[7] An amateur troupe organized by Radio Television Hong Kong and sponsored by the Hong Kong government performed about ten times a month free to the public. Such performances were usually held at playgrounds near public housing estates in various urban areas in Hong Kong. Usually the actors, musicians and workers received low pay and the performing expenses were funded indirectly by the government. Thus, in the 1980s, the major employment opportunities for the professional performers and workers were in the amusement park, as well as in theatrical and ritual performances.[8]

The amateur troupe organized by Radio Television Hong Kong is the only one in the territory that has a stable, if not permanent, personnel. Before it closed down in 1985, the theatre located in the Lai Yuen Amusement Park 荔園 used to hire troupes to perform on a monthly basis. Most other Cantonese operatic troupes are more temporary, organized for a series of performances lasting two to seven days or sometimes longer, then disbanded after the series. A series of performances is referred to as a *toi* 台 (stage) in the profession. From August 1984 to the end of July 1985, thirty-four troupes performed eighty-seven "stages," totalling 415 days; each stage lasted 4.77 days on average. Among the thirty-four troupes, nineteen performed only one stage and only seven performed more than two stages. Only four troupes of the seven had regular principal male and female actors in their performances. Only one troupe of the four had regular accompanying musicians, actors for the major, secondary and minor roles, as well as backstage workers.[9]

In organizing a troupe, referred to as a *ban* 班 (group of people), the *ban zy* 班主 (impresario) will first look for the actors playing the principal male and female roles, referred to in the profession as *men mou seng* 文武生 (civil-military role) and *zing jen fa dan* 正印花旦 (principal female role). In a ritual series taking place in the rural and suburban areas, actors of these two roles are usually assigned or *deing* 定 (booked) by the *zy wui* 主會 (host organization), which is comprised of representatives of the community that wishes to hire a troupe to perform for the celebration of their ritual. The *zy wui* also has the right to choose the performance repertory. After the actors for the principal male and female roles are found, the impresario will look for the other four major role, the secondary role and the minor role actors. The other four major roles are *siu seng* 小生 (young male role, or support-ing male role), *ji bong fa dan* 二幫花旦 (supporting female role), *cau seng* 丑生 (comic role) and *mou seng* 武生 (military role).[10] Together with the principal male and female roles, they are known as *luk cy* 六柱 (six pillars, or the six major roles) in the community of Cantonese operatic employees. The impresario is also responsible for hiring the accompanying musicians, the backstage workers, and the actors playing secondary and minor roles (see Chapter 3).

Ritual Performance

In Hong Kong, Cantonese opera is staged for three types of ritual celebra-tions: *zit* 節 (festival), *dan* 誕 (birthday) and *da ziu* 打醮 (rite of purifica-tion).

Yung (1976a:62–63) mentions that operas have traditionally been staged in festivals such as the Lunar New Year and Dragon Boat Festival; however, in the years 1984 and 1985, while operas were still being staged for the Lunar New Year, few communities staged operas for the Dragon Boat Festival. Most of the ritual performances are still staged for the celebration of the birthdays of deities worshipped in Hong Kong. Though most of these deities are worshipped by people living in both urban and rural areas, most of the ritual performances occur in rural or suburban areas because space for building the large temporary performance halls is only available there. However, such birthday series are often referred to as "festivals."

The temporary halls for ritual performances are constructed with bamboo poles and tin sheets. The size of the performance hall built for staging operas depends on the funds available to the community holding the ritual (see Chapter 3), but it also depends on the importance of the ritual. Rituals of purification are held every year during the *Jy Lan Zit* 盂蘭節 (Festival of Hungry Ghosts, or simply Ghost Festival) in both urban and rural areas. Operas for this festival are usually staged in small temporary halls with no seats provided for the audience. Only small troupes are hired for these one to three-day performances. People understand that such operas are staged chiefly for the deities and ghosts.

An elaborate ritual of purification, known as *tai ping cing ziu* 太平清醮 (purification for peace), is held by some rural or suburban communities once every three, five, seven, eight or ten years. A large performance hall is often built for a five to ten-day operatic series, and a large troupe is hired.

In rituals held for celebrating the birthdays of deities, large halls are usually built, and at least a medium-sized troupe is hired for the birthday series of Tin Hau 天后 (the Queen of Heaven), the chief patron of fishermen and most of the rural, suburban and even urban communities in Hong Kong. Besides the Queen of Heaven, some communities have their own special patron deities. However, the degree of elaboration in the celebratory activities, as well as the size of the performance hall and the troupe, all depend on the funds available. The names of the deities that are patrons of some of the communities in Hong Kong are listed below:

1. Hung Sing 洪聖: Deity of the South Seas
2. Tou Dei 土地: Village Deity
3. Jyn Tin Soeng Dae 玄天上帝: King of the Abstruse Heaven
4. Bek Dae 北帝: Lord of the North
5. Tam Gung 譚公: Revered Tam
6. Zen Gwen Dai Dae 眞君大帝: The Real and Great King
7. Tin Hau 天后: Queen of Heaven
8. Fan Sin 樊仙: Deity of Bowl-making
9. Gwan Dae 關帝: Deity of War and Righteousness
10. Hau Wong 侯王: The Marquis
11. Gwun Jem 觀音: Goddess of Mercy

According to some informants, the King of the Abstruse Heaven, Lord of the North and the Real and Great King were the same deity but worshipped in different titles by different communities.

Theatrical Performance

Performances staged in permanent halls other than the amusement park are known as theatrical performances. In the Cantonese operatic community, people make sharp distinctions between ritual, theatrical and amusement park performances.

From the 1960s to the time of the present study, there has been no theatre in Hong Kong that solely stages Cantonese opera. Most of the theatrical performances are staged in cinemas that show movies as their main business. For example, the Paladium Opera House produces a series of Cantonese operas every month, usually in the evenings and on Sunday afternoons, but shows movies the rest of the time. Other Cantonese operatic performances are staged in concert halls, community halls and stadiums that are mostly run either directly or indirectly by the Hong Kong government. While in ritual series only old plays are performed, new works are sometimes introduced in theatrical performances. A series including a new play usually lasts more than five days, sometimes even two weeks. However, it is rare to have more than one new opera staged within a series.

Yung (1976a:97; 1989:33) noticed that theatrical performances are often technically more sophisticated and experimental, and are widely considered to have higher artistic value than ritual performances. Many actors and accompanying musicians say they pay more attention to theatrical performances since such performances establish their reputations.

The Sizes and Cost of Troupes

In the profession of Cantonese opera, troupes are classified into large, medium and small sizes. The criteria of classification include the fame of the principal male actor and supporting male actor, the number of backstage workers, the number of accompanying musicians and the price of hiring the troupes. Some of the informants say that a large troupe in the mid-1980s should have as its principal one of the top four male actors, who were Sen Ma Si-zeng 新馬師曾 , Lem Ga-sing 林家聲 , Lo Ga-jing 羅家英 and Lung Gim-seng 龍劍笙 . Even the supporting male actor should have had the experience of acting the principal male role in medium and small troupes.

According to some backstage workers, a large troupe should have eight workers responsible for providing costumes for actors who do not own their private costumes (see Chapter 3); a medium troupe should have six such workers and a small troupe should have four. According to some informants, the cost of hiring a large troupe to perform for one day in 1985 ranged from about HK$20,000 (about US$2,500) to HK$30,000 (about US $3,750); the price for a medium troupe varied from about HK$10,000 (about US$1,250) to HK$15,000 (about US$1,875) and the price for a small troupe from about HK$7,000 (about US$875) to HK$8,000 (about US$1,000). According to some instrumentalists, a large troupe should be supported by sixteen instrumentalists, a medium troupe should have twelve and a small troupe should hire nine. However, I once observed a small orchestra of seven players; the orchestra of the Chor Fung Ming 雛鳳鳴 (singing of the young phoenix) Opera Troupe, in which Lung Gim-seng acted the principal male role, and which is widely considered to be a large troupe, only had thirteen players when it performed in Tai O at Lantau Island from 21 to 25 July 1985 (see Chapter 3).

Admission is charged for theatrical performances. In 1986, the price of tickets ranged from HK$30 (about US$3.75) to HK$130 (about US $16.25) for performances by large troupes. A medium troupe only charged from HK$30 to HK$100 (about US$12.5). For amusement park performances (in 1985), seats at the back of the small auditorium were free for the public, who only paid admission upon entering the park; other tickets cost HK$8 (about US$1) and HK$10 (about US$1.25). Amusement park performances were staged exclusively by small troupes, which had even fewer members than most of the small troupes performing in ritual series.

Cantonese Operatic Music

Cantonese operatic music, including both Cantonese opera and its subgenre, operatic song (which lacks costumes, stage settings and acting), comprises both instrumental music and oral deliveries. Instrumental playing is composed of melodic and percussion music; oral deliveries include both speech and vocal music.

Cantonese operatic song usually employs only brief spoken deliveries. Songs are written for either one or two voices with orchestral accompaniment. While songs for one voice can be written either for male or female voice, almost all duets are written for a male and a female voice, referred to as *seng* 生 (male actor) and *dan* 旦 (female actor) respectively.

Voice production in Cantonese operatic music is referred to as *hong hau* 腔口, which is also known as *hau* 喉 (throat). In modern performances, only three kinds of *hong hau* are used. According to Yung (1976a:80), *Ping hau* 平喉 is a natural voice production; the vocal range is approximately from C below middle C to G above middle C. *Zi hau* 子喉 is a falsetto voice production and its vocal range is from middle C to high G. *Dai hau* 大喉 has

A scene from the play *The Royal Beauty* featuring two principal actors of the Singing of the Young Phoenix Cantonese Opera Troupe. (14 September 1987, Lee Theatre, Causeway Bay, Hong Kong)

a vocal quality rougher than the *Ping hau* and its vocal range is approximately a fourth or fifth higher than that of *Ping hau*. In performances of Cantonese opera, all male role actors (including females in these roles) use *Ping hau* except for the military role actor who sometimes sings in *Dai hau*; all female role actors sing in *Zi hau* except that an actor should employ *Ping hau* if he or she impersonates an aged woman. In operatic song performances, usually only *Ping hau* and *Zi hau* are used. For convenience of discussion in this study, *Ping hau* is referred to as male voice and *Zi hau* is referred to as female voice.

The accompanying orchestra in Cantonese operatic music comprises a melodic and a percussion section. Both sections participate in the accompaniment for vocal singing, acting, stylistic gestures, stage movements and dance. However, only percussion instruments accompany the performance of acrobatics and martial arts, which are also important elements of Cantonese opera. The percussion music for such purposes is played in patterns known as *lo gwu dim* 鑼鼓點 (percussion pattern) in the profession. Percussion patterns are also played as preludes for singing, speech delivery and stage movements. Short patterns of percussion music are played to accompany certain types of speech delivery.

The three most common types of vocal music are *Bong wong* 梆黃 (music in the modes of *Bong zi* 梆子 and *Ji wong* 二黃), which is also known as *Ban hong jem ngok* 板腔音樂 (aria type music);[11] *syt coeng* 說唱 (spoken and sung), story-telling music, referred to as singing narrative in the present study; and *kuk pai* 曲牌 (tune title or tune with title), here referred to as fixed tune. Modern Cantonese opera employs about thirty different aria types (Yung, 1981:670) and each one has its own music and textual structures. Four kinds of Cantonese singing narratives are frequently used in Cantonese opera: *Nam jem* 南音 (southern song), *Muk jy* 木魚 (wooden fish), *Lung zau* 龍舟 (dragon boat) and *Ban ngan* 板眼 (beat). Fixed tunes are composed of *Siu kuk* 小曲 (little tune) that are preexistent or pre-composed tunes that mostly have been borrowed from Cantonese instrumental music or which have been specially composed for new plays of Cantonese opera, and *Pai zi* 牌子 (title), which is a special collection of tunes believed to have originated from *kwen keik* 昆劇 (*kwen* opera) of the Ming and Qing dynasties. In the present study, *Siu kuk* and *Pai zi* are referred to as fixed tunes because they have relatively identifiable preexistent or pre-composed melodies. The number of such tunes used in Cantonese operatic music is unknown.

Yung (1989:69–71) points out that the identity of a certain aria type does not depend on its specific melodic contour. Yung's studies of passages belonging to the same aria type, but containing different texts, reveal that the identity of a certain aria type depends on five factors: the text's verse structure, the metrical pattern and syllable placement, the line-ending notes, the *sin* 線 (mode) and the instrumental accompaniment.

However, different aria types do share some characteristics. Theoretically, the basic unit of all aria types is a couplet, which is composed of an upper line and a lower line. In practice, any aria type passage can appear in a single line (either upper or lower), in a couplet (often a lower line followed by an upper line), or in any number of lines. According to Yung (1983a:32), the basic musical unit of any aria type is the two-line melody (upper and lower lines) that may be sung once or repeated any number of times in a passage depending on the number of textual lines. If the passage only contains one textual line, either the upper or the lower line melody (or its variant) is used. If a passage contains more than two lines of text, the two-line melodic structure is repeated, its pitch contents changing to fit the linguistic tones of the different texts. An aria type is defined by the five factors (listed above) that form its structural framework. Singers can perform an aria type passage without written notation if they are given the name of the aria type, the text and the rhythmic notation. Professional singers are able to sing even without the rhythmic notations.

The role of the scriptwriter in both Cantonese opera and operatic song is different from that of the librettist or composer in Western European art music (Yung, 1983a:31; 1989:42–43). To write a new operatic song or a scene within an opera, the scriptwriter chooses the aria types, fixed tunes and singing narratives and writes text to fit them. Occasionally a scriptwriter composes a new *Siu kuk* and sets text to his own tune (see Chapter 5). In Cantonese opera, the vocal passages are often interpolated with speech deliveries. Yung has translated into English the names of seven types of speech delivery: plain speech, supported speech, percussion speech, poetic or versified speech, rhymed speech, patter speech and comic rhymed speech (1976a:121; 1989:57).

The scriptwriter often starts an operatic scene or operatic song with an aria type passage that contains only one upper line or an odd number of lines. He is responsible for setting the text in a linguistic tonal scheme so that the singer can identify whether a line is upper or lower. As a rule, the upper line ends with a syllable in an oblique tone and the lower line ends with a syllable in an even tone (Yung, 1981:673; see Chapter 8). The rule for writing the opening aria type passage in an odd number of lines assumes that the passage ends with the upper line. When the operatic scene or song starts with speech, a fixed tune or singing narrative, the passage does not have to follow the aria type line scheme. In fixed tune passages neither the textual nor the melodic lines are identified as upper or lower lines. Passages of singing narratives contain upper and lower lines, but they do not form couplets with the lines of aria type passages.

The opening passage can be followed by acting, or by speech, fixed tune, singing narrative, or other vocal passage in the same or different aria type. If a fixed tune or a singing narrative follows the opening aria type passage, it does not have to continue the preceding passage with a lower line. Only when an opening aria type is followed by another one does the first line of the following passage have to start with a lower line to complete the couplet. Unless the second of these passages is the last one in the operatic scene or song, it must end with an upper line. In other words, the last aria type passage within a scene or a song can contain a single lower line, or an odd number of lines ending with a lower line. Most operatic scenes or songs end with an aria type passage; some end with a fixed tune passage. The practice of ending aria type passages with upper lines (except in closing aria type passages) serves to maintain the musical continuity of the aria type music within an operatic scene or song.

The criteria for defining a certain kind of singing narrative are the same as those for defining an aria type. Hence, singing narratives are sometimes considered to be a kind of aria type music (*ban hong jem ngok*).

Terms Used in the Analyses and Discussion

A play in Cantonese opera is divided into several acts, but, unlike Western drama, it is not further divided into scenes. In this study, the terms scene, passage and segment are employed for convenience of discussion. Scenes are marked by the entrance or exit of a character: it starts after at least one character has entered the stage, or after the departure of one or more characters, and usually ends with one or all of the characters leaving the stage.

A "passage" of vocal music or speech delivery in either opera or operatic song is one single, complete aria type, *Siu kuk*, singing narrative or particular type of speech delivery, whether long or short. Thus, one passage ends with the start of a different aria type, *Siu kuk* tune, singing narrative or speech delivery, even though the two passages might be delivered or sung by the same actor. If two actors, A and B, are each responsible for delivering some of the phrases or lines within a single passage, the passage is said to be composed of two segments.[12] If A's segment is followed by B, and A delivers another segment, the passage is said to be composed of three segments. Short speech deliveries such as exclamations are not counted as passages or segments.

Most of the operatic songs are not separated into scenes because there is usually no entrance and exit of singers except at the end of the song. In other words, a song is similar to an operatic scene. A song is separated into segments and passages in the same way as Cantonese opera scenes are.

Throughout the present work, the term "melody" denotes successions of at least two notes; the corresponding Cantonese term is *hong* 腔 (notes).

Notes

1. The *Asian Arts Festival* bulletin (1980) contains an article reporting an interview with the renowned Cantonese opera actor Lem Ga-sing (known as Lam Kar-sing in Hong Kong). Lem points out ways of improving the genre, including the assignment of an artistic director, the reinforcement of backstage management, the elimination of improvised comic episodes and the creation of new scripts. In 1982, when Lem was interviewed by a local newspaper, he added that rehearsal and pre-performance discussion should also be reinforced. In fieldwork research in Hong Kong during December 1982, I interviewed several active performers. Their ideas on revitalizing the genre included the assignment of a director, more uses of pre-composed tunes, control over improvising comic episodes, the assignment of a vocal music designer to pre-compose the vocal music, the assignment of a conductor and the use of more musical notation in the script. These ideas will be discussed in Chapters 3 and 4.
2. Such a troupe was the Zyn Sek 鑽石 (diamond) Cantonese Opera Troupe, which performed at Sha Lo Wan 沙螺灣 on Lantau Island for the celebration of the birthday of the Deity of the South Seas, from 16 to 20 August 1984.
3. Stage settings usually involved slides projected on the backdrop, pictures painted on screens and wooden boards, and wooden chairs and tables.
4. In the 1980s, the performances of operatic songs in tea houses did not last long. Tea houses where such performances took place were first and foremost restaurants. In 1985, there were two such restaurants that staged operatic songs in the afternoons; another one staged evening sessions.
5. Sometimes singers were hired to perform opera and operatic song at private banquets held at restaurants.

6. These data were obtained from the record of the *jem ngok bou* 音樂部 (guild of instrumentalists, which is officially known as the Hong Kong Po Fook Tong Cantonese Opera Musicians' Association) of the *Bat Wo Wui Gwun* 八和會館 (society of the eight harmonies, but officially known as the Chinese Artists Association of Hong Kong), which is an umbrella organization and a kind of work union of the profession, though it is not formally registered as a union under the Hong Kong government (see Yung, 1976a:106–7 and 1989:42). A limited number of performances may not have been represented in these data, however, the *Bat Wo* archives remain the only database of this kind in Hong Kong.

   There is a big difference between Ward's figures (1985:162–63) and the figures obtained from the record of the "guild of instrumentalists." Keeping in mind that Ward's data were collected in the 1970s, the difference reflects either a rapid decrease of productions from the 1970s to the mid-1980s, or an inaccurate estimation by Ward. The number of series reported by Ward was obtained from the Royal Hong Kong Police Force that kept such records because it was their responsibility to issue permits for the erection of the temporary theatres. Such records are not generally accessible to the public.

7. Usually the singers received no pay in amateur or semi-professional music clubs. In the semi-professional music clubs, the instrumentalists were paid by the singers on an hourly basis. I interviewed an accompanying musician in 1985 who played about nine sessions a week and received just over HK$3,000 (about US$375) a month. He told me that there was a great increase in the number of music clubs then, which explained the rise in the demand and hence the pay for accompanying musicians at the time.

8. The Bat Wo Cantonese Opera Troupe, organized by the *Bat Wo Wui Gwun*, sometimes performed under the sponsorship of the Urban Services Department. However, these performances were not recorded by the "guild of instrumentalists."

9. In 1985, the four troupes that had regular actors playing the principal male and female roles were the Lae Kwen 勵羣 (to encourage the people) Cantonese Opera Troupe (formally known as the Reckoners Cantonese Opera Company in Hong Kong), the Jing Bou 英寶 (Jing and Bou are names of the principal actors) Cantonese Opera Troupe, the Zung Sen Sing 頌新聲 (celebrate the new sound) Cantonese Opera Troupe, and the Chor Fung Ming Cantonese Opera Troupe. The last one was the only troupe that had regular performers and backstage workers. Lae Gwen and Jing Bou had the same two actors playing the principal roles, but they were operated by different impresarios.

10. *Cau seng* and *mou seng* literally mean "male comic role" and "male military role" respectively to contrast with the female comic and female military roles. As the latter role types have ceased to be used since the 1930s, *cau seng* and *mou seng* are simply referred to as "comic role" and "military role" respectively in the present study.

11. The term *ban hong* literally means "beat and melody." Tunes in this style are rhythmically and melodically related. Liang (1985:233) describes *ban hong* as a "melo-rhythmic motivic type of vocal composition," and discusses the use of this

style in Peking opera (1985:243–53). Due to the drastic changes in the music of Cantonese opera that took place in the 1920s and 1930s, this "melo-rhythmic motivic" nature can no longer be clearly demonstrated in its *ban hong* style. Hence, to follow Yung's practice, the present work employs the term "aria type" for "*ban hong*."

12. The term "segment" in the present work has a different usage from that in this writer's previous study of *nam hei* 南戲 (Southern Drama) of the Song dynasty (960–1279) (Chan, 1984). In *nam hei*, the demarcation of segments is related to the dramatic content of the play.

2. Improvisation in Cantonese Opera and World Musics

Improvisation in Cantonese Operatic Music

According to many experienced actors, accompanying musicians and teachers of Cantonese opera, improvisation was important in both opera performances and operatic song singing from before 1930 into the 1950s. Since then, changes in style and taste have led to a decrease in improvisation in the genre. From the 1950s to the present, employees in Cantonese opera and operatic song have widely believed that the genre is declining in popularity because of stiff competition with various other forms of popular entertainment. They have suggested the elimination of improvisatory practices to revitalize the genre.[1]

Extensive fieldwork for this study revealed that, while improvisation still exists to a limited extent in theatrical performances and operatic song singing, it remains important in the creative process of operatic performances that occur in ritual contexts.[2]

Hong Kong was chosen as the site for research because ritual performances are staged frequently both in the urban and rural areas of the city. In mainland China, in contrast, troupes rely on government sponsorship, and stylistic changes in the performances are accordingly prescribed by the cultural policies of the government. Influenced by Western drama and opera and Peking opera, troupes performing in the permanent theatres of the cities in China often involve directors who supervise the rehearsals, and the use of improvisation is cut down to the minimum. Rural performances that still feature a certain degree of improvisation are not easily seen by outsiders.[3]

While improvisation plays an important part in the performance of Cantonese operatic music, no scholarly research devoted to this topic has yet appeared. This study aims at developing an ethnography of improvisation in Cantonese operatic performances. It investigates the following issues: what is the definition of the term "improvisation" in Cantonese operatic music? how many different kinds of improvisation are used in the genre? what are the criteria for determining the medium in which improvisation is realized? what are the obligatory, optional and forbidden materials involved in performance and improvisation? how do the performers learn to improvise? what are the performers' attitudes towards improvisation? how do the performers coordinate their improvisation? in sum, what is the contextual significance of improvisation in Cantonese opera?

Previous Studies of Cantonese Opera

Two earlier Master's degree theses have discussed the music of Cantonese opera. They are C.P. Lin's "The Two Main Singing Styles in Cantonese Opera /bɔŋ dʒî / and / jⁱ wɔŋ /" (1973) and N. Yeh's "The Yüeh Chü Style of Cantonese Opera With an Analysis of *The Legend of Lady White Snake*" (1972). Daniel Ferguson's doctoral dissertation "A Study of Cantonese Opera: Musical Source Materials, Historical Development, Contemporary Social Organization, and Adaptive Strategies" focuses on the ethnography of the genre in the city of Guangzhou, which was once a stronghold of Cantonese opera.

Published studies of Cantonese operatic music written in English are exclusively by Bell Yung. His dissertation, "The Music of Cantonese Opera" (1976a), contains three parts that discuss the role of music in Cantonese operatic performance, the historical and recent development of the genre in Hong Kong and its social contexts, and technical aspects of speech types, fixed tunes, aria types and uses of padding syllables. The three chapters on fixed tunes, aria types and padding syllables were revised and later published as separate articles (Yung, 1981, 1983a, 1983b and 1983c). The first article discusses the identity of an aria type; the second deals with the role of linguistic tones in the creation of the melodic tones during performances; the third focuses on the vocalists' setting of the texts in singing a fixed tune; and the last discusses various types of padding syllables used in singing. The revised versions of such articles have become the main body of Yung's book *Cantonese Opera: Performance as Creative Process* (1989). Though improvisation is mentioned only briefly in Yung's studies (1976a:70 and 169; 1989:42, 63, 72 and 104–5), his emphasis on the creative process of the genre has laid the foundation for the present study.

Other English publications approach the genre from the sociological and anthropological angles. Most significant are two articles by Barbara Ward, "Not Merely Players: Drama, Art and Ritual in Traditional China" (1979) and "Regional Operas and Their Audiences: Evidence from Hong Kong" (1985). Ronald Riddle's *Flying Dragons, Flowing Streams: Music in the Life of San Francisco's Chinese* (1983) contains a social history of Cantonese opera in San Francisco from the 1950s to the present time. Studies of Chinese regional theatrical genres in Japanese by Tanaka Issei (1981, 1985 and 1989) include extensive discussion of Cantonese opera in its ritual context.

Three Chinese monographs on the genre have also contributed significantly to the present study. The *Jyt kuk se coeng soeng sik* 粤曲寫唱常識 (*Guide to Writing and Singing Cantonese Opera*, 1952) by Cen Coek-jing 陳卓瑩 discusses the musical and textual structures of most of the types of music employed in the genre. The author's approach is "prescriptive" rather than "descriptive," as he wrote all the music and text examples to illustrate the structures; the monograph is intended to be a handbook to guide the writing and singing of the music. The *Jyt keik lo gwu gei bun zi sik* 粤劇鑼鼓基本知識 (*Guide to Percussion Music of Cantonese Opera*, 1979) by Sou Men-bing 蘇文炳 and Ng Gwok-ping 吳國平 is also intended to be used as a guide, but to the playing of the percussion instruments. Besides the drills provided for practising each of the instruments, the monograph also gives the rhythmic notations of the commonly used percussion patterns and briefly discusses the dramatic function and vocal music associated with each pattern. The sources of the examples cited in the book are not given; they are probably not transcriptions of actual performances. The third work, *Jyt keik coeng hong jem ngok koi loen* 粤劇唱腔音樂概論 (*Introduction to Vocal Music of Cantonese Opera*, 1984) edited by the *Guangdong sang hei keik jin gau set* 廣東省戲劇研究室 (Guangdong Province Institute of Drama Research), contains chapters on the history of the genre from the late Ming dynasty to the 1980s; the historical development of aria type music, stylistic characteristics of the music, and the different modes and "sub-modes" employed; the textual and musical structures of the aria types and singing narratives used in the genre, how aria types and fixed tunes are connected to form a sequence of passages, the instruments, instrumentation and the playing of the accompaniment; and music examples of aria types and fixed tunes. Only the last book among the three uses a descriptive approach and cites transcriptions of actual performances as music examples.

Most studies of Cantonese opera published in Chinese focus on the historical aspects of the genre (see "Bibliography" in Yung, 1976a). Several such articles and a monograph have appeared since the completion of Yung's dissertation. Soeng (1981) and Gim (1980) discuss the development of the genre in the 1920s and 1930s respectively. The series of articles entitled *Jyt keik luk sep lin* 粵劇六十年 (*Sixty Years of Cantonese Opera*), dictated by the renowned actor Cen Fei-lung 陳非儂 and written by Jy Mou-wen 余慕雲, were first published in the *Dai sing zap zi* 大成雜誌 (*Dai Sing Magazine*) in 1979 and later published as a monograph (n.d., probably 1982). The monograph contains a memoir of Cen and articles on the history and performance practices of the genre.

Jyt keik jin gau tung loen 粵劇研究通論 (*An Introduction to the Study of Cantonese Opera*, 1982) by Loeng Pui-gem 梁沛錦 is essentially a historical study of Cantonese opera with a brief introduction to the cultural aspects of the Cantonese speaking community, and a discussion of the spread of the genre to Asian countries and the Americas. Chapter 1 discusses the *dek zet zing sen* 特質精神 (the essential spirit) of the genre, and describes its "long standing tradition," "ability to synthesize different styles," "wide spread acceptance," "frequent involvement in political revolutions," "strong creativity" and capabilities of reflecting "regional" and "epochal" characteristics (Loeng, 1982:5–11). Loeng discusses the genre's essential spirit in a historical context, but does not mention contemporary performances, particularly the stylistic characteristics of the genre. However, attributes quoted in his book, such as the "ability to synthesize different styles," "regionalism," and "strong creativity" could be applied to certain aspects of the contemporary style. Yet, such characteristics also exist in many other regional theatrical genres in China and do not form part of Cantonese opera's unique "essence."

Jyt keik ngae soet jen soeng 粵劇藝術欣賞 (*The Appreciation of the Art of Cantonese Opera*, 1981) by Wae Hin 韋軒 briefly discusses the history, role distribution, aspects of singing, stage movements, martial arts, speech delivery, stage setting, face painting, costume, accompaniment and the literary styles of the texts. Chapters 2 and 3 discuss the appreciation and the *ngae soet dek sik* 藝術特色 (artistic characteristics) of the genre (1981:5–12). Wae points out that the artistic characteristics include the syntheses of different elements from other Chinese and Western musical and theatrical genres, the rich varieties of music, the large repertory and constant appearance of new plays, the use of both Western and Chinese musical instruments and the "plain meanings" of the texts (1981:11). However, the attribute "constant appearance of new plays" does not apply to productions in Hong Kong in recent years, where new plays are rarely staged. (No new play was staged during the period of the fieldwork research for this study from July 1984 to December 1985; two plays advertised as

Mek Siu-ha (1903–1941), himself a leading scriptwriter of the 1930s and an amateur actor as well, wrote the first extensive study on the history of Cantonese opera which was published in 1940. (c. 1940, venue unknown, Hong Kong)

"new" were adaptations of old scripts.) Many new plays staged on the mainland are not performed by local troupes in Hong Kong.

Jyt keik dik coeng wo zou 粵劇的唱和做 (*Singing and Acting in Cantonese Opera*, 1957) by Lei Ngan 李雁 gives musical examples of aria types and briefly discusses the techniques of Cantonese operatic singing. According to Lei, the uniqueness of the genre lies in the "refinement and intensification of its means of presentation" (1957:89). However, Wae (1981:8–10) says this is only one characteristic shared by many regional theatrical genres in China.

Studies of the Use of Improvisation in World Musics

The present study aims at establishing a theory of improvisation in the context of Cantonese operatic music. Before this is approached, a brief survey of different studies of improvisation in world musics will provide a useful conceptual background.

Thurston Dart's *The Interpretation of Music* is one of the earlier scholarly works that devotes serious attention to improvisation, which often appears interchangeably with the term "extemporization." According to Dart (1963:62–63), while improvisation played an important role in European art music until late eighteenth century, it was the "pedants" of this period who "turned counterpoint and harmony into 'paper work'" and subsequently they were responsible for breaking the links that once held composer, performer and listener in a "single musical chain."

Philip Alperson's article "On Musical Improvisation" (1984) discusses the philosophical and aesthetic aspects of improvisation that is used mainly in Western European art music. It identifies improvisation as both a product and an action.

Jeff Pressing's article "Improvisation: Methods and Models" (1988) approaches improvisation from the disciplines of cognitive psychology and physiology and attempts to establish a theory of improvisation that may answer these questions: how do people improvise? how do people teach and learn to improvise? what is the origin of improvisatory behaviour? Though the article does not deal with improvisation in different musical cultures, it discusses the related concepts of oral tradition, folklore, intuition and creativity. Pressing's study contains an extensive list of published works on the use of improvisation in world musics.

Derek Bailey's *Improvisation: Its Nature and Practice in Music* (1980) is, so far, the only book wholly devoted to the discussion of the topic. (While David Sudnow's *Ways of the Hand:The Organization of Improvised Conduct* (1978) gives an account of the author's "acquisition" of jazz improvisation.) Not intended to be an academic study, Bailey's book contains interviews with established musicians of several different musical cultures and genres including North Indian music, flamenco, Western European art music, rock, jazz and twentieth-century free improvisatory music. Bailey does not attempt to define the term or provide music examples, but gives the musicians' descriptions of the concept in "abstract terms" (1980:4). In fact Bailey himself is not sure if "improvisation" should be used as a term of reference (1980:5).

Besides distinguishing between idiomatic and non-idiomatic improvisation, where the former concerns the "expression of an idiom—such as jazz, flamenco or baroque" and the latter is what is usually found in "free" improvisatory music (1980:4–5), Bailey gives some valuable insights through the interviews with musicians. According to Bailey (1980: 15–16), a player's improvisatory ability can be developed when he is familiar with the context of the performance, has a strong desire to improvise, has an improviser who he admires and wants to emulate this performance. He also has to improvise by accident, so that he can improve his art by trial and error. Bailey's observation is found applicable to my interviews with actors who describe the acquisition of improvisation techniques in Cantonese opera (see Chapters 4, 8 and 9).

Many articles have been published on the use of, or topics related to, improvisation. These works discuss such musical cultures and genres as jazz (Byrnside, 1975), Latin American music (Béhague, 1980), Turkish classical music (Signell, 1974), Middle Eastern classical music in general (Touma, 1971), Southeast Asian classical music (Hood, 1975), and North Indian classical music (Datta and Lath, 1967; Wade, 1973). The use of improvisation in Western European music, Southeast Asian music, South Asian music and Middle Eastern music is also discussed in the article "Improvisation" in *The New Grove Dictionary of Music and Musicians* (1980). The topic is studied in books such as *Daramad of Chahargah: A Study in the Performance Practice of Persian Music* (1972) by Nettl and Foltin, and *Classical Persian Music: An Introduction* (1973) by Zonis. Signell's *Makam: Modal Practice in Turkish Art Music* (1977) and Wade's *Music in India: The Classical Traditions* (1979) contain brief accounts of improvisation.

Literature on jazz improvisation is abundant, but most focus on the teaching of improvisation and the personal styles of established jazz musicians.

Intended to be a teaching and learning manual, Jerry Coker's *Improvising Jazz* identifies five important factors in the playing of improvisation: intuition, intellect, emotion, sense of pitch, and habit (1987:3). In suggesting that early jazz had a closer connection with African drumming than with Spanish music, Gunther Schuller points out that improvisation in the latter involves primarily elaboration and embellishment, but variation plays an important role in the former, where the "expositional material" is "varied, manipulated, augmented, diminished, fragmented, regrouped into new variants" (Schuller, 1986:58).

In Byrnside's "The Performer as Creator: Jazz Improvisation" (1975:223), the author defines "improvisational composition" as a piece being "composed and performed almost simultaneously" and which could only be created once.

Byrnside later points out that "fixed" and "improvised" music only differ in a matter of degree, and complements his definition by describing the role of the improviser-composer (1975:225): "... the improviser is a creator of non-fixed and essentially non-duplicatable music, who composes with reference to some pre-planned idea and structure, which he borrows from another source."

"Swing" is discussed by Byrnside as a performance practice, and techniques of improvisation are specifically used by jazz musicians when they "swing" a tune. It consists of artistic skills such as adding notes to the tune, omitting notes, replacing notes by others or by rests, changing rhythm (which includes syncopation), and changing timbre (1975:230–32). A closer study of improvised passages reveals that the improviser can develop musical fragments by repetition and constant variation, and build the improvised materials around a "small set of compact germinal ideas" (1975: 241–43).

Byrnside's definition of improvisation resembles that in *The New Grove* (1980, Vol. 9:31–32). According to the *Grove* definition, improvisation is both a creative and performing process; it appears in a continuum with "immediate composition" and "elaboration or adjustment of the framework" as its two extremes. Apparently this definition is too general to make any specific sense, but it is the only one available in recent works published on the topic. Although the term (or concept) is only generally defined, the writers mentioned above, except Nettl and Foltin, have employed it in their studies.

Hood's "Improvisation in the Stratified Ensembles of Southeast Asia" (1975:25) starts with a critique of the definition of improvisation given in the *Harvard Dictionary of Music*. Later, Hood points out that the general nature of the process of improvisation involves both kinetic and abstract memory and it is difficult to draw a line between improvisation and composition, though the former process could be documented and described in detail.

Hood (1975:29) then points out the nine levels of reference for the "comprehension of group improvisation in Javanese gamelan"; they are the tuning system, the form, the abstraction of the fixed melody, the fixed melody, the instrumental or vocal idiom, the local or regional style, the group empathy, personal style, and—with particular emphasis—the mode, which has a role as a regulator of improvisation.

Hood (1975:31) follows with a description of the traditional role of improvisation in some of the Southeast Asian music cultures, and the changes in that role that have already taken place or which might occur in the future.

Though Cantonese operatic music does not contain a "highly stratified" texture and performance practice, the weakening of the employment of improvisation in the 1980s, particularly in performances staged by mainland Chinese troupes and theatrical performances produced in Hong Kong, could be observed at least as a result of a "preoccupation with innovation" which in some ways presumes Western opera and Peking opera as models and views improvisation as an old-fashioned and aesthetically inferior practice (see Chapters 1 and 4). Whether other factors mentioned by Hood will contribute to changes in Cantonese opera awaits further research.

Improvisation in North Indian Classical Music

Both Bailey (1980:7–20) and Datta and Lath (1967:27–34) use abstract terms to describe improvisation in North Indian classical music. Neither work includes musical examples. Bailey (1980:13 and 18) points out that improvisation in this genre includes determination of the size of the *sruti* (the smallest interval used), change of the sub-division of a beat, use of the "'feel' of the rhythm," and the exploration of the melodic possibilities in a *raga*. Datta and Lath (1967:27–28 and 32) mention the terms "elaboration," "unfoldment," and "manipulation" of formulae and patterns, and further clarify the point that elaboration includes melodic development, melodic variation and rhythmic variation. Bailey and Datta and Lath agree that the purpose of improvisation in the genre is to intensify or build up the mood or structure of a *raga*.

Jairazbhoy uses music examples to illustrate improvisatory techniques such as melodic elaboration, expansion and variation in the article "Improvisation" in *The New Grove* (1980, Vol. 9:53–54). His music examples show the improvisatory repetition of melodic fragments, retrograde order of some notes and the addition of pitches to the basic motives.

A detailed description of the use of improvisation in North Indian classical music is written by Powers in *The New Grove* article on "India" (1980, Vol. 9:107–13). The key words are still "combining motives," "develop," "elaborate" and "variation." Powers, however, notices the role of register as part of the framework that regulates improvisation.

Wade's *Music in India: The Classical Traditions* (1979) does not describe the performance practice of improvisation in detail, but defines and briefly discusses terms related to improvisation. In the performance of Hindustani instrumental *gat* (a piece of composition), the *jawāb-sawāl* (question-answer) technique involves a phrase played by the melodic soloists and then a rhythmic or melodic reproduction of the phrase by the drummer (1979:187). In *dhrupad* (a genre of vocal composition) performance, *bolbant* is the rhythm-oriented "playing with the words" and *boltan* is the improvisation of fast melodic figures by using the words as rhythmic reference (1979:168).

Improvisation in Middle Eastern Music

Several articles and books have contributed to the understanding of the use of improvisation in Middle Eastern classical music, which embraces Persian, Turkish and Arabic music, but none of these works attempts to define the term either explicitly or implicitly.

Touma (1971:47) states that improvisation in the three musical cultures is limited only to the handling of the rhythmic-temporal elements when a performer bases his performance on the modal materials of a *dastgah*, *makam* or *maqam*, which are the collections of modes in Persian, Turkish and Arabic classical music respectively. Touma points out that both composed and improvised music play important roles in these three cultures.

Of improvisation as a term and a concept, Touma (1971:38 and 47) emphasizes "creativeness," "new composition re-created every time" and "free organization of the rhythmic-temporal factor" as the constituents. Yet, besides reporting that a musician can improvisatorily determine the time duration for presenting a tone-level (1971:43), Touma does not further explain the actual use of the rhythmic-temporal improvisation, nor does he compare different versions of the same *taqsim* (musical work). Though Touma has not illustrated how tonal-spatial materials can be executed through improvisation, his description of the "combinations and repetitions" of tone-levels, the "departure from and return to the first tone-level" and the proceeding to the highest tone-level, suggest the use of improvisation.

Signell (1974) describes some constraints imposed on the use of improvisation by the traditional model of Turkish classical music, as well as some variable materials that could be executed improvisatorily. The constraints discussed in detail include the intervallic structure, the melodic progression and the tessitura of the *makam*-s (the plural form of *makam*). Other elements discussed briefly by Signell include the proportion of the phrases and the idiomatic exploitation of the instrument's technical capabilities. The variable elements of execution discussed both in detail and in brief include the creation or borrowing of phrases, modulation from one *makam* to another, the creation of tension and resolution, as well as the creation of rhythmic interest. Though he does not define the term "improvisation," Signell emphasizes that the application of improvisation in performances shows the creative ability of a performer (1974:45).

In another study, Signell describes a kind of improvisation that is applied to the musical genre *fasıl*, a semi-classical and nightclub version of classical Turkish music. Without the help of musical examples, Signell briefly writes (1977:12) that, "[T]he musician who specializes in this music is fond of filling in short rests in the melody with his own *keriz* (improvisation), a practice currently frowned on in strictly classical circles."

Nettl and Foltin (1972:11–13) explain that the concept of improvisation does not provide insight into the study of the nature of Persian music. First, a large portion of Persian classical music is not improvised, but composed. Second, the creative processes or techniques found in improvised music can also be found in composed music. Such processes or techniques include repetition, variation of a motif, extension, sequence and reliance on tetrachords. Third, the concept of improvisation as defined traditionally in

Western European art music is not used in Persian classical music. Finally, a "clear, learned model on which a musician bases his performance," as is found in jazz, is absent in Persian classical music. Hence, these authors' study focuses on the performance practices of the musical genre instead of the use of improvisation.

Zonis (1973) has further systematically studied the handling of improvisation in Persian music, but does not approach her discussion from the definition of the term or concept. However, her general description of the role of improvisation in the performance of the genre does in some ways reveal the connotation of the term in the way she uses it.

Zonis' understanding of improvisation consists of several points:

1. An improviser is both the performer and composer at the same time.
2. In a musical genre that is performed through improvisation, each performance of the same piece is different.
3. An improvisation has to be based on a framework or model, which is part of the musical genre's tradition. A model of framework is not a finished composition.
4. An improvisation may involve the alteration, filling-in, elaboration, extension and embellishment of the framework or model.
5. Originality, creativity and individual expression play important roles in an improvisation. Improvisation should be done intuitively and naturally.
6. To study the uses of improvisation in a musical genre is to study the series of decisions involved in the selection, ordering, alteration, filling-in, elaboration, extension and embellishment of the musical materials provided by the framework or model. These processes finally produce the performance.

Zonis then discusses the primary categories of the techniques employed to elaborate motives and melodies, with musical examples. They include repetition and varied repetition, ornamentation and centonization (which is the "joining together of familiar motives to produce longer melodies"). Repetition includes literal repetition, repetition at different octaves and sequential repetition. Varied repetition includes the rhythmic and melodic modification of the motives when they are repeated. Addition of accessory notes and ornamentation are techniques of melodic modification. Regarding ornamentation, Zonis points out that, in Persian music, "not a single note is left unornamented": for example, "every note longer than an eighth note is strummed, and if a note is not strummed, it is trilled." Besides these, grace notes are often added (1973:105–9).

When a performer intends to create a complete composition, he applies the technique as described above to elaborate on the nuclear theme and creates short pieces that finally "make up the sub-section of the *dastgah* called the *gusheh*" (1973:115).

Zonis discusses the practices for facilitating coordination among the singer and the accompanists during an improvised performance (1973:124). In short, the performers coordinate through preparations before an improvised performance, through the heterophonic accompaniment played by the instrumentalist who follows the singer closely, and by reserving improvisation in the accompaniment for sections so designated. Cantonese opera employs a different system of coordination, but the two genres share the basic principle that requires the accompanists to respond to the singer's improvisation.

To summarize, Zonis uses the term improvisation as a performing and creative activity, and the term composition as a pre-performance process, despite questions raised by Nettl and Foltin (1972) and Nettl (1974) about the appropriateness of employing the concept "improvisation" in musicological and ethnomusicological studies. The concept of improvisation can be significant in understanding the nature of a musical genre, if the framework or model that regulates the application of improvisatory practices is made clear and the extent and limitation of the use of improvisation comprehensible.

The Definition of Improvisation

Here, I accept the definition of "improvisation" given by *The New Grove* in a general sense (see previous sections of the present chapter), but I will attempt to refine the term by clarifying some aspects of the concept in the context of Cantonese operatic music.

While Nettl (1974:6) insists that "improvisation" does not have any significant difference from "composition," John A. Sloboda (1988:139) identifies "improvisation" as a "performing" process and further points out that "what distinguishes improvisation from composition is primarily the pre-existence of a large set of formal constraints which comprise a 'blueprint' or 'skeleton' for the improvisation." By comparing story-telling to musical improvisation, Sloboda (1988:139–40) discusses some important characteristics of the latter, which, as shown below, are also reflected in the definition of the term in the context of Cantonese operatic music (also see Chapter 4).

While oral tradition plays an important role in Cantonese operatic music, playwrights make use of the written medium to compose plays or new tunes. The term "composition" would better be understood as the creation of music through the written medium. A performance may be an improvisation or an aural realization of a composition. And improvisation is the creative process by which a performer realizes his musical ideas through the aural media. Improvisation, realization and performance take place at the same time, and the realizer and the performer are the same person: the improviser.

Improvisation in Cantonese operatic music exists at different degrees or levels, from improvising an entire opera, a whole act or a scene, to a sung or spoken passage, a martial arts or comic episode, a melody or an ornament. The present study mainly focuses on the improvisation involved in spoken and vocal passages.

This book will emphasize two types of improvisation used in the genre: improvisatory realization, in which the performer interprets the suggestions in the scripts, without departing from them; and improvisatory deviation, in which the performer adds, deletes and replaces musical material, departing from the script's suggestions. Deviation can take place at a macro or micro level, that is involving whole passages of vocal, instrumental or spoken performance, or simply details within passages suggested by the script. The actor's choice is regulated by a systematic set of performance practice rules.

Notes

1.   In his discussion of the improvisatory aspects of Chinese music, Liang (1985:21) has also pointed out the impact of Westernization:

Traditionally the performer has a minor role as a composer since a successful performance is judged not only on the performing ability of a particular piece of music, but also on the ability to semi-improvise on the given material. The addition of the performer's personal interpretation through semi-improvisation was permitted in traditional and other repertory except in works which have been composed since the second half of the twentieth century when, generally speaking, the role of the composer and the compositional process began to resemble practices in Western serious music.

2. The fact that an improviser would normally limit his improvisation when perform-ing in a formal context is also noticed by Sloboda (1988:149), who advises the readers to find "real improvisatory jazz" at the "late-night backroom informal sessions," whereas on the concert-hall platform, the improviser "is often 'playing safe' by using improvisatory devices which have worked well in other circumstan-ces, so as to create the best effects he knows how." John M. Chernoff's *African Rhythm and African Sensibility* (1979) also gives a detailed account of how the improvising drummers react to the changing elements in the performance contexts.

3. Ward (1985:162) states that operatic performances in the traditional ritual context no longer exist in mainland China. However, in recent years, an increasingly tolerant attitude of the Chinese authorities towards traditional customs, especially religious practices, is observed. Lai and Wong (1988:2) point out that at present there are more than seventy professional, and numerous amateur, Cantonese opera troupes actively performing in Guangdong Province. It is believed that most of these troupes are hired in a ritual context. In 1989, my fieldtrips to several rural communities in southern China revealed that, though operatic troupes were still being hired for the celebration of traditional festivals, the organizers and audience did not emphasize the religious and ritual functions of these performances to avoid being criticized as "superstitious" and "feudalistically minded."

3. Ritual Performance

The Performances Studied

Since a large proportion of the Cantonese operatic productions in Hong Kong are ritual performances, this chapter is devoted to the discussion of performances staged in the ritual context. Materials used in the present chapter are mostly from a series performed by the Coi Lung Fung 彩龍鳳 (colourful dragon and phoenix) Cantonese Opera Troupe for celebrating the birthday of Fuk Dek Gung 福德公 (Deity of Virtue and Fortune) from 10 to 13 March 1985, at Tai O on Lantau Island. The second day within the series was chosen by the community to be the *zing dan jet* 正誕日 (the real or chosen birthday of a deity, also referred to as main festival day), which featured particularly elaborate celebrating activities. Besides data collected from this series, I will also refer to materials collected from the following ritual performances:

1. The Diamond Cantonese Opera Troupe's (see Note 2, Chapter 1) series from 16 to 20 August 1984 at Sha Lo Wan on Lantau Island, for the birthday of the Deity of the South Seas. The main festival day was 19 August, which was the twenty-third day of the seventh month of the lunar calendar.
2. The Gem Fung Wong 錦鳳凰 (beautiful phoenix) Cantonese Opera Troupe's series from 20 to 23 March 1985 at Bun Lou Pang 半路棚 on Lantau Island, for the birthday of the Village Deity. The main festival day was 22 March, which was the second day of the second month of the lunar calendar.
3. The Dai Hung Wae 大雄威 (tremendous heroic strength) Cantonese Opera Troupe's series from 19 to 23 April 1985, for the birthday of the King of the Abstruse Heaven at Tung Wan 東灣 on Cheung Chau Island. The main festival day was 22 April, which was the third day of the third month of the lunar calendar.

4. The Gem Lung 金龍 (golden dragon) Cantonese Opera Troupe's series from 21 to 25 April 1985 for the birthdays of the Lord of the North and Revered Tam at Happy Valley on Hong Kong Island. The main festival day is unknown.

5. The Jing Bou Cantonese Opera Troupe's (see Note 9, Chapter 1) series from 1 to 5 May 1985 for the birthday of the Real and Great King at Tsing Yi Island. The main festival day was 3 May, which was the fourteenth day of the third month of the lunar calendar.

6. The Tremendous Heroic Strength Cantonese Opera Troupe's series from 9 to 13 May 1985 for the birthday of the Queen of Heaven at Po Toi Island. The main festival day was 12 May, which was the twenty-third day of the third month of the lunar calendar.

7. The Hei Lem Mun 喜臨門 (fortune arrives at door) Cantonese Opera Troupe's series from 10 to 14 May 1985 for the birthday of the Queen of Heaven at Aberdeen on Hong Kong Island. The main festival day was 12 May, which was the twenty-third day of the third month of the lunar calendar.

8. The Sing Wae 聲威 (great fame) Cantonese Opera Troupe's series from 10 to 14 May 1985 for the birthday of the Queen of Heaven at Tai Po. The main festival day was 12 May, which was the twenty-third day of the third month of the lunar calendar.

9. The Jing Bou Cantonese Opera Troupe's series from 31 May to 4 June 1985 for the birthday of the Queen of Heaven at Sai Kung. The main festival day was 2 June, which was the fourteenth day of the fourth month of the lunar calendar.

10. The Reckoners Cantonese Opera Company's series (see Note 9, Chapter 1) from 9 to 12 June 1985 for the birthday of the Queen of Heaven of the temple located in the Fan Lau area, at Tai O. The main festival day was 11 June, which was the twenty-third day of the fourth month of the lunar calendar.

11. The Singing of the Young Phoenix Cantonese Opera Troupe's (see Chapter 1) series from 28 June to 2 July 1985 for the birthday of Revered Tam at Shaukeiwan. The main festival day was 30 June, which was the third day of the fifth month of the lunar calendar.

12. The Colourful Dragon and Phoenix Cantonese Opera Troupe's series from 29 June to 3 July 1985 for the birthdays of the Deity of Bowl-making and Deity of War and Righteousness at Wun Yiu

The major part of the temporary performance hall built for the birthday series of the Queen of Heaven. The structure is supported by bamboo poles erected upon a cliff to allow the stage to face the deity's temple. (19 April 1987, Po Toi Island, Hong Kong)

碗窰 of Tai Po. The main festival days were 30 June and 3 July, which were the thirteenth and sixteenth days of the fifth month of the lunar calendar.

13. The Singing of the Young Phoenix Cantonese Opera Troupe's series from 21 to 25 July 1985 for the birthday of the Marquis deity at Tai O. The main festival day was 23 July, which was the sixth day of the sixth month of the lunar calendar.

14. The Hing Nin Wa 慶年華 (celebrate the nice years) Cantonese Opera Troupe's series from 2 to 6 August 1985 for the birthday of the Goddess of Mercy at Pak Sha Wan of Sai Kung. The main festival day was 5 August, which was the nineteenth day of the sixth month of the lunar calendar.

15. The Lei Sing 梨聲 (singing of the "pear," an allusion to the fact that Chinese opera professionals refer to themselves as "sons and brothers of the pear garden") Cantonese Opera Troupe's series from 9 to 12 September 1985 for the ritual of purification held for the Ghost Festival at Shaukeiwan. The date of the main festival day is unknown.

Since traditionally only one day is designated to be the birthday of a certain deity, a single day is chosen to be the main festival day in each series of celebrating activities. With few exceptions, the main festival day is the day of the deity's birthday. However, a community may also choose to celebrate the deity's birthday months after the day. In such cases, it still has to choose a main festival day in the series. For example, the birthday of the Queen of Heaven is traditionally the twenty-third day of the third month of the lunar calendar, yet series nine and ten above were held long after that day. According to many informants, all of the series listed above had been held annually for decades.

Ritual Performances at Tai O

Tai O is a fishing town located in the northeastern region of Lantau Island. During the last decade, according to most sources, there were usually eight series of ritual performances held in different regions of the town each year, for the birthdays of deities of different regions and communities. The eight series were:

1. The Fuk Dek Gung series. Fuk Dek Gung is one of the most important village deities in Tai O and is also the patron deity of the fishermen there.
2. The birthday series of the Village Deity of the Cong Lung Se 創龍社 (society of the creative dragon), which was, and still is, a voluntary organization supported by some of the residents of Tai O.
3. The Bun Lou Pang series as described above.
4. The Queen of Heaven series.
5. The Deity of the South Seas series.
6. The Deity of War and Righteousness series.
7. The birthday series of Lady Golden Flower, a child-giving deity that is particularly worshipped by people of the Sen Cyn 新村 region.
8. The birthday series for the deity known as the Marquis.

In 1983 and 1984, series 2 and 5 were not held. For series 3, no formal troupe was hired by the community at Bun Lou Pang in the years 1981, 1982, 1983 and 1984. In 1981, 1982 and 1983, the community staged Cantonese operatic song singing as the major event in the celebrations. In 1984, amateur actors and musicians were hired to perform a celebratory operatic series. According to Mr. Wen Sing 溫勝 , who was the leader of the *zy wui* at Bun Lou Pang, since the establishment of the village deity's temple in 1967, ritual operatic performances were staged every year except from 1981 to 1983, when the community could not afford to stage operatic performances for economic reasons.

In 1984, of the five series staged in Tai O, which were series 1, 4, 6, 7 and 8, two performed for five days and three performed for four days, making a total of twenty-two days.

Besides hiring a troupe to perform ritual operas, the *zy wui* also organizes various celebratory activities, including banquets, offerings to the deity, distribution of roast pork and red-coloured eggs among the people in the community, auctions of sacred objects, and the contest of snatching the *fa pao* 花炮 (floral firecracker; see below).

A sequence of celebratory activities usually starts one or two days before the main festival day. Operatic presentations are often considered the high points in each day's celebration. In the Fuk Dek Gung series, an evening performance preceded the main festival day. During the main festival day and the following two days, both afternoon and evening shows were staged. A total of seven plays, including four in the evening and three in the afternoon sessions, were produced in the series. According to some sources at Tai O, since Fuk Dek Gung had a lower rank compared to the Queen of Heaven and the Marquis, his birthday series usually had only seven plays performed on four days. Mr. Wong Loi-men 黃來敏 , who was the leader of the *zy wui* for the Fuk Dek Gung series, noted that this had long been a tradition. However, according to some actors, instrumentalists and impresarios, the number of plays and days of performance within a series would depend on the funds raised in the community and would have nothing to do with the importance of the deity. Though there are divergent views on the factors that determine the number of performances for various festivals, the availability of funds is certainly an important one (see Chapter 1).

The *Zy Wui*

The troupe members refer to the few "on-duty" representatives of the community who actually negotiate with, and hire, them as *zy wui*. The people living in the community refer to such representatives as *zik lei* 值理 (people on duty), and refer to the group of residents who financially support the celebrating activities by contributing a definite amount of money as *zy wui*. In the Fuk Dek Gung series of 1985, there were 141 residents who each paid HK$250 to support the celebrating activities. Such people were therefore called *zy wui* by the local residents. The 250 dollars include fees for attending a banquet and the seven operatic performances.

The *zy wui* of the celebrating series held at Bun Lou Pang in 1985 consisted of 324 people. Each of them paid HK$220, either in installments or in a lump sum in advance. The payment entitled them to the seven operatic performances and a banquet, as well as a piece of roast pork and seventeen red-coloured eggs. Bun Lou Pang had about 1,100 residents at the time, so there was probably at least one *zy wui* member in every household in that year's, as in the other years', celebrating series.

The Decision to Stage Opera

In order to show their respect to the deities, the *zik lei* responsible for organizing a certain birthday celebration usually request advice of the deity through a ritual process of *dep bui* 碟杯 (to drop two pieces of wood), which is carried out in front of the altar of the deity.

Usually, after a series, it is customary for the *zik lei* to go to the temple again and ask the deity whether they should stage operatic performances next year. Now, *dep bui* is performed with two identical pieces of wood, flat on one side and round on the other in front of the altar. One of the *zik lei* is responsible for dropping the two pieces of wood from two to three feet above ground. The oracle is *bou bui* 寶杯 (precious *bui*) if the round side of both pieces turn upward, or *joeng bui* 陽杯 (sun *bui*) if both of the round sides turn downward. It is called *sing bui* 聖杯 (sacred *bui*) if the wooden pieces turn upward, one flat and one round. Only when the oracle shows "sacred *bui*" can the deity's agreement be deemed to have been obtained.

In 1984, after the celebrating series was over, the *zik lei* of Fuk Dek Gung series went to Fuk Dek Gung's temple and got the deity's approval for them to spend about HK$70,000 to HK$80,000 (about US$9,000 to $10,000) to stage a series of operatic performances in the next year's celebrating series. The *zik lei* of Bun Lou Pang also performed *dep bui* after the 1984 series, but they did not get the sacred *bui* from the Village Deity. They then went to the temple of the Marquis deity and obtained the advice that they might face some financial difficulty in the coming year's celebration, but they could overcome the difficulty at last. The *zik lei*, thus, decided to stage another series of operatic performances in the next year's celebration.

Mr. Wen, forty-five years of age in 1985 and the leader of the *zik lei* at Bun Lou Pang, said he did not like Cantonese opera himself. He contributed both his effort and money to organizing celebratory activities in the last twelve years only to please the deity. Before Mr. Wen volunteered to work for the village deity of Bun Lou Pang, his children were always troubled by sickness. Soon after he started serving the deity, his children's health improved. He also told me that several years ago he once discovered that the temple of the village deity was slightly damaged. Though he had promised himself, he still forgot to hire workers to fix the damage. He then fell ill until he finally remembered what he should have done to the temple. Since this incident, Mr. Wen became deeply convinced of the supernatural power of the village deity of Bun Lou Pang and is wholeheartedly devoted to serving the temple.

Mr. Wong, forty-two years of age in 1985 and the leader of the *zik lei* of the Fuk Dek Gung's celebrating series, also claimed that he was not a fan of Cantonese opera. He contributed his wealth and effort only because he deeply believed that ritual performances of Cantonese opera would bring peace, prosperity and fortune to his and the community's business.

Mr. Wen and Mr. Wong both pointed out that their leadership did not result from any formal appointment or election. They gained trust from the people in their communities and were then recognized as the decision makers for the celebration series. Neither of them held an official post in their communities.

Financial Sources and Expenditure

There are usually five sources that the *zy wui* can collect money from. In 1985, the Fuk Dek Gung series raised a total of HK$138,775 (about US $17,800). Such sources are (all in Hong Kong dollars):

1. Contributions by the *zy wui* members: 141 persons at $250 each, for $35,250.
2. Admissions to operatic performances: tickets were sold at three different prices. Each ticket allowed the bearer to attend all seven performances. Excluding tickets assigned to the 141 *zy wui* members, six were sold for $200 each, fifty-eight were sold for $150 each and forty-six were sold for $100 each. Total income from admissions was $14,500.
3. Donations for general activities: donations ranged from less than a

hundred dollars to three thousand, and totalled $78,475.

4. Donations from the *fa pao* snatching contest: during such a contest, which is held on the main festival day, a certain number of *fa pao* are projected into the sky one after another. Whoever snatches a *fa pao* can obtain a small statue of the deity and has the right to keep it for a year in his household. It is commonly believed that the deity will protect the household of those who keep his statue in their houses. The contestants who snatch the *fa pao* also have to donate a certain amount to support the celebratory activities. The money donated is referred to as *pao gem* 炮金 (*pao* money).[1] A total of $5,850 was collected.

5. Donations for the purchase of joss stick, candles and incense as offerings to the deity, known as *hoeng jau cin* 香油錢 (incense and oil money): its donors include local residents and the audience of operas from other nearby areas. The exact amount was not recorded in the Fung Dek Gung series.

There are also indirect donations from local residents in every ritual series. Sometimes people make votive oaths, promising to offer money or eggs if the deity grant them their wishes. Such requests usually include fortune in business, or the good health of one's relatives, or children. These donations were not formally recorded in the Fung Dek Gung series.

The total expenses for the celebrations consisted of the following items (in Hong Kong dollars):

1. Construction of the temporary opera hall, $27,500.
2. *Hei gem* 戲金 (opera money, which is the fee for hiring a troupe for operatic performance), $77,000.
3. Transportation of the troupe's stage property, costumes and miscellaneous items, $5,600.
4. Gifts presented to the major role actors and impresario, $540.
5. Setting of electric lights and fans in the operatic hall and nearby areas, $3,000.
6. Making of *fa pai* 花牌 (flower pendant), which bear Chinese characters giving the title of the deity, the name of the community that organizes the series, the name of the troupe, the names of the major role and some of the secondary role actors. They are often decorated with live or plastic flowers, and are usually hung above the entrances of the operatic hall. The *fa pai* cost $1,600.

7. Offerings to the deity, $2,000.
8. Banquet, $17,500.
9. Gifts, $100.
10. Deposit (purpose uncertain, probably for the electric appliances provided), $3,000.
11. Miscellaneous entries, $2,500.

The total expenditure was HK$140,340 (about US$18,000). A deficit of HK$1,565 was recorded for the series, but because a surplus of HK$42,000 remained from earlier years, the celebratory series of 1985 left a surplus balance of HK$40,435.

Expenditure items one through six were related to the staging of the operatic performances. They totalled HK$115,240 (about US$15,000), over 80 percent of the funds expended for the celebration. In terms of expenses, it was evident that operatic performances were the core of the series of celebrating activities.

The Formation of the Troupe

Immediately after the celebration series of 1984, the *zik lei* of Fuk Dek Gung's birthday celebrations decided to stage operatic performances the next year. Seven months later, Mr. Wong, previously mentioned, contacted Mr. Loeng Ben 梁品, who was the impresario of the troupes hired for the last few years' celebration. Mr. Wong told Mr. Loeng that his community would like to spend HK$70,000 to HK$80,000 on a series of four-day performances.[2] Mr. Wong also told Loeng the names of the principal male and female actors they would like to hire. Mr. Loeng then started to contact the actors, musicians and workers. Meanwhile, the *zik lei* at Tai O had to arrange for the following:

1. To hire workers to build a temporary performing hall.
2. To engage a transport company to move the troupe's costumes, stage property and miscellaneous items to Tai O. Such items are stored in wooden trunks known as *hei soeng* 戲箱 (drama trunk).
3. To hire workers to install electric lights and fans at the performing hall and places where celebration activities would be held at night.
4. To put up posters on streets and in public places such as restaurants and stores.

Mr. Loeng Ben is a well-known impresario in Hong Kong. Two of the five series of ritual performances staged in the previous year (of the lunar calendar) in Tai O were organized by him. Members of the *zy wui* believed that the price as proposed by Loeng was reasonable, and that Loeng's troupes usually would provide better stage settings than other operatic companies.

After negotiating with the *zy wui* at Tai O, Loeng contacted the principal male and female actors that the *zy wui* wanted to hire. He told these actors the dates of performances and discussed salary. Loeng later recruited the four actors for the other major roles: the supporting male and female roles, the military and comic roles. Loeng often uses the name Coi Lung Fung as the *ban pai* 班牌 (name of troupe) for his companies, and invariably so for the annual Fuk Dek Gung series at Tai O. For the series staged at Bun Lou Pang seven days after the Fuk Dek Gung series, Gem Fung Wong was the *ban pai* used. According to Loeng, a different *ban pai* would provide "fresh attraction" for a community that lived nearby.

No matter what *ban pai* Loeng uses for his troupes, he always hires the same accompanists. In his troupes, most of the actors other than the ones taking the six major roles have worked with Loeng as his basic cast for several years.

The six major role actors in a Cantonese operatic troupe only perform in the evenings and in the afternoon on the main festival day. Actors, other than the six major ones, are known as *ban dae* 班底 (base of the troupe): these include the six actors for major roles in afternoon performances, except the main festival day, referred to as *ji bou zem* 二步針 (second cast); and the category of actors known as *ha lan jen* 下欄人 (actors of minor roles). Usually all actors participate in evening performances and the afternoon performance on the main festival day; the "second cast" actors only play roles of secondary importance in such productions. Afternoons, other than that of the main festival day, and occasional all-night performances feature the "base" of the troupe. Among actors of minor roles, female actors are known as *mui hoeng* 梅香 (maid); male actors are known as *lai ce* 拉扯 (dragger) and *sau ha* 手下 (one who works under somebody). *Mui hoeng* and *sau ha* are actors of the lowest rank in a troupe; they are the ones who get the lowest pay.

Besides the actors, ten accompanists played at the Fuk Dek Gung series and there were twenty-three backstage workers responsible for dressing the actors, controlling the sound and lighting systems, setting and managing the stage, cooking meals and handling miscellaneous work. The entire troupe for the Fuk Dek Gung series was made up of fifty-seven members, including twenty-three actors, twenty-three workers, ten accompanists and the impresario.

About the organization of the troupe, several points should also be noted: First, one of the *lai ce* actors was engaged by the military role actor as his costume servant, known as *ji soeng* 衣箱 (costume trunk). Second, role distribution among actors of the "second cast" and minor roles is often flexible. With the permission from the impresario or *tae coeng* 提場 (play reminder), some actors can be absent from an afternoon performance and sometimes from an evening performance. Hence, sometimes *lai ce* actors take major roles in the afternoon performances. Third, the play reminder in the evening performances acted the supporting male role in the afternoon performances except on the main festival day. The play reminder in the afternoon performances, except on the main festival day, acted as *lai ce* in the evening performances and the main festival day. Fourth, role and work distribution in the main festival day afternoon performance was the same as in the evening performances. As well, in most of the troupes, usually only one worker is responsible for controlling the sound system. In the troupe for the Fuk Dek Gung series, Loeng Ben's son sometimes helped the worker as a second sound system controller. In addition, Loeng Ben's wife was responsible for cooking meals.

The Accompanying Orchestra

The accompanying orchestra used in Cantonese opera is known as *pang min* 棚面 (front of the performance hall), because, before the 1920s, it was situated at the back part of the stage, in front of the backdrop and facing the audience (Yung, 1976a:82). According to Yung (1976a:83), the instrumentalists have played on stage right since the 1920s. In theatrical performances, the orchestra is sometimes placed in the orchestra pit.[3]

In the profession, the orchestra is also known as *zung sae ngok* 中西樂 (Chinese and Western music). Beginning in the 1920s, most of the melodic instruments used in the orchestra have been borrowed from Western music. Such instruments include the violin, cornet, banjo, xylophone, saxophone and guitar (Yung, 1976a:76). Thus, the melodic instrumental section in the orchestra is referred to as *sae ngok* 西樂 (Western music); the percussion section is known as *zung ngok* 中樂 (Chinese music) because it is composed

A ritual opera performed on the stage in front of the Queen of Heaven's temple. The Door Deities painted on the temple's wooden doors are seen in the foreground. (20 April 1987, Poi Toi Island, Hong Kong)

of traditional Chinese instruments. Today, even when some Chinese melodic instruments are employed, the terms *sae ngok* and *zung ngok* are still used, not just as the names of the two sections, but also to refer to the players in each of the sections.

Each section has its leader. The leader of the melodic section is known as *sae ngok ling dou* 西樂領導 (leader of the Western instrumentalists) or *tau ga* 頭架 (head melodic instrumentalist). Since he either plays the two-string fiddle or the violin, the leader of the melodic section is referred to as "fiddler" in this work. The leader of the percussion section is known as *zung ngok ling dou* 中樂領導 (leader of the Chinese instrumentalists) or *zoeng ban* 掌板 (player in charge of the beat, where *ban* means both the beat and the large woodblock played by him). Yung (1976a:27) mentions that this player is also called *za zuk* 揸竹 (one holds the bamboo sticks) and *da gwu lou* 打鼓佬 (drummer); here, this leader is referred to as "woodblock player."

Table 3.1 shows the instrumentation in thirteen series of ritual performances, some of which were listed at the beginning of the present chapter.

Table 3.1 Musical instruments used in thirteen ritual series

Troupes, Dates & Places of Performances	Instruments Used*																		Number of Players
	1	2	3	4	5	6	7	8	9	10	11	12	13	14	15	16	17	18	
1. Colourful Dragon and Phoenix. 10–13 March 1985, Tai O	×		×	×		×	×		×					△	△	×	×	×	10
2. Diamond, 16–20 August 1984, Sha Lo Wan	×		×	×		×		△		×			×	△	△	×	×	×	10
3. Tremendous Heroic Strength, 19–23 April 1985, Tung Wan of Cheung Chau	×		×	×		×	×		△					△	△	×	×	×	9
4. Golden Dragon, 21–25 April 1985, Happy Valley	×		×	×		⊗								⊗	△	×	×	△	7
5. Jing Bou, 1–5 May 1985, Tsing Yi Island	×		×	×	×	×						×		△	△	×	×	×	10
6. Tremendous Heroic Strength, 9–13 May 1985, Po Toi Island		×	×	×		×			△					△	△	×	×	×	8
7. Fortune Arrives at Door, 10–14 May 1985, Aberdeen		×	×	×		×	×	×			⊗	⊗		△	△	×	×	×	11

* For the names of the instruments, see Table 3.2.

Table 3.1 Musical instruments used in thirteen ritual series (cont'd)

Troupes, Dates & Places of Performances	Instruments Used*																		Number of Players
	1	2	3	4	5	6	7	8	9	10	11	12	13	14	15	16	17	18	
8. Encouraging Sound, 10–14 May 1985, Ping Che	x		x			x	x			x	x			△	△	x	x	x	10
9. Colourful Dragon and Phoenix, 29 June to 3 July 1985, Wun Yiu of Tai Po	x		x	x		x	x		△					△	△	x	x	x	9
10. Singing of the Young Phoenix, 21–25 July 1985, Tai O	x		x	x		x		x	x	x	x	x		△	△	x	x	x	13
11. Celebrate the Nice Years, 2–6 August 1985, Pak Sha Wan		x	⊗	x		x	x	x						⊗	△	x	x	△	9
12. National Pioneer, 26–29 August 1985, Chai Wan		x	△				x							△	x	x	x	x	7
13. Brilliant Sound, 4–6 September 1985, Sai Ying Pun	x	⊗	⊗	x			x			x				⊗	△	x	x	△	8

* For the names of the instruments, see Table 3.2.

Sometimes, the same orchestra or same group of players would appear in troupes with different names. For example, series 1 and 3 had the same members in their orchestras. However, though the two troupes for series one and nine had the same name, the members of their orchestras were not exactly the same. Table 3.2 shows the names of the instruments represented by the arabic numerals in Table 3.1. The number of instrumentalists in each orchestra ranges from seven to thirteen. In Table 3.1, crosses indicate the presence of the instruments. Crosses not put in circles or triangles indicate that each of the instruments is played by one player. Two or more checks put in a circle or triangle indicate that the instruments are used by just one player.

Every troupe has the same set of percussion instruments including *siu lo* 小鑼 (small gong), *bet* 鈸 or *ca* 查 (cymbals), *lo* 鑼 (gong), *buk jy* 卜魚 or *ban* 板 (large and hollow woodblock), *bong gwu* 梆鼓 (medium woodblock), *sa dik* 沙的 (small woodblock), *dai gwu* 大鼓 (big drum), *zin gwu* 戰鼓 (war drum), *pung ling* 碰鈴 (bells) and *muk jy* 木魚 (wooden fish). The large and small woodblocks are used for maintaining the pulse in vocal music. The medium woodblock is for playing the percussion patterns together with the large woodblock, war drum, gongs and cymbals. The bells and wooden fish are specially used for accompanying the singing of *Siu kuk* tunes. One performer is responsible for playing the gongs, which appear in different shapes and sizes. Another player is responsible for the cymbals, which are also of different sizes (Yung, 1976a:28–29). The small gong is not considered as part of the category of "gongs" because it has a different timbre; the player responsible for the small gong usually also performs the instrument called *so nap* 嗩吶 or *dai deik* 大笛 (a double-reed instrument with a conical pipe), which belongs to the percussion, rather than the melodic, section. Sometimes he also plays the bells. The rest of the percussion instruments described above are usually played by the woodblock player; they are, thus, grouped under number 18 in Table 3.2. In performances of small troupes, and the afternoon performances, apart from the main festival day, for the rest of the troupes, the woodblock player also plays the small gong, which is then suspended horizontally on a wooden or metallic frame supported by rubber bands. In such cases, the saxophone player also plays the *so nap*. Thus, only three percussionists are needed.

It is also common for players to perform more than one instrument in the melodic section. The instruments most often used in this section are the violin, melody (C tenor) saxophone, *joeng kem* 洋琴 (dulcimer played with

**Table 3.2 Names of instruments used in the thirteen ritual series
listed in Table 3.1**

	Instruments	Description
1	violin	
2	*gou wu* 高胡	high two-string fiddle
3	melody (C tenor) saxophone	
4	*joeng kem* 洋琴	dulcimer
5	*dai jyn* 大阮	large round-shaped lute
6	*zung jyn* 中阮	medium round-shaped lute
7	steel guitar	
8	*zung wu* 中胡	medium two-string fiddle
9	*hau gwun* 喉管	double-reed straight pipe
10	*pei pa* 琵琶	four-string pear-shaped lute
11	cello	
12	*deik zi* 笛子	horizontal flute
13	portatone	portable electronic keyboard
14	*so nap* 嗩吶	double-reed conical pipe
15	*siu lo* 小鑼	small gong
16	*bet* 鈸	cymbals
17	*lo* 鑼	gongs
18	*buk jy* 卜魚	large hollow woodblock
	bong gwu 梆鼓	medium woodblock
	sa dik 沙的	small woodblock
	zin gwu 戰鼓	war drum
	dai gwu 大鼓	big drum
	pung ling 碰鈴	bells
	muk jy 木魚	wooden fish

a pair of thin bamboo sticks), *zung jyn* 中阮 (medium sized *jyn*, which is a round, four-string plucked lute) and steel guitar. Other instruments often appearing are the *gou wu* 高胡 (high-pitched two-string fiddle), *zung wu* 中胡 (medium-pitched two-string fiddle), *hau gwun* 喉管 (double-reed instrument with a straight pipe) and *pei pa* 琵琶 (four-string and pear-shaped lute).

Within the melodic section, players of the dulcimer, melody saxophone, steel guitar and *jyn* usually concentrate on just one instrument during the performance, except that sometimes the saxophone player also plays the *so nap*. The fiddler either plays the *gou wu* or violin, but occasionally performs both.[4] The violin is tuned to the pitches F, C, G and D, but, as other melodic instruments, it is usually tuned twenty vibrations per second higher than the same pitches on a piano in modern Western equal-tempered tuning (see Chapter 5). Since some players employ more than one instrument, it is difficult to determine exactly how many different instruments are used in a performance.

The role of the woodblock player is relatively important in providing accompanying music for the performances. In Cantonese opera, percussion music precedes the actor's entrance and exit, accompanies the actor's gestures and stage movements, introduces vocal and speech passages and melodic instrumental accompaniment, and closes all passages, episodes, scenes and acts. Each of the percussionists has to listen carefully and watch the woodblock player's playing and gestures in order to be able to play the correct percussion pattern in the right time. Usually the woodblock player sits behind the melodic players and in front of the gong and cymbal performers. (The role of the woodblock player will be further discussed in Chapters 6 and 7.)

Similarly, the fiddler is watched, and listened to, by other melodic instrumentalists. As the woodblock player does, he too reads the script and observes the acting in order to play the appropriate accompaniment at the right moment. The other melodic instrumentalists only function to enrich and reinforce the fiddler's playing.[5] Only two to three copies of the script are used in the orchestra: the fiddler reads one copy, the woodblock player reads another, and usually the saxophone and dulcimer players share an additional one, if it is available.

Instruments such as the *joeng kem*, *gou wu*, *jyn*, *pei pa* and violin are often amplified by contact microphone attached to the sound boxes of the instruments. With the help of stroboscope, the two strings of the fiddles and the two higher strings of the violin are tuned to twenty vibrations higher than the pitches G and D used in the Western art music system. As a rule, only the actor who gets the highest pay in the troupe, usually the principal male role actor, has the right to change the tuning (see Chapter 5).

The members of the orchestra are usually employed by an impresario in one of the three ways. If the principal male role actor that the impresario or *zy wui* chooses has a fiddler and a woodblock player who usually work with him, the impresario will hire these leaders and let them recruit members of their individual sections. If the principal male actor does not have any preference, but the impresario has such leading instrumentalists who usually perform in his troupes, he will use these players and let them hire the rest of their partners. In case neither the principal male role actor nor the impresario has players who usually work with them, the impresario will look for leaders of the two sections, telling them the total salary and the number of players to be engaged in each section, and let the leaders hire members of their sections.

The wages of the players are more or less fixed by the "instrumentalists' guild" of the Chinese Artists Association of Hong Kong (see Note 6, Chapter 1). In 1985, the minimum wage that a player got for a day's performance (including afternoon and evening shows) was HK$200 (about US$25). The minimum wage for the woodblock player was about HK$400 (about US$50). The fiddler could get from HK$600 to HK$1,000 a day (about US$75 to US$125).

The wages are higher during the third month of every lunar year, when people in all parts of Hong Kong celebrate the birthday of the deity Queen of Heaven. Usually no fewer than ten troupes are hired in various areas in Hong Kong and Macau[6] to stage ritual performances. During this period, the "instrumentalists' guild" allows non-members to perform and be paid the same wages as the members. The minimum wage is usually raised in this period.

All members and non-members of the guild who have participated in performances have to pay *fuk lei fae* 福利費 (welfare fee) to the guild, at HK$2 (about US$0.25) for each day they had performed in 1985.[7]

All employees of Cantonese opera are paid daily, according to the number of days they participate in performance. Rehearsals are held only for theatrical performances; usually no one is paid for the first day of rehearsal, but accompanying players can get half for rehearsals on the second day and afterwards.[8]

According to the interviews I conducted, most of the instrumentalists who are members of the guild have full-time or part-time jobs other than playing in troupes. Most of them consider playing in troupes as their part-time job.[9]

Preparation for Performance

Actors of the six major roles and some of the secondary roles have their own costume trunks that are stored in warehouses when there are no performances. After they have been hired by the impresario, they will tell him the address of the warehouses and the numbers of the trunks they need, and the impresario will then send labourers to transport the trunks, together with other trunks containing stage properties, instruments and miscellaneous items, to the backstage of the performance hall.

Every actor of a major role hires a costume servant to take care of his costumes, boil water, make tea, wash clothes and perform other services for him during the days of performances. In order to keep his expenditure low, an actor sometimes has his wife, student or friend carrying out these duties. Sometimes two actors share one servant; sometimes an actor hires another minor role actor to serve him. In smaller troupes, some actors of the major roles do not hire costume servants.

The trunks of the actors, workers and instrumentalists arrive at the performance hall before the afternoon of the first evening performance. The costume servants choose the dressing compartments backstage for the actors they work with.[10] The one who serves the principal male actor has the first priority, followed by the one who works for the principal female actor, and then servants of the other major role actors.

One of the backstage workers hired by the impresario, the play reminder, performs as a stage manager (or "prompter" as in Western opera). His main duty is to read the script and remind each of the actors when to enter the stage during the performance. He is also responsible for preparing a *tae gong* 提綱 (outline), which is somewhat like a summary of the script, giving instructions for stage setting, stage properties, the characters played by each of the actors, and the percussion patterns for accompanying the entrance of the actors. The outline is posted backstage for the troupe members' reference. Without reading the script, most of the actors and workers are able to perform their duties with the instructions given by the outline. The play reminder is also responsible for distributing the dressing

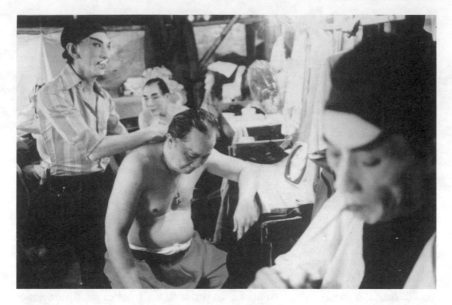

Four actors, with their facial makeup complete, take a rest backstage before putting
on their costumes. (9 March 1987, Kau Sai Wan, Kau Sai Island, Hong Kong)

compartments among the minor role actors. Dressing compartments also
serve as sleeping spaces for most of the actors. Workers and instrumentalists who do not have dressing compartments have to sleep on the stage.
However, if transportation or a hotel is available, most of the major role
actors and instrumentalists will not stay at the performance hall overnight.
The play reminder writes on posters the location of each actor's dressing
compartment, the time to start the afternoon and evening performances, and
the time for meals; these posters are put up backstage for the troupe
members' reference.

After arriving at the performance hall, the impresario and the major
role actors, accompanied by some musicians who take instruments such as
so nap, gongs and cymbals with them, go to offer incense to the deity whose
birthday is to be celebrated. During the ceremony, *so nap* and percussion
music is played. Later, the troupe members offer incense to the deities Wa
Gwong 華光 , or Tin 田 and Dau 竇 , the patron deities of the Cantonese
opera employees, whose shrines are placed backstage.[11] If a Cantonese
opera employee has died and his grave is located nearby, the troupe offers

incense and plays music to show their respect. This ritual is known as *zae sin jen* 祭先人 (offering to the ancestors). At the end of this, all the troupe members attending ritualistically shout "*sing jem hoeng loeng*" 聲音響亮 (to have a loud and bright sound), in anticipation of good performances. Usually a simplified version of *zae sin jen* is also held before the second evening's performance. Sweets used as offerings in the ritual are distributed among the actors, who believe that they will produce a good sound after eating them. Actors offer incense at the edge of the stage before the start of each of the performances.

After the offerings, the major role actors go to their dressing compartments and start reading the script of the play that they will perform in the evening. Since no new plays are staged in ritual performances, rehearsal is seldom necessary. In case there are scenes featuring dance or martial arts, those involved, usually including the principal male and female role actors, will rehearse with the woodblock player who, instead of playing the instruments, vocally utters mnemonics of the percussion patterns to provide accompaniment. In such rehearsals, these principal actors may tell the woodblock player the percussion patterns to be used to accompany each gesture in the series of stage movements in the performance. The instructions given by them often deviate from what is written in the script. If the play contains tunes that are not well known to an actor, he will rehearse singing them with the fiddler.

The cooks start preparing meals in the early afternoon, as the troupe members will eat their dinner at about 5 p.m. Usually the major role actors and instrumentalists do not take the meals provided by the troupe if there is a restaurant nearby.

Actors who participate in the opening scenes of the evening's performance have to start their makeup at about 7 p.m. The play reminder runs around every corner of the backstage, instructing the workers to set the stage, prepare the stage property and lighting system, as well as telling the secondary role and minor role actors the appropriate costumes to wear. The instrumentalists start to tune their instruments with stroboscope and set their amplifiers. The martial arts performers warm up on the stage behind the curtain. People begin to gather around the performance hall, talking excitedly, not forgetting to offer incense and donate money to the deity in the temple. Merchants and pedlars are busy selling food and drink at stores and stalls situated near the performance hall. Employees of the gambling dens nearby show their customers the way to try their luck.[12] The festive

mood gets stronger and stronger every minute before the evening's performance starts.

Simple patterns of percussion music are usually played an hour or so
before the start of the afternoon performances. The music is known as *fat
bou gwu* 發報鼓 (signalling drumming), and serves to notify the backstage
workers, actors, instrumentalists and audience that the performance will
start after a certain period of time. Traditionally, the drumming started
around 11 a.m. and was divided into four sections. The fourth section
coincided with the first ritualistic operatic piece that started at 2 p.m.
(Au-joeng, 1954:139). However, this practice is no longer strictly observed
by contemporary troupes. Nowadays there are usually three sections of
signalling drumming, each one lasting ten to fifteen minutes. The drumming stops half an hour or so before the start of the ritualistic play, and
recorded music is played through speakers to fill in time.

The Ritual Playlets

Several hours before the first evening's performance of the Fuk Dek Gung
series, some local villagers of Tai O told me that there would be a ritual of
sacrificial offering to the White Tiger before the performance. I then visited
the backstage and asked the actors if there would be such a ritual. The
atmosphere backstage was generally indifferent, and no one knew if the
troupe would perform the ritual. According to a minor role actor, the ritual
would be necessary for the safety of the troupe members if the performance
hall was built on a piece of land that had never been used for such a purpose.
The ritual is referred to as *zae bak fu* 祭白虎 (offering to the White Tiger),
zae toi 祭台 (offering to the stage) or *po toi* 破台 (breaking or initiating the
stage) in the profession.

In the Fuk Dek Gung series, the ritual of sacrificial offering to the
White Tiger was not seen before the troupe began the evening performance
with the play *Luk gwok dai fung soeng* 六國大封相 (*The Grand Six
Countries Invest a Chancellor*), sometimes known as *Luk gwok fung soeng*
六國封相 (*Six Countries Invest a Chancellor*) or *Cet coi luk gwok fung
soeng* 七彩六國封相 (*The Colourful Six Countries Invest a Chancellor*).
Later a member of the *zik lei* told me that the land used this year had been
used for a performance several years ago, so no White Tiger ritual was
needed.

It was at the ritual series held on Tsing Yi Island that I witnessed the

White Tiger ritual. When I visited the backstage about two hours before the opening evening's performance, the workers and actors whom I knew well maintained silence and avoided talking to me. The military role actor Ziu Sek-men 招石文 waved his hand and let me enter his dressing compartment. In a low voice, he told me that the performance hall was a "new" one (which actually means that it was built on a piece of land which has not been initiated for this purpose), and nobody should speak before the White Tiger ritual. Like Ziu, most of the other actors hid themselves in their dressing compartments, which were closed with curtains. The solemn atmosphere backstage resembled what Ward had experienced (1979:30):

> Early on the opening night of the festival operas at Tuen Moon [Tuen Mun], Castle Peak (April/May 1975), Mr Leung and I went to visit some actor friends backstage. Usually on such occasions one is made very welcome, even effusively so. This time it was different. There were no greetings, almost everyone sheered away. Although politeness forbade our being asked to leave, it needed no special sensitivity to make us decide to do so at once.

According to an experienced accompanying musician Wong Jyt-seng 王粵生 (see Note 15), before the execution of the *zae bak fu* ritual, troupe members in the "new" performance hall could easily be hurt by the White Tiger. The White Tiger was capable of making use of a member's mouth to hurt another member, in that the words uttered by one member could become a curse and anybody who answered such an utterance might meet with bad fortune. According to Wong, accidents had taken place in the past which were believed to have been caused by the White Tiger, including fire backstage and the collapse of the performance hall.

The performance of the sacrificial ritual that witnessed by the present writer is similar to what Ward describes (1979:30–31):

> The audience was still coming in. Suddenly the musicians broke into a distinctive rhythm on percussion alone and a black-faced, black-bearded, male-role figure entered stage right bearing aloft in his right hand a three foot stave from which dangled a string of exploding fire crackers.... He ran straight across (upstage, in front of the backcloth), off stage left and then immediately round backstage and on again stage right, without the firecrackers, to take up a pose on top of the table (centre front stage) facing stage left with the stave held at the ready. (Posing on a table on entry normally indicates that the character is a god just descended from Heaven.)
>
> There then entered, stage left, a crouching figure clad in a fairly close-fit-

ting yellow costume with a long tail and a grinning cat-like mask: the White Tiger. Running on all fours, the Tiger came down stage left to the front where he discovered a piece of raw pork and mimed eating it. Meanwhile the god descended from his mountain and took up an attacking pose and the two proceeded to fight until the blackfaced figure overcame the Tiger, bestrode his prostrate body, and then fitting his mouth with a kind of bit made of metal chain … rode him off backwards, up stage left. As the two disappeared, a rather ragged shout came from behind the backcloth, the property man came forward to remove a row of chairs which had been placed along the front of the stage, and the orchestra immediately struck up the first notes of the usual opening performance.

Though itself a ritual, the *zae bak fu* is sometimes considered to be one of the ritualistic playlets that are performed to precede the main operatic items within a ritual series. Other ritual playlets are the *Six Countries Invest a Chancellor*, *Bat sin ho sau* 八仙賀壽 (*A Birthday Greeting from the Eight Immortals*), *Tin gei sung zi* 天姬送子 (*The Heavenly Maiden Offers Son*), and *Ga gwun* 加官 (*Promotion to the Rank of an Official*) also known as *Tiu ga gwun* 跳加官 (*Dance of Promotion*). As mentioned above, if a ritual operatic series last for four days, a total number of seven performances of different plays will be staged: the seven performances are staged in four evening and three afternoon shows. Similarly, if a ritual operatic series last for five days, nine performances of different plays will be staged: the nine performances include five evening and four afternoon shows. Such plays are referred to as *Zing bun hei* 正本戲 (main operatic items) and they do not include the ritualistic playlets.

With rare exceptions, the opening evening's performance usually starts with the *Six Countries Invest a Chancellor*. In addition to the regular acting members of the troupe who all participate in the playlet in their best costumes, the impresario always hires four to six martial arts performers to add special spectacles to the playlet. As noted by Yung (1976a:64), the playlet is mainly composed of stylistic movements and gestures with some singing. It is a common practice for the troupe to display its cast and costumes in order to attract the audience with this playlet.

The playlets *The Heavenly Maiden Offers Son* and *A Birthday Greeting from the Eight Immortals* are often performed in sequence, and thus are usually known as *Ho sau sung zi* 賀壽送子 (*Birthday Greeting and Offering of a Son*). Before the main operatic item starts in the afternoon of the main festival day, an elaborate version of *Birthday Greeting and Offering of a Son*, which together last about eighteen minutes, is performed by both the major and secondary role actors. Sometimes this elaborate version is performed in the evening. For example, on the opening evening of the series performed by the Tremendous Heroic Strength Cantonese Opera Troupe at Po Toi Island, instead of staging the *Six Countries Invest a Chancellor*, the troupe performed the *Birthday Greeting and Offering of a Son* with the major role actors. Another example was the ritual series performed on Tsing Yi Island: on the opening evening, the troupe performed the elaborate version of *Birthday Greeting and Offering of a Son* with the major role actors, after the sacrificial offering to the White Tiger. Later they performed the *Six Countries Invest a Chancellor* and the main operatic item of the evening. However, except on the main festival day, some troupes perform the simplified version of the *Birthday Greeting and Offering of a Son* by actors of secondary roles before each of the main operatic items in the afternoons; often the playlet lasts three minutes and no singing is used.

In operatic series performed for the Ghost Festival, troupes sometimes stage the ritualistic playlet *Birthday Greeting and Offering of a Son*, though the festival is not related to any birthday. It can be said that the ritualistic item is indispensable in any ritual operatic series. The performance is a ritual by itself. The actors, who are hired by the community to be its representatives, offer birthday or festival greetings to the deities and ghosts through the performance of the ritualistic playlet.

The playlet *Promotion to the Rank of an Official*, which usually lasts about half a minute, is often performed after either the simplified or elaborate version of *Birthday Greeting and Offering of a Son*.

Besides the main operatic items and ritualistic playlets, sometimes the *zy wui* requires a troupe to perform *Tin gwong hei* 天光戲 (dawn show, meaning all-night performance) after a certain evening's or after each of the evening performances. An all-night show often starts within one hour after the evening's main operatic item and lasts for about four hours. According to some actors, it is often staged roughly and improvisatorily, not based on a script, but on an outline prepared by the play reminder, in a style somewhat close to the improvisatory plays of the pre-1930 period (see Chapter 4). At the present time, an all-night performance is rarely staged, except occasionally in the Purification for Peace series.

A series of performances, disregarding the type of context, is always concluded with a brief ritual playlet called *fung toi* 封台 (to seal a stage). The playlet is usually performed shortly after the end of the last main operatic item of the series, and involves only one actor who wears a white mask and goes through a short sequence of stylistic movements, which lasts for about ten seconds.

Improvisatory Comic Episodes

Improvisatory comic episodes are widely considered as the trademark of Cantonese opera in Hong Kong. With the common aim of evoking laughter from the audience, and sometimes even from fellow performers, such comic episodes are improvised by the comic role actor as well as actors of other roles. The techniques of evoking laughter are categorized into six types:

1. Insertion of English words. Referred to as "cheap" by critics, the insertion of English words in speech and sung passages is often used as a comic technique. In the 1980s, while this technique rarely occurred in theatrical performances, it sometimes appeared in ritual shows, mostly in afternoon productions staged by the actors of secondary and minor roles. English words such as "hello" and "good-bye" were often used and mixed with Cantonese. Expressions with additions of English words commonly used were: "hello, *lei hou ma* 你好嗎 " (hello, how are you?), "good-bye, *zoi gin la* 再見啦 " (good-bye, see you later) and "*deng ngo dei jet cae* 等我哋 一齊 enjoy *ha la* 吓啦 " (let us enjoy ourselves).

2. Strategically positioned pauses in speech. An example of this took place in a ritual performance in May 1985. In the scene when the comic role actor reported to the official that somebody had molested his daughter, he said, "*key tiu hei ngo*" 佢調戲我 (he molested me), paused for a moment which aroused laughter from the audience, and added, "*ngo go ney*" 我個女 (my daughter).

3. Use of traditional Cantonese jokes. One example took place in a performance staged for the Ghost Festival in 1985 at Shaukeiwan. In a scene where the official (acted by the comic role actor) told the prince (acted by the principal male role actor) that his present father was not his real father, he said, "*lei lou dau ngo*" 你老豆我 (your father, me), which is a common expression of abuse in Cantonese dialect. Later the official explained that the father of the prince was someone greatly respected by him. Another expression of the similar type is *lei mg sae fong* 你唔駛慌 which has a double meaning of "do

not be afraid" and "do not expect too much." It is often used in episodes where one character is about to cheat another in the play. The actor playing the deceiving character often adds the expression after he has made a promise, in order to create a comic atmosphere.

4. Making use of the performance context. This is one of the most common ways to amuse the audience. An example took place in the ritual performance staged at Pak Sha Wan. In a scene where a female character asked her aunt why she remained single, the comic role actor who acted the aunt answered, "I was very good looking when I was young ... even the actor Men Cin-sey (name of the principal male role actor in the same troupe) courted me...." Loud laughter from the audience was inevitable. Another example took place in a ritual performance staged for the Ghost Festival at Shaukeiwan. In the last scene where all the major characters in the play were waiting for the witness to report the true story, the comic role actor urged the witness character to tell the truth as soon as possible because the play was going to end, causing laughter from the audience. Sometimes the actors mention the name of the village, region or community where the ritual performance is staged, in order to provoke laughter. For example, once within a performance staged in a community at Lantau Island, the comic role actor portraying a bandit told the audience that the base of his fellow bandits was located at a mountain in Lantau Island. In another performance staged on Lantau Island, an actor in the role of the emperor designated another character in the play to be his son-in-law, according to the instructions given by the script. Later he improvisatorily added that his son-in-law would be the official in charge of Lantau Island. Such mention of local names and objects always pleases the audience.

5. Puns. One example took place in the performance of the play *Pei pa san soeng jing hung hyt* 琵琶山上英雄血 (*The Heroic Blood Sheds on Mount Pei Pa*). When the mistress (acted by the comic role actor) was stepping out of the house to see her son returning home, the maid told her to be careful because she was *sam bou bet coet gwae mun* 三步不出閨門 (has never walked three steps beyond the bedroom, where *gwae mun* means the door of a woman's bedroom). However, the comic role actor replied, "*met je sam bou bet coet gae mun?*" 乜嘢三步不出雞門 (What do you mean by saying I had never walked three steps beyond the door of the *gae mun*?), where *gae*

mun means either the door of a chicken shed, or the door of a brothel.

6. Foul language. In general foul language expressions in Cantonese are of two types, one with sex-related meaning, the other not. A common expression by Cantonese people in Hong Kong, "*diu lei*" □你 (fuck you), is of the first kind, "*hem ga can*" □家產 (may your whole family be ruined) is of the second. All foul language expressions employed by actors in Cantonese opera as a means of evoking laughter are of the second type. Expressions commonly used are *hem ga can, puk gai* 仆街 (drop flat on the street) and *hem ga fu gwae* □家富貴 (good fortune to your family, which, by inversion of meaning, is the same as of *hem ga can*). Probably because this kind of expression is commonly used by people living in the rural areas of Hong Kong, their use, mostly by the comic role actors, often succeeds in arousing laughter from the audience.

Mistakes and Casual Aspects of the Performances

Mistakes can often be observed during the performances of the main operatic items within a ritual series, mainly because the performances are usually staged with only brief rehearsals, if any. Actors of the major roles often receive the scripts of the planned repertory several days before they arrive at the performance hall. For plays that are frequently performed, the actors often receive the scripts after they have arrived at the hall. As mentioned above, the only rehearsal often takes place several hours before the performance starts, and then only in episodes, often in scenes involving martial arts.

Since most of the troupes performing for ritual and festival series are temporary, both the accompanists and actors are aware of the need of adjusting themselves to work with different fellow performers every time they participate in a series of performances. They also are aware that minor mistakes in the performances are inevitable. According to the performers, and confirmed by my observation, the most common mistakes are forgetting one's cues and forgetting some words in one's speech or vocal passage. As a result, sometimes two actors start to sing or speak at the same time. To avoid further complications caused by a mistake, other actors on the stage might improvisatorily remind the forgetful actor by asking him a question. The techniques of covering up a mistake are known as *dau zy* 兜住 (wrap-up) in the profession. Mistakes that are difficult to wrap up include starting to sing together at the same time, or disconnections in the performance of martial arts. Actors often remind themselves that even when they commit such mistakes they have to continue to perform. Quick reaction and improvisation are often needed. The improvisatory reaction performed after a mistake is known as *zep sang* 執生 (to deliver a child or to stay alive) in the profession. *Dau zy* and *zep sang* are similar in concept. In practice, the former is often applied in speech and the latter is applied in gesture and stage movement.

During the performances of the ritual playlets, such as the *Six Countries Invest a Chancellor* and others, and occasionally during the performances of the main operatic items, the backstage workers often step onto the stage, move the stage properties, carry the actors' colourful flags and perform other minor duties. Audiences who are not familiar with ritual performances are often surprised at the backstage workers' appearance at the performances. According to some of the workers, in the past it was common for them to step onto the stage to perform their duties. Since the 1970s, the practice has become less common because it was regarded as disturbing the performances.

However, I have seen at least one backstage worker appear during the performance of a main operatic item. The incident took place in one of the performances staged in the ritual series held at Happy Valley. During the second act, when the princess (portrayed by the supporting female actor) in the play got drunk and threw a wine glass to the floor, a backstage worker came to the stage, picked up the glass and returned to the backstage. The appearance of the worker immediately aroused laughter from the audience.

Besides the play reminder, every worker in the troupe is prepared to remind the actors and workers of things that should be done during the performance to avoid making mistakes. One example was witnessed in a ritual performance staged at Cheung Chau. During the third act of the play *Jin gwae jen mei gwae* 燕歸人未歸 (*The Swallow Returns*), the workers responsible for providing stage properties were supposed to make a pair of mechanical swallows "fly" in front of the backdrop, to accompany the principal female role actor's singing. Seeing that the stage property workers had forgotten to provide this special effect, the sound system controller yelled loudly to remind them. Another example was seen in the fourth act of the same play. When the comic role actor forgot his cue, a musician yelled "*Sem go*" 森哥 (brother Sem, Sem is the name of the actor) to remind him. From these two examples, it is obvious that both the workers and accompanying musicians pay close attention to the performance on the stage, all feeling somewhat responsible for reminding their colleagues.

With the practices of improvising comic episodes, wrapping up mistakes and staying alive after mistakes are committed, as well as the appearance of backstage workers during the performance, ritual performance often gives an impression of being spontaneous, highly improvisatory, casual and even sloppy. However, for most of the people who live in the rural and suburban areas of Hong Kong, who regularly hire troupes to perform during their religious festivals, Cantonese opera is still one of the most popular and enjoyable forms of entertainment.

Profiles of Some Members of the Troupe

Interviews with members of the troupe performing for the Fuk Dek Gung series revealed some important information concerning their backgrounds and attitudes towards their profession.

1. Loeng Ben. Loeng, the impresario, had worked in this capacity for the past forty years, and was sixty years old at the time of the interview in 1985. He organized an average of about forty series of performances every year, most of them in the ritual context.[13] Loeng's father worked in Cantonese opera troupes as a martial arts performer, but he died when Loeng was thirteen years old. Because of his poverty, Loeng could only afford two years of formal education. During the Sino-Japanese War, Loeng fled from Guangzhou to Hong Kong, worked as an office boy for the famous Cantonese opera playwrights Lei Siu-wen 李少芸 and Tong Dik-seng 唐滌生 , and at the same time had the chance to learn scriptwriting under these two masters. Since then he has been deeply involved with Cantonese opera.

2. Loeng Wae-hung 梁威熊 . Eighteen years of age in 1985, he is the eleventh and youngest son of Loeng Ben. He began to work under his father in the troupes when he was nine years old. In this troupe, he was responsible for controlling the sound system, performing martial arts and acting minor roles. Two of his brothers were also performers of martial arts in Cantonese opera troupes. His sister (see below) sometimes took the principal female role in small troupes. Loeng Wae-hung confessed that he did not enjoy Can-

tonese opera, but worked in the profession only to help his father. When working in his father's troupes, he and his brothers and sister usually received no salary. In this way, Loeng Ben was able to reduce his cost of production and could, therefore, offer a lower price to the *zy wui* that hired his troupe. However, according to Loeng Wae-hung, his father always lost money from his troupe business. Besides working for his father, he also worked in other troupes. His daily wage, if and when he was paid, was HK$150 (about US$19) in 1985. Sometimes he took up temporary jobs that were not related to Cantonese opera.

3. Loeng Gyn-gyn 梁娟娟 . Originally she was not a member of the present troupe, but took the place of the principal female role in the second cast on the third day of the series. Besides performing in troupes, she was sometimes hired to sing operatic songs and perform operatic excerpts at banquets held in restaurants. The latter type of performance is known as *tong hei* 堂戲 (opera at a dining-hall) in the profession. In 1985, Loeng usually received HK$500 (about US$63) a show.

4. Tim 添 . About twenty years of age in 1985, Tim's main income was derived from working as a labourer on construction sites. He entered the profession six years ago because of his acquaintance with Loeng Ben, who had treated him as his son. When Loeng required his services, Tim would take leave from his main job and served as sound system controller for the troupe.

5. *Ce* Sem 扯深 . Since he usually played the part of *lai ce* in troupes, he was known as *Ce* Sem in the profession though his legal name was Cen Hoi-sem陳開深. Forty-three years old in 1985, his main occupation was selling clothes and groceries as a street hawker. In the present troupe, he also worked as the dressing servant to the military role actor besides playing the *lai ce* role. *Ce* Sem studied Cantonese opera at the *Guangzhou nam key ngae soet hok hao* 廣州南區藝術學校 (The Guangzhou Art School of the Southern District) in Guangzhou in the 1950s and had performed the comic role, the military role, the supporting male role and the principal male role after graduation. He and his family moved to Hong Kong in 1965, where he could only take the minor roles in the profession. He performed an average of about forty days a year and collected about HK$100 a day in 1985. He was very interested in the genre

and had tried his best to attend every performance, either as actor or in the audience. When hired for ritual performance, he would move his business to the place where the performances were due to be staged a few days before the performance series started. During these few days, he would sell his goods on the street as a hawker, and would go fishing and swimming after his work. Sometimes he would bring his children and wife to watch his performances, and stay with them in the performance hall during the days of the series. When he did not have a stage part to play in the afternoon performance, he would join the musicians to play accompaniment. He deeply enjoyed working and living with a troupe.

Ce Sem believed that Cantonese opera was not declining in popularity, but that the economic situation in Hong Kong was the major explanation for the slight decline of the profession. He said if the economy improved, there would be more ritual performances and, hence, more employment. He believed that the genre had its own unique artistic value and would always be appreciated by people in Hong Kong.

6. Fung Jip-cyn 馮業全 . Fifty years of age at the time of the inter-view, Fung, also known as Fung Cyn in the profession, was born in Macau. He had been working in the profession for thirty years. As a teenager, Fung studied Cantonese opera in Guangzhou and per-formed minor roles in some troupes. Gradually he was promoted to the principal male role in the second cast and later even in the evening performances of some small troupes. However, because of his poverty, Fung could not afford his own costume. Having to wear old and dirty costumes that belonged to the troupes, accord-ing to Fung, was the reason why he had never been taken seriously by the audience or the troupe administrators. He had tried to perform all male role types, but never became famous. In recent years his income came mainly from serving as a play reminder in troupes performing in amusement parks. He also took the role of *tung tin wae* 通天位 (all purpose position), which meant that he would stand in for any absent actor of any role. Besides working in the theatre and at the amusement parks, he performed an average of about seventy days in troupes, mostly those organized by Loeng Ben. He was a regular member of Loeng's troupes, where he worked as a play reminder in the afternoon shows that were not on

the main festival days and played the minor roles in the evening performances and the afternoon show on the main festival day. He received a daily wage of about HK$150 in 1985. Fung said his income could barely pay for his living expenses. Yet, since he was single and had only his mother to support, he did not have to worry about money too much. His mother was a fan of Cantonese opera, who always attended Fung's performances and lived in the opera hall with Fung during the performance days. Fung owned an expensive Sony Walkman Professional portable tape recorder and enjoyed recording live performances of Cantonese opera.

7. Joeng Ping 楊平 . Sixty-three years of age at the time of the interview, Joeng was also known as Joeng Gim-ping 楊劍平 in the profession. He became a regular member of Loeng Ben's troupes in 1983 and mostly performed minor roles. Joeng performed an average of about 130 days every year and collected a daily wage of HK$100 to HK$150 in 1985.

Before the establishment of the People's Republic of China, Joeng's father was a warlord in Yunnan 雲南 Province. His mother played various kinds of instruments and taught him to play, beginning when he was five years old. When he was fifteen, he joined the political work section of the army of the Republic of China, studied in the army school and performed music, drama and opera to entertain the soldiers. His formal education ended after he had finished primary school. Joeng came to Hong Kong in 1949 and acted in movies and Cantonese opera during the 1950s.

According to Joeng, he was quite well received as an actor of the principal male role in the 1950s. He became famous, but his addiction to opium also began at that time. At a time when the price of the drug was extremely high, some famous actors tried to show that they were wealthy by using it.[14] So, Joeng's fortune did not last. Soon he found himself performing only secondary and minor roles, as he did at the time. In 1980 Joeng gave up opium. As an actor who was once famous, Joeng sighed frequently and expressed many regrets during the interview. He said that the performing life of an actor was extremely short. If an actor could not acquire fame and fortune in the days when he was at his best, total failure would follow. He would then be forgotten by his audience.

Success, he observed, did not solely depend on one's artistic merit, but largely on his luck.

Joeng said he enjoyed his present job because he found pleasure in performing and had a lot of free time when he did not have to perform. He was mainly supported by his children; he performed just to pass the time.

Joeng believed that Cantonese opera was declining in the sense that it was out of fashion and its performance involved organizing work that was too complicated. He thought that the high rent of the theatre, the lack of enthusiastic audiences, the falling quality of performance and the absence of a young generation of performers were responsible for the decline. He added that solid training for an actor would take eight to ten years and it would be too much of a risk for a young person to enter the profession.

8. Jing 英 . About forty years old at the time of the interview, Jing was the dressing servant to the actress who took the supporting male role in the troupe. She also worked regularly as dressing servant to two other well-known actors. She entered the profession and began acting when she was a teenager. Later she changed her position to that of dressing servant because, according to Jing, her performance was not outstanding. She had been in this position for more than twenty years.

9. *Luk go* 六哥 (the sixth elder brother). His legal name was unknown to most of the people in the profession, where he was known as *luk go*. As did Jing, he entered the profession as an actor, but switched to dressing servant when he became older. In the present troupe, he was responsible for taking care of the costumes, providing stage properties and dressing the actors of the secondary and minor roles who did not have their own costumes. In other troupes, *luk go* also worked as private dressing servant for actors. He worked about eighty days a year and got a fixed wage of HK$155 a day in 1985. He said that he was chiefly supported by his children and he worked only to earn extra income and to while away his leisure time.

10. Gwok 國 . About fifty years of age at the time of the interview, he was also working as a dressing servant for the actors who did not possess their own costumes. According to Gwok, most of the

dressing servants entered the profession as actors and changed their job because of old age and he was no exception. Gwok mentioned that the guild of the costume and stage property makers under the Chinese Artists Association of Hong Kong had at one time about 100 members, but more than half of them had left the profession. Some retired and some took up other jobs. Most of those remaining had either part-time or full-time jobs in addition to working in operatic troupes. Their daily wage was fixed by the guild at HK$155 (about US$19) in 1985. Gwok also worked as a private dressing servant and was sometimes employed as a cashier in a food store. He was employed by the troupes for about 100 to 120 days a year.

11. Ling Fung 凌鳳 . Ling was a graduate of the *Bat wo jyt keik hok jyn* 八和粵劇學院(The Bat Wo Institute of Cantonese Opera). She had been working in the profession for more than one year by the time of the interview. Besides acting secondary roles in troupes, she also sang operatic song at Jung Sy Tau 榕樹頭 , a public thoroughfare and flea market in Kowloon where Cantonese operatic singers gathered and sang, in the open air, in the evenings.

12. Four female actors in minor roles. The four teenagers were the only players in the troupe who had never performed in Cantonese opera before. Two of them were students, one worked in a factory and another worked as a shop assistant. They were all part-time and temporary players and were engaged in movies and television commercials. The impresario Loeng Ben hired them through an entertainment agency. While Loeng offered each of them a daily wage of HK$100, the agency took a commission of $30 and, hence, each of the girls received only HK$70 (about US$9) a day.

13. Jy Gai 羽佳 . Jy was the principal male role actor in the troupe. Forty-nine years old in 1985, he was born to an operatic family in Guangzhou and came to Hong Kong when he was one or two years old. Since his grandfather, father and mother were all actors and performers of martial arts, Jy began learning the martial arts and basic performing skills from his father, and singing from his mother, as a child. He started to perform at seven and since then had played exclusively the principal male role in operatic troupes, appearing alongside famous players in the profession. He had also taken part in several Cantonese movies and had made stage ap-

pearances in Canada, the U.S.A. and several Southeast Asian countries.

In 1981 he made an attempt to launch a career as a singer of Cantonese popular songs at nightclubs in Singapore, yet his limited repertory and the audience's mediocre acceptance made him decide to remain in the Cantonese operatic profession. In recent years he performed mainly in Malaysia with local players, and appeared in only two to three series a year in Hong Kong. In 1984 he performed about 110 to 120 days, which was unusually busy for him.

Jy pointed out that the popularity of Cantonese opera was declining mainly due to high rentals at theatres and the resultant high ticket prices. Stiff competition among different types of entertainment also pulled the audience away from the genre. However, a fatal problem which had existed since the 1970s was a lack of playwrights, and, hence, the lack of new operas. According to Jy, the latest works in his repertory were written in the 1960s and early 1970s. Since then, he had not taken up any new ones because he could not find a qualified playwright. It should be noted that in the profession, it is usually the principal male actor who is responsible for hiring a playwright and for commissioning new plays from him.

Jy noted that, though most people in Hong Kong and the Southeast Asian countries did not consider the genre as art, Cantonese opera was an art form that was extremely difficult to learn. A successful actor had to be accomplished in singing, acting, speech delivery and martial arts; he should also have outstanding *sing* 聲 (quality of voice), *sik* 色 (appearance) and *ngae* 藝 (art). Above all, he had to be sociable in order to maintain good relations with the impresarios and theatre owners, so that he could have good employment opportunities. According to Jy, to become famous, one also had to possess *wen hei* 運氣 (fortune).

Jy did not teach his art to any student because he thought the future prospect of the genre was uncertain. An actor could only perform for a limited number of days a year, and, though a principal male role actor should be able to earn a considerable amount of money, the net income would still be low with the costs of performances deducted. Such costs that an actor had to take care of include rent for storing costume trunks in a warehouse and wages for dressing servants. An established actor sometimes had to donate to the *zy wui* and give *lae si* 利是 (red packets containing money) to the backstage workers of the troupe.

Jy also mentioned that the audience in Hong Kong only attended performances of their "idols." To be popular, an actor had to organize his "fan club" and maintain good relations with the fans. Most fans of well-known actors did not care about the quality of the performances, but would attend their idols' shows and neglect others. Jy said since he was not sociable and did not have a fan club, his opportunities for stage success were limited.

While the social status of Cantonese operatic actors remained low until late imperial China, Jy noticed that the situation had improved in modern day Hong Kong. He also believed that Peking opera actors had a better social standing than their Cantonese brethren. As an enthusiast, Jy thought that Peking opera was the most "artistic" among the Chinese regional theatrical genres.

When Jy was asked to give the names of his favourite actors, he was reluctant to speak and said he did not want to criticize his colleagues since politics had always been complicated in the profession. Later he confessed that the late comic role actor Loeng Sing-bo 梁醒波 , who was well known for his improvisation, was his most admired actor. To end the interview, Jy added that people within the profession should rally to strive for a bright future for the genre.

14. Men Bou-sem 文寶森 . Forty-nine years of age in 1985, Men was also known, as a singer of Cantonese operatic songs, by the stage name Men Coi-sing 文彩聲 (where *coi sing* means colourful voice). He was born in Shanghai and moved to Taiwan shortly before the establishment of the People's Republic of China. His family later moved to Macau when he was about twelve years old. Men recalled that at that time his family was extremely poor and he almost had to beg on the streets. Having no skills, he joined a Cantonese opera troupe when he was sixteen or seventeen. He had acted the minor roles in various troupes until he was twenty-two or twenty-three, when he became a lorry driver. At that time, he also performed in comic spoken drama in an amusement park in Hong Kong. Men re-entered the profession in 1976 when he joined a troupe as the comic role actor and toured Singapore. In recent

years, besides performing in opera, he sometimes sang operatic songs at banquets and had made recordings. Now he was mainly supported by his children and he treated acting and singing as his hobbies.

According to Men, he had always been eager to perform the comic role since he was a child and the renowned Loeng Sing-bo was also his most favourite actor. He had never studied under any teacher, but learned to improvise by watching Loeng and other performers, and his singing, acting and performing skills were all self-taught. He thought Cantonese opera was only a form of entertainment and not art. Though he deeply enjoyed performing, he could not stand the idea of watching a performance sitting among the audience. Besides performing, Men's other hobbies were watching comic movies and playing the electronic keyboard.

Men performed an average of about eighty days a year and received a wage fixed by himself: it ranged from HK$600 to HK$700 a day in 1985. When he performed, his wife would be his dressing helper.

Men was never worried about the future of the genre, and he was ready to change his job at any time.

15. Ziu Sek-men. Forty years old in 1985, Ziu was the actor of the military role in the troupe. He started his career as an amateur actor and began to perform professionally in the 1970s. Later he joined a troupe which toured several cities in the U.S.A.

Ziu pointed out that the present popularity of the genre was an improvement on the situation in the 1970s and he did not think that the genre was declining in popularity. In recent years he usually performed an average of 100 days a year and obtained a flexible wage from HK$400 to HK$1,000 per day. He thought that his income was sufficient to support his family. When his wife was interviewed, she said that Ziu's income from performing was not even enough to cover his performance expenses, which also included the cost of ordering new costumes. She added that their livelihood was mainly supported by their business in Singapore.

16. Nam Fung 南鳳 . Nam, whose legal name was Gou Pui-wa 高佩華 , was the supporting female role in the troupe. At the start of her career, she performed minor roles under the principal female actor Nam Hung 南紅 , who suggested *nam* 南 (south) as the first char-

acter of her stage name. Nam's cousin Gou Lae 高麗 was also a
popular actress in the profession. Nam's husband was another
well-known actor of major roles.

Nam was attracted by the colourful costumes of Cantonese
opera when she was a child. In 1963, she was led by her friends to
learn operatic song singing under the well-known teacher Wong
Jyt-seng,[15] who was also teaching Nam Hung. In 1966, Wong
invited Nam Fung to perform minor roles in Nam Hung's troupes.
Nam left school after completing the second year of her secondary
education and started performing professionally.

From 1974 to 1980 she worked in a television station and
performed in programs mostly unrelated to the genre. During this
period, she participated in opera only occasionally. In recent years,
she usually performed about eighty days a year, two-thirds of them
in the supporting female role, the other third as principal female
role. She said that she was still not considered a player of the
principal female role in the profession because she had never taken
the role in theatrical productions. Compared to other female actors
who looked forward to gaining this status, Nam thought she was
the most patient one. She believed that she had adequate artistic
ability to handle the role. However, even if the opportunity came
along, she felt she would not accept it hastily. She stressed that
failure at one performance would completely ruin the future of an
actor, and artistic ability alone could not guarantee success. As Jy
Gai and Joeng Ping said, Nam believed that fortune was very
important for reaching an attainment.

She agreed that Cantonese opera was declining in popularity,
mainly due to the lack of solidarity among people in the profession, a shortage of theatres and new plays, the fact that fans only
cared for their idols' performances, and the genre's failure to
appeal to the tastes of the broader public. In order to counter these
problems, she made some suggestions.

According to Nam, first of all, every performer in the profession should respect his job and be serious in his performances. A
well established performer should understand that it would cost a
large sum of money to organize a troupe and should not merely
think of raising his own wage. Second, the practice of writing plays
on the basis of the six major roles, known as *luk cy zae* 六柱制

(six-major-role formula) in the profession, should be abolished. She believed that such a practice usually produced plays with formulaic plots that often failed to attract contemporary audiences. Also the formula makes organizing a troupe expensive. Third, more melodious tunes should be incorporated into new plays. Even the tunes of popular songs could be adopted if they would fit the dramatic context. Aria type music, which often featured the singing of long melismatic phrases, should be reduced in new plays. Patternized episodes (see Chapter 4), which were abundant in the existing repertory, should be delivered in Cantonese instead of the old stage dialect used extensively before the 1920s. And fourth, she thought that duets involving two melodies in contrapuntal texture, as well as simple harmonic devices, should be introduced to the genre.

Nam Fung had not considered leaving the profession, but was thinking of starting her own business in a few years. In 1985 she and her husband founded a school to train Cantonese opera performers.

17. Cen Gim-sing 陳劍聲 . Cen was a female actor who played the supporting male role in the troupe. Due to her family's poverty, she was only educated to primary school standard. She started learning Cantonese opera in private institutes in 1970 and was soon given minor roles in some troupes. Later she was promoted to the principal male role in the afternoon performances not held on the main festival day.[16] In recent years, she usually performed the supporting male role in large troupes and the principal male role in medium and small troupes. While she mostly acted with troupes in Hong Kong, she also performed in Malaysia during the seventh month of the lunar calendar, when many troupes were hired to stage operas for the Ghost Festival. Occasionally she sang operatic songs at private banquets.

Actors' Attitudes towards Ritual Performance

Though the majority of the performers' income comes from participating in ritual performances, most of the performers are more interested in theatrical, than ritual, performances. Some of them refer to ritual performance as *Lok hoeng hei* 落鄉戲 (rural performance) and think that it is an informal context that, therefore, does not demand a high standard of performance. This attitude can be clearly seen in three practices in the profession. First, as mentioned before, an actor is considered qualified to execute a certain role only if he has fulfilled that role in a theatrical performance. For example, according to the comic role actor Men Bou-sem, since he had never performed the comic role in the theatrical context, he was not considered a qualified actor for this role; he could only perform the role in ritual series and, hence, could not demand a high wage. Second, a new play is never premiered in ritual performance. Third, no rehearsal is deemed necessary before the performers arrive at the opera hall in ritual performances.

According to some accompanying musicians, even some well established actors do not take ritual performances seriously. For example, when an actor enters the stage, usually he is supposed to go through a series of stylized movements and gestures which are accompanied by percussion music. But some actors sometimes omit these stylized movements, step to the microphone and stand in front of it to wait for the end of the percussion pattern.

According to some members of *zy wui*, some actors treat the audience of the ritual context as *hoeng ha jen* 鄉下人 (rural people) and suppose that they do not know how to appreciate opera. Such actors sometimes do not have adequate preparation before the performance and commit mistakes frequently. Performers who are not serious sometimes delete or shorten the scenes and they are reluctant to improvise comic episodes. In order to avoid these, most *zy wui* demand that, while intermissions between acts are included, a play should last for at least four hours. Following this rule, a play reminder sometimes requires the actors to improvise more in order to satisfy the *zy wui*.

The Religious Aspects of Ritual Performances

Ritual performance of Cantonese opera is not only "ritual," but highly religious, involving as it does offering of incense to temple deities, the patron deities of the Cantonese opera employees and their "ancestors," as well as the sacrificial offering to the White Tiger and the performance of *A Birthday Greeting from the Eight Immortals*. Above all, members of the troupe, the *zy wui*, and the audience are all aware that the operas are staged for entertaining not only the people, but also the deities. Concerning the religious context of ritual performances, Ward writes:

Traditional Chinese social custom does indeed give high significance to the performance of mutual services and the exchange of gifts, especially gifts of food and entertainment. As with his human relationship, so with his gods: a traditional Chinese villager grapples them to him with services, gifts and entertainment. Thus, together with the roast pigs and the incense, the operas are offerings to the god—as any member of the audience will agree. (Ward, 1979:24)

This is no accident: the stage is deliberately placed in such a position that the god (who is assumed to descend spiritually into his image—for which reason some part of every temple is always unroofed) can 'see the operas'. Again all informants are agreed, and any continuing scepticism as to their seriousness is dispelled when one visits festivals at places where local topography makes it impossible to erect the stage directly in front of the temple or where local custom for one reason or another decrees that the god needs a closer view. In such places, when the temporary theatre is put up, either a kind of temporary temple facing the stage is also constructed, or, occasionally, a sort of 'royal box' is slung below the roof over the heads of the audience. Hither the image is escorted with due ceremony and installed (literally 'in the gods') for the duration of the festival. (Ward, 1979:25)

Sometimes the *zy wui* also invite deities other than the one whose birthday is being observed to enjoy the operas. In such cases the portable shrines, known as *heng gung* 行宮 (temporary palace), of the various deities are escorted from their temples to the performance hall, in a ritual known as *ceing sen* 請神 (to invite the deity). The shrines containing the statues of the deities are then placed at the "temporary temple" or "royal box" known as *sen pang* 神棚 (shed for the deity), which is built inside the performance hall to face the stage. For example, in the opera series staged from 9 to 12 June 1985 at Tai O when the birthday of the Queen of Heaven was celebrated, various deities from temples in Tai O were invited to the *sen pang*. The statue of the Queen of Heaven was placed in the middle; on its right were statues of the Village Deity from Fan Lau and the Queen of Heaven from the temple at Sen Cyn; on its left were statues of the Deity of the South Seas, the Deity of War and Righteousness and the Marquis.

When the operatic performances are over, the statues of the various deities are escorted back to their temples, in a ceremony known as *sung sen* 送神 (to escort the deity home) among the local people. It should be added that the statues of the deities placed at the altars of the temples are not moved by the people; they are known as *zo gung* 座宮 (pedestal palace).

As mentioned in Chapter 1, ritual performance is called *sen gung hei*

The shrine of the patron deities of Cantonese operatic employees is placed backstage. (20 April 1987, Po Toi Island, Hong Kong)

(performance for the deities as a charitable and pious deed) in the profession of Cantonese opera, where *sen gung* means "charitable and pious deeds performed for the deities." For the people who hold festivals, birthday celebrations for the deities and rituals of purification, besides staging operas, *sen gung* activities also include: the *fa pao* snatching contest, offerings to the deities, carving the sacrificial roast pigs and distributing the pork to members of the community, elaborate sacrificial offerings to the deities on the main festive days, as well as escorting the statues of deities from their temples to the performance hall and from the hall back to the temple. Moreover, as the main item in every series of celebrating activities, ritual Cantonese opera can be seen not only as a performing event and religious activity, but also as a customary and secular function.

The sacrificial offering to the White Tiger reveals the religious connotation in the custom of staging operas in festivals and for celebrating the birthdays of the deities. According to an informant who is a Taoist priest, the White Tiger is considered a fierce demon in Chinese belief. The White Tiger opens its mouth (that is, is ready to hurt people) from the third solar term *ging zik* 驚蟄 (the waking of insects), which comes before the solar term vernal equinox, usually in early March. It then makes use of rats, snakes and insects to harm people and their animals. Thus, many decades ago, this gave rise to the custom of hiring troupes to perform operas at that time of the year, in order to scare the harmful insects and animals away through the festive mood, the firecrackers and the music (particularly the percussions). Sacrificial offering to the White Tiger was also performed, primarily for protecting local people, and, secondarily, for protecting the actors from harming the local people when they "opened their mouths" during their performances. It is believed that the practice of the sacrificial offering to the White Tiger dates from the early stages of Cantonese opera.

Ward (1979:32) notes that the sacrificial offering to the White Tiger is an "exorcistic act" that can also be staged in a context other than operatic performance:

> Indeed, actors may well be especially requested to carry out similar acts of exorcism on behalf of their clients, just like priests. In 1975 at Sai Kung, in Hong Kong's New Territories, a development comprising several modern blocks of shops and high-rise flats was declared open in an official ceremony, which included the (also symbolic but hardly magical) act of cutting a red, white and blue ribbon performed by a high-ranking member of the British administration. On the preceding evening the actors already engaged to per-form operas in the town in connexion with a temple festival were asked to perform *The White Tiger*, and they did so in exactly the same manner as in the performance seen two weeks before. The sole difference was that the second performance was for the purpose of exorcising evil forces from the new buildings, which stood on recently reclaimed land where people had never lived before.

This suggests a close relationship between some Chinese regional operatic genres and religious rituals. Tanaka Issei (1989:162) states:[17]

> From a historical point of view, the cross-fertilization between Taoism and Chinese folk literature can be traced back to the Song [960–1279] and Yuan [1279–1368] dynasties.... For example, many Taoist plays were used for popularizing Taoism in the Yuan dynasty. The term *fo* 科 or *fo fan* 科範 [acting] used frequently in Song dynasty plays was a technical term originated from the Taoist rituals. To summarize, Taoism and Chinese drama were developed from the same ethnographic base. They share the same fundamental ritualistic and musical structures. This common foundation has constantly promoted exchan-ges between Taoism and Chinese drama.

Concluding Notes

Whenever there is a ritual performance, there are temporary stores and stalls selling food, drinks, and toys in areas around the performance hall, mostly at the entrance of the hall. There are also gambling stalls operating secretly. The owners of such businesses are often contributors to, or patrons of, the celebrating series; they hope that they can make more than they have donated.

The people who attend the operatic performances also offer incense and donate money to the temple. They stroll around the stalls and stores, looking for entertainment and talking to one another. In fact, ritual performances accompany many different kinds of secular activities. Above all, one can easily see that the community that holds the celebrating series is actually intent on displaying its wealth and the solidarity of its people, through the size of the troupe, the price of hiring the troupe, the dimensions of the performance hall, the luxurious stage setting and costumes, as well as the fame of the principal male and female role actors.

From the various kinds of religious and secular events, as well as from the performing activities that take place on the stage, we can understand that it is the genre's unique and all-inclusive stylistic characteristics that enable Cantonese opera to become the main item in the celebrating series. To begin with, the noisy and deafening sounds of the percussion music, the colourful stage setting and costumes, as well as the brilliantly illuminated performance hall and the nearby areas create a strong festive mood. The comic episodes in the plays provide entertainment. The audience is mostly familiar with the stories of the plots, and the usually slow development of the plots enables the people to follow the stories without spending all of their time in their seats. Those who only enjoy vocal music may well join other activities during passages of speech delivery. Whether they are gambling, offering incense at the temple, talking to fellow-villagers or dining at stalls outside the performance hall, they can tell from the duration and loudness of the percussion music when the principal actors are entering the stage or the play has reached its climax. They can always get back to their seats in time to catch such episodes. The highly improvisatory performance creates spontaneous dramatic effects, which are readily enjoyed by local opera goers, who appreciate spontaneity more than urban audiences do.

In the performance hall, hardly anybody stays quietly and statically in his seat. People laugh loudly, talk about the story and the performance, or eat the food that they bring with them. Usually about a dozen people, mostly teenage girls, take photographs of their favourite actors and ask for the actors' signatures at the backstage. The moral messages conveyed by the plays—such as "good will be rewarded with good and evil with evil," "where there is a will there is a way," "filial piety can move the deities," and the happy reunions that conclude the plays—all serve to reinforce the people's confidence in their future, symbolizing that the deities will allow them a good life in return for their charitable and pious deeds.

Notes

1. Before firework were banned by the Hong Kong Government in the late 1960s, the contest involved the firing of paper cartridges into the air for the villagers to snatch. From the 1980s on, small bamboo pieces have been projected upward by rubber band for the same purpose. To avoid violence caused by the contest, *fa pao* are often distributed among the participants by drawing lots. See Blake (1981) for further details on the subject.

2. According to some actors, when a performance contract is signed between the *zy wui* and the impresario, the impresario has to pay a contract fee to the Chinese Artists Association of Hong Kong. However, some impresarios refuse to observe the rule. All impresarios I interviewed avoided mention of the contract and contract fee.

3. However, in performances staged at the Paladium Opera House, the orchestra is placed at the corner of the balcony, close to the stage.

4. When the fiddler plays both the violin and the *gou wu*, the criteria for choosing one instrument over the other to accompany the vocal music vary according to different players. The *je wu* 椰胡 (coconut-shell fiddle) is usually used to accompany the singing of *nam jem*, which is a kind of singing narrative.

5. During ritual performances, while the leaders of the melodic and percussion sections have to concentrate on observing the actors' gestures and movements and the instructions given by the script, the rest of the players sometimes smoke, drink soda and talk to one another, though quietly. The players often dress casually and some of them wear bedroom slippers during the performances.

6. Macau is a Portuguese dependency on the coast of southern China about forty miles from Hong Kong. Cantonese operatic troupes from Hong Kong are sometimes hired to perform there. Macau is not known to have any local Cantonese opera troupes.

7. As mentioned by Yung (1976a:107), every employee in the profession of Cantonese opera, but not operatic song, belongs to one of the six guilds of the Chinese Artists Association of Hong Kong. There are only six guilds because "through the years, some of the guilds within the society were merged, some were made obsolete, or changed...." Every employee has to pay a fee to his guild for welfare purpose, based on the number of days he has been hired by a troupe. In 1989, the fee for the

instrumentalists' guild was raised to HK$4 (about US 50¢) for each day of performance, while their daily wage remained the same.

8. Some instrumentalists say they are not willing to participate in rehearsals because of the low pay.

9. The instrumentalists whom I have interviewed work full-time as policemen, labourers, movie extras and factory workers. Some instrumentalists earn their income mainly from teaching Cantonese operatic singing and playing in operatic song clubs.

10. Concerning the assignment of dressing compartments, Yung (1976a:84) writes:

    ... the rule for room assignment, according to the type of role played by the individual actor, is quite rigid. For example, the actor of the Principal Male Role occupies the room next to the Tiger Gate; the actress for the Principal Female Role occupies the room next to the Fox Hole; and the actor for the Principal Military Role occupies the room at the very center of the backstage.

    The practice described by Yung was no longer strictly observed in the years from 1984 to 1990. However, the practice described by Ward (1979:27–28) of the male actors using the dressing compartments backstage right and the female actors using the compartments backstage left is still observed to this day.

11. In the profession, Wa Gwong (Deity of Fire) is the patron of all the employees, particularly the instrumentalists. The deities Tin (a field) and Dau (a hollow) are patrons of the actors and martial arts performers. According to a legend widely known among Cantonese operatic employees, in the early days of Cantonese opera, actors only performed simple routines of martial arts, known as *nam pai* 南派 (southern style). The new style of martial arts, known as *bek pai* 北派 (northern style), was introduced to Cantonese opera by the deities Tin and Dau, long before the 1920s. It was said that some actors and martial arts performers once saw two children fighting on a footpath between some fields. The two children fought from evening to dawn and later entered a hollow in the field and disappeared. The actors and martial arts performers, thus, realized that the two fighters were deities who came to teach them a new style of martial arts. However, according to Jy (1982: 5–7), the northern style of martial arts was introduced by the actor Cen Fei-lung to Cantonese opera in the 1920s. Jy also says that Cen learned the style from an actress of Peking opera. Mek (1941:162) identifies several Cantonese opera actors who were responsible for introducing the northern style of martial arts from Peking opera to Cantonese opera; Cen is not identified as one of them (see Yung, 1976a:86–87).

12. Most types of gambling are illegal in Hong Kong. The gambling stalls located near the performance halls are operated secretly.

13. However, according to the records of the guild of instrumentalists, Loeng organized only twenty-one series of ritual performances during the period August 1984 to July 1985.

14. One established actor in Hong Kong told me that he used opium for medicinal purposes.

15. Mr. Wong Jyt-seng (1919–1989) was one of the top melodic instrumentalists in Cantonese opera, and the teacher of many established actors and accompanists in the profession. He taught Cantonese operatic singing at the Department of Music, The Chinese University of Hong Kong from 1976 until his death.

16. According to the actor Jy Gai, there was a fixed promotion system governing role distribution among actors in the early period of Cantonese opera. For example, a male novice had to start acting the minor roles, first the *sau ha* and then the *lai ce* role. Later, he could be promoted to play the sixth supporting male role. Further promotion led to the fifth, fourth and, later, the third supporting male role, which was, and still is, the principal male role of the afternoon performances, aside from those on the main festival day. He could then be promoted to the "second male role," which is known as the supporting male role in this study. However, in practice, no actor is known to have gone through all the steps to take the principal male role.

17. The passage is translated from Chinese to English by the present writer.

4. Improvisatory Concepts among Performers

The Performers' Conceptualization of Improvisation

Many actors and instrumentalists told me that the essence of Cantonese opera performance lay in the fact that the same script, if performed by two different troupes, or even by the same troupe in two different performances, would be rendered very differently. In other words, each performance is unique in itself. Some remark that Cantonese opera is a difficult art because performers have to create during the performances to enable each performance to be different from others. Some claim that Cantonese opera is art, in the sense that "art" should be defined in terms of "changes," "adjustment," and "variation."

To explain the notion of "creation during performance," most of the actors and instrumentalists do not use any of the Cantonese words that translate as "improvisation." Some actors, mostly of the younger generation and those about forty years of age, use the term *zik hing* 即興 to describe the creative process during their performances. According to established actors Jyn Siu-fae 阮兆輝 and Gwan Hoi-san 關海山 , *zik hing* plays an important role in the performance of Cantonese opera and includes elaboration on acting, singing, speech delivery and stage movements. Such elaborations are based on the structural framework of the oral deliveries and accompanying music which have been selected by the scriptwriter and specified in the scripts. *Zik hing* elaborations also include the addition, during the performance, of stage movements, gestures, and singing or spoken passages which are not written in the script. Actors who adopt the use of *zik hing* tend to be extensively read in books on theatrical theories both Eastern and Western, and often know something about the different stylistic characteristics of Western theatre and Cantonese opera and of Peking and Cantonese opera. Their reading has led some of them to believe that Western opera and Peking opera are more "sophisticated" because they employ less improvisation.

In Chinese, the word *zik* 即 means "instant" or "immediate," and the word *hing* means "to build," "to start," or "an impulse." Together, the term *zik hing* can be translated as "an immediate creation." Other Chinese terms that have similar or related meanings are *zik zik* 即席 (on the spot, at once and extempore), *zik ging* 即景 (to compose poems with the scenery one is looking at as theme) (Liang *et al.*, 1971:24), *zik hing fu si* 即興賦詩 (to write poems on the spur of the moment) (Lin, 1972:1322). According to the Chinese dictionary *Ci Hoi* 辭海 (*The Sea of Words*) (1979:932), *zik hing biu jin* 即興表演 means "performance deviating from the script or staged with no rehearsals," *zik hing* meaning "to create in terms of the immediate feeling," and *zik hing hei keik* 即興喜劇 is the Chinese translation of *commedia dell' arte* or *commedia all' improviso*. Another Chinese-English dictionary explains *zik hing* as "*ad libitum*" (Liu, 1978:205). Judging from the various connotations of the term *zik hing*, it would best be translated as "improvisation."

Within the profession, the Cantonese term *bao tou* 爆肚 (to explode one's belly or stomach) refers to the use of materials in acting, stage movement, singing or speech that deviate from the instructions written in the script. Hence, *bao tou* is a particular kind of improvisation. However, most of the audience in Hong Kong only recognize the term as denoting improvised comic episodes. Since, up until the 1970s most such comic episodes involved foul language, innuendoes and jests (see Chapter 10), the term sometimes has a negative meaning. Audiences in Hong Kong often fail to observe the use of different kinds of improvisation besides *bao tou*. Hence, for many people, to improve Cantonese opera would often involve the elimination of *bao tou*.

The Improvisatory Play

When actors and instrumentalists were asked to talk about improvisation in Cantonese opera during fieldwork for this study, they invariably mentioned the form of Cantonese operatic performance popular in the pre-1930 period, when no script was used. The play reminder, referred to as *hoi hei si je* 開戲師爺 (play initiator) in the troupe, was responsible for preparing an outline with cues for the actors' entrances and exits. The outline also contained instructions for stage settings and stage properties, some notes concerning the plot of the play, the names of the characters played by each actor and the types of percussion music to accompany the entrance of the actors. The outline was written in a brief, economical style and each actor had to perform in a highly improvisatory manner. This form of performance was referred to in the 1980s as *Bao tou hei* 爆肚戲 (play performed by exploding belly), *Tae gong hei* 提綱戲 (outline play) or *Pai coeng hei* 排場戲 (episodic play) by members of the profession. Whether these terms existed in the 1930s and before is uncertain. Throughout this book, this form of performance is referred to as "improvisatory play."[1]

Most troupes have ceased to perform improvisatory plays from the 1930s. Nowadays, they are staged only in occasional all-night shows in Hong Kong and afternoon shows in Singapore and Malaysia.[2] Though modern troupes usually perform with scripts, the use of improvisation still has a limited existence in contemporary performances of Cantonese opera.

In earlier times, the outline's notes concerning the plot usually stated only the titles of the *pai coeng* 排場 (patternized episode), and the actors would provide the relevant text, gestures, and the highly stylized patterns of stage movement that they had acquired in their training. An opera performance might involve several acts; each act would have several patternized episodes. Each episode was associated with a definite basic set of text, gestures and stage movements. For example, in the scene where an official had to advise his emperor, the title of the patternized episode *Gan gwen pai coeng* 諫君排場 (the patternized episode of advising the emperor) would be stated in the outline. An actor who played the character of an official would then apply the appropriate gestures and stage movements and the relevant text in his performance. The text is quoted as follows.

Lei Bak coi gou wae zau song.

李　白　才　高　為　酒　喪

The poet Lei Bak had high talent but died of excessive alcohol.

Zau wong tam sik bai san gong.

紂　王　貪　色　敗　山　江

The emperor Zau lost his nation because he was too fond of women.

Tin si fen coi Ging Co song.

田　氏　分　財　荊　楚　喪

The Tin family divided wealth among themselves and destroyed the Co Kingdom.

Zau Jy sam hei sei Cai Song.

周 瑜 三 戲 死 柴 桑

The hero Zau Jy died at Cai Song after he had been tricked three times.

zau sik hoi jen jy dou joeng.

酒 色 害 人 如 刀 樣

Women and alcohol can harm people as a knife can.

jing hung nan gwo mei jen gwan.

英 雄 難 過 美 人 關

No hero can survive a sex-trap.

While the text of each patternized episode is more or less fixed, the actor who is responsible for performing them can still choose the appropriate form of oral delivery, subject to his own improvisation with limited choices. As described by Yung (1976a), each type of oral delivery has its textual and musical structures. In order to apply a certain type of oral delivery to present the text of a patternized episode, the actor has to know that the structure of the text fits the textual structure of the oral delivery. This will be further discussed in Chapter 8 of the present study. The structure of the text of the *Gan gwen pai coeng* quoted above is suitable for several types of oral delivery. If the actor chooses to use speech delivery, he can use patter speech, poetic speech, or even plain speech with some textual modification. If the actor chooses musical delivery, he can use *Cet zi cing* 七字清 (seven-word air), *Kwen fa* 滾花 (rolling flower), *Fai zung ban* 快中板 (fast aria type with moderate tempo), *Muk jy* or *Nam jem*.[3]

Besides memorizing the relevant gestures, stage movements and text of each patternized episode, actors also have to acquire two sets of sign language, which are referred to as *sau jing* 手影 (hand shadow) and *jing tau* 影頭 (head of the shadow or, better, gestic hint) in the profession. Hand shadows show the types of oral delivery which the actor will perform. Gestic hints are usually used to show the type of stylistic movement that the actor will employ. For example, an actor who intends to present the *Gan gwen pai coeng* in the form of poetic speech has to show a fist-like hand shadow to the accompanying musicians in order to stop the accompanying melodic and percussion music and make his speech delivery, because poetic speech is delivered with no accompaniment at its beginning. The fist-like hand shadow is known as *sau gwet* 收掘 (to end). If the actor wants to present the same text in the aria type *Kwen fa*, which is sung in flexible tempo and free rhythm, he has to shake his index finger in order to instruct the accompanists to play the appropriate percussion pattern and melodic prelude. Hand shadow and gestic hint are discussed in detail in Chapter 6.

Performers' Attitudes towards Improvisation

One actor made an analogy between the employment of improvisation and cooking. He said that an actor was like a cook; the instructions written in the script were the main ingredients of the dish, yet the actor had to add improvisation to enrich the performance, just as the addition of spices and sauce would enrich the taste of the dish. It is interesting to note that actors of Cantonese opera are not the only ones who consider improvisatory performance akin to cooking; Bell Yung, in his article "Reconstructing a Lost Performance Context: A Field Work Experiment" (1976b:125–26), writes:

> The improvisatory nature of Nam Jem is further evidenced by what Dou [Dou Wun 杜煥] told me one day. When I expressed surprise and admiration at the large number of songs that he claimed he knew, his response was something like this: "I don't really know all these songs by heart. Most of them are quite similar to each other, sharing standard episodes like a wedding, a quarrel, or a love scene. All I need to remember are these episodes, and I use them when they are suitable. My singing is like cooking. A chef has a limited amount of ingredients and spices. He mixes them in different ways and orders, and can produce a very large number of different dishes."

Some actors noted that they had to observe certain rules when they improvised; random improvisation would only produce confusion in the performance. The first rule is to use the appropriate hand shadow or gestic hint before one improvises. But, actors also deem it appropriate to try their best to cover their hand shadows with their sleeves, or show hand shadows at their backs, so that the audience's attention is not disturbed. Since each gestic hint is itself a stylistic gesture incorporated into the acting, actors do not perform them under cover.

In case an actor wants to prolong the duration of a performance to satisfy an enthusiastic audience, sung passages instead of spoken passages will usually be added. The main reason is that it is extremely difficult to improvise well-organized spoken passages; loosely improvised spoken passages would make the audience wonder whether the performance has been deliberately prolonged.[4] On the other hand, since most of the operatic audience does not know operatic music well, some mistakes could be allowed in improvised vocal passages.

The well-known actor Jyn Siu-fae once told me about his experience in making use of hand shadows and adding aria type passages to prolong his performance. Jyn, another male actor, and a female actor were in the last act of a play. Suddenly the female actor fell down on the stage, became unconscious and was carried backstage by the other male actor. In order to sustain the performance, Jyn improvised a series of aria types, hoping that the two actors could return to the stage and continue the play. In his improvised episode, he put in action suggesting that the character was recalling what had previously happened in the play, and before each of the aria type vocal passages he showed the corresponding hand shadow to communicate with the instrumentalists. The two actors did not return, and after about fifteen minutes, the play reminder finally announced that the troupe had to cut the performance short due to the female actor's sickness.[5]

Many actors believe that every actor should possess the ability to improvise, particularly actors of the comic role. In order to improvise well, one has to possess a quick mind and deep knowledge of the structures of the various aria types, singing narratives and speech deliveries. Above all, one has to be equipped with some knowledge of Chinese literature, as well as the system of rhyming. In improvising aria type vocal music, the added passage has to rhyme with the text preceding and following it.

According to many actors, improvisation is never explicitly taught to them by their teachers. Most of the actors learn to improvise by trial and error only after they have been learning to sing and act for a long period of time. The comic role actors Men Bou-sem and Cen Zi-hung told me that they had learned improvisation from watching the performance of other actors, particularly the performances of the late renowned actor Loeng Sing-bo, who was well known for his improvisation, especially *bao tou.* Loeng is admired not only by comic role actors, but also by many contemporary actors of various roles. However, he is sometimes criticized for overdoing his improvisation, which often resulted in breaking the dramatic continuity, disturbing the concentration of the actors onstage and distracting the audience's attention from the other actors.

It is difficult to find a commonly accepted criterion to evaluate the appropriateness of improvisation. Jyn believes that good improvisation must be consistent with the dramatic mood. On the other hand, some actors, especially those in comic roles, believe that, since the function of Cantonese opera is to entertain the public, improvised comic episodes could be added even to scenes with a sad mood to arouse laughter among the audience.

Different performers often have different concepts concerning the role of improvisation. While some of the young and educated actors recognize the importance of improvisation, some older actors think that the different kinds of improvisation are residues of improvisatory play of the 1930s and before, and that both improvisatory play and improvisation, being out of fashion, should be eliminated. However, such actors count *bao tou* as the only kind of improvisation.

Jyn Siu-fae (b. 1945), an actor active in the principal and supporting male roles, is very much respected in the profession for his serious attitude towards performance. He is also well known for his improvisation. (18 February 1988, the New Village of Sam Mun Tsai, New Territories, Hong Kong)

From the 1930s to 1980s, Westernization and influences from other performing arts caused rapid changes in ideology and taste among both audience and performers of Cantonese opera. The transformation from improvisatory play to script-oriented play was one result of this change. Westernization of the genre brought Western instruments to the accompanying orchestra, as well as Western stories in the plays during the 1930s; improvisation also came under increased control in this period. Influences from Peking opera can be seen in the incorporation of percussion instruments from that genre. In the 1980s, improvisation was further controlled when innovation in, and revitalization of, Cantonese opera became a controversial topic.

Notes

1. It is too early to determine whether improvisatory play exists in other theatrical genres in China. Some performers mentioned that the Cantonese improvisatory opera originated in an early period, but failed to specify even an approximate date. Yet in as early a play as *Sae soeng gei* 西廂記 (*Story of the Western Mansion*), written by Lei Jet-wa 李日華 in the Ming dynasty, the playwright gives instructions that resemble patternized episodes. For example, in scene 10, an instruction reads *cey ji zou dou coeng gai zung* 隨意做道場介衆 (casually set the stage as a place to hold a Taoist ritual, actors act in the place). In scene 31, the playwright only put down one line of instruction, which reads *ban hao si cey ji ziu soeng zou gai* 扮考試隨意照常做介 (casually play sitting an examination, as usual). In these scenes, the playwright does not provide details concerning the types of oral delivery, stage movement, gesture or music required. These examples are from *Luk sep zung kuk* 六十種曲 (*A Collection of Sixty Operatic Scripts*, 1958).
2. Future research should include fieldwork and detailed studies of improvisatory plays performed in Singapore and Malaysia.
3. An actor told me that the text would have to be modified if he were to sing this patternized episode using *Muk jy* or *Nam jem*, but he did not demonstrate.
4. However, a passage of improvised patter speech was recorded in my fieldwork. It is cited in Chapter 8.
5. The incident took place about twenty years ago when Jyn was in a performance of the play *Soeng lung dan fung ba wong dou* 雙龍丹鳳霸王都 (*Two Dragons and the Loyal Phoenix at the Heroic Capital*).

5. Communication before Performance

The author of a Cantonese opera or an operatic song is known as the *zan kuk* 撰曲 (author of the *kuk*), where *kuk* literally means "music" or "song." Yet the *kuk* that the *zan kuk* writes contains little musical notation; the music is usually not composed, but only set by the author who chooses the appropriate types of music. For convenience of discussion, the written words used for performances of Cantonese opera and for singing Cantonese operatic song are referred to as script and *kuk* respectively, and the authors are referred to as scriptwriter and *kuk*-writer.

The Roles of the Scriptwriter and *Kuk*-Writer

Whereas in Western European art song or opera, a lyricist or librettist, or even the composer himself, writes the text, and a composer creates the music, in Cantonese opera, the scriptwriter usually produces just the text, but chooses the types of music and speech delivery from an existent repertory, and gives instructions concerning stage setting, stage properties and acting. As pointed out by Yung (1983a:31), the music in most Cantonese opera is drawn from a common pool of "preexistent materials" (see Chapter 2 of the present book). A scriptwriter or *kuk*-writer may sometimes modify the structures of these preexistent musical materials in his play or song. He may also compose *Siu kuk* for some of the scenes, or, more often, he may assign this task to other people. Hence, a script might contain newly created music, but this music is not by the scriptwriter.

For musical types that are commonly known to the actors and accompanying musicians through oral tradition, musical notation of pitch and rhythm is not written in the scripts. It is usually provided, however, for newly composed tunes and for modified preexistent musical materials, as well as when, occasionally, some modern *kuk*-writers and scriptwriters specially arrange or compose melodies for part of the text in an aria type or singing narrative.

The Cantonese operatic songs and operas written in the 1980s, especially those by mainland Chinese writers, often contain musical materials not commonly used in the genre. The sources of these musical materials include *tan ci* 彈詞 (a kind of Chinese singing narrative popular in Suzhou and the nearby areas) and *fan jem* 梵音 (Buddhist chants).[1] These works often feature more musical notation than the ones written before the 1980s. They point to a new creative direction, valuing originality in the writing of songs and operas.

The concept of originality certainly exists in the tradition of Cantonese operatic music, but it has not been emphasized in the writing of the scripts or *kuk*. Rather, it is through the realization of the materials suggested by the scripts or *kuk*, and, most importantly, through improvisation, that originality is created. As mentioned in Chapter 4, both the accompanying musicians and the actors in Cantonese opera emphasize their view that each individual performance should be unique in itself, even though the play has been performed many times.

Because Cantonese operatic song has mainly been disseminated through amateur performances and professional commercial recordings since the 1960s, little is known about the role of improvisation and the concept of originality in its modern professional performances. Certainly, improvisation plays only a marginal role. Hence, in the songs at least, there has been a shift in emphasis from improvisation to greater creativity in the writing of the *kuk*, while maintaining the central concept of originality as part of the tradition of Cantonese operatic music. This change of attitude is one of the outcomes of influences from Peking opera and probably also from Western European art music as mentioned in Chapter 4.

The Script as a Suggested Framework of Performance

The script of a play is the means of communication between the scriptwriter and the troupe members who collaborate to stage a performance. Yung (1989:43–44) has described how a troupe prepares the first performance of a play, beginning with *gong hei* 講戲 (discussing the opera), revisions of the script, group and individual rehearsals and *dok kuk* 度曲 (realizing or designing the song orally). Yung also mentions the possible revisions of the script that result from the discussion held among the scriptwriter, the major role actors, the impresario, the play reminder, the fiddler and the woodblock player. Such revisions include altering some of the oral delivery types, changing the text, and determining various aspects related to the singing and accompaniment as well as stage movements. Yung also notices that changes are often introduced to the script without consulting the scriptwriter.

In the profession, the first performance of a play is known as *hoi san* 開山 (to found). A performance by a troupe which is not the founder of the play is known as *zep lae zou* 執嚟做 (an adopted performance).[2] Whether the troupe is staging a first performance or an adopted one, the performers choose appropriate ways of modifying, adding and deleting some of the materials written in the script. In practice, such changes include the deletion of acts and passages of oral delivery, in whole or in part, the addition of passages or segments of oral delivery, as well as adjustments of role distribution, stage setting, the accompanying music, the tuning of the accompanying instruments, and aspects of singing. Such changes, as discussed below, are often determined shortly before the performance starts or even improvisatorily during the performance.

The *zy wui* often require the troupes to shorten the duration of afternoon shows staged within a series of ritual performances because part of the temporary auditorium may be used for other celebratory activities such as a banquet or ritual offerings. One example occurred during the ritual series staged at Sha Lo Wan on Lantau Island when the Diamond Cantonese Opera Troupe performed an afternoon show on 19 August 1984. Since the villagers had to set up dining tables at the performance hall to prepare for the banquet held in the evening, a complete act from the script was deleted to enable the performance to end an hour earlier. A similar example took place within the Ghost Festival series staged at Shaukeiwan. During the last evening's performance of the play *Adultery Is the Chief of All Crimes*, a whole act from the play was deleted because the troupe was required by the nearby police station to conclude the performance before 11 p.m.

An example of adjusting the stage setting took place on 3 July 1985 at Wun Yiu village in Tai Po when the Colourful Dragon and Phoenix Cantonese Opera Troupe was performing within the ritual series. During the intermission before the last act, a stage worker came to the dressing compartment of the principal male role actor to ask if she would like the stage setting as written in the script. This female actor who played a male role expressed no preference, but the supporting male role actor told the worker that the setting should be simplified to allow himself adequate space to perform the martial arts. The worker later followed the supporting actor's instruction.

A potential change in the accompaniment was observed on 9 May 1985 on Po Toi Island within the Tremendous Heroic Strength Cantonese Opera Troupe's ritual series. During an intermission, the dressing servant of the supporting male role actor Kong Wae-lung 鄺威龍 suggested that Kong tell the percussionists to play the long pattern *dai sau ban* 大首板 (grand introduction) at the beginning of the next act, before his entrance, so that he could have more time to change his costumes. Kong told the present writer that in the past it was common for the major role actors to require the percussionists to prolong the percussion prelude of the coming act to allow the actors enough time to prepare. However, in order not to cause the percussionists additional work, Kong did not take the advice.

As mentioned in Chapter 3, the melodic instruments in the accompanying orchestra are normally tuned to twenty vibrations per second higher than the pitches within the equal-tempered system. According to some operatic song teachers, this tuning projects the singers' voices better. In a troupe, only the principal male and female role actors have the right to change the tuning to fit the conditions of their voices. One example took place on 14 May 1985 when the Fortune Arrives at Door Cantonese Opera Troupe staged a ritual performance at Aberdeen. A few minutes before the performance started, the principal male role actor told the fiddler to tune the two strings of his instrument to *jet ban sin* 一板線 (a system of strings, which is equivalent to the interval of a major second) higher than the standard tuning during a certain vocal passage within the play. Other melodic instruments also had to be re-tuned.

The addition and deletion of phrases or passages of oral delivery, as well as changes concerning the singing and accompaniment, are often improvisatorily determined during the performance; such aspects are discussed in Chapters 7, 8 and 9. Changes concerning role distribution are discussed in Chapter 10.

Besides the kinds of adjustments mentioned above, the names of the plays and the performing repertory can also be altered.[3] Generally speaking, the troupe members who collaborate to stage a performance only treat the contents of a script as suggestions and not prescriptions, whether the play is founded or adopted by the troupe.

The Sources of Script and *Kuk*

Today, in Hong Kong, the reproduction of scripts and *kuk* is not governed by copyright laws. Printed text of *kuk* and scripts can be found in the program notes accompanying commercial recordings, and are published in the newspaper and collections of opera and operatic song. However, because of misprints, the total lack of musical notation and occasional absence of the titles of the oral delivery and percussion patterns, these three sources of *kuk* and scripts are rarely used in actual performances.[4]

Another source of *kuk* is transcriptions from commercial recordings. Students, singers and teachers of operatic song who need *kuk* for singing, performing and teaching purposes can pay professional transcribers to write out the song text and titles of oral delivery and percussion patterns for the pieces they need. Such transcriptions are often supplemented with necessary rhythmic and scale degree notations. Other sources of *kuk* include transcriptions prepared by operatic-song teachers and students themselves, by photocopying the available *kuk,* and obtaining copies from the *kuk*-writer.

For operatic performances, after the repertory for a certain series has been determined, the principal male and female actors are each responsible for providing copies of the scripts to the troupe members. The supply of scripts by the two principal actors is known as *gao hei* 交戲 (to hand over a play).

Every actor of the principal male or female role has his own performing repertory, which is composed of a number of plays. An actor has to prepare about twenty copies of each script within his repertory. If he should have to supply the scripts of any of the plays in a ritual series, he would distribute the copies among the actors, the play reminder and some of the instrumentalists. Of the instrumentalists, as mentioned in Chapter 3, usually only the woodblock player and fiddler receive copies of the scripts; if a third copy is available, it is usually shared by the dulcimer and saxophone players. The other instrumentalists listen and watch the leaders of the melodic and percussion sections carefully. The play reminder is the only backstage worker who receives a copy of the script. For the actors who do not sing or speak, and for the backstage workers, the play reminder is responsible for writing an outline based on the instructions given by the script (see Chapter 6).

If the play is familiar to most of the actors, the copies of the script will be distributed only several hours before the performance starts; if the play is relatively new to them, or if it is to be staged in a permanent theatre and rehearsals are needed, the copies will be distributed several days before the performance or rehearsal. Except for the first performance of an opera, the musicians and play reminder usually do not receive their copies until several hours before the curtain rises. The copies of the script are collected by the play reminder immediately after every performance and are handed back to the owner.

A new script is given by the scriptwriter to the one who commissions it, usually the principal male role actor, but, sometimes, the impresario. The one who receives the original script, usually in the scriptwriter's manuscript, will make copies for each of the participating actors, the two leading instrumentalists and the play reminder, and will distribute the copies, through the play reminder, several days before *gong hei* and rehearsals.

The modern ways of reproducing a script include photocopying, mimeographing and copying by hand. While photocopying is extremely popular in Hong Kong, the copies of scripts are not always made by this method, for reasons discussed later. In the 1960s, there was at least one company in Hong Kong that printed copies of scripts for performers of Cantonese opera.

Because the fee for commissioning a scriptwriter to create a new play is extremely high, only a few established principal actors can afford to have plays founded by themselves within their personal repertories. Most of the other principal actors' repertories contain adopted plays exclusively.

In practice, every principal actor tries his best to avoid having his plays adopted by other actors. The main way to achieve this is to protect against copies of the script being lost or reproduced. On the other hand, every principal and potential principal actor tries his best to obtain copies of scripts from other principal actors to enlarge his own repertory. Technically, any experienced actor can perform a play by reading the script, so successfully adopting a play into his repertory depends on gaining possession of a copy.

Most of the principal actors begin their careers by acting minor or supporting roles in different troupes. An ambitious performer of one of these roles who plans to become a principal actor will try his best to obtain a copy of the script of the play in which he takes part. Similarly, if the script is supplied by the principal male role actor, the principal female role actor

Two pages from the script of the play *The Heroic Blood Sheds on Mount Pei Pa*.
(1987, Hong Kong)

who has not yet adopted the play into her repertory will also try her best to
obtain a copy for her own use.

One usual form of precaution is that the principal actor supplies the
minimum quantity of copies needed, and numbers each one. Although the
contents of the copies are exactly the same whether they are given to the
two leading instrumentalists, the participating actors or the play reminder,
each copy is marked with the name of the character in the play, position of
the instrumentalist or the "play reminder" to whom it is given. Usually
either the troupe member signs his name on the cover of the copy that he
uses, or the play reminder writes the names on the copies.

If the play is unfamiliar to most of the actors, the principal actor has to
take the risk of distributing the copies at least one day before the performing
day. Sometimes, to minimize the risk, the principal actor prepares copies
that are blurred so that they cannot easily be photocopied, although this
does not prevent copying by hand. Another tactic is to distribute copies of
the complete script only to the instrumentalists, the six major role actors

and the play reminder, and to provide only the appropriate excerpts of the play for the other actors.

In brief, every actor guards his scripts as valuables, and each one tries to seize as many valuables as he can. However, this is but only one form of guerrilla battles that are constantly fought among the actors. Other aspects of the politics within a troupe are discussed in detail in Chapter 10.

The Form of Notation in Scripts

Most scripts indicate the text and the musical accompaniment without using musical notation. The script reproduced in Figure 5.1 for the play *Tit ma ngen fen* 鐵馬銀婚 (*Iron Horse and Silvery Marriage*) is typical. It is to be read from top to bottom, right to left.

There are twelve columns in the figure. The first three Chinese characters in the first column indicate "act I" of the play. The following six characters give instructions for stage setting: the act should start with a *jy fa jyn* 御花園 (a royal garden) and later *zyn* 轉 (to switch) to the setting of a *gem din* 金殿 (a royal court). The characters given in parentheses at the beginning of the second, third, fifth, sixth, seventh, eighth, tenth and eleventh columns are instructions for the actors and accompanying musicians concerning the types of oral delivery, percussion patterns and stage movements used in the scene. In the profession, instructions regarding gestures and movements are known as *gai* 介 (acting),[5] the instructions concerning oral deliveries are known as *hau* 口 (mouth), and the two kinds of instructions are known collectively as *gai hau* 介口 (instructions for acting and oral deliveries). The Chinese characters following the instructions are the text of the oral deliveries. The various instructions given in Figure 5.1 are explained as follows:

1. *Pai zi tau hoi bin hei mok* 排子頭開邊起幕 (column 2).[6] *Pai zi tau* 排子頭 and *hoi bin* 開邊 are both names of percussion patterns that are often used at the beginning of an opera act or operatic song. The two Chinese characters *hei mok* 起幕 (to raise the curtain) indicate that the percussion pattern *hoi bin*, which follows *pai zi tau*, is played when the curtain rises. In modern day performances, the complete *pai zi* percussion pattern is rarely played, and only the *pai zi tau* (the opening section of the *pai zi* pattern) is used.

2. *Pok deng ngo* 撲燈蛾 (column 3).[7] Translated as "moth on the

Figure 5.1 Excerpt of script from *Iron Horse and Silvery Marriage*

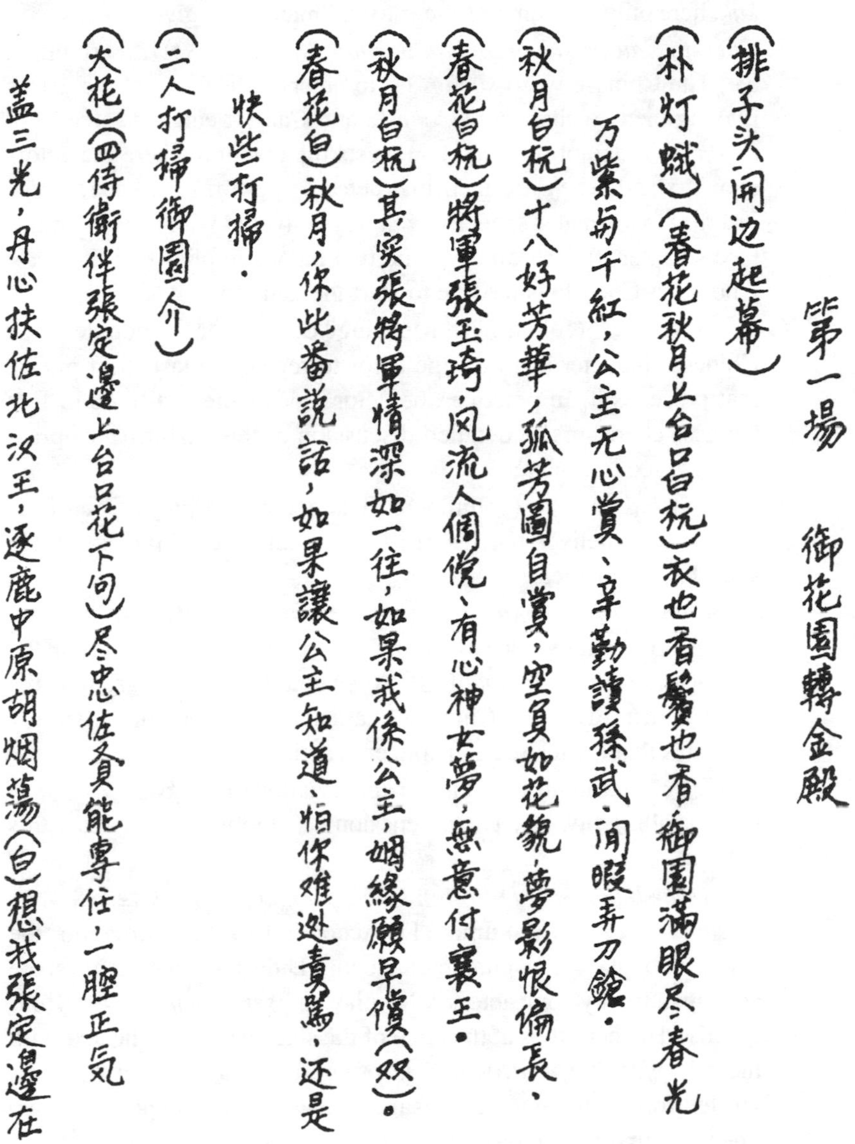

第一場　御花園轉金殿

(排子头開边起幕)

(朴灯蛾)(春花秋月上台口白杬)衣也香鬢也香，御園滿眼尽春光

万紫与千紅，公主无心賞、辛勤讀孫武，閒暇弄刀鎗。

(秋月白杬)十八好芳華，孤芳圖自賞，空負如花貌，夢影恨偏長、

(春花白杬)將軍張玉琦，风流人倜傥，有心神女夢，無意付襄王。

(秋月白杬)其实張將軍情深如一往，如果我係公主，姻緣願早償(双)。

(春花白)秋月，你此番說話，如果讓公主知道，怕你难逃責罵，还是

快些打掃。

(二人打掃御園介)

(大花)(四侍衛伴張定邊上台口花下句)尽忠佐貟能專任，一腔正気

蓋三光，丹心扶佐北汉王，逐鹿中原胡烟蕩(白)想我張定邊在

lamp," it is the name of a percussion pattern that usually precedes and introduces patter speech. As in many instructions in scripts and *kuk*, here only the name of the musical material is given.

3. *Coen-fa Cau-jyt soeng toi hau bak lam* 春花秋月上台口白欖 (column 3).[8] The Chinese word *soeng* 上 (to enter) indicates that the actors playing the two characters Coen-fa and Cau-jyt enter the stage. *Toi hau* 台口 (edge of the stage) suggests the position where the actors should stand. They are then instructed to perform the speech type *bak lam* 白欖 (patter speech), which is delivered with a steady pulse (see Chapter 9). The order of the two names implies that the actor who plays Coen-fa is the one to start the delivery.

4. *Soeng* 双（雙）(column 7).[9] Meaning "double" or "to double," this Chinese character instructs the actor to repeat the last short phrase that precedes it. In practice, the actor repeats the last three to five Chinese characters. A detailed discussion of this performance practice is given in Chapter 9.

5. *Coen-fa bak* 春花白 (column 8). The actor who plays Coen-fa is supposed to deliver the text in the speech type of *bak* 白 (plain speech; see Chapter 9).

6. *Ji jen da sou jy jyn gai* 二人打掃御園介 (column 10). *Ji jen* 二人 (two people) refer to the two actors. According to the instruction, the two actors start to *da sou* 打掃 (to sweep the floor or ground) the royal garden. The last Chinese character, *gai* 介 (acting), simply indicates that the instruction concerns acting.

7. *Dai fa* 大花 (column 11). It is the abbreviation of *dai kwen fa* 大滾花 (grand rolling flower). The percussionists are instructed to play this pattern.

8. *Sei si wae bun Zoeng Ding-bin soeng toi hau fa ha gey* 四侍衛伴張定邊上台口花下句 (column 11). According to the instruction, the actor who plays the character Zoeng Ding-bin enters the stage accompanied by four actors who play the *sei si wae* 四侍衛 (four guards). He then stops at the edge of the stage and sings the text with the aria type *Kwen fa*, which is often abbreviated as *fa* 花 in its written form. The musical passage of *Kwen fa* is composed of two lines: the first two phrases belong to the first line and the next two phrases belong to the second line. The Chinese characters *ha gey* 下句 (lower line) indicate that the first line is sung as a "lower line." It is then understood that the second line should be sung as an upper

line. The difference between a lower and upper line lies in the cadential notes. Since the vocal passage is to be sung after the percussion pattern *Dai fa*, which literally means "big" or "grand" *Kwen fa*, the actor is supposed to sing the passage in the vocal style of *Dai hau*. As mentioned in Chapter 2, this vocal style features a relatively rougher vocal quality and higher pitches. If the scriptwriter wants the actor to sing the *Kwen fa* passage in an ordinary male voice, the instruction *Dai fa* will be omitted. By this it is also understood that the percussionists are supposed to play the percussion pattern *Kwen fa* to precede the singing. *Kwen fa* passages are sung in one of three different modes. However, if the mode is not specified in the script, it is understood that the passage is sung in the mode of *Si gung* 士工 , which is also known as *Bong zi* 梆子 . A detailed discussion of the structure of *Kwen fa* is given in Chapter 7.

9. *Bak* 白 (column 12). According to the instruction, the actor is supposed to deliver the text in plain speech after he has finished the *Kwen fa* singing.

As we see from the above description, the instructions given in the script are often brief and economical. Most of the instructions concerning accompanying music are for the percussionists, as melodic preludes often follow the percussion patterns. By specifying the type of vocal music, the script enables the melodic instrumentalists to play the appropriate prelude and accompaniment. Musical notation is usually not used for aria type and singing narrative passages.

The notation of musical rhythm and pitch in the script can be seen in Figure 5.2, which is reproduced from a portion of pages eighteen and nineteen of the script for the same play.

There are four columns in the figure. Instructions are given at the beginnings of columns 1 and 3. Ngen-ping 銀屏 and Wen-lung 雲龍 are the names of two characters in the play;[10] *Jet zi mui* 一枝梅 (*A Twig of Plum Blossom*) is the name of a *Siu kuk*. According to the instruction, the actor who plays Ngen-ping is supposed to sing a segment of the *Siu kuk*, and the actor who plays Wen-lung will *zip* 接 (to follow) with a different segment of the same *Siu kuk*.

The type of musical notation used in script and *kuk* is known as *gung ce pou* 工尺譜 (*gung ce* notation, where *gung* and *ce* are names of two scale degrees in the notation). The relatively small Chinese characters written

Figure 5.2 Excerpt of script that contains pitch symbols, from
Iron Horse and Silvery Marriage

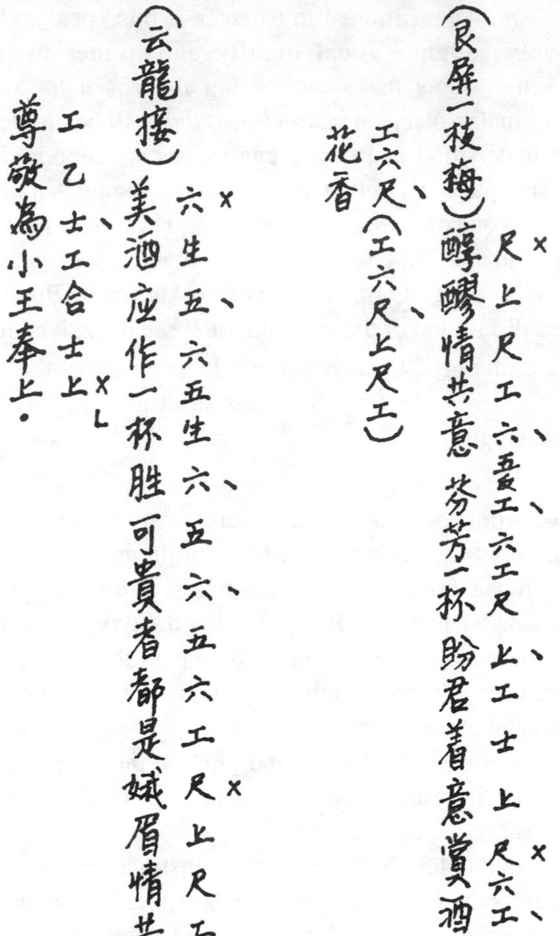

（良屏一枝梅）醇醪情共意　芬芳一抔　盼君着意賞酒

尺上尺工六㐄工、六工尺上工士　上　尺六工尺

工六尺（工六尺上尺工）

花香

（云龍接）美酒应作一杯胜　可貴者都是娥眉情共意　輕舒

六生五、六五生　六、五六、五六工尺上尺工六㐄工六

工乙士工合士上

尊敬為小王奉上．

beside the text are scale degree symbols.[11] The actor is supposed to sing each of the text characters at the pitch or pitches represented by these symbols: the first syllable of the text, *soen* 醇 (mellow or rich), is sung to *ce* 尺 ; the second syllable *lou* 醪 (wine) is sung to *sang* 上 , and so on. The fifth syllable of the song text, *ji* 意 (feeling), is sung to a sequence of *liu* 六 , *wu* 五 and *fan* 反 . The group of symbols in parentheses at the end of column 2 indicate scale degrees that are supposed to be played by the melodic instrumentalists as an interlude between the singing of the first and second phrases.

The small symbols "✗" and " ↘ " (sometimes notated as " ↗ ") beside some of the scale degree symbols denote the pulses. Theoretically, an "✗" indicates that the woodblock player hits a stroke on the large woodblock; the symbol is known as *ban* 板 , which is another name for the large woodblock. A " ↘ ," *ding* 叮 , indicates that the woodblock player hits a stroke on the small woodblock. The strokes of *ban* and *ding* as notated on the script or *kuk* have equal time durations; *ban* and *ding*, thus, serve as beats or pulses. The concept of *ban* being equivalent to a strong beat and *ding* being equivalent to a weak beat is questionable. In my interviews, intensive listening and participation in the singing of operatic songs confirm that *ban* and *ding* in their various combinations in practice function as conceptual pulse-regulators and serve as rhythmic references only. Cantonese operatic music combines *ban* and *ding* in three different ways. The first, known as *jet ban jet ding* 一板一叮 (one *ban* and one *ding*), forms a pattern of two pulses, articulated by alternating strokes on the large and small woodblocks. The second combination, known as *jet ban sam ding* 一板三叮 (one *ban* and three *ding*), combines one *ban* and three *ding* to form a pulse pattern. Both of these patterns can be repeated for any number of cycles. The third combination, *lau sey ban* 流水板 (water flowing beats), uses strokes played only on the large woodblock to articulate the pulses. Since the Western musical term "metre" implies a pattern of accents, the three kinds of pulse patterns used in Cantonese operatic music are not described in terms of "metre" here. A piece of music set in one *ban* and one *ding* is not necessarily transcribed as a duple metre; similarly, a piece set in one *ban* and three *ding* is not necessarily transcribed as a quadruple metre.

The symbol " ↳ " appearing at the end of column 4 is known as a *dae ding* 底叮 (bottom-*ding*). In notation, the symbol is used if the *ding* does not fall on the attack of a note. Similarly, the *dae ban* 底板 (bottom-*ban*) symbol, written as "✗," is used if the *ban* symbol does not fall on the attack of a note. Figure 5.2 does not contain a *dae ban*. *Dae ding* and *dae ban* usually occur where there is a rest or a sustained note.

The aspect of *sin* 線 (string) is often implied, but not explicitly specified, in the notation. *Sin* has two meanings in Cantonese operatic music: the first refers to the relationship between the tuning of the fiddler's two-string *gou wu* (or his violin's two highest strings) and the naming of the pitches. As mentioned above, the two strings are always tuned twenty vibrations per second higher than the pitches G and D in Western tuning.[12] In *Zing sin* 正線 (original naming of the strings) tuning, the two pitches are named *ho* 合 and *ce* 尺 and this tuning is also called *Ho ce sin* 合尺線 (strings in *ho* and *ce*). The names of the pitches played by all melodic instruments in *Zing sin* tuning are given in Music Example 5.1 (see p. 111). In *Fan sin* 反線 (reversed naming of the strings) tuning, the two strings are still tuned to G and D, but they are renamed *sang* and *liu*, and, thus, it is also known as *Sang liu sin* 上六線 (strings in *sang* and *liu*). The tuning involves a "reverse" of naming because the scale degrees *ho* and *liu* are considered to be the same note, but an octave apart. The names of the other pitches in *Fan sin* tuning are given in Music Example 5.2 (see p. 111).

The second meaning of the term *sin* is that of mode, which is a complicated issue: only a preliminary study is presented here. According to the *Jyt keik coeng hong jem ngok koi loen* (*Introduction to Vocal Music of Cantonese Opera*, 1984:35–48), seven modes are identified in the music of Cantonese opera, yet they can be grouped under four categories: *Ji wong* 二黃 , *Bong zi* (or *si gung*), *Fan sin* 反線 and *Ji fan* 乙反 . Only the *Fan sin* mode is played with *Sang liu sin* tuning; the other three modes are played with *Zing sin* tuning.

For convenience of discussion, the seven modes identified by Jyt (1984) are referred to as sub-modes, and are further grouped under the four modes *Ji wong*, *Bong zi*, *Fan sin* and *Ji fan*. *Ji wong* has two sub-modes: the first is G-heptatonic; the second is G-hexatonic combined with D-hexatonic. *Bong zi* has only a C-pentatonic sub-mode. Two sub-modes, a G-heptatonic and a G-pentatonic combined with a D-pentatonic, are grouped under *Fan sin*. The only sub-mode under *Ji fan* is a G-pentatonic. The final sub-mode, A-tetratonic, is not grouped under any mode; it is used only in the singing narrative *Ban ngan*.

Each of the sub-modes is used in one or more aria types and singing narratives. Table 5.1 shows the scale degrees in each of the seven sub-modes and the aria types and singing narratives they each are used for. The

Table 5.1 A classification of aria types and singing narratives by sub-modes

Name of sub-modes	Pitches used in sub-mode	Names of aria types and singing narratives
G-heptatonic	56712345 G = 5	*ji wong man ban* 二黃慢板 *coeng gey ji wong man ban* 長句二黃慢板 *nam jem* 南音 *gam zi fu jung* 減字芙蓉 *fu jung zung ban* 芙蓉中板 *coeng gey ji lau* 長句二流 *ji wong sau ban* 二黃首板
G-hexatonic combined with D-hexatonic	56712356712 G = 5	*ji wong kwen fa* 二黃滾花 *ji lau* 二流
C-pentatonic	123561 C = 1	*bong zi sau ban* 梆子首板 *bong zi man ban* 梆子慢板 *bong zi zung ban* 梆子中板 *bong zi kwen fa* 梆子滾花
G-heptatonic	12345671 G = 1	*fan sin zung ban* 反線中板 *fan sin fu jung* 反線芙蓉
G-pentatonic combined with D-pentatonic	12356123 G = 1	*fan sin ji wong man ban* 反線二黃慢板
G-pentatonic	571245 G = 5	all aria types and singing narratives in *ji fan* mode
A-tetratonic	61356 A = 6	*ban ngan* 板眼

pitches are represented in the table by cipher notation: the arabic numerals denote the scale degrees with the pitch of the first note given below the scale; dots below the numerals indicate the lower register; dots above the numerals indicate the higher register; numerals with no dots belong to the middle register.

According to Yung (1981:674), there are several heptatonic scales in Cantonese operatic music, with different combinations of pitches. Music Example 5.3 (see p. 111) shows the sets of pitches emphasized in the three modes *Bong zi*, *Fan sin* and *Ji fan*. Though Yung uses the term *Zing sin* instead of *Bong zi*, his studies are based on analyses of the aria types *Cet zi cing* and *Bong zi zung ban* 梆子中板 (*Zung ban* in the mode of *Bong zi*) in which the mode *bong zi* is used.

Interviews reveal that singers of Cantonese operatic music are often conscious of the fact that each aria type belongs to a particular kind of mode, but they are not aware of the sub-modes. Singing narratives are sung and played in *ho ce sin* tuning. For example, *nam jem* (southern song) can be performed in either *Ji wong* (but usually referred to as "*Zing sin*" in *nam jem* singing) or *Ji fan* mode. *Kuk pai* tunes are not restricted to specific modes or sub-modes, and can be sung and played with either *ho ce sin* or *fan sin* tuning.

In scripts and *kuk*, if no specification is given, *ho ce sin* tuning is used for both the vocal and instrumental music. The names of the modes are not often specified; players and singers know which modes are required from the names of the aria types. For example, the aria types *Bong zi kwen fa* and *Bong zi zung ban* are frequently used, often written in abbreviated forms as *Kwen fa* or simply *Fa* and *Zung ban* respectively, with the mode *Bong zi* understood. The aria type *Fa* called for in Figure 5.1 is actually *Kwen fa* sung (in *dai hau* voice production) to the mode of *Bong zi* and played in *ho ce sin* tuning (see instruction number eight above). Similarly, the aria types *Ji wong man ban* and *Coeng gey Ji wong man ban* are often abbreviated to *Ji wong* and *Coeng ji wong* respectively (see Chapter 8).

Since the script in Figure 5.2 (see p. 100) does not specify the *sin*, *ho ce sin* is used. Music Example 5.4 (see p. 112) is a transnotation of the pitches shown in Figure 5.2. Both the singers and the players are supposed to perform the same pitches as those written in the script, but in performance they usually add ornaments to the music, often resulting in a heterophonic texture.

The Form of Notation in *Kuk*

The written notation for music and text in *kuk* is based on the prior practices for opera scripts with no significant difference.

Figure 5.3 is part of the *kuk* of the song *Lau ngae cyn sy* 柳毅傳書 (*Lau Ngae Delivers the Letter*) (given in column 1). The two Chinese characters *sung bit* 送別 (Farewell) given in parentheses are the subtitle of the piece. Some of the instructions in rectangular or circular windows are explained as follows:

1. *Dan pai zi hei Ciu-gwen jyn cing coeng jen zi* 旦排子起昭君怨清唱 引子 (column 2). In opera, *dan* is the generic term for all female roles; in operatic song it refers to the female voice. *Pai zi* is the name of the percussion pattern that starts the piece. After the *Pai zi* is played, the female-voice singer is supposed to *cing coeng* 清唱 (to sing without accompaniment) the opening phrase of the *Siu kuk* tune *Ciu-gwen jyn* 昭君怨 (*Regrets of Ciu-gwen*) as an introduction to the whole piece. *Jen zi* refers to the opening phrase of an operatic song or operatic scene. Though there are rhythmic notations written beside the text, they will be executed flexibly in the performance because *Jen zi* is often sung to a free tempo and rhythm.

2. *Hoi bin* 開邊 (column 2).[13] It is suggested that the percussionists play this percussion pattern after the *Jen zi* is sung. The scale degree symbols that follow the instruction are to be played on the melodic instruments.

3. *Ji fan ji wong* 乙反二黃 (column 4).[14] As mentioned above, *Ji wong* is the abbreviation of the term *Ji wong man ban*, which is the name of an aria type. The text following this instruction is supposed to be sung to the aria type *Ji wong man ban* in the mode of *ji fan*.

4. *Seng coeng zey* 生唱序 (column 4). *Seng* is the abbreviated form of *siu seng*, the supporting male role in Cantonese opera, and the male voice in operatic song. *Coeng* means to sing. *Zey* refers to melodic instrumental interludes in Cantonese operatic music. Sometimes such interludes are also set with text intended to be sung. According to this instruction, the text following it is to be sung to the melodic instrumental interlude used in the aria type *Ji fan ji wong man ban* (*Ji wong man ban* in *Ji fan* mode).

Figure 5.3 Excerpt of *kuk* from *Lau Ngae Delivers the Letter*

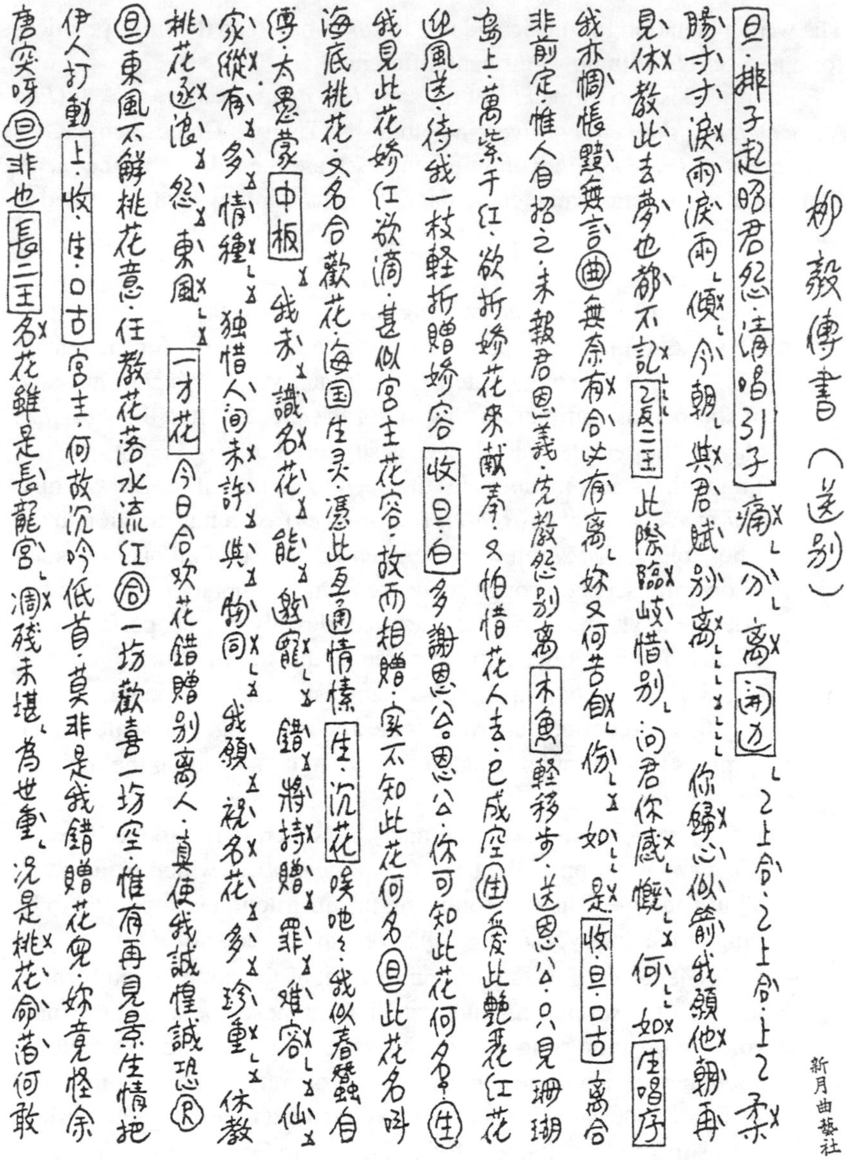

柳毅傳書（送別）

旦．排子起 昭君怨．清唱引子　瘋、分、離　開邊、乙上尺乙上尺上乙柔

眼才才淚雨淚、倆、今朝、與君賦別離、　你歸心似箭我願他朝再

見、休教此去夢也都不記　反二王　此際臨岐惜別．問君你感慨、何如　生唱序

我亦惆悵暨無言　曲　無奈叔令也有離　妳又何苦做、如、是　收旦口古　離合

非前定、惟人自招之．未報君恩義．怎教怨別離　木魚　輕移步、送恩公．只見那江花

島上萬紫千紅．欲折嬌花來戴養．又怕惜花人去．已成空　生　愛此艷死江花

迎風送．待我一枝輕折贈嬌容　收旦白　多謝恩公恩公．你可知此花何名　生

我見此花嬌紅欲滴．甚似宮主花容．故而相贈．實不知花何名叫

海底桃花．又名合歡花．海国生灵．憑此夏通情愫　生、沉花　唉吔々、我似春蠶自

傳、大愚蒙　中板　我未、識名花、能、邀寵．錯將持贈、罪難容．仙主

家縱有、多情種、独惜人間未許、共物同、我顏、祝名花、多、珍重、休教

桃花逐浪、怨東風　才花　今日合欢花錯贈別離人．真使我誠惶誠恐　尺

旦　東風不解桃花意．任教花落水流紅　合　一坊歡喜一坊空．惟有再見景生情把

伊人打動　上收生口古　宮主．何故沉吟低首．莫非是我錯贈花兒．妳竟怪余

唐突呼　旦　非也　長二王　名花雖是長龍宮．凋殘未堪、為世重．況是桃花命洏何敢

新月曲藝社

5. *Kuk* 曲 (column 5). *Kuk* (song) here refers to the aria type *Ji fan ji wong man ban*. After the melodic instrumental interlude has been sung, the male-voice singer is instructed to continue the aria type *Ji fan ji wong* for the text following the instruction.

6. *Sau, dan hau gwu* 收‚且口古(column 5). *Sau* 收 (to end or to take away) here indicates that the instrumental accompanying music should cease when the male-voice singer finishes singing. The female voice performer then makes a speech, delivered in the form of *hau gwu* 口古 (rhymed speech). (A detailed discussion of this type of speech is presented in Chapter 9.)

7. *Jet cey fa* 一錘花 (column 13).[15] According to this instruction, the percussion patterns *jet cey* 一錘 (one-stroke) and *Kwen fa*, and a melodic prelude precede the singer's performance of the text in the aria type *Kwen fa*.

8. *Ce* 尺 (column 13). The symbol *ce* here indicates that the preceding syllable should be sung to the note *ce* or sung to a melisma that ends on *ce*. The symbol *sang* 上 in column 15 has a similar function.

As Figure 5.3 illustrates, musical notation, especially pitch-related notation, is sparse in *kuk*. In *kuk*, and scripts used by experienced and professional singers, rhythmic and pitch-related notation indicating the cadential notes of singing passages is usually missing. As we have seen, these notations are only used for modified aria types, *kuk pai* tunes that are unfamiliar or modified, or *Siu kuk* tunes that are newly composed.

Implicit Information in Script and *Kuk*

Beyond the explicit instructions given in *kuk* and scripts, certain kinds of information are implied, however. First of all, the rhythmic symbols written in *kuk* and scripts provide only a rhythmic reference and do not indicate an exact time value or proportion of time value for each of the notes that are sung or played. As shown in column 2 of the *kuk* in Figure 5.3, dots can be put below notes to indicate that they should be played a longer time, but the exact time values are not given. The *dae ding* at the beginning of the phrase indicates that the melodic instrumentalists are supposed to play the phrase a little bit after the pulse, which is not necessarily articulated by the woodblock player. In practice, a short rest often results. In actual performance, the notated phrase can be realized in many different rhythms. Four possible ways, as I have seen demonstrated by accompanists, are transcribed in Music Example 5.5 (see p. 113).

Second, the scale degree symbols give only a melodic framework. In actual performance, the melodic instrumentalists are allowed to ornament the pitches (see Chapter 7). No matter whether pitch-related notation is provided in the *kuk* or script, both singers and instrumentalists apply improvisation in the realization of the pitches during the performances.

For the instrumental accompaniment, the *kuk* and script sometimes name the specific percussion patterns to be played, but sometimes give only the names of the aria types, singing narratives, fixed tunes and speech deliveries without specifying the percussion patterns. As has been noted above, however, in the tradition of Cantonese operatic music each type of vocal music is associated with a percussion pattern and a melodic instrumental prelude, and, by recognizing the name of the musical type in the *kuk* or script, the percussionists will first play its appropriate pattern followed by the melodic instrumentalists playing the appropriate prelude. For example, while the *kuk* in Figure 5.3 only states the use of *Ji fan ji wong* in column 4, both the singers and the instrumentalists understand that a percussion pattern and a melodic instrumental prelude precede the singing. (The names of the percussion patterns associated with each of the commonly used vocal music types are given in Chapter 6. The accompaniment in Cantonese operatic music is also discussed in Chapter 7.) If the scriptwriter or the *kuk*-writer wishes to omit the percussion and melodic instrumental preludes, he specifies this with the Chinese characters *tuk tau* 禿頭 (bald), *gen zip* 緊接 (to connect tightly) or *zik zyn* 直轉 (to change directly).

The sung and spoken passages in the written *kuk* and scripts are only a textual framework, and the performers are not expected to follow them strictly. While textual deviation in sung and spoken passages is rare in both amateur and professional circles of operatic song singing, it is common in opera performances, particularly in spoken segments. (The improvisatory delivery of spoken text is discussed in Chapter 9. Textual deviations used in vocal music are analyzed in Chapter 8.)

Concluding Notes

The form of expression in Cantonese operatic *kuk* and scripts is highly economical and condensed. The reasons for this characteristic lie in the nature of the sources of *kuk* and scripts, and in the role of improvisation in the genre.

Because hand-writing and copying by hand are the chief ways of producing the original or copies of *kuk* or scripts, the scriptwriters, *kuk*-writers and transcribers employ a sparse form of expression to save time and effort. A comparison of different *kuk* for the same operatic song reveals that the versions intended for teaching contain more music notation, while those used by experienced and professional singers are highly economical, some containing only text.

On the other hand, since the genre is performed in a highly improvisatory manner, an elaborate form of expression would only limit the actors' and musicians' scope and freedom of improvisation. Scripts, though, can reflect changes through improvisation; the actor Jyn Siu-fae told me that some scripts of Cantonese opera incorporate episodes that had been added improvisatorily in a performance. One example can be found in the script of the play *Adultery Is the Chief of All Crimes*.[16]

To summarize, it is difficult to draw a distinction between "cause" and "result" in the relationship between improvisation and form of expression. In any case, the improvisatory nature of Cantonese operatic performances is reinforced by its economical form of expression and notation.

Notes

1. Among the numerous *kuk*-writers, Cen Gwun-hing 陳冠卿 is the one best known for employing rare musical types in operatic songs. For example, he uses a *tan ci* passage in the piece *Zae juk ho* 祭玉河 (*Memorial Ceremony for Jade River*).
2. According to scriptwriter Sou Jung 蘇翁, the troupe members who give the first performance of a play always follow the scriptwriter's original ideas. This statement is questionable, in the light of Yung's research (1976a and 1989) and my interviews. Sou also pointed out that the scriptwriter can do nothing to prevent his script from being altered in adopted performances. Another scriptwriter, Jip Siu-dek 葉紹德, claimed that he had secured the copyright of all of his works through his lawyer, and that he would have the right to sue any troupe that tried to perform his works as adopted performances without his permission. However, no court case is known to have been filed concerning the unauthorized performance of a Cantonese opera.
3. Usually the *zy wui* and the principal male and female actors have the right to change plays a few hours before the performance starts. The impresario or play reminder can change the title of a play shortly after the repertory for a series is decided. In ritual performance, titles containing words associated with blood, death and bad

fortune are usually avoided. For example, the play *King gwok king sing bik hyt fa*
傾國傾城碧血花(*Blood Shed for the Woman Who Caused the Fall of the Nation*),
where *bik hyt* means "blood shed in a just cause," had its title changed to *King gwok
king sing bing tae fa*傾國傾城並蒂花where *bing tae fa* means "twin flowers on one
stalk," when the play was staged in a ritual performance during the Fuk Dek Gung
series at Tai O on 9 March 1985.

4. In 1981, a collection of operatic-song *kuk* was published with the title *Tong si Jyt
   kuk Coeng bun* 唐氏粵曲唱本 (*Tong's Book of Cantonese Operatic Song*). In this
   collection, rhythmic notations are indicated in all the vocal passages, and pitch-related notations are frequently employed. The collection is intended to be used by
   amateur singers.

5. In the scripts, the word *gai* also refers to special audio and visual effects. For
   example, in the third act of the script for the play *The Swallow Returns*, the
   instruction *dai deik dau gwun giu gai* 大笛斗官叫介 tells the double-reed pipe
   instrumentalist to play music imitating the crying of a baby.

6. Operatic scripts and *kuk* feature many Chinese characters in substitute, abbreviated,
   simplified and condensed forms. The word 辺 usually appears as 邊 in a standard
   dictionary.

7. The word *pok* 朴 should be written as 撲 .

8. The form 杬 is a simplified character commonly used in the People's Republic of
   China and Hong Kong; it is also written as 欖 .

9. The form 双 is a simplified character; it is also written as 雙 .

10. The word *ngen* 艮 should be written as 銀 ; the form 云 is a simplified character; it
    is also written as 雲 .

11. As these symbols only indicate the scale degrees, their function is similar to that of
    the tonic sol-fa system. For convenience, they are also referred to as "pitch" or
    "pitch-related" notation.

12. Before Western musical instruments were introduced to Cantonese opera, the tradi-
    tional Chinese melodic instruments employed in the accompanying orchestra had a
    limited range of pitches. Hence, high notes that exceeded the range of a certain
    instrument would be replaced by the playing of their equivalent notes at a lower
    octave. While a difference in twenty vibrations per second can be found in music of
    the middle register, the discrepancy doubles in the higher but lessens in the lower
    register. As mentioned previously, throughout this book, for convenience of discus-
    sion and notation, these differences are disregarded in both transcription and
    transnotation, which is the translation from one kind of musical notation to another.

13. The form 开 is a simplified character; it is also written as 開 .

14. The word 黃 as in *Ji wong* 二黃 is commonly substituted by 王 .

15. The word *cey* 才 should be written as 鎚 .

16. This comic episode cannot be quoted because the script is not available to me.
    However, it was included in three different performances of the same play that I
    attended.

Music Example 5.1 Names of pitches in *Zing sin*

Music Example 5.2 Names of pitches in *Fan sin*

Music Example 5.3 Pitches emphasized in the three modes

Music Example 5.4 Transnotation of the vocal passage in Figure 5.2 from *gung ce* to staff notation

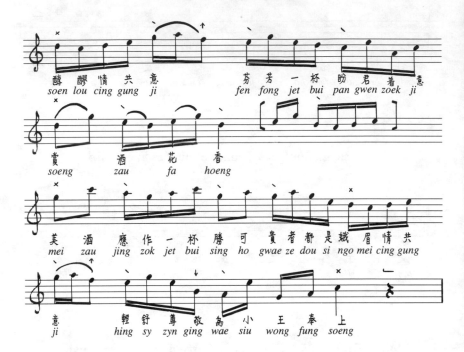

Music Example 5.5 Four ways of realizing the rhythmic and scale
degree notations in Figure 5.3

6. Communication during a Performance

The Stage Plan

The backstage is screened from the audience by curtains. It includes a corridor directly behind the backdrop, dressing compartments, and spaces at stage left and right (see Figures 6.1a and 6.1b). Stage left is known as *ji bin* 衣邊 (costume side), and it is here, at one end of the corridor, that the costume trunks for the secondary and minor role actors are placed. Stage right is called *zap bin* 雜邊 (miscellaneous side); the accompanists sit here and face stage left, and trunks of stage property, tools for setting the stage, and miscellaneous objects are placed here.

The accompanists usually sit and stand in four rows: the fiddler, the saxophonist and the dulcimer players sit in the front, the other supporting melodic instrumentalists in the second, the woodblock player in the third, and the other percussionists either sit or stand in the last row. Since the front-row seats are often on the stage and the rest of the seats are on the miscellaneous side, the accompanying orchestra is located partly onstage and partly backstage. Figure 6.1b shows the plan of a stage proper.[1] According to Yung (1976a:81–82), the doorway at stage right, known as *fu dou mun* 虎道門 (tiger gate), is for actors entering the stage; the doorway on stage left, *wu lei dung* 狐狸洞 (fox hole), is for exiting from the stage. Troupe members in Hong Kong nowadays often refer to both of these doorways simply as the tiger gate. The doorways are actually gaps between the backdrop and the wing curtains that mark the side of the stage. In modern performances, actors enter and leave the stage from either doorway depending on the dramatic context. For example, a character who approaches the courtyard of a house (located onstage symbolically) will enter from stage right. The actor exits from stage right when he is supposed to leave the courtyard and the house; he leaves the stage from the left doorway when the story line requires him to go inside the house.

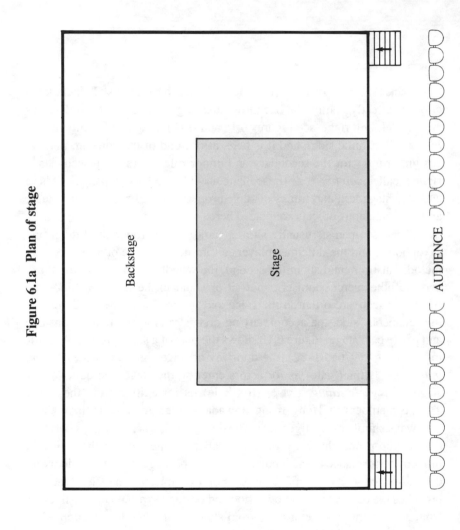

Figure 6.1a Plan of stage

Figure 6.1b Plan of stage

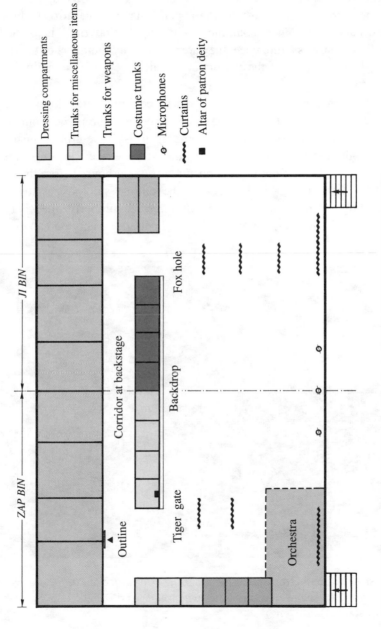

Dressing compartments

Trunks for miscellaneous items

Trunks for weapons

Costume trunks

Microphones

Curtains

Altar of patron deity

ZAP BIN

JI BIN

Corridor at backstage

Outline

Backdrop

Fox hole

Tiger gate

Orchestra

AUDIENCE

Communication Backstage

Figure 6.2 diagrams the various means of communication employed by the troupe members backstage during a performance. The arrows show the means and directions of communication. The "scriptwriter" is provided in the figure only as a reference: they are not actually members of the troupes and seldom appear at the performance hall except occasionally for first performances.

The three groups within a troupe who communicate with one another actively are the actors, the backstage workers and the percussionists. The play reminder moves among the members of the three groups, instructing and reminding them of the details of the performance. He is also responsible for writing the outline and posting it several hours before the performance starts. (As described below, the outline summarizes the script, including instructions for stage setting, stage property, the characters played by each actor, the order of actors' entrances, and the names of the

The stage is viewed from the costume side: a performance of *The Swallow Returns* is taking place before an enthusiastic audience. (9 April 1989, Tung Wan, Cheung Chau Island, Hong Kong)

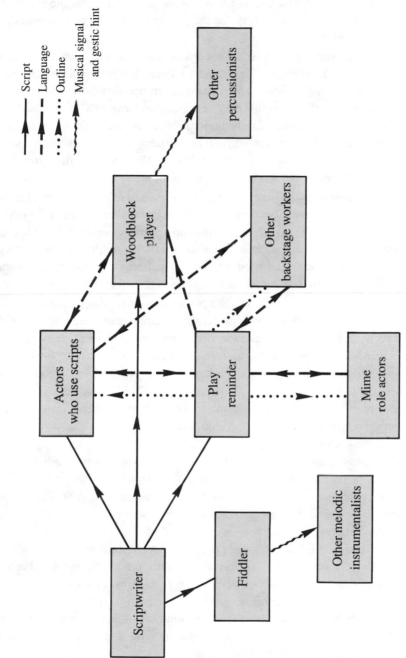

Figure 6.2 A diagram of backstage communication

Script

Language

Outline

Musical signal and gestic hint

Other percussionists

Woodblock player

Other backstage workers

Actors who use scripts

Play reminder

Mime role actors

Scriptwriter

Fiddler

Other melodic instrumentalists

percussion patterns that accompany the entrances.) The outline is a written means of communication between the play reminder and both the backstage workers and the actors.

Mime role actors, who do not speak, sing, or act, other than making routine stage movements, do not read a script, but refer only to the outline to prepare for their performance. The other troupe members who constantly consult the outline are the play reminder and the rest of the backstage workers. Only the actors for the major roles and some of the secondary ones have to consult the script when they prepare for the performances. The major role actors usually do not read the outline because they are always prompted to enter the stage by the play reminder.

The names of the percussion patterns used to accompany the entrances of the actors are usually copied from the script and recorded in the outline. An actor waiting to go on stage at the miscellaneous or costume side enters when he hears the appropriate percussion pattern. Actors have to be able to identify the most often used percussion patterns, but the play reminder sometimes has to tell the actors to enter at the correct moment.

If a major role actor wants the percussionists to play a pattern different from the one prescribed or to prolong a certain pattern, the actor can either directly notify them, or ask the play reminder to inform the woodblock player. When a major role actor is ready to enter the stage, the play reminder sometimes notifies the woodblock player by yelling "hey" loudly. Thus, spoken word and yelling are the means of communication used between the play reminder and the percussionists. There is little verbal communication between the actor or the play reminder and the melodic accompanists during a performance.

The woodblock player is the only percussionist who reads the script during a performance. He communicates the percussion patterns to the other percussionists by different ways of beating strokes on the three woodblocks and through gestures known as gestic hints. For example, to signal a short one-stroke pattern composed of a simultaneous attack on the small gong, cymbals and the gong, the woodblock player will make a downward motion with the drum stick in his left hand, somewhat like a cue gesture made by conductors of Western orchestras. For a long one-stroke pattern, the player rolls his sticks on the medium woodblock and the other percussionists follow with the appropriate strokes on their instruments. Music Example 6.1 (see p. 137) shows the typical rhythms played for the short and long one-stroke patterns.

Two common gestic hints are used to notify the other percussionists to play the patterns *Sin fung ca* 先鋒查 (vanguard cymbal) and *Hoi bin* (starting). The *Sin fung ca* pattern is often used to accompany the action of one actor holding the wrist of another and dragging him to the edge of the stage, in an attempt to interrogate him, usually in front of the microphone. To signal this pattern, the woodblock player points his left stick vertically downward, then moves his right stick close to the left one and points it slanting downward. For the *Hoi bin* pattern, which is used at the beginning of an act, the player strikes the large woodblock with both of the sticks simultaneously and then moves the sticks away from the instrument horizontally in opposite directions.

Some percussion patterns have short fragments that can be repeated an unlimited number of times to prolong the pattern for accompanying an actor's stage movements. Paying close attention to the actor, the woodblock player determines when to stop the repetition and signals his cue to the other percussionists by yelling "hey." Although yelling is spoken communication, the woodblock player's use of it is considered a kind of gestic hint.

The Outline

The outline is normally posted near the tiger gate. Often it is hung with strings from a bamboo stand, beside the curtain concealing the corner dressing compartment at backstage right. The play reminder is responsible for posting the outline several hours before the performance starts. Often the outline is written by the reminder, but occasionally by the impresario. Some outlines are used over and over again whenever the same play is performed, in which case the names of the actors are not identified in the outline, but on another piece of paper posted alongside the outline.

Figure 6.3a, copied from the original by the present writer, is the outline of the play *The Swallow Returns*, used by the Celebrate the Nice Years Cantonese Operatic Troupe when it performed the play on 4 August 1985. The circled arabic numerals indicate the acts, of which there are four. Act I is translated in Figure 6.3b.

In Figure 6.3a, the Chinese characters underlined by a wavy line are the title of the play. The other underlined characters indicate the stage setting. To the left of these groups of characters, the word *noi* 內 (inside) identifies the list of stage properties that should be prepared backstage and brought

Figure 6.3a Outline of the opera *The Swallow Returns*

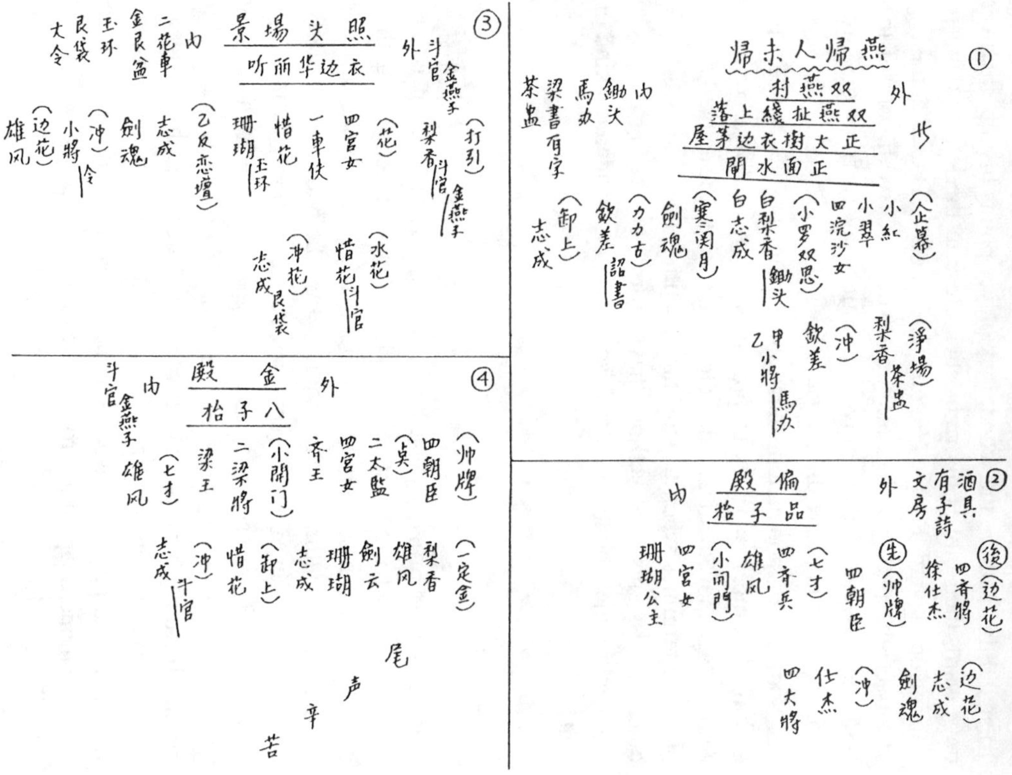

Figure 6.3b Translation of Act I from Figure 6.3a

The Swallow Returns

The Two Swallows Village
Two mechanical swallows
controlled by strings
Big tree at middle and
a hut near *Ji bin*
water gate at middle

outside   ①

basket

$$\left(\begin{array}{cc} kei \\ mok \end{array}\right)$$

four   Siu-cey   Siu-hung
girls
wash
clothes

$$\left(\begin{array}{cc} siu \\ lo \quad soeng \\ si \end{array}\right)$$

Bak   Bak
Zi-sing   Lei-hoeng
| hoe

royal   Lei-hoeng
official | tea-cup

$$\left(\begin{array}{c} zing \\ coeng \end{array}\right)$$

junior   royal $\left(cung\right)$
generals
A and B
| horse-whip

$$\left(\begin{array}{c} hon \\ gwan \\ jyt \end{array}\right)$$

Gim-wen   inside   hoe

horse-   letter
whip   with
  words

$$\left(\begin{array}{c} lak \\ lak \\ gwu \end{array}\right)$$

royal
official
| royal
| letter

tea-
cup

$$\left(\text{enters quietly}\right)$$

Zi-sing

onstage by the actors when they enter. On the opposite side, the word *ngoi* 外 (outside) indicates the stage properties that should be placed on the stage before the act starts. For Act I, a hoe, a horsewhip, a letter with words copied from the script, and a tea-cup are needed for "inside"; only a basket is needed for "outside."

Many Chinese characters in outlines appear in abbreviated forms that are rarely used in contexts other than those related to the genre. Many of these abbreviated forms are considered wrong characters. For example, in Act I, the character *lam* 艹 will appear as 籃 in a standard dictionary; the character *bin* 办 will appear as 鞭. Similarly, in Act II, the character *zi* 子 in the phrases *ben zi toi* 品子枱 and *jau zi si* 有子詩 should be written as 字. In Act III, the character *teing* 㕔 in *ji bin wa lae teing* 衣边华丽㕔 should be written as 廳; the character *ngen* 艮 in *gem ngen pun* 金艮盤 and *ngen doi* 艮袋 should be written as 銀.

Below the underlined Chinese characters in the same figure, there are two rows of characters, each intended to be read from top to bottom and from right to left. (The translation in Figure 6.3b should also be read this way.) The words in parentheses are instructions summarized and copied from the script. The relatively smaller characters with lines drawn on their left sides indicate the stage properties that the actors should bring onto the stage. The other Chinese characters show the names of the characters in the play.

According to the outline, in Act I the actors playing Siu-hung 小紅, Siu-cey 小翠 and the four girls who wash clothes should be present on the stage before the curtain rises. No percussion pattern is needed to accompany their entrance onto the stage, and no pattern is indicated in the outline. The outline briefly summarizes the instructions written in the script, which are *Siu-hung Siu-cey jy sei cyn ney tung kiu dae jyn sa gai* 小紅小翠與四村女同橋底浣紗介 (Siu-hung, Siu-cey, and four village girls wash clothes under the bridge) and *Hoi bin hei mok* 開邊起幕 (the percussion pattern *Hoi bin* is played; curtain). According to the script, the six actors should leave the stage before the next two actors enter the stage, but their exit is supposed to be understood by the six actors and, thus, is not indicated in the outline. This is typical for all outlines, which give only instructions concerning the actors' entrances, but not their exits.

The second instruction in the outline, *siu lo soeng si* 小鑼相思, is the name of the percussion pattern that accompanies the two actors' entrance. The character Bak Lei-hoeng is supposed to carry a hoe. In the script, the instruction is given as *Siu lo soeng si Bak Lei-hoeng, Bak Zi-sing na dai bao fuk, co tau tung soeng gai* 小鑼相思白梨香，白志成拿大包袱，鋤頭同上介 (the percussion pattern *siu lo soeng si* is played, Bak Lei-hoeng and Bak Zi-sing enter the stage, carrying a big cloth-wrapped bundle and a hoe). In this particular performance, the play reminder decided to omit the stage property *dai bao fuk* 大包袱 (a big cloth-wrapped bundle) and, thus, did not include it in the outline. However, the actor who plays Bak Zi-sing can still bring the *dai bao fuk* onto the stage if he wants. In writing an outline, the play reminder does not have to follow the script strictly, and can sometimes omit minor details.

The third instruction, *Hon gwan jyt* 寒關月 (*Moon Over the Cold Mountain Pass*), is the name of a *siu kuk* tune that is to be sung by the actor playing Ngae Gim-wen 魏劍魂 shortly after he has entered the stage. The instructions in the script read *man coeng cey, Ngae Gim-wen soeng gai* 慢長錘，魏劍魂上介 (the percussion pattern *man coeng cey* (slow and long strokes) is played, Ngae Gim-wen enters the stage) and *Gim-wen toi hau hei Hon gwan jyt* 劍魂台口起寒關月 (Ngae Gim-wen starts singing the tune *Hon gwan jyt* at the edge of the stage). The outline in Figure 6.3a only gives the name of the *siu kuk* tune to remind the actor that he has to sing shortly after he has entered the stage.

The fourth instruction, *lak lak gwu* 叻叻古, sometimes written as 叻叻鼓, is the name of the percussion pattern that is to be played when the actor in the role of the *jem cai* 欽差 (royal official) enters the stage. The actor is supposed to bring a royal letter with him. The instruction written in the script reads *lak lak gwu jem cai soeng gai* 叻叻古欽差上介 (the percussion pattern *lak lak gwu* is played, the royal official enters).

The fifth instruction, *se soeng* 卸上 (entering the stage without notice by the characters on the stage), says that no percussion pattern is to be played when the actor playing Zi-sing enters the stage. In the script the instruction reads *Zi-sing se soeng tau teing gai* 志成卸上偷聽介 (Zi-sing enters and listens to the dialogue without notice by the characters).

The sixth instruction, *zing coeng* 淨場 (silent moment), sometimes written as 靜場, also implies that no percussion pattern is needed to accompany the actor's entrance. However, the script suggests that the percussion pattern *dei gem* 地錦 should be played. According to an experienced actor, the *zing coeng* instruction is intended to remind the actor that no vocal passage follows his entrance onto the stage.

The last instruction, *cung* 冲, is an abbreviated form of the percussion pattern *cung tau* 沖頭 , which is often used when a character enters the stage with an urgent message. In the script, the instruction reads *cung tau, jem cai, sei dai zoeng dai loeng ma pet soeng gai* 沖頭 , 欽差 , 四大將帶兩馬匹 上介 (the percussion pattern *cung tau* is played, the royal official and four senior generals bring two horses, enter). The "four senior generals" in the script are changed to "junior generals A and B" in the outline; "two horses" become simply a "horsewhip," which symbolizes a horse in the tradition of Cantonese opera as in many other Chinese regional operatic genres. Again, we can see that the play reminder has the freedom to simplify and change the instructions given by the script, if the instructions are not essential to the plot. Such adjustments often cater the size of, and the stage properties available to, the troupe.[2]

While most troupes employ outlines written in the form shown in Figure 6.3a, some troupes use a simplified outline for particularly familiar plays. This form of outline gives only the names of the characters, the names of the actors and the numbers of the acts in which the secondary and minor role actors participate. Figure 6.4 is a simplified outline, reproduced from a handwritten copy, of the play *Zi cai gei* 紫釵記 (*Story of the Purple Hairpin*) used by the Singing of the Young Phoenix Cantonese Opera Troupe when they performed the play on 25 July 1985. The Chinese words at the beginning of the first row, *keik zung jen* 劇中人 (people in the play), indicate that the names in this row are characters in the play. The second row, *dong keik ze* 當劇者 (people serving the play), indicates the names of the actors playing the characters written above. In the third row, *coeng ci* 場次 means the numbers of acts in which the actors participate. Acts I, II, III, V, VI, VII and finale are shown by the Chinese numerals 丨 , 刂 , 刂丨 , 夕 , 亠 , 亠, and the word *mei* 尾 (tail or end) respectively. Act IV does not appear in the outline because it involves only major role actors.

Communication Onstage

When the performance is in progress onstage, troupe members cannot rely on the spoken word to communicate with one another because talking might disturb the performance. Instead, the actors, play reminder and other backstage workers employ six other methods of communication as diagrammed in Figure 6.5.

When necessary, the play reminder or any backstage worker stands behind one of the wing curtains at the miscellaneous and costume sides,

Figure 6.4 A simplified outline of the opera *Story of the Purple Hairpin*

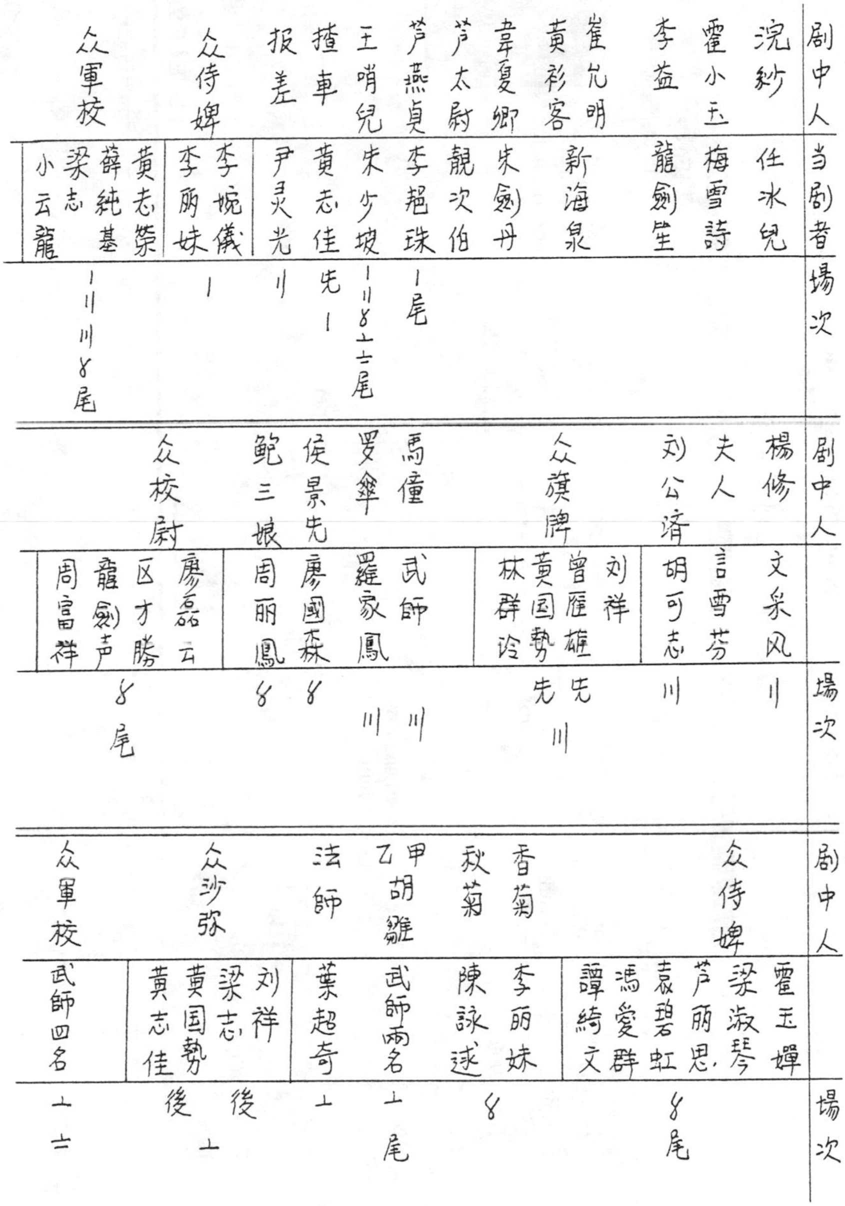

剧中人	当剧者	场次
浣纱	任冰儿	
霍小玉	梅雪诗	
李益	龙剑笙	
崔允明	新海泉	
黄衫客	宋(剑)丹	
韦夏卿	宋少伯	
芦燕贞	李超珠	一尾
芦太尉	靓次伯	
王哨儿	宋少坡	一丨8土六尾
揸车	黄志光	丨
报差	尹灵光	丨
众侍婢	李婉仪、李丽妹	丨
众军校	小云龙、梁志龙、薛纯基、黄志荣	丨丨丨8尾

剧中人		场次
杨修	文汝风	丨
夫人	言雪芬	丨
刘公济	胡可志	丨丨
众旗牌	林群玲、曾雁雄、黄国势、刘祥	先丨丨
马僮	武师	丨丨
罗伞	罗家凤	丨丨
侯景先	廖国森	8
鲍三娘	周丽凤	8
众校尉	周富祥、龙剑声、区才胜、廖嘉云	8尾

剧中人		场次
众侍婢	霍玉婵、梁淑琴、芦丽思、袁碧虹、冯爱群、谭绮文	8尾
香菊	李丽妹	8
秋菊	陈咏逑	
乙甲胡雏	武师两名	土尾
法师	叶超奇	后
众沙弥	刘祥、黄国势、黄志佳	后土
众军校	武师四名	土二

Figure 6.5 A diagram of onstage communication

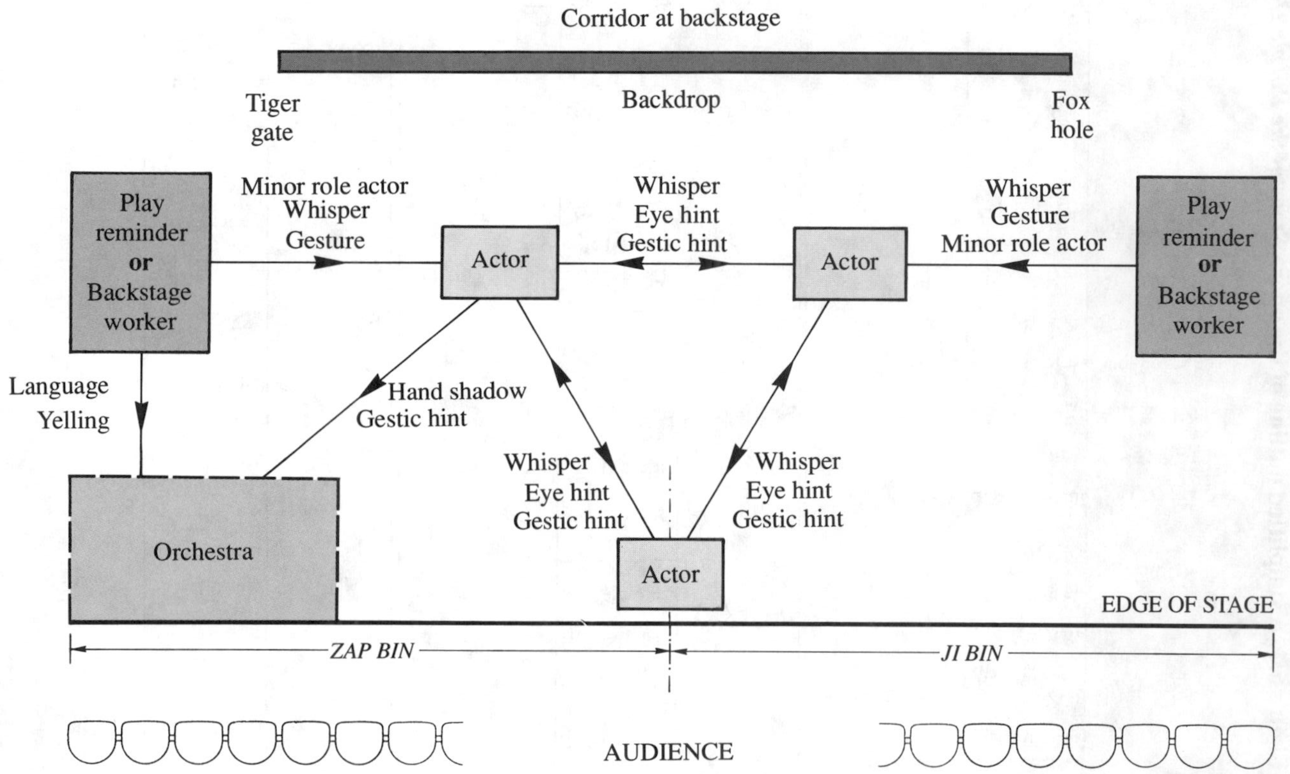

quite close to the actor concerned, to deliver a message to him, in whisper or gesture. Sometimes a backstage worker might send a minor role actor dressed in the costume of a guard or maid onstage to whisper a message to an actor.

Among the actors, messages at the rear of the stage are often delivered in a whisper so that the main performing activities will not be disturbed. Another means of communication is the eye hint, which is referred to as *ngan sik* 眼色 in the profession. An example occurred in a theatrical performance on 17 December 1984, when the New Joyful Popular and Excellent Cantonese Opera Troupe performed the play *Blood Shed for the Woman Who Caused the Fall of the Nation*. In one scene, a hairpin accidentally fell on the stage from the coiffure of the principal female role actor. In order to avoid disturbing stage movements, which would occur if an actor were to step on the hairpin, the supporting male role actor delivered an eye hint to a minor role actor who was portraying a maid. The minor role actor stepped forward, picked up the hairpin, and returned to the rear of the stage.

The main means of communication onstage during a performance are the two sets of sign language known as gestic hint and hand shadow. In the profession of Cantonese opera, the two sets of sign language are sometimes referred to collectively as gestic hint. However, there are some differences between the two. While gestic hint is employed by actors and the woodblock player, hand shadow is only used by the actors. Among the actors, gestic hints are used to deliver various messages to other actors and to the accompanists; hand shadow is mainly used for notifying the accompanists, especially the woodblock player, about the kind of oral delivery to expect and the percussion patterns to be used. A gestic hint may be made by bodily movements; hand shadow involves only the hand. Some "oral" hints are considered to be gestic hints, but hand shadow is purely a sign language. Except for the gestic hints used by the accompanists and play reminder, those employed by the actors are often integrated into the performance as part of the stylized stage movements and gestures. Hand shadows, however, are not considered part of the performance; actors always try to hide the hand shadows from the audience by covering them with their sleeves or showing them to the musicians behind their backs.

Gestic Hint

The most common gestic hint is the one used to prevent more than one actor from starting to sing or speak at the same time. An actor who is ready to begin an oral delivery sways his sleeve, touches his beard or hat, or moves one step forward towards the microphone. In scenes that involve only one actor, he can move and stand in front of the microphone before he makes an oral delivery so that the musicians can play the appropriate percussion and melodic preludes in time to accompany his delivery.

Another commonly used gestic hint is the utterance of the syllable "*a*" 呀 (ah) at the end of a speech delivery to notify the accompanists that the actor is ready to sing the prescribed vocal passage following, or to improvise one.

Some gestic hints are used to call for specific percussion patterns to accompany particular stage movements. As we have seen, the percussion pattern *sin fung ca* is often used to accompany the stage movement of one actor dragging another to the edge of the stage for an interrogation. To call for this percussion pattern, the actor has to step towards the other actor, raise one of his arms vertically and stretch out his fingers. Another signal concerns *sey bo long* 水波浪 (waves), which is the name of a percussion pattern and a series of stage movements. To call for this percussion pattern, an actor has to look forward, and then move several steps backward.

Hand Shadow

Tables 6.1a, 6.1b and 6.1c show the commonly known hand shadows used by actors to notify the accompanists of the oral deliveries and stage movements they intend to employ and to signal the moment to stop the accompaniment. As shown in the tables, each hand shadow calls for a particular percussion pattern; the only exception is hand shadow 26, *tuk tau*, which requires the accompanists to stop for a moment.

Hand shadow is a direct communication between the actor and the woodblock player. Theoretically the melodic accompanists listen to the percussion pattern and play the appropriate melodic prelude associated with the pattern. In practice the fiddler also pays close attention to the hand shadow, and listens carefully to the percussion pattern being played. He is usually the first melodic instrumentalist to react, and closely followed by the other melodic instrumentalists.

Hand shadows 16, 21 and 27 in the three tables have the same name and gesture, but different functions. Since the deliveries of rhymed speech, plain speech, poetic speech and comic rhymed speech do not need accom-

Table 6.1 Hand shadows: gestures, corresponding percussion patterns and indications

A. Hand shadows related to aria types

Gesture	Name of Hand Shadow	Corresponding Percussion Pattern	Aria Types Indicated
1. point thumb down	*dou ban* 倒板	*dou ban* 倒板	*si gung dou ban* 士工倒板 *ji wong dou ban* 二黃倒板
2. point thumb up	*sau ban* 首板	*sau ban* 首板	*si gung sau ban* 士工首板 *ji wong sau ban* 二黃首板
3. shake index finger	*kwen fa* 滾花	5-stroke	*si gung kwen fa* 士工滾花 *ji wong kwen fa* 二黃滾花 *ji fan kwen fa* 乙反滾花 *sat ban* 煞板
4. shake left and right index fingers alternately	*cem fa* 沉花	heavy 1-stroke	*cem fa* 沉花
5. bend index and middle fingers	*huk soeng si* 哭相思	*huk soeng si* 哭相思	*huk soeng si* 哭相思
6. bend index finger	*tan ban* 嘆板	5-stroke followed by 1-stroke	*tan ban* 嘆板
7. point index, middle and ring fingers downward	*sam goek deng* 三腳櫈	*dik dik* 的的	*sam goek deng* 三腳櫈

A. Hand shadows related to aria types (cont'd)

Gesture	Name of Hand Shadow	Corresponding Percussion Pattern	Aria Types Indicated
8. stretch out thumb and index fingers	*dik dik* 的的	*dik dik* 的的	*gam zi fu jung* 減字芙蓉 *sam goek deng* 三腳凳 all aria types and *siu kuk* tunes that start with *ban* of the pulse pattern
9. stretch out and keep close middle and index fingers	*zung ban* 中板	*zung ban* 中板 (*zong dim tau* 撞點頭)	*si gung zung ban* 士工中板 *cet zi cing* 七字清 *sep zi cing* 十字清
10. same as above, roll hand from left to right	*fan sin zung ban* 反線中板	*zung ban* (*zong dim tau*)	*fan sin zung ban* 反線中板
11. same as 9, bend index finger slightly	*ji fan zung ban* 乙反中板	*zung ban* (*zong dim tau*)	*ji fan zung ban* 乙反中板
12. stretch out and separate index and middle fingers	*ji lau* 二流	*zong dim* 撞點	*ji lau* 二流
13. stretch out thumb, index and little fingers	*cet cey* 七鎚	*cet cey* 七鎚 (*fai zung ban* 快中板)	*fai zung ban* 快中板 *fai ji lau* 快二流
14. point index finger forward	*man ban* 慢板	*man ban* 慢板	*man ban* 慢板 in *si gung* 士工, *ji wong* 二黃, *fan sin* 反線 or *ji fan* 乙反 mode

B. Hand shadows related to *siu kuk*, *pai zi*, speech deliveries and singing narratives

Gesture	Name of Hand Shadow	Corresponding Percussion Pattern	Oral Deliveries Indicated
15. stretch out thumb and little fingers	*nam jem* 南音	*gwak dik* 摑的 *dyn tau zung ding* 段頭中叮	*nam jem* 南音
16. hold a fist or five finger tips stay together, point upward	*sau gwet* 收掘	3-stroke followed by 1-stroke	*muk jy* 木魚 *lung zau* 龍舟
17. point middle finger forward	*zung ding* 中叮	*dyn tau* 段頭	all aria types and *siu kuk* tunes that start with the middle *ding* of the one *ban* and three *ding* pulse pattern
18. point all fingers down except thumb	*pai zi tau* 睥子頭	*pai zi tau* 睥子頭	*pai zi* tunes
19. hold right arm upward vertically, put the left palm under the right elbow	*sau tok* 手托	*pai zi tau* 睥子頭 1-stroke	*sau tok* 手托 (a *pai zi* tune)
20. keep five fingers close and bend palm or stretch out fingers except thumb, move up and down alternatively	*pok deng ngo* 撲燈蛾	*pok deng ngo* 撲燈蛾	patter speech

C. Hand shadows related to stage movements and ending of accompaniment

Gesture	Name of Hand Shadow	Corresponding Percussion Pattern	Indication
21. same as 16	*sau gwet* 收掘	3-stroke followed by 1-stroke	poetic speech rhymed speech plain speech comic rhymed speech
22. point all fingers upward except thumb	*sei gwu tau* 四鼓頭	*sei gwu tau* 四鼓頭	martial arts movements
23. point index finger upward	*cung tau* 沖頭	*cung tau* 沖頭	an actor enters stage hastily to report on something
24. point index finger downward	*dei gem* 地錦	*dei gem* 地錦	without haste, an actor enters stage to report on something
25. touch the left palm with the right fist	*da jen* 打引	*da jen* 打引	a major role actor enters stage in a quiet scene
26. keep fingers close, palm flat, stay horizontally	*tuk tau* 禿頭	no percussion pattern is needed as prelude	the actor starts a vocal passage with no instrumental preludes
27. hold a fist or keep five finger tips together and point upward	*sau gwet* 收掘	3-stroke followed by 1-stroke	the accompaniment stops temporarily after the percussion patterns
28. stretch out all fingers	*sat fo* 煞科	long 1-stroke	end of an act or operatic song

paniment at the beginnings (see Chapter 9), and the singing narratives *muk jy* and *lung zau* are sung without accompaniment, the same hand shadow *sau gwet* is used for these four kinds of speech delivery and two kinds of singing narratives. The basic meaning of the hand shadow is to notify the accompanists to stop playing temporarily.

The hand shadows listed in the three tables were collected from interviews with several operatic song teachers, professional melodic accompanists and both professional and amateur woodblock players. While they are the most commonly known hand shadows, some of them are no longer frequently employed. I have witnessed the use of hand shadows 1, 3, 5, 8, 9, 10, 11, 13, 14, 15, 16, 17, 18, 20, 21, 26, 27 and 28 in opera performances, operatic song performances and teaching demonstrations.[3] Different accompanists, singers, actors or singing teachers might use slightly modified systems of hand shadows.[4] I believe that there were more hand shadows and gestic hints employed in the previous decades, but some of them are no longer known by people in the profession.[5]

Hand shadows are occasionally seen in the singing sessions held at amateur and semi-professional operatic song clubs. Each singer is usually responsible for preparing several copies of the *kuk* he chooses to sing and these will be distributed to the accompanists. Yet, sometimes the singer cannot provide a copy of *kuk* for the accompanists, or can provide only one copy that is usually read by the fiddler. In such cases, the accompanists have to watch the hand shadows employed by the singer. Among the many reasons for providing a limited number of copies of the *kuk* are that a singer may not want other people to know his repertory, or a visiting singer (who does not belong to the music club) fails to bring with him enough *kuk* copies when he is requested to sing.[6]

Hand shadows are commonly used in operatic performances, especially those in the ritual context, but they are often not easily seen since actors usually take pains to hide them. One could only detect them by observing at the "miscellaneous side" backstage. An experienced professional woodblock player told me that hand shadows were often given in the situation when an actor was unsure of the order of the oral deliveries he is going to make. He would show hand shadows before each oral passage to assure that, even if he delivered the passages in a different order, the accompanists could still follow him. In addition to such situations, hand shadows are made when actors improvisatorily add passages of oral delivery to the performance. Examples that I observed are described in

Chapters 8 and 9; another example of using hand shadows to coordinate improvisation is cited in Chapter 4.

Notes

1. Instead of having three fixed microphones located at the edge of the stage, large and medium troupes performing in the peak season sometimes have only one movable microphone controlled by the sound system worker through a string and pulley system. Small troupes usually have one fixed microphone.

2. The last four Chinese characters in the outline, *mei sing sen fu* 尾聲辛苦, sometimes written as *mei sing sen fu dai ga* 尾聲辛苦大家, literally mean "the end, thanks for everybody's laborious work."

3. A hand shadow called *lou sy mei* 老鼠尾 (tail of a rat), shown by stretching out the little finger, is not listed in Table 6.1 since its actual use is unclear.

4. For example, many singers and accompanists use only hand shadow 9 to call for the aria type *Zung ban* in *Si gung, Fan sin* or *Ji fan* mode. When the hand shadow is shown, the percussionists play the *Zung ban* percussion pattern and the melodic accompanists play the melodic prelude that precedes *Zung ban* in the *Si gung* mode. The musicians then stop for a short moment to listen to the singer's first syllables in order to know the mode chosen by him. It is a common performance practice that the first syllables of any *Zung ban* passage are sung without accompaniment.

5. It is interesting to note that the improvisatory practice of calling for percussion patterns is also used in *ping keik* 評劇, a regional opera genre in northern and northeastern China. We can see this described in the autobiography of the well-known actress Sen Fung-ha 新鳳霞 (Sen, 1982:181–82) (my translation):

    > After elder sister Ling-ha 靈霞 had sung the first line, we entered the stage with her in front of me. I accidentally kicked off one of her shoes shortly after we had entered the stage.... Elder sister Ling-ha could walk no more, but the percussion pattern *gep gep fung* 急急風 (a sudden wind) was being played and we were supposed to walk around the stage! The elder sister scolded me in a low voice when we were walking.... I said to her, "Wait," picked up the shoe and said, "Follow me." I called for the playing of the percussion pattern *lyn cey* 亂錘 (random strokes), helped her to sit in the middle of the stage, put on the shoe for her and helped her to stand up.... I then called for the percussion pattern *gep gep fung* to return to the play. No audience could detect the flaw.

6. For example, during a singing session held at the members' lounge of the "instrumentalists' guild" of the Chinese Artists Association of Hong Kong, on 17 November 1984, the singer Zoeng Jim-hung 蔣艷紅 had only one copy of the *kuk* for herself when she sang the song *Lem Doi-juk zyt ming ci* 林黛玉絕命詞 (*Lem Doi-juk's Dying Poem*), and she used hand shadows to communicate with the accompanists. After singing, she refused to let me look at the *kuk*. Another example of the use of hand shadows in operatic song performance took place in an amateur music club; it is cited in Chapter 7.

Music Example 6.1   The short and long one-stroke patterns

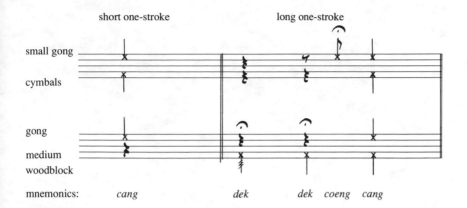

7. Improvisation in Instrumental Accompaniment

This chapter describes the improvisatory practices used by the instrumental musicians accompanying the singing of Cantonese operatic music. The most involved interaction between singer and accompanists generally occurs in the aria type *Kwen fa*, which is sung with no steady pulse and in free tempo; the temporal elements often being determined improvisatorily by the singer.

The *Kwen fa* examples selected for this study were all sung in the *Si gung* mode. *Kwen fa* can be sung to other modes such as *Ji wong* or *Ji fan*, but studies show that the improvisatory practices in the accompaniment in all three modes are similar.

The Performance Contexts

The first examples are three different singers' versions of the same *si gung Kwen fa* passage in the operatic song *Juk lei wen* 玉梨魂 (*The Soul of Jade Pear*). *The Soul of Jade Pear* was originally a song from an opera of the same name. It is often performed today as an independent operatic song, and the opera is rarely staged. The song features three vocal passages that each uses a different aria type: *Man ban* in *Si gung* mode, *Zung ban* in *Fan sin* mode, and *Kwen fa* in *Si gung* mode.

Music Example 7.1 (see pp. 157–58) transcribes a commercial tape by the renowned Cantonese opera actor and operatic song singer Sit Gok-sin 薛覺先 (1904–1956), who was active in the 1930s and 1940s. The date of recording is not given on the tape, but it is believed to be a reissue of a recording made in the 1930s. *The Soul of Jade Pear* in this tape was recorded as an independent operatic song. The accompanying instruments include violin, xylophone, banjo, woodblocks of different sizes, acoustic guitar and perhaps a clarinet or *hau gwun*. No cymbals or gongs are used and the woodblocks are totally absent from the *Kwen fa* passage that ends the song.

Music Example 7.2 (see pp. 159–60) was recorded in a Cantonese operatic-song class taught by Wong Jyt-seng at the Music Department of The Chinese University of Hong Kong in 1984. The song was performed by Wong, who showed the appropriate hand shadow before each passage, played the violin and uttered the mnemonics of the percussion patterns to accompany his singing. This manner of self-accompaniment is intended for class demonstration, and is typical of singing classes for operatic song currently practised in Hong Kong.

Music Example 7.3 (see pp. 161–63) was recorded in a singing session held on 26 May 1985 at the *Sen jyt kuk ngae se* 新月曲藝社 (new moon singing club, formally known as the Crescent Cantonese Opera Society), one of the many music clubs in Hong Kong that has Cantonese operatic song singing as its main activity. *The Soul of Jade Pear* was sung by Deng Juk-fae 鄧旭輝 who was a businessman and amateur singer. He was not a

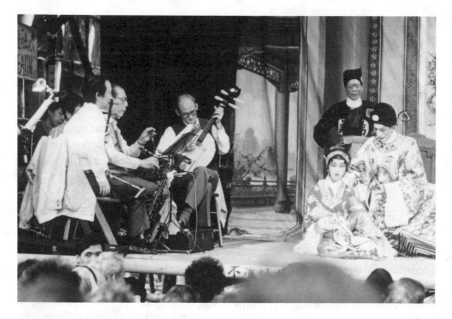

Accompanists on stage are playing for a performance by a small troupe. Melodic instruments seen include a medium-size round-shaped *jyn*, a high-pitch fiddle and a melody saxophone. (21 March 1990, Ping Shek, Kowloon, Hong Kong)

regular member of the club, but happened to be visiting and was asked by some of the members to perform. The accompanying instruments were the high two-string fiddle, vertical flute, dulcimer, the medium two-string fiddle, banjo, *dai wu* 大胡 (low two-string fiddle), large round-shaped lute and percussion instruments played by three performers.

Only two copies of the *kuk* were available, one brought by Deng and the other by the present writer. Deng read his own copy, which contained only the text, and informed the accompanying musicians the different aria types he would use before he began singing. The *kuk* that I provided contained the text, names of the aria types, as well as rhythmic, and some pitch, notations. With the exception of a few syllables, the texts of the two copies were basically the same. My copy of the *kuk* was shared by the fiddler and the player of the vertical flute. During the singing, Deng showed the corresponding hand shadows before some of the passages. The musicians who did not have the *kuk* watched and listened carefully to the leaders of the melodic and percussion sections, as well as to the singer.

Both Wong and Deng confessed that their singing is deeply influenced by Sit Gok-sin. Transcriptions of the three performances provide a backdrop against which we can examine the similarities and differences in the three accompaniments, the extent to which the accompanists followed the traditional, obligatory materials, and the accompanists' choices when handling optional materials.

This chapter focuses on the relation between the vocal line and the aggregate accompaniment. Therefore, while in common practice the various instruments play in a heterophonic texture, the music examples contain the vocal melody and a composite of the accompanying instruments. The method of transcribing the composite accompanimental line in music examples cited here is shown in Music Example 7.4 (see p. 164). If more than one note is played at a time by the different instruments, the one played by the *gou wu* or violin is notated.

Music Examples 7.1 to 7.3 are divided into thirteen divisions. The divisions do not correspond with the textual structure, but are arbitrary divisions of comparable length. Table 7.1 lists the texts and the musical materials in each of the divisions in the examples. Except for some syllables, the texts in the three music examples are nearly identical. A translation and romanization of the text in Music Example 7.1 are as follows:

Table 7.1 Texts and musical materials used in the thirteen divisions of Music Examples 7.1 to 7.3

Divisions	Music Example 7.1	Music Example 7.2	Music Example 7.3
1	*tung si jet joeng* 同是一樣	(same)	(same)
2	*cae loeng cam cong* 淒涼惨愴	(same)	(a) *cae loeng* 淒涼 (b) melodic interlude (c) *cam cong* 惨愴
3	melodic interlude	(a) 4-stroke pattern (b) melodic interlude	(a) 1-stroke pattern (b) 5-stroke pattern (c) melodic interlude
4	*ngo hung wae hung lau peng diu* 我空為紅樓憑弔	(a) (same) (b) melodic interlude	(a) (same) (b) (same)
5	*sey liu ngo bei bou juk* 誰料我比寶玉	(a) (same) (b) melodic interlude	(a) (same)
6	*geng cing soeng* 更情傷	(same)	(a) (same) (b) 1-stroke pattern
7	melodic interlude	(same)	(same)

Table 7.1 Texts and musical materials used in the thirteen divisions of Music Examples 7.1 to 7.3 (cont'd)

Divisions	Music Example 7.1	Music Example 7.2	Music Example 7.3
8	*ley sa sae fung* 淚灑西風	(a) (same) (b) melodic interlude	(a) (same) (b) (same)
9	*gao bet sey cing si man zoeng* 絞不碎情絲萬丈	(a) *gao bet tyn cing si* 絞不斷情絲 (b) melodic interlude (c) *man zoeng* 萬丈	(a) *zin bet dyn cing si* 剪不斷情絲 (b) same (c) same
10	(absent)	4-stroke pattern	(a) 1-stroke pattern (b) 5-stroke pattern
11	melodic interlude	(same)	(same)
12	*hon kem jit ley* 寒衾熱淚	(a) *hon kem jim ley* 寒衾浸淚 (b) melodic interlude	(a) *hon kem jit ley* 寒衾熱淚 (b) (same)
13	*pou hen fong coeng* 抱恨方長	(a) *pou hen* 抱恨 (b) melodic interlude (c) *fong coeng* 方長	(a) *pou hen fong coeng* 抱恨方長 (b) 1-stroke pattern

(line 1: half line)

tung si jet joeng cae loeng cam cong.

同 是 一 樣 淒 涼 慘 愴

It is the same misery and tragedy.

(line 2)

ngo hung wae hung lau peng diu,

我 空 爲 紅 樓 憑 弔

I vainly lament for the red mansion,

sey liu ngo bei Bou-juk geng cing soeng.

誰 料 我 比 寶 玉 更 情 傷

Nobody knows my love is more desperate than that of Bou-juk.

(line 3)

ley sa sae fung, gao bet sey cing si man zoeng.

淚 灑 西 風 絞 不 碎 情 絲 萬 丈

I shed tears in the west wind, I cannot wring the long silken rope of love into pieces.

(line 4)

hon kem jit ley, pou hen fong coeng.

寒 衾 熱 淚 抱 恨 方 長

The warm tears wet my cold quilt; I shall bear regret for a long time.

Music Examples 7.1 and 7.3 start with two short phrases sung to the text *fa jau hen* 花有恨 (the flower regrets) and *jin mou ga* 燕無家 (the swallow is homeless). According to the *kuk*, these are the first two phrases of a line sung rhythmically in the aria type *Fan sin zung ban*;[1] the last two phrases of this line are sung as one phrase in the *Kwen fa* aria type. Beginning with the syllables *tung si jet joeng* 同是一樣 (it is the same), the singers are to begin singing non-metrically. (The singer in Music Example 7.3 starts the non-metrical singing with the syllables *jin mou ga*.) For purposes of comparison, we will consider the *kwen fa* passage that starts with the syllables *tung si jet joeng* in the three music examples. The text preceding these four syllables is not shown in Music Example 7.2.

Musical Structure of *Si gung kwen fa*

The most prominent features of a *kwen fa* passage are the free tempo and non-pulsatory singing. As in other aria types, a *kwen fa* passage is usually composed of one or more couplets; occasionally, only one line is used. However, the passage taken from *The Soul of Jade Pear* has slightly less than two couplets: the first half of the first line is missing because it was originally set to a different aria type.

According to Cen (1952:243), most *si gung kwen fa* passages have seven-syllable lines; each seven-syllable line has two phrases, with four and three syllables respectively. In a special type of *si gung kwen fa*, the two phrases within a line have the same number of syllables (1952:246–47); this type, thus, does not have seven-syllable lines. Except for the padding syllables shown in parentheses in the text below, the *kwen fa* passage in the three music examples has a total of seven phrases, all in four-syllable structure. There are four lines, but the first one is actually a half-line.

Upper line: *FAN SIN ZUNG BAN fa jau hen jin mou ga,*   (3)

                  花　有　恨　燕　無　家

       KWEN FA (tung si jet joeng) cae loeng cam cong.   (2)

            （同　是一　樣）　凄　涼　惨　愴

Lower line: *(ngo hung wae) hung lau peng diu,*   (1)

       （我　空　爲）　紅　樓　憑　弔

       (sey liu ngo bei) Bou-juk (geng) cing soeng.   (1)

      （誰　料我　比）　寶　玉　（更）　情　傷

Upper line: *ley sa sae fung,*   (3)

       淚　灑　西　風

       (gao bet sey) cing si man zoeng.   (2)

      （絞　不　碎）　情　絲　萬　丈

Lower line: *hon kem jit ley,*   (6)

       寒　衾　熱　淚

       pou hen fong coeng.   (1)

       抱　恨　方　長

The arabic numerals at the end of the phrases indicate the cadential pitches (in cipher notation) as performed in the three music examples. Since *The Soul of Jade Pear* is sung by a male character in the play, the passage is known as *Ping hau si gung kwen fa* 平喉士工滾花 (*Si gung kwen fa* sung by a male voice). In *Si gung kwen fa*, the cadential patterns for the male voice differ from those for the female voice: by tradition, the male-voice upper line ends on the pitch *ce* (which is transcribed as the pitch D), and the lower line ends on *sang* (transcribed as C). Comparison of the line-ending notes used in the three music examples with the pattern allowed in tradition categorizes the phrases into upper and lower lines, as shown above.

Melodic interludes precede each of the *Kwen fa* lines. According to Cen (1952:241), six different interludes are used in *Si gung kwen fa*. Though ornaments can be added, each of such interludes has a more or less fixed melody that is identified by their cadential notes. They are given in Music Example 7.5 (see p. 164) in *gung ce*, cipher and staff notations.

Since Music Examples 7.1, 7.2 and 7.3 are all male-voice *Kwen fa* in the mode of *Si gung*, they use only the *sang* and *ce* interludes (see below). The *sang* interlude also often appears as a prelude for a *Kwen fa* passage sung in *Si gung* mode, but in these examples the *Fan sin zung ban* passage connects directly to the *Kwen fa* passage and, thus, no prelude is played.

Besides the fixed melodic interludes, the melodic instrumentalists are responsible for playing interludes that imitate the vocal melodies. This

A closer look at a saxophone player. (8 June 1987, Wun Yiu, New Territories, Hong Kong)

practice is known as *zey hong* 追腔 (chasing the notes in the vocal line) in the profession.

Percussion instruments such as woodblocks, which accompany the singing of metrical types, are not used during the singing of the non-pulsatory *Kwen fa*, except in percussion interludes played on the cymbals, gongs, large woodblock and medium woodblock between phrases and lines. It is a common practice for the percussionists to play the one-stroke pattern after the upper, and the two-stroke pattern after the lower, line.

Obligatory and Optional Accompaniment Practices

The selection of the fixed melodic interlude depends on the final pitch of the vocal line just concluded. If the line ends on the pitch *sang*, a *sang* interlude should precede the next line. The mode of the interlude must be the same as that of the *Kwen fa* passage. In Music Examples 7.1 to 7.3 the melodic accompanists played *sang* interludes of the *Si gung* mode, as appropriate, and not a different mode.[2]

The melodic accompanists pay close attention to the vocal line so they can support it during the singing. In their imitative melodic interludes, the accompanists do not have to imitate the vocal line strictly. As long as the identity of the vocal line is maintained, the melodic accompanists can play a free imitation. Apparently, imitative melodic interludes are not obligatory, and they are not played in Music Example 7.2.

A vocal line begins unaccompanied in its opening syllables, then the accompanists add support towards the end of the line. For instance, in line 2 (divisions 4 to 6) of Music Example 7.2, the melodic instrumentalists play the supporting accompaniment only for the singer's last three syllables. In line 3 (divisions 8 to 9) of the same example, the melodic accompanists support the singer's last two syllables. In Music Example 7.3, the same practice can be seen in divisions 4 to 6, 8 to 9 and 12 to 13. The technique is somewhat different in Music Example 7.1; the musicians start playing the supporting accompaniment after the singer has finished the padding syllables, when he is about to start the main syllables of the phrase. In divisions 8, 12 and 13, the accompanists slightly delay playing the supporting accompaniment.

In the percussion accompaniment for the three music examples, the practice of playing the one-stroke pattern after the upper line and the two-stroke pattern after the lower line is not consistently observed. This practice seems to be optional rather than obligatory.

If there is a break between the vocal passages the instrumentalists must play appropriate percussion and melodic preludes to introduce the singing. The percussion prelude is usually the *mg cey* 五錘 (five-stroke, also known as *Kwen fa*) pattern and the melodic prelude is one of the six fixed melodic interludes. In Music Examples 7.2 and 7.3, four-stroke and five-stroke pattern interludes are played in divisions 3 and 10, to precede lines 2 and 4, but not line 3.

The playing of percussion interludes to precede lines is, in fact, determined by the singer. In practice, the singer indicates the end of a passage of vocal music by singing a more elaborate melody on the last syllable. Thus, at the end of lines 1 and 3 in Music Examples 7.2 and 7.3, both singers showed the *Kwen fa* hand shadow, indicating the continuation of the *Kwen fa* passage and to call for percussion music. Upon seeing the hand shadow, the percussionists played the five-stroke or four-stroke pattern, and then the melodic accompanists followed with the melodic prelude. If a *Kwen fa* passage is to be sung in a relatively faster tempo, the four-stroke pattern is played instead of the five-stroke. The practice of singing the last syllable of a line to an elaborate melody and, thereby, calling for the percussion interlude is often used in an operatic performance, when an actor wants to make stage movements after singing a line of *Kwen fa*. The stage movements are then accompanied by the percussion interlude. In operatic song, while usually no stage movement is required, however, the practice is employed to allow the singer a break.

Line 2 in Music Examples 7.2 and 7.3 ends with only a short melody, which informs the instrumentalists that the singer will continue in *Kwen fa* aria type and does not need a percussion interlude.

Though line 4 ends with an elaborate melody, the singers in examples 7.2 and 7.3 gave the *sau gwet* hand shadow indicating the end of the piece. A one-stroke pattern is played after line 4 in Music Example 7.3. The playing of this pattern to end a song is optional.

Music Example 7.1 contains no percussion preludes and interludes. According to Wong (personal conversation, 22 October 1985), the omission of percussion preludes and interludes in performances of operatic songs is rare. It is occasionally found in commercial recordings, in which the percussion preludes are sometimes shortened, or even omitted, to accommodate the time limit of the tape or record.

To summarize, the obligatory practices in playing accompaniment to *Kwen fa* aria type are as follows:

1. Except after the line that ends a passage, the melodic instrumentalists play the appropriate fixed melodic interlude after each line. The end of a passage may be indicated by the *kuk*, the singing, or hand shadow.
2. Supporting melodic accompaniment should be played at least towards the end of a line. The singer indicates the end of a line by singing the last few syllables to a slightly more elaborate melody.
3. Imitative melodic interludes are not obligatory. However, if they are played, they must maintain the identity of the vocal melody.
4. If a break between the last vocal passage and the coming *kwen fa* passage is required, the singer signals the break either by an elaborate melody on the last syllable of the passage, temporarily stopping, or showing the *Kwen fa* hand shadow. The percussionists play a five-stroke or four-stroke pattern, and the melodic instrumentalists play a melodic prelude before the singer starts singing again.

Improvisatory Practices: Multi-Part Relation and Temporal Aspects

The melodic accompanists of Cantonese operatic music can produce different relationships between the vocal melody and the composite instrumental accompaniment by starting their playing at different points in the piece. Here, the term "multi-part relation" equates with "texture."

The multi-part relation, used in a broad sense, is monophonic in division 1 of Music Examples 7.1 to 7.3. In Music Example 7.2, the voice and instruments are in unison; in the other two examples the voice is unaccompanied. The melodic accompanists can produce a monophonic multi-part relationship by either playing with the vocal line in unison or allowing the singing to be unaccompanied.

Divisions 4 and 5 of Music Example 7.1 show clearly the supporting accompaniment appearing as a free imitation of the vocal melody by the use of rhythmic diminution, with an effect close to the free imitative counterpoint of Western European art music. Yet, conceptually and practically, the melodic instrumentalists only delay the playing of the heterophonic supporting accompaniment for a few notes. We can refer to this relationship as "delayed heterophony."

Divisions 4 and 5 of Music Example 7.2 show a different technique, in which the accompanists wait until the singer ends a phrase before they begin to imitate the vocal melody. Since the instrumental and vocal lines are monophonic in texture but imitatively related, we shall call this type of multi-part relationship "imitative monophony" in the present study. Imitative monophony is not uncommon in Cantonese operatic music, even though the accompanying orchestra is usually composed of more than one melodic instrument, because the accompaniment sometimes is provided by only the leader of the melodic section. Music Example 7.6 (see p. 165), which is transcribed from a live field recording of a performance of the play *Adultery Is the Chief of All Crimes*,[3] shows another use of imitative monophony. The fiddler probably signalled the other melodic accompanists to stop and imitated the vocal melody on his instrument all by himself.

Moments of delayed heterophony also occur in divisions 2, 8, 9, 12 and 13 of Music Example 7.1, but more straightforward heterophony is used towards the ends of divisions 2, 5, 9, 12 and 13, and division 6 is all heterophonic. These examples show that the melodic accompanists often use delayed heterophony at the beginning, and simple heterophony towards the end, of a phrase or line. A similar practice can be seen in division 13 of Music Example 7.2, and divisions 5 to 6, 9 and 13 of Music Example 7.3. However, monophony (in unison) is played towards the end of lines 3 and 4 in divisions 9 and 13 of Music Example 7.2, but imitative monophony is played at the beginning of lines 2 and 3. Thus, the melodic accompanists have the option to choose playing either delayed heterophony or monophony at the beginning of a phrase or line, and heterophony or monophony towards the end of a phrase or line. The different types of multi-part relationship that occur in Music Examples 7.1 to 7.3 are shown in Table 7.2.

Although the accompanists have a certain amount of freedom in choosing the multi-part relation for their accompaniment, they are never conscious of making such a selection. The different multi-part relationships are rather the result of the conscious decisions of when to start playing the supporting accompaniment or imitative melodic interlude. In other words, the different multi-part relationships result from entrances occurring at different points of time. If the accompanists choose to play an imitative melodic interlude after the singer has finished a phrase or fragment, imitative monophonic multi-part relation is produced. If the accompanists choose to support the vocal melody strictly in unison, monophonic multi-

Table 7.2 Types of accompaniment in Music Examples 7.1 to 7.3

Divisions	Music Example 7.1	Music Example 7.2	Music Example 7.3
1	monophony: single line	monophony: 2 identical lines	monophony: single line
2	heterophony delayed heterophony	monophony: 2 identical lines	imitative monophony delayed heterophony
3	FMI*: *ce* interlude	4-stroke pattern FMI: *ce* interlude	1-stroke pattern 5-stroke pattern FMI: *ce* interlude
4	delayed heterophony	imitative monophony	imitative monophony
5	delayed heterophony	imitative monophony	delayed heterophony
6	heterophony	heterophony	delayed heterophony 1-stroke pattern
7	FMI: *sang* interlude	FMI: *sang* interlude	FMI: *sang* interlude

* FMI stands for Fixed Melodic Interlude.

Table 7.2 Types of accompaniment in Music Examples 7.1 to 7.3 (cont'd)

Divisions	Music Example 7.1	Music Example 7.2	Music Example 7.3
8	delayed heterophony	imitative monophony	imitative monophony
9	delayed heterophony heterophony	imitative monophony monophony	delayed heterophony
10	(absent)	4-stroke pattern	1-stroke pattern 5-stroke pattern
11	FMI*: *ce* interlude	FMI: *ce* interlude	FMI: *ce* interlude
12	delayed heterophony	heterophony monophony	imitative monophony
13	delayed heterophony heterophony	imitative monophony monophony	delayed heterophony heterophony 1-stroke pattern

* FMI stands for Fixed Melodic Interlude.

part relation results. The latter multi-part relationship rarely occurs in actual performance, except when a singer accompanies himself. Heterophonic multi-part relationship often results when the instrumentalists choose to play a supporting accompaniment and start playing when the singer starts singing, or one or more notes after the singer has started singing.

These different multi-part relationships are only theoretical; in actual performance, they exist in a continuum and are not distinct from each other. Similarly, the production of different multi-part relationships is unconscious; it is only a by-product of an improvisatory practice. On the other hand, the conscious determination to play an imitative melodic interlude or supporting accompaniment at a particular time, and the selection of tempo for the fixed and imitative melodic interludes, are improvisatory.

Improvisation in the tempo and in the time to start playing is related to the dramatic effect of the text. If the text involves an intense dramatic mood, the imitative and fixed melodic interludes will be played faster, with fewer ornaments added. In such cases, except towards the end of a line, supporting accompaniment is usually not played, and the imitative melodic interlude features a faster, shortened or simplified version of the vocal melody. In Music Example 7.7 (see p. 166), a *Si gung kwen fa* from the play *Adultery Is the Chief of All Crimes*,[4] the imitative melodic interlude begins before the singer has finished the vocal melody. Later, the singer, who in the drama forces his daughter to abandon her lover, a blind man, also starts before the accompanists have finished the interlude. Similar practices can be observed in Music Example 7.8 (see p. 167), from the commercial tape *Dae ney fa* 帝女花 (*The Royal Beauty*), where, dramatically, the actor who portrays the Han prince asks the Manchurian emperor to give in.[5] These recordings illustrate that the more intense the dramatic mood, the faster the tempo taken by the singer and accompanists, resulting in fewer notes in the accompaniment, and less heterophonic multi-part relationship.

Improvisatory Ornamentation

The concept of ornamentation is based on the recognition of a "skeletal melody," with "extra notes" added to it either in writing or improvisation. The study of ornamentation in Cantonese operatic music is difficult because the "skeletal melody," if such a concept does exist in the genre, is often impossible to obtain in any type of vocal or instrumental music. Even with *siu kuk* tunes, which consist of more relatively preexistent melodies than those of aria types and singing narratives, the singers' extensive ornamentation often obscures the "skeletal" version. The published versions of tunes cannot represent the skeletal form because they are often transcriptions of the performed versions. Sometimes they are edited drastically by established players, singers or teachers.

The concept of ornamentation nevertheless exists in Cantonese opera. In percussion music, for example, a gong player plays a five-stroke pattern by hitting the gong five times. Additional strokes are referred to as *fa* 花 (flower); the practice of adding extra strokes is known as *da fa* 打花 (to beat flowers). In vocal and instrumental music, extra notes added to the singing or playing are referred to as *fa jem* 花音 (flower notes) and the addition of such notes is known as *ga fa* 加花 (to add flowers). However, singers and instrumentalists often fail to verbalize the actual uses of *ga fa*, nor can they distinguish between *fa jem* and skeletal notes when they are asked to do so, even with the help of transcriptions.

An experimental approach is employed in this chapter for studying ornamentation used in accompanimental music. Music Example 7.9 (see p. 168) juxtaposes and compares the different versions of the two fixed melodic interludes used in Music Examples 7.1 to 7.3. The *ce* and *sang* skeletal melodies emerge after the extra notes are removed. They correspond to the pitch-contents of the two fixed melodic interludes identified by Cen (1952).

Music Example 7.9 contains twenty-seven uses of ornaments in the fixed melodic interludes. Their effects approximate those of ornaments and non-harmonic tones in Western European music (from which the following terms are borrowed). As shown in Music Example 7.10 (see p. 169), these ornaments include passing tones (five times), tremolos (eight times), escape tones (three times), effects close to acciaccatura (ten times), and one unclassified example. The unclassified ornament (note C in division 7 of Music Example 7.1) might be considered a prolonged escape tone or a long acciaccatura: the note with a dotted quaver appears to be an ornament, but its time value is much longer than the note D in the skeletal melody.

Notes appearing in the imitative melodic interludes and the supporting melodic accompaniment but not in the vocal melodies are also considered ornaments. Music Example 7.11 shows various types of ornaments used in portions of Music Examples 7.1 to 7.3, including acciaccatura, slide, escape tone and tremolo.

Improvisation in the playing of the imitative melodic interlude should also be discussed briefly. The melodic accompanists create free imitative interludes by adding ornaments to the line sung by the vocalist, by omitting the ornaments used in the vocal line, or by repeating the vocal line with certain notes omitted.

Improvisatory Percussion Music

Five examples of *kwen fa* passages in *si gung* mode from the play *Adultery Is the Chief of All Crimes* (Music Examples 7.7, 7.12, 7.13, 7.14 and 7.15)[6] illustrate the percussionists' practice of playing the one-stroke pattern after the upper line of text and the two-stroke pattern after the lower line. Music Examples 7.7 and 7.14 are sung by male voice, Music Examples 7.12, 7.13 and 7.15 by female voice. In Music Example 7.12 (see pp. 171–72), a two-stroke pattern is played after the first line, a lower line according to its cadential note. A long one-stroke pattern is played after the upper line that follows. In addition, a short form of the same pattern appears after both three-syllable fragments within the same line. In a different performance of the passage (not transcribed in this example),[7] imitative melodic interludes were played after both fragments, instead of the one-stroke patterns. These one-stroke patterns in Music Example 7.12 are added improvisatorily by the percussionists. The long unidentified percussion pattern after the *Kwen fa* passage in the same example accompanies stage movements by the female actor. The percussionists, who pay close attention to the actions onstage, improvisatorily determine the number of repetitions of the fragments in the pattern.

In Music Example 7.13 (see p. 173), the one-stroke pattern is played after the *Kwen fa* line, an upper line according to its cadential note. Music Example 7.14 (see p. 174) starts with a lower line followed by the two-stroke pattern, and ends with an upper line and the one-stroke pattern. Music Example 7.15 (see p. 175) contains only an upper line. The one-stroke pattern follows the first sung phrase and the end of the line.

To summarize, then, the playing of one-stroke and two-stroke patterns after the upper and lower lines respectively is common, but is neither obligatory nor improvisatory. However, percussionists can add short patterns such as the one-stroke to enhance the dramatic effect within a line; and fragments within a certain percussion pattern can be improvisatorily repeated.

Notes

1. As mentioned in Chapter 5, the metrical concept and practice in Cantonese operatic music are unlike that of Western art music. The rhythmic singing here does not follow a strong-and-weak pattern of accents.

2. In *Kwen fa* singing of a different mode, a different set of fixed melodic interludes is used. For example, for a *sang* interlude in *Si gung kwen fa*, the accompanists would not play the interlude that belongs to the system of *Ji wong kwen fa* (*Kwen fa* in *Ji wong* mode). The *sang* interlude of *Ji wong kwen fa* is composed of this succession of pitches: DGBAC.

3. The play was performed by the Sen Ma 新馬 (new horse) Cantonese Opera Troupe led by the renowned actor Sen Ma Si-zeng 新馬師曾 on 15 November 1984 in the Sunbeam Theatre. The music example is transcribed from a live recording of the performance that I made.

4. Ibid.

5. The excerpt was sung by Jem Gim-fae 任劍輝 , Hong Kong Crown Records (n.d., no tape number given).

6. Sen Ma Cantonese Opera Troupe, 15 November 1984 (see Note 3 above).

7. The commercial tape contains operatic excerpts from the play *Adultery Is the Chief of All Crimes* sung by Sen Ma Si-zeng and Ng Gwen-lae 吳君麗 , Hong Kong Wing Cheung Records Co., TL-1002 (n.d.).

Music Example 7.1 *Kwen fa* passage of *Juk lei wen*, sung by Sit Gok-sin

Music Example 7.1 *Kwen fa* passage of *Juk lei wen*, sung by Sit Gok-sin (cont'd)

Music Example 7.2 *Kwen fa* passage of *Juk lei wen,* sung by
Wong Jyt-seng

Music Example 7.2 *Kwen fa* passage of *Juk lei wen*, sung by
Wong Jyt-seng (cont'd)

Music Example 7.3 *Kwen fa* passage of *Juk lei wen*, sung by Deng Juk-fae

Music Example 7.3 *Kwen fa* passage of *Juk lei wen*, sung by
Deng Juk-fae (cont'd)

Music Example 7.3 *Kwen fa* **passage of** *Juk lei wen*, **sung by**
Deng Juk-fae (cont'd)

Music Example 7.4 Method of notating a composite line

Music Example 7.5 Fixed melodic interludes used in *Si gung kwen fa*

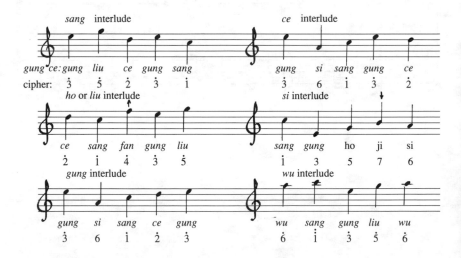

Music Example 7.6   Vocal passage using imitative monophonic multi-part relationship

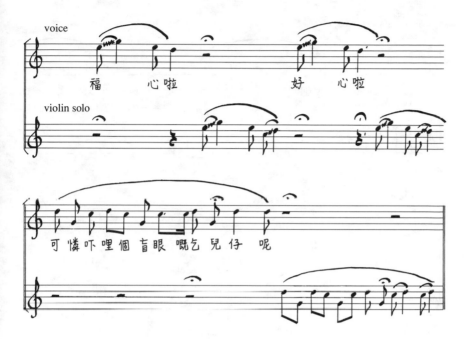

Music Example 7.7 *Si gung kwen fa* **passage from** *Adultery Is the Chief of All Crimes*

Music Example 7.8 *Si gung kwen fa* passage from *The Royal Beauty*

Music Example 7.9 Different versions and skeletal melodies in
the fixed melodic interludes

Music Example 7.10 Ornaments used in the fixed melodic interludes

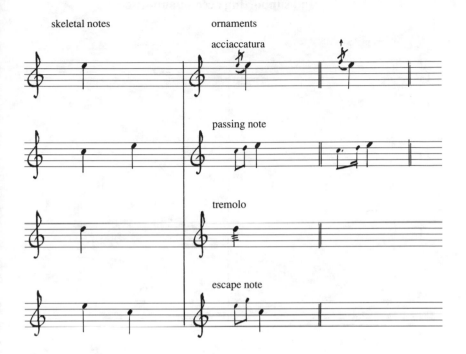

Music Example 7.11 Ornaments used in the imitative melodic interludes
and supporting accompaniment

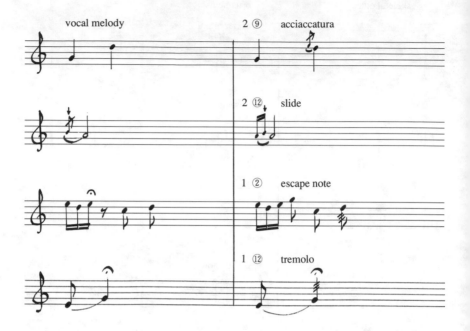

Music Example 7.12 *Si gung kwen fa* **passage from** *Adultery Is the Chief of All Crimes*

Music Example 7.12 *Si gung kwen fa* **passage from** *Adultery Is the Chief of All Crimes* (cont'd)

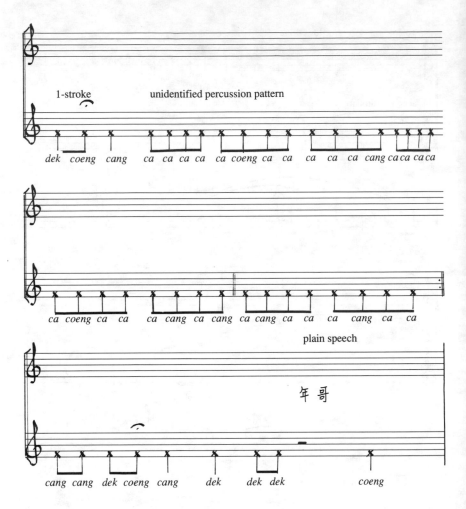

Music Example 7.13 *Si gung kwen fa* passage from *Adultery Is the Chief of All Crimes*

Music Example 7.14 *Si gung kwen fa* **passage from** *Adultery Is the Chief of All Crimes*

Music Example 7.15 *Si gung kwen fa* **passage from** *Adultery Is the Chief of All Crimes*

8. Improvisation in Singing

Improvisation in vocal music exists at both the macro and micro levels. The improvisatory practices at the macro level include addition and deletion of vocal passages and replacement of oral delivery. Improvisatory practices of musical details—micro improvisation—include pitch selection in realizing the vocal melody, adding melismas, ornamentation, the replacement of syllables, adding and deleting *lap zi* 擸字 (grasp syllables), and deleting vocal phrases and lines.

Addition of Vocal Passages

Vocal passages are often added to the prescribed text in a performance of Cantonese opera to prolong a scene or to allow for behind the scenes activities. Music Example 8.1 (see pp. 200 202), a passage of the aria type *Gam zi fu jung* 減字芙蓉 (abbreviated *Fu jung*) from a performance of the play *Blood Shed for the Woman Who Caused the Fall of the Nation*,[1] appeared in a scene towards the end of Act V and involved the son of the general and his maid. The male actor, as the son, showed the hand shadow for *dik dik* 的的 and sang the passage *Gam zi fu jung* with the maid. After the performance, the fiddler told me that the vocal passage was added to the scene to allow enough time for the principal female role actor to change costume before her entrance at the beginning of the next act.

Music Example 8.2 (see pp. 203–11) transcribes a long passage of the aria type *Cet zi cing* 七字清 (seven-word air), from a performance of *The Courtship of the Phoenix by the Side of Lake Peach Blossom*.[2] A long passage of patter speech (discussed in Chapter 9) was also improvised before the addition of this *Cet zi cing* passage. According to the comic role actor who initiated both passages, they were added to prolong the performance and satisfy the enthusiastic audience.

The police authorities at Happy Valley, where this performance took place, had originally allowed the troupe to perform until 11 p.m. (Police authorities have the right to determine when performances of this kind should end, so as to make sure that the music and noise will not disturb the neighbourhood.) Since this was the last performance of the ritual series, the *zy wui* requested the police to grant approval for prolonging the performance by ten to fifteen minutes. During the final act, a representative of the *zy wui* notified the troupe that they were permitted to lengthen the play.

Towards the end of the act, while the major characters of the play were on stage ready to uncover the one who had had a secret affair with the younger sister (played by the supporting female role actor) of the empress (played by the principal female role actor), the comic role actor showed a

The principal male and female actors in a duet from the play *The Courtship of the Phoenix by the Side of Lake Peach Blossom*. (19 April 1987, Po Toi Island, Hong Kong)

Pok deng ngo hand shadow and started a long passage of patter speech, in which all the major role actors onstage participated. In the last segment of this passage, the comic role actor showed a *Zung ban* 中板 hand shadow and started the *Cet zi cing* passage, in which the military role actor, the supporting male role actor, the principal female role actor, the supporting female role actor and the principal male role actor each sang a segment. The principal male actor then connected his *Cet zi cing* segment to a line of *Si gung kwen fa* 士工滾花 .

Music Example 8.2a (see pp. 203–5) shows the vocal melody, but the plain speech and the melodic accompaniment to the singing are omitted. A translation of the text, including that of the spoken segments, is given in Music Example 8.2b (see pp. 206–10).

An actor communicates with the accompanying instrumentalists and his fellow actors by using the appropriate hand shadow and gestic hint so that no confusion results from his improvisation. Analysis of Music Examples 8.1 and 8.2 shows that there are structural devices in oral deliveries to indicate the ending of a segment, so that another actor can follow with a new segment in time. In Music Example 8.2, the final syllables in the various segments are all sung to melismas that last from two to three quarter notes. As in other aria types, the relatively longer melismas are used to indicate the end of a segment. In addition to this, in *Cet zi cing* aria type singing, while normally the fourth syllable should be placed on the upbeat, the same syllable of a segment's last line is always sung on the beat, and is followed by a rest of one quarter note or slightly less. This device is clearly shown in the segment sung by the military role actor in Music Example 8.2c (see p. 211): with the padding, nonsense and particle syllables put in parentheses, the fourth structural syllable *ming* 明 (clear) in the last line is sung on the beat, then followed by a quarter note rest. In this same line, a melisma that lasts for two quarter notes is set to the last syllable *siu* 笑 (to laugh). This technique is also employed in the following three segments.

Since the melodic interludes in *Siu kuk* passages have definite but usually short duration, it is uncommon for singers to add speech or stage movements when such interludes are being played. In the performance represented by Music Example 8.1 (which is an aria type), the addition of spoken words within the sung vocal passage did not disturb the playing of the interlude. During the singing, the instrumentalists closely observed, and listened to, the singer. They understood that the singer would normally start singing a line on the strong beat after the short instrumental interlude of four quarter notes. But, when the singer did not start on the strong beat, choosing instead to speak or make stage movements, the fiddler began the short interlude on the upbeat to accompany the speech or stage movements. The interlude was repeated somewhat like an ostinato until the actor resumed singing.

The stylistic characteristic of setting the last syllable of a segment to a relatively longer melisma, and the repetition of a short instrumental interlude that starts with the upbeat, all facilitate the improvised addition of vocal passages in the tradition of Cantonese opera.

Deletion of Vocal Passages

Deletion of a single vocal passage within a scene or act is not commonly found in operatic performances, but complete acts can be cancelled. Even when an actor fails to remember the text of a vocal passage, usually he can still recall part of the lyrics and deliver it in speech. This is a kind of wrap-up used to cover up an actor's memory lapse, problem or mistake. One example occurred in the 1985b performance of the play *The Swallow Returns* (see below and Note 11). During the second scene of Act I, the comic role actor omitted the sung passage of the *Coeng gey kwen fa* 長句滾花 aria type, but delivered some of the text in a passage of plain speech. This use of improvisation can be considered either a deletion of a vocal passage (or part of one) or the employment of a different oral delivery.

Replacement of Oral Delivery

Chapter 4 has already discussed the way in which the text of a certain patternized episode can be presented in different forms of oral delivery. Usually a singer chooses an appropriate form of oral delivery during his performance and shows hand shadows to inform the accompanists and fellow performers of his choice. Traditional Cantonese opera allows a singer to use the text as written, but to employ an aria type, singing narrative or speech delivery not suggested by the script. The singer often adds or deletes syllables to fit the chosen form of presentation.

Fieldwork research in modern opera and operatic song performances in Hong Kong can rarely find improvisatory replacement of oral delivery. The operatic song instructor at The Chinese University of Hong Kong, Wong Jyt-seng, said that this practice was widely used from the 1930s to 1950s when Cantonese operatic song reached its peak of popularity in Hong Kong and in Saigon (now officially known as Ho Chi Minh City), Vietnam. During this period, tea houses staged daily singing sessions and singers were hired for private gatherings and banquets. For each such performance, several different singers, mostly female, were hired, each of them responsible for one or two operatic songs in a session. Female professional singers were referred to, then as now, as *ney ling* 女伶 (female artiste) in Hong Kong.

According to Wong, Saigon became the centre of operatic song after the Japanese invasion and occupation of Hong Kong in December 1941. During this period, he taught operatic singing and played professionally in singing sessions and night clubs in Saigon. Singers took lessons before, and during, their professional careers and were always eager to learn songs that had become popular in the city through commercial recordings and radio broadcasting.

In those days, teachers of operatic songs often hired transcribers to write out the text, names of oral deliveries and certain musical notation of the popular repertory as *kuk* for teaching purposes. In order to maximize their profit, transcribers often sold the same *kuk* to several teachers, who then had to adjust some of the contents of the *kuk* to ensure that their students' singing would vary from other singers. During a performance, a singer had to be prepared to sing a variety of songs, because the ones she had planned to sing might have already been performed by the previous singers. Further, to avoid comparison, a singer would refrain from using an oral delivery that had been employed several times by other performers in the same session, even if in different songs with different texts. Thus, every singer had to learn a wide repertory, besides singing minor variations, to cope with the stiff competition among singers and teachers.

Singing teachers gave intensive training to their students in improvisatory practices. Among the various techniques, the ability to choose alternative aria types for those given in the *kuk* was regarded as very important.

The improvisatory practice of replacing an aria type with another is seldom known among singers in modern Hong Kong: the number of tea houses that stage operatic song singing is on the decline, and the audience's taste has changed. The listeners nowadays have more exposure to commercial recordings than live performances, and are probably less demanding than the audiences of the 1930s to the 1950s. In the 1980s, Cantonese operatic song singing had become essentially an amateur activity.

The adoption of an alternative oral delivery was witnessed twice during fieldwork for this study, on both occasions in comic episodes of opera performances. The first was in a performance of the play *Adultery Is the Chief of All Crimes*.[3] In a scene where the script instructed the comic role actor to sing a passage of *Muk jy*, he, who had already appeared onstage, told the musical accompanists loudly that he did not have to sing what the script prescribed, but would sing a passage of *Lung zau* 龍舟 instead; he then proceeded to do so.[4]

The second occurrence was in a ritual performance of the same play.[5] In a scene after the comic role actor had sung two syllables, *ngo soeng* 我想 (I think), the instrumentalists played an imitative interlude, and another actor onstage interrupted the comic role actor and asked him what he was thinking. Using plain speech, the comic role actor loudly complained about the interruption and questioned the instrumentalists as to why they played the imitative interlude as if they accompanied the *Zung ban* aria type. He said he was not going to sing *Zung ban* but would sing a passage of *Muk jy* instead, and then did so.

Most of the other examples of this improvisatory practice collected for the present study occurred not in live performances, but in the Cantonese operatic singing classes taught by Wong at the Music Department, The Chinese University of Hong Kong. I attended these classes from September 1984 to May 1985, and from October to December 1985. The discussion here would, thus, reflect the more theoretical and academic aspects rather than the practical ones.

Music Example 8.3a (see p. 212) shows the text and rhythmic notation written in the *kuk* of the song *Lau toi wui zi zey zau* 樓台會之醉酒 (the *Drunk* Episode from *Story of the Butterfly Lovers*). Music Example 8.3b (see p. 213) transcribes Wong's singing of the *Cet zi cing* and *Si gung kwen fa* passages as prescribed in the *kuk*. Music Example 8.4 (see p. 214) illustrates how a singer can use the *Si gung kwen fa* aria type to sing the text that are originally set to the *Cet zi cing* aria type, and later use plain speech to deliver the text that are originally set to *Si gung kwen fa*. The singer must indicate his intentions. Before starting to sing the first three lines in *Kwen fa*, he has to show the *Kwen fa* hand shadow to call for the appropriate percussion pattern and melodic prelude, which are, however, omitted from the music example. After the *Kwen fa* lines, he has to show a *sau gwet* hand shadow to stop the accompanying music before he begins his speech delivery (see Chapter 6).

The time duration of Music Example 8.4 is slightly longer than that of Music Example 8.3b. If the singer wishes to prolong this passage even further, he can use the aria type *Ji wong lau sey ban* (abbreviated as *Ji lau*). Since it is common practice for instrumentalists to play a longer prelude and interludes in this aria type, the overall time duration is longer. Music Example 8.5 (see p. 215) shows the singing of the first line in *Ji lau*, but omits the opening percussion pattern, the melodic prelude and the supporting melodic accompaniment.

Music Example 8.6a (see p. 216) illustrates the use of poetic and plain speech to deliver the same text; Music Example 8.6b (see p. 216) shows this text as performed in poetic speech and *Si gung kwen fa*. Passages of poetic speech often have an even number of lines. If only two lines are used in such a passage, the first one has to end with a syllable in an oblique tone, and the second one has to end in an even tone (see Note 6). If an actor chooses to deliver the text in poetic speech, this performance practice causes him to handle the text of the script in a special way: to reverse the order of the opening two lines and omit the third one.

The particle "*a*," which appears in both Music Examples 8.6a and 8.6b, has two uses. When a spoken passage is coming to an end, but is not connected to a singing passage, the "*a*" syllable has to be delivered before the last syllable of the spoken passage to notify the accompanists that they do not have to play music after the speech. If a spoken passage is connected to a singing passage, it has to be uttered after the last syllable of the speech to notify the accompanists that they have to get ready to play the supporting accompaniment. No percussion pattern or melodic prelude will be performed if the singer does not show an appropriate hand shadow. The *Kwen fa* in Music Example 8.6b is a "bald" passage (see Chapter 5).

An oral delivery chosen to replace the one suggested by the script must have a textual structure compatible to that of the script's text. In theory, an oral delivery structured in seven-syllable lines can be replaced by any other oral delivery that also has seven syllables in each line; the same applies for oral deliveries with ten-syllable lines. In fact, however, while aria types with seven-syllable lines are all structured into two-phrase lines and the phrases have four and three syllables respectively (Yung, 1981:673), aria types that have ten-syllable lines do not always have the same number of phrases nor are the phrases of equal length. For example, each line in the aria type "abbreviated *fu jung*" has two phrases and each phrase has five syllables. The ten-syllable lines in *Fan sin zung ban* have four phrases, which have three, three, two and two syllables respectively. Hence, a singer who applies the improvisatory practice of replacement of oral delivery for aria types of ten-syllable lines has to consider both the number of phrases and syllables per phrase in each line.

Within this practice singers need not adjust the verse structure of the text at the end of the lines. The placement of the rhyming syllables as well as the line-ending syllables (which have to follow the rules of linguistic tones) are basically the same among all of the commonly used oral deliveries that have the same number of syllables and the same number of phrases in each line. The singer only has to adjust the line-ending notes, and sing the vocal melodies in the chosen mode.

Operatic song employs the same techniques for substituting oral delivery. The song *Gwae jyn* 歸怨 (*Resentment of Return*) has an excerpt of two lines, each having two phrases, and each phrase having four and six syllables respectively. While the original type of oral delivery set for the text is not known, a singer can treat the syllables and phrases with a certain degree of flexibility and sing the text in several different aria types, according to Wong.

Music Example 8.7a (see p. 217) transcribes Wong's demonstration of singing the text in aria type *ji wong man ban* with eight-syllable lines. There are three phrases in each line of this kind of *ji wong man ban*; in the first line the four syllables *kuk gei* 曲寄 (to send a song) and *zing jen* 征人 (the person in the battle) are sung as the first phrase, *fen fu* 吩咐 (to order) are sung as padding syllables, and the last four syllables *Hung Kiu* 洪喬 (the name of a person) and *fong bin* 方便 (to help) are sung as two phrases respectively. A similar grouping of syllables is used in the second line. The first line ends with the syllable *bin* 便 , which belongs to the oblique tone and ends on the note *sang* (transcribed as C); the second line ends with the syllable *min* 綿 , which belongs to the even tone and ends on the note *ho* (transcribed as G), to conform to the line-ending pattern of the aria type. In this example, the first and second lines are sung as an upper and lower line respectively.

If this same text were to be sung in the aria type *Fan sin zung ban* in ten-syllable lines, the singer would then have to change the original textual structure. For *Fan sin zung ban*, he would add a three-syllable phrase to the beginning of both lines, making four phrases with three, three, two and two syllables respectively in each line. Music Example 8.8 (see p. 219) shows the demonstration sung by Wong. The first phrase of the upper line, *bik wen tin* 碧雲天 (a sky with blue cloud), is added to the original text. The second syllable *gei* 寄 (to send) in the second phrase, and the first two syllables of the following phrase, *fen fu* (to order), are sung as padding (or grasp) syllables. Similarly, the first phrase of the lower line, composed of the syllables *tan jen seng* 嘆人生 (to sigh for life), is added to the original text. The second syllable *cey* 隨 (to follow) in the second phrase is sung as a padding syllable; the following two syllables, *ding gao* 定敎 (will certainly), are also treated as padding syllables.

The text of the excerpt can also be sung to the aria types *Ji wong kwen fa* and *Si gung kwen fa* without modification of the textual structure. Though the two aria types often appear in lines of seven syllables, they are in free tempo and so the number of syllables in each line is often flexible. Music Examples 8.9 (see p. 220) and 8.10 (see p. 221) show the demonstration sung by Wong in these two aria types respectively. In Music Example 8.9a (see p. 220), a relatively more elaborate melody is sung to the last syllable of the passage to notify the accompanists and fellow singers or actors that the passage is approaching its end. If there is at least one line of the same aria type following the syllable *min* (long lasting), a less elaborate melody will be sung to the syllable, as shown in Music Example 8.9b (see p. 220). As their names indicate, the main difference between the two aria types lies in the modes used. *Ji wong kwen fa* uses a combination of two hexatonic modes that is similar to a heptatonic scale in sound. *Si gung kwen fa* uses basically a pentatonic mode, but allows other notes to appear for passing or decorating effect (see Chapter 5). Other differences include the line-ending-note patterns and the use of particular melismas in the singing.

Vocal Improvisation in *Si gung kwen fa*

A comparison of various performances of the same opera text reveals variants attributable to improvisation. Alteration of musical details—micro-improvisation—is discussed here with the transcriptions of free-tempo aria type, an aria type with a regular pulse, and a *Siu kuk* passage.

Si gung kwen fa is a free-tempo aria type. Three different versions of a *si gung kwen fa* passage from the operatic song *The Soul of Jade Pear*, performed by three different singers, are transcribed in Music Example 8.11 (see pp. 222–24 and Chapter 7 for the performance contexts). The three versions are vertically juxtaposed, omitting the accompaniment, to reveal the variants. The pitches sung in each of the versions do not differ drastically from other versions except in the relatively longer melismas that are located mostly at the end of a phrase or line. The melodic lines in the three versions sometimes also differ in the use of ornaments.

Since the singers did not use musical notation during the performance and no "pre-meditation" on the use of pitches was made by Wong and Deng before their performances, the differences in singing were essentially the result of improvisation. Because it is not known whether preparation of this kind was made before the recording of Sit's version, it is difficult to estimate the role of improvisation in this performance.

The realization of the vocal melody is itself an improvisatory practice. The singer has to determine continuously the pitch for each syllable or melisma. In *Kwen fa* singing, most of the syllables are sung syllabically, except for melismas on syllables at the end of a line. In other aria types, melismas connect one syllable to another, or to the line-ending note.

According to Yung (1989:83–86), while there is no absolute match between the linguistic tones and the melodic pitches, melodic aspects such as tonal inflection, duration, pitch levels and melodic contours are directly related to the linguistic tones of the text.

In the Cantonese operatic profession, the practice of realizing the melodic tones based on the syllables' linguistic tonal properties is known as *men zi lo hong* 問字攞腔 (to derive pitches from the syllables) and *ji zi heng hong* 依字行腔 (to determine pitches by following the syllables), though singers never analytically conceptualize the role of linguistic tones and the overall creative process. A singing style is called *Lou zi* 露字 (displaying the syllables or words), if the meaning of the sung syllables are easily understood by the listeners. Analysis shows that *Lou zi* can only be achieved by projecting the tonal inflections of the sung syllables in the vocal melodies. In the tradition, it is widely accepted that a good singer should maintain this kind of style in the singing of all types of music and *Lou zi* is taken as one of the essential elements in a good style of singing.

Music Example 8.12 (see pp. 225–26) shows the pitches chosen by each of the singers to enunciate the syllables in the three versions of *Si gung kwen fa*, shown in Music Example 8.11. Ornaments close in effect to acciaccatura appear in Music Example 8.12, prompted by the linguistic tonal inflection of the syllables. Among the eleven occurrences of these ornaments in the example, nine are descending ones used for enunciating syllables that have a descending tonal inflection; one descending ornament enunciates a syllable with a level tonal inflection; and one ascending ornament is set to a syllable with descending tonal inflection.

Table 8.1 shows the nine tones and tonal symbols in the Cantonese dialect. As explained by Yung (1989:158–59), the vertical line of the tonal symbols represents a pitch axis, which is divided into five pitch levels, 1 to 5. The horizontal and slanted lines, as well as the dots, represent the tonal inflections. For example, the tonal symbol " ˥ " designates a linguistic tone that starts at pitch level 5 and descends to level 3,[6] and this tonal inflection is also represented by a pair of arabic numerals: 53. In Music Example 8.12, tonal symbols and arabic numerals under each of the syllables show their linguistic tones. It is evident that the linguistic tonal contour of the text, which is formed by joining the tonal inflections of the syllables, is basically the same as the three melodic contours. The similarity of the two contours demonstrates that, except in some spots, a *Lou zi* effect is generally achieved in the three versions.

Table 8.1 Linguistic tonal symbols of the Cantonese dialect

upper even	upper rising	upper going	upper entering
˥	˧˥	˧	˙˥
53	35	33	5
			middle entering
			˙
			3
lower even	lower rising	lower going	lower entering
˩	˨˧	˨	˙˨
21	23	22	2

Excluding ornaments, each of the versions in Music Example 8.12 contains forty-three notes, which are numbered for easy reference in the following discussion. Except for notes 29, 31 and 38, each is associated with a single syllable used in all of the three versions. At note 29, Versions 1 and 2 have the syllable *gao* 絞 (to cut repeatedly) but Version 3 has *zin* 剪 (to scissor); the two syllables are sung to the same linguistic tone. At note 31, the performers of Versions 2 and 3 sing the syllable 斷 (cut or broken) to the linguistic tones 23 and 22 respectively. This is because, in everyday Cantonese speech, the syllable is spoken in two different ways: *tyn* with linguistic tone 23 and *dyn* with linguistic tone 22. Version 1 at the same note has the syllable *sey* 碎 (broken in fragments), which has a similar meaning to *tyn*. In the other instance, at note 38, Versions 1 and 3 have the syllable *jit* 熱 (hot), instead of *jim* 染 (to wet) as used in Version 2.

Among the three versions, twenty-six of the forty-three pitches are identical, and seventeen are different. Of this latter group, three (notes 39, 42 and 43) differ in the use of ornaments. The differences in these pitches show that a singer has some degree of flexibility in the choice of the pitches even when the tonal inflections of the text have to be taken into consideration.

The sixteen pitches that vary in the versions of this example are all within a minor third with note 37 as an exception, where a perfect fourth interval occurs. Thus, although the actual pitch content differs in the three versions, they all have the same melodic contour.

The use of melisma in the three versions can be seen in Music Example 8.13 (see pp. 227–229), which compares all syllables sung to more than one note. In the profession, multiple notes sung to one syllable are known as *hong* 腔 (notes). Since the term "melisma" in Western music usually refers to a group of more than two notes, the melodic fragments listed in Music Example 8.13 are better referred to as *hong*. In the music example, single notes with stems in parentheses are not *hong*, but are provided for reference; notes in parentheses, but without stems, are notes that the *hong* connect to. When the *hong* occurs at the end of a line, the last note of the line is part of the *hong*; as mentioned above, in *Si gung kwen fa* singing, the male-voice singer has to end the upper line with the note D and end the lower line on C. (*Hong* made up only of ornaments are not listed in the music example as they have already been discussed above.)

The overall melodic contours of the *hong* are related to the notes that they connect to. For example, in *hong* 12, the syllable *geng* 更 is sung on the note B and connects to a G; in its descending melodic contour, an A fills in between the two notes. More often the direction of the melodic contour is not so straightforward, but the *hong* still leads towards the connecting note. *Hong* 15 has an arch shape, leading from the enunciation pitch G to a C, but first outlining a fifth and filling in all the notes except the C.

Of the thirty-five *hong* listed in Music Example 8.13, twenty-four have melodic contours derived from the melodic direction between the enunciation notes and the notes they connect to.[7] *Hong* 18, 19, 20, 30, 31 and 32 have melodic contours related to both the connecting notes and the tonal inflections of the syllables. Among the other eleven *hong*, four have melodic contours related only to the linguistic tonal inflections of the syllables sung to the enunciation notes.[8] For example, in *hong* 5, the syllable *cam* 慘 has a tonal inflection of 35, so an ascending *hong* is sung.

The seven remaining *hong* have melodic contours independent of the notes they connect to and the tonal inflections of the syllables.[9] Three of these (*hong* 33, 34 and 35) are on the last syllable of a passage, where the singers follow the practice of singing a relatively more elaborate *hong*.

Vocal Improvisation in *Ji wong man ban*

Ji wong man ban is a commonly used aria type that has a relatively steady pulse and is regulated by the rhythmic pattern of "one *ban* and three *ding*" (see Chapter 5). It falls into three categories according to the number of syllables and their placement patterns in the lines. In its *coeng gey* 長句 (extended line) form, two of the phrases within the line can be repeated an indefinite number of times in theory, but usually one to three times in practice. It is often connected to another form that has eight structural-syllables in each line. The third form of *Ji wong man ban* has ten-syllable lines and it is rarely used in contemporary Cantonese operatic performances.

Music Example 8.14 (see pp. 230–42) juxtaposes four versions of a *Ji wong man ban* passage sung by Jem Bing-ji 任冰兒 who is one of the most active actresses in the supporting female role in Hong Kong.[10] As this discussion aims at exploring the micro-improvisation employed by a singer in singing different versions of the same vocal passage, transcription of the accompaniment are not shown in the music examples to avoid complication.

The passage is composed of two lines: the first one is set to the form of *coeng gey* and the second is in an eight-syllable structure. According to the rhyming scheme of the two ending syllables, where the first one is in an even and the second in an oblique tone, the first line is a lower and the second an upper line. The two lines also follow the usual line-ending pattern of *Ji wong man ban*, such that the first one ends on G and the second on C.

While there are five factors that define an aria type, the structure of *Ji wong man ban* can best be identified by its patterns of syllable placement. Figure 8.1a gives the pattern of the *coeng gey* form and Figure 8.1b gives that of the eight-syllable form, with arabic numerals indicating the positions and order of the structural syllables. The roman numerals in the figure stand for the order of phrases in the syllable-placement scheme.

In the *coeng gey* form, there is a minimum of seven phrases, and additional structural syllables can be set to the sub-pattern formed by joining phrases III and IV. For example, in Music Example 8.14a (see pp. 230–34), both phrases 3 to 4 and 5 to 6 are set to the sub-pattern, but phrase III or IV would not be repeated individually.

Figure 8.1a Syllable placement patterns of *Coeng gey ji wong man ban*

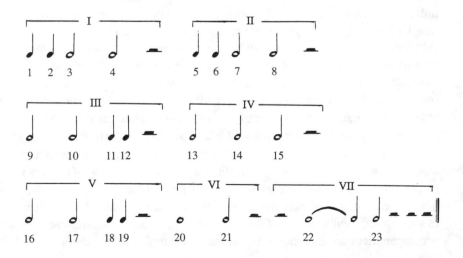

Figure 8.1b Syllable placement patterns of eight-syllable
Ji wong man ban

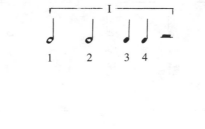

Figure 8.2 illustrates the syllable placement of the nine phrases from line 1 of Version 1 as shown in Music Example 8.14b (see pp. 234–42), with the padding and nonsense syllables in parentheses. The arabic numerals represent the order of phrases that appear in the music example.

With roman numerals standing for each of the phrases within the syllable-placement pattern, the *Coeng gey* line in the music example is represented by this sequence: I II III IV III IV V VI VII, where the sub-phrase of III plus IV is repeated once.

As a flexible number of structural syllables can be accommodated in a *Coeng gey* line, the form often appears in a single line. If other dramatic ideas are to be expressed within the same vocal passage, the *Coeng gey* line is often connected to another line of *Ji wong man ban* that has an eight-syllable structure. Since the syllable-placement scheme in phrases V to VII of the former is exactly the same as that of phrases I to III of the latter, the transition always takes place smoothly.

As shown in Figure 8.2, though most of the structural syllables follow the placement pattern, there are, however, two exceptions. Both the syllables *kei* 其 (in phrase 2 of line 1) and *loeng* 梁 (in phrase 6 of line 1) are

**Figure 8.2 Syllable placement of line 1 from version 1 of
Music Example 8.14**

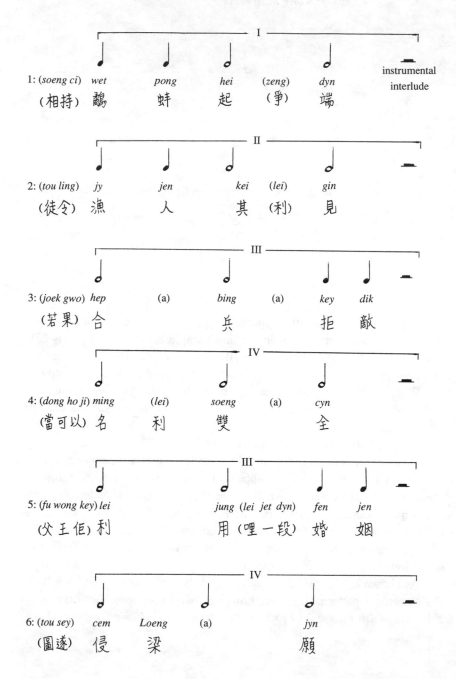

Figure 8.2 Syllable placement of line 1 from version 1 of Music Example 8.14 (cont'd)

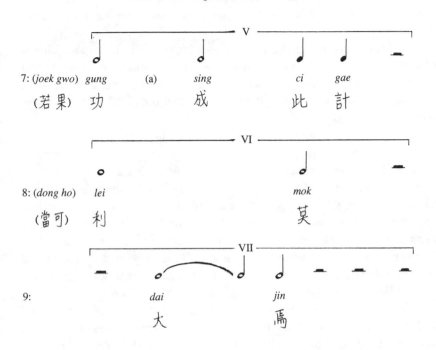

sung on the upbeat, and the singer delayed *kei*, but anticipated *loeng*. Further, as Music Example 8.14 shows, the same syllables in the other three versions are handled in the same way.

Besides the manner of handling the two syllables mentioned above, the four versions also share some obvious similarities including the number of syllables in each phrase and line, the overall syllable placement, the rhyming scheme, the style of accompaniment (which is not shown in the transcription), the use of the G-heptatonic mode, and the overall meaning of the text. The first five factors are responsible for maintaining the identity of the aria type, and the last factor enables the four versions to serve the same dramatic function within the same scene. An example of textual deviation, however, occurs in phrases 2 to 3 in line 1 of Version 2, where, semantically, the text deals with "receiving the state guests" rather than the "sheer infatuation." Above all, among the 12 phrases shown in Music Example 8.14b, the four versions sound most alike in phrases 1, 2 and 6 of line 1.

The obvious differences noticed in the four versions include the tempo, the use of ornaments, and the relative duration of some notes and rests. Phrase 2 of line 2 of the various versions shows the most prominent difference.

The deviations in the choice of notes have much to do with the choice of syllables. Pitch-difference of this type can take place on an individual syllable level or a phrase level. Music Examples 8.15 (see p. 243) and 8.16 (see pp. 244–46) respectively give fragments that suggest deviations of this type on both levels.

Several other fragments demonstrate that, in handling the four versions, the singer can choose different notes for the same syllables. Some of these deviations are produced by the adding of notes that are of an ornamental nature, as in Music Example 8.17 (see p. 247), but others, as shown in Music Example 8.18 (see p. 248), can only be described by taking into consideration the combined role of time duration, ornament and other factors. For example, the pitch difference between Versions 1 and 3 in fragment *a* of Music Example 8.17 can only be explained by the use of ornament, but note-sustaining certainly plays a part in producing the deviation between Versions 1 and 4 in fragment *f* of Music Example 8.18.

The third type of difference, as shown in Music Example 8.19 (see p. 249), is that of syllables that are set to the same notes in different versions. Evidently, this is only possible when the different syllables or sequence of syllables share the same linguistic tone or sequence of linguistic tones, so that the linguistic tonal inflections would not be violated when the different syllables or sequence of syllables are sung to the same notes or sequence of notes. For example, the linguistic tones of the two syllables *sem* 心 (in fragment *c* of Version 1) and *ben* 賓 (in fragment *c* of Version 2) are both well projected, though they are both set to the note E, because they belong to the same tonal category of upper even. Similarly, the two sequences of syllables in Versions 2 and 3 of fragment *a* can be sung to the same succession of notes because they share the same sequence of linguistic tones. On the other hand, the sequence of syllables in Versions 1 and 3 of fragment *b* does not share the same sequence of linguistic tones, but the tonal levels of the two linguistic tones (lower entering and lower going) are so similar that setting them to the same pitches is possible.

Besides the third type, the first two types of deviations in notes or syllables within the various versions of the same passage can also be discussed from the aspect of linguistic tone. For example, the two different *hong* used in Versions 1 and 4 in fragment *d* of Music Example 8.15 are created respectively from the two syllables *soeng* and *ho*. Because the former syllable is in an upper even tone, which has a descending tonal inflection from level 5 to 3, the singer chose a straight descending *hong* to project the syllable. In contrast, an ascending melodic motion is set to the latter syllable since it has an ascending tonal inflection from level 3 to 5. Fragment *h* in the music example also illustrates the same point: note D is set to the syllable *jen* 姻 that has a 5 to 3 tonal inflection, whereas a lower note G is sung to the syllable *meng* 盟 that inflects from 2 to 1.

In Music Example 8.16, certain syllables in each of the fragments clearly reflect the role of linguistic tones in the singer's process of realizing the vocal melody. Similarly, in Music Example 8.17 which gives samples of pitch-syllable deviations of the second type, it is also evident that linguistic tones of the text play an important part in fragments *a*, *b*, *c* and *d*.

Improvisation in *Siu kuk*

As mentioned in Chapter 1, *Siu kuk* tunes have relatively more stable and invariable melodic contents than an aria type, but none of the *Siu kuk* tunes has a standard version. Different singers might have slightly different versions of the same tune in their mind, and they add extensive ornamentations in their performances.

Five different performed versions of a passage of *Siu kuk* entitled *Hon gwan jyt* 寒關月 (*Moon Over the Cold Mountain Pass*) illustrate the improvisatory practices. They are taken from five performances of the play *The Swallow Returns* (1975, 1976, 1980, 1985a and 1985b).[11] Each version was sung by the principal male role actor of the troupe. Music Example 8.20 (see pp. 250–61) juxtaposes the vocal melodies and texts of the five versions, with the accompaniment omitted.

The realization of the melody in *Siu kuk* follows a similar process to that in aria type. Since the script[12] states only the text without pitch notations, the singer first improvises the vocal melody, based on the pitch levels and the inflections of the linguistic tones of the text, over the skeletal structure of the tune *Hon gwan jyt*. Here the improvisation only involves ornamentation, choosing an appropriate version of the *Siu kuk* tune and rhythmic variations. As the realization of the vocal melodies is regulated by the *Siu kuk* tune, different performers' versions differ only in details.

In addition to the realization of the vocal melody, other improvisatory aspects can be seen in the same music example. The 1975 and 1976 versions have only two notes, rather than long instrumental melodic preludes preceding the singing. According to many actors and operatic song teachers, the presence or absence of a long melodic prelude is the result of an improvisatory practice. After the appropriate percussion pattern is played, the melodic instrumentalists start to play the brief version of the prelude. If the singer does not begin immediately after this, the melodic instrumentalists will continue to play. Thus, the short prelude is actually the beginning portion of the longer version. This long melodic prelude can be repeated several times until the singer starts to sing. This sort of practice to determine the duration of a melodic prelude is also used in singing aria type passages.

Some of the phrases in Music Example 8.20a (see pp. 250–57) have different numbers of syllables. The text also has meaningless syllables such as "*a*" and "*e*," which are not written in the script, but some of them are, however, transcribed in Music Example 8.20b (see pp. 258–61). Meaningful syllables sung to an upbeat are known as "grasp syllables": the term refers to single syllables sung to the upbeat of a *ding* or *ban* (beat or pulse, transcribed as a quarter note in Music Example 8.20a; see Chapter 5) and to syllables sung to the upbeat when multiple syllables are set to a *ding* or *ban*. For example, the second, third and fourth syllables sung within the first beat of measure 12, as well as the syllable *gung* 共 (together) in the first beat of measure 13, are all grasp syllables.

Yung has studied the use of padding syllables in Cantonese operatic music, and has distinguished between "base syllable" and "padding syllable" from a performance approach (Yung, 1989:93). However the singers interviewed for this study are often not aware of using padding syllables in their performances, but are always conscious of the use of grasp syllables.[13] Of course, many grasp syllables function as padding syllables in the context of Yung's study. Further research is needed to relate the concept of padding syllables to the actual performance practices.

Many grasp syllables are written in the script, but the singers also have the freedom to add or delete them during the performance. In phrase 2 (measures 6 to 8) of the singing in Music Example 8.20a, the singer of Version 1985b adds grasp syllables *ngo* 我 (I or me) at the beginning in measure 5, and *zin* 戰 (to fight or a battle) after the second syllable in measure 6. The addition of the syllables *je dek* 惹得 (to bring upon) in measure 7 of the same version produces a different syllable placement, causing the syllable *set* 失 (to lose or a loss) to be sung as a grasp syllable. On the basis of the script alone, which gives no rhythmic notation, it would be difficult to say that the syllable placement used in the other four versions is the "basic" pattern and Version 1985b the deviant one.

In the third phrase (measures 10 to 11), grasp syllables have been added in different spots in the five versions. At the end of the second beat in measure 10, the grasp syllable *key* 佢 (she) is added in Versions 1975, 1976 and 1985b. In the fourth beat of the same measure, the pair of padding syllables *lei go* 哩個 (this one) is added to Versions 1975, 1980 and 1985a. In Version 1985a, the grasp syllable *ngo* (I or me) is added together with *lei go*. In Version 1985b, the grasp syllable *dek* 得 (to succeed) is added after the fifth syllable.

In the fourth (approximately the first half of measure 12) and fifth phrase (approximately from the second half of measure 12 to measure 14), most of the grasp syllables sung in Versions 1975, 1976 and 1980 are written in the script. They are intended to be sung as grasp syllables according to the melodic contents and contour of the *Siu kuk* tune. Versions 1985a and 1985b include some of these and other grasp syllables: *ngo* (I or me) is added in the third beat of measure 12, and *zen* 眞 (true) is added in the second beat of measure 13. The first syllable in measure 13 of Versions 1975, 1976, 1980 and 1985a, *gung* (together), does not appear in the two versions of the script used in this study; it is also a grasp syllable added improvisatorily in the performances.

Analyses of other *Siu kuk* passages show that deleting grasp syllables is one of the improvisatory practices, even though it does not appear in this example.

Another improvisatory practice in the singing of *Siu kuk* passages is the replacement of syllables. Music Example 8.20b shows that singers do not strictly follow the text written in the script. For example, in measure 6, Versions 1980 and 1985a follow the script, but the singer of Version 1985b replaces the syllable *sen* 新 (of the recent past) by *co* 初 (the first time), and the singers of the other two versions use the syllable *bing* 兵 (military). The meanings are similar, but while the script and Versions 1980 and 1985a say *sen bai* 新敗 (the loss in the recent past), Version 1985b has *co zin bai* 初戰敗 (the first lost battle), and Versions 1975 and 1976 have *bing bai* 兵敗 (the military loss).

The melodic accompanists' improvisatory practices (which are not shown in Music Example 8.20) are limited to the addition of ornaments when they support the vocal melodies. They are also responsible for performing the melodic interludes that are phrases of the *Siu kuk* tune that are not set with text. While the vocal melody and the accompaniment maintain a heterophonic multi-part relationship, usually no imitative melodic interlude or percussion pattern occurs within a passage of *Siu kuk* singing.

Notes

1. The performance was staged by the New Joyful Popular and Excellent Cantonese Opera Troupe on 17 December 1984 at the Paladium Opera House.
2. The performance was staged by the Golden Dragon Cantonese Opera Troupe on 24 April 1985 in Happy Valley.
3. The performance by the Bat Wo Cantonese Opera Troupe took place on 11 September 1984 at the Ko Shan Theatre in Kowloon.
4. As mentioned in Chapter 1, both *Muk jy* and *Lung zau* are genres of singing narratives often used in Cantonese operatic music. Their textual structures are similar, but melodic details differ. This improvisatory practice of replacing one singing narrative passage with one from a different genre is similar to that of replacing one suggested aria type with another.
5. The performance by the Singing of the Pear Cantonese Opera Troupe took place on 12 September 1985, during a ritual performance held in Shaukeiwan.
6. According to Yung, some of the syllables classified under the category of upper even have a tonal inflection of 55, represented by the tonal symbol " ˥ ". Upper and lower even tones belong to the "even" tone category; the rest of the tones belong to the "oblique" tone category.
7. They are *hong* 1, 2, 3, 7, 8, 9, 10, 11, 12, 13, 14, 15, 16, 18, 19, 20, 21, 22, 24, 25, 29, 30, 31 and 32.
8. These are *hong* 4, 5, 6 and 17.
9. These are *hong* 23, 26, 27, 28, 33, 34 and 35.
10. Version 1 is taken from a set of two commercial tapes made in 1976 (Wen Sing Recordings Company, tape number WS203), with no date of performance. Version 2 is from another set of commercial recordings made by Zung Sing 鍾聲 Recordings Company (tape number BR-432). Without any date, it is believed to have been recorded around 1976. Versions 3 and 4 are respectively taken from the 1980 and 1985b performances to be discussed in the next section on *Siu kuk* (see Note 11). Here the four versions' dates of performance or production are referred to as 1976, c.1976, 1980 and 1985 respectively.
11. The five live performances are recorded on five different sets of tapes. Set I consists of two commercial tapes made in 1976 by the Wen Sing Recordings Company (see Note 10). Sets II and III record two performances on 2 May 1975 and 11 February 1980 respectively (the latter from a radio broadcast). Both sets were recorded by Bell Yung in Hong Kong. Sets IV and V were ones that I made: IV contains a performance from 23 April 1985; V contains a performance of 4 August 1985. Sets

I to III were performed by the Dai Lung Fung 大龍鳳 (huge dragon and phoenix) Cantonese Opera Troupe, with Mek Bing-wing 麥炳榮 and Fung-wong Ney 鳳凰女 acting the principal male and female roles. Set IV was performed by the Tremendous Heroic Strength Cantonese Opera Troupe, with Loeng Hon-wae 梁漢威 and Nam Fung 南鳳 in the principal male and female roles. Set V was by the Celebrate the Nice Years Cantonese Opera Troupe, with Men Cin-sey 文千歲 and Ze Syt-sem 謝雪心 in the principal male and female roles.

12. Two versions of the script were obtained for this study. Version A is a photocopy of the script that was used by the fiddler of the Huge Dragon and Phoenix Cantonese Opera Troupe, and I believe that this was the version used in the performances of 1975, 1976 and 1980. However, the tapes of 1976 contain only excerpts of the performance. Version B is a photocopy of the script used by the fiddler performing for the Celebrate the Nice Years Cantonese Opera Troupe for 1985b. The two versions show only minor differences. The 1985a performance probably used a script that did not differ significantly from the two available versions.

13. In the profession, non-structural syllables in vocal music are rarely referred to as *cen zi* 襯字 (decorating syllables) but are called *me zae zi* 孭仔字 (syllables carried on one's back, where *me zae* literally means to carry a baby on one's back) or *lap zi* (grasp syllables where *lap* 擸 literally means to grasp something quickly). Yung's approach presents some difficulties in this study because the meaningless syllables, syllables of interlude fillers and syllables in the added phrases—identified by Yung as three of the six types of padding syllables—are not considered to be *cen zi, me zae zi* or *lap zi* in the profession.

Music Example 8.1a A passage of *Gam zi fu jung*

Music Example 8.1a A passage of *Gam zi fu jung* (cont'd)

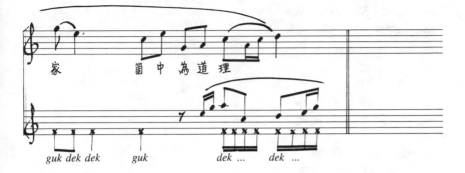

Music Example 8.1b The text of Music Example 8.1a

(male actor makes a *Dik dik* hand shadow)
(the percussion pattern *Dik dik* is played, short melodic prelude is played)

(male actor sings *Gam zi fu jung*)
(line 1, phrase 1)
hou sem mg pa zou,
好　心　唔　怕　做
Don't be afraid of doing good.

(female actor continues)
(line 1, phrase 2)
ngo Coen- hoeng ze pa jen jin a a,
我　春　香　姐　怕　人　言　呀
I, Coen-hoeng, am afraid of people's gossip.

(male actor speaks plain speech)
nei wa pa? zou jen ne, mg ho ji mg bong jen ga.
你　話　怕　做　人　呢　唔　可　以　唔　幫　人　㗎
Did you say you were afraid? But as a human being
one should help others.

bong dek jen do ne, zi jin jau hou bou go bo.
幫　得　人　多　呢　自　然　有　好　報　個　嘴
If you have helped many people, naturally you will be rewarded.

Music Example 8.1b   The text of Music Example 8.1a (cont'd)

hou   sem   jau   hou   bou   lok,

好　心　有　好　報　咯

If a good heart can bring good return,

ngo   ne,   bou   jau   nei   sang   fan   go   hou   zae.

我　呢　保　祐　你　生　番　個　好　仔

Then I pray that you have a good son.

(female actor speaks plain speech)
ngo   zau   la,   ngo   zau   la.

我　走　啦　我　走　啦

I am leaving, I am leaving.
(unclear speech, omitted)
(male actor sings *Gam zi fu jung*)

(line 2, phrase 1)
jau   gwok   zi   jau   ga,

有　國　至　有　家

Family comes after the country,

(line 2, phrase 2)
go   zung   wae   dou   lei.

箇　中　為　道　理

this is the truth.

Music Example 8.2a A *Cet zi cing* passage

comic role actor sings

愛 河 情 海 泛 情 e 潮   叫 句 阿 成

來 心 e 照 呀 你 原 來 a 想 佢 a 做 鵲 a 橋

我 叫 句 王 侄 a 兒 a   你 有 何 a 心 了

military role actor sings

呢 問 a 明 白 誰 個 把 情 描   誰 是 e 姦 夫 a   唔

plain speech, omitted

military role actor sings

誰 a 是 e 姦 夫 應 心 a 照 u ua 查 明 a 查 白

免 嬌 a 嬈   怨 着 查 a 明 a   無 須

恥 a 笑 a   plain speech, omitted

Music Example 8.2a A *Cet zi cing* passage (cont'd)

Music Example 8.2a A *Cet zi cing* passage (cont'd)

Music Example 8.2b The text of Music Example 8.2a

(the comic role actor makes a *Zung bang* hand shadow)
(the percussion pattern *Zung ban* and the melodic prelude of *Zung ban*
in the mode of *Si gung* are played simultaneously)

(comic role actor sings *Cet zi cing*)
ngoi ho cing hoi fan cing e ciu.
愛　河　情　海　泛　情　　潮
Waves are aroused in the river of love and sea of affection.

giu gey a Sing loi sem e ziu a.
叫　句　阿　成　來　心　　照　呀
Ah Sing, you should open your heart to me.

nei jyn loi a soeng key a zou zoek a kiu.
你　原　來　　想　佢　做　鵲　　橋
Originally you wanted her to serve as your match-maker.

ngo giu gey wong zet a ji a nei jau ho a sem liu?
我　叫　句　王　侄　兒　你　有　何　　心　了
My royal nephew, what do you want?

(the military role actor continues)

ne men a ming bak, sey go ba cing miu.
呢　問　明　白　誰　個　把　情　描
Let's clarify the matter, and uncover the one who was involved
in the secret relation.

sey si e gan fu a mg
誰　是　姦　夫　唔
The secret lover, could not...

(speaks in plain speech)

mg dek liu a.
唔　得　了　呀
could not avoid serious trouble.

Music Example 8.2b The text of Music Example 8.2a (cont'd)

(comic role actor speaks plain speech)

nei gem sey la, siu ngo, ae ja, jung je lei siu ngo.
你 咁 衰 啦 笑 我 哎 吔 用 嘢 嚟 笑 我
You are bad, you laughed at me, you made excuses to laugh at me.

(the military role actor speaks plain speech)

ai, ngo hok nei a ma! (sings)
唉 我 學 你 吖 嘛
I was just imitating you.

(the military role actor sings the syllable *ciu* to a short melody,
the comic role actor then speaks plain speech)

ngo zap zy,
我 閘 住
Stop.

ngo dei ney zae gong je, nei jau hok jen, cau gwai a!
我 哋 女 仔 講 嘢 你 又 學 人 醜 怪 呀
You imitated the way we girls speak. Shame on you!

(plain speech between the comic role and military role actors, omitted)
(the military role actor sings *Cet zi cing*)

sey a si e gan fu jing sem a ziu u ua.
誰 是 姦 夫 應 心 照
The secret lover should know in his own heart.

ca ming a ca bak min giu a jiu.
查 明 查 白 免 嬌 嬈
We will not blame the lady after we have found out the truth.

fet zoek ca a ming a mou sey ci a siu a.
忽 著 查 明 無 須 恥 笑
We will not sneer at her when the truth is revealed.

Music Example 8.2b The text of Music Example 8.2a (cont'd)

(the comic role actor speaks plain speech)

bin go hae nei go cing fu a?
邊 個 係 你 個 情 夫 呀
Who is your secret lover?

(supporting male role actor sings *Cet zi cing*)

ney giu a jiu, zau zey a zi si nei cing bet e hiu.
女 嬌 嬈 酒 醉 之 時 你 情 不 曉
Lady, you could not control your passion when you were drunk.

fu long sey go min gem ma ziu.
夫 郎 誰 個 免 今 朝
Who then is your lover?

ca tam dong a si zen cing zoen ziu.
查 探 當 時 真 情 盡 照
Let us investigate now to reveal the truth.

(the principal female role actor sings *Cet zi cing*)

ci jen a zoi hen gei do a ciu?
此 恩 再 恨 幾 多 朝
For how much longer does my love have to be expressed as hatred?

jet dim ci sem tin fu a siu.
一 點 痴 心 天 苦 笑
The heavens laugh bitterly at my infatuation.

jy long a git hep dou lam a kiu.
與 郎 結 合 渡 藍 橋
I only hope that I could marry the one I love.

hen a dong co nei sy bet ciu.
恨 當 初 你 殊 不 肖
I regret that you behaved badly at the beginning.

Music Example 8.2b The text of Music Example 8.2a (cont'd)

men zoeng goi wun fu sat ney giu jiu.

文　章　改　換　苦　煞　女　嬌　嬈

You changed the words in my letter and caused me anxiety.

si men gem ma ciu jing e zik ziu.

試　問　今　　朝　應　　直　照

I am asking you now, tell us the truth.

(speaks plain speech)

nei tung bin go jem gwo zau?

你　同　邊　個　飲　過　酒

Who did you drink with?

jem zey zau zi hau nei jau dim a?

飲　醉　酒　之　後　你　又　點　呀

What happened to you after you were drunk?

(the supporting female role actor sings *Cet zi cing*)

ci si ci zae ngat sem ziu.

此　時　此　際　壓　心　焦

I feel extremely anxious now.

gek dek dong co sem soeng ziu.

記　得　當　初　心　相　　照

I remember that we loved each other at the beginning.

pou tou soeng zeng zi tin jiu.

葡　萄　相　　贈　指　天　遙

We exchanged wine and swore that we would stay in love.

gung a juk e cing ho sem soeng ziu.

共　浴　　情　河　心　相　　照

Then we bathed in the river of love and opened our hearts to each other.

Music Example 8.2b The text of Music Example 8.2a (cont'd)

cing ho ngoi hoi loeng cing miu.
情 河 愛 海 雨 情 苗
We were two love buds in the river of affection and sea of love.

fa lok sey ga nan soeng ziu.
花 落 誰 家 難 相 照
But I still don't know whom I should marry.

(several actors speak plain speech, omitted)

(the principal male role actor sings *Cet zi cing*)

nei hey hau e ngo bin bit giu jiu
你 去 後 我 便 別 嬌 嬈
We parted after you left.

ci zae ci si ngo nan syt e hiu.
此 際 此 時 我 難 説 曉
I can hardly explain to convince you now.

ngo zi zi jyn ley mou giu a jiu.
我 只 知 園 裏 方 嬌 嬈
I only know that the lady was not there in the garden.

(sings *Si gung kwen fa*)

ci gan nan zok gan fu soeng.
此 間 難 作 姦 夫 相
I can hardly admit that I was the secret lover.

Music Example 8.2c Rhythmic scheme of the military role actor's
segment in Music Example 8.2a

(military role actor sings *Cet zi cing*)
(line 1)

(ne) men (a) ming   bak   sey (go) ba   cing   miu

(line 2, interrupted)

sey   si   (e) gan   fu (a)   mg   (plain speech,
                                                    omitted)

(line 2, in its complete form)

sey (a) si (e) gan   fu   jing   sem (a) ziu (u   ua)

(line 3)

cu   ming (a) ca   bak   min   giu   (a) jiu

(line 4)

fet   zoek   ca (a) ming (a)   mou (sey)   ci (a) siu (a)

Music Example 8.3a Two passages of text taken from *Story of the Butterfly Lovers*

(the male actor enters with the percussion patters *Dai zong dim* , sings *Cet zi cing* which starts with the lower line)

(lower line)

ꭓ   ꭓ   ꭤ   ꭤ   ꭓ   ꭤ

bet   ci   bet   sit   wae   jen   jyn.

不　辭　跋　涉　為　姻　緣

Having taken a long trip for the prospect of marriage.

ꭤ   ꭓ   ꭤ   ꭤ   ꭓ   ꭤ

juk   dip   e   jet   soeng   sing   mei   gyn.

玉　蝶　一　雙　成　美　眷

This pair of jade butterflies will make a perfect couple.

ꭤ   ꭓ   ꭤ   ꭤ   ꭓ

lam   kiu   jau   lou   fong   sen   sin.

藍　橋　有　路　訪　神　仙

The blue bridge leads me to visit the nymph.

(sings *Si gung kwen fa*)

ji   dou   Zuk   ga,

已　到　祝　家

I have arrived at Zuk's home.

mong   jy   gwu   jen   wui   min.

忙　與　故　人　會　面

I am in a hurry to see my old friend.

Music Example 8.3b Passages of *Cet zi cing* and *Si gung kwen fa*

Music Example 8.4 Passages of *Si gung kwen fa* and plain speech

Music Example 8.5 A line sung to *Ji lau*

Music Example 8.6a Passages of poetic and plain speech

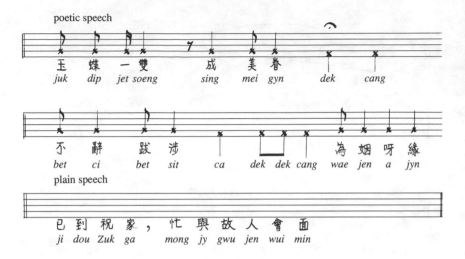

Music Example 8.6b Passages of poetic speech and *Si gung kwen fa*

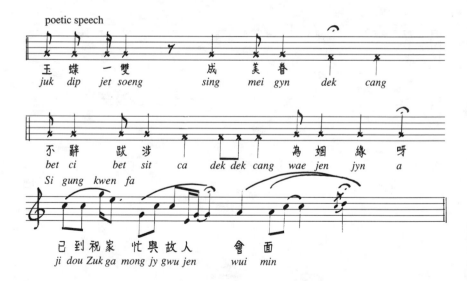

Music Example 8.7a A passage of *Ji wong man ban*

Music Example 8.7b The text of Music Example 8.7a

(line 1)

kuk gei zing jen,

曲　寄　征　人

I sent a song to the one in the battle,

fen fu Hung Kiu fong bin,

吩　咐　洪　喬　方　便

I asked Hung Kiu to help.

(line 2)

sy cey sey hey,

書　隨　水　去

The letter was gone with the river,

ding gao ci hen min min.

定　教　此　恨　綿　綿

my desperate wish will never be realized.

Music Example 8.8 A passage of *Fan sin zung ban*

Music Example 8.9a A passage of *Ho ce kwen fa*

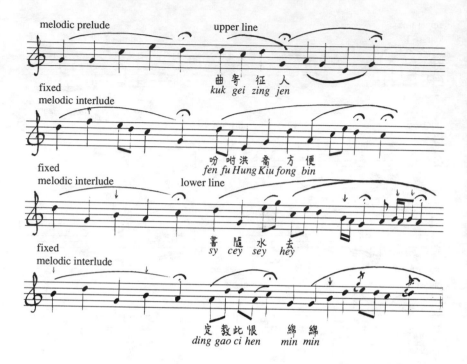

Music Example 8.9b Short melisma sung to the last syllable

Music Example 8.10 A passage of *Si gung kwen fa*

Music Example 8.11 Three versions of a *Si gung kwen fa* passage

Music Example 8.11 Three versions of a *Si gung kwen fa* passage (cont'd)

Music Example 8.11 Three versions of a *Si gung kwen fa* passage (cont'd)

Music Example 8.12 Enunciation notes used in the three versions of a *Si gung kwen fa* passage

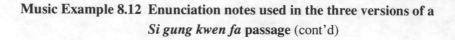

Music Example 8.12 Enunciation notes used in the three versions of a
Si gung kwen fa **passage** (cont'd)

Music Example 8.13 *Hong* in the three versions of a *Si gung kwen fa* passage

Music Example 8.13 *Hong* **in the three versions of a** *Si gung kwen fa* **passage** (cont'd)

Music Example 8.13 *Hong* **in the three versions of a** *Si gung kwen fa* **passage** (cont'd)

Music Example 8.14a Four versions of a *Ji wong man ban* passage

Music Example 8.14a Four versions of a *Ji wong man ban* passage (cont'd)

Music Example 8.14a Four versions of a *Ji wong man ban* passage (cont'd)

Music Example 8.14a Four versions of a *Ji wong man ban* passage (cont'd)

Music Example 8.14a Four versions of a *Ji wong man ban* passage (cont'd)

Music Example 8.14b The texts of Music Example 8.14a

(line 1, phrase 1)
(Script)
soeng   ci   wet   pong   hei   zeng   dyn.
相　持　鷸　蚌　起　爭　端
grapple   sandpiper   clam   arise   dispute
When the sandpiper grapples with the clam, a dispute arises.

Version 1 (1976)
(same as the script)

Version 2 (c. 1976)
(same as the script)

Music Example 8.14b The texts of Music Example 8.14a (cont'd)

Version 3 (1980)
(same as the script)

Version 4 (1985)
soeng ci wet a pong hei zeng dyn.
相　持　鷸　　蚌　起　爭　端
When the sandpiper grapples with the clam, a dispute arises.
(*a* is a nonsense syllable)

(line 1, phrase 2)
(Script)
si si　　　jy jen　　kei　　lei　　gin.
師　事　　　漁　人　其　利　見
learn from   fisherman   his   interest   see
To learn from the fisherman, we can see our interest.

Version 1 (1976)
tou ling　　jy jen kei　　lei　　gin.
徒　令　　　漁　人　其　利　見
only enable   fisherman   his   interest   see
It only enables the fisherman to see his interest.

Version 2 (c. 1976)
ci hau jy jen kei lei gin.
此　後　漁　人　其　利　見
After that, the fisherman sees his interest.
(*ci hau*: after that)

Version 3 (1980)
(same as Version 1)

Version 4 (1985)
tou ling jy jen kei lei a gin.
徒　令　漁　人　其　利　　見
It only enables the fisherman to see his interest.
(*a* is a nonsense syllable)

Music Example 8.14b The texts of Music Example 8.14a (cont'd)

(line 1, phrase 3)
(Script)
loeng gwok hep bing   po   dik.
兩　國　合　兵　破　敵
two   nation unite troops defeat enemy
The two nations unite their troops to defeat the enemy.

Version 1 (1976)
joek gwo hep a bing a key   dik.
若　果　合　兵　拒　敵
　　if　unite　troops　resist　enemy,
If the troops are united to resist the enemy,
(*a* is a nonsense syllable)

Version 2 (c. 1976)
loeng gwok hep a bing e po dik.
兩　國　合　兵　破　敵
The two nations unite their troops to defeat the enemy.
(*a* and *e* are nonsense syllables)

Version 3 (1980)
joek si sing a gung jet zin.
若　是　成　功　一　戰
if it is success   one battle
If a single battle will bring success.
(*a* is a nonsense syllable)

Version 4 (1985)
soeng a ci zung a jet.
相　持　終　日
The grapple lasts for a whole day.
(*a* is a nonsense syllable; *zung jet*: a whole day)

(line 1, phrase 4)
(Script)
ngo bin ming lei soeng cyn.
我　便　名　利　雙　全
　I will　fame　interest　both　complete gain
I will have a complete gain of both fame and interest.

Music Example 8.14b The texts of Music Example 8.14a (cont'd)

Version 1 (1976)
dong   ho   ji   ming   lei   soeng   a   cyn.
當　可　以　名　利　雙　　全
certainly   can   fame   interest   both   complete gain
Both fame and interest can certainly be completely gained.

Version 2 (c. 1976)
ngo   bin   ming   lei   soeng   a   cyn.
我　便　名　利　雙　　全
I will have a complete gain of both fame and interest.
(*a* is a nonsense syllable)

Version 3 (1980)
(same as Version 1)

Version 4 (1985)
zi   jau   ming   a   lei   ho   a   jin.
自　有　名　利　可　言
will surely have   fame   interest   can   say
(We) will surely have fame and interest to talk about.
(*a* is a nonsense syllable)

(line 1, phrase 5)
(Script)
fu   wong   lei   jung   fen   jen.
父　王　利　用　婚　姻
father   emperor   exploit   marriage
Father-emperor exploits the marriage,

Version 1 (1976)
fu   wong   key   lei   jung   lei   jet   dyn   fen   jen,
父　王　佢　利　用　哩　一　段　婚　姻
father   emperor   he   exploit   this   marriage
He, (my) father-emperor, exploits this marriage,

Version 2 (c. 1976)
(same as the script)

Music Example 8.14b The texts of Music Example 8.14a (cont'd)

Version 3 (1980)
fu   wong   lei   a   jung   lei   jet   dyn   fen   jen,
父　王　利　　用　哩　一　段　婚　姻
Father-emperor exploits this marriage,
(*lei jet dyn*: this; *a* is a nonsense syllable)

Version 4 (1985)
　fu　　　wong　lei　jung　lei　jet　dyn　　fen　　a　　meng,
父　　　王　利　用　哩　一　段　婚　　　盟
father   emperor   exploit   this   marriage   agreement
Father-emperor exploits this marriage-agreement,
(*a* is a nonsense syllable)

(line 1, phrase 6)
(Script)
wae   sey   cem   　　loeng   　jyn.
為　遂　侵　梁　顧
for   satisfy   encroach   the Loeng kingdom   wish
to satisfy his wish of encroaching upon the Loeng kingdom.

Version 1 (1976)
　tou　　sey　　cem　　loeng　　a jyn.
圖　遂　侵　梁　顧
attempt   satisfy   encroach   the Loeng kingdom   wish
attempts to satisfy his wish of encroaching upon the Loeng kingdom.

Version 2 (c. 1976)
(same as the script)

Version 3 (1980)
tou sey cem loeng a a jyn.
圖　遂　侵　梁　顧
attempts to satisfy his wish of encroaching upon the Loeng kingdom.
(*a* is a nonsense syllable)

Version 4 (1985)
(same as Version 3)

Music Example 8.14b The texts of Music Example 8.14a (cont'd)

(line 1, phrase 7)
(Script)
mong   gwen   nei   jyn sing   gae wak,
望   君   你   完   成   計   劃
hope gentleman you accomplish   plan
(I) hope that you gentleman will accomplish the plan,

Version 1 (1976)
joek gwo gung a   sing   ci   gae,
若   果   功   成   此   計
    if   success achieve this plan
If this plan can be successfully achieved,
(*a* is a nonsense syllable)

Version 2 (c. 1976)
(same as the script)

Version 3 (1980)
joek si   hep a   bing a   tey   dik,
若   是   合   兵   退   敵
if   it is unite   troops   repel enemy
If the troops are united to repel the enemy,
(*a* is a nonsense syllable)

Version 4 (1985)
joek si   gung e   sing   jet e   zin,
若   是   功   成   一   戰
    if   it is success achieve one   battle
If a single battle can achieve success,
(*e* is a nonsense syllable)

(line 1, phrases 8 and 9)
(Script)
  dong   jau   lei   mok dai   jin.
  當   有   利   莫   大   焉
certainly   has   interest utmost   (a particle)
the utmost interest will certainly be there.

Music Example 8.14b The texts of Music Example 8.14a (cont'd)

Version 1 (1976)
dong   ho   lei   mok   dai   jin.
當　可　利　莫　大　馬
certainly   can   interest   utmost   (a particle)
the utmost interest can certainly be there.

Version 2 (c. 1976)
(same as the script)

Version 3 (1980)
fong   ho   ji   ming   a   lei   soeng   cyn.
方　可　以　名　利　雙　全
then   can   fame   interest   both   complete gain
then (we) can have a complete gain of both fame and interest.
(*a* is a nonsense syllable)

Version 4 (1985)
dong ho   lei   a   mok   dai   jin.
當　可　利　莫　大　馬
the utmost interest can certainly be there.
(*a* is a nonsense syllable)

(line 2, phrase 1)
(Script)
gwen   ci   fen   dip   lin   hoeng.
君　似　粉　蝶　憐　香
gentleman   seem   white butterfly   pity   flower
It seems that you gentleman are a white butterfly that pities a flower.

Version 1 (1976)
jau joek   fen   a   dip   lin   hoeng.
有　若　粉　蝶　憐　香
resemble   white butterfly   pity   flower
(You) resemble a white butterfly that pities a flower.
(*a* is a nonsense syllable)

Music Example 8.14b The texts of Music Example 8.14a (cont'd)

Version 2 (c. 1976)
gem   nei   jet   a   pin   ci   cing.

感 你 一 片 痴 情
feel you   sheer   infatuation
(I) can feel your sheer infatuation.
(*a* is a nonsense syllable)

Version 3 (1980)
(same as Version 1)

Version 4 (1985)
nei   jau   joek   fen   e   dip   lin   a   hoeng.

你 有 若 粉 蝶 憐 香
You resemble a white butterfly that pities a flower.
(*nei*: you; *e* and *a* are nonsense syllables)

(line 2, phrase 2 and 3)
(Script)
ngo   gem   nei   ci   cing   jey   pin.

我 感 你 痴 情 一 片
I feel you   infatuation   sheer
I can feel your sheer infatuation.

Version 1 (1976)
gem   ze   nei   ci   sem   jet   i   pin

感 謝 你 痴 心 一 片
  thank   you   infatuated heart   sheer
(I) thank you for your sheer infatuated heart.
(*i* is a nonsense syllable)

Version 2 (c. 1976)
sin   ba   gwok   ben   zip   gin.

先 把 國 賓 接 見
first (a preposition)   state guest   receive
Firstly, (let us) receive (our) state guests.

Music Example 8.14b The texts of Music Example 8.14a (cont'd)

Version 3 (1980)

ngo gem nei ci a cing jet i pin.

我　感　你　痴　情　一　　片

I can feel your sheer infatuation.

(*a* and *i* are nonsense syllables)

Version 4 (1985)

gwu fu nei cing a a a coeng jet a pin.

辜　負　你　情　　　　長　一　　片

(I) disappointed your sheer and lasting affection.

(*a* is a nonsense syllable; *gwu fu*: to disappoint; *coeng*: long)

Music Example 8.15 Deviations in notes as a result of text-difference: syllable level

Music Example 8.16 Deviations in notes as a result of text-difference:

phrase level

Music Example 8.16 Deviations in notes as a result of text-difference: phrase level (cont'd)

Music Example 8.16 Deviations in notes as a result of text-difference: phrase level (cont'd)

difference in pitches are not
related to the difference in syllables

Music Example 8.17 Deviations in notes as a result of adding ornaments

**Music Example 8.18 Deviations in notes resulted from addition of
                      ornaments, rhythmic variations and
                      other factors**

Music Example 8.19 Different syllables set to the same notes

Music Example 8.20a Five versions of a *Siu kuk* passage

Version 1 (1976)

Version 2 (1975)

Version 3 (1980)

Version 4 (1985a)

Version 5 (1985b)

Music Example 8.20a Five versions of a *Siu kuk* passage (cont'd)

Music Example 8.20a Five versions of a *Siu kuk* passage (cont'd)

Music Example 8.20a Five versions of a *Siu kuk* passage (cont'd)

Music Example 8.20a Five versions of a *Siu kuk* passage (cont'd)

Music Example 8.20a Five versions of a *Siu kuk* passage (cont'd)

Music Example 8.20a Five versions of a *Siu kuk* passage (cont'd)

Music Example 8.20a Five versions of a *Siu kuk* passage (cont'd)

Music Example 8.20b The texts of Music Example 8.20a

(phrase 1)
(Script)
wu   ga   cey   po   san   ho   sey.
胡 笳 吹 破 山 河 碎
The blowing of the Huns' pipes shatters my country into fragments.

Version 1 (1976)
(same as the script, with the nonsense syllables disregarded)

Version 2 (1975)
(same as the script, with the nonsense syllables disregarded)

Version 3 (1980)
(same as the script, with the nonsense syllables disregarded)

Version 4 (1985a)
(same as the script, with the nonsense syllables disregarded)

Version 5 (1985b)
(same as the script, with the nonsense syllables disregarded)

(phrase 2)
(Script)
sen   bai   ho   hem   bei   set   ji.
新 敗 何 堪 悲 失 意
How can I bear the sad frustration caused by the recent loss.

Version 1 (1976)
bing   a   bai   ho   hem   fung   a   set   a   ji.
兵   敗 何 堪 逢   失   意
How can I face the frustration caused by the military loss.

Version 2 (1975)
bing   a   bai   ai   ho   hem   bei   set   ji.
兵   敗   何 堪 悲 失 意
How can I bear the sad frustration caused by the military loss.

Music Example 8.20b The texts of Music Example 8.20a (cont'd)

Version 3 (1980)
sen e bai ai ho hem tung zi zey (speaks) *ai.*
新 敗 何 堪 痛 知 最 唉
How can I bear the feeling, which I know is the bitterest,
caused by the recent loss. Alas!

Version 4 (1985a)
sen a bai ho hem bei set a a ji.
新 敗 何 堪 悲 失 意
How can I bear the sad frustration caused by the recent loss.

Version 5 (1985b)
ngo co a zin bai ho hem je dek bei a set ji.
我 初 戰 敗 何 堪 惹 得 悲 失 意
I lost my first battle. How can I bear the sad frustration
which I brought upon myself.

(phrase 3)
(Script)
juk jen wan gau mong zung jy.
玉 人 挽 救 網 中 魚
The nice lady saved the fish from the net.

Version 1 (1976)
juk a jen e key wan gau a mong zung a jy.
玉 人 佢 挽 救 網 中 魚
She, the nice lady, saved the fish from the net.

Version 2 (1975)
juk a jen e key wan gau a lei go mong zung a jy e.
玉 人 佢 挽 救 哩 個 網 中 魚
She, the nice lady, saved this fish from the net.

Version 3 (1980)
juk a jen e wan gau lei go mong zung jy.
玉 人 挽 救 哩 個 網 中 魚
The nice lady saved this fish from the net.

Music Example 8.20b The texts of Music Example 8.20a (cont'd)

Version 4 (1985a)
juk e jen wan a gau a ngo lei go mong zung jy.
玉　人　挽　救　我　哩　個　網　中　魚
The nice lady saved me, who was a fish in a net.

Version 5 (1985b)
juk a jen key soeng dek gau e mong a zung a jy.
玉　人　佢　相　得　救　網　中　魚
She, the nice lady, succeeded in saving the fish from the net.

(phrase 4)
(Script)
ze gwo cong tin hao ci loeng jyn.
謝　過　蒼　天　巧　賜　良　緣
Thank heaven which graciously bestowed on me a good marriage.

Version 1 (1976)
ze gwo cong tin hao cit loeng a jyn.
謝　過　蒼　天　巧　設　良　緣
Thank heaven which graciously ordained a good marriage.

Version 2 (1975)
ze gwo cong tin hao git loeng a jyn a.
謝　過　蒼　天　巧　結　良　緣
Thank heaven which graciously brought us together in a good marriage.

Version 3 (1980)
(same as Version 2, with the nonsense syllables disregarded)

Version 4 (1985a)
(same as Version 2, with the nonsense syllables disregarded)

Version 5 (1985b)
ngo ze gwo cong tin hao ci loeng jyn.
我　謝　過　蒼　天　巧　賜　良　緣
I thank heaven which graciously bestowed on me a good marriage.

Music Example 8.20b The texts of Music Example 8.20a (cont'd)

(phrase 5)
(Script)
jy Lei Loeng git jyn ley.
與 梨 娘 結 篤 侶
Lady Lei and I became a couple.

Version 1 (1976)
jy Lei a Loeng gung git jyn a ley.
與 梨 娘 共 結 篤 侶
Lady Lei and I together became a couple.

Version 2 (1975)
(same as Version 1, with the nonsense syllables disregarded)

Version 3 (1980)
(same as Version 1, but no nonsense syllable is used)

Version 4 (1985a)
ngo gung Lei e Loeng gung git jyn a ley.
我 共 梨 娘 共 結 篤 侶
Lady Lei and I together became a couple.

Version 5 (1985b)
ngo jy Lei Loeng git zen jyn a ley.
我 與 梨 娘 結 真 篤 侶
Lady Lei and I became a true couple.

9. Improvisation in Speech Delivery

Yung (1989:57–66) identifies seven types of speech delivery used in Cantonese opera: *bak* 白 (plain speech), *long ley bak* 浪裏白 (supported speech), *lo gwu bak* 鑼鼓白 (percussion speech), *si bak* 詩白 (poetic or versified speech), *hau gwu* 口古 (rhymed speech), *bak lam* 白欖 (patter speech) and *wen bak* 韻白 (comic rhymed speech). This chapter will examine the use of improvisation in the major types of speech delivery. Because percussion speech and comic rhymed speech are not often used, and, since in supported speech "the vocal part is practically identical with that of plain speech, except that a melodic instrumental accompaniment constantly accompanies the spoken word" (Yung, 1976a:125), the following discussion will focus on the four types of delivery that are the most prevalent and distinct ones.

Poetic Speech

Poetic speech, also known as *nim bak* 念白 (recited speech), has a verse form resembling that of *zyt gey* 絕句 , a poetic genre popular in the Tang dynasty (618–907) (Yung, 1976a:127). A passage of poetic speech is usually composed of sets of four lines of equal length, each containing either five or seven syllables. The last syllables of the second and fourth lines must belong to the even tone category and must rhyme. The ending syllables of the first and third lines are in the oblique tone and may or may not rhyme. As in patter and rhymed speech, performers are allowed to add particles, nonsense and exclamatory syllables after rhyming end syllables.

Example 9.1 (see pp. 282–84) shows a poetic speech passage from the script of the play *The Swallow Returns*, and from four versions of the same passage derived from different performances (1976, 1980, 1985a and 1985b). Comparison of the four performed versions with the script shows that improvisation occurs only in the addition of grasp syllables and the replacement of syllables. Grasp syllables appear in lines 3 and 4 of Version 2 and in line 2 of Version 3; the syllables, *ngo* 我 (I or me) and *key* 佢 (he or him), are all pronouns. The improvised syllables that replace the ones written in the script occur in line 3 of Version 1 and line 4 of Versions 3 and 4. Actors invariably keep the ending syllable the same (*gwae*, in this case), so that the rhyming scheme is not violated.

A seven-syllable line of poetic speech is segmented into three phrases, with respectively two, two and three syllables. Though there is no melodic accompaniment, the percussionists play the one-stroke pattern after each of the first three lines and also between the second and third phrases of the last line of the passage. According to Wong Jyt-seng,[1] an actor who improvisatorily adds a passage of poetic speech has to pause shortly after the second phrase of the last line, so that the percussionists know the passage is coming to an end and can respond by playing a one-stroke pattern. The particle "*a*" 呀 ('ah') used at the end of Versions 1, 3 and 4 is slightly prolonged, and its use at the end of a spoken passage is often accompanied with a stylistic gesture as a kind of gestic hint to notify the accompanists that the actor is ready to sing a vocal passage (see Chapters 6 and 8). Hence, the appearance of a one-stroke percussion pattern between the second and last phrase of the last line and the recitation of the syllable "*a*" at the end of a passage of poetic speech are improvisational characteristics.

Patter Speech

The most prominent feature of patter speech is the reciting of syllables in even pulses that are regulated by strokes played on the large woodblock. The lines are organized into rhyming couplets; the second line of each couplet maintains a rhyme, and sometimes the first line of the couplet shares in the rhyme. However, as Yung noted (1976a:130), the scriptwriters sometimes do not follow the rhyme scheme strictly. Performers sometimes add particles, exclamatory and nonsense syllables to the end of lines after the rhyming syllables.

Example 9.2 (see pp. 285–96) shows a long passage of patter speech from the play *The Courtship of the Phoenix by the Side of Lake Peach Blossom*[2] with interpolated plain speech. According to the comic role actor who started the passage, it was added to prolong the performance in order to satisfy the enthusiastic audience. When the major characters were on

stage towards the end of the final act, the comic actor made a *Pok deng ngo*
hand shadow. The *Pok deng ngo* percussion pattern was played, and the
comic role actor improvised three couplets of patter speech. He was followed in order by actors of the principal male role, principal female,
supporting male, military, second-supporting female, supporting female
and finally the comic role again. In the last segment of the entire passage,
the comic role actor recited two lines of patter speech and made a *zung ban*
hand shadow to start another improvised vocal passage (see Chapter 8).

In this performance, the segments improvised by the various actors—
except the supporting female role—are all in couplets. The supporting
female actor did not produce syllables with the correct rhyme at the end of
her lines. Upon hearing her mistake, the military role and comic role actors
improvised lines of plain speech to allow her a break and to distract the
audience's attention from the error. This is an example of wrap-up. After the
break, the supporting female actor was able to catch up and succeeded in
improvising a couplet that followed the rhyming scheme.

The function of repeating the last phrase of a segment is to enhance the
coordination of the spoken and instrumental segments. The last phrase is
repeated in segments recited by the principal female, supporting male,
military and the second-supporting female role actors in Example 9.2. An
actor is expected to repeat the last short phrase if the segment is ending, so
that another actor can follow with a new segment in time, or the percussionists can play the appropriate pattern. When the comic and principal
male role actors failed to observe the practice, as in Music Example 9.2, this
resulted in some irregularities. There is no speech during the three
woodblock strokes after the comic role actor's segment, and one stroke
after the principal male role actor's segment, probably because the other
actors did not realize that they had finished their segments. The practice of
repeating a short phrase to indicate the end of a segment or passage is also
used in singing of *Nam jem* and *Muk jy*.

Yung (1989:63–64) mentions that lines of patter speech often have five
or seven syllables. As we can see from the examples in this chapter, the
actual number of syllables in each line is often far from regular, but, when
grasp syllables, nonsense syllables and particles are excluded, most of the
lines follow Yung's description.[3]

To examine the uses of improvisation in patter speech, four versions of
another passage from the play *The Swallow Returns* are transcribed and
juxtaposed in Example 9.3 (see pp. 297–311), along with two versions of

the script. Since the script does not contain rhythmic notation, the performers had to improvise the placement of the syllables.

Version 3 (1985a) departs the most from the script. In Segment 1 recited by female actor A, the second line in the script was deleted in the performance. In Segment 3 by the same actor, a completely different line was improvised to replace the second one in the script, and an additional short line was improvised in the performance. Afterwards, female actor A made the *sau gwet* hand shadow to stop the accompanying percussion music. She took a short break, apparently to allow herself time to recall the text written in the script. Then she showed the *Pok deng ngo* hand shadow to notify the percussionists that she would continue the patter speech delivery. After the percussion pattern *Pok deng ngo* was played, she recited two lines to conclude the passage.

Besides the improvisatory realization of the placement of syllables, Table 9.1 shows three more kinds of improvisation that are used in Example 9.3: the replacement, addition and deletion of syllables, phrases and lines.

One way to add phrases, as noted above, is to repeat the last phrase of a segment to notify other performers that the segment is ending. This occurs in all but three of the segments in Example 9.3. A variation takes place at the end of the passage in the 1985a and 1985b versions, where the actors repeated the whole line instead of only the last phrase. The absence of the repeated phrase (in Segment 1 of Version 3, Segment 2 of Versions 3 and 4) caused no disturbance in the performance, probably because the actors knew the text well as the play was frequently performed and the scene involved only two actors.

Though probably subconsciously, the actors who deliver passages of patter speech determine the relative duration of each line by adding, deleting and grouping syllables together. The delivery of the text is regulated by the woodblock strokes, and the time span of each line can be expressed in terms of the number of strokes or beats. Table 9.2 shows the lengths of all fifty-six lines in the four versions, in terms of the number of strokes accompanying their delivery. Excepting the added short line in Version 1985a, all lines have three to seven strokes, and most (thirty-three of fifty-six) in four strokes. Of the thirteen lines that have more than four strokes, nine appear at the ends of segments. Interestingly, nine of the twelve segments are structured in a progressively increasing number of strokes per line.

Table 9.1 Uses of improvisation in passages contained in Example 9.3

Version 1

Segments	Lines	realization	addition	deletion	replacement
Segment 1	1	x			
	2	x			
	3	x			x
	4	x	x		
Segment 2	1	x			
	2	x			
	3	x	x		
	4	x		x	
	5	x			
	6	x			
Segment 3	1	x			
	2	x	x		
	3	x	x		x
	4	x	x		

Version 2

Segments	Lines	realization	addition	deletion	replacement
Segment 1	1	x			
	2	x			
	3	x			x
	4	x	x		
Segment 2	1	x			
	2	x			
	3	x			
	4	x		x	
	5	x			
	6	x	x		
Segment 3	1	x		x	
	2	x	x		
	3	x			
	4	x	x		

**Table 9.1 Uses of improvisation in passages contained in
Example 9.3** (cont'd)

Version 3

Segments	Lines	realization	addition	deletion	replacement
Segment 1	1	x	x		
	2				
	3	x			
	4	x	x		x
Segment 2	1	x			
	2	x			
	3	x			
	4	x			x
	5	x			
	6	x	x		
Segment 3	1	x	x		
	2	x			x
	added	x	x		
	3	x	x	x	
	4	x			

Version 4

Segments	Lines	realization	addition	deletion	replacement
Segment 1	1	x			
	2	x			x
	3	x			x
	4	x	x	x	
Segment 2	1	x			
	2	x			
	3	x	x		
	4	x	x		
	5	x			
	6	x	x		
Segment 3	1	x	x		x
	2	x	x		
	3	x			x
	4	x	x	x	x

**Table 9.2 Number of woodblock strokes in segments
contained in Example 9.3**

Segments	Lines	Versions			
		Version 1 (1975)	Version 2 (1980)	Version 3 (1985a)	Version 4 (1985b)
Segment 1	1	4	4	4	4
	2	4	4	0	4
	3	4	5	4	5
	4	6	7	4	5
Segment 2	1	3	3	3	3
	2	4	5	4	4
	3	4	4	4	4
	4	4	4	4	4
	5	4	4	4	4
	6	6	6	4	4
Segment 3	1	3	3	4	5
	2	3	3	4	3
	added	0	0	2	0
	3	4	4	4	4
	4	6	7	6	6

One to four syllables are grouped in each woodblock stroke (see Table 9.3). Forty-five strokes have only one syllable spoken either short or long. About two-thirds of the strokes have two syllables, in five different rhythmic patterns. There are twenty-seven strokes with three syllables, in four rhythmic patterns. Only eleven strokes have four syllables, all in the same rhythm. Though only thirty-seven of the 256 strokes in Table 9.3 have syncopated rhythmic patterns (♪, ♫, ♫, ♫), such groupings contrast with the prevailing onbeat formation. Seven of these syncopated groupings occur towards the ends of segments, when the last short phrase or the whole line is repeated. For rhythmic variety, each of the fifty-six lines in the four versions employs more than one pattern of syllable placement.

Rhymed Speech

Rhymed speech has no regular structure in respect to the number of syllables, phrases and lines, and is delivered with no regular pulse and no

Table 9.3 Rhythmic patterns of syllable grouping used in segments contained in Example 9.3

	Number of syllables in a stroke										
	1 syllable in a stroke		2 syllables in a stroke				3 syllables in a stroke				4 syllables in a stroke
rhythmic patterns	♩	♪	♫	♫.	♫.	♫	♫	♫	♫	♫.	♫♫
number of occurrences in each pattern	38	7	123	23	3	2	3	19	4	1	11
total number of occurrences	45		153				27				11

instrumental accompaniment, except that the last syllables of the lines have to rhyme. As in poetic and patter speech, nonsense and exclamatory syllables can be added after the rhyming ones; each line is then punctuated by a one-stroke percussion pattern. Example 9.4a shows two segments from a passage of rhymed speech, from the script of the play *The Swallow Returns*, as well as four performed versions (1976, 1980, 1985a and 1985b). According to the script, the first segment is to be recited by the actor of the principal male role, the second by the actor playing the official. Each segment has only one line, typical for a rhymed speech passage.

The principal female actor recites a passage of poetic speech in the opening of Act III of *The Swallow Returns*. (9 April 1987, Tsing Yi Island, Hong Kong)

The script prescribes five phrases in Segment 1 and six phrases in Segment 2 and such phrases are separated by commas in Example 9.4a (see pp. 312–17). The two versions of the script differ in only one syllable: the syllable *ming* 命 (to order) in the third phrase of Segment 2 in Version A is absent from Version B. Thus the phrase in Version A is translated as "he ordered this minor official to observe publicly and investigate privately," while Version B says "this minor official observed publicly and investigated privately."

The percussion pattern *Sin fung ca* written in the script is intended mainly to accompany the stage movements: the principal male role actor drags the actor who plays the official to the edge of the stage to question him. Rhymed speech is only occasionally preceded by this percussion pattern.

The phrase divisions in the four transcribed versions are determined by the actors' pauses. The two segments in Version 1 have seven and six phrases respectively (the plain speech interpolated in Segment 1 and the exclamation added in Segment 2 are not counted). In Version 2, the two segments each have five phrases. In Version 3, the two segments have five and six phrases respectively (the short plain speech phrase interpolated in Segment 1 is not counted). The two segments of Version 4 are of six and five phrases respectively. The order and contents of the phrases in the four performed versions, however, are different from each other and from the script. Example 9.4b (see pp. 317–20) juxtaposes phrases with similar meaning from Segment 1.

Changes found in Example 9.4 were produced improvisatorily, by adding, deleting and replacing syllables and phrases. These same practices have already been discussed in the sections above, on poetic and patter speech, so a systematic analysis is not repeated here.

An instance of added syllables and phrases can be seen in phrases 3 and 4, Segment 1, Version 1 in Example 9.4b. This version omits phrases 2 and 3 of the script. Version 4 includes a replacement phrase in Segment 1: the script's phrases "three months ago we made a sneak attack on the Huns" and "escaped individually" are replaced by a single phrase, "I was separated from my father-emperor." The rhyming scheme is kept in all versions, even when ending syllables are replaced: in Version 2 of Segment 1, the actor replaced the syllable *cy* 處 (a place) by *zy* 住 (to live); in Version 3 Segment 1, the actor used *ci* 此 (this place).

Most of the phrases in these versions are more or less based on the script. The exceptions are the first three phrases in Version 4 of Segment 1, and the last phrase of Version 3 in Segment 1. The actor in Version 4 deletes the phrase "official" and adds the phrases "I have told you not to address me in this way," "you address me as 'Your Highness' even when somebody is around," and "yes." The actor in Version 3 changes the last phrase from "how do you know the living place of this young prince" to "how did you follow my trail and come to this place?"

In Segment 1, phrases other than the first and last ones carry the main ideas and were performed variably by different actors. They are referred to as the "inner" phrases. To facilitate analysis, the inner phrases in the script and four performance versions have been syntactically separated into groups. Example 9.5 (see pp. 321–27) contains these groups and a detailed translation of the texts.[4] Comparison shows that an individual version may contain some of the textual groups written in the script, delete some of the groups, or add different groups. The result is that the overall ideas are presented in performance, but the actors' versions may well become quite different from the written text.

The actors in Cantonese opera handle the textual groups written in the script in the same way a composer of Western European art music handles motives. Table 9.4 compares nine textual groups from the script in Example 9.4b; these are the "basic motives," while the groups added by the actors are "additional motives." Textual groups with similar meaning are listed under the same motive in the table. As the table shows, within Segment 1, the actor of Version 1 used five additional motives and three basic motives, but deleted six basic motives. The actor who delivered Version 2 used four additional motives and four basic motives, but deleted five basic motives. The actor who performed Version 3 used three additional motives and all nine basic motives. And the actor in Version 4 used two additional motives and two basic motives, but deleted seven basic motives. Version 3 deviates least from the script, Version 4 deviates the most.

Percussion patterns play a significant part in the accompaniment; their use during the delivery of rhymed speech segments must be noted. The script calls for a one-stroke percussion pattern at the end of the third phrase of Segment 1, but this is not observed in any of the performed versions. However, the one-stroke pattern appears at the end of Segment 1 in all four versions, as well as after the interpolated exclamation in Version 1 Segment 2, and at the end of Segment 2 in Versions 3 and 4. As noted in Chapter 7, the percussionists can always improvisatorily add the one-stroke pattern at

Table 9.4 The use of motives in the texts of Example 9.5

	additional motive 1	additional motive 2	basic motive 1	additional motive 2	basic motive 2	basic motive 3
Script			*sam jyt cin* 三月前		*tau zap* 偸襲	*wu jing* 胡營
Version 1	*gei dek* 記得	*ngo* 我	*samgojytcin* 三個月前			
Version 2	*gei dek* 記得	*ngo dei* 我哋	*samgojytcin* 三個月前			
Version 3			*sam jyt zi cin* 三月之前	*ngo dei* 我哋	*tau zap* 偸襲	*wu jing* 胡營
Version 4	*soeng* 想		*samgojytcin* 三個月前			

	basic motive 4	additional motive 3	basic motive 5	additional motive 4	basic motive 6	additional motive 5
Script	*zung liu* 中了		*hung nou* 匈奴		*mai fuk* 埋伏	
Version 1						
Version 2		*bei* 彼	*dik jen* 敵人		*so kwen* 所困	
Version 3	*zung zo* 中咗		*hung nou* 匈奴	*ge* 嘅	*mai fuk* 埋伏	
Version 4						*ngo tung ngo fu wong* 我同我父王

Table 9.4 The use of motives in the texts of Example 9.5 (cont'd)

	additional motive 6	basic motive 7	additional motive 7	basic motive 8	additional motive 8	basic motive 9
Script				*gok zi* 各自		*tou mong* 逃亡
Version 1	*tung nei* 同你	*set san* 失散				*tou mong* 逃亡
Version 2		*set san* 失散				*tou mong* 逃亡
Version 3		*set san* 失散	*zi hau* 之後	*gok zi* 各自	*lok fong* 落荒	*tou mong* 逃亡
Version 4		*set san* 失散				

	additional motive 9	additional motive 10
Script		
Version 1	*ngo dai soeng dou ci* 我帶嚐到此	*jau heng dek key dei hing mui leong jen* … 尤幸得佢哋兄妹兩人…
Version 2		
Version 3		
Version 4		

appropriate moments to enhance the dramatic effect.

Actors can improvisatorily add plain speech and exclamation within a segment of rhymed speech. Instances are found in Example 9.4a, Version 1, Segments 1 and 2, and Version 3 Segment 1. Normally, plain speech is interpolated only in rhymed speech passages and rarely in other speech types. Its occurrence in poetic or patter speech is merely for wrapping up mistakes or improvising comic episodes.

Plain Speech

In Cantonese opera, plain speech is vernacular Cantonese, in a style delivered slowly and with exaggerated intonation to enable the audience to hear clearly through the amplifying system.

Plain speech text written in scripts are not structured in lines. Practically no actor follows the script exactly; improvisatory practices of addition, deletion and replacement of syllables are more frequently employed here than in other speech types. Thus plain speech seems always to be delivered freely, rather than according to a given structure.

As mentioned earlier,[5] actors often spontaneously improvise plain speech within passages and segments of rhymed speech, and sometimes even in patter speech. Furthermore, while plain speech is not frequently added improvisatorily in sung passages or segments, actors often improvise plain speech within a passage or segment of *Kwen fa* singing, although rarely into other kinds of sung passages because the non-pulsatory nature of *Kwen fa* is more compatible to the free structure of plain speech. Another possible occurrence of improvised plain speech is during a long melodic instrumental interlude within a vocal passage. In such cases, however, the improvised words become supported speech because it is then accompanied by melodic instrumental music.

Example 9.6 (see pp. 328–29) shows a *Kwen fa* segment from the script and from the 1985a performance of the play *The Swallow Returns*. As the example shows, the actor added plain speech to the sung segment and, thus, created a dramatic dialogue between speech and singing.

Plain speech is often used to enhance comic episodes. Example 9.7 (see pp. 330–31) illustrates the comic function, by comparing the script and two performance versions of a *Muk jy* segment from the play *The Heroic Blood Sheds on Mount Pei Pa*.[6] The actor in Version 1 followed the script closely, replacing some syllables in line 2 and changing the older reference to

Marilyn Monroe to the more current one of Bo Derek. The actor in Version 2 made even greater changes, deleting line 1 and replacing it with a segment of plain speech, to prepare for the improvisation that took place in the singing of line 2.

Plain speech is also used to wrap up mistakes. Example 9.8 (see p. 332) is from the 1985a version of the play *The Swallow Returns*.[7] As mentioned above, the female actor had difficulty continuing the patter speech in the segment, and then made the *sau gwet* hand shadow to allow herself a break for recalling the text. Towards the end of the same scene, before she and the other female actor left the stage, she improvised the segment of plain speech shown in Example 9.8. Even though no one in the audience was able to detect her problem during the patter speech, because she wrapped up the problem with a break, she added the plain speech segment to confess her problem, probably not to the audience but to her fellow actor and the accompanists.

This example is consistent with other instances observed during fieldwork for this study. Actors always confessed their mistakes and problems to their fellow actors and accompanists through improvised plain speech, and did not consider committing a mistake or having a problem as losing face. It seems one would truly lose face if he could not even detect his problem or mistake.

Plain speech can be inserted to solve other performance problems. Example 9.9 (see pp. 333–34) shows a plain speech passage from the play *The Courtship of the Phoenix by the Side of Lake Peach Blossom* performed by the Golden Dragon Cantonese Opera Troupe on 24 April 1985 in Happy Valley. At the beginning of Act V, the principal female role actor playing the empress escaped from the battlefield, performed *jiu sey fat* 搖水髮 (to sway one's hairpiece) which is a stylistic, continuous, circular movement of the neck and head that makes an actor's long hairpiece swinging in the air. It is a common practice that, in scenes featuring the arrest, defeat or conviction of characters, the performers have to take off their hats and then sway their heads and hairpiece to symbolize their strain and distress. Performers usually try their best to sway as many times as they can to gain applause from the audience. In this particular performance, the actress swayed more than three hundred times and earned loud applause. Following *jiu sey fat*, a short melodic prelude was struck up by the accompanists. Upon hearing that, she showed a gestic hint to notify the accompanists that she would make some stylistic movements on the stage. The melodic instrumentalists, thus, stopped, and the percussionists started to accompany her movements. A moment later, the performer moved to the edge of the stage and stood in front of the microphone. The melodic instrumentalists played the previous melodic prelude again, but were soon stopped by the actress who made a *sau gwet* hand shadow. She then spoke in plain speech, as transcribed in Example 9.9. The melodic prelude was again played following her speech, and she began to sing the *Siu kuk* tune *Fo zung lin* 火中蓮 (*Lotus in Fire*).

When I interviewed the performer the next day, she told me that the stylistic movements and the passage of plain speech were added after the energy-consuming *jiu sey fat* performance, to give herself a respite before starting the *Lotus in Fire*. The melodic accompanists, assuming she would start the tune right after the *jiu sey fat*, played the short melodic prelude. The gestic hint and *sau gwet* hand shadow functioned to stop the melodic music, but notified the percussion musicians to start their accompaniments. The percussionists were attentive during the plain speech—which, though improvised, was closely related to the plot in content—and played two one-stroke patterns within the passage. After the delivery of the plain speech, the melodic instrumentalists played the short prelude again, and the actor sang. In this way, we can observe the role of gestic hint and hand shadow in coordinating the accompanists during the performance of improvised passages.

Plain speech is also used to elaborate on details in the plot. Example 9.10 (see pp. 335–38) shows a passage of plain speech from the script and a performance (1985a) of *The Swallow Returns*. While the passage written in the script contains only seven phrases in one segment, the passage in the performed version is composed of three segments with thirty-seven phrases. In Segment 1, the comic role actor spoke eleven phrases, was interrupted by the principal female role actor's exclamation, and continued with another nineteen phrases. In Segment 2, the principal female actor spoke two phrases as a response to the comic role actor. The comic role actor then spoke four phrases in Segment 3, which are connected to a *Coeng gey kwen fa* singing segment. Besides the addition and replacement of syllables and phrases, two phrases in the script were omitted. The deletion was probably improvised to avoid repetition, as the following *Coeng gey kwen fa* segment would start with a similar text.

The plain speech delivery of text intended to be sung is illustrated in

Example 9.11 (see pp. 339–41). The texts are a group of segments from the script and a performed version of the play *Story of the Purple Hairpin*.[8] The text of the *Muk jy* (a kind of singing narrative) segment in the script is delivered as plain speech in the performed version. In practice, the actor who delivered the plain speech did not have to make a *sau gwet* hand shadow to stop the melodic instrumentalists before he started the delivery, because *Muk jy* is supposed to be sung without accompaniment.

Besides *Muk jy*, sometimes actors use the text of *Kwen fa* or *Coeng gey kwen fa* segments for plain speech delivery. Example 9.12 (see pp. 342–43) shows the script and a performed version of a *Coeng gey kwen fa* segment from *The Swallow Returns*.[9] The segment in the script was intended to be sung in the performance, but part of its text was delivered as plain speech, so that the *Coeng gey kwen fa* segment was, in part, replaced by plain speech.

Concluding Notes

In all, speech delivery involves six kinds of improvisation. They are first, the addition; second, the deletion; third, the replacement of syllables, phrases and lines; fourth, the addition of a whole passage of speech delivery; fifth, the use of vocal text for speech delivery; and, sixth, realization of syllable grouping. The last kind is unique to patter speech because of its steady pulse; the fifth kind is found only in plain speech; the first and third are present in all four types of speech delivery discussed here; the second kind is used in patter, rhymed and plain speech; and the fourth is usually used in patter and plain speech. The first three and the sixth kinds, which are micro-improvisation, are the ones most often used. Both the fourth and the fifth kinds involve whole passages, and are macro-improvisation.

The first three kinds of micro-improvisation are employed most in plain speech and rhymed speech, less in patter speech, and least in poetic speech. The textual structure of poetic speech is the strictest, followed by patter speech, then rhymed speech, and the freest structure, plain speech. Hence, we see that the stricter the textual structure, the more limited the application of micro-improvisation. As a corollary, the use of improvisation is constrained by the textual structure in speech delivery.

The dramatic functions of the four types of speech delivery can also be profiled, according to Yung (1989:62): poetic speech is often used as a soliloquy when a certain character enters the stage; patter speech is often used as narration; rhymed speech and plain speech are used as dialogues. Moreover, poetic speech and rhymed speech are often used in scenes with a more or less serious context or mood, such as in court or in a palace; rhymed speech is often used in dialogues between officials, members of the royal family, and educated persons. Patter speech and plain speech are used more in scenes with a casual context, or in scenes involving characters who belong to a lower social class. Hence, the extent to which the three kinds of micro-improvisation are utilized is also related to the dramatic contexts of the performance. The more serious and intense the context or mood, the less micro-improvisation. However, my observation reveals that, although micro-improvisation in speech deliveries diminishes in serious scenes, improvisation of gestures and movements generally occurs more.

The dramatic context's association with each of the four types of speech delivery is, of course, not without exceptions. For example, the patter speech in Example 9.2, although a conversation among royal personages and, therefore, supposedly serious, was in fact only a comic episode used by the actors to prolong the duration of the performance. Another exception is the passage of plain speech cited in Example 9.9, spoken by the empress as an expression of regret: the main function of the improvisation was nothing more than a breather for the actor after a tiring *jiu sey fat* performance.

Although motivic analysis is applied only to the delivery of rhymed speech here, it is evident that motivic treatment is used in all four types of speech delivery under study. In Chapter 5 we have noted the economical form in which the scripts of Cantonese opera are often written. The motivic analysis shows that the texts are written in a highly condensed and economical form: only the important ideas are given in the script and actors are expected to elaborate on the details. To prepare for a speech, an actor has only to memorize the basic ideas or motives and the rhyming scheme, but not necessarily words of the text. Improvisation, involving addition, deletion and replacement of syllables, phrases and lines, plays an important role during the performance. An actor who recites from the script performance after performance is not considered wrong, but certainly regarded as inadequate. Hence, the improvisatory practices of addition, deletion and replacement can be seen as the necessary means of realizing speech delivery from the written scripts.

Notes

1. Information given by Wong at a class in The Chinese University of Hong Kong.
2. The performance was staged by the Golden Dragon Cantonese Opera Troupe on 24 April 1985 in Happy Valley. See discussion of the performance context in Chapter 8.
3. As mentioned previously, spoken Cantonese syllables that have no corresponding written forms are romanized with no Chinese characters provided.
4. Phrases 3 and 4 of Version 1 are not separated into textual groups because the other three versions do not contain phrases with similar meanings and separation is, thus, insignificant to the present comparison.
5. Improvised comic episodes are often composed of plain speech; see the discussion of various kinds of comic episodes in Chapter 3.
6. Version 1 is taken from the performance staged by the Colourful Dragon and Phoenix Cantonese Opera Troupe on 3 July 1985 at Tai Po; Version 2 is taken from the performance staged by the Jing Bou Cantonese Opera Troupe on 12 October 1985 at Shek O.
7. See the discussion of the performance context in Chapter 8.
8. Version 1 was performed by the Sing Lei Nin 勝利年 (year of victory) Cantonese Opera Troupe at the Paladium Opera House on 16 June 1984.
9. See the discussion of the performance context in Chapter 8.

Example 9.1   The texts of a passage of poetic speech from
The Swallow Returns

(line 1)
(Script)
cae   loeng   ci   mou   ting   ji   tae.
淒　涼　慈　母　聽　兒　啼
A sobbing, loving mother is listening to her baby's cry.

Version 1 (1976)
(same as the script) (one-stroke)

Version 2 (1980)
(same as the script) (one-stroke)

Version 3 (1985a)
(same as the script) (one-stroke)

Version 4 (1985b)
(same as the script) (one-stroke)

(line 2)
(Script)
cam   cit   jau   jy   wun   fu   gwae.
慘　切　猶　如　喚　夫　歸
(The baby) cries sorrowfully as if calling (my) husband to come home.

Version 1 (1976)
(same as the script) (one-stroke)

Version 2 (1980)
(same as the script) (one-stroke)

Version 3 (1985a)
cam   cit   jau   jy   ngo   wun   fu   gwae. (one-stroke)
慘　切　猶　如　我　喚　父　歸
(The baby) cries sorrowfully as if I were calling (his) father to come home.

Version 4 (1985b)
(same as the script) (one-stroke)

Example 9.1 The texts of a passage of poetic speech from
           The Swallow Returns (cont'd)

(line 3)
(Script)
bit   si   jep   men   gwae   ho   jet.
別   時   泣   問   歸   何   日
At the time (we) separated, (I) weepingly asked when (he) would return.

Version 1 (1976)
bit   si   dae   men   gwae   ho   jet.   (one-stroke)
別   時   低   問   歸   何   日
At the time (we) separated, in a low voice, (I) asked when
(he) would return.

Version 2 (1980)
ngo   bit   si   jep   men   gwae   ho   jet.   (one-stroke)
我   別   時   泣   問   歸   何   日
I, at the time (we) separated, weepingly asked when (he) would return.

Version 3 (1985a)
(same as the script) (one-stroke)

Version 4 (1985b)
(same as the script) (one-stroke)

(line 4)
(Script)
zuk   hau   long   gwae   zoi   jin   gwae.
囑   候   郎   歸   在   燕   歸
(He) told (me) to expect his return when the swallow returns.

Version 1 (1976)
zuk   hau   long   gwae (one-stroke)   *zoi   jin   gwae   a.* (one-stroke)
囑   候   郎   歸   在   燕   歸   呀
(He) told (me) to expect his return when the swallow returns. Ah!

Example 9.1 The texts of a passage of poetic speech from
         The Swallow Returns (cont'd)

Version 2 (1980)

key zuk hau long gwae (one-stroke) *zoi jin gwae.* (one-stroke)

佢　嘱　候　郎　歸　　　　　在　燕　歸

He told (me) to expect his return when the swallow returns.

Version 3 (1985a)

dae si jin gwae (one-stroke) *mei gin ngo long gwae a.*

底　是　燕　歸　　　　未　見　我　郎　歸　呀

(one-stroke)

The fact is that the swallow returns
without seeing my husband coming home. Ah!

Version 4 (1985b)

zuk hau jin gwae (one-stroke) *si long gwae a.* (one-stroke)

嘱　候　燕　歸　　　　是　郎　歸　呀

(He) told (me) to wait for the swallow's return and he will also return. Ah!

Example 9.2 An improvised passage of patter speech from *The Courtship of the Phoenix by the Side of Lake Peach Blossom*

(the comic role actor makes a *Pok deng ngo* hand shadow)
(the percussionists play the *Pok deng ngo* pattern)
(the comic role actor recites patter speech)

(line 1)

(woodblock strokes)

(speech rhythm)
(romanizations)   giu   gey   a   Sing,

(Chinese characters)   叫   句   阿   成

(translation of the line)   Let me talk to you, Sing,

(line 2)

dai   ga   zau   jiu   sem   ziu   a.
大   家   就   要   心   照   呀
let us open our hearts to each other.

(line 3)

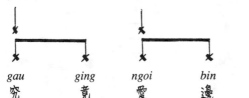

gau   ging   ngoi   bin   go?
究   竟   愛   邊   個
Which one do you like?

(line 4)

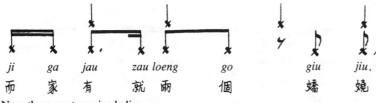

ji   ga   jau   zau loeng   go   giu   jiu.
而   家   有   就   兩   個   嬌   嬈
Now there are two nice ladies.

Example 9.2 An improvised passage of patter speech from
The Courtship of the Phoenix by the Side of
Lake Peach Blossom (cont'd)

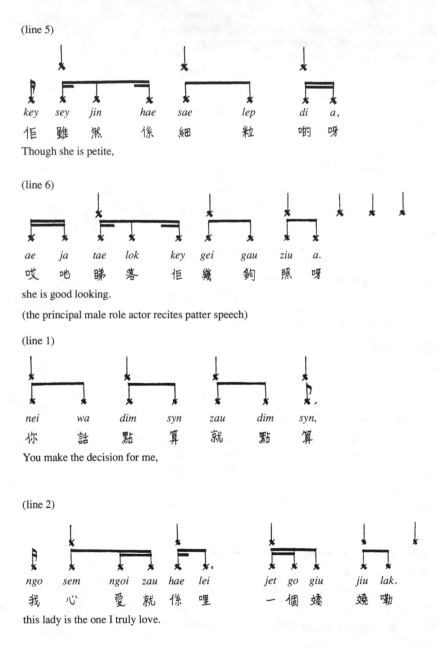

(line 5)

key   sey   jin   hae   sae   lep   di   a,
佢   雖   然   係   細   粒   啲   呀
Though she is petite,

(line 6)

ae   ja   tae   lok   key   gei   gau   ziu   a.
哎   吔   睇   落   佢   幾   夠   照   呀

she is good looking.

(the principal male role actor recites patter speech)

(line 1)

nei   wa   dim   syn   zau   dim   syn,
你   話   點   算   就   點   算
You make the decision for me,

(line 2)

ngo   sem   ngoi   zau   hae   lei   jet   go   giu   jiu   lak.
我   心   愛   就   係   哩   一   個   嬌   嬈   嘞

this lady is the one I truly love.

Example 9.2 An improvised passage of patter speech from *The Courtship of the Phoenix by the Side of Lake Peach Blossom* (cont'd)

(the principal female role actor recites patter speech)

(line 1)

giu　　sing　　a　　Hung-　　lyn,
叫　　聲　　阿　　紅　　鸞

Let me talk to you, Hung-lyn,

(line 2)

jau　　gin　　si　cing　zau　hou　　gen　　jiu　a.
有　　件　　事　情　就　好　　緊　　要　呀

there is an important matter.

(line 3)

wae,　　　dong　jet　go　sau　　　cing　　si,
喂　　　當　日　個　首　　　情　　詩

Hey, the love poem that day,

(line 4)

ming　　ming　hae　se　　　sam　　gang.
明　　明　係　寫　　　三　　更

I had clearly written (that I would meet him at) the fifth hour (of the night).

Example 9.2 An improvised passage of patter speech from
The Courtship of the Phoenix by the Side of
Lake Peach Blossom (cont'd)

(line 5)

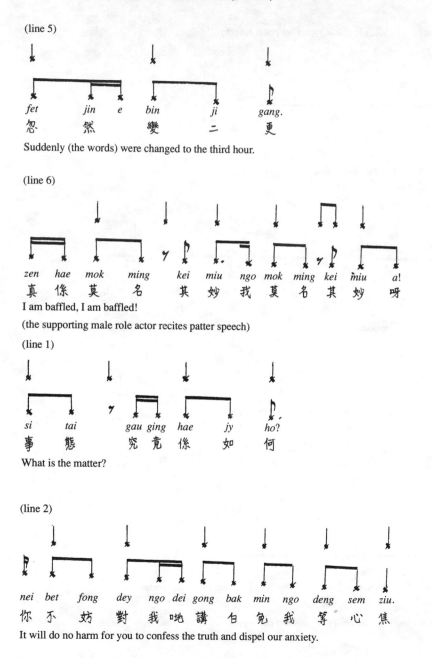

fet   jin   e   bin   ji   gang.
忽   然   變   二   更

Suddenly (the words) were changed to the third hour.

(line 6)

zen hae mok ming   kei miu ngo mok ming kei miu   a!
真   係   莫   名   其   妙   我   莫   名   其   妙   呀

I am baffled, I am baffled!

(the supporting male role actor recites patter speech)

(line 1)

si   tai   gau ging hae   jy   ho?
事   態   究   竟   係   如   何

What is the matter?

(line 2)

nei   bet fong   dey   ngo dei gong bak min ngo deng sem ziu.
你   不   妨   對   我   哋   講   白   免   我   等   心   焦

It will do no harm for you to confess the truth and dispel our anxiety.

Example 9.2 An improvised passage of patter speech from
**   *The Courtship of the Phoenix by the Side of***
**   *Lake Peach Blossom* (cont'd)**

(line 3)

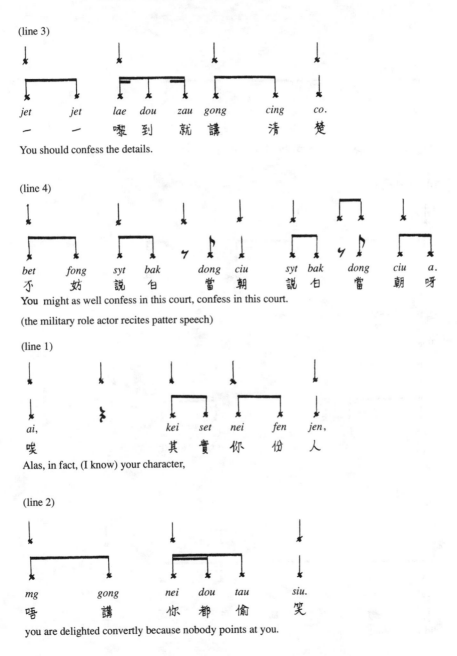

| jet | jet | lae | dou | zau | gong | cing | co. |
| 一 | 一 | 嚟 | 到 | 就 | 講 | 清 | 楚 |

You should confess the details.

(line 4)

| bet | fong | syt | bak | dong | ciu | syt | bak | dong | ciu | a. |
| 不 | 妨 | 説 | 白 | 當 | 朝 | 説 | 白 | 當 | 朝 | 呀 |

You might as well confess in this court, confess in this court.

(the military role actor recites patter speech)

(line 1)

| ai, | | kei | set | nei | fen | jen, |
| 唉 | | 其 | 實 | 你 | 份 | 人 |

Alas, in fact, (I know) your character,

(line 2)

| mg | gong | nei | dou | tau | siu. |
| 唔 | 講 | 你 | 都 | 偷 | 笑 |

you are delighted convertly because nobody points at you.

Example 9.2 An improvised passage of patter speech from
The Courtship of the Phoenix by the Side of
Lake Peach Blossom (cont'd)

(line 3)

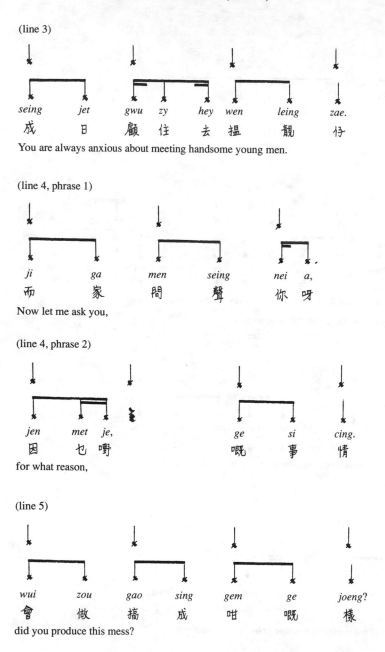

seing   jet   gwu   zy   hey   wen   leing   zae.
成   日   顧   住   去   搵   靚   仔
You are always anxious about meeting handsome young men.

(line 4, phrase 1)

ji   ga   men   seing   nei   a,
而   家   問   聲   你   呀
Now let me ask you,

(line 4, phrase 2)

jen   met   je,   ge   si   cing.
因   乜   嘢   嘅   事   情
for what reason,

(line 5)

wui   zou   gao   sing   gem   ge   joeng?
會   做   搞   成   咁   嘅   樣
did you produce this mess?

Example 9.2 An improvised passage of patter speech from
       The Courtship of the Phoenix by the Side of
       Lake Peach Blossom (cont'd)

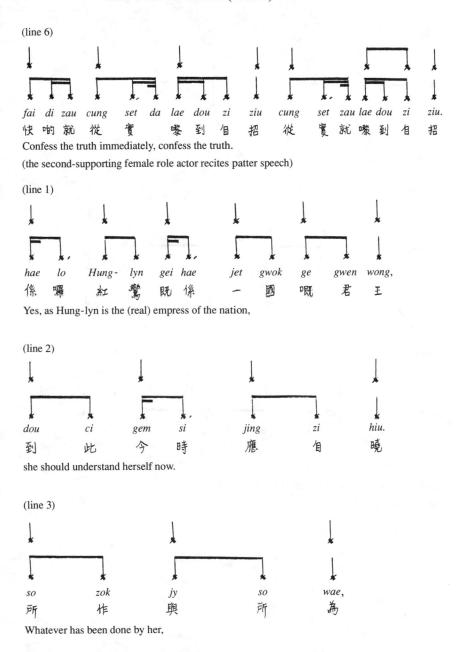

(line 6)

fai di zau cung set da lae dou zi ziu cung set zau lae dou zi ziu.

快 啲 就 從 實 嚟 到 佢 招 從 實 就 嚟 到 佢 招

Confess the truth immediately, confess the truth.

(the second-supporting female role actor recites patter speech)

(line 1)

hae lo Hung- lyn gei hae jet gwok ge gwen wong,

係 嚹 紅 鸞 既 係 一 國 嘅 君 王

Yes, as Hung-lyn is the (real) empress of the nation,

(line 2)

dou ci gem si jing zi hiu.

到 此 今 時 應 自 曉

she should understand herself now.

(line 3)

so zok jy so wae,

所 作 與 所 為

Whatever has been done by her,

Example 9.2 An improvised passage of patter speech from
The Courtship of the Phoenix by the Side of
Lake Peach Blossom (cont'd)

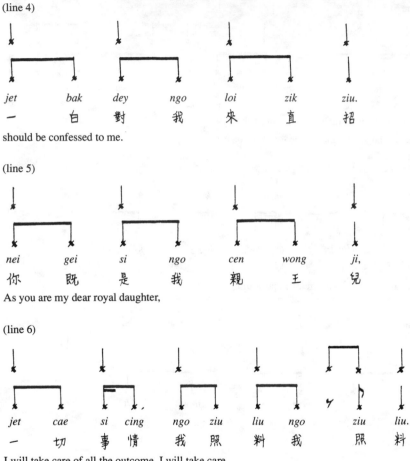

(line 4)

jet   bak   dey   ngo   loi   zik   ziu.
一   白   對   我   來   直   招

should be confessed to me.

(line 5)

nei   gei   si   ngo   cen   wong   ji,
你   既   是   我   親   王   兒

As you are my dear royal daughter,

(line 6)

jet   cae   si   cing   ngo   ziu   liu   ngo   ziu   liu.
一   切   事   情   我   照   料   我   照   料

I will take care of all the outcome, I will take care.
(speak plain speech)

nei   gong   la.
你   講   啦

You speak.

Example 9.2 An improvised passage of patter speech from *The Courtship of the Phoenix by the Side of Lake Peach Blossom* (cont'd)

(the supporting female role actor recites patter speech)

(line 1)

e   e,   ngo   zi   si   sem   zok   sey.

嗯   嗯   我   自   私   心   作   祟

It was my selfishness that caused trouble.

(interpolated plain speech, omitted)

(line 2)

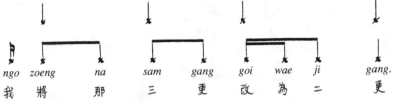

ngo   zoeng   na   sam   gang   goi   wae   ji   gang.

我   將   那   三   更   改   為   二   更

I changed the fifth hour to the third hour.

(line 3)

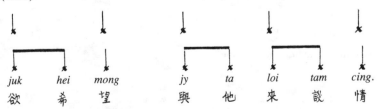

juk   hei   mong   jy   ta   loi   tam   cing.

欲   希   望   與   他   來   談   情

I planned to talk about love to him.

Example 9.2 An improvised passage of patter speech from
The Courtship of the Phoenix by the Side of
Lake Peach Blossom (cont'd)

(the military role actor speaks plain speech)

sam gang goi ji gang.
三　更　改　二　更
To change from three points (on the domino) to two points,

joek gwo tey pai gau zou zong ai sei fo la zen hae.
若　果　推　排　九　做　莊　哎　死　火　啦　真　係
you would certainly be dead if you were the banker in *pai gau* (domino) gambling.

(the comic role actor speaks plain speech)

gem mae bin zo ji sam gang?
咁　咪　變　咗　二　三　更
Would it then become two and three points?

ae ja zou dei zong dou sei jen la zen hae.
哎　吔　做　地　莊　都　死　入　啦　真　係
You would be dead even if you were only the co-banker.

(the supporting female role actor recites patter speech)

(line 4)

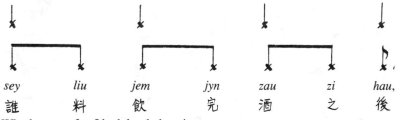

sey　　*liu*　　*jem*　　*jyn*　　*zau*　　*zi*　　*hau,*
誰　　料　　飲　　完　　酒　　之　　後
Who knows, after I had drunk the wine,

Example 9.2 An improvised passage of patter speech from
          The Courtship of the Phoenix by the Side of
          Lake Peach Blossom (cont'd)

(line 5)

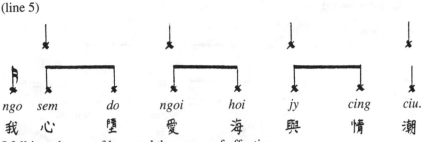

ngo	sem	do	ngoi	hoi	jy	cing	ciu.
我	心	墮	愛	海	與	情	潮

I fell into the sea of love and the waves of affection.

(the comic role actor speaks plain speech)

mg hae jem zo zau sem bep bep tiu a ma?
唔 係 飲 咗 酒 心 　　跳 吖 嘛
Did your heart beat fast after you had drunk the wine?

(the supporting female role actor speaks plain speech)

jau tiu jau, jau siu la.
又 跳 又 又 笑 啦
My heart beat fast, and, and I laughed.

(the comic role actor speaks plain speech)

so ji wa nei siu ney sem,
所 以 話 你 少 女 心
That is why I say you young girls,

Example 9.2 An improvised passage of patter speech from
The Courtship of the Phoenix by the Side of
***Lake Peach Blossom* (cont'd)**

(recites patter speech)

(line 1, phrase 1)

jem   zo   zau   a   go   sem   zau bep   bep   tiu   a,
飲   咗   酒   個 心   就   跳   呀

your hearts beat fast after you have drunk wine,

(line 1, phras 2)

gin   nam   zae   a   ae   ja   gwa   gwa   giu   a.
見   男   仔   哎 吔 呱   呱   叫   呀

you scream when you see young men.

(line 2)

"key fu   zy   ngo   gem zau   mg   dek   liu   a."
佢 扶   住   我   咁   就 唔   得   了   呀

"I became wild when he propped me up."

Example 9.3 Four versions of a patter speech passage from *The Swallow Returns*

(female actor A recites patter speech)
(segment 1, line 1)

Script, Version A
Soeng   Jin   Cyn   hou   ging   zi.
雙　燕　村　好　景　緻
There is nice scenery at *Two Swallows Village.*

Script, Version B
(same as Version A)

Version 1 (1975)

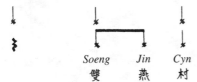

Version 2 (1980)

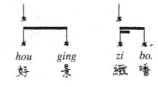

Version 3 (1985a)

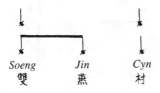

(syllables not in script: *bo* is a particle)

Version 4 (1985b)

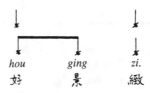

Example 9.3 Four versions of a patter speech passage from
The Swallow Returns (cont'd)

(segment 1, line 2)

Script, Version A
ce   ting   nei   nam   soeng   jin   jy.
且 聽 呢 喃 雙 燕 語
Please listen to the sweet songs of the two swallows.

Script, Version B
(same as Version A)

Version 1 (1975)

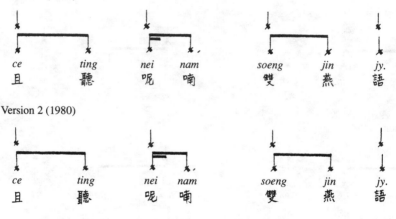

Version 2 (1980)

Version 3 (1985a)

(line deleted)

Version 4 (1985b)

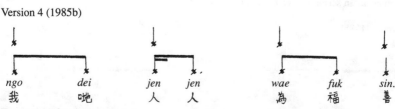

Every one of us is doing good.

Example 9.3 Four versions of a patter speech passage from
The Swallow Returns (cont'd)

(segment 1, line 3)

Script, Version A
zi cung Hung Nou cem fan hei fung jin,
自 從 匈 奴 侵 犯 起 烽 烟
But, since war started with the Huns' invasion.

Script, Version B
(same as Version A)

Version 1 (1975)

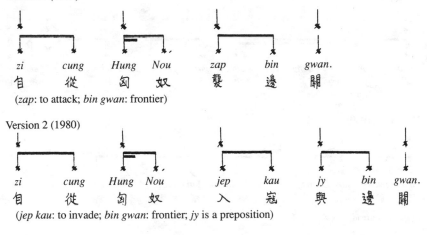

zi   cung   Hung Nou   zap   bin   gwan.
自   從   匈   奴   襲   邊   關
(*zap*: to attack; *bin gwan*: frontier)

Version 2 (1980)

zi   cung   Hung Nou   jep   kau   jy   bin   gwan.
自   從   匈   奴   入   寇   與   邊   關
(*jep kau*: to invade; *bin gwan*: frontier; *jy* is a preposition)

Version 3 (1985a)

zi   cung   Hung   Nou   cem   fan   hei   fung   jin,
自   從   匈   奴   侵   犯   起   烽   烟

Version 4 (1985b)

zi   cung   Hung Nou   cem   fan   hei   bin   gwan.
自   從   匈   奴   侵   犯   起   邊   關
(*bin gwan*: frontier)

Example 9.3 Four versions of a patter speech passage from
The Swallow Returns (cont'd)

(segment 1, line 4)

Script, Version A
ngo Sae Loeng coet bing gai set lei .
我　西　梁　出　兵　皆　失　利
Our (nation) Western Loeng has lost all the battles.

Script, Version B
(same as Version A)

Version 1 (1975)

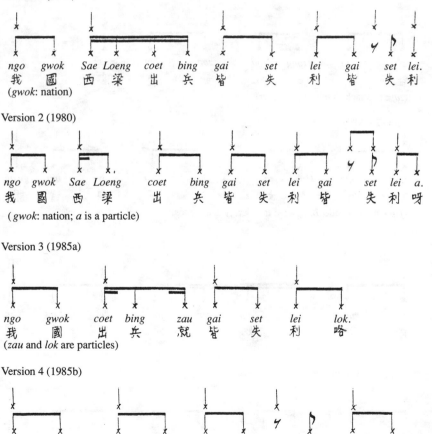

Version 2 (1980)

Version 3 (1985a)

Version 4 (1985b)

Example 9.3 Four versions of a patter speech passage from *The Swallow Returns* (cont'd)

(female actor B recites patter speech)
(segment 2, line 1)

Script, Version A
gei dek zoi sam jyt cin,
記　得　在　三　月　前
(I) remember three months ago,

Script, Version B
(same as Version A)

Version 1 (1975)

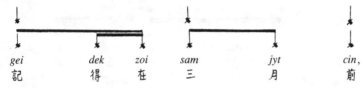

Version 2 (1980)

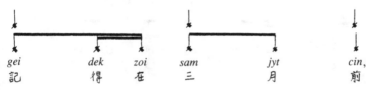

Version 3 (1985a)

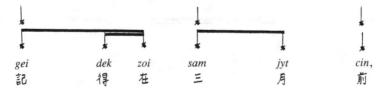

Version 4 (1985b)

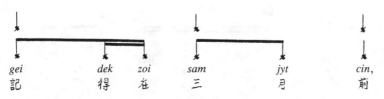

Example 9.3 Four versions of a patter speech passage from
The Swallow Returns (cont'd)

(segment 2, line 2)

Script, Version A
ngo gwen tau zap wu jing ging ci dei.
我　軍　偷　襲　胡　營　經　此　地
Our army passed by this village to give the Huns a sneak attack.

Script, Version B
(same as Version A)

Version 1 (1975)

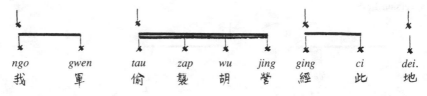

Version 2 (1980)

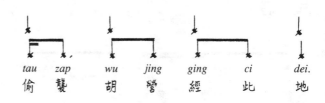

Version 3 (1985a)

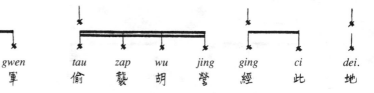

Version 4 (1985b)

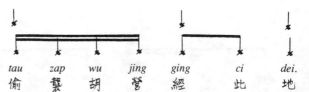

Example 9.3 Four versions of a patter speech passage from
The Swallow Returns (cont'd)

(segment 2, line 3)

Script, Version A
cyn zung jau wae Bak Lei- hoeng,
村　中　有　位　白　梨　香
In the village there was a girl called Bak Lei-hoeng,

Script, Version B
(same as Version A)

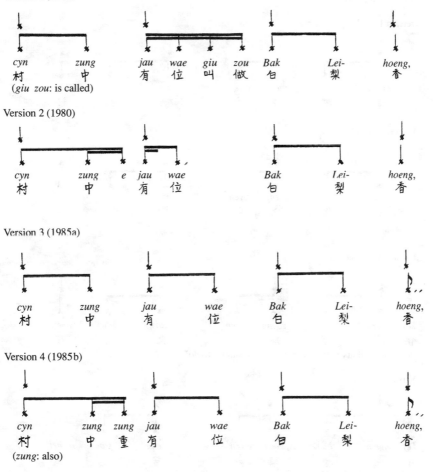

Version 1 (1975)

cyn   zung   jau wae giu zou Bak   Lei-   hoeng,
村   中   有   位   叫   做   白   梨   香
(*giu zou*: is called)

Version 2 (1980)

cyn   zung   e jau wae   Bak   Lei-   hoeng,
村   中   有   位   白   梨   香

Version 3 (1985a)

cyn   zung   jau   wae   Bak   Lei-   hoeng,
村   中   有   位   白   梨   香

Version 4 (1985b)

cyn   zung zung jau   wae   Bak   Lei-   hoeng,
村   中   重   有   位   白   梨   香
(*zung*: also)

Example 9.3 Four versions of a patter speech passage from
The Swallow Returns (cont'd)

(segment 2, line 4)

Script, Version A
key ngem ba zoeng gwen ceng gau hei.
佢 暗 把 將 軍 曾 救 起
she secretly rescued the general.

Script, Version B
key ba zoeng gwen ceng gau hei.
佢 把 將 軍 曾 救 起
she rescued the general.

Version 1 (1975)

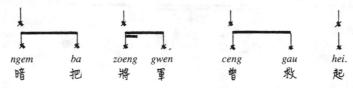

Version 2 (1980)

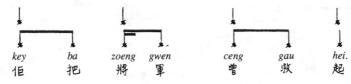

Version 3 (1985a)

(*loi* is an auxiliary verb, approximately meaning 'to do')

Version 4 (1985b)

Example 9.3 Four versions of a patter speech passage from
The Swallow Returns (cont'd)

(segment 2, line 5)

Script, Version A
liu soeng sam jyt loeng cing hin.
療　傷　三　月　雨　情　牽
They fell in love during the three months of recuperating.

Script, Version B
(same as Version A)

Version 1 (1975)

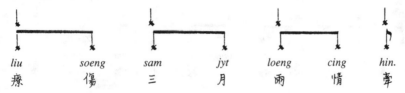

Version 2 (1980)

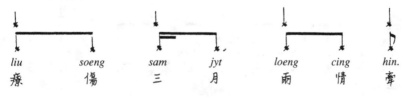

Version 3 (1985a)

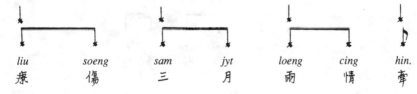

Version 4 (1985b)

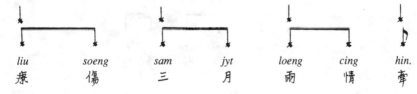

Example 9.3 Four versions of a patter speech passage from
The Swallow Returns (cont'd)

(segment 2, line 6)

Script, Version A
ho wae jet gin zung cing tim wen si.
可　謂　一　見　鍾　情　添　韻　事
Their falling in love at first sight can well be called a romantic story.

Script, Version B
(same as Version A)

Version 1 (1975)

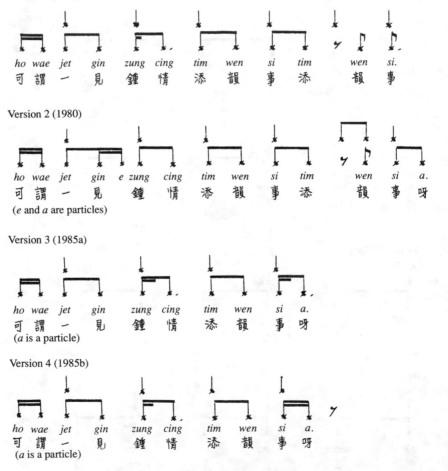

Version 2 (1980)

(*e* and *a* are particles)

Version 3 (1985a)

(*a* is a particle)

Version 4 (1985b)

(*a* is a particle)

Example 9.3 Four versions of a patter speech passage from *The Swallow Returns* (cont'd)

(female actor A recites patter speech)
(segment 3, line 1)

Script, Version A
nei ho bit sin mou jen,
你 何 必 羨 慕 人
You don't have to admire them,

Script, Version B
nei nei nei ho bit sin mou jen,
你 你 你 何 必 羨 慕 人
You, you, you don't have to admire them,

Version 1 (1975)

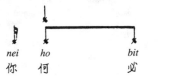

Version 2 (1980)

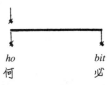

Version 3 (1985a)

nei jau ho bit sin mou jen zek,
你 又 何 必 羨 慕 人 唶
(*jau* and *zek* are particles)

Version 4 (1985b)

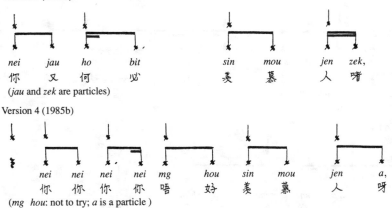

nei nei nei nei mg hou sin mou jen a,
你 你 你 你 唔 好 羨 慕 人 呀
(*mg hou*: not to try; *a* is a particle)

Example 9.3 Four versions of a patter speech passage from
The Swallow Returns (cont'd)

(segment 3, line 2)

Script, Version A
ci nai ngae him si.
此 乃 危 險 事
this is a dangerous matter.

Script, Version B
(same as Version A)

Version 1 (1975)

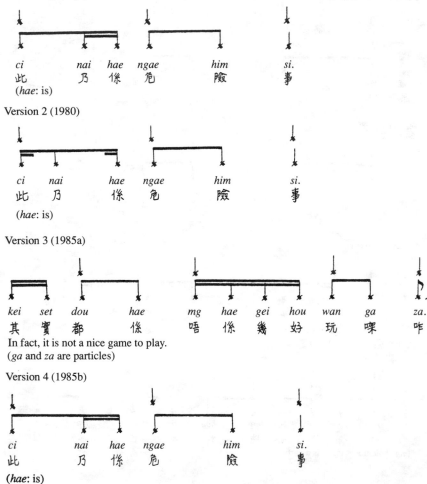

Version 2 (1980)

Version 3 (1985a)

Version 4 (1985b)

Example 9.3 Four versions of a patter speech passage from
The Swallow Returns (cont'd)

(segment 3, line 3)

Script, Version A
joek bei Hung Nou key ca zi , (one-stroke)

若　被　匈　奴　佢　查　知

If the Huns discover this,

Script, Version B
(same as Version A)

Version 1 (1975)

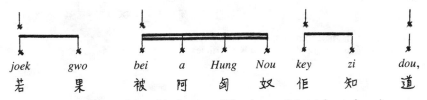

joek   gwo   bei   a   Hung   Nou   key   zi   dou,

若　　果　　被　　阿　　匈　　奴　　佢　　知　　道

(*joek   gwo*: an alternate form of *joek*, means 'if'; *a* is a particle; *zi dou*: to know)

Version 2 (1980)

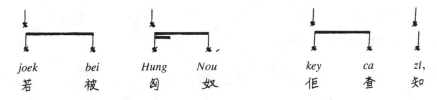

joek   bei   Hung   Nou   key   ca   zi,

若　　　被　　　匈　　奴　　　佢　　　查　　　知

Version 3 (1985a) (an additional line)

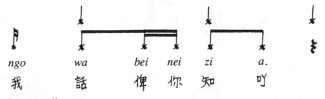

ngo   wa   bei   nei   zi   a.

我　　話　　俾　你　　知　　吖

Let me tell you.

(*a* is a particle)

Example 9.3 Four versions of a patter speech passage from
The Swallow Returns (cont'd)

(female actor A makes a *Sau gwet* hand shadow)
(two-stroke percussion pattern played by the percussionists)
(female actor A makes a *Pok deng ngo* hand shadow)
(*Pok deng ngo* percussion pattern played by the percussionists)
(female actor A recites patter speech)

(line 3)

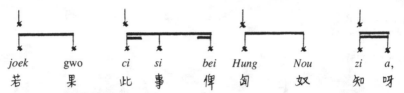

joek   gwo   ci   si   bei   Hung   Nou   zi   a,
若   果   此   事   俾   匈   奴   知   呀

(*joek gwo*: an alternate form of *joek*; *ci si*: this matter;
bei 俾: an alternate form of *bei* 被; *a* is a particle)

Version 4 (1985b)

joek   bei   Hung Nou   key   zi   men   a,
若   被   匈   奴   佢   知   聞   呀

(*zi men*: to hear about; *a* is a particle)

Example 9.3 Four versions of a patter speech passage from *The Swallow Returns* (cont'd)

(segment 3, line 4)

Script, Version A
hung pa seing cyn dou bei key ley hei. (repeat last phrase)
恐 怕 成 村 都 俾 佢 累 起
I am afraid the whole village will be implicated.

Script, Version B
(same as Version A)

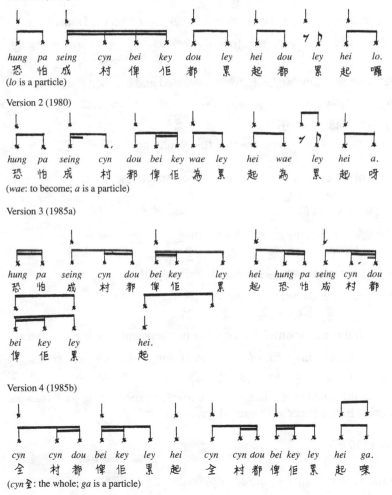

Version 1 (1975)

hung pa seing cyn bei key dou ley hei dou ley hei lo.
恐 怕 成 村 俾 佢 都 累 起 都 累 起 囉
(*lo* is a particle)

Version 2 (1980)

hung pa seing cyn dou bei key wae ley hei wae ley hei a.
恐 怕 成 村 都 俾 佢 為 累 起 為 累 起 呀
(*wae*: to become; *a* is a particle)

Version 3 (1985a)

hung pa seing cyn dou bei key ley hei hung pa seing cyn dou
恐 怕 成 村 都 俾 佢 累 起 恐 怕 成 村 都
bei key ley hei.
俾 佢 累 起

Version 4 (1985b)

cyn cyn dou bei key ley hei cyn cyn dou bei key ley hei ga.
全 村 都 俾 佢 累 起 全 村 都 俾 佢 累 起 㗎
(*cyn* 全: the whole; *ga* is a particle)

Example 9.4a The texts of a rhymed speech passage from
           The Swallow Returns

Script

(the percussion pattern *Sin fung ca* is played)
(the principal male role actor recites rhymed speech, segment 1)

(line 1, phrases 1 to 5)

dai fu, sam jyt cin tau zap wu jing,
大 夫 三 月 前 偷 襲 胡 營
Official, three months ago (we) made a sneak attack on the Huns,

zung liu Hung Nou mai fuk, (one-stroke) *set san gok zi tou mong,*
中 了 匈 奴 埋 伏   失 散 各 自 逃 亡
(we) fell into the Huns' ambush, were separated and escaped individually,

ho ji nei dek zi siu wong gey cy?
何 以 你 得 知 小 王 居 處
how do you know the living place of this young prince?

(the actor playing the official recites rhymed speech, segment 2)

(line 1, phrases 1 to 6)

din ha je, nei fu wong bing zung,
殿 下 爺 你 父 王 病 重
Your Highness, your father-emperor is seriously ill,

(ming) mei sen ming ca ngem fong,
命 微 臣 明 查 暗 訪
(he ordered) this minor official to observe publicly and investigate privately,

hau dek cyn ney tung zi, dek loi cem fong, dai loi jet zi ziu sy.
後 得 村 女 通 知 特 來 尋 訪 帶 來 一 紙 詔 書
Later I was informed by a village girl, I come here specially to look for you,
and to bring here a paper with a royal message.

Version 1 (1976)

(the percussion pattern *Sin fung ca* is played)
(the principal male role actor recites rhymed speech, segment 1)

Example 9.4a The texts of a rhymed speech passage from
The Swallow Returns (cont'd)

(line 1, phrase 1)

dai   fu,
大　夫
Official,
(the actor playing the official speaks plain speech)

din   ha   je.
殿　下　爺
Your Highness.
(the principal male role actor continues rhymed speech)

(line 1, phrases 2 to 7)

gei dek ngo sam go jyt cin tung nei set san tou mong,
記　得　我　三　個　月　前　同　你　失　散　逃　七
I remember three months ago we were separated in our escape,

ngo   dai   soeng   dou   ci,
我　帶　傷　到　此
I came here with my wounds,

jau heng dek key dei hing mui loeng jen zoeng ngo wan gau,
尤　幸　得　佢　哋　兄　妹　兩　人　將　我　挽　救
fortunately I was saved by that woman and her elder brother,

dim gai nei, fet jin jau zi dou, ngo zoi ci gey cy le? (one-stroke)
點　解　你　忽　然　又　知　道　我　在　此　居　處　呢
how do you suddenly know my living place here?

(the actor playing the official recites rhymed speech, segment 2)

(line 1, phrases 1 to 2)

ngo ben soeng a din ha je, nei ge fu wong bing zung a!
我　稟　上　阿　殿　下　爺　你　嘅　父　王　病　重　呀
I report to your Highness, your father-emperor is seriously ill!
(the principal male role actor speaks)

Example 9.4a The texts of a rhymed speech passage from
The Swallow Returns (cont'd)

ha! (one-stroke)

吓

Hah!

(the actor playing the official continues rhymed speech)

(line 1, phrases 3 to 6)

giu   mei   sen   ming   ca   ngem   fong,

叫 微 臣 明 查 暗 訪

told this minor official to observe publicly and investigate privately,

hau   dek   jet   wae   cyn   ney   gou   zi,

後 得 一 位 村 女 告 知

later I was informed by a village girl,

lae   dou   lei   dou   zi   wen   dou   nei   a,

嚟 到 哩 度 至 搵 到 你 呀

I found you when I got here,

nei   fu   wong   giu   mei   sen   dai   loi   jet   zi   ziu   sy   a!

你 父 王 叫 微 臣 帶 來 一 紙 詔 書 呀

your father-emperor told this minor official to bring here a paper with
a royal message!

Version 2 (1980)

(the percussion pattern *Sin fung ca* is played)
(the principal male role actor recites rhymed speech, segment 1)

(line 1, phrases 1 to 5)

dai   fu,   gei   dek   ngo   dei   sam   go   jyt   cin   bei   dik   jen   so   kwen,

大 夫 記 得 我 哋 三 個 月 前 被 敵 人 所 困

Official, remember three months ago we were surrounded by enemies,

lok   fong   tou   mong,

落 荒 逃 亡

(we were) defeated and fearfully fled,

dim   gai   nei   jau   zen   zi   dou,   ngo   zoi   ci   gey   zy   le? (one-stroke)

點 解 你 又 真 知 道 我 在 此 居 住 呢

how do you really know that I live here?

(the actor playing the official recites rhymed speech, segment 2)

Example 9.4a The texts of a rhymed speech passage from
The Swallow Returns (cont'd)

(line 1, phrases 1 to 5)

ai a din ha je,
唉 阿 殿 下 爺
Alas your Highness,

ngo fong coi a, dek dou go cyn ney tung zi,
我 方 才 呀 得 到 個 村 女 通 知
a while ago, I was informed by a village girl,

nei fu wong ji ga bing zung a,
你 父 王 而 家 病 重 呀
your father-emperor is now seriously ill,

key ming ngo dai loi jet fung ge ziu sy.
佢 命 我 帶 來 一 封 嘅 詔 書
he ordered me to bring here a royal message.

Version 3 (1985a)

(the percussion pattern *Sin fung ca* is played)
(the principal male role actor recites rhymed speech, segment 1)

(line 1, phrase 1)

dai fu,
大 夫
Official,
(the actor playing the official speaks plain speech)

hae dou.
喺 度
Here.
(the principal male role actor continues rhymed speech)

(line 1, phrases 2 to 5)

sam jyt zi cin ngo dei tau zap wu jing,
三 月 之 前 我 哋 偷 襲 胡 營
three months ago we made a sneak attack on the Huns,

zung zo Hung Nou ge mai fuk,
中 咗 匈 奴 嘅 埋 伏
fell into the Huns' ambush,

Example 9.4a The texts of a rhymed speech passage from
The Swallow Returns (cont'd)

set   san   zi   hau   gok   zi   tou   mong,
失　散　之　後　各　自　逃　亡
we escaped individually after we had separated,

dim   gai   nei   jau   wui   zey   zung   zi   ci   ne? (one-stroke)
點　解　你　又　會　追　蹤　至　此　呢
how did you follow my trail and come to this place?
(the actor playing the official recites rhymed speech, segment 2)

(line 1, phrases 1 to 6)

din   ha   je,   nei   fu   wong   bing   zung,
殿　下　爺　你　父　王　病　重
Your Highness, your father-emperor is seriously ill,

ming   ngo ... [unclear recording], *ming   ca   ngem   fong,*
命　我　　　　　　明　查　暗　訪
ordered me ..., to observe publicly and investigate privately,

ne   ne   ne,   ji   ga   dai   loi   jau   jet   zi   ge   ziu   sy. (one-stroke)
呢　呢　呢　而　家　帶　來　有　一　紙　嘅　詔　書
here, now I bring here a paper with a royal message.

Version 4 (1985b)

(the percussion pattern *Sin fung ca* is played)
(the principal male role actor recites rhymed speech, segment 1)

(line 1, phrases 1 to 6)

giu   zo   nei   mg   hou   gem   cing   fu   ngo   ga   la,
叫　咗　你　唔　好　咁　稱　呼　我　㗎　啦
I have told you not to address me in this way,

jau   jen   hoeng   dou   nei   jau   cing   fu   ngo   din   ha   je,
有　人　响　度　你　又　稱　呼　我　殿　下　爺
you address me as "Your Highness" even when somebody is around,

hae   ne,   soeng   sam   go   jyt   cin,   ngo   tung   ngo   fu   wong   set   san,
係　呢　想　三　個　月　前　我　同　我　父　王　失　散
yes, I recall three months ago, I was separated from my father-emperor,

Example 9.4a The texts of a rhymed speech passage from
The Swallow Returns (cont'd)

nei jau dim wui ... [unclear recording] *zi ngo gey cy?* (one-stroke)
你 又 點 會　　　　　知 我 居 處
how do you ... know the place I live?
(the actor playing the official recites rhymed speech, segment 2)

(line 1, phrases 1 to 5)

din ha je, nei fu wong bing zung a,
殿 下 爺 你 父 王 病 重 呀
Your Highness, your father-emperor is seriously ill,

ming mei sen sei wae ming ca ngem fong,
命 微 臣 四 圍 明 查 暗 訪
ordered this minor official to observe publicly and investigate privately
in many areas,

hau loi jau cyn ney tung zi,
後 來 有 村 女 通 知
later a village girl informed me,

ngo dai loi jet zi ziu sy a. (one-stroke)
我 帶 來 一 紙 詔 書 呀
I bring here a paper with a royal message.

Example 9.4b The texts of a rhymed speech segment from
Example 9.4a

(the percussion pattern *Sin fung ca* is played)
(the principal male role actor recites rhymed speech, segment 1)

(line 1, phrases 1 and 2)
Script
dai fu, sam jyt cin tau zap wu jing,
大 夫 三 月 前 偷 襲 胡 營
Official, three months ago (we) made a sneak attack on the Huns,

Example 9.4b The texts of a rhymed speech segment from
Example 9.4a (cont'd)

Version 1 (1976)

dai   fu,

大　夫

Official,

(the actor playing the official speaks plain speech)

din   ha   je.

殿　下　爺

Your Highness.

(the principal male role actor continues rhymed speech, line 1, phrase 2)

gei dek ngo sam go jyt cin tung nei set san tou mong,

記　得　我　三　個　月　前　同　你　失　散　逃　亡

I remember three months ago we were separated in our escape,

Version 2 (1980)

dai fu, gei dek ngo dei sam go jyt cin bei dik jen so kwen,

大　夫　記　得　我　哋　三　個　月　前　被　敵　人　所　困

Official, remember three months ago we were surrounded by enemies,

Version 3 (1985a)

dai   fu,

大　夫

Official,

(the actor playing the official speaks plain speech)

hae   dou.

喺　度

Here.

(the principal male role actor recites rhymed speech)

sam   jyt zi cin ngo dei tau zap wu jing,

三　月　之　前　我　哋　偷　襲　胡　營

three months ago we made a sneak attack on the Huns,

**Example 9.4b The texts of a rhymed speech segment from
Example 9.4a** (cont'd)

Version 4 (1985b) (phrases 1, 2, 3 and 4)

giu zo nei mg hou gem cing fu ngo ga la,

叫 咗 你 唔 好 咁 稱 呼 我 㗎 啦

I have told you not to address me in this way,

jau jen hoeng dou nei jau cing fu ngo din ha je,

有 人 响 度 你 又 稱 呼 我 殿 下 爺

you address me as "Your Highness" even when somebody is around,

hae ne, soeng sam go jyt cin,

係 呢 想 三 個 月 前

yes, I recall three months ago,

(segment 1, line 1, phrases 3, 4 and others with similar meaning)

Script

zung liu Hung Nou mai fuk, (one-stroke) *set san gok zi tou mong,*

中 了 匈 奴 埋 伏　　　失 散 各 自 逃 亡

(we) fell into the Huns' ambush, were separated and escaped individually,

Version 1 (1976)

ngo dai soeng dou ci, jau heng dek key dei hing mui loeng

我 帶 傷 到 此 尤 幸 得 佢 哋 兄 妹 兩

jen zoeng ngo wan gau,

人 將 我 挽 救

I came here with my wounds, fortunately I was saved by
that woman and her elder brother,

Version 2 (1980) (phrase 3 only)

lok fong tou mong,

落 荒 逃 亡

(we were) defeated and fearfully fled,

Example 9.4b The texts of a rhymed speech segment from
Example 9.4a (cont'd)

Version 3 (1985a)
zung zo Hung Nou ge mai fuk, *set san zi hau gok zi tou mong*,
中 咗 匈 奴 嘅 埋 伏 失 散 之 後 各 自 逃 亡
fell into the Huns' ambush, we escaped individually after we had separated,

Version 4 (1985b) (phrase 5)
ngo tung ngo fu wong set san,
我 同 我 父 王 失 散
I was separated from my father-emperor,

(segment 1, line 1, phrases 5, 6, 7 and others with similar meaning)

Script (phrase 5 only)
ho ji nei dek zi siu wong gey cy?
何 以 你 得 知 小 王 居 處
how do you know the living place of this young prince?

Version 1 (1976)
dim gai nei, fet jin jau zi dou, ngo zoi ci gey cy ne? (one-stroke)
點 解 你 忽 然 又 知 道 我 在 此 居 處 呢
how do you suddenly know my living place here?

Version 2 (1980) (phrases 4 and 5 only)
dim gai nei jau zen zi dou, ngo zoi ci gey zy ne? (one-stroke)
點 解 你 又 真 知 道 我 在 此 居 住 呢
how do you really know that I live here?

Version 3 (1985a) (phrase 4 only)
dim gai nei jau wui zey zung zi ci ne? (one-stroke)
點 解 你 又 會 追 踪 至 此 呢
how did you follow my trail and come to this place?

Version 4 (1985b) (phrase 6)
nei jau dim wui ... [unclear recording] *zi ngo gey cy*? (one-stroke)
你 又 點 會   知 我 居 處
how do you ... know the place I live?

**Example 9.5 Syntactical grouping of the texts in phrases 2 to 4 of
segment 1 from Example 9.4b**

Script

(phrase 2, group 1)
(romanizations)   *sam*   *jyt*   *cin*
(Chinese characters)   三   月   前
(syllable translation)   three   month   before
(group translation)   three months ago

(group 2)
tau   *zap*
偷   襲
steal   attack
sneak attack

(group 3)
wu   *jing*
胡   營
foreign tribes   camps
the Huns' base

(phrase 3, group 1)
zung   *liu*
中   了
fall into   (a particle)
fell into

(group 2)
Hung *Nou*
匈   奴
Huns
the Huns

(group 3)
mai *fuk*
埋   伏
ambush
the ambush

**Example 9.5 Syntactical grouping of the texts in phrases 2 to 4 of
segment 1 from Example 9.4b** (cont'd)

(phrase 4, group 1)
set   san
失   散
lose   separated
got separated

(group 2)
gok   zi
各   自
each   self
individually

(group 3)
tou   mong
逃   亡
escape   die
fled for one's life

Version 1 (1976)
(phrase 2, group 1)
gei   dek
記   得
remember
remember

(group 2)
ngo
我
 I
 I

(group 3)

sam   go   jyt   cin
三   個   月   前
three   (an article) month   before
three months ago

Example 9.5 Syntactical grouping of the texts in phrases 2 to 4 of segment 1 from Example 9.4b (cont'd)

(group 4)
tung   nei
同   你
with   you
with/and/from you

(group 5)
set   san
失   散
lose   separated
got separated

(group 6)
tou   mong
逃   亡
escape die
fled for one's life

(phrase 3, group 1)
ngo   dai   soeng   dou   ci
我   帶   傷   到   此
I   carry wound arrive here
I came here with my wounds

(phrase 4, group 1)
jau heng dek key dei   hing   mui   loeng   jen
尤   幸   得   佢 哋   兄   妹   兩   人
luckily   to have they   brother and sister   two persons

zoeng   ngo   wan gau
將   我   挽   救
(a preposition) I   to save
Fortunately, I was saved by that woman and her elder brother

Example 9.5 Syntactical grouping of the texts in phrases 2 to 4 of
segment 1 from Example 9.4b (cont'd)

Version 2 (1980)
(phrase 2, group 1)
gei   dek
記   得
remember
remember

(group 2)
ngo   dei
我   哋
we
we

(group 3)
sam   go   jyt   cin
三   個   月   前
three   (an article)   month   before
three months ago

(group 4)
bei
被
by
by the

(group 5)
dik   jen
敵   人
enemy
the enemies

(group 6)
so   kwen
所   困
(an adverb)   surround
be surrounded

Example 9.5 Syntactical grouping of the texts in phrases 2 to 4 of
segment 1 from Example 9.4b (cont'd)

(phrase 3, group 1)
lok   fong
落   荒
fearfully
fearfully

(group 2)
tou   mong
逃   亡
escape die
fled for one's life

Version 3 (1985a)
(phrase 2, group 1)
sam   jyt   zi   cin
三   月   之   前
three   month   (a particle)   before
three months ago

(group 2)
ngo   dei
我   哋
we
we

(group 3)
tau   zap
偷   襲
steal   attack
sneak attack

(group 4)
wu   jing
胡   營
foreign tribes   camp
the Huns' base

**Example 9.5 Syntactical grouping of the texts in phrases 2 to 4 of
segment 1 from Example 9.4b** (cont'd)

(phrase 3, group 1)
zung   *zo*

中   咗

fall into   (an adverb, a colloquial form of *liu* 了)
fell into

(group 2)
Hung   Nou

匈   奴

Huns
the Huns

(group 3)
ge

嘅

(a particle used after a noun as a possessive marker;
for example, *Hung Nou ge* means "the Huns'")

(group 4)
mai   fuk

埋   伏

ambush
the ambush
(translation of the phrase: fell into the Huns' ambush)

(phrase 4, group 1)
set   san

失   散

lose   separated
got separated

(group 2)
zi   hau

之   後

(a particle)   after
after

Example 9.5 Syntactical grouping of the texts in phrases 2 to 4 of segment 1 from Example 9.4b (cont'd)

(group 3)
gok   zi

各   自

each   self
individually

(group 4)
tou   mong

逃   亡

escape   die
fled for one's life

Version 4 (1985b)
(phrase 4, group 1)
soeng

想

recall
recall

(group 2)
sam   go   jyt   cin

三   個   月   前

three   (an article)   month   before
three months ago

(phrase 5, group 1)
ngo   tung   ngo   fu   wong

我   同   我   父   王

I   and   my   father   emperor
my father-emperor and I

(group 2)
set   san

失   散

lose   separated
got separated

Example 9.6 The texts of a *Kwen fa* segment from *The Swallow Returns*

Script

(the principal female actor sings the lower line of *Kwen fa*)

(lower line)

key tin cy men gae hei mou gim,
佢　天　曙　聞　雞　起　舞　劍
He heard the cock's crow at dawn and woke up to practice his swordplay,

lik mau zoi gey hau loeng gei.
力　謀　再　舉　候　良　機
plans to wait for a good opportunity to strike back.

(upper line)

long ngoi gwok, jau hung sem,
郎　愛　國　有　雄　心
My husband loves his nation, he has a heroic ambition,

nan dek key hung wai dai zi,
難　得　佢　胸　懷　大　志
the fact that he bears a great ideal in his bosom is rare.

The Performed Version

(the principal female actor sings *Kwen fa*)

(lower line)

tin cy men gae key hei mou gim,
天　曙　聞　雞　佢　起　舞　劍
Hearing the cock's crow at dawn he woke up to practice his swordplay,

(the comic role actor speaks plain speech)

jau hey hau san lin gim?
又　去　後　山　練　劍
He went to the other side of the hill to practice his swordplay?

Example 9.6 The texts of a *Kwen fa* segment from
The Swallow Returns (cont'd)

(the principal female actor speaks plain speech)

hae   a.
係　呀
Yes.

(the principal female actor sings *Kwen fa*)

(lower line, continued)

lik   mau zoi cey hau si gei.
力　謀　再　取　候　時　機
plans to wait for an opportunity to strike back.

(the comic role actor speaks plain speech)

gem   a,   jing   goi,   jing   goi,   jing   goi,   jing   goi,
咁　呀　應　該　應　該　應　該　應　該
I see, he should, he should, he should, he should.

(the principal female actor sings *Kwen fa*)

(upper line)

long   ngoi   gwok,   key   jau   hung   sem,
郎　愛　國　佢　有　雄　心
My husband loves his nation, he has a heroic ambition,

ji   ce   zung   hung   wai   dai   zi
而　且　重　胸　懷　大　志
He also bears a great ideal in his bosom.

(the comic role actor speaks plain speech)

a   hae,   gem   zi   hae   nam   jen   dai   zoeng   fu   a   ma.
呀　係　咁　至　係　男　人　大　丈　夫　吖　嘛
I see, it shows that he is a real man.

Example 9.7 The texts of a *Muk jy* segment from *The Heroic Blood Sheds on Mount Pei Pa*

Script

(the comic role actor sings *Muk jy*)
(line 1)
Siu- guk bing fei joeng fa sey sing.

小　菊　並　非　楊　花　水　性

Siu-guk is not changeable.

(line 2)
wen fan go Ma- tae- ling Mung- lou zung hou sen coi.

搵　番　個　馬　蹄　檸　檬　露　重　好　身　材

Get one with a figure better than that of Marilyn Monroe.

Version 1
(the comic role actor sings *Muk jy*)
(line 1)
Siu- guk bing fei joeng fa sey sing.

小　菊　並　非　楊　花　水　性

Siu-guk is not changeable.

(line 2)
ngo tung nei cey go bei Bou Doi-lae geng hou sen coi.

我　同　你　娶　個　比　寶　黛　麗　更　好　身　材

I will help you to marry one with a figure better than that of Bo Derek.

Version 2
(the comic role actor speaks plain speech)
na, Siu- guk mg hae gei hou joeng ze.

哪　小　菊　唔　係　幾　好　樣　啫

See, Siu-guk is not really good looking.

hae mae a? gem sau.

係　咪　吖　咁　瘦

Isn't she? So skinny.

jau met hou zi dek gak?

有　乜　好　至　得　㗎

What is so good about her?

Example 9.7 The texts of a *Muk jy* segment from *The Heroic Blood Sheds on Mount Pei Pa* (cont'd)

nei   jau   sou   loi   hae   zan   a   ma   hou   ge.

你　又　素　來　係　讚　阿　媽　好　嘅

And you always praise your mother as being terrific.

(sings *Muk jy*, line 2)

mg   ngam   deng   ngo   tung   nei   hey   met   sik   jet   go,

唔　啱　等　我　同　你　去　物　色　一　個

Or I will recruit for you one,

(the comic role actor adds comic gestures, sings)

(line 2, cont.)

hou   ci   a   ma   gem   ge   sen   coi.

好　似　阿　媽　咁　嘅　身　材

with a figure like that of your mother.

Example 9.8 The text of an improvised plain speech segment from
            The Swallow Returns

(female actor A speaks plain speech)

mg   hou   gong   gem   do   la.
唔　好　講　咁　多　啦
Don't say any more.

hei,   gong   dou   ngo   zi   gei   dou   jet   gau   gau.
唏　講　到　我　自　己　都　一　舊　舊
Hey, my words messed me up.

fan   uk   kei   ba   la.
返　屋　企　罷　啦
(I) better go home.

Example 9.9   The text of an improvised plain speech passage from
The Courtship of the Phoenix by the Side of
Lake Peach Blossom

(the principal female actor speaks plain speech)

cing,   si   tim   wan   si   fu   ne?
情　是　甜　還　是　苦　呢
Love, is it sweet or bitter?

wan   gei   tou   lem   jet   zik,
還　記　桃　林　一　夕
I can still remember the evening with peach blossom,

syn   zeng   gem   ngen   biu.
選　贈　金　銀　鏢
I selected them to receive my gold and silver darts.

go   cing   hae   tim   ga.
個　情　係　甜　㗎
Love was sweet.

dan   hae   ngo   jau   wae   zo   jet   go   cing   zi,
但　係　我　又　為　咗　一　個　情　字
But merely for love,

lung   dou   gwok   po   ga   mong.
弄　到　國　破　家　亡
I ruined my nation and family.

lung dou ngo, soeng, dey bet hei sin wong mou hau. (one-stroke)
弄　到　我　上　對　不　起　先　王　母　后
It made it difficult for me to face my late emperor and
my mother-empress above me.

ha,   ngo   dey   bet   hei   lae   men   bak   sing.
下　我　對　不　起　黎　民　百　姓
Below me, I had let my people down.

Example 9.9 The text of an improvised plain speech passage from
   The Courtship of the Phoenix by the Side of
   Lake Peach Blossom (cont'd)

mou   hau   cyn   sau   ngo   ge   gong   san,
母　右　傳　授　我　嘅　江　山
The nation handed to me from my mother-empress,

ngo   zep   zoeng   dou   bet   dou   jet   bak   jet,
我　執　掌　都　不　到　一　百　日
I have ruled for less than a hundred days,

zau   lung   dou   ze   bun   tin   dei   lo! (one-stroke)
就　弄　到　這　般　田　地　囉
I produced this kind of situation!

hai!
唉
Alas!

Example 9.10   The texts of a plain speech passage from
                              The Swallow Returns

Script

(the comic role actor speaks plain speech)

ce, Lei- hoeng, ngo dei loeng hing mui,
嗐　梨　香　我　哋　兩　兄　妹
Hey, Lei-hoeng, we brother and sister,

zi jau fu mou soeng mong,
自　幼　父　母　雙　亡
our parents passed away when we were kids,

zing lok do siu tin dei,
剩　落　多　少　田　地
left us some crop fields,

key hae ngo mui fu, mou gae ge
佢　係　我　妹　夫　冇　計　嘅
he is my brother-in-law, I won't be mean.

The Performed Version (1985a)

(the comic role actor speaks plain speech)

(segment 1)
ngo wa nei dou so so dei ge,
我　話　你　都　傻　傻　地　嘅
I think you are a little bit silly,

ngo dei loeng hing mui a,
我　哋　兩　兄　妹　呀
we brother and sister,

dit gem dai go a,
哋　咁　大　個　呀
since we were kids,

a go za ji ging hae hou ngoi seik nei ga lak.
阿　哥　咋　已　經　係　好　愛　錫　你　㗎　嘞
your elder brother has been treating you nicely.

Example 9.10 The texts of a plain speech passage from
The Swallow Returns (cont'd)

zi cung a de a ma loeng go mg hoeng dou zi hau,
自 從 阿 爹 阿 媽 兩 個 唔 响 度 之 後
Since dad and mom passed away,

nei zi ma, a go mui jau hae nei,
你 知 嘛 阿 哥 妹 又 係 你
do you know, I treat you as my younger sister,

ga ze jau hae nei,
家 姐 又 係 你
and treat you as my elder sister,

a ma jau dong hae nei,
阿 媽 又 當 係 你
and also treat you as my mom,

a ba jau dong hae nei,
阿 爸 又 當 係 你
and also treat you as my dad,

lou po jau hae nei,
老 婆 又 係 你
and also treat you as my wife,

(the principal female actor speaks)

wae!
喂
Hey!

(the comic role actor speaks plain speech)

mg hae, mg hae, lou, lou po mg hae.
唔 係 唔 係 老 老 婆 唔 係
no, no, you are not my wife.

zen hae dou dong zy sai!
真 係 都 當 住 晒
I treat you as everything!

Example 9.10 The texts of a plain speech passage from
The Swallow Returns (cont'd)

ngo wae zo nei dou gem jet ngo dou mg soeng git fen,

我　為　咗　你　到　今　日　我　都　唔　想　結　婚

Because of you, I haven't felt like marrying anybody up till today,

zau hae geing git zo fen lok,

就　係　驚　結　咗　婚　咯

I am afraid if I get married,

cou go a sou fan lae ha nei ga ma.

草　個　阿　嫂　返　嚟　蝦　你　㗎　嘛

your sister-in-law who marries me will treat you badly.

ma, loeng hing mui,

嘛　兩　兄　妹

See, we brother and sister,

ngo dei ji ga jau mg hae wa sik mg dou,

我　哋　而　家　又　唔　係　話　食　唔　到

jau mg hae wa zoek mg dou,

又　唔　係　話　着　唔　到

now we don't have any problem in food, and clothing,

ngo dei a de a ma zing dou gem do tin dei,

我　哋　阿　爹　阿　媽　剩　到　咁　多　田　地

our dad and mom left us so many crop fields,

a go ji ga dou mg sae dim zou ga,

阿　哥　而　家　都　唔　駛　點　做　㗎

your brother doesn't have to work too much,

kau kei tae zy go pun sang ji zau dek,

求　其　睇　住　嗰　盤　生　意　就　得

I merely have to keep an eye on our business.

cey zi ngoi gang tin a, wak ze cap joeng,

除　之　外　耕　田　呀　或　者　插　秧

Example 9.10　The texts of a plain speech passage from
The Swallow Returns (cont'd)

joeng gae joeng ngap,
養　雞　養　鴨
Other than that, for jobs such as plowing the fields, transplanting the rice
seedlings and raising chickens and ducks,

ngo dou hae ceing gung jen ga,
我　都　係　請　工　人　㗎
I hire workers to take care of them,

jau gung jen jau fo gei jau sae met zi gei juk sau?
有　工　人　有　伙　記　又　駛　乜　自　己　郁　手
We have servants and workers, why do you still bother to work?

nei jau sae met dam sem a go joeng nei dei
你　又　駛　乜　擔　心　阿　哥　養　你　哋
mg hei dek ga. (one-stroke)
唔　起　得　㗎
You don't have to worry about your brother's capacity to support you.

(the principal female actor speaks plain speech)

(segment 2)
mg hae ne, mg hou ji si a ma.
唔　係　呢　唔　好　意　思　吖　嘛
No, I just feel sorry about that.

(the comic role actor speaks plain speech)

(segment 3)
met je giu zou mg hou ji si?
乜　嘢　叫　做　唔　好　意　思
What does it mean by feeling sorry?

so ge! na, a mui, nei zi ma?
傻　嘅　嗱　阿　妹　你　知　嘛
Silly! See, my sister, do you know?

Example 9.11 The texts of a plain speech passage from *Story of the Purple Hairpin*

Script

(the military role actor speaks plain speech angrily, with gestures)

hei, ngo ca men ta jen ming sing dou bet si jy
唏 我 查 問 他 人 名 姓 都 不 是 與
nei da gao cing,
你 打 交 情
Hey, I only asked you about the name of that person
and I am not trying to befriend you,

nei wan bet fai ba siu jy seng sing si gong zoeng coet loi?
你 還 不 快 把 小 儒 生 姓 氏 講 將 出 來
Why don't you tell me the name of that young Confucian scholar?

(the comic role actor speaks plain speech)

tai wae je je cing ting.
太 尉 爺 爺 請 聽
Please listen, master Military Commissioner.

(the comic role actor sings *Muk jy* in the mode of *Ji fan*)

(line 1)
key ga zoi Lung Sae lem Gong Ha.
佢 家 在 隴 西 臨 江 夏
His native home is located at Longxi near Jiangxia.

(line 2)
hae coet sin ciu zoi soeng ga.
系 出 先 朝 宰 相 家
His lineage can be traced back to the prime minister of
one of the previous emperors.

(line 3)
Sep- long Lei Jik jen siu sa.
十 郎 李 益 人 瀟 灑
His name is Lei Jik Sep-long and he is a man of spontaneity.

Example 9.11 The texts of a plain speech passage from *Story of the Purple Hairpin* (cont'd)

(line 4)

wae loek hung coi zoeng soeng nga.

偉 略 雄 才 將 相 芽

He has great talent, intelligence and the potential to become
a general or prime minister.

(line 5)

fu hao Coeng On ging si ba.

赴 考 長 安 經 試 罷

He came to Changan city and has already sat for the examination.

(line 6)

Ci Jen Zi noi zam cae nga.

慈 恩 寺 內 暫 棲 鴉

He temporarily lodges at the Ci Jen Temple.

(line 7)

joek hey coi long fui tin ha,

若 許 才 郎 魁 天 下

If this talented person is allowed to come first and
overwhelm other people,

(line 8)

bet zoi zeng mun him fan ca.

不 再 僧 門 欠 飯 茶

he does not have to owe the temple food and tea.

The Performed Version

(the military role actor speaks plain speech angrily)

ta dou dae sing sem ming sey?

他 到 底 姓 甚 名 誰

So, then, what is his name?

**Example 9.11 The texts of a plain speech passage from *Story of
the Purple Hairpin* (cont'd)**

nei fai gong coet lae!
你 快 講 出 嚟
You tell me immediately!

(the comic role actor speaks plain speech)

dai jen, gong coi sep gen go wae sau coi ne,
大 人 剛 才 拾 巾 嗰 位 秀 才 呢
Master, the scholar who picked the kerchief up a moment ago,

hae Lung Sae jen si,
係 隴 西 人 士
is a native Longxi,

sing Lei ming Jik, bit zi Gwen- jy.
姓 李 名 益 別 字 君 虞
His family name is Lei, his given name is Jik, his other name is Gwen-jy.

**Example 9.12 The text of a sung segment delivered as plain speech
from *The Swallow Returns***

Script

(the comic role actor sings the lower line of *Coeng gey kwen fa*)

(lower line)
mui fu hae zi gei jen, ho bit fen bei ci.
妹 夫 係 自 己 人 何 必 分 彼 此
Brother-in-law one of us, we shouldn't make
a distinction between him and us.

do go jen sik fan do soeng fai zi.
多 個 人 食 飯 多 雙 筷 子
An additional person at the dining table merely means
adding a pair of chopsticks.

ngo fu dam key seng wut coek coek jau jy.
我 負 擔 佢 生 活 綽 綽 有 餘
I have more than enough to support him.

ho fong nei dei sam jyt jen cing fa git zi.
何 況 你 哋 三 月 恩 情 花 結 子
Not to say your three-month love has yielded a seed.

dan kau mui nei zung sen heng fuk.
但 求 妹 你 終 身 幸 福
I only hope that you will be happy for the rest of your life.

a go zi dong zoen lik wae ci.
阿 哥 自 當 盡 力 維 持
Your elder brother will try his best to handle things.

(upper line)
nei fong sem jau joeng mok cou lou. (one-stroke)
你 放 心 休 養 莫 操 勞
You relax, rest and don't work hard.

Example 9.12 The text of a sung segment delivered as plain speech from *The Swallow Returns* (cont'd)

ho ji bet gin zoeng gwen key pui bun nei?
何 以 不 見 將 軍 佢 陪 伴 你
Why can't I see the general accompanying you?

The Performed Version (1985b)

(the comic role actor speaks plain speech)

gem nei zau mg hou hey la.
咁 你 就 唔 好 去 啦
Thus you shouldn't go.

hae ne, a mui a, gong gong ha ngo dou mg gei dek tim,
係 呢 阿 妹 呀 講 講 吓 我 都 唔 記 得 添
Yes, younger sister, I just keep talking and forget.

dim gai gem ziu zou mg gin zo a a mui fu ne?
點 解 今 朝 早 唔 見 咗 阿 阿 妹 夫 呢
why is brother-in-law not seen this morning?

(the principal female role actor speaks plain speech)

key a?
佢 呀
He?

ngo wa nei zi la go.
我 話 你 知 啦 哥
I will tell you, elder brother.

10. Jests, Jokes and Tricks

Perhaps because musicians have an exceptionally good sense of humour, ethnomusicologists have often noticed the occurrences of jests, jokes and tricks in the music of many cultures: R.D. Trimillos mentions that Filipino jaw's harp players are apt to flirt with their female listeners through their musical utterances;[1] W. Anku reports how an Akan drummer, through his drumming, may ask his audience to buy him a drink to quench his thirst.[2] Jokes and tricks in Cantonese opera, however, reflect something more than the musicians' humour. A detailed study of such practices, both onstage and off, will help to shed light on aspects such as the organization of Cantonese opera troupes, the performers' attitudes towards their profession, and the improvisatory nature of their performances.

While some tricks are spontaneously made, many are pre-meditated. One who intentionally plays tricks on his fellow performers usually covers them in jests and jokes, and pretends to execute them in a casual and improvisatory manner so as to avoid being blamed. Tricks and hoaxes, no matter whether they are spontaneous or pre-planned, are collectively known as *zing gwu* 整蠱 (creating confusion), though practically everybody in the profession understands that such actions are often consciously thought out to upstage, or to bring harm to, others. Here, *zing gwu* is referred to as "trick" or "hoax." Because jests, jokes and tricks often involve conflicts and politics among Cantonese operatic performers, the informants whom I interviewed for the present study will not be identified.

The Comic Role Actor's Jokes and Jests

Jokes and jests in comic episodes are frequently played by the comic role actor. Sometimes the episodes are called for in the scripts, sometimes the actor improvises them.

In one performance, an actor of the comic role was about to sing a passage of *Muk jy* as prescribed by the script. After he heard the percussion prelude he shouted to the accompanying musicians that he was not going to sing the *Muk jy*, but would sing a passage of *Lung zau* using the same lyrics. He even asked the musicians how they knew he was supposed to have sung *Muk jy*, thus provoking laughter among the musicians and the other performers on stage, as well as the audience.[3]

In another performance, after hearing the beginning of the instrumental prelude, the comic role actor shouted to the musicians that he had not finished his improvised speech; this aroused laughter, and he continued to talk with the performers on the stage, and later sang the prescribed passage.[4]

These incidents show that the comic role actor has the freedom to improvise comic speech and does not have to follow the script strictly, as long as he evokes laughter from the audience. Some critics of Cantonese opera do not approve of such improvisations, especially those which involve English or vulgar, and even foul language, and blame them for drawing out and vulgarizing the plays and unduly lengthening the duration of performances.[5] Through interviews with viewers of Cantonese opera, I have found that such improvisatory jokes are welcomed by the older members of the audience, but young people, and especially those who are educated, often dislike them.[6]

Performers of the other roles usually do not have strong opinions about jokes and tricks such as those cited above. There are, however, jokes and tricks played by the comic role actors that are intensely disliked by fellow performers. Once in a scene within a sad play, the character played by a female actor left the stage in tears, walking in special steps symbolic of her grief. Seeing that, the comic role actor imitated her movements on the stage and commented that she walked like a corpse. Laughter was provoked in the audience and the sad mood was, thus, changed into a comic one.[7] In another play the next day, the same two actors were to appear in a scene involving another male actor, the locale being the garden. Dramatically, the female actor was attracted by the male actor, but was urged by the comic role actor to leave. The script prescribed that the comic role actor should drag her by pulling her sleeve, but instead he mischievously pulled her hair. The audience laughed but the female actor was angered.[8] When she was interviewed, she expressed her displeasure. She had talked with the comic role actor and asked him not to make similar jests after the first night of the series, but he kept making them. She also complained that, since the troupe was an *ad hoc* group and the comic role player was experienced, she dared

not voice her grievance too strongly for fear of creating conflicts.[9] A critic
later commented in the press that the comic role actor was not serious in his
performance and advised him to change that attitude for the sake of the art
of Cantonese opera.[10] The comic role actor told me that he did not care
about performing Cantonese opera too much since he had already switched
to being a movie and television actor.

As the number of Cantonese opera productions decreased sharply in
the 1960s and 1970s, this comic role actor was only one of the many
operatic actors who had switched to other media. He said that acting in
movies and television was now his major career, and that he had no time to
care about Cantonese opera, besides occasionally participating in performances.[11]

A comic role actor impersonates the aunt of the prince in *The Courtship of the
Phoenix by the Side of Lake Peach Blossom.* (19 April 1987, Po Toi Island, Hong
Kong)

The Principal Male Actor's Tricks

Tricks involving the principal and supporting male role actors were often heard. (Some supporting female role actors also reported being tricked by the principal female role actors.) Since a troupe is often identified by its principal male role actor and most troupes are set up only for an occasion, people are often less attracted by the name of the troupe than by the reputation of the principal male actor.[12] It is understandable that he usually gets the highest pay of all troupe members. In 1982, a famous actor in this role might get as much as HK$4,800 (about US$600) for a day's performance, while the lowest paid member in a troupe received HK$100 (about US$12.50).[13] In 1984, the lowest pay for a troupe member was still HK $100. An unconfirmed source suggested that the highest pay for a principal male role actor was HK$12,000 (about US$1,500) for a day's performance in the same year.[14]

Besides getting the highest pay, an actor in this role dominates in his troupe; even the impresario and scriptwriter have to obey him. It is widely known that actors in the principal male role play tricks on other performers, especially the supporting male role actors. The following story was told by a young performer (A) who had once played the supporting male role under a principal male role actor (B), in a series of ritual performances. The first evening, A got more applause, arousing B's jealousy. Soon afterwards, B announced backstage that he had decided to change the play for the next day's performance. However, he produced only one copy of the script, a clipping from a newspaper. Mr. A told me that B was aware that all of the performers in the troupe except him knew that play well because A had only been in the profession for a few years. A had to share the clipping with the other performers, but studied it diligently and succeeded in performing the play after hours of preparation memorizing the text.

Later performer A had a chance to perform with B in another ritual performance. B selected a play that required A to appear onstage for less than one minute. Sensing that this was another trick against him, A informed his singing teacher of the situation. To give him as much exposure before the audience as possible, the teacher found a passage of vocal music that was suitable for the occasion in the plot and told A to sing it during his appearance. Every performer was surprised by this addition and B was greatly annoyed. The next day, B told A shortly before the night's performance that he would perform the supporting male role and A was required to take the principal male role. Fortunately, A had performed in the same play as principal male role before, or the trick would have caused him much trouble and embarrassment. After this series of tricks, A decided to avoid performing under B.

Performer A remarked that almost all the present principal male role actors played tricks on the supporting male role actors in their troupes. He pointed out that the stiff competition between actors of the two roles often prompted the principal male role actor to suppress his rivals' opportunities to please the audience, thereby to preserve his own status. Such actors treasure their fame more than the quality of the productions. Performer A also noticed that this bad attitude was responsible for the uneven quality of operatic performances as well as for the public's hesitation in accepting the genre.[15]

Sometimes the principal male role actor plays tricks on all the other actors in order to project himself. In one instance the principal male role actor surprised all of his fellow actors during a ritual performance. Since, in a ritual series, the performance hall is usually a temporary structure, performers are often worried about water seeping through the roof when it rains. In this incident, shortly before the evening performance, the principal male role actor told the other actors that it was going to rain that night so they had better wear their old costumes. In the opening scene of the play, when the other actors were already on stage, the principal male role actor appeared in a brand new costume, and was accordingly greeted with loud applause.

An established performer (C), said to have always tricked the supporting male role actors who performed under him, told me that most established performers were selfish, narrow-minded, jealous of other performers' talent, and, above all, bossy. None of them would permit other performers to have much opportunity to sing or act, for fear of competition. He did not mention whether he had tricked others when he was performing the principal male role, but he recalled that, throughout his career, he had suffered a great deal of frustration due to the constant suppression of his singing and acting opportunities, before he had established his fame as a leading actor.

Performer C recalled that he was once the victim of a trick that involved the traditional stylistic movement *jiu sey fat*. (As mentioned in Chapter 9, in order to gain applause from the audience, performers usually attempt to sway their hairpiece as many times as they can manage.) Mr. C was to sway *sey fat* together with his fellow principal male role actor. They were supposed to conclude at the same moment, but the principal male role actor slowed his sway, pretended to stop, then kept swaying after C had paused. He remarked that established performers were always pleased to see their fellow performers' mistakes, as they cared about the projection of their personal images more than anything else.

Another trick mentioned by performer C took place in 1968 during a series of New Year performances. He was playing the supporting male role under a principal male role actor who was well known for his tricks. In the second act of the play, C was required by the script to appear on stage to sing three vocal passages introducing the character's background. In the opening evening's performance, he got loud applause from the audience after the three vocal passages, and, thus, aroused the principal male actor's envy. After the performance, the principal male role actor told him to cancel the first vocal passage in the next evening's performance; several nights later, he told performer C to cancel the second vocal passage as well. In the remaining performances, performer C had to act with little self-introduction, and many in the audience were dissatisfied with his performance.[16]

Another experienced performer (D) interviewed for this study was reluctant to mention the tricks he had experienced in his career, though he said they were countless. He did not mention specific incidents because he was still in the profession and did not want to be in conflict with his colleagues. His seriousness was evident when he asked me to show my identification, because he did not believe that I was really a researcher and not a "spy." After I had shown him my student identity card, he told a brief story, illustrating that principal male role actors could themselves be victims of tricks.

Mr. D was once performing the principal male role with another male performer. The script required his colleague to spill tea on D's arm, but the performer intentionally spilled it on his own arm, thus disturbing the development of the plot. Performer D was forced to cut the speech he was supposed to say after the spilling of the tea.

Performer D added that tricks could be played in many different ways, and he found it extremely difficult to escape from them. The most common form was that tricky performers talked to other troupe members onstage while D was singing or speaking; they might even improvise jokes to distract the audience's attention from him. He admitted that Cantonese opera in Hong Kong was declining and one of the main reasons for this decline was the competition among performers by means of tricks, rather than art.[17]

Concluding Notes

The motivations behind the *zing gwu* examples cited in the present chapter are all similar: the tricksters want to project themselves, please the audience, embarrass fellow-performers, and gain an advantage over their competitors.

When he was asked to comment on the tricks played by established performers on their supporting actors, performer C mentioned that a director should be assigned to a troupe to solve such problems and to counter the dominance of the principal male role actor. Yet for many reasons, among them cost and the lack of qualified personnel, none of the troupes in Hong Kong but one currently employs a director.[18] Other troupes refer to their play reminders as "directors" and some troupes hire "artistic consultants," but the principal male role actors are still the ones to make the final decisions. The dominance of the principal male role actor is deeply rooted in the tradition of the genre; it will no doubt continue, and tricks both backstage and onstage will continue to occur from time to time, at least during the near future.

The thirty interviews with actors of Cantonese opera conducted for this study indicate one further major factor affecting attitudes towards jokes and trickery. Most of the performers are self-deprecating and have an inferiority complex. Forty percent of them claimed that they entered the profession because of their poverty. They started to learn singing and acting because they wanted to acquire a skill. Most of them had only a few years' formal education, and learned their first Chinese characters from the scripts they had to perform with. They are very conscious that the social status of the Cantonese operatic performers was low in the past and is not much improved at present. Some of them quoted Cantonese sayings popular in the past such as *mg kung mg hok hei* 唔窮唔學戲 (one would not learn opera if he is not poor) and *soeng toi hei zi lok toi het ji* 上台戲子落台乞兒 (an artiste onstage is a beggar after he has left the stage).

Their sense of inferiority is reinforced by their belief that the genre has declined in popularity, and further by the notion that Peking opera is the most representative form of Chinese opera and that Cantonese opera is only a regional genre that lacks artistic value.

When asked if Cantonese opera was an art, some replied negatively and referred to the performance as a "game." Some of them claimed that the genre was art, but productions by local Hong Kong troupes were not. Most of those in the operatic profession who were interviewed said that the genre was art, but many added that they performed to make a living and not for the sake of art. Few could define art when they were questioned further; some claimed that the genre was art just as television and movies were. Their answers give me a strong impression that the term "art" is foreign to the profession. Most of the performers believe that they are not artists and that most of the audience does not treat the genre as "art." One of the leading playwrights once told me that he could hardly respect his job and that he earned his living like a beggar.

In a Westernized community like Hong Kong, Cantonese opera is not art in the same sense that European opera is art. The symbolic and ritualistic natures, improvisation, tricks and the sense of inferiority among the practitioners do not exist in the Western European art music traditions, or, if they do, certainly not to the same degree.

Notes

1. Trimillos, lecture on Filipino music at University of Pittsburgh, 1982.
2. Anku, drumming demonstration at University of Pittsburgh, 1984.
3. The joke occurred in a performance staged by the Bat Wo Cantonese Opera Troupe on 11 September 1984, Hong Kong.
4. The joke occurred in a performance staged by the Dai Hung Wen 大鴻運 (big fortune) Cantonese Opera Troupe on 27 August 1984, Hong Kong.
5. This point was made by Tong Gin-wun 唐健垣 , a critic, Cantonese operatic song teacher and ethnomusicologist, in a seminar on Cantonese opera at the Hong Kong Arts Centre (n.d.). Loeng (1982:326) reproduces a cartoon, originally published in the *Sing Tao Wan Pao* 星島晚報 (*Sing Tao Evening Post*) on 29 November 1969, which also criticized random improvisation.
6. The interviews were held on 17 and 28 August, 1 and 10 October and 31 December 1984. The interviewees included secondary school and university students, factory workers and professional actors of Cantonese opera, all members of Cantonese operatic song clubs.
7. The jest took place in a performance staged by the Big Fortune Cantonese Opera Troupe on 27 August 1984, Hong Kong.
8. The jest occurred in a performance staged by the Big Fortune Cantonese Opera Troupe on 28 August 1984, Hong Kong.
9. The female actor was interviewed on 26 October 1984.

10. The article was published in *Wah Kiu Yat Po* 華僑日報 (*Wah Kiu Daily News*) on 9 September 1984.
11. Interview, 17 November 1984.
12. Sometimes an impresario may use the principal male role actor's name as the name of the troupe. For example, the Lae Ga-bou 黎家寶 Cantonese Opera Troupe, led by Lae Ga-bou in the principal male role, performed from 26 to 28 March 1984.
13. Interview, 22 December 1984.
14. To avoid income tax problems, employees in the profession—impresarios, actors and instrumentalists alike—seldom mention their income to anybody, even to their colleagues. This information was obtained in an interview on 22 October 1984.
15. Interview, 18 November 1984.
16. Interviews, 16, 17 and 18 August 1984.
17. Interview, 12 December 1984.
18. The one troupe with a director in 1985 was the Singing of the Young Phoenix Cantonese Opera Troupe.

Conclusion

Having discussed the history, performance contexts and the systems of communication in Cantonese operatic music, questions concerning the function and the purpose of improvisation remain.

Improvisation in modern practice functions to make every performance unique, in order to fulfil an aesthetic purpose. Performers also improvise to give contrast and variation to each performance, not merely for entertaining the audience, but as well to make the play interesting and enjoyable for themselves. Further, they improvise to respond to other performers' improvisation, to "wrap up" mistakes committed by themselves and other performers, and to handle unexpected incidents. During the 1930s and before, actors and accompanists had to apply improvisation in "outline plays" when elaboration, deviation, addition, deletion and replacement were not optional, but obligatory, elements in productions. The use of improvisation functions to resolve problems and provide response to demands brought forth by the performance environment, and the ritual context in which most of the performances take place.

Yung (1989:91) points out that the practice of deriving the melodic tones from the linguistic tones of the text enables the singers to spend little time preparing for performance. This practice facilitates the use of improvisation, which, in turn, facilitates preparation for performance. Many actors told me that actors learned patternized episodes and the contents of the scripts aurally and orally in the past. The system of improvisation was, and still is, built on gesture (the uses of hand shadow and gestic hint), language and minimal writing (as in the outline), rather than on the written medium. Hence, the profession can admit employees of relatively low literacy. Now, though the performances are more script-oriented, a high degree of literacy is still not an essential qualification for actors.

Like other musical cultures where improvisation plays an important part, all performers in Cantonese operatic music have to absorb the basic

With the help from a cassette tape player, a play reminder supervises the rehearsal of a dance scene. (12 March 1987, Kau Sai Wan, Kau Sai Island, Hong Kong)

rules and performance practice before they can improvise. The realization of materials from the framework provided by the script, and the creation or organization of materials that deviate from the script are regulated by rules governing performance practice. These rules involve gestures, stage movements, the textual and musical structures of different aria types, singing narratives, fixed tunes, speech deliveries, and the dramatic functions and structure of the percussion patterns. Future research may focus on components in the stylized gestures and stage movements, each of the oral delivery types and percussion patterns. Studies should involve documentation, transcriptions, analyses and comparison of different versions of performances both by the same performer and by different performers, in order that a comprehensive description of the traditional practices of Cantonese operatic music, in terms of the obligatory, optional and forbidden materials, may be derived.

Cantonese opera and operatic song will face drastic changes in the near future because ideas about innovating and revitalizing the genre tend to put greater esteem on theatrical performance, rather than ritual performance and to value planning, rehearsing, directing, and controlling improvisation more than elaborating individual talent. In the 1990s, though various theatrical troupes have already attempted to realize such ideals, the traditional stylistic characteristics that have been accumulated in the tradition of the genre to facilitate improvisation still exist in such troupes' productions, but are no longer employed consciously and intentionally by performers as performance practices to achieve improvisatory functions.

Such stylistic characteristics did not come into being incidentally. We can hardly account for why the genre has accumulated and has been keeping such traditional performance practices when they are isolated from the context of improvisation.[1] In ritual performances, such characteristics and practices are still employed in their improvisatory context.[2] Hence, if the genre is to maintain an improvisatory nature, the innovations should include educating the genre's employees and audience in the concepts of improvisation,[3] as well as improving its use so that improvisation will always enhance the dramatic effect.

The dance scene in the actual performance. (12 March 1987, Kau Sai Wan, Kau Sai Island, Hong Kong)

Notes

1. Thurston Dart (1963:61) puts forward a similar argument in his discussion of extemporization in J.S. Bach's music:

   This tradition of extemporizing slow movements is no doubt the explanation of the two chords which separate the first and second movements of Bach's third Brandenburg concerto; as Tovey pointed out long ago, these are quite meaningless in themselves. But if it be supposed that a slow movement was to be interpolated at this point, perhaps extemporized by the leader, the continuo-player and a string bass, then the chords make sense; for they are clearly designed to lead back from a slow movement in the relative minor towards the home key of the 12/8 finale.

2. It is also possible that the structural devices that facilitate the use of improvisation were not formed for this purpose, but only preserved in the tradition to achieve improvisation.

3. While most Chinese scholars (both in mainland China and Hong Kong) and employees of the Cantonese opera profession discourage improvisatory practices, in the Western world, several teaching and learning manuals on the use of improvisation in theatre, dance and music have been published in recent years. They include John Hodgson and Ernest Richards' *Improvisation* (1966, reprinted in 1974), Viola Spolin's *Improvisation for the Theater* (1963, updated and reprinted in 1987), Joyce Morgenroth's *Dance Improvisations* (1987), and Mildred Portney Chase's *Improvisation: Music from the Inside Out* (1988), to name only a few.

Glossary

bak 白		plain speech.
bak lam 白欖		patter speech.
ban 班		a troupe.
ban 板		1. a pulse or beat articulated by a stroke played on the large woodblock. 2. the large woodblock; also known as *buk jy*.
ban dae 班底		actors in the troupe other than those playing the six major roles.
ban hong 板腔		"beat and melody," referred to as aria type in the present study.
ban ngan 板眼		a kind of Cantonese singing narrative.
ban pai 班牌		the name of a troupe.
ban zy 班主		impresario.
bao tou 爆肚		the term used by some contemporary performers to denote improvisation which deviates from the script; also the general public's term for comic episodes added in a play.
bao tou hei 爆肚戲		"belly-exploding play," referred to as improvisatory play.
bek pai 北派		the style of martial arts used in Peking opera and several other northern Chinese regional operatic genres; it was introduced to Cantonese opera in the 1920s.
bet 鈸		cymbals.
bong gwu 梆鼓		medium woodblock used for the playing of percussion patterns.
bong wong 梆黃		music in the modes of *bong zi* and *ji wong*; in Cantonese opera, it is the equivalent of *ban hong* or aria type.
bong zi 梆子		the name of a mode; also known as *si gung*.
bong zi zung ban 梆子中板		the name of an aria type; also known as *si gung zung ban* or simply *zung ban*.
buk jy 卜魚		large and hollow woodblock used for maintaining pulse in

		vocal music and for performing the percussion patterns; also known as *ban*.
ca	查	1. cymbals; 2. the mnemonic for the playing of cymbals.
cang	撐	the mnemonic for the sounding together of cymbals and gong.
cau seng	丑生	comic role.
ceing sen	請神	to escort the portable figure of the deity from the temple to other places.
cen zi	襯字	syllables that are of relatively little semantic importance; referred to as "padding syllables" in the present study.
cep	揖	the mnemonic for two strokes played simultaneously on the medium woodblock.
cet zi cing	七字清	the name of an aria type.
cing coeng	清唱	to sing without accompaniment.
coeng	唱	to sing.
coeng	場	an act in a play.
coeng	昌	the mnemonic for the playing of the small gong.
coeng ci	場次	the order of acts in a play.
coeng zey	唱序	to sing text set to a melodic interlude.
cung tau	冲頭	the name of a percussion pattern.
da fa	打花	to hit ornamental percussion strokes.
da gwu lou	打鼓佬	the drummer, who is the leader of the percussion section; referred to as the "woodblock player" in this book.
da ziu	打醮	rite of purification.
dae ban	底板	a symbol indicating that the large woodblock stroke does not fall on the attack of a note.
dae ding	底叮	a symbol indicating that the small woodblock stroke does not fall on the attack of a note.
dai deik	大笛	double-reed conical pipe.
dai fa	大花	1. name of a percussion pattern; 2. *kwen fa* aria type sung with *dai hau*.
dai gwu	大鼓	big drum.
dai hau	大喉	the style of voice production sometimes used by the military role actor and occasionally by the supporting and principal male role actors in vocal passages with an agitated dramatic expression; it features a natural voice of a rough quality.

dai hei   大戲   an alternate name of Cantonese opera in Hong Kong.

dai sau ban   大首板   the name of a percussion pattern.

dan   誕   birthday.

dan   旦   a female role.

dau zy   兜住   to cover up a mistake or problem.

dei gem   地錦   the name of a percussion pattern.

deing   定   to book, engage or to reserve.

dek   得   the mnemonic for the playing of the medium woodblock.

dep bui   碟杯   the ritual of dropping two pieces of oracular wood as a means to seek advice from a deity.

dik   的   the mnemonic for the playing of the small woodblock.

ding   叮   a pulse or beat articulated by a stroke played on the small woodblock.

dok kuk   度曲   realizing or designing the song; usually done orally with no use of musical notation.

dong keik ze   當劇者   the actors who are assigned by the play reminder to participate in a performance.

fa   花   1. the abbreviated form of *kwen fa*; 2. ornaments.

fa jem   花音   ornamental notes.

fa pai   花牌   boards decorated with flowers and hung above the entrances of a temporary or permanent performance hall; painted on these boards are the name of the troupe, the major role actors and some of the secondary role actors.

fa pao   花炮   usually a small piece of bamboo projected upward by rubber band, which people participating in the contest will scramble for.

fai zung ban   快中板   the name of an aria type.

fan jem   梵音   Buddhist chants.

fan sin   反線   the two strings of the fiddle (or the higher strings of the violin) are named *sang* and *liu* respectively; also known as *sang liu sin*.

fu dou mun
虎道門   doorways between the backstage and the stage at stage right and left.

fuk lei fae   福利費   welfare fee.

ga fa   加花   to add ornaments.

gai   介   instructions for stage movements.

gai hau   介口   instructions for stage movements and oral deliveries.

*gam zi fu jung*減字芙蓉the name of an aria type.

gan gwen pai coeng   the patternized episode of offering advice to the emperor.
諫君排場

gao hei   交戲   to supply the scripts.

gen zip   緊接   to connect directly to the following vocal passage with no instrumental prelude.

ging zik   驚蟄   the third solar term of the lunar year.

go tan   歌壇   tea houses and restaurants where singing of Cantonese operatic song is staged.

gong hei   講戲   discussing the opera.

gou wu   高胡   high two-string fiddle.

guk   局   the mnemonic for the playing of the large woodblock.

gung ce pou   工尺譜   a notational system of traditional Chinese music which is also used in scripts and *kuk* of Cantonese opera.

ha gey   下句   lower line.

ha lan jen   下欄人   actors playing the minor roles.

hau   口   instructions for oral deliveries.

hau   喉   ways and styles of voice production with a particular reference to style of singing.

hau gwu   口古   rhymed speech.

hau gwun   喉管   double-reed straight pipe.

hei gem   戲金   fee for hiring a troupe to perform.

hei jyn hei   戲院戲   theatrical performance.

hei mok   起幕   to raise the curtain.

hing   興   to build, to start or an impulse.

ho ce sin   合尺線   also known as *zing sin*.

hoeng ha jen   rural people.
鄉下人

hoeng jau cin   money donated to a temple for purchasing incense and oil.
香油錢

hoi bin   開邊   percussion pattern often played at the beginning and end of an act or operatic song.

hoi hei si je   the writer of the outline for an improvisatory play; some-
開戲師爺   times referred to as the play reminder in the profession nowadays.

hoi san   開山   to stage the first performance of a play.

hong   腔   1. to the Cantonese operatic performers a single note or a succession of notes; 2. in this study, it means a succession of two or more notes.

hong hau   腔口   ways and styles of voice production.

je wu   椰胡   coconut-shell fiddle.

jem ngok 音樂	1. music; 2. the melodic accompaniment; 3. a melodic accompanist.
jen zi 引子	the opening phrase of an operatic song or operatic scene.
jet ban jet ding 一板一叮	a pulse pattern composed of two beats played on the large and small woodblocks respectively.
jet ban sam ding 一板三叮	a pulse pattern composed of four beats: the first one on the large and the rest on the small woodblock.
jet ban sin 一板線	the interval of a major second.
jet cey 一錘	the one-stroke percussion pattern.
ji bin 衣邊	area left of the backstage.
ji bong fa dan 二幫花旦	supporting female role.
ji bou zem 二步針	major role actors of the non-main-festival-day afternoon shows.
ji fan 乙反	the name of a mode.
ji fan ji wong 乙反二黃	the name of an aria type.
ji soeng 衣箱	an actor's personal costume servant who is also responsible for all miscellaneous services.
ji wong 二黃	1. the name of a mode; 2. an abbreviated form of *ji wong man ban*.
ji wong man ban 二黃慢板	the name of an aria type.
ji zi heng hong 依字行腔	the performance practice of creating the vocal melody by following the tonal inflections of the syllables in the lyrics.
jing tau 影頭	gestic hint.
jiu sey fat 搖水髮	an actor's stylistic movement of swaying his hairpiece circularly.
joeng kem 洋琴	dulcimer played with a pair of thin bamboo sticks.
jyt keik 粵劇	Cantonese opera; commonly known as *dai hei* in Hong Kong.
jyt kuk 粵曲	Cantonese operatic song.
keik zung jen 劇中人	the characters in a play.
kuk 曲	1. the text used for performing Cantonese opera and operatic song; 2. in the present study: the text for performing operatic song; 3. in other contexts: a piece of music or a song.

kuk pai　曲牌　　　　a collection of tunes that have relatively identifiable pre-
　　　　　　　　　　　existent melodies; in Cantonese opera, it includes both
　　　　　　　　　　　siu kuk and *pai zi*.

kwen fa　滾花　　　　the name of an aria type.

lae si　利是　　　　　"red packet" which contains money.

lai ce　拉扯　　　　　the relatively more experienced male minor role actors.

lak lak gwu　　　　　the name of a percussion pattern.
叻叻鼓

lap zi　擸字　　　　　syllables in vocal music which are sung on the upbeat of a
　　　　　　　　　　　ding or *ban*; referred to as "grasp syllable" in the
　　　　　　　　　　　present study.

lau sey ban　　　　　a pulse pattern having continuous beats played on the
流水板　　　　　　　　large woodblock.

lo　鑼　　　　　　　　gong.

lo gwu bak　　　　　　a kind of speech delivery; referred to as percussion speech.
鑼鼓白

lo gwu dim　　　　　　percussion pattern.
鑼鼓點

lok hoeng hei　　　　rural performance.
落鄉戲

long ley bak　　　　　a kind of speech delivery; referred to as supported speech.
浪裏白

lou sy mei　　　　　　the name of a melodic prelude and a hand shadow.
老鼠尾

lou zi　露字　　　　　to display the words; generally considered to be an essen-
　　　　　　　　　　　tial element in stylish singing.

luk cy　六柱　　　　　the six major roles.

luk cy zae　六柱制　　the practice of writing plays centred on the six major roles.

lung zau　龍舟　　　　a kind of Cantonese singing narrative.

man coeng cey　　　　the name of a percussion pattern.
慢長錘

me zae zi　預仔字　　syllables sung on the upbeat; an equivalent of *lap zi*.

men mou seng　　　　principal male role.
文武生

men zi lo hong　　　　the performance practice of creating the melodic tones
問字攞腔　　　　　　　based on the linguistic tonal inflections of the lyrics.

mg cey　五錘　　　　the name of a percussion pattern, also known as *kwen fa*;
　　　　　　　　　　　referred to as five-stroke.

mou seng　武生　　　military role.

mui hoeng　梅香　　　female minor role actors.

muk jy 木魚		1. a kind of Cantonese singing narrative; 2. a wooden percussion instrument.
nam jem 南音		a kind of Cantonese singing narrative.
nam pai 南派		the traditional style of martial arts used in Cantonese opera.
ney ling 女伶		female professional singers of Cantonese operatic song.
ngae 藝		art.
ngan sik 眼色		eye hint.
nim bak 念白		poetic or versified speech.
pai coeng 排場		patternized episodes.
pai coeng hei 排場戲		"episodic play"; also referred to as improvisatory play.
pai zi 牌子		1. a kind of fixed tune; 2. the name of a percussion pattern.
pai zi tau 牌(排)子頭		the opening section of the *pai zi* percussion pattern.
pao gem 炮金		money donated by the winning contestants of the *fa pao* snatching contest.
pei pa 琵琶		four-string pear-shaped lute.
ping hau 平喉		the *hau* used by all male role actors; it features a natural voice production.
po toi 破台		the ritual of initiating a stage; it involves the sacrificial offering to the White Tiger in Cantonese opera.
pok deng ngo 撲燈蛾		percussion pattern which is always played to precede patter speech.
pong 旁		the mnemonic for the playing of one of the gongs excluding the small gong.
pung ling 碰鈴		bells.
sa dik 沙的		small woodblock used for maintaining pulse in vocal music.
sae ngok 西樂		1. the melodic instruments; 2. the melodic instrumentalists; 3. Western music; 4. the melodic music.
sae ngok ling dou 西樂領導		the leader of the melodic section.
sang liu sin 上六線		also known as *fan sin*.
sau 收		to end.
sau gwet 收掘		hand shadow used to stop the accompaniment.
sau ha 手下		male minor role actors.
sau jing 手影		hand shadow.
se soeng 卸上		to enter the stage without being noticed by the characters on stage; usually no percussion pattern is played.
sen gung hei 神功戲		ritual performance.

seng   生   a male role.

sey bo long   the name of a percussion pattern and a series of stage
水波浪   movements.

sey fat   水髮   hairpiece worn by actors.

si bak   詩白   a kind of speech delivery; referred to as poetic or versified
                              speech.

si gung   士工   name of a mode; also known as *bong zi.*

sik   色   1. appearance; 2. colour.

sin   線   1. the systems of tuning and pitch-naming; 2. mode.

sin fung ca   the name of a percussion pattern.
先鋒查

sing   聲   voice quality.

siu kuk   小曲   pre-composed or preexistent tunes; a kind of fixed tune.

siu lo   小鑼   small gong.

siu lo soeng si   the name of a percussion pattern.
小鑼相思

siu seng   小生   supporting male role.

so nap   嗩吶   double-reed conical pipe; also known as *dai deik.*

soeng   雙   1. a pair; 2. to deliver twice.

soeng   上   to enter the stage.

soeng gey   上句   upper line.

sung sen   送神   to escort the deity's portable figure back to the temple.

syt coeng   說唱   a musical genre used for story-telling; referred to as singing
                              narrative in the present study.

tae coeng   提場   play reminder.

tae gong   提綱   outline.

tae gong hei   提綱戲   "outline play"; also referred to as improvisatory play.

tan ci   彈詞   a kind of Chinese singing narrative popular in Suzhou and
                              the nearby areas.

tau ga   頭架   the leader of the melodic section.

tin gwong hei   all-night performance.
天光戲

toi   台   1. the stage; 2. a series of Cantonese operatic performan-
                              ces.

toi hau   台口   the edge of the stage.

tong hei   堂戲   the performance of operatic excerpts in restaurants.

tuk tau   禿頭   a vocal passage with no instrumental prelude.

wen bak   韻白   a kind of speech delivery; referred to as comic rhymed
                              speech.

wen hei   運氣   luck or fortune.

wu lei dung 狐狸洞	doorway between the backstage and the stage at stage left; a term rarely used nowadays.
za zuk 揸竹	the leader of the percussion section.
zae bak fu 祭白虎	the sacrificial offering to the White Tiger.
zae toi 祭台	the ritual of offering to a stage; it involves the White Tiger ritual in Cantonese opera.
zap bin 雜邊	stage right of the backstage area.
zep lae zou 執嚟做	1. an adopted performance; 2. to adopt a performance.
zep sang 執生	to continue to perform despite a mistake or problem.
zey 序	melodic interlude or prelude.
zey hong 追腔	the practice of playing an imitative melodic interlude.
zi 字	literally a "word"; referred to as "syllable" in the present study.
zi hau 子喉	the *hau* used by all young female role actors; it features a falsetto voice production.
zik 即	immediate.
zik ging 即景	to compose poems with the scenery one is looking at as theme.
zik hing 即興	improvisation.
zik hing biu jin 即興表演	to give a show on the spur of the moment; performance which deviates from the script or which is staged with no rehearsals.
zik hing fu si 即興賦詩	to write poems on the spur of the moment.
zik hing hei kek 即興喜劇	*commedia dell'arte* or *commedia all'improviso*.
zik lei 值理	the representatives of a community that holds a festival celebration.
zik zyn 直轉	to connect directly to the following vocal passage with no instrumental prelude.
zin gwu 戰鼓	war drum.
zing bun hei 正本戲	main operatic items.
zing coeng 淨(靜)場	no percussion pattern is needed to accompany an actor's entrance to stage.
zing dan jet 正誕日	the real or chosen birthday of a deity (main-festival-day) within a celebratory series which last for several days; also referred to as *zing jet*.
zing gwu 整蠱	to play tricks on somebody.
zing jen fa dan 正印花旦	principal female role.

zing jet 正日	the main day.
zing sin 正線	the two strings of the fiddle (or the two higher strings of the violin) are named *ho* and *ce* respectively; also known as *ho ce sin*.
zit 節	festival.
zo gung 座宮	the deity's fixed statue in the temple.
zoeng ban 掌板	the leader of the percussion section; referred to as the woodblock player.
zung jyn 中阮	medium sized *jyn*, which is a round, four-string plucked lute.
zung ngok 中樂	1. the percussion instruments; 2. the percussionists; 3. Chinese music; 4. percussion music.
zung ngok ling dou 中樂領導	the leader of the percussion section.
zung sae ngok 中西樂	1. the orchestra; 2. the accompanists; 3. Chinese and Western music; 4. the melodic and percussion music.
zung wu 中胡	medium two-string fiddle.
zy wui 主會	1. to the troupe members: representatives of a community that hires a troupe to perform; 2. to the local people: residents of a community who financially support the celebratory activities for a traditional ritualistic event.

References

A. Chinese and Japanese Works

Au-joeng, Jy-sin 歐陽予倩 (1954). "Si tam Jyt keik" 試談粵劇 (A Preliminary Study of Cantonese Opera). In *Zung gwok Hei kuk jin gau zi liu co cep* 中國戲曲研究資料初輯 (*The First Collection of Research Materials for the Study of Chinese Opera*), edited by J. Au-Joeng. Hong Kong: Hei keik ngae soet se 戲劇藝術社, pp. 109–57.

Cen, Coek-jing 陳卓瑩 (1952). *Jyt kuk se coeng soeng sik* 粵曲寫唱常識 (*Guide to Writing and Singing Cantonese Opera*), 2 volumes. Guangzhou: Nam fong tung zuk coet ban se 南方通俗出版社.

Chan, Sau Y. (1985). "Nam jem jem ngok jen loen: jet, kuk sik" 南音音樂引論:(一) 曲式 (Introduction to the Music of *Nam Jem*: Form). In *Jem ngok jy ngae soet* 音樂與藝術 (*Music and Art*), October 1985, pp. 43–46.

——— (1988). *Hong Kong Jyt Keik jin gau (soeng gyn)* 香港粵劇研究 (上卷) (*A Study of Cantonese Opera in Hong Kong, Volume I*). Hong Kong: Wide Angle Press.

——— (1990). *Hong Kong Jyt Keik jin gau (ha gyn)* 香港粵劇研究 (下卷) (*A Study of Cantonese Opera in Hong Kong, Volume II*). Hong Kong: Chinese Opera Research Project, Society of Ethnomusicological Research in Hong Kong.

The Editors for *Ci Hoi* (1979). *Ci hoi* 辭海 (*The Sea of Words*), 3 volumes. Shanghai: Shanghai ci sy coet ban se 上海辭書出版社.

Gim, Fung (1980). "Dey sam sep nin doi Jyt keik ping ga dik cin gin" 對三十年代粵劇評價的淺見 (Preliminary Criticism on Cantonese Opera of the 1930s). In *Hei keik jin gau zi liu* 戲劇研究資料 (*Drama Research Materials*), number 2 (1980), pp. 43–50.

Guangdong Sang Hei Keik Jin Gau Set 廣東省戲劇研究室 (Guangdong Province Institute of Drama Research) (1984). *Jyt keik coeng hong jem ngok koi loen* 粵劇唱腔音樂概論 (*Introduction to Vocal Music of Cantonese Opera*). Beijing: Jen men jem ngok coet ban se 人民音樂出版社.

Jau, Kwen-loeng 邱坤良 (1983). *Jin doi se wui dik men zuk kuk ngae* 現代社會的民

俗曲藝 (*Ethnic Music in Modern Society*). Taipei: Jyn lau coet ban si jip gwu fen jau han gung si 遠流出版事業股份有限公司 .

Jy, Mou-wen 余慕雲 [n.d.]. *Jyt keik luk sep nin* 粵劇六十年 (*Sixty Years of Cantonese Opera*). Hong Kong: Ng hing gei sy bou se 吳興記書報社 .

Lai, Bak-goeng 賴伯彊 and Wong, Geing-ming 黃鏡明 (1988). *Jyt keik si* 粵劇史 (*A History of Cantonese Opera*). Beijing: Zung gwok hei keik coet ban se 中國戲劇出版社 .

Lei, Ngan 李雁 (1957). *Jyt keik dik coeng wo zou* 粵劇的唱和做 (*Singing and Acting in Cantonese Opera*). Guangzhou: Jy nga se 爾雅社 .

Lei, Jet-wa 李日華 [n.d.]. "Sae soeng gei" 西廂記 (Story of the Western Mansion). In *Luk sep zung kuk* 六十種曲 (*A Collection of Sixty Operatic Scripts*) [1958]. Beijing: Zung wa sy guk 中華書局 .

Liang, Shih-chiu 梁實秋 , et al (1971). *A New Practical Chinese-English Dictionary*. Taipei: Far East Book Company Limited.

Lin, Yu-tang (1972). *Chinese-English Dictionary of Modern Usage*. Hong Kong: The Chinese University Press.

Liu, Dah-jen (1978). *Chinese-English Dictionary*. Taipei: Wa Jing Publishing Company.

Loeng, Pui-gem 梁沛錦 (1982). *Jyt keik jin gau tung loen* 粵劇研究通論 (*An Introduction to the Study of Cantonese Opera*). Hong Kong: Lung mun sy dim 龍門書店 .

Mek, Siu-ha 麥嘯霞 (1941). "Guangdong Hei keik si loek" 廣東戲劇史略 (A Brief History of Cantonese Opera). In *Guangdong men met* 廣東文物 (*Cultural Relic of Guangdong*), Volume 9, pp. 141–85.

Sen, Fung-ha 新鳳霞 (1982). *Ngae soet seng ngai* 藝術生涯 (*My Artistic Life*). Hong Kong: Sam lyn coet ban se 三聯出版社 .

Sin, Juk-cing 冼玉清 (1963). "Cing doi luk sang hei ban zoi Guangdong" 清代六省戲班在廣東 (A Study of the Opera Troupes from Six Outside Provinces in Guangdong During the Qing Dynasty). In *Zhongshan dai hok hok bou* 中山大學學報 (*The Journal of Zhong Shan University*) 3 [1963], pp. 105–26.

Soeng, Je 尚耶 (1981). "Ji sep nin doi jyt keik dik sing zau bet jung mut sat" 二十年代粵劇的成就不容抹煞 (The Achievement of Cantonese Opera in the 1920s Cannot be Obliterated). In *Hei keik jin gau zi liu* 戲劇研究資料 (*Drama Research Materials*), number 6 (1981), pp. 71–73.

Sou, Men-bing 蘇文炳 and Ng, Gwok-ping 吳國平 (1979). *Jyt keik lo gwu gei bun zi sik* 粵劇鑼鼓基本知識 (*Guide to Percussion Music of Cantonese Opera*). Guangzhou: Guangdong jen men coet ban se 廣東人民出版社 .

Tanaka, Issei (1981). *Chugoku saishi engeki kenkyu* 中國祭祀演劇研究 (*Ritual Theatres in China*). Tokyo: Institute of Oriental Culture, University of Tokyo.

———— (1985). *Chugoku no sozoku to engeki* 中国の宗族と演劇 (*Lineage and Theatre in China*). Tokyo: Institute of Oriental Culture, University of Tokyo.

——— (1989). "Dou gao ji lae jy zi sen Hei keik zi gan dik gwan hae" 道教儀禮與祀神戲劇之間的關係 (The Relation Between Taoist Rituals and Ritual Drama). In *Studies of Taoist Rituals and Music of Today*, edited by P.Y. Tsao and D. Law. Hong Kong: The Chinese Music Archive, Music Department, The Chinese University of Hong Kong and Society of Ethnomusicological Research in Hong Kong, pp. 155–65.

Tong, Gin-wun 唐健垣 (1980). *Tong si Jyt kuk coeng bun* 唐氏粤曲唱本 (*Tong's Book of Cantonese Operatic Song*). Hong Kong: Hong Kong sy dim 香港書店.

Wae, Hin 韋軒 (1981). *Jyt keik ngae soet jen soeng* 粤劇藝術欣賞 (*The Appreciation of the Art of Cantonese Opera*). Nanning: Guangxi jen men coet ban se 廣西人民出版社.

Wong, Lik 王力 (n.d./1957). *Guangzhou wa cin syt* 廣州話淺說 (*Introduction to Cantonese*). Hong Kong: Weng tou coet ban se 宏圖出版社. (The same title has been published in 1957 in Beijing.)

Zoeng, Gung-seng 張賡生 (1982). *Zung gwok hei kuk ngae soet* 中國戲曲藝術 (*The Art of Chinese Opera*). Tianjin: Bak fa men ngae coet ban se 百花文藝出版社.

B. English Works

Alperson, Philip (1984). "On Musical Improvisation." In *The Journal of Aesthetics and Art Criticism*, Volume XLIII, number 1, pp. 17–29.

Asian Arts Festival, Hong Kong (1980). *Asian Arts Festival.* Hong Kong: Urban Council.

Bailey, Derek (1980). *Improvisation: Its Nature and Practice in Music.* London: Moorland Publishing in association with Incus Records.

Becker, Judith (1969). "The Anatomy of a Mode." In *Ethnomusicology*, number 2 (1969), pp. 267–79.

Béhague, Gerard (1980). "Improvisation in Latin American Music." In *Music Educators' Journal*, 66 (5), pp. 118–25.

Blake, C. Fred (1981). *Ethnic Groups and Social Change in a Chinese Market Town.* Honolulu: The University Press of Hawaii.

Byrnside, Ronald (1975). "The Performer as Creator: Jazz Improvisation." In *Contemporary Music and Musical Cultures*, edited by C. Hamm., B. Nettl and R. Byrnside. Englewood Cliffs: Prentice-Hall, pp. 223–51.

Chan, Sau Y. (1984). "Tune Arrangements in *Nanxi* (Southern Drama) of the Song Dynasty." Unpublished M.A. Thesis, University of Pittsburgh.

——— (1986). "Improvisation In Cantonese Operatic Music." Unpublished Ph. D. Dissertation, University of Pittsburgh.

Chase, Mildred Portney (1988). *Improvisation: Music from the Inside Out.* Berkeley: Creative Arts Book Company.

Chernoff, John Miller (1979). *African Rhythm and African Sensibility.* Chicago,

London: University of Chicago Press.

Coker, Jerry (1987). *Improvising Jazz*. New York: Simon and Schuster,Inc.

Dart, Thurston (1963). *The Interpretation of Music*. New York, Hagerstown, San Francisco, London: Harper and Row.

Datta, Vivek and Lath, Mukund (1967). "Improvisation in Indian Music." In *The World of Music*, number 1 (1967), pp. 27–34.

Davis, Nathan T. (1985). *Writings in Jazz*. Scottsdale: Gorsuch Scarisbrick Publishers.

Ferguson, Daniel (1988). "A Study of Cantonese Opera: Musical Source Materials, Historical Development, Contemporary Social Organization, and Adaptive Strategies." Unpublished Ph.D. Dissertation, University of Washington.

Hodgson, John and Richards, Ernest (1974). *Improvisation*. New York: Grove Weidenfeld.

Hood, Mantle (1975). "Improvisation in the Stratified Ensembles of Southeast Asia." In *Selected Reports in Ethnomusicology*, Volume II, number 2, pp. 25–33.

Hsu, Francis L.K. (1983). *Exorcising the Trouble Makers: Magic, Science and Culture*. Westport, London: Greenwood Press.

Jairazbhoy, Nazir, et al (1980). "Improvisation." In *The New Grove Dictionary of Music and Musicians*, 6th Edition, edited by S. Sadie, Volume 9, pp. 31–56.

Kwok, Helen (1984). *Sentence Particles in Cantonese*. Hong Kong: Centre of Asian Studies, University of Hong Kong.

Liang, Mingyue (1985). *Music of the Billion: An Introduction to Chinese Musical Culture*. New York: Heinrichshofen Edition.

Lin, Chew-pah (1973). "The Two Main Singing Styles in Cantonese Opera / bɔŋ dʒí / and / ji wɔŋ /." Unpublished Master Thesis, University of Washington.

Luke, Kang Kwong (1990). *Utterance Particles in Cantonese Conversation*. Amsterdam: John Benjamins Publishing Company.

Morgenroth, Joyce (1987). *Dance Improvisations*. Pittsburgh: University of Pittsburgh Press.

Nettl, Bruno (1974). "Thoughts on Improvisation: A Comparative Approach." In *Musical Quarterly*, Volume 60, pp. 1–19.

Nettl, Bruno and Foltin, Bela, Jr. (1972). *Daramad of Chahargah: A Study in the Performance Practice of Persian Music*. Detroit: Information Coordinators, Inc.

Powers, Harold (1980). "Mode." In *The New Grove Dictionary of Music and Musicians*, 6th Edition, edited by S. Sadie, Volume 12, pp. 376–450.

Powers, Harold, et al (1980). "India, Subcontinent of." In *The New Grove Dictionary of Music and Musicians*, 6th Edition, edited by S. Sadie, Volume 9, pp. 69–166.

Pressing, Jeff (1988). "Improvisation: Methods and Models." In *Generative Processes in Music*: *The Psychology of Performance, Improvisation and Composition*, edited by J.A. Sloboda. Oxford: Oxford University Press, pp. 129–78.

Riddle, Ronald (1983). *Flying Dragons, Flowing Streams*: *Music in the Life of San Francisco's Chinese*. Westport, London: Greenwood Press.

Schuller, Gunther (1986). *Early Jazz*: *Its Roots and Musical Development*. New York, Oxford: Oxford University Press.

Signell, Karl (1974). "Esthetics of Improvisation in Turkish Art Music." In *Asian Music*, V-2 (1974), pp. 45–49.

——— (1977). *Makam*: *Modal Practice in Turkish Art Music*. Seattle: Asian Music Publications.

Sloboda, John A. (1988). *The Musical Mind*: *The Cognitive Psychology of Music*. Oxford: Clarendon Press.

Spolin, Viola (1987). *Improvisation for the Theater*. Evanston: Northwestern University Press.

Sudnow, David (1978). *Ways of the Hand*: *The Organization of Improvised Conduct*. Cambridge: Harvard University Press.

Thompson, Laurence G. (1989). *Chinese Religion*: *An Introduction*. Belmont: Wadsworth Publishing Company.

Touma, Habib Hassan (1971). "The *Maqam* Phenomenon: An Improvisation Technique in the Music of the Middle East." In *Ethnomusicology*, number 1 (1971), pp. 38–48.

Wade, Bonnie (1973). "*Chīz* in *Khyāl*: The Traditional Composition in the Improvised Performance." In *Ethnomusicology*, number 3 (1973), pp. 443–59.

——— (1979). *Music in India*: *The Classical Traditions*. Englewood Cliffs: Prentice-Hall.

Ward, Barbara (1979). "Not Merely Players: Drama, Art and Ritual in Traditional China." In *Man*, March (1979), pp. 18–39.

——— (1985). "Regional Operas and Their Audiences: Evidence from Hong Kong." In *Popular Culture in Late Imperial China*, edited by D. Johnson, A.J. Nathan and E.S. Rawski. Berkeley, Los Angeles, London: University of California Press, pp. 161–87.

Witzleben, John Lawrence (1983). "Cantonese Instrumental Ensemble Music in Hong Kong: An Overview With Special Reference to the *Gou Wuh* (*Gao Hu*)." Unpublished M.A. Thesis, University of Hawaii.

——— (1987). "Silk and Bamboo: Jiangnan Sizhu Instrumental Ensemble Music in Shanghai." Unpublished Ph.D. Dissertation, University of Pittsburgh.

Yeh, Nora (1972). "The *Yüeh Chü* Style of Cantonese Opera With an Analysis of 'The Legend of Lady White Snake.'" Unpublished M.A. Thesis, University of California at Los Angeles.

Yung, Bell (1976a). "The Music of Cantonese Opera." Unpublished Ph.D. Dissertation, Harvard University.

——— (1976b). "Reconstructing a Lost Performance Context: A Field Work Experiment." In *Chinoperl Papers*, number 6 (1976), pp. 120–43.

——— (1981). "Music Identity in Cantonese Opera." In *IMS: Report of the Twelfth Congress, Berkeley 1977*, edited by D. Heartz and B. Wade. Berkeley: University of California Press, pp. 669–75.

——— (1983a). "Creative Process in Cantonese Opera I: The Role of Linguistic Tones." In *Ethnomusicology*, number 1 (1983), pp. 29–47.

——— (1983b). "Creative Process in Cantonese Opera II: The Process of *T'ien Tz'u* (Text-Setting)." In *Ethnomusicology*, number 2(1983), pp. 297–318.

——— (1983c). "Creative Process in Cantonese Opera III: The Role of Padding Syllables." In *Ethnomusicology*, number 3 (1983), pp. 439–56.

——— (1984). "Model Opera as Model: From *Shajiabang* to *Sagabong*." In *Popular Chinese Literature and Performing Arts in the People's Republic of China, 1949–1979*, edited by B.S. McDougall. Berkeley, Los Angeles, London: University of California Press, pp. 144–64.

——— (1989). *Cantonese Opera: Performance as Creative Process*. Cambridge: Cambridge University Press.

Zonis, Ella (1972). Book review of Nettl and Foltin's *Daramad of Chahargah: A Study in the Performance Practice of Persian Music*. In *Asian Music*, IV-1, pp. 67–68.

——— (1973). *Classical Persian Music: An Introduction*. Cambridge: Harvard University Press.

Index